FUNDAMENTALS OF

OPERATIVE SURGERY

SECOND EDITION

FUNDAMENTALS OF OPERATIVE SURGERY

SECOND EDITION

Vipul D Yagnik MBBS, MS, FMAS, FIAGES, FAIS, FISCP

Consultant Endoscopic and Laparoscopic Surgeon
Ronak Endo-Laparoscopy and Surgical Hospital
Patan, Gujarat

Formerly
Assistant Professor
Pramukhswami Medical College
Karamsad, Gujarat
and
Shree Krishna Hospital
Karamsad, Gujarat

Publishing Manager: Dr Vandana Mittal
Senior Production Editor: Nayan Gogoi
Assistant Manager Manufacturing: Sumit Johry

10th Floor, Tower C, Building No. 10, Phase – II, DLF Cyber City
Gurgaon, Haryana - 122002

Second Edition, 2018

ISBN: 978-93-87506-81-7

Published by Wolters Kluwer (India) Pvt. Ltd., New Delhi
Compositor: Design Modus, New Delhi (www.designmodus.in)
Printed and bound at Sanat Printers, Haryana

For product enquiry, please contact – Marketing Department (marketing@wolterskluwerindia.co.in) or log on to our website www.wolterskluwerindia.co.in.

Dedicated to

My mother (Narmadaben), Father (Dahyalal), wife (Parul), daughter (Nishtha), son (Vansh), and brothers (Alpesh and Bhargav)

Foreword

It is with great pleasure that I introduce the second edition of 'Fundamentals of Operative Surgery' by Vipul Yagnik. The first edition occupied place of pride in my library for close to a decade, and it is a strong indication of a textbook's vibrancy and viability that its second edition is being published.

As an MBBS student, during my operation theatre postings, I always wished for a handy, concise book that not only explained the principles and background of the fascinating surgical procedures, but also suited the syllabus and covered the practical aspects of what would feature in the examinations. This book abundantly fulfils that need. Much of the undergraduate practical surgery training is unstructured and impromptu that, despite the best efforts of busy surgeon–teachers, often leaves the beginner bewildered. A *vade mecum* of this nature would help students make sense of what goes on in the operating room, and add substance to their experiences of observation and participation during this valuable and often inspiring phase of their education.

Dr Vipul Yagnik has an enviable track record of research and publication; I have collaborated with him on several occasions and was always impressed with his academic dedication, diligence, and attention to detail. He brings to this book his wide experience of surgical teaching and practice, distilled and presented in a manner ideal for undergraduate medical students. He has described the various commonly seen operative procedures in adequate detail with relevant background information and illustrative photographs. Yet, the various descriptions maintain an immediacy and brevity that will help the beginner become familiar with practical aspects of surgery, both in the operating room and the wards and clinics. Even the advanced students of surgery would find this book of interest and it would help to conform their grasp of fundamental principles.

The second edition of the book has been expanded with the addition of chapters on fundamentals of minimal access surgery, operations for benign anal conditions, written informed consent, surgical incisions, anesthesia, and postoperative complications. There are new sections on breast surgery, thyroid surgery, and urology including TURP, PCNL and URS, to complete the list of procedures an MBBS student may see in the operating room, or would be required to know about. Notably, the chapter on radiology has been updated with information on modern imaging modalities and nuclear medicine. There is also a useful chapter on emergency drugs and antibiotics written from a surgical perspective. Highlights of this book include a chapter on FAQs and salient points which appear as 'pearls' in most of the chapters and help retention.

The content reflects the scope of MBBS practical and viva-voce examinations in Surgery in several universities, especially across the Indian subcontinent. Moreover, the content has been updated to include recent advances in concepts and techniques relevant to the undergraduate student of surgery. In addition, the book has been extensively rewritten to make the matter lucid and academically more relevant. Most of the photographs have been replaced by more illustrative versions. Information has been curated in simple clear language with logical progression that will aid comprehension and retention.

As a result, this reincarnation is perfectly tailored to the needs of the undergraduate students of surgery. It would complement voluminous formal textbooks and help the student make sense of, and profit from, their time spent in the operating room, as well as face the viva and practical component of the MBBS examinations with more knowledge and confidence.

Sushil Dawka, MBBS, MS, EMBA, ELS
Academic Programme Director and Professor of Surgery
Sir Seewoosagur Ramgoolam Medical College
Mauritius

Preface to the Second Edition

Following the popularity of the first edition of *Fundamentals of Operative Surgery*, a second edition was inevitable. Built on the foundation of the previous edition, this edition incorporates suggestions from students as well as faculty members.

As with previous edition, this book presents the operational steps in a lucid manner. Although this book is not a textbook on operative surgery, it includes sufficient details on the subject to be of value to the undergraduate students and post graduate residents in surgery.

There are significant changes in this edition with the inclusion of many new topics such as laparoscopic cholecystectomy, benign perianal operations, PCNL, URS, and TURP, thyroidectomy and modified radical mastectomy. Also, there is inclusion of new and essential chapters such as written informed consent, anesthesia, abdominal incisions, fundamentals of minimal access surgery, general postoperative complications, and drugs. Minimally invasive surgery, which had not been there in the first edition of the book, is now dealt with concisely and adequately in appropriate chapters. Virtually all the chapters have been updated or extensively rewritten.

Wolters Kluwer India has done a magnificent job in producing the second edition that is an even more beautiful tome to read. I sincerely hope that this book finds a place in the bookshelves of all undergraduate students as well as junior residents of surgery.

Vipul D Yagnik

Preface to the First Edition

Surgery is a rapidly expanding branch of medical profession. With the introduction of minimally invasive surgery and other newer diagnostic and therapeutic modalities, the importance of open surgery is decreasing. But it remains essential for an undergraduate/postgraduate student of surgery to acquire basic knowledge of open surgical techniques.

During my final year of M.B.B.S, I encountered many difficulties in preparing for operative procedures. The idea behind writing this book is to help students overcome such difficulties.

In no way does this book pretend to be a comprehensive textbook of surgery. It is aimed to be a concise, yet useful aid to the students, covering basic operative procedures step by step and thus helping students during their exams. To my knowledge, no standard textbook has adopted such an approach of describing procedures step by step, right from indications to post-operative managements, along with basic knowledge of relevant anatomy or physiology and commonly asked practical questions.

I have tried to provide adequate information on basic operative procedure as well as instruments, solutions and X-rays, endoscopy, sterilization techniques and basic ward procedures. Original photographs of the procedures are included to reinforce understanding of details by the students. Lastly, I have included some important questions with answers that might help the students in the theory as well as viva voce examinations.

I have made utmost efforts to make this book as concise as possible without compromising the accuracy of the material. Although primarily designed for final year M.B.B.S students, this book will be beneficial to junior residents in surgery also in understanding various surgical procedures. Despite my best efforts, some errors might have crept in. Constructive criticism and valuable suggestions are always welcome.

I would like to thank Dr. B.C. Sharma, Senior Commissioning Editor, and Mr. Yagnesh Pandya, sales executive (Ahmedabad Branch) of B.I. Publications for their sincere efforts and constant support due to which publication of this book has become a reality.

Vipul D Yagnik

Acknowledgments

I would like to express my deepest appreciation to my family members. My mother (Narmadaben) and father (Dahyalal) have always been a great source of inspiration for me; without their blessings this project would not have been completed. My lovely wife (Parul), daughter (Nishtha), and son (Vansh) were always there with me throughout the journey of writing this book, and I will never forget the sacrifices they made for this project. I can also not forget the help of my brothers (Alpesh and Bhargav), my sister, brother in law, nephews (Kailash, Vikram kumar, and Mrunal), and my in-laws (Jagdish Chandra and Amrutaben). Without their steadfast support, this book would not have become a reality.

I would like to thank my colleagues and seniors, Dr Jignesh Rathod (Professor of Surgery), Dr Jitesh Desai (Professor of Surgery), Dr Shirish Srivastav (Professor of Surgery), from the Department of Surgery, Pramukhswami Medical College and Shree Krishna Hospital, Karamsad, and Dr Paresh Patel (Consultant Surgeon) from Shraddha Hospital, Borsad. I would also like to acknowledge the help provided by the management of Pramukhswami Medical College and Charutar Arogya Mandal, Karamsad, without which the first edition of this book might not have been possible. I am also thankful to the staff of the department of Pathology at Pramukhswami Medical College for helping me in the chapter on specimens. I would also like to express my gratitude to Dr Chirag Prajapati (Associate Professor of Surgery) and Dr Palekar (Professor of Surgery) at GMERS Medical College, Dharpur, Patan (Gujarat) for their help in the chapter on specimens.

A special thanks to Dr Dhaval Shah (Consultant Radiologist) at Sankar X-ray and Sonography Clinic, for his valuable help in preparing the chapter on radiological investigations. I would also like to acknowledge the help provided by Dr Jayesh Modi and the staff of Ronak Hospital (Rohit, Tofik, Suresh, Bharat, and Savita) for capturing the high-quality images during the operative procedures. I express my sincere thanks to Dr Gautam Suthar for providing images for chapter on minimal invasive urological procedures such as PCNL, URS, and TURP.

Moreover, I would like to acknowledge my friends, especially Dr Rajesh Bhanushali, Dr Ashwin D Patel, Rakesh Patel, Dr Deepak Mudgal, Dr Mansur Momin, Dr Mayank Patel, Dr Rajesh Oza, Dr Kamal Gupta, Dr Vismit Joshipura, and Dr Sunil Prajapati who had always been there to encourage me.

Finally, I would like to acknowledge the help of Dr Sushil Dawka, Academic Program Director and Professor of Surgery at SSR Medical College, Mauritius, who has been a great motivator and constant source of inspiration for me throughout the journey of writing this book. He has always been a great help to me whenever required.

Last but not the least I would like to thank the publisher, Wolters Kluwer, and in particular Sangeetha Parthasarathy (Publishing Manager), Dr Vandana Mittal (Publishing Manager), and Nayan Gogoi (Senior Production Editor), for their unwavering support during the lengthy time of development of this book. Their guidance and suggestions helped me overcome the many hurdles encountered during the process of publishing such a book.

To all those who have participated directly or indirectly in the creation and publication of this book, I thank you very much.

Vipul D Yagnik

Table of Contents at a Glance

Detailed Table of Contents

CHAPTER 1

Preoperative Preparation

PURPOSE

Before any operation, certain preoperative preparations are mandatory. Physical and psychological preparations are made according to the individual needs of the patient as well as the type of surgical procedure to be undertaken. Preoperative procedures are designed to improve the outcome of the surgery, decrease the risk for complications, and make the surgery as safe and effective as possible. In this chapter, we will discuss the general preoperative preparations needed to be carried out prior to a surgery.

CLASSIFICATION OF SURGERIES

Surgical procedures may be classified according to their seriousness (minor/major), urgency (elective/urgent), purpose (diagnostic/therapeutic), and specialty (neurosurgery/general surgery). A classification based on urgency may be made as described in Table 1.1.

PREOPERATIVE EVALUATION

Preoperative evaluation aims at assessing the condition of the patient on the basis of thorough history taking and examination, and preparing him/her for anesthesia administration and actual surgery. The ultimate goals of preoperative assessment are to reduce the patient's surgical and anesthetic perioperative morbidity or mortality, and to return him to desirable functioning as quickly as possible. Preoperative testing identifies patients with associated comorbidities who need further evaluation or treatment that helps in optimizing them for surgery. Preoperative assessment is based on careful history, a complete physical examination, and laboratory investigations.

History

Careful history includes the following: History of preexisting medical illness (especially cardiovascular and respiratory), history of operation, and operative complications. It also includes history of tobacco, alcohol, and/or drug use as well as the history of allergy. Inquire about use of anesthetic drugs and any adverse reaction to anesthetics during previous surgery, if any. A history of risk factors for deep vein thrombosis (DVT) should be taken. Patients with a high risk for DVT are those with the following:

- Major orthopedic surgery (hip and pelvic surgery)
- Oncosurgery
- Lower limb paralysis
- Major lower extremity amputation
- Heart failure and recent myocardial infarction (MI)
- Nephrotic syndrome, polycythemia, and homocystinemia

Table 1.1 Classification of Surgeries on the Basis of Urgency

Type of surgery	Description	Example
Emergency surgery	Operation is to be carried out immediately, along with resuscitation for life-threatening conditions	Rupture of aortic aneurysm
Urgent surgery	Operation should be carried out after resuscitation is over for potentially life-threatening conditions	Intestinal obstruction
Scheduled surgery	Early operation is required, but it is not an immediate threat to life	Cancer surgery
Elective surgery	Operation should be done at a time that is convenient to both the patient and the doctor	Lipoma excision

- Obesity, pregnancy, puerperium, and previous history of DVT or pulmonary embolism (PE)
- Hormone replacement therapy (HRT)
- Oral contraceptive pills (OCPs)

Clinical Examination

Medical examination includes the following:

- *Airway assessment*: See Chapter 3, *Anesthesia*
- *General examination*: Pallor; cyanosis; edema in feet, bone, joints, and spine; clubbing; jaundice; lymphadenopathy; and source of infection (leg ulcer, feet, etc.)
- *Cardiovascular system examination*: Along with routine cardiovascular examination such as pulse, blood pressure, heart sound, and bruits, signs of congestive cardiac failure (CCF), peripheral vascular (arterial and venous) disease, and valvular heart disease are specifically looked for
- *Respiratory system examination*: Respiratory rate, air entry, foreign sound, percussion note, and oxygen saturation
- *Abdominal system*: Lump, ascites, external genital, hernia, and bowel sounds
- *Neurological examination*: Consciousness level, muscle power, tone, and reflexes
- *Clinical findings*: The site and side of the surgery noted and the findings of the radiological investigation related to the pathology for which surgery is going to be carried out confirmed

Investigations

Low-risk procedures do not require routine investigations unless patients have an associated comorbid condition. The preoperative investigations depend on expected surgical blood loss during a procedure, age of the patient, presence of any existing medical condition, and history of medications. The recommended investigations are as follows:

- *Hematological*: Complete blood count (CBC), erythrocyte sedimentation rate (ESR), blood grouping and cross-matching, and coagulation studies
- *Biochemistry and urine analysis*: Blood sugar, renal function tests, liver function tests
- *Microbiology*: Sputum, methicillin-resistant *Staphylococcus aureus* (MRSA) screen, virology (HIV, HBsAg [surface antigen of the hepatitis B virus])
- *Radiological*: X-ray, ultrasound, computed tomography (CT), magnetic resonance imaging (MRI)
- *Pulmonary functions*: Pulmonary function tests, arterial blood gases (ABGs)
- *Cardiovascular function tests*: Electrocardiogram (ECG), echocardiogram, exercise testing

Hematological assessment

- *CBC*: It gives an idea about anemia, infection, and thrombocytopenia. It is indicated in patients with a history suggestive of underlying anemia, age >65 years, expected substantial blood loss (all intermediate and major surgeries in which estimated blood loss >500 mL), bleeding disorders, liver disease and splenomegaly, cardiac disease, recent chemotherapy, and chronic illness.
- *ESR*: It is performed to rule out chronic pathology.
- *Blood grouping and cross-matching*: If the risk of bleeding is:
  - *Low*: None required
  - *Low to moderate*: Type and screen required
  - *Moderate to high risk* (>500 mL): Type and cross-match required
- *Coagulation studies* are indicated in patients with:
  - Personal or family history of bleeding disorders
  - Conditions associated with an increased risk of bleeding:
    - History of alcohol abuse
    - Liver disease
    - Cholestasis
    - Eclampsia
    - Sepsis
  - History of treatment with anticoagulant or antithrombotic agents
  - Procedures with high expected blood loss such as craniotomy, cardiothoracic, and vascular procedures
  - Prior to epidural analgesia

The coagulation profile can be judged on the basis of:

- *Bleeding time, clotting time, prothrombin time (PT), and activated partial thromboplastin*

time (aPTT): To detect clotting disorders; corrected accordingly
- *Fibrinogen, fibrin degradation products, and D-dimer*: In case of suspected disseminated intravascular coagulation

Biochemistry

- *Tests for assessment of diabetic status*: These are blood sugar (fasting and postprandial) and glycated hemoglobin (HbA1c). These should be performed in patients with diabetes and other endocrine disorders. HbA1c gives an idea about control over a longer duration (120 days; red blood cell life span). Normal value or reference range is 4.8–5.9%.

Persistent hyperglycemia is associated with an increased risk of septic complications, vascular complications, and a longer hospital stay.

- *Renal function tests*
  - *Serum creatinine and blood urea*: To assess the function of kidney (70% of nephrons must be damaged to elevate serum creatinine); must be done in patients who satisfy the following requirements:
    - Age >50 years
    - Dehydrated
    - Genitourinary pathology, especially kidney
    - Major surgery
    - Hepatic, renal, and cardiac diseases
    - Long-term use of drugs such as digoxin, diuretic, angiotensin-converting enzyme (ACE) inhibitor, and nonsteroidal anti-inflammatory drugs (NSAIDs)
    - All vascular procedures
  - *Serum electrolytes*: Must be done in patients with:
    - Excessive vomiting and profuse diarrhea
    - Suspected significant blood loss
    - Major respiratory problem
    - Altered renal function
    - CCF
- *Liver function tests*: Must be done in patients with:
  - Significant alcohol consumption
  - Suspected liver pathology (primary)
  - Malignancy to rule out secondaries in liver
  - Biliary tract disorder
  - Known or suspected hepatitis
  - Poor nutritional reserve

  Some liver function tests are as follows:
    - Serum bilirubin, serum glutamic pyruvic transaminase (SGPT) or alanine aminotransferase (ALT), serum glutamic oxaloacetic transaminase (SGOT) or aspartate aminotransferase (AST), serum alkaline phosphatase. Serum bilirubin indicates the presence or absence of jaundice. Raised SGPT suggests hepatocellular pathology while raised alkaline phosphatase suggests obstructive jaundice.
    - *Serum protein*: It gives an idea about the nutritional status.
- *Urine analysis*: It is not a routine investigation. It should be done in patients with suspected genitourinary pathology. It should be done in the following cases:
  - To detect urinary tract infection (UTI)
  - Presence of bile salts and bile pigments
  - Glycosuria
  - Specific gravity
  - Urinary pH

  The interpretation of tests is performed as follows:
  - *Proteinuria*: Intrinsic renal disease and congestive heart failure (CHF)
  - *Urinary glucose*: Diabetes
  - *Ketones*: Starvation
  - *Microscopic hematuria*: Infection, calculi, and vascular disease
  - *Gross hematuria*: Malignancy
  - *Epithelial cells*: Poorly collected sample
  - *Pus cells*: Few in a female is normal but an increased number suggests infection
  - *β-Human chorionic gonadotropin* (pregnancy testing): Menstruating woman unable to assure that they are pregnant or if >30 days have passed since last menstrual period

Microbiology

- Serology for HbsAg and HIV: It is required in the following cases:
  - All high-risk patients
  - Patients who suffer from percutaneous exposure to HIV-infected blood (risk of transfusion: 0.25–0.30)
- Screening for MRSA from nostril, perineum, and axilla performed through swab: MRSA is associated with increased hospital morbidity

and mortality, prolonged hospitalization, and increased healthcare cost. Decolonization with antibacterial shampoo or soap and cream for 5 days is indicated in a positive case.

Radiological

Chest X-ray: Not indicated as a routine investigation. It is required in a patient with known or suspected pulmonary pathology or disease. X-ray may demonstrate:

- Chronic obstructive pulmonary disease (COPD)
- Pneumonia
- Atelectasis
- Pleural effusion

Radiological investigations are discussed in Chapter 9.

Cardiovascular

- *ECG*: It should be done in the following cases:
  - All patients older than 50 years
  - Family history of cardiac disease in a young adult
  - Patients with diabetes and hypertension
- *Noninvasive test*: It is done in patients who are at a risk of developing adverse cardiac event such as patients with peripheral vascular disease (PVD) diabetes, unexplained chest pain, and ECG abnormality.
  - Exercise stress test: Patients with exercise-induced ECG changes or inability to perform a modest level of activity have a high risk of a cardiac adverse event.
    - Rope jumping is excellent functional capacity while jogging and calisthenics are indicative of good functional status.
    - Moderate functional status or capacity is climbing a flight of steps, bicycling, and sexual activity.
    - Inability to perform daily routine activity indicates poor functional status.
  - Dobutamine stress echocardiography provides superior prognostic accuracy.
- *Invasive test*: Those who are identified as a high risk on noninvasive test should undergo angiography.

Pulmonary function tests

These are done to evaluate patients with unexplained dyspnea, chronic lung disease, and significant smoking. Tests are the following:

- Forced vital capacity (FVC) and forced expiratory volume during first second of FVC (FEV1). These tests are controversial and probably not required in stable patients undergoing nonthoracic surgery.
- *Preoperative pulmonary evaluation*: It is done as a part of history and clinical evaluation. In otherwise healthy patients, routine X-ray chest is not recommended. X-ray is suggested for acute symptoms, severe COPD, cardiac failure, lung cancer, metastasis, or effusion.
- *ABGs*: These are indicated in chronic lung disease, lung resection, preexisting hypoxia, or hypercapnia.

Preoperative risk assessment

The aim is to assess physical status. Various scoring systems are used:

- American Society of Anesthesiologists (ASA) classification
- Fleischer Risk Index for cardiac disease
- Child–Pugh scoring system for liver disease
- Goldman index for cardiac disease
- Glasgow Coma Scale for head Injury
- New York Heart Association (NYHA) scoring for heart disease

The most commonly used classification is ASA, which is the simplest. It has the following subclassifications:

- *ASA 1*: No systemic illness
- *ASA 2*
  - Mild to moderate systemic disturbance
  - Social alcohol drinker
  - Pregnancy
  - Well-controlled diabetes/hypertension
  - Obesity (30 < BMI < 40)
  - Old age
- *ASA 3*
  - Severe systemic illness
  - Angina
  - Alcohol dependence
  - Cardiac failure (moderate reduction of ejection fraction)
  - Uncontrolled DM/HT
  - BMI >40

- History (>3 months) of MI, cerebrovascular accident (CVA), transient ischemic attack (TIA), or coronary artery disease (CAD)/stents
- *ASA 4*
  - Life-threatening severe systemic illness
  - Not always correctable by operation
  - Liver failure
  - Respiratory failure
  - History (<3 months) of MI, CVA, TIA, or CAD/stents
  - Marked cardiac insufficiency (severe reduction of ejection fraction)
- *ASA 5*: Moribund—very low possibility of survival even after operation

For emergency operation, the letter E is added after the numerical classification.

PREMEDICATION

- *Inj. tetanus toxoid 0.5 mg intramuscular* (IM): It is given as a prophylaxis against tetanus
- *Tab. bisacodyl* (Dulcolax[R]) *2 HS* ('hora somni'; at the hour of sleep): It is a laxative. It is given to prevent contamination of the operative site/theater by passing of stools on the operative table, because anesthesia leads to relaxation of anal sphincter.
- *Tab. diazepam 1 HS*: It provides relief from apprehension and anxiety.
- *Inj. atropine 0.6 mg 30 minutes before operative procedure* (for minor procedures): It reduces salivary and bronchial secretion, prevents laryngospasm, and prevents vasovagal attack.

Glycopyrronium bromide can be used instead of atropine, especially in patients with tachycardia and cardiac problems, and in children.

Advantages over atropine are as follows:

- Does not cross blood–brain barrier
- Less tachycardia and arrhythmia
- Better suppression of gastric acid
- More potent in drying salivary secretion (dose: 0.2–0.4 mg)

- *Antibiotics*: If antibiotics are given as a prophylaxis, they should be used when local wound defenses are not established (the decisive period).

  Preoperative intravenous (IV) antibiotics are administered within 60 minutes before skin incision (120 minutes for vancomycin and fluoroquinolones).[1] Single dose is usually sufficient. Repeat dose at appropriate intervals, usually 3 hours for abdominal operation.
  - Optimal timing to administer preoperative antibiotic is controversial. According to National Institute for Health and Care Excellence (NICE) guidelines, antibiotics should be administered at the time of induction of anesthesia. Repeat dose is given if the duration of surgery is longer than half life of the antibiotic.[2]
  - In clean, nonprosthetic surgery, no antibiotic prophylaxis is required.
  - Antibiotic prophylaxis is indicated in most clean-contaminated and contaminated cases.
  - Antibiotics for dirty surgery are therapeutic rather than prophylactic.
  - Antibiotics used for prophylaxis should be safe and narrow spectrum.
  - There is no conclusive evidence that further dose of antibiotic as a prophylaxis after surgery is of any value and it should not be used beyond 24 hours.
- *Stress ulcer prophylaxis* (Histamine H2-receptor antagonist or proton pump inhibitor): It is to be given at the time of induction. Routine use is not recommended in elective operation when patients are not critically ill except in patients with hiatus hernia, obesity, pregnancy, and diabetes.

Specific Preoperative Premedication

Preparations specific to the operation are as follows:

- Upper gastrointestinal tract (GIT)
  - *Patient may be anorexic*: Correction of nutritional status and electrolyte imbalance
  - *Patient may have persistent vomiting*: Correction of nutritional status, dehydration, and electrolyte imbalance
  - *Perforation and obstruction*: Nasogastric tube
- Large bowel surgery
  - Bowel preparation. It is contraindicated in perforation and obstruction.
  - Explain the risk of pelvic nerve injury in rectal surgery.
  - Explain about the possible need of colostomy or ileostomy.

- Liver, pancreas, and biliary tract
  - Patients with long-term jaundice may have deficiency of fat-soluble vitamins including vitamin K. Deficiency of vitamin K–dependent coagulation factors may lead to bleeding problems, so injection of vitamin K is required.
  - Routine preoperative drainage of biliary system in obstructive jaundice is not indicated except in symptomatic hyperbilirubinemia.
  - To prevent hepatorenal shutdown, adequate preoperative hydration is mandatory.
  - Antibiotic prophylaxis is routine in obstructive jaundice patients to prevent postoperative infection.
  - Cholangitis needs urgent biliary drainage (endoscopic retrograde cholangiopancreatography [ERCP] or percutaneous transhepatic biliary drainage [PTBD]).
  - In patients with cirrhosis, correct coagulopathy with vitamin K or fresh frozen plasma (FFP). Avoid operating on decompensated cirrhosis.
  - In major pancreatic surgery, consider giving octreotide.
- Thyroid surgery
  - Preoperative antithyroid drugs to prevent thyrotoxic crisis
  - Laryngoscopy to check vocal cord movement
  - CT scan for retrosternal goiter

PREOPERATIVE PREPARATION OF THE PATIENT

- In preoperative preparation, the patient needs to be cleaned. A minimum preoperative hospital stay is advised. The steps given in the next subsections are recommended.
- Written and informed consent should be obtained (to be taken by surgical team, preferably by the operating surgeon). It is explained in Chapter 2, *Written Informed Consent*.
- The patient should be given a preoperative shower with chlorhexidine the night prior and few hours of the surgery.
- There should be no intake by mouth from 10 pm on the day before surgery if surgery is planned in the early morning and/or for at least 6 hours for solids and semisolids and 2–4 hours for liquids (isotonic drinks and water). Infants are allowed mother's milk up to 4 hours and cow's milk up to 6 hours before surgery.
- Patients on antihypertensive or anti-ischemic drugs, respiratory medicines, anticonvulsants, and antipsychotic drugs should take the medication with sips of water on the morning of surgery.
- Soap water enema should be given on the night before surgery and early in the morning (to prevent contamination of the operative site/theater by passing of stools on the operative table), because anesthesia leads to relaxation of anal sphincter.
- Do not remove hair from the operative site unless necessary to execute the surgery. Preoperative shaving on the day before surgery may lead to laceration and infection; so, if hair removal is required, it is advisable to do shaving on the operation table, or use clipper or depilation cream for hair removal. Clipper is preferred.
- Preoperative painting with antiseptic solution. Painting includes skin incision site as well as a wide area around it. It starts from the incision site and working away from it. Contaminated area such as groin, perineum, umbilicus, and axilla should be painted last.
- Prepping with chlorhexidine–alcohol scrub is superior to prepping with povidone–iodine scrub. It decreases both superficial and deep wound infections.
- Drapes should be handled by scrubbed personnel. Once in place, drapes should not be disturbed. They should allow full access to the incision and possible extension too.
- Adherent plastic film placed on the exposed skin reduces the chance of contamination from the surrounding skin.
- Preoperative order should mention the time at which the patient is to be shifted to the operation theater.
- The patient should be wearing operative dress and not his/her own clothes.

PREOPERATIVE PREPARATION FOR THE SURGEON

Special care has to be taken in maintaining sterilization with regard to disinfection of hands, dress for the operation theater, and surgical instruments. Most infections in the hospitals are transferred from the hands; so hand washing is the best, safest, cheapest, and simplest way of controlling the infections.

Disinfection of Hands

- Hands should be washed thoroughly and properly before and after removal of gloves (Fig. 1.1).
- Upper extremity should be thoroughly washed from hand to elbow, with removal of soap in the direction from hand to elbow.
- Use a liquid soap or a detergent cream containing hexachlorophane 2–3%, or wash with povidone–iodine surgical scrub for 3–5 minutes. Washing hands with detergents cleans the hands and reduces the germ count by a factor of 100. Long-time and vigorous scrubbing may damage the skin and increase the risk of infections.
- After washing, any remaining soap is rinsed off thoroughly and the hand dried gently with a clean, dry, and, if possible, autoclaved towel. After that, apply a disinfectant such as a combination of ethanol, 1-propanol, and 2-propanol at a level of 80% (v/v), to which skin care components are added.

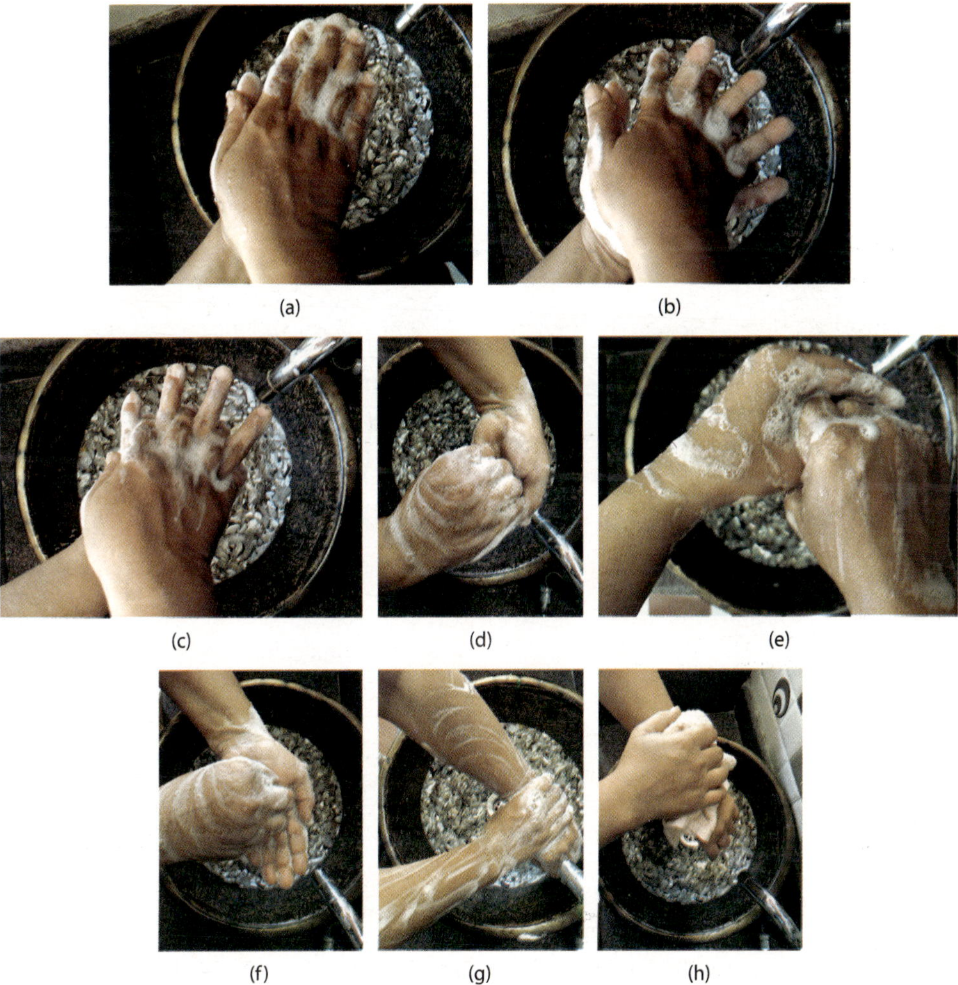

Figure 1.1 Steps in hand washing. (a) Rub palms together, (b) rubbing palms with fingers interlaced, (c) rub palms over the dorsum with fingers interlaced, (d) interlock fingers and rub back of the fingers, (e) rotational rubbing of thumb, (f) rotational rubbing of backward and forward of finger tips, (g) rubbing of wrist with hand, (h) dry with clean sterile towel.

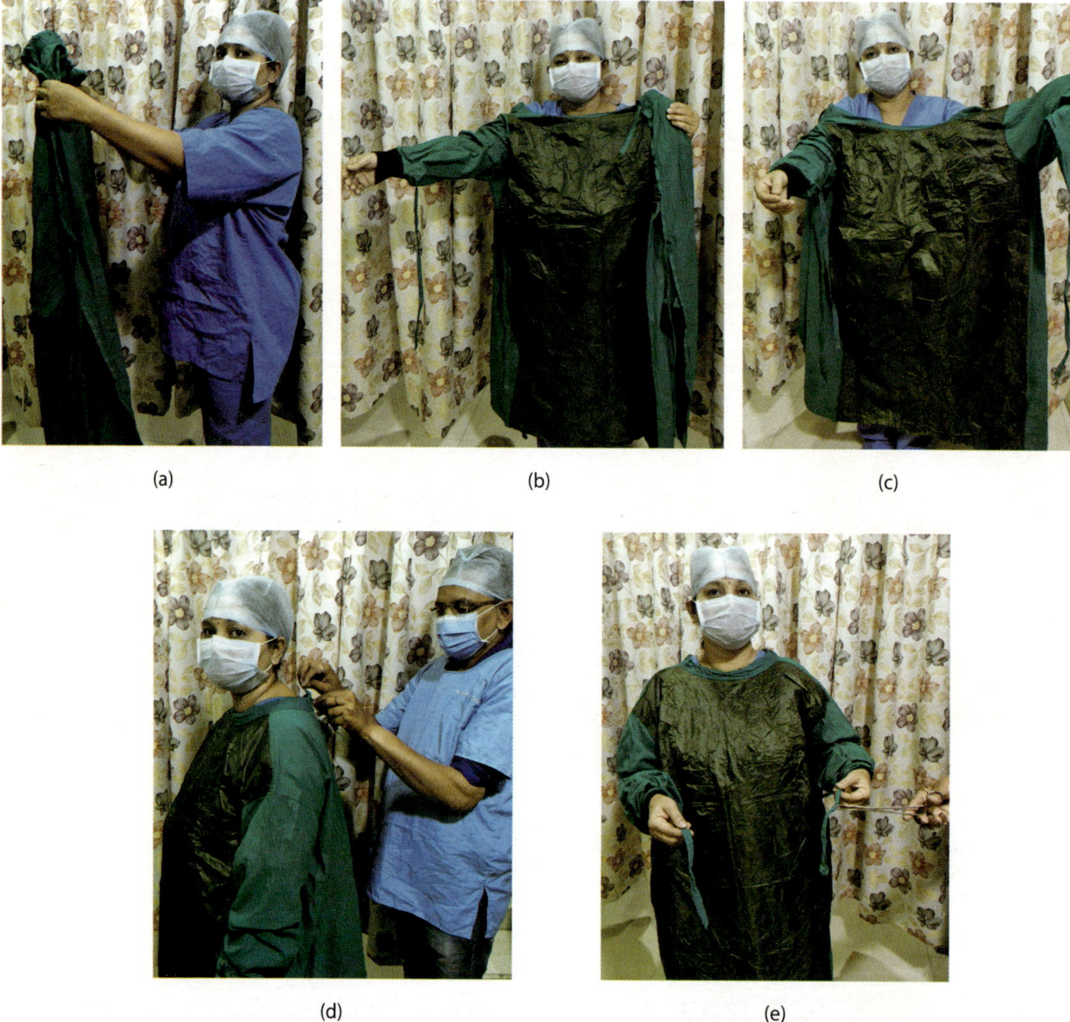

(a) (b) (c) (d) (e)

Figure 1.2 Gown wearing procedure. (a) Unfold the gown and hold it from back, (b) place hands and arms through the sleeves, (c) place opposite hand and arm through sleeve, (d) an assistant fastens the neck tie, (e) close gowning—the sterile tie is grasped by the surgeon or scrubbed nurse and other sterile tie is given by the assistant.

Dress

Surgeons and operative auxiliaries must wear newly laundered dress, gowns, face masks, caps, and rubber operating boots or special overshoes in the operating theater.

Wearing the gown

A special procedure is used for wearing the gown to maintain sterilization (Fig. 1.2). The gown is held at an arm's length with inner surface facing the operator. First one arm and then the other is thrust into the sleeves, followed by slipping the gown on, without touching its external surface with the bare hands. Then waist tapes are seized by a nurse and tied behind the back of the surgeon without touching the gown.

Hand gloving procedure

While gloving the hands, first the left glove is picked up, where the cuff is folded back on itself (Fig. 1.3). Using the right hand, the glove is slipped

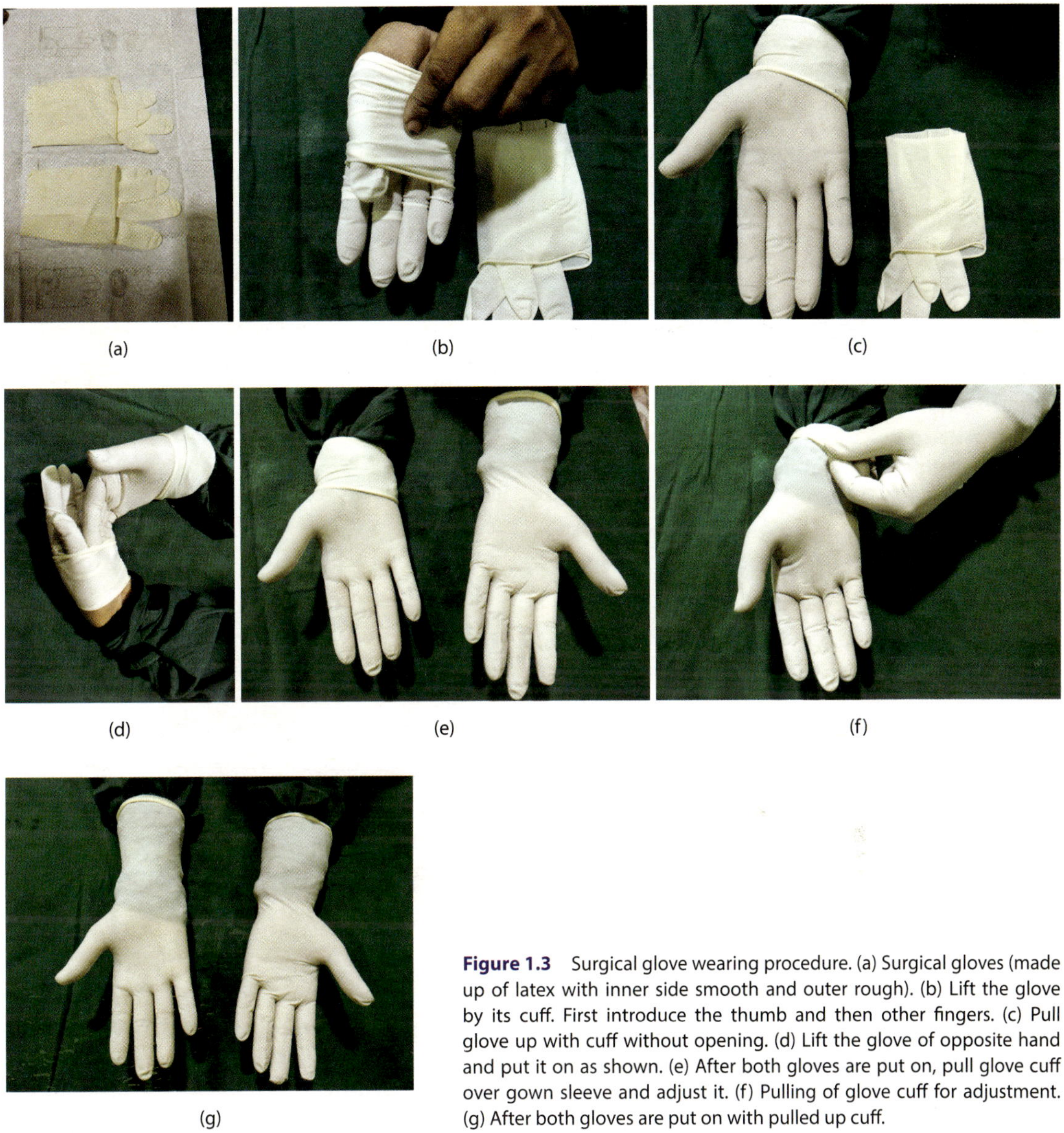

(a) (b) (c)

(d) (e) (f)

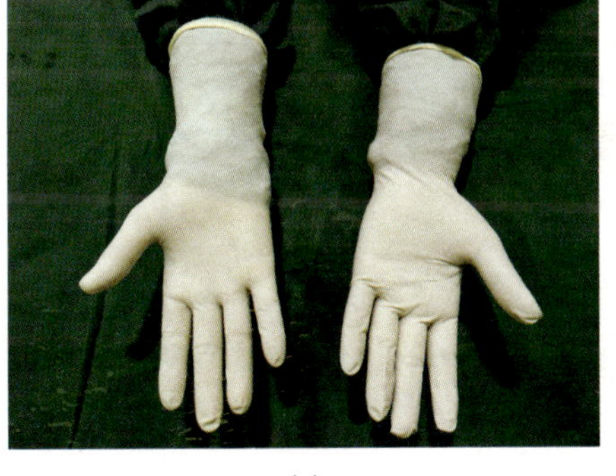

(g)

Figure 1.3 Surgical glove wearing procedure. (a) Surgical gloves (made up of latex with inner side smooth and outer rough). (b) Lift the glove by its cuff. First introduce the thumb and then other fingers. (c) Pull glove up with cuff without opening. (d) Lift the glove of opposite hand and put it on as shown. (e) After both gloves are put on, pull glove cuff over gown sleeve and adjust it. (f) Pulling of glove cuff for adjustment. (g) After both gloves are put on with pulled up cuff.

over the left hand leaving the cuff over the palm of the glove. Then, the right glove is grasped with the right hand at the folded cuff and the gloved fingers of the left hand slided between the palm of the glove and the cuff by thrusting the right hand into the glove. Then the sleeve of the gown is folded and adjusted on the left side and the cuff is drawn back over the sleeve at the wrist. The same procedure is repeated for the right cuff and glove.

Gloves are important as they prevent contamination of wounds and protect the surgical team from blood and body fluids of patients. They should be changed if there is suspicion of perforation.

Surgical instruments

Use a separate set of well-sterilized/disinfected instrument (explained in Chapter 10, *Sterilization*).

STANDARD PRECAUTIONS IN PATIENTS WITH HIV OR HBsAg[3]

The Centers for Disease Control and Prevention (CDC) has developed a strategy of universal precautions, which state that all patients coming for invasive procedures should be considered potentially infective.

Universal precaution is applied only to the blood and body fluids such as semen and vaginal secretions that have been implicated in the transmission of blood-borne infections. It does not apply to the feces, urine, nasal secretion, sweat, and vomitus, which were later included under the term body substance isolation (BSI).

Standard precautions include universal precautions as well as BSI.

- Hand washing: Hands must be washed with soap and water before and after contact with the patient.
- Protective barrier
  - Impervious gloves
  - Eye protection with spectacles
  - Mask
  - Face shield
  - Impervious gown
  - Shoes
- Sharp handling
  - Used needles should not be recapped.
  - All used sharps should be placed in a puncture-resistant box that should not be overfilled.
  - Use an instrument to grasp the needle, retract the wound, and load and unload the needle.
  - Avoid hand-to-hand passage (use kidney tray).
  - When appropriate, use alternating cutting methods such as electrocautery.
  - Use newer techniques such as needle-less system, retractile lancet, and closed blood collecting system.
- Patient care equipment
  - Patient care equipment and linen soiled with blood and other body fluids should be handled in a manner that prevents skin and mucous membrane exposure.
  - Reusable instruments should not be used until they have been properly cleaned and reprocessed.
- Patient placement: The patient should be placed in a private room.

Additional precautions required are as follows:

- Minimum surgical assistants
- Meticulous hemostasis
- Operation to be performed in a slow and methodical manner
- Use of staple device instead of suturing
- Operation theater staff should be informed about the high-risk patients and they are expected to maintain a high degree of discipline.
- Senior and experienced staff should be scrubbed and unnecessary instruments must be removed from the field.

SPECIFIC PREOPERATIVE PROBLEMS AND MANAGEMENT

Cardiac Disease

Those patients who have a good effort tolerance such as climbing a flight of stairs without getting breathless or having chest pain have a lower perioperative cardiac morbidity and mortality than those who do not have such tolerance.

Risk factors for cardiac morbidity

The American College of Cardiology (ACC) and the American Heart Association (AHA) in 2007 stratified cardiac risk factors into three categories:

1. Factors that need further evaluation
   - Unstable coronary syndrome
     - Unstable angina: Elective operation must be postponed.
   - *Decompensated heart failure*: Patients should be treated and optimized before surgery.
   - *Significant arrhythmias*: Supraventricular and ventricular arrhythmias have been identified as independent risk factors. Cardiac output can increase by 15% once sinus rhythm has been restored.
   - Severe valvular heart disease such as severe aortic and mitral stenosis may benefit from valvuloplasty before undergoing elective noncardiac surgery. All patients must take antibiotic prophylaxis to prevent infective endocarditis.
2. Factors that may affect outcome
   - History of ischemic heart disease
     - *Recent MI*: Elective surgery should be postponed for 3–6 months.

- History of CVA: History of TIA or stroke
- Compensated or previous heart failure
- Renal insufficiency: Serum creatinine >2 mg/dL
- Diabetes

3. Factors not proven to increase the risk
   - Advanced age
   - Abnormal ECG
   - Rhythm other than sinus
   - Uncontrolled systemic hypertension (blood pressure should be controlled to near 160/90 mmHg)

Preoperative management in cardiac patients

- Patients with pacemaker
  - Turn the pacemaker to uninhibited mode.
  - Use bipolar cautery.
  - If unipolar is a must, then ground plate should be as far as possible from the heart.
- Internal defibrillator: It should be turned off.
- Beta-blockers, digoxin, and calcium channel blocker should be started preoperatively in order to control the rate and possible rhythm in dysrhythmias. Beta-blockers reduce perioperative ischemia and may reduce the risk of MI and cardiovascular death in high-risk patients (POISE trial). Dose should be titrated to maintain heart rate between 60 and 80/min in the absence of hypotension.
- Patients with angioplasty: Postpone nonurgent surgery in case of balloon angioplasty <14 days, bare metal stent <6 weeks, and drug-eluting stent <12 months.
- Symptomatic heart block and asymptomatic second- and third-degree blocks will require temporary cardiac pacemaker insertion.

Renal Evaluation

Underlying conditions leading to chronic renal failure, such as diabetes and hypertension, should be stabilized prior to elective surgery. Serum creatinine level of 2.0 mg/dL or more is an independent risk factor for cardiac complications. It is also associated with an increased risk of MI, CAD, delayed wound healing, wound infection, platelet dysfunction, and bleeding.

UTI should be treated before embarking on elective surgery where infection carries dire consequences such as surgery where prosthesis is required.

History

- Cardiac risk
- Sign of fluid overload such as raised JVP and pulmonary crepitations
- Timing of last dialysis
- Preoperative weight
- Amount of fluid removed

Investigations

- CBC: Anemia
- Serum creatinine
- Blood urea nitrogen (BUN)
- Electrolytes: Sodium, potassium, bicarbonate, calcium, phosphorus, and magnesium

Management

Appropriate arrangement should be made to treat acid–base and electrolyte imbalance.

In dialysis-dependent patients, it should be performed few hours before surgery and after last dialysis, blood sample should be sent for CBC and urine examination.

Invasive monitoring is required in major surgery as both hypovolemia and volume overload are poorly tolerated.

Anemia associated with chronic renal failure is well tolerated and usually perioperative blood transfusion is not required.

Factors associated with an increased risk of renal dysfunction are the following: Bleeding, hypovolemia, cardiac failure, intraoperative hypotension, sepsis, use of nephrotoxic drugs, contrast media, aortic cross-clamping, myoglobinuria, preoperative elevated BUN and/or creatinine, and postrenal obstruction.

Prevention

Adequate hydration is the most important preventive measure because all mechanisms of renal failure are exacerbated by renal hypoperfusion.

Contrast-induced nephropathy can be prevented by the following: Adequate hydration, low-osmolality agents, a bicarbonate drip, and oral *N*-acetylcysteine.

Avoid nephrotoxic drugs such as NSAIDs and aminoglycoside.

Diabetes

- In case of diabetes, perform preoperative assessment of cardiac risk, wound infection, renal function, and blood pressure changes (due to autonomic neuropathy). Diabetic patients experience more infectious complications and have delayed wound healing.

- Any history of hyperglycemic and hypoglycemic episodes and hospital admissions should be noted.
- Diabetes and associated complications should be as near normal level as possible before elective surgery.
- Statins (lipid-lowering agents) should be added if the patient has a high risk for cardiovascular complications.
- Diet-controlled diabetic patients can be safely managed without food and infusion of glucose.

For management of adults with diabetes undergoing surgery and elective procedures, ensure that glycemic control is optimized prior to surgery, aiming for an HbA1c of less than 69 mmol/mL (8.5%), if it is safe to do so.[4]

Type I patients

- Whenever possible, diabetic patients should be first on the list of patients to be operated to minimize the period of fasting (minimal disruption of their diet and medications).
- Optimal perioperative blood sugar is <180 mg/dL.
- For patients receiving once-daily injection (morning or evening), reduce dose by 20% the day prior to surgery. For those who are on more than twice-daily injection, no dose adjustment is required on the day before surgery.
- On the day of surgery (am or pm surgery), for patients receiving injection
  - *Once daily:* For evening regimen, check glucose; for morning regimen, reduce dose by 20% and check glucose.
  - *Twice daily*: Halve the usual morning dose and check glucose.
  - *Twice-daily separate injections* (short acting and intermediate acting): Calculate the total dose of both morning insulins and give half as intermediate acting only in the morning. Check blood glucose on admission.
- Standard combination of 16 units short-acting insulin + 20 mEq KCl in 500 mL 10% glucose is infused at 100 mL/hour during surgery.
- Depending on the blood sugar monitoring every 1 hour, additional insulin can be given.
- Postoperative insulin is maintained until the patient is able to eat.
- Glucose level is checked every 1–2 hours.

Type II patients

- On the day prior to surgery (oral antidiabetics): Take medication as normal.
- On the day of surgery
  - For early morning or am surgery
    - Omit morning dose of acarbose, meglitinide, metformin, sulfonylurea, and SGLT-2 (sodium/glucose cotransporter 2) inhibitors (e.g., dapagliflozin, canagliflozin, empagliflozin).
    - Take the following as normal: Pioglitazone, dipeptidyl peptidase IV (DPP IV) inhibitor (e.g., sitagliptin, vildagliptin, saxagliptin, alogliptin, linagliptin), and glucagon-like peptide 1 (GLP-1) analog (e.g., exenatide, liraglutide, lixisenatide, dulaglutide).
  - For pm surgery
    - Take as normal: Pioglitazone, DPP IV inhibitor (e.g., sitagliptin, vildagliptin, saxagliptin, alogliptin, linagliptin), and GLP-1 analog (e.g., exenatide, liraglutide, lixisenatide, dulaglutide)
    - Omit on day of surgery: SGLT-2 inhibitors (e.g. dapagliflozin, canagliflozin, empagliflozin), metformin, sulfonylurea
    - If patient is not NBM: Acarbose and meglitinide given
- Patients with fasting blood sugar (FBS) <144 mg/dL can be treated as nondiabetic (only for preoperative purpose). Patients with FBS <126 mg/dL are considered nondiabetic as a standard definition.
- Other precautions are similar to those for type I patients.

Infection

Classification of surgical wounds

Surgical wounds are classified as shown in Table 1.2.

The following are the high risk factors for developing surgical site infection: Extremes of age, length of preoperative stay, diabetes, smoking (nicotine use), steroid, obesity, remote active infection, malnutrition, chronic illness, immunosuppression, preoperative nares colonization with *S. aureus*, and perioperative leukocyte containing allergenic blood transfusion

Table 1.2 Classification of Surgical Wounds*

Type of wound	Surgery/procedure	Infection rate (%)	Antibiotic prophylaxis
Clean: Clean surgery, no viscus opened	Hernia, lumpectomy or wide excision for breast lumps, thyroid surgery, etc.	1–2	No antibiotic; indicated only in patients in whom prosthesis is required
Clean contaminated: Viscus opened, with minimal contamination	Esophagogastric and biliary surgery, hysterectomy, elective colon resection	<10	Preoperative single-shot antibiotic and no evidence that supports continuation of antibiotic after skin closure
Contaminated: Viscus opened, with gross spillage	Peritonitis (biliary), penetrating abdominal trauma, rectal surgery, perforated appendix, and resection of unprepared bowel	15–20	Single-dose antibiotic and need for continuation of antibiotic tailored according to the patient's wound condition
Dirty: Gross contamination	Incision and drainage for abscess, debridement for necrotizing wound, fecal peritonitis	<40	Skin closure generally not recommended; therapeutic antibiotic for 5 days

*Defined by American College of Surgeons National Surgical Quality Improvement Program (ACS NSQIP).

Operative issues leading to SSI are as follows: Preoperative shaving, preoperative skin preparation, skin antisepsis, duration of scrub and hand washing, operating room ventilation, duration of operation, and poor surgical technique (poor hemostasis, failure to obliterate dead space, etc.), drain placement, inadequate antibiotic prophylaxis, and hypothermia.

Types of surgery are also correlated with wound infection: Clean surgery has an infection rate of 1–2% while in dirty surgery it may reach up to 40%.

CDC guidelines for prevention of surgical site infection should be followed along with few additional factors.

Preoperative measures

- Regular and timely surveillance for operating room ventilation and instrument sterilization
- Identification and treatment of remote infection before surgery
- Minimum preoperative stay
- Hyperglycemia controlled in the perioperative period
- Tobacco smoking ceased 30 days prior to surgery
- Antiseptic shower night prior to surgery

In operation theater

- Hospital staff with open and infected skin lesion should not be allowed in the theater.
- The number of staff and movement in and out from the theater should be kept to minimum.
- Do not remove hair routinely; use electric clipper if it is required.
- Hand scrub practice should be followed by the surgical team.
- Appropriate antimicrobial prophylaxis should be provided.
- Surgical barriers such as gloves and gown should be used.
- Antiseptic skin preparation should be present.
- Avoid hematoma and dead space.
- There should be limited electrocautery use.
- Avoid hypothermia and give supplemental oxygen in the recovery room.
- Do not close contaminated skin incision.

Antibiotic prophylaxis

The type of surgical wound determines the need for antibiotic prophylaxis. Usually broad-spectrum antibiotics are used. For details, see Table 1.2.

Coagulation and Antithrombotic Medication

The British Committee for Standards in Hematology does not recommend routine preoperative coagulation testing. Indications for testing have been already discussed.

The primary indications for chronic anticoagulation include the following:

- Atrial fibrillation
- Embolism associated with mechanical heart valve
- Venous thromboembolism

It is advisable to keep preoperative international normalized ratio (INR) <1.5. For those who are on anticoagulation and whose INR is maintained between 2.0 and 3.0, withhold medication for 4–5 days, and patients with INR of >3 are required to withhold medication for a few more days. In high-risk patients, get the INR done on the day before surgery. In emergency operation where there is no time to reverse the effect of anticoagulant, FFP must be administered. Bridging anticoagulation is recommended in those who are on oral anticoagulants. Either low-molecular-weight heparin (LMWH) or unfractionated heparin (UFH) is given when oral anticoagulant is stopped and required to withhold as suggested in Table 1.3.

Aspirin should be withheld especially in surgery where risk of hemorrhage is high such as transurethral resection of the prostate (TURP) and where small hemorrhage would have catastrophic consequences such as retinal surgery (also see Table 1.3).

Patients with bare metal stent <6 weeks and drug-eluting stent within 12 months of surgery should continue aspirin and clopidogrel as the risk of thrombosis and infarct is very high.

Medication associated with an increased risk of bleeding should be withheld for a variable period of 5–7 days (e.g., aspirin, clopidogrel).

Antithrombotic prophylaxis should be commonly started, in case of major surgery, with low-molecular-weight heparin (LMWH), unfractionated heparin (UFH), or fondaparinux.

Venous thromboembolism prophylaxis guidelines in surgical patients are as follows:

- *Low-risk patients* (such as minor surgery in fully mobile patients and major surgery in patients <40 years of age with no risk factors): Early aggressive ambulation
- *Moderate-risk patients* (major surgery in patients >40 years of age and with associated risk factors, and minor surgery in patients with a previous history of DVT or PE): LMWH, UFH, or fondaparinux and mechanical (external pneumatic compression) thromboprophylaxis
- *High-risk patients* (major orthopedic surgery, oncosurgery, major trauma, lower limb major amputation, lower limb paralysis): LMWH, fondaparinux, and warfarin; mechanical (external pneumatic compression)

Table 1.3 Withhold Interval for Anticoagulant Drugs

Drugs	Withhold interval
Aspirin and clopidogrel	5–7 days (at least 5 days)
Warfarin	5
Low-molecular-weight heparin	24 hours
UFH	4–6 hours

Anemia and Blood Transfusion

Need for perioperative blood transfusion should be tailored according to patients. However, the general recommendation according to the ASA states that blood transfusion is almost always required when hemoglobin value is <6 g/dL and is usually not required if hemoglobin is >10 g/dL. Some authorities recommend blood transfusion at the hemoglobin level of <8 g/dL in major surgery. Follow restrictive transfusion policy at a concentration of 8 g/dL in most patients (Table 1.4).

In patients with ongoing ischemia, it is recommended to maintain hemoglobin at 10 g/dL or greater.

Transfusion recommendations in acute anemia are as follows:

- Up to 30% blood loss (up to 1.5 L): Transfusion unnecessary unless preexisting anemia or cardiac problem exists
- Thirty to 40% (1.5–2 L): Transfusion probably required
- >40% (>2 L): Transfusion required.

AABB guidelines also state that decision to transfuse blood should not be based only on hemoglobin level but should incorporate individual patient characteristics and clinical symptoms.

Nutritional Status

Poor nutritional status is associated with delayed wound healing, increased risk of infection, prolonged hospital stay, delayed recovery of bowel function, and increased incidence of mortality.

Table 1.4 Guidelines for Blood Transfusion in Hemodynamically Stable Patients (Not Actively Bleeding)[5]

Hemoglobin level	Transfusion
<6 g/dL	Transfusion recommended
6–7 g/dL	Transfusion almost always indicated
7–8 g/dL	Transfusion may be indicated in patients undergoing orthopedic surgery, cardiac surgery, or any major surgery as well as patients with stable cardiovascular problem
8–10 g/dL	Transfusion generally not indicated, but should be considered in symptomatic anemia, ongoing bleeding, ongoing ischemia, and severe thormbocytopenia
10 g/dL	Transfusion generally not indicated except in exceptional circumstances

Undernutrition

BMI <18.5 indicates nutritional impairment and <15 is associated with significant postoperative mortality. Whenever possible, at least 2 weeks of nutritional support should be given preoperatively. Morbid obesity, BMI >35, is associated with significant postoperative morbidity and mortality. If possible, the patient is advised to lose weight. If this does not work, prophylactic measure for acid suppression and DVT should be taken care of and explained to the patient.

Preoperative hypoalbuminemia is associated with postoperative morbidity and mortality. Correction of albumin level is associated with a significant survival advantage.

Oral nutritional supplementation for 5–7 days is given to those patients who are nutritionally at risk.

Surgery is postponed for those patients who are at a severe nutritional risk (BMI <18.5 kg/m^2, weight loss >10–15% within 6 months, and serum albumin <30 g/L) until nutritional deficit is corrected.

Enteral is the preferred route whenever feasible. Parenteral nutrition is used in case of nonfunctioning bowel and short gut syndrome.

Irrespective of the baseline nutritional status, supplementation of immunomodulating substances such as arginine (stimulates T-cell function and improves microcirculation), glutamine (source of metabolic fuel and T-lymphocyte response preserved), and omega-3 fatty acid (anabolic effect) improves surgical outcome.

Obesity

The goal is to identify and modify the risk factors for better perioperative management.

In patients with BMI >40 or >35 kg/m^2 with comorbid condition, perioperative mortality risk is very high.

Take at least X-ray chest and 12-lead ECG.

Obese patients are more likely to have essential hypertension, left ventricular hypertrophy, ischemic heart disease, and congestive heart failure.

Obesity is also a risk factor for surgical site infection, DVT, and PE.

Adrenocortical Suppression

Those patients who are on long-term oral steroids will require adrenocortical suppression and extra dose of steroid should be given around the time of surgery to prevent Addisonian crisis.

Management options for the steroid replacement in the perioperative period are as follows:

- Hydrocortisone 25 mg IV at the time of induction followed by 100 mg IV infusion over 24-hour period
- Hydrocortisone 100 mg IV before, during, and after surgery

Neurological and Psychiatric Problems

Anticonvulsant and antiparkinson drugs should be continued and lithium should be stopped 24 hours prior to surgery. Anesthesiologists should be made aware about the psychiatric medications taken by the patient as many psychiatric drugs such as tricyclic antidepressants and monoamine oxidase inhibitors interact with anesthetic drugs.

Those who are having a previous history of stroke or neurological problem and are on antiplatelets and anticoagulants should follow the guidelines given earlier.

The risk factors that make a patient high risk for CVA are the following: Previous history of CVA, hypertension, smoking, cardiovascular disease, diabetes, etc. Elective surgery in a patient with recent CVA should be delayed for at least 4–6 weeks.

References

1. Anderson DJ, Podgorny K, Berríos-Torres SI, et al. Strategies to prevent surgical site infections in acute care hospitals: 2014 update. Infect Control Hosp Epidemiol 2014;35(6):605–27.
2. https://www.nice.org.uk/guidance/CG74/chapter/1-Guidance#preoperative-phase. Last accessed on 30th March, 2018
3. Bolyard EA, Tablan OC, Williams WW, et al. Guideline for infection control in health care personnel, 1998. Available at https://www.cdc.gov/hicpac/pdf/infectcontrol98.pdf. Last accessed 30th March, 2018, pp 291–354.
4. Dhatariya K, Levy N, Flanagan D, et al. Joint British Diabetes Societies for Inpatient care (JBDS-IP): Management of adults with diabetes undergoing surgery and elective procedures: Improving standards (revised March 2016). Available at https://www.diabetes.org.uk/professionals/position-statements-reports/specialist-care-for-children-and-adults-and-complications/management-of-adults-with-diabetes-undergoing-surgery-and-elective-procedures-improving-standards. Last accessed 30th March, 2018.
5. Carson JL, Guyatt G, Heddle NM, et al. Clinical Practice Guidelines From the AABB: Red Blood Cell Transfusion Thresholds and Storage. JAMA 2016;316(19):2025.

CHAPTER 2

Written Informed Consent

CONSENT (SECTION 13 OF INDIAN CONTRACT ACT, 1872)

When two or more persons agree upon the same thing in the same sense, they are said to consent. Consent is a must for all medical examinations, investigations, and procedures. It may be simple verbal consent for examination or informed written consent for procedures. Consent is not only a formality but also a legal requirement. It is a process, not a single event. We should give sufficient time to the patients whenever possible to retain, process, understand, and weigh up information to give valid consent. Oral consent is a good consent but it is very hard to prove in retrospect while written informed consent provides a record. The term informed consent was first used in 1957 by California appellate court.

Various sections dealing with consent in Indian Penal Code (IPC) are the following:

- *IPC Sections 87 and 88*: Harm is done in good faith and for the benefit of the consenting individual (exemption of liability).
- *IPC Section 89*: Act is done in good faith for the benefit of a child or an insane person. Consent is given by the guardian or a person who has an authority to give consent.
- *IPC Section 90*: If consent is obtained by coercion (fear of injury), undue influence, misrepresentation or misconception, and fraud, it is not valid.
- Consent given by a person is not valid if he/she is of unsound mind, intoxicated, or of an immature age (<12 years) as he/she is incapable of understanding the nature and consequences of the act for which consent is given.
- *IPC Section 92*: It deals with emergency cases. Consent need not be obtained if circumstances are such that it is impossible for that person to give consent.
- *CrPC Section 53(1)*: An arrested person can be examined without consent if requested to do so by a police officer not below the rank of a Sub-Inspector. Examination of an arrested person can lead to vital evidence related to the commission of crime.
- *CrPC Section 54*: An arrested person can also request to be examined by the doctor.
- *Criminal Law (Amendment) Act, 2013 (Amendments to Criminal Procedure Code, 1973), 357C*: All hospitals shall immediately provide first aid or medical treatment, free of cost, to the victims of any offence covered under Section 326A, 376, 376A, 376B, 376C, 376D, or 376E of the IPC, and shall immediately inform the police of such offence.
- *Indian Contract Act (Section 11)*: Every person who is of the age of majority is competent to contract.
- *Indian Majority Act (Section 3 [1])*: Every person attains the age of majority on his/her completion of age of 18 years.

TYPES OF CONSENT

- *Implied*: When a patient comes to the OPD, pays the professional fees, and waits for his/her turn to come, he/she has consented for the treatment and this allows physical examination in the form of inspection, palpation, percussion, and auscultation. This consent is not written. It is the most common type of consent and is legally effective. There is a scope for misunderstanding between doctors and patients on what was implied by the patient's action.
- *Expressed*: It is required for minor examination as well as for procedures. Oral consent for minor examination such as per rectal and per vaginal is sufficient. It should be taken in the presence of a disinterested party (nurses, pharmacist) and not the patient's relatives. Properly witnessed oral consent is as safe as written consent. Written informed consent is a must for all major procedures or minor interventions.

- *Presumed consent*: It is for emergency cases where consent cannot be taken.

GUIDELINES FOR CONSENT

- Consent should be procedure specific. The consent taken for a diagnostic procedure is not valid for a therapeutic procedure. A common consent for diagnostic as well as therapeutic operative procedures may be taken where they are contemplated.
- Consent should be procedure specific and general consent, for example, 'I so and so allow the doctors to perform surgery in course of my treatment,' is not valid (blanket consent).
- Consent for illegal procedures is not valid, for example, criminal abortion.
- Fresh consent should be obtained for a repeat procedure.
- Surgical consent does not cover anesthesia consent or risk and it should be obtained separately.
- Consent of one spouse is not necessary for operation of another. However, for sterilization procedure, consent of both is required.
- According to the Indian Medical Council (Professional Conduct and Ethics) Regulations, 2002, before performing an operation, written consent should be obtained. Unilaterally executed consent is not valid (signed by the patients but not by the doctors).
- Even after consent is taken, the examination should be done in the presence of a third party (nurse or female attendant) while examining a female patient.

WHO SHOULD TAKE THE CONSENT?

Operating surgeon or clinician or assistant doctor involved in the procedure who is having sufficient knowledge about the procedure and risks and benefits involved in the procedure should take the consent.

PRINCIPLES OF VALID CONSENT

- It must be voluntary.
- It must be informed.
- The patient must be competent.
- The consent must be procedure specific.
- Separate consent should be obtained for blood transfusion.
- It should contain significant disclosure of information.
- It should be understood, processed, and evaluated.
- Consent for surgery is not sufficient to cover anesthetic risk.
- Consent taken during an operative procedure is not valid.

WHO CAN GIVE THE CONSENT?

A competent adult can give consent. In India, the legal age for consent is 18 years. According to IPC Section 89, a child older than 12 years of age can give consent for physical as well as medical examination. In case of minors, being younger than 18 years of age in Indian law and <16 years of age in British law, consent should be obtained from the person with parenteral responsibility. An incompetent person cannot give valid consent so in that case consent should be obtained from a decision maker next to kin (parents/spouse).

No one can consent on behalf of a competent adult. In some cases, additional consent of the spouse is required: Procedure likely to cause sexual dysfunction or sterility operation. In children, in elective cases parents can give consent. However, in emergency, the person in charge of the child can give consent in the absence of parents (loco parentis).

In emergency, treatment will be provided by the doctors without documented consent to save the patient's life or to prevent the occurrence of severe harm. Nonavailability of consent does not preclude the doctors to treat the life-threatening emergency. Only documented refusal of the patients is valid for not treating a life-threatening emergency.

Witnessed consent is more dependable: The role of a witness is more important when the patient is illiterate, and one needs to take his/her thumb impression.

WHAT SHOULD BE DISCLOSED?

Disclosure includes diagnosis, treatment, procedure, alternative option or treatment available (if available), prognosis, significant risk, complications, adverse or side effects of the procedure, and adverse consequences of refusing the treatment.

It also includes details of the patients, types of anesthesia, doctor's details, consent for blood transfusion if required, patient's signature, and doctor's signature.

IF PATIENTS REQUEST A TREATMENT THAT IS NOT IN LINE WITH STANDARD GUIDELINES

- *Peptic perforation with peritonitis*: The doctor wants to perform emergency surgery but the patient wants nonoperative management. In such a case, patients cannot use their wish of nonoperative management. If the doctor feels that operative procedure is correct and appropriate, this should be explained to the patients. The doctor's aim is to explain the advantages and risks of the alternative treatment. He/she should be in a position to explain why the suggested approach is superior. If patients remain unconvinced, it is better to offer them a second opinion.
- *Jehovah's witnesses*: They are a group and refuse to accept the administration of blood products, no matter how serious the problem is and even when consequences include death or severe irreversible injury. Their refusal must be carefully documented.

WITHDRAWAL OF CONSENT

A patient may withdraw consent at any stage of treatment.

- *If patients are not giving consent for general anesthesia*: The procedure is cancelled and an alternative, less invasive procedure or conservative management is suggested.
- *If under local anesthesia*: If the patient demands withdrawal during a procedure, the procedure should be abandoned. If the patient is still not willing, re-explain the procedure.
- If stopping procedure at a point puts the patient's life in danger, the doctor may continue with the procedure till the risk is over.
- *A patient has the right to refuse treatment even in emergency*: In such a condition, informed refusal must be obtained and documented, over the patient's witnessed signature.

CONSENT NOT REQUIRED

- Medicolegal cases brought by police, in which consent is implied under CrPC Section 53
- Medical examination and issuing of certificate for insurance policy
- Cases where it is issued in the interest of community
- Notifiable disease
- Prisoners
- Examination under the court order

ANESTHETIC CONSENT

It is the responsibility of the anesthetist.

It should disclose application of monitor, insertion line, method of induction, method of airway management, recovery, and postoperative management.

Potential benefits and risks of anesthesia should be explained.

CONSENT FOR RESEARCH

Helsinki Declaration

It is the doctor's duty to ensure that all patients subjected to research are adequately informed about the aim of the study, methods, anticipated benefits, and potential hazards of the research study and the discomforts it may entail. The patient should be informed that he/she has a liberty to abstain from involvement in the study and that he/she is free to withdraw his/her consent to participate at any time during the research study. The doctor should preferably obtain written informed consent.

- Separate consent should be obtained.
- Local ethics committee should be involved.
- The consent must be written and well informed.
- Performa of the research should be disclosed. Aim, methodology, risks, and benefits of the study should be disclosed.
- Randomization is also important and it should be disclosed to the patient.

COMMON AND FREQUENT MISTAKES MADE BY DOCTORS

- Consent is not taken considering a minor procedure.

- General consent is taken instead of procedure-specific consent.
- Consent of the relative is taken even when the patient is competent.
- Consent lacks physician's and/or doctor's signature.
- There is no witnessed consent.
- Consent for blood transfusion is not obtained.
- Alteration in form is done without prior permission of the patient.
- Sufficient disclosure of information is not followed.
- Fresh consent is not obtained for a repeat procedure.

CHAPTER 3

Anesthesia

> Surgeons should not demand or insist on particular technique of anesthesia, as he may not know the limitations of the technique or the capability of the anesthesiologist to manage the particular technique.
>
> *John Alfred Lee*

The term 'anesthesia' refers to a carefully controlled reversible modification, modulation, or suppression of various functions of the nervous system such as CNS, ANS, and peripheral nervous system by using small, incremental, titrated doses of various drugs to achieve a specific desired physiological goal. The goal is protection of patients from various unwanted or undesirable side effects of pain of operation, handling of tissue or organ, and retraction of various muscles, especially skeletal muscles.

The anesthetist must be informed about preexisting medical history and medication. The medicines that need to be stopped preoperatively have been discussed in Chapter 1, *Preoperative Preparation*.

PREANESTHETIC MEDICATION

It refers to the medicine to be administered prior to surgery or during surgery. Preanesthetic medication is given to relieve pain, to support pain relief during anesthesia (background analgesia), and to induce sleep before anesthesia (basal narcosis).

The aims of preanesthetic medication are as follows:

- *Avoid fear*: Lorazepam or diazepam can be given on the night prior to surgery to avoid fear; they also help to have a sound sleep.
- *Suppress secretion*: Atropine and glycopyrrolate are used to reduce the secretion, especially salivary secretion that helps in airway management during induction and surgery. Secretions may interfere with the gaseous exchange. These drugs are antimuscarinic, given IM or IV. Glycopyrrolate is more potent and long-acting, and produces less tachycardia as compared to atropine.
- *Increase pH and reduce gastric secretion*: Preanesthetic medication is given to prevent aspiration. PPI and H2 antagonists are used. Prokinetic such as metoclopramide can be given 0.5 hour before surgery to speed up the gastric emptying. It also increases the tone of LES. A combination of H2 blocker and prokinetic is more effective. Ondansetron can be given to prevent vomiting. 5-HT3 blocker reduces the incidence of postanesthetic nausea and vomiting. It is practically devoid of side effects and is an antiemetic of choice for the anesthetist. The chance of reflux damage to the lung is minimal if gastric volume is <25 mL and pH >3.5.
- It helps to prevent vagal stimulation by suppression of reflexes.

The timing of administration is as follows:

- *Oral*: 2 hours prior to induction
- *Intramuscular*: 45 minutes prior to induction
- *Intravenous*: Just before induction

Two classes of drugs are available:

1. *Anticholinergic*: Atropine and glycopyrrolate
2. *CNS depressant*: Benzodiazepines, barbiturates, and opioid

Important points that should be remembered regarding premedication are as follows:

- Five rights of medication should be followed: Right drugs, right patient, right time, right dose, and right route.
- After premedication, sufficient time should be given prior to induction for drugs to achieve their effective blood concentration (2 hours for oral, 45 minutes for intramuscular).
- In patients with severe pain, opioid analgesics are given along with premedication.
- Fasting guidelines are given in Table 3.1.

Emergency rapid sequence intubation is followed for those who have not fasted and emergency intervention is required.

Table 3.1 Fasting Intervals Prior to Induction of Anesthesia

Oral intake	Fasting interval prior to induction
Solid foods, milk, and infant formula	6 hours
Breast milk	4 hours
Clear liquid	2 hours
Fried, fatty food or meat	8 hours

STAGES OF ANESTHESIA

Guedel's stages of induction of anesthesia are classically divided into the following:

- *Stage 1*: Analgesia. The patient becomes drowsy.
- *Stage 2*: Excitement. There is involuntary muscle contraction; respiration becomes irregular, and reflexes are active like cough.
- *Stage 3*: Surgical anesthesia. In the initial phase, respiration becomes regular and progresses to complete loss of respiration (medullary depression); there are no reflexes, and muscles are relaxed.
- *Stage 4*: Respiration and vasomotor tone are completely lost; spontaneous respiration ceases, and death occurs within minutes.

TYPES OF ANESTHESIA

There are three main categories of anesthesia, each having many forms and uses. They are as follows:

1. *General* (GA): Patient is unconscious and has no awareness or other sensations.
    - Inhalational
        - *Volatile liquids*: Ether, halothane, enflurane, sevoflurane, isoflurane, and desflurane
        - *Gas*: Nitrous oxide
    - Intravenous: Ketamine (dissociative anesthesia), midazolam, propofol, thiopental sodium, and fentanyl
2. *Regional*: The anesthetic is injected near a cluster of nerves to numb a specific area of the body; it may be spinal, epidural, nerve block, field block, and eutectic mixture of local anesthetics (EMLA). The patient may remain awake, or may be given a sedative.
3. *Local*: The anesthetic drug is usually injected into the tissue to numb just the specific location of the body requiring minor surgery.

CHOICE OF ANESTHESIA

Following factors need to be considered:

- *Age*: For children and infants, GA is the preferred choice. For adults, depending on condition, GA or regional anesthesia can be used.
- *Types and duration of surgery*: GA is preferred for a longer procedure, a procedure performed in a prone or lateral position, and abdominal (especially upper abdominal surgery) and laparoscopic surgery.
- *Physical condition of the patient*: In patients with a neuromuscular problem such as polio and myasthenia, it is better to avoid muscle relaxants. Patients on anticoagulants or blood-thinning agents are better managed by GA than by regional anesthesia. Uncooperative and mentally disturbed or emotional patients are managed by GA.
- Patient's wish should be taken into account.
- Preference of surgeons as well as anesthetist should be considered.

PROPERTIES OF AN IDEAL ANESTHETIC

- Should be pleasant and nonirritating
- Should have smooth onset and recovery, and not cause postoperative nausea and vomiting
- Should provide adequate analgesia, immobility, and muscle relaxation
- Should involve easy and controllable administration
- Should have a wide therapeutic index
- Should be potent and allow rapid adjustment of depth of anesthesia
- Should not affect heart and liver function
- Should be cheap, easily available, safe, and easily stored
- Should be noninflammable and nonexplosive

INDUCTION OF ANESTHESIA

It is the time period between administration of anesthetic drugs and development of effective surgical anesthesia. It depends on how quickly drugs reach the brain. Depth of anesthesia is directly related to partial pressure of oxygen in the brain. Certain factors that decide the induction and recovery (time between cessation of anesthetic drugs and consciousness of the patient) are as follows:

- *Solubility of anesthetic*: It determines the transfer of drug from the alveolar air to the blood and is expressed as blood–gas partition coefficient. The lower the blood–gas partition coefficient, the more rapid is the onset and recovery from anesthesia. Halothane has a higher solubility and high blood–gas partition coefficient; it dissolves completely (so requires a large amount to raise the arterial tension) and indicates slow induction and slow recovery. Nitrous oxide has low blood solubility and has a rapid induction and fast recovery.
- *Rate of ventilation*: The rate of delivery of drugs to the alveoli is determined by rate and depth of ventilation. The effect of increased ventilation is significant in drugs with a high blood–gas partition coefficient and insignificant in drugs with a low blood–gas partition coefficient.
- *Alveolar blood flow*: More the flow, rapid will be the induction and recovery and vice versa.
- *Concentration in inspired gas mixture*: Rapid induction is possible in the presence of increased concentration of drugs in the inspired gas mixture. For drugs with a high solubility in the blood, rapid induction is achieved by concentrations that are higher than those required for maintenance. Halothane 2–4% is used for rapid induction and 0.5–1% for maintenance.

MAINTENANCE OF ANESTHESIA

Inhalation anesthesia is preferred.

Minimum alveolar concentration (MAC) is the concentration of drug required to prevent movement on painful stimulation (incision) in 50% of experimental subjects.

The smaller the MAC value, the more potent is the anesthetic. The higher the lipid solubility, the greater is the potency and lower is the MAC. Inhalational anesthetics exhibit synergism. 0.5 MAC of two anesthetics will produce 1 MAC of anesthesia.

ELIMINATION

All volatile anesthetics are eliminated through lungs (once the anesthetic is discontinued, the channel of absorption becomes the channel of elimination). Most general anesthetics are eliminated unchanged. In case of a prolonged procedure, recovery is delayed because a large quantity of anesthetics enters muscles and fat and is released slowly.

SYSTEMIC EFFECTS

All inhalational agents cause the following:

- *Systemic hypotension*: Myocardial depression and vasodilatation
- *Increased cerebral blood flow*: Cerebrovascular dilatation and loss of coupling
- Decreased renal blood flow and GFR up to 50%
- *Hypothermia*: Patients made vulnerable to hypothermia by anesthetics, which is due to combination of cold operation theater environment and redistribution of heat from the core to the periphery (core temperature control is lost) and open body cavity.

MANAGEMENT OF AIRWAY DURING ANESTHESIA

Airway management is a crucial skill for the clinical anesthesiologist. It is an integral part of general anesthesia, allowing ventilation and oxygenation as well as a mode for anesthetic gas delivery.

Use of muscle relaxant does not allow patients to breathe spontaneously and hence the patients require artificial ventilation. Chin lift, jaw thrust, and head tilt along with oropharyngeal airway allow bag and mask ventilation. This method is short term and is used where no aid is available.

Usually airway is approached through either supraglottic route such as laryngeal mask airway (LMA) or endotracheal intubation.

Assessment of Airway

This forms a part of preoperative evaluation. Preoperative airway assessment is very crucial to determine which device is most appropriate and to predict difficult airway. In addition to standard devices such as facemasks, laryngoscopes, oral and nasal airways, supraglottic airway, and a bougie, alternative devices such as video laryngoscope and flexible intubating scope, as well as other emergency airway equipment, should be kept ready. Position of the head is sniffing position.

Two systems of classification are used to grade the adequacy of airway:

1. Samson–Young modification of Mallampati classification, oropharyngeal view, is as follows:
   - *Class I*: Uvula, faucial pillars, and soft palate visible
   - *Class II*: Faucial pillars and soft palate visible
   - *Class III*: Soft and hard palate visible
   - *Class IV*: Only hard palate visible
2. Cormack and Lehane classification (laryngoscopic view) is as follows:
   - *Grade 1*: Most of the glottis is visible.
   - *Grade 2*: Only posterior portion of glottis is visible.
   - *Grade 3*: The epiglottis is seen but no part of glottis is seen.
   - *Grade 4*: No airway structure is visualized.

Difficult airway

Difficult airway (defined as more than three attempts, or taking longer than 10 minutes) is a major factor in anesthesia morbidity. Conditions that influence airway management or indicate difficult intubation are as follows:

- Congenital: Trisomy 21, Turner syndrome, Treacher Collins syndrome, and Klippel–Feil syndrome
- Acquired
  - Infections: Epiglottitis, croup, abscess (submandibular, Ludwig angina), and tetanus
  - Trauma: Cervical spine injury, mandibular and maxillary injury, and laryngeal fracture
  - Neoplastic: Neoplastic upper airway obstruction
  - Connective tissue disorder: Scleroderma, sarcoidosis, and ankylosing spondylitis
  - Endocrine disorder: Acromegaly, thyromegaly, hypothyroidism, and diabetes (may have decreased mobility of atlanto-occipital joint)
  - Obesity
  - Postradiation

Aims of Airway Management

- Maintain and protect airway
- Zero incidence of aspiration of material into the respiratory tract

Steps of Airway Management

- *Preoxygenation*: It allows replacement of lung nitrogen with oxygen and provides oxygen in the alveolar capillary bed after the onset of apnea.
- *Support of the airway*: Following induction of anesthesia, support with ventilation and oxygenation is provided by either LMA or endotracheal intubation.
  - Endotracheal intubation: It is considered in every patient receiving GA. With the help of laryngoscope, endotracheal tube is passed through glottis until 2 cm proximal to proximal end of cuff and is allowed to be in the midtrachea.
    - Fiber-optic endotracheal intubation: This method is employed when difficult intubation by laryngoscopy is anticipated.
    - Nasal fiber-optic intubation: This method is used when there is inability to intubate through oral cavity due to restricted mouth opening.
  - Supraglottic airway or LMA
    - It is an invaluable tool in managing difficult airway.
    - The distal tip of the cuff should be against the upper esophageal sphincter.
    - The lateral edges rest on the piriform sinuses.
    - The proximal end seats under the base of the tongue.
- *Extubation*: It must be performed when patients are either deeply anesthetized or fully awake. Extubation in light plane of anesthesia is associated with laryngospasm.

STEPS OF ANESTHESIA

- *Induction*: Avoid stage 2 or excitatory phase (seen usually with slow-onset anesthetics). IV anesthetics such as thiopental sodium that produces unconsciousness within 25 seconds avoid this stage. Additional IV or inhalation drug is given to achieve desired depth of surgical anesthesia. A skeletal muscle relaxant such as pancuronium, rocuronium, atracurium, and succinylcholine (SCh) is coadministered to facilitate intubation and relaxation. In children without IV access, halothane or sevoflurane is used to induce general anesthesia (inhalation induction). *Triad of anesthesia* includes hypnosis, analgesia, and reflex suppression.
- *Maintenance of anesthesia*: Volatile anesthetic is used. It provides good minute-to-minute control over depth of anesthesia. Monitor vital signs and

Box 3.1 Criteria for full recovery

- Patient must be fully awake and fully oriented.
- Patient must have active protective reflexes.
- Patient must not suffer severe pain and complete reversal of muscle relaxant as indicated by spontaneous breathing without assistance while maintaining adequate ventilation and oxygenation and follows commands such as eye opening.

response to various stimuli to carefully balance the amount of drug inhaled or infused.

- *Recovery*: The anesthesiologist withdraws the anesthetic mixture and monitors the return of patient's consciousness. It is reverse of induction and is due to redistribution of the drug from the site of action. Recovery from neuromuscular blockers takes considerable time, even with vecuronium (relatively short half-life). Its antagonists such as neostigmine, pyridostigmine, and edrophonium raise the concentration of neurotransmitter acetylcholine to a higher level than neuromuscular blockers. Patients should be monitored till the full recovery of physiological functions, for example, patients may be able to start breathing on their own (Box 3.1).

AGENTS USED IN ANESTHESIA

Induction

- Propofol is the drug of choice for outpatient ambulatory surgery.
- Lorazepam and diazepam are rarely used for induction because of their slow onset of action.
- Midazolam has a slightly rapid onset of action and can be used as an induction agent. It is helpful in special situations where nitrous oxide is contraindicated or as a part of total intravenous anesthesia (TIVA). It is used in combination with propofol or ketamine. It facilitates the onset and reduces the intraoperative recall. Cardiostimulatory response and psychomimetic reaction to ketamine is decreased.
- Ketamine is used as an induction agent in patients with reactive airway.

Maintenance

Maintenance of anesthesia can be done by either continuous infusion of IV agents or volatile anesthetics.

Muscle relaxation: neuromuscular blocking agents

Patients must be anesthetized properly before administration of muscle relaxant. The muscle relaxant should not be administered in awake patients. It does not have amnestic, hypnotic, and analgesic properties. Inhalation agent may produce all the components of GA, but the depth of anesthesia required to produce profound muscle relaxation is much deeper than that required to produce amnesia and hypnosis. Addition of muscle relaxant along with small dose of inhalation agents and IV anesthetics will help to achieve satisfactory operating condition. Nerve stimulator is the best to monitor intraoperative immobility and postoperative residual paralysis.

There are two types of neuromuscular blocking agents:

1. *Depolarizing* (noncompetitive): SCh
2. *Nondepolarizing* (competitive): Pancuronium, vecuronium, rocuronium, and mivacurium

Reversal

- *Reversal agents*: These include neostigmine, edrophonium, and pyridostigmine.
- *Mechanism of action*: These agents increase the acetylcholine levels by inhibiting acetylcholinesterase.
- All muscles are not equally sensitive to muscle relaxants. Diaphragm is the most resistant and neck and pharyngeal muscles are the most sensitive.
- *Uses*: Reversal is indicated in most patients who receive a nondepolarizing neuromuscular blocking agent. Reversal is not required in patients who received SCh. Reversal agents are also used when intraoperative relaxation is required to facilitate the surgical exposure.
- *Indicators for reversal*: Reversal is indicated by an increase in the tidal volume, hand grip, vital capacity, and head lift. The definitive clinical test for complete reversal is the patient's ability to sustain head lift from bed for 5 seconds. Peripheral nerve stimulator is used to assess depth and reversal of motor blockade.

GENERAL ANESTHETIC DRUGS

Commonly Used Intravenous Agents

- Sodium thiopental
  - It mimics the action of GABA by activating chloride channel and is a competitive inhibitor of *N*-acetylcholine receptor.
  - It is ultrashort acting and highly lipid soluble.
  - It reduces cerebral metabolic rate of oxygen ($CMRO_2$) and cerebral blood flow and lowers intracranial pressure.
  - It improves cerebral perfusion pressure as decrease in systemic vascular resistance is less than ICP.
  - It is neuroprotective and acts as a potent anticonvulsant.
  - It produces dose-dependent respiratory depression.
  - It decreases cardiac output, and is systemic and peripheral vascular resistant.
  - Adverse drug reactions: These are respiratory depression, laryngospasm, and bronchospasm. Extravasation at local site leads to tissue necrosis and gangrene.
  - Dose is 3–5 mg/kg in adults.
- Ketamine
  - It produces functional dissociation between thalamocortical and limbic systems. The term used for this type of anesthesia is dissociative anesthesia.
  - It inhibits *N*-methyl-D-aspartate (NMDA) receptor and produces dissociative anesthesia with profound analgesia.
  - Patients remain in cataleptic state with eyes remaining open and nystagmic gaze.
  - Ketamine is a potent bronchodilator and preserves respiratory drive. It decreases postoperative dose or requirement of opiate.
  - It is an ideal induction agent for patients in shock, significant hypovolemia, and cardiac tamponade. It is useful in children, elderly, and asthmatics.
  - Undesirable side effects are: Dose-dependent unpleasant psychomimetic action such as hallucination (but it can be minimized by administration along with benzodiazepines), increased cerebral blood flow, increased oral secretions, direct myocardial depression, increased cardiac work, increased mean arterial pressure, and increased cardiac output (sympathetic outflow is increased).
  - Dose: 1- to 2-mg/kg IV injection induces patients within 60 seconds and a 5- to 10-mg/kg IM injection within 2–4 minutes.
  - Contraindications: Upper airway obstruction, raised intracranial pressure, and raised intraocular pressure are absolute contraindications. Ketamine is also contraindicated in epilepsy and hypertension. It is relatively contraindicated in patients with IHD.
- Etomidate: It augments GABA-gated chloride current (indirect modulation) and in high dose evokes chloride current in the absence of GABA (direct activation).
- Propofol
  - It is a $GABA_A$ receptor agonist. Its mechanism of action is the same as that of sodium thiopental.
  - In addition, it possesses ion channel blocking effects in cerebral cortex and nicotinic acetylcholine receptors, as well as an inhibitory effect on lysophosphatidate signaling in lipid mediator receptors.
  - It has a rapid induction within 30 seconds and awakening in 4–8 minutes after single bolus dose.
  - It is the only IV anesthetic with antiemetic action. It is provided in emulsion.
  - It is associated with anaphylactoid reaction in patients with egg allergy and pain on injection, and triglyceride level may increase on prolonged infusion.
  - It decreases $CMRO_2$, CBF, and ICP and is neuroprotective.
  - It decreases mean arterial pressure through its effect on systemic vascular resistance (vasodilatation).
  - It is a myocardial depressant. In high doses, it augments central vagal tone and causes bradycardia, conduction abnormalities, and asystole.
  - It produces dose-dependent respiratory depression. It is an effective induction agent for reactive airway disease.
  - It is the induction agent of choice in patients prone to malignant hyperthermia.

- It is mostly used in ambulatory surgery because of its short duration, faster recovery, and early discharge from the hospital.
- Adverse effects: Contaminated propofol causes sepsis and death. Propofol syndrome is seen in critically ill pediatric patients receiving a high dose. It is characterized by myocardial failure, metabolic acidosis, and rhabdomyolysis. It is because of large lipid load.
- Dose is 1.5–2.5 mg/kg.

- Midazolam
  - It enhances the binding of GABA to its receptors. GABA activates the chloride channel and hyperpolarizes neuron, thereby inhibiting it.
  - Twenty percent receptor occupancy leads to anxiolysis, 30–50% to amnesia and sedation, and 60% to hypnosis (or unconsciousness).
  - It produces minimal myocardial depression with no effects on mean arterial pressure and cardiac output. It produces dose-dependent respiratory depression.
  - Dose is 0.1–0.2 mg/kg.
- Fentanyl
  - It is a potent opioid analgesic. Its analgesic action is 75–125 times more as compared to that of morphine.
  - It is short acting. Its main use is as a supplement to balance anesthesia.
  - In combination with benzodiazepines, it obviates the need for inhaled anesthetics.
  - It is used in diagnostic, endoscopic, and angiographic procedures, burns dressing, and other minor procedures.

Volatile Anesthetics

- Ether
  - It is the safest agent in an untrained hand.
  - There is no renal and liver toxicity
  - Disadvantages of ether are as follows:
    - Explosive with air and oxygen
    - Slow induction and slow recovery
- Halothane
  - Potent anesthetic
  - Volatile liquid with sweet odor
  - Onset 2–5 minutes
  - Two to 4% used as induction and 0.5–1% used for maintenance through special vaporizer
  - Wide safety margin
  - Noninflammable, nonexplosive, and nonirritant to pulmonary tract, and no bronchospasm
  - Laryngeal and pharyngeal reflex abolished, and cough reflex suppressed, but causes bronchodilation and is preferred in asthmatics
  - Recovery smooth and reasonably quick
  - Nausea and vomiting rare
  - Is suitable in children for induction as well as maintenance and in adults used for maintenance anesthetics after IV induction
  - Disadvantages of halothane are as follows:
    - Hepatotoxic and cardiotoxic
    - Poor analgesic and poor muscle relaxation (this property is compensated by use of N_2O or opioid or neuromuscular blocker in combination with halothane)
    - Raised intracranial pressure and potentiation of action of antihypertensive medications
    - Rare complication: Malignant hyperthermia
- Nitrous oxide
  - Laughing gas
  - Colorless, odorless, and heavier than air
  - Rapid induction
  - Is effective as an analgesic in low dose
  - Low potency, hence usually combined with other agents such as halothane
  - Generally used as a carrier and used in combinations such as 70% N_2O + 25–30% O_2 + 0–2% another potent anesthetic
  - Advantages of nitrous oxide are as follows:
    - Noninflammable, nonexplosive, nonirritant to respiratory tract, and noncardiotoxic
    - Rapid and smooth induction
    - Good analgesic
  - Disadvantages of nitrous oxide are as follows:
    - Low potency, poor relaxation, hypoxia, possible mutagenic, powerful greenhouse gas, increases the size of air bubble causing adverse effects and postoperative nausea and vomiting
- Isoflurane: Less reduction of cardiac output, less sensitization, minimal metabolism, less sensitization to arrhythmogenic effects of stress hormones, and minimum metabolism; little increase in ICP; causes tachycardia
- Sevoflurane
  - The MAC value of sevoflurane with O_2 is 2 and with 70% N_2O is 0.8. MAC value

decreases with increasing age. In neonates it is 3.3 and in adults 1.48. The MAC value also decreases with other hypnotics. Sevoflurane is excreted unchanged through lungs. Blood gas partition coefficient is 0.6 so alveolar anesthetic concentration is rapidly achieved. Sevoflurane has fast induction, within 5 minutes. Due to lower distribution coefficient, recovery is also fast. Sevoflurane is a nonirritant to upper airway.

- Effects
  - *CVS*: Minimal tachycardia, decreased pulmonary arterial pressure, and systemic vascular resistance; also leads to decreased cardiac contractibility and cardiac output
  - *RS*: Nonirritant to airway and pleasant to smell, respiratory depressant, and bronchodilator
  - *CNS*: Vasodilatation, minimal increase in cerebral flow, and cerebral metabolic rate decreased
- Advantages: Sevoflurane is good for induction of anesthesia in pediatric patients. It has good hemodynamic stability. It is environment friendly. It is well suited for *out*patient surgery, mask induction, and maintenance of patients with bronchospastic condition.

Muscle Relaxants

Depolarizing agents

Succinylcholine

- *Mechanism of action*: It binds to acetylcholine receptors on postjunctional membrane in neuromuscular junction and produces depolarization of muscle fiber. It initially produces contraction (fasciculation) followed by profound relaxation. It has a rapid onset (<1 minute) and short duration of action (5 minutes). It is rapidly metabolized by *pseudocholinesterase*. Because of short duration of action, mask ventilation is performed in patients who cannot be successfully intubated. Patients with low *pseudocholinesterase* level should preferably avoid SCh.
- *Adverse reactions*: These include postoperative pain and aches, bradycardia, hyperkalemia (in patients with burns and massive traumatic injury, it may produce dangerous hyperkalemia leading to arrhythmia and cardiac arrest), malignant hyperthermia, and increased intraocular and intragastric pressure. Because of multiple problems with SCh, some anesthesiologists reserve it for rapid sequence induction.

Nondepolarizing agents

Nondepolarizing agents bind to postsynaptic terminal in neuromuscular junction in a reversible manner and prevent acetylcholine from depolarizing the muscle.

- *Short acting*: Mivacurium (metabolized by plasma cholinesterase)
- *Intermediate acting*: Rocuronium and vecuronium (metabolized by the kidney and liver), and atracurium (metabolized by Hoffmann elimination)
- *Long acting*: Pancuronium (excreted unchanged by kidney) and tubocurarine

LOCAL ANESTHESIA

It provides anesthesia and analgesia. It is used either alone or as an adjunct to GA.

Various types include the following:

- Topical
- Local infiltration

Topical Anesthesia

- *EMLA*: It is applied over skin to produce topical anesthesia prior to venipuncture, especially in children. It is a combination of lidocaine and prilocaine.
- *Cocaine* (Moffett solution): It is used in the operation of nose to produce anesthesia and vasoconstriction.
- *Lidocaine 4% spray*: It anesthetizes the airway before fiber-optic intubation.

Local Infiltration

The mechanism of action of local anesthetics is dose-dependent blockage of sodium current in nerve fibers.

Blocking potency of commonly used local anesthetic drugs is as follows:

- *Low*: Procaine
- *Intermediate*: Prilocaine and lidocaine
- *High*: Bupivacaine and tetracaine

Subcutaneous infiltration is performed to achieve local effect. Addition of epinephrine will prolong the effect of local anesthetics. Epinephrine produces local vasoconstriction, limits uptake of local anesthetics, and prolongs the duration of action as well as reduces the toxicity of local anesthetics. It is contraindicated in digital blocks and areas with poor collateral circulation.

The choice of drug and dose depends on the extent of the area to be anesthetized and duration of the procedure.

A large volume of diluted drugs is required for a large surface area.

Lidocaine is effective in diluted solutions up to 0.3–0.5%.

Pain after injection is because of acidic nature of the solution and can be minimized by neutralization of lidocaine by sodium bicarbonate immediately before injection.

Complications of local anesthesia are the following:

- Pain at injection site
- Burning sensation at injection site
- Hematoma at local site
- Allergic reaction
- Infection
- Paresthesia

Systemic toxicity

Inadvertent intravascular injection can lead to systemic toxicity:

- Neurological: This includes tingling and numbness around tongue, metallic taste, light headache, tinnitus, and visual disturbance.
- Disorientation and convulsion may also develop.
- Convulsion is treated with benzodiazepines or thiopental and maintenance of airway.
- Persistent seizure requires endotracheal intubation.
- Cardiac: Bupivacaine is more cardiotoxic. It is more lipid soluble as compared to lidocaine; it binds tightly to sodium channels and is known as fast-in, slow-out anesthetic. Toxic dose is 3 mg/kg.
- Hypertension, tachycardia, ventricular dysrhythmias, and decreased cardiac contractility and output occur.
- Very high dose can lead to cardiovascular collapse.

How to prevent toxicity

- Aspirate before injecting to check for unplanned vascular entry.
- Have knowledge of maximum safe dose of drugs.
- Adding epinephrine will slow the absorption and will decrease the likelihood of toxic reaction secondary to rapid absorption.

REGIONAL NERVE BLOCK

- *Superficial cervical plexus block*: It is used in carotid surgery and superficial neck surgery.
- *Interscalene brachial plexus block*: It is used in shoulder, humerus, and elbow surgery.
- *Vertical infraclavicular block*: It is used in forearm, wrist, and hand surgery.
- *Coracoid block*: It is used in elbow, wrist, and hand surgery.
- *Thoracic paravertebral block*: Analgesia and anesthesia are given for breast surgery and analgesia for open cholecystectomy, renal surgery, and fractured rib.
- *Inguinal field block*: For surgery of inguinal hernia, orchidopexy, and hydrocele. Ilioinguinal and iliohypogastric nerves are blocked.
- *Transverse abdominis plane block*: The anterior abdominal wall is innervated by anterior rami of T6–L1. The T6–L1 segmental nerve enters the triangle of Petit just medial to the anterior axillary line. The triangle is above the iliac crest with anterior border formed by external oblique and posterior border by latissimus dorsi. The nerve lies between internal oblique and transverse abdominis. Injection of local anesthetic into the fascial plane between the internal oblique and the transverse abdominis muscle provides very good anesthesia for anterior abdominal wall. Ultrasound may be used to achieve the block.
  - *Local anesthetic dose*: 30 mL per side. Volume is more important than concentration. Take care about maximum safe dose.
  - *Complications*: These include bowel puncture, and intrasplenic and intrahepatic injection.
- *Rectus sheath block*: Analgesia is given for midline abdominal incision and anterior laparoscopic port.
- *Fascia iliaca block*: Analgesia is given for fracture neck femur and combined with spinal or GA for hip surgery.
- Intravenous regional anesthesia (Bier block)
  - It is most commonly used for upper limb surgery but may be effectively used for surgery on lower limb also.

- First, inflate proximal cuff of double tourniquet. Injection prilocaine is given on the back of the hand on which operation is planned. After 5–10 minutes, distal cuff is inflated and proximal cuff is deflated. The cuff is kept inflated even if surgery is over.
- It allows the drug to be bound to tissue and hence prevents systemic circulation of drug.
- Prilocaine is the most preferred agent for this because of high therapeutic index. Lidocaine is a safe alternative.
- Compared to 0.2% lidocaine, 0.375% ropivacaine is associated with prolonged and improved analgesia.
- It is cost-effective as compared to GA in outpatient hand surgery.
- Various adjuvants are used to decrease tourniquet pain, improve the quality of block, and prolong analgesia after cuff deflation.
- Lornoxicam improves postoperative analgesia and decreases tourniquet pain.
- Dexamethasone and dexmedetomidine (alpha-receptor agonist) improve quality of block and postoperative analgesia.

Central Neuraxial Block

Spinal anesthesia

It refers to injection of local anesthetics with or without opioids in subarachnoid space. It provides excellent motor and sensory block below the level of injection.

Indications are the following:

- Various urological surgeries such as TURP, URS, VIU, and open prostate or bladder surgery
- Lower abdominal surgery such as hysterectomy and LSCS
- Lower limb surgery
- Perineal surgery
- Orthopedic surgery

Drugs used include lidocaine, tetracaine, and bupivacaine. Bupivacaine and tetracaine have a longer duration of action as compared to lidocaine (maximum 200 minutes vs. 60 minutes).

The mixture of drug used may be *hypobaric, isobaric, or hyperbaric*. Plain drug is isobaric, drug mixed with water is hypobaric, and drug mixed with dextrose is hyperbaric. Baricity influences the distribution of anesthetic; hyperbaric solutions tend to 'sink' within the CSF, and hypobaric solutions rise relative to the site of injection. Hyperbaric solutions are associated with rapid onset and greater extent and shorter duration of block compared with isobaric solutions.

Factors affecting the duration and onset of SA are as follows:

- Choice of local anesthetic drugs: Bupivacaine and tetracaine have a longer duration of action as compared to lidocaine.
- Volume and speed of injection: Greater the volume, more are the chances of spread and rapid injection leads to turbulent flow and unpredictable onset.
- Addition of vasoconstrictor agent or opioid: Vasoconstrictor agent increases the duration of block and opioid increases the duration of analgesia.
- Position of the patient: Allow the patient to be in supine and sitting position till the drug is fixed. It will lead to more intense block below the level of block. Changing position before the fixing of drugs leads to cephalad spread and possibility of total spinal anesthesia. CSF has a low specific gravity and hypobaric solution ascends within CSF.
- Patients who are obese, pregnant, and those with increased intra-abdominal pressure can have a higher level of spinal anesthesia than expected.

Structures encountered during spinal anesthesia are as follows:

- Skin
- Subcutaneous tissue
- Supraspinous ligament
- Interspinous ligaments
- Ligamentum flavum
- Dura mater
- Arachnoid mater

Levels of block for common surgeries are the following:

- *Kidney and LSCS*: Up to T6
- *Prostate, testis, and hernia*: Up to T10
- *Appendix*: T8–T10

Advantages are as follows:

- Complications associated with endotracheal intubation and general anesthesia are avoided.
- Awake surgeries in endourology such as TURP will allow assessment of TUR syndrome and bladder perforation.

- Analgesia is better with combined use of opioid.
- Postoperative CNS complications such as confusion and delirium are less as compared to those with GA.
- Spinal anesthesia is easy to perform.
- It has a rapid onset.
- It leads to dense surgical anesthesia.

Disadvantage is as follows:

- Prolonged procedure cannot be performed because of limited duration of block.

Contraindications are as follows:

- Patient's refusal
- Local infection
- Sepsis and shock
- Coagulopathy
- Increased ICP

Complications are as follows:

- Hypotension: It is because of autonomic sympathetic blockade particularly if level of block is above T10. Care must be taken in patients with hypovolemia and cardiovascular disease. Patients must be adequately prehydrated. If required, at least 1–1.5 L fluid should be given preoperatively. Treatment includes administration of IV fluid and vasopressors such as ephedrine and mephentermine.
- Headache: It is because of dural puncture. It usually develops after 48 hours and mainly in the occipital region. Diameter and configuration of needle is an important factor and can be reduced to 1% by using 25G and 27G needle. Minimum puncture and fine-bore pencil-tip needles that split the dura rather than cut help to minimize the problem of headache. Patients should lie in supine position for at least 24 hours and should avoid pillow. Treatment includes administration of analgesics, IV or oral fluids, and injection dextran.
- Urinary retention: It is the most common postoperative complication.
- Backache can occur.
- There may be hematoma and infection at the local site.
- Transient neuropathy may occur.
- High spinal: If it is up to cardioaccelerator fiber, then bradycardia and hypotension develop and if it involves cervical diaphragmatic, paralysis occurs.
- There may be cardiorespiratory arrest.
- Rare complications include the following:
  - Cauda equina syndrome
  - Paraplegia
  - Sixth cranial nerve palsy
  - Meningitis

Epidural anesthesia

Indications are the following:

- Thoracic operative procedure
- Abdominal operation (GI surgery)
- Surgery on lower extremity (surgery for peripheral vascular disease)
- For pain management in flail chest

Mainly it is used as an adjunct to GA or for postoperative pain management.

Epidural space is located with 19-gauge introducer needle and loss of resistance technique. Once space is located, 21-gauge catheter is introduced by the previously placed needle. Confirm that it is not placed in intrathecal space and check for intravascular injury. After localization, local anesthetic with or without opioids is injected in epidural space with the help of epidural catheter in place. Catheter is placed for several days. It is usually not used for surgery at or below knee because it fails to block the sacral nerve root.

Location is the following:

- Thoracic or lumbar epidural space

Drugs used are the following:

- Dilute local anesthetic with vasoconstrictors or opioids

Advantages are the following:

- Onset of block can be well controlled; because of its slower onset, resultant hypotension because of sympathetic blockade can be better controlled and can reduce blood loss.
- Lengthy procedure can be performed as it allows repeated dosing due to catheter in place.
- Postoperatively better analgesia is present.
- It involves early ambulation and less postoperative ileus in GI surgery.
- Postoperative pulmonary function is better and there are less chances of pneumonia.
- There are decreased chances of DVT.
- There is decreased 30-day mortality and pneumonia as compared to that in GA.

Complications are the following:

- Nerve damage

- Accidental dural puncture and injection of large volume of drugs
- Spinal injuries
- Epidural hematoma
- Infection
- Complications of spinal anesthesia if dural puncture

Contraindications are the same as for spinal anesthesia.

Special care needs to be taken for those who are on anticoagulant therapy because of risk of spinal hematoma.

LMWH should not be started before 6 hours of placement of catheter and the catheter should be removed at least 12 hours after the last dose of LMWH. Epidural catheter should be placed at least 24 hours after the last dose of LMWH.

Patients should watch for signs of spinal hematoma such as back pain, lower limb motor and sensory dysfunction, and bowel and bladder dysfunction.

Caudal block

It is used mainly in children for perineal surgery. Drugs such as lidocaine are injected in sacral hiatus.

CHAPTER 4

Abdominal Incisions

Pray before surgery but remember God will not alter a faulty incision.

Keeney's dictum

INCISION

An ideal incision must provide access to the site of pathology and should allow easy extension if required. The choice of incision also influences the rate of surgical site infection, wound dehiscence, and hernia formation. The incision should be executed in such a fashion that it allows secure closure of wall and interferes very little with the function and cosmesis of the abdominal wall. It is the only portion of the surgeon's works that is accessible to the patients for examination. It is also called the signature of the surgeon.

Langer's lines, sometimes called *cleavage lines*, are topological lines drawn on a map of the human body. These correspond to the natural orientation of the collagen fiber in the dermis, and are generally parallel to the orientation of the underlying muscle fiber. Wounds against Langer's lines have been described to have a poorer final cosmetic appearance compared to those along Langer's lines.

Incision should be made with either 20 or 22 blade using a scalpel.

The blade is firmly pressed at right angles to the skin and drawn across the skin in the predetermined directions to execute the operation safely.

There should be no hand-to-hand passing of scalpel or sharp instrument to avoid injury.

Diathermy should be used for incision of deeper structures as it reduces blood loss and may reduce postoperative pain.

The length of suture material should be at least four times the wound to be closed to minimize the wound complications.

RELEVANT ANATOMY

- Flat muscles
  - External oblique
    - Largest flat muscle, fibers transversely oriented
    - Origin: External surface and inferior border of lower eight ribs
    - Insertion: Iliac crests
    - Aponeurosis ending medially in linea alba
  - Internal oblique
    - Fibers at right angle to the external oblique fiber (vertical)
    - Origin: Upper surface and lateral two-third of the inguinal ligament, anterior two-third of the iliac crest, and the thoracolumbar fascia
    - Insertion: Lower three ribs and their costal cartilage
    - Aponeurosis enveloping the rectus muscle and anterior bend with the external oblique aponeurosis and posterior portion along with transversus abdominis aponeurosis forming a posterior rectus sheath
  - Transverse abdominis
    - Origin: Same as internal oblique plus lower costal cartilage, fibers are transversely oriented.
    - In aponeurosis, upper three-fourth goes behind rectus and lower one-fourth in front of rectus.

Aponeurosis of each of these three flat muscles joins the rectus muscle to form linea alba.

- Vertical
  - Rectus abdominis
    - Origin: Two heads, from the front of the symphysis pubis and pubic crests
    - Insertion: Xiphoid process and fifth, sixth, and seventh costal cartilages
    - Is enveloped by aponeurosis of three flat muscles

- Pyramidalis
  - Triangular, vestigial muscle
  - Origin: Symphysis pubis
  - Insertion: Linea alba

Important Landmarks

These are as follows:

- Linea alba: Midline between two rectus muscles
- Fusion of three flat muscle aponeurosis: Is in the midline. Aponeurosis of the three flat muscles join the rectus muscles to form linea alba.
- Arcuate line of Douglas: It is a sharp concave line that occurs bilaterally half way between symphysis pubis and umbilicus
- Below the arcuate line posterior rectus sheath absent

TYPES OF INCISIONS[1]

- Vertical (Fig. 4.1)
  - Midline
  - Paramedian: Right and left

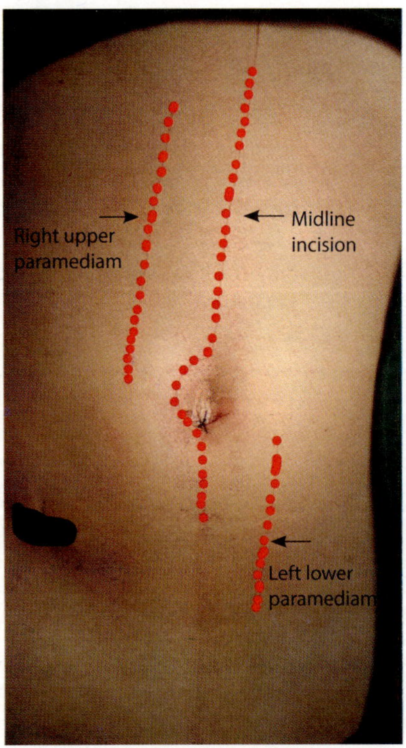

Figure 4.1 Midline incision, right upper paramedian, and left lower paramedian.

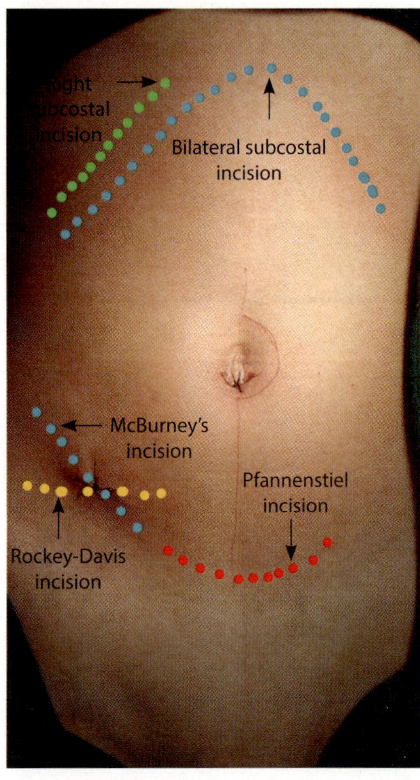

Figure 4.2 Right subcostal, bilateral subcostal, McBurney's, Rockey–Davis, and Pfannenstiel incisions.

- Transverse and oblique (Fig. 4.2)
  - Rooftop
  - Maylard
  - Cherney
  - Pfannenstiel
  - Subcostal
  - McBurney's

  Transverse incision is preferred if adequate exposure can be obtained. This is because it involves better cosmesis and fewer respiratory complications. Transverse incision is parallel to Langer's line of skin, inflicts less tension on suture line, and runs parallel to important structures such as nerves and blood vessels.
- Retroperitoneal
- Thoracoabdominal
- Separate thoracic and abdominal

FACTORS AFFECTING CHOICE OF INCISION

- It should provide adequate exposure.

- It should cause minimal damage to the deeper structures.
- It should be readily extendable, if required.
- It should cause minimal interference with abdominal wall function (injury to the motor nerve and muscle).
- It should provide sound and secure closure.
- It should be cosmetically acceptable. For better cosmesis, incision should be parallel to the line of dermal collagen fibers (Langer's line). In some cases, dog ear at the end of incision develops; skin hook is used to elevate the dog ear and cut it parallel to the skin for a satisfactory cosmetic result.
- An elliptical incision must be at least three times as long as it is wide for allowing tension-free closure.
- In *reoperation*, same incision is ideal. Care must be taken to avoid injury to the underlying structure due to possibility of adhesion. Never put an incision parallel to another incision because of risk of necrosis in between.

MIDLINE INCISION

Indications

- Upper midline: Surgery involving
  - Esophageal hiatus and abdominal esophagus
  - Stomach
  - Duodenum
  - Liver
  - Pancreas
  - Spleen
- Lower midline
  - Lower abdominal and pelvic organ

In some cases, incision can be extended superiorly up to xiphoid process and inferiorly up to symphysis pubis (major trauma).

Layers Cut

- Skin
- Subcutaneous tissue
- Linea alba
- Preperitoneal fat
- Peritoneum

Advantages

- Rapid
- Better exposure
- Little blood loss
- No muscle fiber and no nerve is cut
- Good access on both sides

It is an ideal incision for emergency surgery (abdominal trauma, acute abdomen, major hemorrhage).

Disadvantage

It is cosmetically ugly and risk of acute wound failure is high.

Procedure

While taking entry near the umbilicus, pick up the peritoneum with artery forceps, palpate in between, and carefully incise fold with scalpel (avoid injury to the intestine). Opening is widened to admit two fingers that are used to protect the underlying bowel or viscera.

The falciform ligament is best avoided by taking entry into the peritoneum either left or right of the midline.

Curve the incision around the umbilicus to avoid dividing it and for better exposure.

In case of a previous surgery, incision should begin 3–4 cm beyond the scar to avoid injury to the underlying structure.

Closure

- Nowadays, mass closure using no. 1 nylon, polypropylene, or polydioxanone (PDS) is preferred. There is still controversy between multilayer closure and en mass closure. Some studies show that multilayer closure is associated with increased wound complications while others show no difference. The ease with which fascia is closed and time required for closure in en mass closure allow it to be the method of preference for closing the incision.
- Continuous running closure with delayed absorbable suture is preferred. Advantage of continuous suture is even distribution of tension throughout the suture line and disadvantage is its dependence on a single suture. Nonresorbable or delayed resorbable suture is preferred to minimize the risk of wound complications.
- Two size 0 looped or 1 size nonlooped suture is used. Principle of 1 is followed; suture is passed 1 cm from the wound edge and at 1-cm interval.
- Apex and lower end of incision are clearly defined.

- Using delayed absorbable suture on a blunt or taper cut needle, approximate with continuous running stitch using 1:4 wound to suture length ratio. On completion of the half of the incision closure, commence from the opposite side and tie the two sutured segments in the middle with a secure knot.
- Bury the knot under fascial layer to avoid discomfort.

PARAMEDIAN

- It is a vertical incision.
- It is 2.5–4 cm from the midline.
- There is good exposure.
- No muscle, nerve, or vessel is cut.
- It is a physiological incision.

Indications

- *Right upper paramedian*: Stomach, duodenum, gallbladder, and biliary tract surgery
- *Left upper paramedian*: Stomach and splenic surgery
- *Lower paramedian*: Is for pelvic organ; right lower paramedian for cecum and ascending colon and left for sigmoid and descending colon

Layers Cut

- Skin
- Subcutaneous fat
- Anterior rectus sheath
- Muscle separated and retracted laterally (rectus muscle has a segmental nerve supply derived from the intercostal nerve, which enters the rectus from the lateral side)
- Posterior rectus sheath and peritoneum

Closure

- Peritoneum and posterior rectus sheath: These are closed with polyglactin 910 or PDS.
- Allow the rectus muscle to fall back.
- Close anterior rectus sheath with polyglactin 910 or PDS.

Advantages

- Provides access to the lateral structures
- Is theoretically more secure closure

Disadvantages

- Time consuming, not advisable in emergency surgery
- Bilateral access not possible
- Difficult to access superiorly as limited by costal margin

Differences Between Upper and Lower Rectus Sheath

- In upper rectus sheath, there are three tendinous inscriptions: Subxiphoid, umbilicus, and midway between two.
- In lower rectus sheath, posterior rectus sheath is absent below semicircular line of Douglas. Inferior epigastric artery needs to be ligated prior to division.

TRANSVERSE INCISION

- Site
  - It can be placed above and below the umbilicus depending on requirements.
  - Ramstedt pyloromyotomy and transverse colostomy incision is above the umbilicus.
  - Lanz incision and Pfannenstiel incision are below the umbilicus.
  - Split the fascial fiber of the abdominal wall parallel to the long axis of fascia.
- Advantages
  - More anatomically aligned with Langer's line
  - Best cosmesis
  - Closure stronger as compared to that with vertical incision
  - Less wound complications such as wound dehiscence and incisional hernia
  - Associated with less postoperative pain and less pulmonary complications
- Disadvantages
  - It provides limited access to the specific organ.
  - Pathology in the upper and lower abdomen cannot be dealt with.

Pfannenstiel Incision

- Indications
  - Gynecological operation
  - Lower segment Caesarean section
  - Operation on retropubic space
- Advantage
  - Better cosmesis

- Disadvantage
  - Limited access
- Incision is 2–3 cm above the pubic symphysis in interspinous crease.

Layers cut

- Skin
- Subcutaneous fat
- Anterior rectus sheath divided transversely
- Sheath separated from muscle superiorly up to umbilicus and inferiorly up to pubic symphysis
- Muscle retracted laterally
- Peritoneum cut open vertically

Closure

- Peritoneum closed with polyglycolic acid or polyglactin 910 (optional)
- Rectus sheath closed with polypropylene or PDS

Kocher Subcostal Incision

- Indications
  - *Right*: Surgery on the gallbladder and biliary tract
  - *Left*: Splenectomy, and Hassab and Sugiura operations for esophageal varices
  - *Bilateral (Chevron)*: Liver resection, total gastrectomy, pancreatic surgery, and anterior access to both adrenal glands
- Advantage
  - Direct access to gallbladder on right and spleen on left
- Disadvantages
  - Time consuming
  - More bleeding as compared to that with vertical incision
  - Injury to subcostal nerve

Incision is started at the midline two fingerbreadths below xiphoid process and extended laterally and runs 1 inch below and parallel to the costal margin (sufficient fascia must be preserved to allow secure closure so avoid placing too far superior incision).

Layers cut

- Skin
- Subcutaneous fat
- External oblique muscle
- Internal oblique muscle
- Transverse abdominis muscle
- Anterior rectus sheath
- Rectus muscle
- Peritoneum

Rectus and other muscles are divided using electrocautery. It is to control the branches of the superior epigastric artery.

Closure

- Mass closure technique is used to close the incision.
- Technique is as described in closure of midline incision.

Layered closure

- Peritoneum is left to heal by mesothelial cell regeneration.
- Muscles are closed with polyglactin 910, PDS no. 1, and polypropylene no. 1.
- Anterior rectus sheath is closed with no. 1 PDS or polypropylene continuous sutures.

Rockey–Davis Incision

- Modified McBurney's incision
- Cosmetically superior
- Transversely placed

  Indications of Rockey–Davis incision are as follows:
- Appendectomy
- Cecostomy

Layers cut

- Skin
- Subcutaneous tissue
- External oblique aponeurosis
- Internal oblique and transverse abdominis: Split in the direction of muscle fiber
- Tranversalis fascia
- Peritoneum

If more exposure is required, medially rectus sheath is divided and muscle retracted medially and lateral extension is achieved by dividing oblique muscle.

Closure

By either mass closure or layered closure

Other Incisions

Other incisions are not commonly used nowadays in surgery:

- *Maylard*: Same as Pfannenstiel incision except lower flap is not raised and recti are cut transversely
- *Cherney*: Same as Pfannenstiel incision except after raising flap, recti are cut free from the symphysis pubis and retracted upwards
- *Mayo-Robson (hockey stick) incision*: Right paramedian with a medial right subcostal incision

THORACOABDOMINAL INCISION

It enhances the exposure of upper abdominal organ. This incision is reserved for the operations that cannot be safely performed via abdominal incision as it is associated with pulmonary complications and phrenic nerve injury.

- Indications
  - *Right abdominothoracic incision*: It provides good exposure of right hemidiaphragm, esophagus, liver, portal triad, inferior vena cava, right kidney, right adrenal, and head and body of pancreas:
    - Operation on the liver and biliary tract
    - Portocaval shunt
  - *Left abdominothoracic incision*: It provides good exposure of left hemidiaphragm, gastroesophageal junction, gastric cardia, stomach, distal pancreas, left kidney, adrenal, aorta, and spleen:
    - Operation on the lower third esophagus, cardia, and stomach
    - Lienorenal shunt
- Technique
  - It involves corkscrew position with abdomen tilted 45° from the horizontal and thorax is oriented in full lateral position.
  - Midline or paramedian incision is kept, after entering the abdominal cavity; incision is extended laterally and obliquely along the line of eighth intercostal space just beneath the inferior angle of scapula.
  - After entering the abdominal cavity, on oblique extension of incision, the following layers are cut:
    - Skin
    - Subcutaneous tissue
    - Latissimus dorsi
    - Serratus anterior
    - External oblique muscle and aponeurosis
    - Intercostal muscles divided
    - Short segment of costal cartilage
    - Diaphragm incised radially or in curvilinear fashion (avoids injury to phrenic nerve)
- Closure
  - Chest tube kept
  - Diaphragm closed in two layers using nonabsorbable suture
  - Ribs approximated with sutures
  - Chest wall and abdominal wall closure done in layer-wise fashion
- Advantage
  - Good exposure of both peritoneal and pleural cavities
- Disadvantages
  - Time consuming
  - Chances of infection due to opening of both the cavities
  - Pulmonary complications
  - Management of intercostal drainage

RETROPERITONEAL INCISION

Indications

- Surgery involving kidney such as stone surgery
- Ureterolithotomy
- Nephrectomy
- Aortic surgery
- Lumbar sympathectomy

Layers Cut

- Skin
- Subcutaneous tissue
- In posterior part: Latissimus dorsi and serratus posterior inferior muscle
- Periosteum incised
- Free periosteum from surrounding and subperiosteal resection of rib
- Pleura safeguarded
- In anterior part: External oblique muscle, internal oblique muscle, and transversus abdominis muscle
- Peritoneum safeguarded

Closure

- Layered or mass closure using either monofilament PDS no. 1 (monolayer) or polyglactin 910 or 1-0 (layer-wise) closure
- Advantages
  - Postoperative paralytic ileus is reduced (by not entering the peritoneal cavity, manipulation and handling of intra-abdominal viscera is minimal).
  - Hemorrhage is likely to be tamponaded as compared to that with transperitoneal approach.

INGUINAL INCISION

- Indication
  - Repair of inguinal hernia

Details of inguinal incision are given in section 'Hernia' of Chapter 6.

It is sometimes very difficult for the surgeons to decide where to put the incision in case of nontraumatic acute abdomen. It happens that surgeons kept the upper midline incision and pathology is there in the pelvis and he/she needs to extend the incision. In such a situation, equivocal incision is better. Incision is kept 2 inches above and 2 inches below the umbilicus curving around the umbilicus. After entering the peritoneum, carefully inspect the peritoneal cavity and decide in which direction incision needs to be extended. If pathology is in the pelvis or lower abdomen, make it lower midline and if it is in the upper abdominal organ, make it upper midline. Right paramedian incision can also be kept as most pathology leading to acute abdomen and not confidently diagnosed preoperatively is on the right side.

Reference

1. Baker RJ. Abdominal wall incisions and repair. In: Fischer JE, Bland KI, Callery MP, eds. Mastery of Surgery, 5th edn. Philadelphia: Lippincott Williams & Wilkins, 2007, 131–47.

CHAPTER 5

Fundamentals of Minimal Access Surgery

MINIMAL ACCESS SURGERY

Minimal access/invasive surgery[1] is a means of performing major surgeries via small incisions as compared to larger incision needed in traditional laparotomy, often using specially designed instruments and miniaturized, high-tech imaging systems, to minimize the trauma of surgical exposure. Minimal access does not refer to magnitude of invasiveness as the absolute criterion, but invasiveness or accessibility is compared with the conventional open surgery. When the concept of minimal invasive surgery was introduced, it was expected to better or at least equal the results of more traditional procedures. Thirty years after introduction, laparoscopic surgery has fulfilled most expectations. With the introduction of minimal access surgery, the importance of open surgery is decreasing. Nowadays, almost all general surgical operations can be performed using minimal access including procedures in the chest and abdomen.

The main limitations of traditional open surgery are wound size, trauma to tissue by retractors, and exposure of the cavity to the atmosphere. In minimal access surgery, wound-related complications such as infection, dehiscence, and pain are minimal. In laparoscopic surgery, gentle and even retraction is provided by pneumoperitoneum associated with minimal trauma.

Broadly, minimal access surgery can be categorized as follows:
- Laparoscopy
- Thoracoscopy
- Endoluminal endoscopy (upper gastrointestinal endoscopy, colonoscopy, cystoscopy, bronchoscope, natural orifice transluminal endoscopic surgery [NOTES], etc.)
- Perivisceral endoscopy (mediastinoscopy, retroperitoneoscopy, etc.)
- Arthroscopy

Nowadays, most of the procedures can be performed through minimal access surgery. We will concentrate more on laparoscopic surgery in this chapter (Tables 5.1 and 5.2).

Table 5.1 Commonly Performed Laparoscopic Procedures

Basic	Advanced
• Adhesinolysis • Appendectomy • Cholecystectomy • Inguinal hernia repair • Diagnostic laparoscopy	• Antireflux surgery • Bariatric surgery • Splenectomy • Anterior resection • Colectomy • Nephrectomy • Adrenalectomy • Gastrectomy • Gastrojejunostomy

Table 5.2 Contraindications for Laparoscopic Surgery

Absolute	Relative
• Hemodynamic instability • Uncorrected coagulopathy • Inability to give informed consent • Advanced pregnancy • Generalized peritonitis • Abdominal wall infection	• Multiple previous operations • Huge organomegaly • Abdominal aortic aneurysm

ENERGY SOURCES FOR LAPAROSCOPIC SURGERY

Phases of coagulation are the following:
- *Coagulation*: 60°C
- *Vaporization and desiccation*: 100°C
- *Carbonization*: >200°C

The three most commonly used sources of electrosurgery are the following:

1. Monopolar current
    - It is the most commonly used method.

- AC current is generated and travels through active electrode to the tissue at sufficiently high current density. Depending on tissue heating, coagulation, fulguration, or vaporization occurs. The circuit is completed by return of the electron back to the generator by returning electrode or grounding pad.
- Ground plate on the patient's leg or back receives the flow of electron that generates at a point of source (surgical electrode, such as hook, spatula).
- It causes high current density at the site of application and rapid heating of tissue.
- The exposed electrode tip must be under vision whenever the unit is operating, and the tissue has to be placed in tension to achieve cutting.
- Do not use power more than 30 W.
- Prolonged use of current increases the remote site electrical injury.
- Advantages are: Ease of use, better hemostasis, instrument can be used for dissection, and area of coagulates is twice that of the bipolar.

2. Bipolar
   - There is high-frequency, low-voltage current.
   - The electrons flow between two adjacent electrodes and the tissue between the two electrodes is heated and desiccated. They achieve greater hemostasis than monopolar devices.
   - One electrode acts as an active electrode and another electrode acts as a return electrode.
   - No patient return electrode is required.
   - Flow of current beyond field is minimal.
   - It allows small vessel coagulation without thermal injury to the adjacent structure.
   - Advantages are the following: Less lateral spread, safe in patients with pacemakers, and minimal risk of capacitive coupling.
3. Vessel sealing device
   - It consists of low-voltage, high-amperage bipolar instruments that fuse vessel wall and create a permanent seal. It seals up to 7-mm vessel. The seal can withstand three times normal systolic blood pressure.
   - Advantages of vessel sealing energy sources are the following:
     - Up to 7-mm vessel is sealed.
     - A single instrument can grasp, coagulate, dissect, and cut so it can save time by fewer instrument exchanges during the procedure.
     - There is less thermal damage.
     - There is no capacitive coupling.

Ultrasonic Energy Source (Figs 5.1 and 5.2)

(*Synonym*: Harmonic scalpel)

Principle

Electrical energy is converted to mechanical vibration.

One blade of the ultrasonic shears oscillates at 55,000 cycles/second, generating localized heat of 50–100°C. This causes amino acid unwind and reshape and hydrogen bond breaks, resulting in sticky coagulum that seals the vessel. Lateral

Figure 5.1 Harmonic generator.

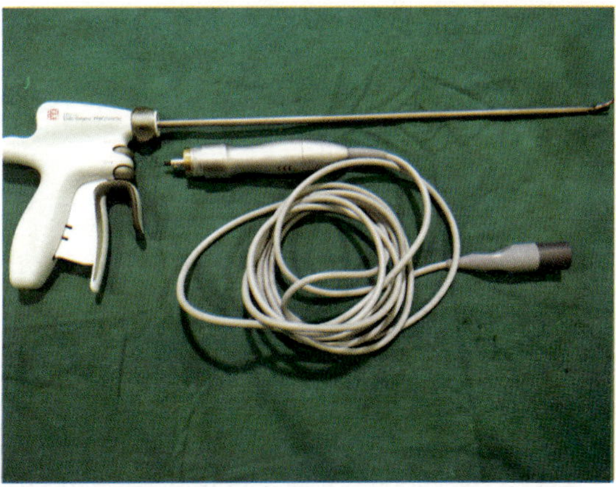

Figure 5.2 Harmonic shear and hand piece.

thermal spread is only 2 mm so it is a very efficient tool for bowel as well as solid organ surgery.

Modes

- *Cutting (maximum)*: Rapid cycling of active blade, precise cutting, less thermal spread, and less hemostasis
- *Coagulating (minimum)*: Slow cycling of active blade, less precise cutting, more thermal spread, and more accurate hemostasis

Advantages

- It is useful to control medium-sized vessels (up to 5 mm) that are too big to control with monopolar cautery.
- A single instrument can grasp, coagulate, dissect, and cut so it can save time by fewer instrument exchanges during the procedure.
- There are no capacitive coupling, minimal thermal damage, and no tissue sticking.
- Very less smoke is generated compared to that with monopolar and bipolar devices.
- Absence of charring of tissue keeps the operative field clear.
- It is safe.

Limitations

Its utility is limited for sealing major or named vessels and active blade remains hot for few seconds so contact with delicate tissue during this time is avoided. Fogging of laparoscope is common as it produces steam and makes the environment humid.

PATIENT PREPARATION

The patient's preparation is the same as that in an open surgery (Chapter 1, *Preoperative Preparation*). However, some important considerations are given in the subsequent text.

Careful History and Physical Examination

- Patients must be fit for general anesthesia and open surgery if required. Coagulation profile needs to be corrected prior to laparoscopic surgery.
- Careful physical examination to rule out severe cardiopulmonary problem and presence or absence of jaundice and abdominal scar needs special attention.

Informed Consent

- Patients must be explained in detail about the pros and cons of laparoscopic surgery. Complications particular to the laparoscopy such as trocar injury, thermal injury, injury to the bile duct, shoulder tip pain, and surgical emphysema need to be explained.
- Patients should know the limitations of laparoscopic surgery and that every laparoscopic surgery has an inherent risk of conversion to open surgery.
- Patients should be explained about the alternative procedure available.

DVT Prophylaxis

- Patients undergoing laparoscopic surgery are at a high risk for developing DVT and high incidence of nausea and vomiting.
- In addition to common factors associated with a high risk for DVT, reverse Trendelenburg position is also associated with a high risk for DVT. Details of DVT prophylaxis have been discussed in Chapter 1.

Postoperative Nausea and Vomiting (PONV)

- Ondansetron is the most effective prophylaxis. Low-dose steroids are also associated with a low incidence of nausea and vomiting without increased the incidence of infectious complications.
- Other preventive measures are: Nasogastric decompression and adequate hydration. Intravenous ketorolac or diclofenac sodium by decreasing the requirement of narcotics may also help to prevent nausea and vomiting. Avoiding GA when possible, use of propofol for induction and maintenance of anesthesia, and avoiding nitrous oxide and volatile anesthetic may also help to prevent PONV.

OPERATING ROOM SETUP

Basic instruments (Fig. 5.3) required for setting minimal access surgery operating room (OR) are as follows:

- Camera
- Telescope
- Fiber-optic cable
- Light source
- CO_2 insufflators

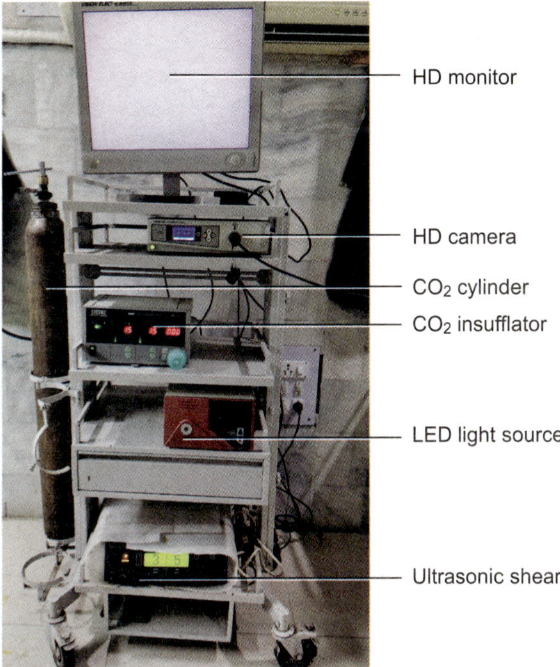

Figure 5.3 Trolley of laparoscopy.

- Monitor
- Hand instruments

One should make the best possible OR and consider between single-chip cameras, halogen light source, and simple TV monitors and three-chip cameras, xenon light source, and medical-grade monitors.

Cleaning of instruments is difficult because their design is complex and they are delicate in nature. Blood and other body fluids also enter the channels of the instrument.

- Operative field should be between the surgeon and the monitor. An LCD or HD monitor is ideal.
- Position of the monitor varies according to surgery, for example, in laparoscopic cholecystectomy the monitor should be at 10 o'clock position at the right side on the shoulder side and the surgeon should be at 4 o'clock position while in pelvic surgery the monitor should be best placed at foot end. The insufflating device and other equipment should be kept opposite to the surgeon so he or she can observe pressure, gas flow, end-tidal CO_2, etc.
- Recording system is desirable to record the procedure.

Van det et al.[2] have provided the following guidelines for optimal laparoscopic surgery suites:

- Monitor is positioned straight ahead of each person in line with the forearm instrument motor axis and it should be at the level of eye (preferable 15° lower).
- *Patient's position*: Arms or legs do not interfere with the surgeon's movement and position of the patients should enable the surgeon's alignment with the operating field (Table 5.3).

Table 5.3 Patient's Position

Position	Procedure
Supine, split leg	Nissen fundoplication, paraesophageal hernia, bariatric surgery, cholecystectomy, liver surgery, splenectomy, gastrectomy
Supine	Appendectomy, adhesinolysis, adrenalectomy, inguinal hernia
Lateral decubitus	Adrenalectomy
Lithotomy	Rectal surgery such as APR, low anterior resection, and total proctocolectomy

- *Equipment position*: Do not disrupt the eye–hand–target axis; there should be no view blockage for the surgeons, OT assistants, and OR nurses, and free axis of rotation should be allowed for the patient's, surgeon's, and assistant's positions.

ANESTHESIA AND SURGERY

- General anesthesia with controlled ventilation is the choice of anesthesia for most minimal invasive surgeries.
- Controlled ventilation helps to counteract hypercapnia and hypoxia, to meet the simultaneously increased ventilatory requirements.
- The anesthetist and the surgeon must communicate properly and effectively during surgery as many complications, especially cardiovascular and pulmonary complications, are readily treatable by releasing pneumoperitoneum.
- As most of the minimal invasive procedures are performed on day care basis, short-acting, well-tolerated anesthetic agents are preferable.
- Nowadays, few studies had been performed where laparoscopic surgeries are performed under spinal anesthesia with low-pressure pneumoperitoneum.

CREATING PNEUMOPERITONEUM

There are three methods:

1. Closed technique with Veress needle
2. Direct trocar technique
3. Open technique with Hasson technique

Veress Needle Technique (Figs 5.4 and 5.5)

It is the oldest and most popular method. Veress needle is a spring-loaded needle, 12 cm in length, with an external diameter of 2 mm. The abdominal wall is relatively thin at the periumbilical area. An adequate incision is made to allow the passage of trocar. The abdominal wall is held with either hand or towel clip. Two distinct pops are felt as the surgeon passes the needle through fascia and peritoneum. The position of the needle should be confirmed. It should move freely about the fulcrum point located within the anterior abdominal wall.

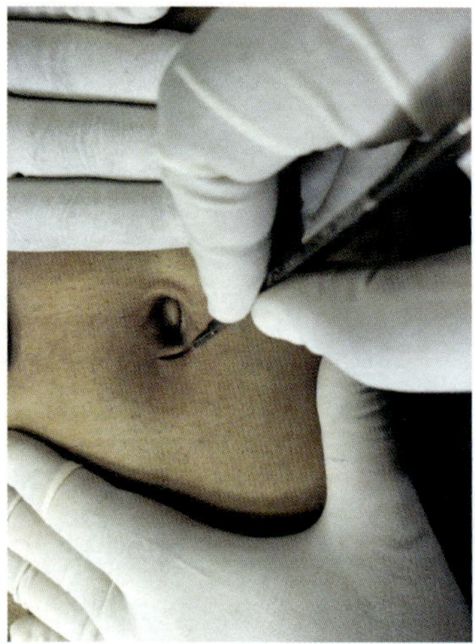

Figure 5.4 Periumbilical skin incision.

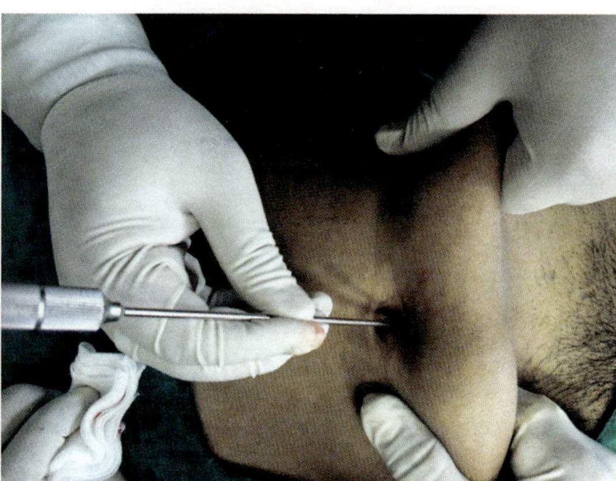

Figure 5.5 Insertion of Veress needle.

Tests to check the position of the needle are the following:

- *Aspirate*: There should be no blood or enteric content. Presence of either of these indicates wrong entry.
- *Inject saline*: It should enter freely.
- *Drop test*: Elevate the abdominal wall; put a drop of saline over the hub of the needle; saline will suck in (Fig. 5.6).

Abdomen is insufflated with CO_2 gas after confirming the position of the needle; pressure is kept around 15 mmHg. Watch is kept on flow rate and abdominal pressure. Zero flow rate and more than 20 mmHg pressure indicate that tip of the needle is not situated freely within the peritoneal

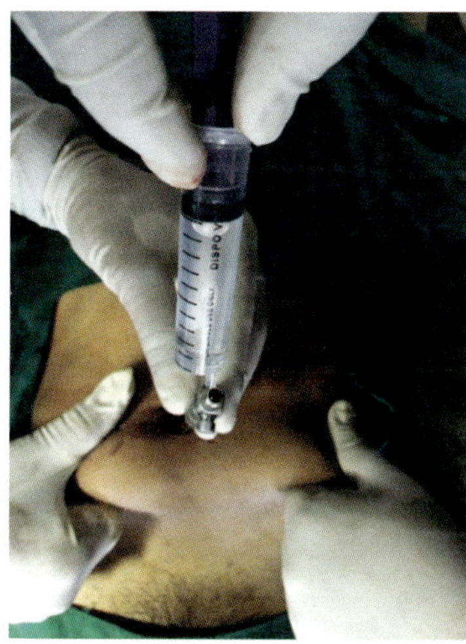

Figure 5.6 Drop test to confirm intra-abdominal placement.

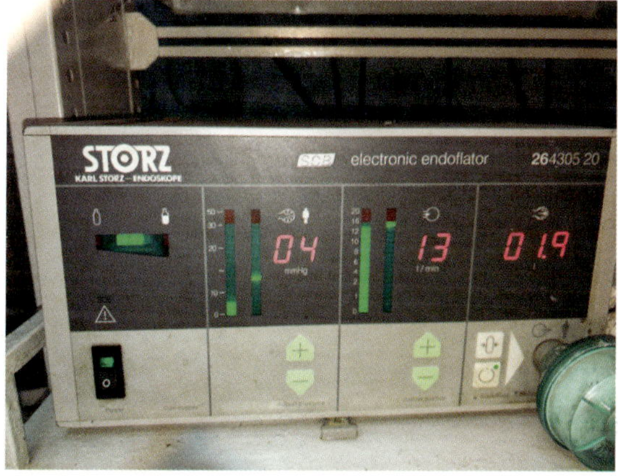

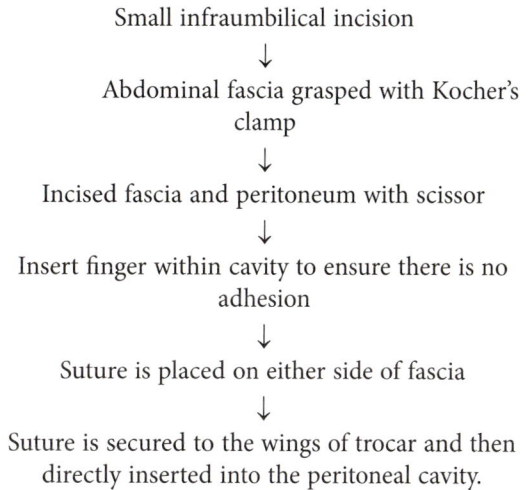

Figure 5.7 Pressure of 4 mmHg on insufflator indicates intra-abdominal placement of needle.

cavity. Pressure below 10 mmHg indicates free position of tip of the needle (strongest predictor of intra-abdominal placement) (Fig. 5.7).

After an adequate volume of gas insufflations, Veress needle is removed and trocar is inserted blindly. Gas tubing is connected to the trocar. Other trocars are inserted under direct vision.

Other techniques are the following: direct trocar insertion and Hasson technique.

Hasson Technique

It is used in case of suspected adhesion or in the presence of suspected obstruction.

Small infraumbilical incision

↓

Abdominal fascia grasped with Kocher's clamp

↓

Incised fascia and peritoneum with scissor

↓

Insert finger within cavity to ensure there is no adhesion

↓

Suture is placed on either side of fascia

↓

Suture is secured to the wings of trocar and then directly inserted into the peritoneal cavity.

FASCIAL CLOSURE

- All ports more than 10 mm need to be closed.
- A 5-mm defect does not require closure.
- It can be closed with a conventional needle. Specialized needle or port closure devices are also available in the market.
- Fascial closure can prevent port site hernia.

PORT PLACEMENT

- Location of port depends on the procedure (Fig. 5.8).
- Usual site for primary port is umbilicus, but it is not mandatory.
- Secondary port needs to be placed according to the site of operation and should not be placed too close to the primary port.
- Secondary port should be placed under vision with transillumination of the abdominal wall to avoid injury to the wall vessels (Fig. 5.9). Secondary trocar should be placed under direct vision to avoid injury to the intra-abdominal organs (Fig. 5.10). The area beneath the primary trocar should be inspected to look for unexpected injuries.
- Trocar for the surgeon's left and right hands should be placed at least 10 cm apart. If possible, orient telescope between these trocars.
- The surgeon should stand behind the telescope for optimal ergonomics.

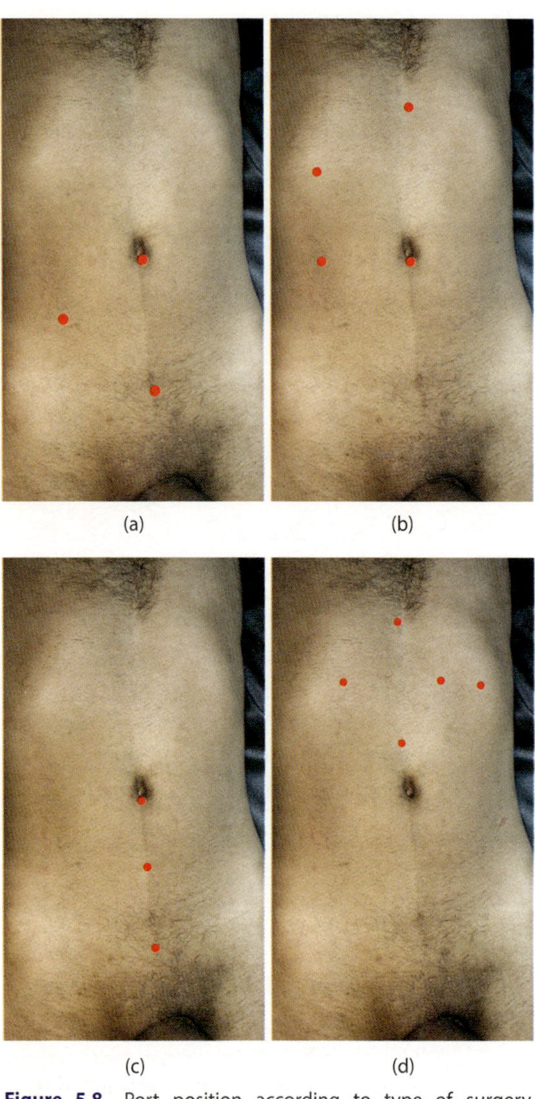

Figure 5.8 Port position according to type of surgery. (a) Laparoscopic appendectomy, (b) laparoscopic cholecystectomy, (c) laparoscopic total extraperitoenal repair of hernia, and (d) laparoscopic Nissen fundoplication port position.

- The optimal pattern of port placement should form a diamond array or an equilateral triangle around the operative field (Fig. 5.11).
- The position of the operating table should allow the surgeon to work with both elbows in at the sides with arm bent at 90° at the elbow joint.
- The fulcrum of the instrument should be 15 cm to produce 1:1 translation movement from the surgeon's hand to the operative field as the standard length of the laparoscopy instrument is 30 cm.

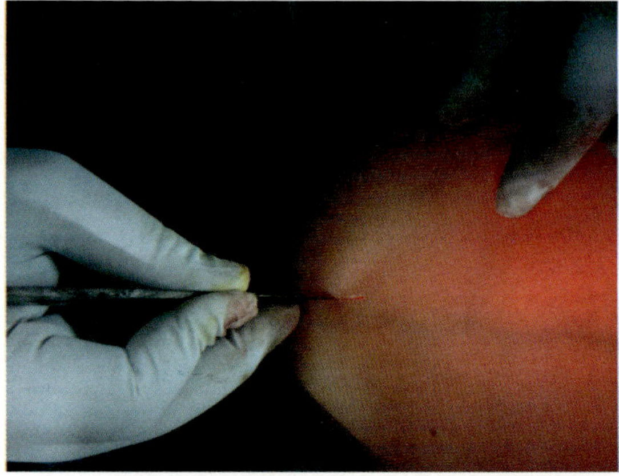

Figure 5.9 Incision for second port with transillumination of the abdominal wall.

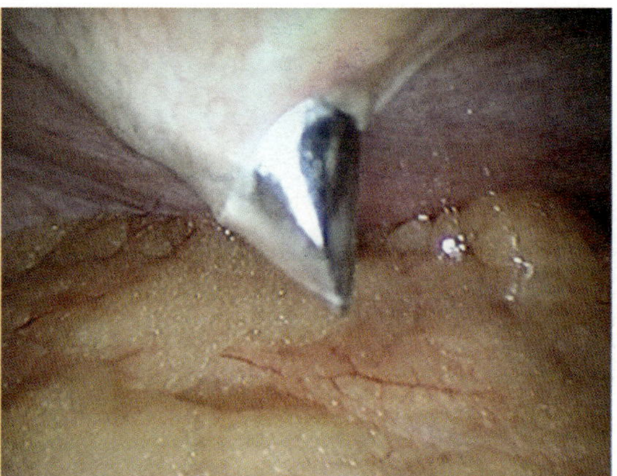

Figure 5.10 Under vision placement of second trocar.

- The angle between two instruments at the target should be optimal (60–90°) to avoid sword fighting.
- Depending on the operation, position of the table needs to be altered such as Trendelenburg or reverse Trendelenburg, head low or head up, and right tilt.

GASES USED IN THE LAPAROSCOPY

These are CO_2, N_2O, helium, and argon. However, CO_2 is the most commonly used.

Advantages of CO_2 are the following:

- Cheap
- Readily available
- Suppresses the combustion
- Easily absorbed by the tissue and quickly released via respiration

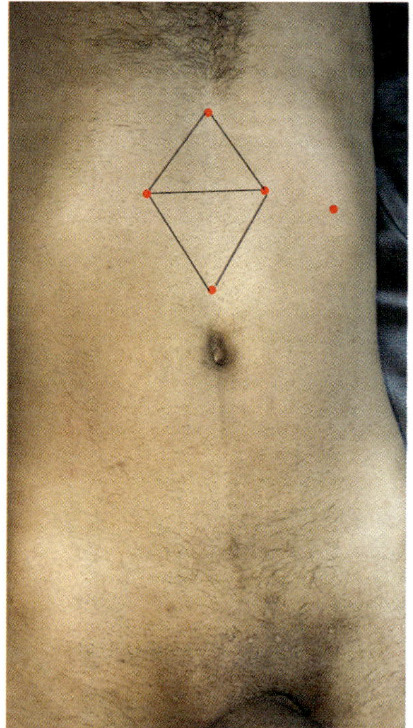

Figure 5.11 Concept of diamond. Trocars for the surgeon's right and left hands are placed 10–12 cm apart. This creates an equilateral triangle, with the sides measuring 10–12 cm, between the right hand, left hand and telescope. Target of operation is at the apex. Telescope is at the lowest port. It provides optimal ergonomics (e.g., laparoscopic fundoplication).

Laparoscopic surgery requires the insufflations of CO_2 into the abdominal cavity.

PHYSIOLOGICAL EFFECTS OF PNEUMOPERITONEUM

- Increased abdominal pressure

  ↓

  Decreased venous return

  ↓

  Decreased cardiac output

  ↓

  Increased heart rate

  ↓

  Increased myocardial oxygen demand

  High-risk patients with cardiorespiratory problem may not tolerate laparoscopy well.

- Pneumoperitoneum

  ↓

  Increased heart rate and systemic vascular resistance

  ↓

  Hypertension and impaired visceral blood flow

- Increased intra-abdominal pressure

  ↓

  Restricted movement of diaphragm

  ↓

  Decreased functional residual capacity and decreased pulmonary compliance

- Increased abdominal pressure

  ↓

  Decreased renal blood flow

  ↓

  Decreased GFR

  ↓

  Decreased urine output

- Increased intra-abdominal pressure

  ↓

  Increased pressure over IVC

  ↓

  Decreased venous return

  ↓

  Increased risk of DVT

STRESS RESPONSE IN OPEN AND LAPAROSCOPIC SURGERIES

There is less stress response and cytokine release is same in both minimal and open surgeries, but normalization occurs more rapidly in minimal access surgery and there is less depression of delayed-type hypersensitivity.

THORACOSCOPY AND EXTRACAVITARY ENDOSCOPIC SURGERY

- Because of bony confines of the thorax, it does not require positive pressure to create working space. By deflating an ipsilateral lung via double-lumen endotracheal tube, working space is obtained. If positive pressure is desirable, one must keep it less than 10 mmHg to avoid developing a tension pneumothorax.

- Extracavitary endoscopic surgeries are associated with subcutaneous emphysema and metabolic acidosis.

COMPLICATIONS

- Insertion of Veress needle and primary trocar accounts for around 40% of all laparoscopic complications.
- Injury to the small bowel is the most common followed by that to the abdominal wall vessel. Other injuries include bladder, major abdominal vessel, and stomach injuries.

Vascular Injury[3]

Major vessel injury

- Incidence of major vascular injury is slightly more common with closed technique. Injuries due to trocar are more obvious and catastrophic. Transmural injury is the rule.
- Once recognized, trocar and cannula are left in place, the abdomen is opened, and vascular repair is performed. In major vessels, iliac artery and iliac vein followed by mesenteric vessels are injured.
- Once bleeding vessel is identified, catch with fingertip grasper; apply either electrocautery or clip depending on the size of the vessel.
- If bleeding vessel is not readily identified due to blood pool, apply compression with either swab or adjacent organ, suck with good-quality suction, and gradually release the compression to locate the bleeding point. Once identified, electrocautery, clip, or repair is performed.
- Surgicel or tissue glues may also be used for hemostasis.
- Abdominal aorta and vena cava injuries are less common.
- For major vessels, rapidly convert to open, ask anesthetist to control volume, and prepare for blood loss. Control inflow and outflow to perform repair.

Trocar site bleeding

- Bleeding from the trocar site can be controlled by applying pressure with trocar upward and laterally.
- If substantial bleeding from either falciform ligament or epigastric vessel is present, passing suture passer needle with monofilament suture from one side of bleeding and exiting it from the other side and applying traction throughout the procedure will suffice. Pressure can also be applied using Foley catheter through trocar site and is left in situ for 24 hours.
- For abdominal wall vessel, it is important to visualize all trocar sites after its removal to minimize abdominal wall vascular complications.

Bleeding from the gallbladder bed

Direct (either hook or ultrasonic shear or with direct grasper) or indirect (apply pressure with blunt, insulated grasper and touch the grasper with another insulated grasper connected with electrocautery) application of electrocautery controls the bleeding.

Evacuation of blood clot

Best strategy is to avoid the formation itself.

How to avoid

- Dissect in a correct plane (gallbladder bed), identifying vessels and its branches (e.g., cystic artery and its branches).
- Using 5000 units of heparin per liter of irrigation fluid helps to prevent clot formation.

Treatment

- Once it is formed, due to either failure of identifying cystic artery or anomalous vessels and not getting proper plane due to severe inflammation, large-bore suction is used to retrieve the blood clot.
- Large-bore suction is used to retrieve the blood clot.
- Care should be taken to avoid suction in close proximity to the clip.

Bowel Injury

Many bowel injuries are not recognized at the time of operation.

Once needle injury is suspected, it should be kept in place and second needle is placed in another location. Once within the abdomen, location is identified and repair performed

Perforation of the Gallbladder

- It is more common in laparoscopy as compared to that in the open counterpart.

- It is usually due to traction on the gallbladder or thermal injury.
- Bile is not sterile even in the absence of cholecystitis so every attempt should be made to close the perforation by either endoclip or Endoloop.
- Bile spillage can prolong the operative time. It usually does not require conversion to open; liberal irrigation and aspiration of the bile suffice.
- Escaped stone is associated with an increased risk of infectious complications such as intra-abdominal abscess and port site abscess so every attempt must be made to retrieve the stone.
- Plastic retrieval bag is recommended to remove large and friable gallbladder.

Electrical or Thermal Injury

Mechanism of electrical injury to nontarget tissue

- *Insulation failure*: Insulating coating of instruments is compromised and it allows dissipation of heat to the other organs in contact with shaft. Insulation failure may be because of manufacturing problem, abrasive cleaning of instruments, and continuous use of high-voltage current.

  Laparoscopic field of view must include all uninsulated portions of the electrosurgical electrodes.

  Integrity of the insulation must be maintained and assured.
- *Direct coupling*: When active electrodes touch other conductive instruments such as clip, laparoscope, metal tip of the other instruments, or stapler within the body. Current may flow from the active electrode of the monopolar instrument to the contiguous conductive instruments that are in contact with bowel or another nontarget tissue.

  Example: Application of cautery close to clip of cystic duct can dissipate energy to the bile duct.
- *Capacitive coupling*: When current is transferred from an active electrode to the adjacent tissue without direct contact in the presence of intact insulation. Normally electrical current disperses from the cannula to the abdominal wall and returns to the passive electrode. A capacitor exists between two conductors separated by insulation (active electrode within cannula). Transfer of unintended energy from the cannula results in injury to the nontarget tissue. Chances increase when hybrid cannulas such as metal and plastic are used.

CO_2-Related Adverse Effects

- Hypercapnia and acidosis:
  - Rapid carbon dioxide absorption from the peritoneal membrane leads to development of hypercapnia and acidosis.
  - In a ventilated patient, increase in minute ventilation or respiratory rate must compensate for hypercapnia and acidosis.
  - Normal physiological buffers can neutralize up to 120 L of carbonic acid. Increase in respiratory rate above 20/minute diminishes time for gas mixing and a large increase in vital capacity may lead to barotraumas.
  - Best treatment is to deflate the abdomen for 10–15 minutes and reinflate; if patients again develop hypercapnia, then change the gas.
- Capnothorax: At the time of transhiatal dissection or through defect in the diaphragm or opening of the pleuroperitoneal duct.
  - Effects
    - Hypoxia
    - Decreased pulmonary compliance
    - Increased end-tidal CO_2
  - Treatment
    - Deflate abdomen.
    - Stop CO_2 administration.
    - Adjust ventilator.
    - Evacuate with the help of red rubber catheter through defect in the pleura and one end should be brought through trocar and kept in water seal till the bubble stops and then the catheter should be removed.
- Carbon dioxide gas embolus: Gases such as CO_2 and N_2O are poorly soluble in blood. Gas embolism develops if gas has direct access to the venous system.
  - Diagnosis
    - Hypotension during insufflations
    - Unexplained hypotension and hypoxia during surgery
    - Mill wheel murmur on auscultation
    - Decrease in end-tidal CO_2 (complete right ventricular outflow obstruction)

    - Transesophageal echocardiography, which is the most sensitive test to detect embolus (other devices used to detect embolus are the following: precordial Doppler, end-tidal nitrogen, end-tidal CO_2, and pulmonary artery catheter)
  - Treatment
    - Hyperventilation
    - One hundred percent oxygen
    - Durant position (left lateral decubitus with head low) that will trap the gas in the apex of right ventricle
    - Central venous catheter to aspirate gas bubble

Conversion to Open From Laparoscopy

It is not a failure for surgeon but is always a wise decision.

- Lack of progression in the surgery
- Hemodynamic instability of patient
- Inability to create or maintain pneumoperitoneum
- Failure of instruments
- Compromise of oncological outcome
- Surgeon's experience
- Uncontrolled hemorrhage

POSTOPERATIVE CARE[3]

Most patients can be discharged within 24 hours.

Laparoscopic surgeries are associated with low incidence of pain and other problems.

Common postoperative symptoms are mild upper abdominal pain, nausea, and shoulder tip pain.

Measures adopted during operation to decrease postoperative pain are as follows:

- Port site instillation of LA
- Leaving 1 L normal saline within peritoneal cavity
- Instillation of local anesthetic into subhepatic space
- One hundred milligram diclofenac suppository

Postoperative pain management includes the following:

- One hundred milligram diclofenac suppository is provided for severe pain.
- For mild pain, 1 g paracetamol is sufficient every 4 hours.
- Opiate should be avoided unless pain is very severe.
- Usually not more than four doses of paracetamol are required. Persistent postoperative severe pain may indicate something is wrong and needs further investigation.
- If nasogastric tube is placed, it should be removed as soon as the operation is over. Oral fluid is started routinely after 6 hours in most procedures; exceptions are the following: Colectomy or resection and anastomosis involving small bowel. Patients can eat a light meal after 6–8 hours if they are not nauseated. They are advised that they can eat a normal diet but they should avoid high-fat meals for the first week and should avoid overeating.
- Urinary catheter, if placed, should be removed before the patient regains consciousness.
- Drain is removed as soon as the purpose is over. If kept to vent the remaining gas and/or peritoneal fluid, it is removed within 1 hour. If kept for bleeding or bile leak, it is removed within 24 hours. Continued blood loss from drain is an indication for re-exploration.

ADVANTAGES AND DISADVANTAGES[1]

Advantages of minimal access surgery are as follows:

- Postoperative pain and wound complications are reduced.
- Postoperative pulmonary complications are reduced.
- Immunosuppression caused by surgery is decreased.
- Wound trauma is decreased.
- Improved vision of the operative field helps the trainers and whole surgical team to have a better visualization of the wound.
- Heat loss is decreased.
- Cosmesis is improved.
- Reduced contact with patients' blood leads to decreased contact with pathogens such as HIV and HBV.
- Hospital stay is short.
- Minimal access surgery aids communications to the patients and their family with the help of recording.

Disadvantages of minimal access surgery are as follows:

- Expensive technology

- Longer operative time, especially during learning curve
- Technical expertise: Reliance on remote vision, loss of tactile feedback, and dependence on hand–eye coordination
- Potential complications related to trocar insertion
- Difficulty in achieving hemostasis
- Greater potential for iatrogenic injury through either surgical disorientation (CBD injury) or unrecognized bowel perforation
- Retrieval of intact organs difficult, particularly for the organ containing malignancy or a large organ

NATURAL ORIFICE TRANSLUMINAL ENDOSCOPIC SURGERY

NOTES combines techniques from both laparoscopy and endoscopy and is performed by making incisions in hollow viscera. There are two categories of NOTES:

- *Hollow-visceral transperitoneal (HVT)*: Transgastric, transcolonic
- *Squamous conduit intraperitoneal (SCI)*: Transvaginal, transanal

NOTES can also be classified as follows:

- *Pure NOTES*: Only natural orifice is used.
- *Rendezvous NOTES*: More than one portal of entry is used to complete the surgery such as transabdominal laparoscopy port.
- *Robotic NOTES*: Da Vinci surgical robot is used to perform various procedures. The most successful route is transvaginal as closure is easy and it is expansile.

SINGLE INCISION LAPAROSCOPIC SURGERY (SILS), LAPAROENDOSCOPIC SINGLE SITE SURGERY (LESS), SINGLE PORT ACCESS SURGERY (SPA)

The basic idea in SILS is to introduce all necessary instruments through a single incision.

SILS can be seen as a bridge between multiport laparoscopy and NOTES.

Potential advantages of SILS are the following:

- Better cosmesis
- Less trauma
- Less risk of port site bleeding
- Less chances of incisional hernia

Main disadvantages over conventional multiport surgeries are the following:

- Loss of triangulation
- Clashing of instruments
- Lack of tissue retraction by assistant surgeon

SILS uses umbilicus as a portal of entry. Transumbilical approach may be associated with high incidence of port site hernia and wound infection. Therefore, remote access laparoscopic surgery (REAL) was developed where the pubic line is used as a distant portal of entry.

Some centers have started cholecystectomy and hernia surgery through this technique.

The main difference between NOTES and SILS is that NOTES leaves no scar, while SILS leaves one small scar at the umbilicus.

ROBOTIC SURGERY

In robotic surgery, the surgeon uses a computer console to manipulate the instruments and a computer transmits the surgeon's movements, which are then carried out on the patient's body by the robot. Robot can be passive, semiactive, or active depending on the functions.

Limitations of laparoscopic surgery have created an interest in robotic surgery:

- Two-dimensional view
- Reduced degree of freedom of movement
- Little or no tactile feedback
- Ergonomically difficult position for the surgeon

Few examples of commercially available and FDA-approved robots are as follows: AESOP system (Computer Motion Inc., Santa Barbara, CA), the comprehensive master–slave surgical robotic systems, Da Vinci (Intuitive Surgical Inc., Mountain View, CA), and Zeus (Computer Motion Inc.).

Telementoring and telerobotics have been combined in SOCRATES (Computer Motion Inc.).

Advantages of assistance of robotic system are as follows:

- Improved vision (three-dimensional vision)
- Increased dexterity
- Elimination of hand tremor allowing greater precision
- Seven degrees of freedom allowed by robotic wrist and complex procedures allowed to be performed

- Decreased learning curve
- Better hand–eye coordination
- Less need of assistance during procedure
- Ergonomic environment with less stress and higher concentration

Disadvantages of robotic system are as follows:

- Cost
- Size of the system
- Lack of compatible instruments and equipment
- Loss of tactile sensation

Minimal access surgery has fundamentally changed surgical technology. In many aspects, minimal access surgery yields better results than its conventional open counterpart. With increasing experience, minimal access surgery offers cost-effectiveness to the health services and to patients by a short hospital stay and early return to work. There are many things that are new in minimal access surgery but only time will tell how much is really better. In the future, minimal access surgery will probably replace traditional open surgery.

References

1. Yagnik V. Minimal access surgery. IJMU 2011;6(2):1–2.
2. van Det MJ, Meijerink WJHJ, Hoff C, et al. Optimal ergonomics for laparoscopic surgery in minimally invasive surgery suites: a review and guidelines. Surg Endosc 2009;23:1279.
3. Ashrafian A, Purkayastha S, Darzi A. Principle of laparoscopic and robotic surgery. In: Bailey and Love Short Practice of Surgery. Williams NS, O'Connell PR, McCaskie, eds, 27th edn. FL: CRC press, Taylor and Francis, 2018, 105–18.

CHAPTER 6

Operative Procedures

APPENDICECTOMY (APPENDECTOMY)

DEFINITION

Surgical removal of appendix is called appendicectomy. The appendix is normally located in the right lower side of the abdomen and its surgical removal is usually carried out on an emergency basis due to inflammation or rupture of the appendix. Acute appendicitis is the most common general surgical emergency worldwide.

RELEVANT ANATOMY

- The appendix consists of a narrow, blind-ended, tubular structure which arises from the posteromedial cecal wall.
- It is derived from the midgut and base is located at the convergence of three tenia at the inferior aspect of cecum.
- Gerlach valve is a mucosal fold covering the appendicular orifice. Adhesion from the right abdominal wall to the anterior tenia of the ascending colon is known as Jackson membrane.
- Inferior ileocecal fold does not contain any vessel and is known as bloodless fold of Treves (ileoappendicular fold of peritoneum) which connects terminal 2.5 cm of ileum to the cecum.
- Layers of appendix are: Mucosa, submucosa, muscularis, and serosa.
- Submucosa of appendix contains lots of lymphoid tissue and its presence is an important etiological factor in the development of appendicitis. Hence, it is known as abdominal tonsil.
- Length of appendix: 2–20 cm (average length is 9 cm).
- Common positions of appendix are given below:
  - Retrocecal (74%)
  - Pelvic (21%)
  - Paracecal (2%)
  - Subcecal (1.5%)
  - Preileal (1%)
  - Postileal (0.5%)
- Blood supply: Appendicular artery is a branch of the lower division of ileocolic artery. It is an end artery.
- Venous drainage: Appendicular vein drains into the ileocolic vein which in turn drains into the superior mesenteric vein.
- Lymphatic drainage: It is through ileocolic node.

ETIOLOGY OF APPENDICITIS

- Infection, either bacterial or viral, leads to inflammation of lymphoid follicle in submucosa and causes swelling and edema that leads to obstruction of lumen. Other etiology is fecalith.
- Diet low in fiber is associated with increased risk and green leafy vegetables are protective.
- In elderly, chronic use of nonsteroidal anti-inflammatory drugs (NSAIDs) is associated with increased risk.
- Histological hallmark of appendicitis is neutrophilic infiltration of muscularis propria.
- Most common bacteria isolated are *Bacteroides fragilis* followed by *Escherichia coli*.

INDICATIONS FOR APPENDECTOMY

- Acute appendicitis: Operate within first 48 hours
- Complicated appendicitis
  - Suppurative
  - Gangrenous
  - Perforated
- Acute recurrent appendicitis
- During pregnancy (first and third trimesters): Operate because of the risk of abortion
- Infants, children, and elderly with acute appendicitis: Early operation carried out
  - Infants, children: High risk of peritonitis

- Elderly: Increased risk of gangrene and perforation because of atherosclerosis of vessels
- Chronic appendicitis and subacute appendicitis
- Adenocarcinoma of appendix, involving only mucosa
- Carcinoid tumor of appendix <2 cm
- Mucocele

Existence of chronic appendicitis has been controversial since long, but nowadays it has been proved by histopathological studies that it exists and, clinically, the patient will have typical but less intense pain which lasts longer.

CONTRAINDICATION

Lump: To be managed by Ochsner-Sherren regimen

DIAGNOSIS

'Appendicitis is a clinical diagnosis' (Box 6.1).

Symptoms

Murphy's Triad

- Pain (periumbilical, dull aching, shift to right iliac fossa, sharp and localized). Localized pain is the most important symptom.
- It is followed by vomiting and nausea (reflux pylorospasm, due to neural stimulation and ileus).

Box 6.1 Alvarado score for diagnosis of appendicitis[1]

• Symptoms	
– Migration of pain	1
– Anorexia	1
– Nausea/vomiting	1
• Signs	
– Tenderness	2
– Rebound tenderness	1
– Elevated temperature	1
• Lab study	
– Leucocytosis	2
– Shift to left	1
Total	10

Score of 5 or 6: Ultrasonography (USG) or computed tomography (CT) scan to confirm the diagnosis. CT is better than USG.
Score 7 or more: It suggests appendicitis.
With the improvement is imaging study, this scoring system plays a limited role.

- This is followed by fever (low grade, due to release of inflammatory cytokines).

- If vomiting, nausea, or fever precedes the pain, suspect medical cause.
- If anorexia is absent, diagnosis is questionable.
- High-grade fever indicates complicated appendicitis. If present along with white blood cell (WBC) count >20,000/cm, it indicates perforation. Site of perforation is usually site distal to the obstruction on antimesenteric border.

Signs

- Tenderness maximal at McBurney's point
- *Psoas sign*: Pain caused by extension of thigh, due to stretching of psoas (retrocecal appendix)
- *Obturator sign*: External rotation of hip causing severe pain and spasm
- *Rovsing sign*: Pain in right iliac fossa, while palpating left iliac fossa (due to shifting of coils of intestine and gas)
- *Blumberg sign*: Rebound tenderness
- *Hyperesthesia*: In the region of T10, 11, and 12 (Sherren triangle)
- *Dunphy sign*: Increased pain with coughing or other movements
- *Ten Horn sign*: Pain caused by gentle traction of right testicle
- *Aaron sign*: Pressure at McBurney's point leading to pain over epigastric region or anterior chest wall
- Possibility of worsening of pain on movement or Valsalva maneuver so patients typically prefer to lie still

Investigations

- Total leukocyte count (TLC), differential leukocyte count (DLC)
  - Leucocytosis: 11,000–17,000/mm^3; if >20,000/mm^3, suspect perforation. High degree of suspicion in case risk factors are present.

Risk factors for perforation: <5 and >65 years, pelvic appendix, immunocompromised state, and fecalith. Site of rupture is distal to obstruction on antimesenteric border.

  - Polymorphs—these are increased.

- Urine: Routine and microscopic
  - Mild pyuria, due to irritation of bladder by pelvic appendix
  - Microscopic hematuria common
  - Ureteral irritation by retrocecal appendix
- Plain X-ray abdomen findings which may suggest appendicitis:
  - Localized ileus
  - Air–fluid level
  - Fecalith
  - Obliteration of psoas shadow
  - Free intraperitoneal air
  - Blurring of right flank stripe
- Ultrasonography (USG)
  - Noncompressible
  - Blind-ended, laminated, tubular
  - Aperistaltic
  - >6 mm lumen and >2 mm thickness of wall
  - Pericecal fluid collection
  - Appendicolith
- Computed tomography (CT) scan
  - Pericecal inflammation
  - Increased density
  - Appendiceal thickening
  - Pericecal adenopathy
  - Pericecal fluid collection
- Magnetic resonance imaging (MRI): Will accurately rule out appendicitis in pregnant women

OPERATIVE TECHNIQUES

There are two main surgical techniques for the removal of appendix: Open and laparoscopic appendectomy. In open appendectomy, an incision is made through the skin, underlying tissue, and the abdominal wall to access the appendix, while in the laparoscopic appendectomy three small incisions are made in the abdomen.

Open Appendicectomy

- *Anesthesia*: Spinal anesthesia (SA) or general anesthesia (GA)
- *Position*: Supine
- *Incision*: Following are the different types of incisions used in appendicectomy (Fig. 6.1):
  - McBurney's or Gridiron—most commonly used (Fig. 6.1*C* and *D*)
  - Rutherford Morrison—chances of incisional hernia high (muscle-cutting incision)

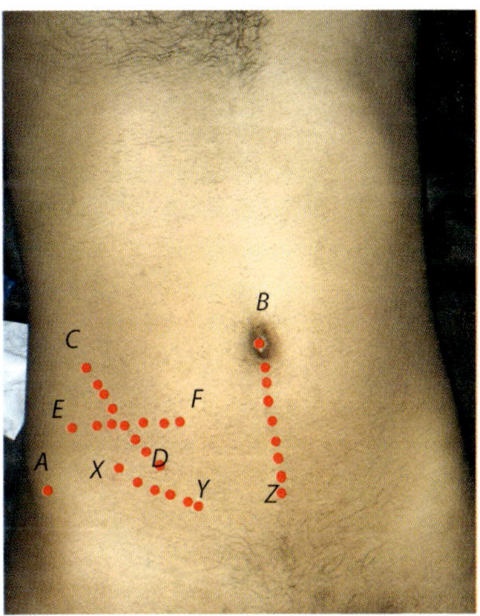

Figure 6.1 Incisions used in appendicectomy.

  - Rockey-Davis incision—cosmetically better (Fig. 6.1*E* and *F*)
  - Lanz incision (Fig. 6.1*X* and *Y*)
  - Lower midline incision—if diagnosis is in doubt, or in female patient in whom gynecological pathology is suspected, or in case of perforated appendix (Fig. 6.1*B* and *Z*)

Emergency appendicectomy

- Incision: McBurney's incision is the most common incision used. Various incisions and their advantages have been summarized in Table 6.1.
- After painting, draping, and isolation of local part, make incision perpendicular to the spinoumbilical line, at the junction of medial two-third and lateral one-third, with D-knife.
- Cut skin and subcutaneous tissue.
- Cut external oblique aponeurosis (in the line of incision or in the direction of muscle fibers) (Fig. 6.2).
- Split internal oblique and transverse abdominis in the direction of the fibers (Fig. 6.3).
- With the help of a retractor, retract internal oblique and transverse abdominis to expose peritoneum (Fig. 6.4).

Catch the peritoneum with mosquito forceps and keep a nick over the peritoneum with D knife or scissor (Fig. 6.5). Then, hold the peritoneum from cut edge with the forceps, and cut with scissors (before putting nick over peritoneum, confirm that there is no structure intervening) (Fig. 6.6).

Table 6.1 Incisions Used in Appendectomy

McBurney's incision	Rockey-Davis incision	Lanz incision	Lower midline incision
• Centered over point of maximal tenderness • Muscle splitting • Oblique • Direction of muscle fiber is perpendicular to each other like the iron-grid bars of deck of the ship (Gridiron incision) • It was first described by McArthur	• Centered over point of maximal tenderness • Muscle splitting • Transverse • Cosmetically more superior	• Cosmetically better • Easier to extend • Muscle splitting • Better exposure	• If diagnosis is in doubt • Provides maximum access to the abdominal cavity

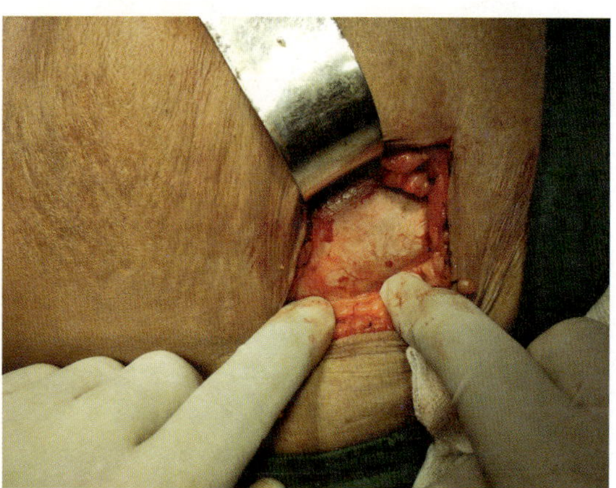

Figure 6.2 Expose external oblique aponeurosis.

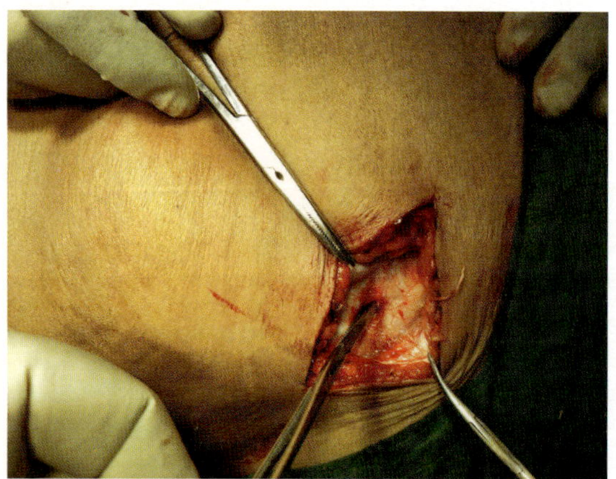

Figure 6.3 Splitting of internal oblique and transverse abdominis.

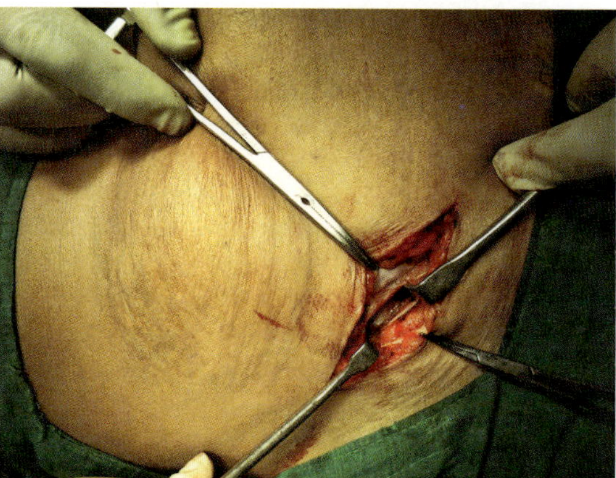

Figure 6.4 Retraction of internal oblique and transverse abdominis.

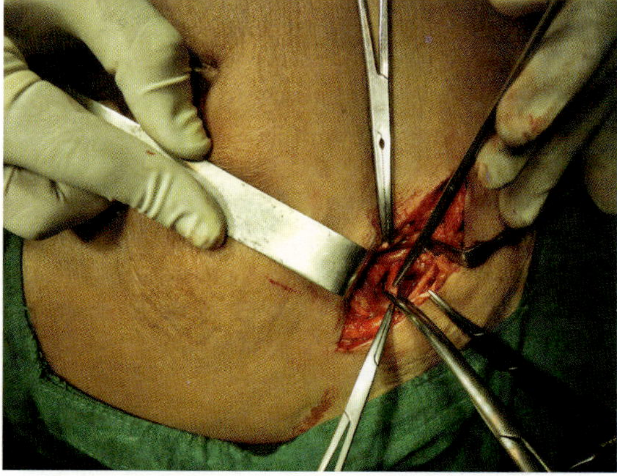

Figure 6.5 Holding of the peritoneum with forceps.

- After opening the peritoneum, if there is pus, then send it for culture and sensitivity.
- Identify cecum by tenia coli and appendices epiploicae.
- Hold tenia with a Babcock's tissue holding forceps and deliver outside.
- Trace the three tenia to reach the appendicular base.

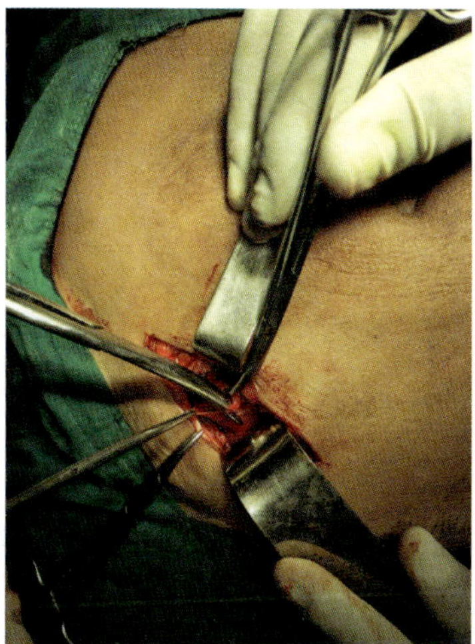

Figure 6.6 Cutting peritoneum with scissor.

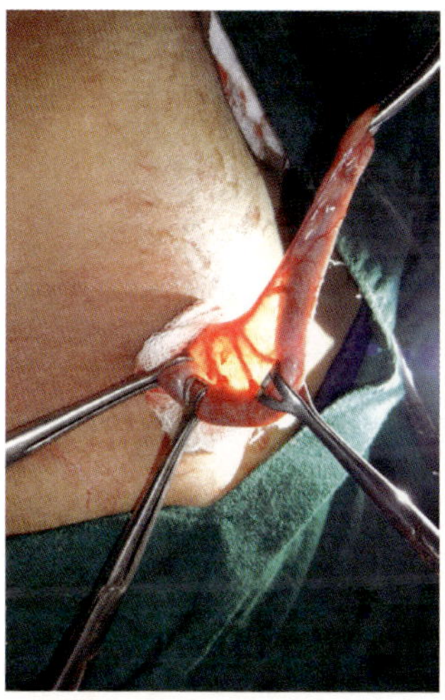

Figure 6.7 Appendicular artery runs over the free border of mesoappendix.

- Identify appendix and hold it with a Babcock's tissue holding forceps.
- Identify appendicular artery (Fig. 6.7), which runs over the free border of mesentery. Make a window near the base of the appendix, into the mesoappendix. Ligate appendicular artery with black silk or polyglactin 910 and cut (Fig. 6.8).
- Crush the appendix 5 mm above the base.
- Ligate with Vicryl (polyglactin [910] 2'0) (Fig. 6.9).
- Apply a straight hemostatic forceps distal to the ligature.

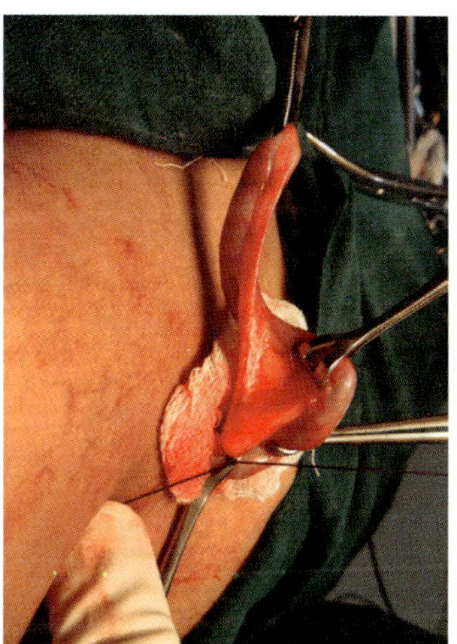

Figure 6.8 Ligation of appendicular artery.

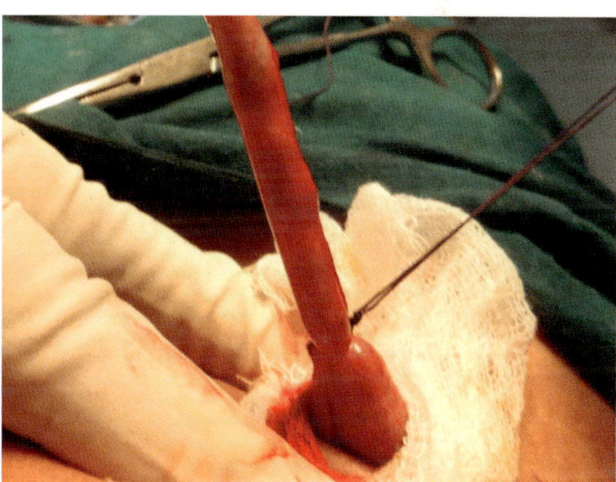

Figure 6.9 Ligation of appendix.

- Cut appendix flush to the hemostat with a stab knife (number 11 knife).
- Discard appendix with hemostat and knife in a separate kidney tray and send for histopathological examination (HPE).
- Apply Betadine, followed by spirit, and again followed by Betadine.
- Burry the stump with purse-string or z-stitch (optional).
- Trace terminal 2 ft of ileum for Meckel's diverticulum.
- Repose ileum and cecum into the peritoneal cavity.
- Check hemostasis with three-swab test (first pelvic cavity, second paracolic gutter, third peritoneal cavity).

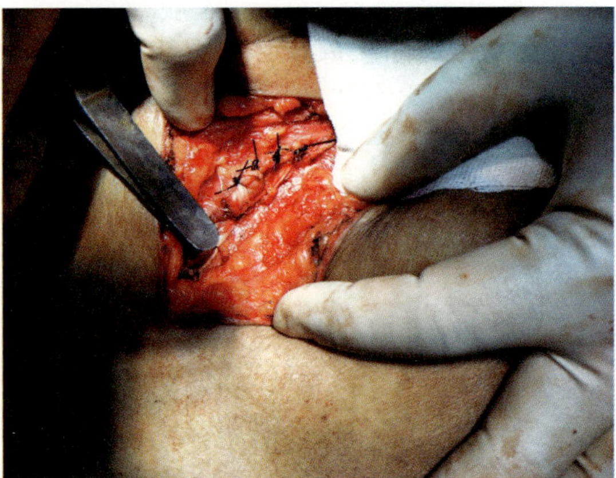

Figure 6.10 Closure in single layer with polydioxanone 1-0.

- In female patients, look for fallopian tube and ovary.
- Closure
  - Peritoneum: It is closed with the help of Vicryl 2-0 continuous locking or running suture (optional).
  - Muscle: Just approximate in the direction of fibers with polyglactin 910 (Vicryl) 2-0 with intermittent stitch.
  - External oblique aponeurosis: Prolene 2-0 (polypropylene) or Ethilon 2-0 (polyamide) continuous locking suture. Some surgeons choose to close in a single layer with polydioxanone 1-0 (Fig. 6.10).
  - Skin: Ethilon 2-0 or 3-0, or Prolene 2-0 or 3-0 vertical mattress stitch. It can be closed with skin stapler also (Fig. 6.11).

In the author's opinion, subcutaneous tissue closure is not advisable, because by closing subcutaneous tissue we are keeping more foreign body inside (increasing risk of infection and sinus formation), and closing of subcutaneous tissue creates a tight compartment, which sometimes may leads to hampering of blood supply to skin. Fat does not contain collagen and does not contribute to healing.

Interval appendicectomy

It is performed between 6th and 10th weeks, following acute attack.

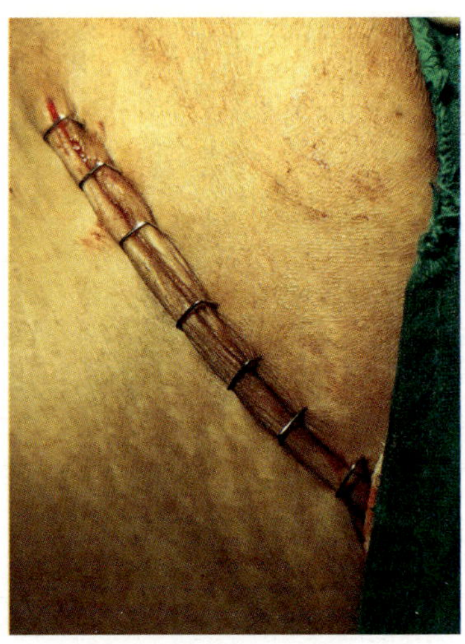

Figure 6.11 Skin closed with skin stapler.

Routine interval appendectomy after initial nonoperative management is not justified because recurrence rate is only 15–20%.

Incidental appendicectomy

- It is removal of appendix at the time of an other operative procedure.
- The practice of incidental appendectomy is controversial and the recent findings of its role in immunity and maintenance of healthy colonic flora make it more controversial.
- As appendicitis is a disease of the young population, the best candidates are people younger than 20 years old. Between 20 and 40 years, it is up to the surgeon's discretion and in those older than 40 years it is best avoided.
- Regardless of the age of the patients, it is recommended in the following conditions:
  - If appendiceal lesion is found at the time of an other operation
  - Noncommunicative patients and in operation where position of appendix is greatly altered by primary operation and makes the future diagnosis very difficult (Ladd's procedure for midgut malrotation)
  - Crohn disease, with cecum free of macroscopic disease
  - Children about to undergo chemotherapy

Problems encountered during appendicectomy

Variations of appendix

- Normal appendix
  - Perform a methodical search for alternate diagnosis.
  - Even a normal-looking appendix should be removed as 25% of macroscopically normal appendix shows microscopic appendicitis.
- Tumor of appendix (carcinoid)
  - If <1 cm—appendicectomy
  - If 1–2 cm with mesentery not involved, at the tip or mid of appendix—appendicectomy
  - If 1–2 cm with mesentery involved, located at the base of appendix, and/or lymph node involvement—right hemicolectomy
  - If >2 cm—right hemicolectomy
- Appendicular abscess
  - Peritoneal toilet
  - Interval appendicectomy
- Absent appendix: Rare
- Extensively inflamed or edematous: Not to be crushed/purse-string suture not applied
- Long retrocecal/subserosal appendix: Retrograde appendicectomy
- Crohn disease
  - Cecal wall healthy at the base: Appendectomy
  - If appendix is involved: Medical management
- Gangrenous base: Two stitches placed through the cecal wall close to the base, amputate flush to the wall, and stitches tied; second layer of interrupted seromuscular stitch taken

Invagination of stump is not mandatory, and may lead to obstruction. Nowadays, most surgeons routinely do not prefer it.

Complications on table

- Hemorrhage
- Injury to surrounding structures—cecum, ileum
- Perforation

Postoperative complications

- Infection: Most common; higher in patients with gangrenous or perforated appendix (anaerobic bacteroides and aerobic coli are the usual cause)
- Pyrexia: Always performed per rectal examination to rule out pelvic abscess (on examination, heat, bogginess, and tenderness; in case of pelvic abscess, drainage is the treatment either per rectal or per vaginal [female] or percutaneous under sonography guidance)
- Ileus: Fever with ileus of more than 5 days' duration suggesting intra-abdominal abscess
- Reactionary hemorrhage: Due to slippage of ligature
- Postoperative adhesions: Treatment being diagnostic laparoscopy and adhesiolysis.
- Stump appendicitis: Can be minimized by accurate visualization of base and keeping <5 mm stump (the best way to avoid stump appendicitis is 'appendiceal critical view': Keep appendix at 10 o'clock, tenia coli at 3 o'clock, and terminal ileum at 6 o'clock and look where tenia merge and disappear as this is paramount to locate and ligating the base; treatment is completion appendectomy)
- Incisional hernia due to damage of iliohypogastric nerve
- Portal pyemia: Clinical symptoms being high-grade fever, rigors, and jaundice (treatment is using antibiotics and percutaneous drainage of abscess)
- Fecal fistula: Usually develops in case of Crohn disease and perforated and gangrenous appendix involving base of appendix, malignancy involving cecum or appendix, ileocecal tuberculosis, and distal obstruction
- Possibility of deep vein thrombosis (DVT) and embolism in very high-risk patients

Acute appendicitis is the most common surgical diagnosis in young patients. Debate remains on whether uncomplicated acute appendicitis should be treated surgically or not. A systematic review with meta-analysis of randomized controlled trials comparing appendectomy and nonoperative management with antibiotics found that appendectomy remains the most effective treatment for patients with uncomplicated acute appendicitis. The subgroups of patients with uncomplicated cases where antibiotics can be more effective should be accurately identified.[3]

Laparoscopic Appendectomy

- Indications: Same as open appendectomy
- Contraindications
  - Inability to tolerate GA

- Uncorrected coagulopathy
- Hemodynamic instability

Operative technique VIDEO

- Supine position, GA, and both arms tucked along the side
- Nasogastric tube and Foley urinary catheter to decompress stomach and urinary bladder, respectively (optional)
- Both surgeon and assistant on the left side
- Monitor on the opposite side of the table at foot end
- Painting, draping, and isolation of part in such a manner that the entire abdomen is exposed
- Small infraumbilical incision placed with stab knife
- Veress needle introduced with the abdomen wall lifted by surgeon and assistant (Fig. 6.12)
- Pneumoperitoneum created with CO_2 gas using insufflator
- Veress needle removed, extension of incision slightly, and introduction of the first trocar (10 mm) directing toward pelvis (Fig. 6.13)
- Introduced 0° or 30° angled scope and connected to monitor
- Whole abdomen inspected
- Other two trocars introduced under vision
- Second 10- or 5-mm trocar kept in the right iliac fossa at the McBurney's point (Fig. 6.14)
- Third 5-mm trocar kept in either suprapubic region or left iliac fossa (Fig. 6.14)

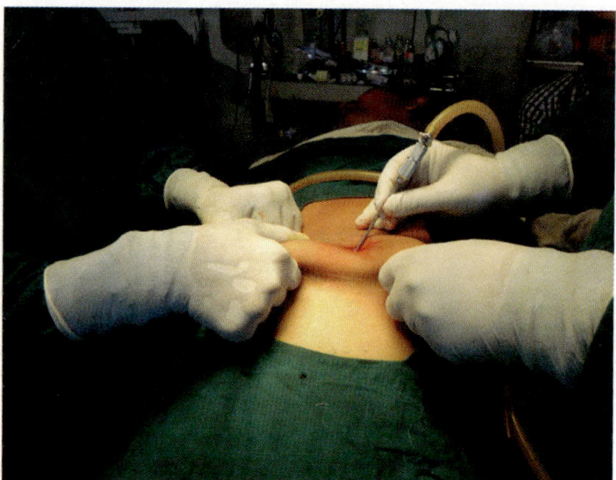

Figure 6.12 Introduction of Veress needle through infraumbilical incision.

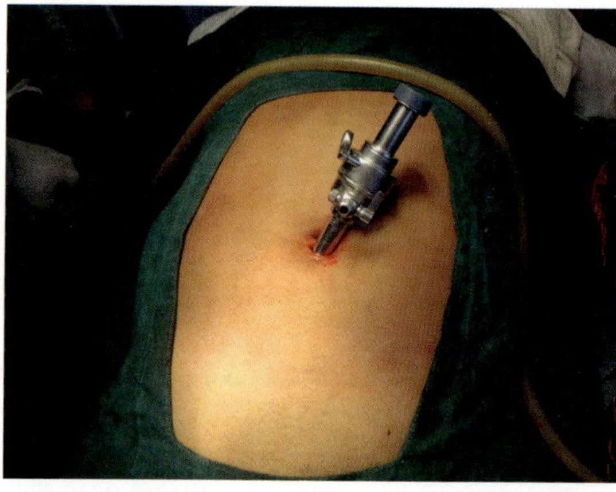

Figure 6.13 Ten-millimeter trocar insertion through infraumbilical incision.

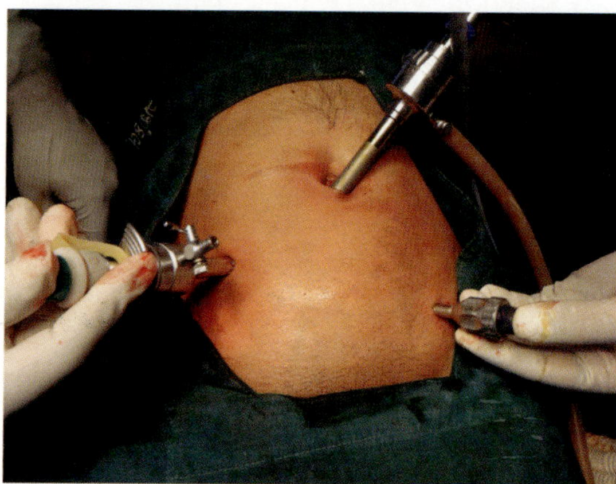

Figure 6.14 Ten-millimeter trocar at McBurney's point. Five-millimeter trocar in left iliac fossa.

- Trendelenburg position with table tilted right side up is adopted
- Appendix exposed and traced to its base on the cecum by using atraumatic grasper
- Appendix grasped at the tip and retracted toward the anterior abdominal wall to expose the mesoappendix (Fig. 6.15)
- A window created between base of appendix and appendicular artery with Maryland forceps
- Appendicular artery ligated with either suture or clip, or cauterized with ultrasonic scalpel (Fig. 6.16)
- Base of the appendix identified, cleared circumferentially, the base doubly ligated with the pretied ligature (Fig. 6.17), and suture

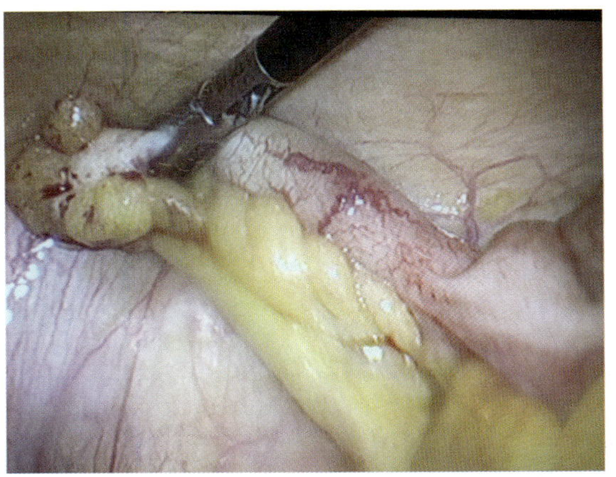

Figure 6.15 Tip of the appendix grasp with grasper.

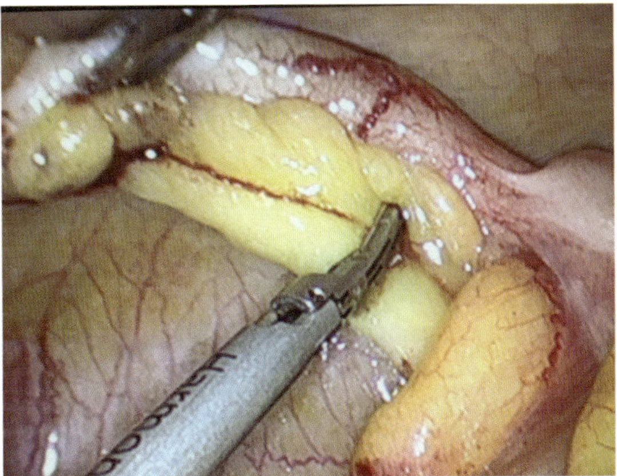

Figure 6.16 Cauterization of appendicular artery with harmonic scalpel.

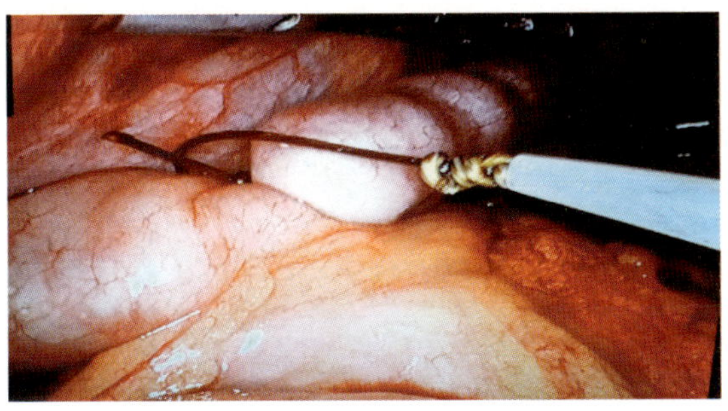

Figure 6.17 Ligation of the appendix with pretied loop.

(Fig. 6.18) as well as appendix cut with the endoscopic scissor (Fig. 6.19)

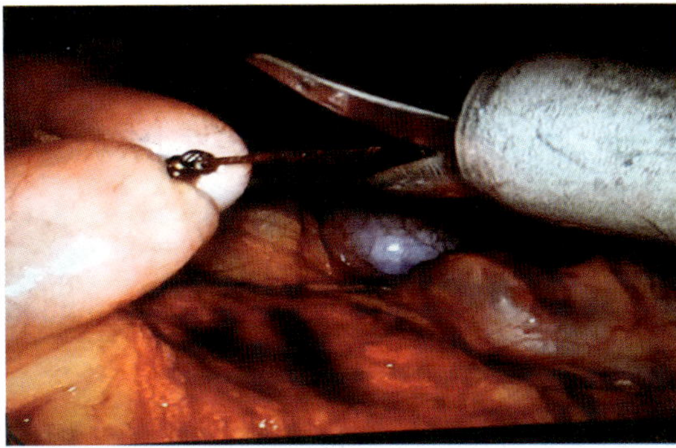

Figure 6.18 Cutting of suture with endoscopic scissor.

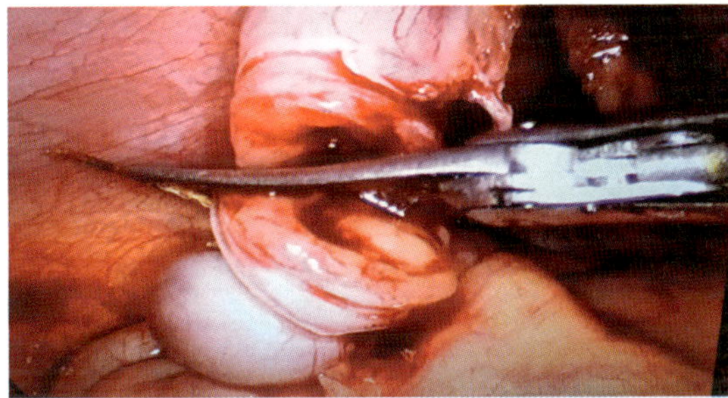

Figure 6.19 Cutting of appendix with endoscopic scissor.

Laparoscopic GIA stapler loaded with internal cartridge is used if available.

- Appendix removed from the 10-mm port (avoid direct contact with abdomen wall, put in a retrieval bag)
- Hemostasis checked at the end
- For 10-mm trocar, close fascia with polyglactin 910, 1-0 suture
- Skin closed with either stapler or nylon 3-0 suture

- In case of retrocecal appendix, mobilize the cecum and ascending colon by dividing lateral peritoneal attachment.
- Bleeding is controlled with gentle pressure, bipolar cautery or harmonic scalpel, or ligation.
- Necrotic base is tackled with excision of the portion of cecum and suturing.
- In case of unexposed tip, perform retrograde appendectomy.

Postoperative care

Same as for open appendectomy

Complications

- Bleeding
- Bowel perforation and peritonitis
- Accidental cautery injury to the bowel or vessels
- Bladder injury
- Stump leak
- Dropped or lost fecalith

Advantages of laparoscopic appendicectomy

- Less pain
- Less risk of adhesions
- Survey of whole peritoneal cavity without excessive handling
- Early mobilization
- Early return to work
- Less risk of wound infection

Disadvantages of laparoscopic appendicectomy

- Complications associated with GA
- Complications associated with pneumoperitoneum

LAPAROSCOPIC CHOLECYSTECTOMY

Laparoscopic cholecystectomy is the removal of gallbladder through laparoscopy. Most cholecystectomies are performed laparoscopically nowadays. In the USA, 90% of the procedures are performed laparoscopically. The main advantages of laparoscopy are less postoperative pain, shorter hospital stay, and better cosmesis. However, major complications remain higher in laparoscopy group than in open cholecystectomy.

INDICATIONS

- Symptomatic gallstone
- Acute or chronic cholecystitis
- Empyema of gallbladder
- Acalculous cholecystitis
- Asymptomatic gallstone with high risk for complications or who are at high risk for developing carcinoma of gallbladder (anomalous pancreatic ductal drainage, large gallstone [>3 cm], porcelain gallbladder, gallbladder polyp >10 mm)

CONTRAINDICATIONS

- Hemodynamic instability
- Uncorrected coagulopathy
- Inability to tolerate GA
- Suspected carcinoma of the gallbladder

PREOPERATIVE INVESTIGATIONS

- Laboratory investigations: Routine blood investigations plus liver function tests. In suspected pancreatitis, *S. amylase* and *S. lipase* should also be assessed.
- Radiological investigations
  - *USG of the abdomen*: It helps in detecting gallstones as well as common bile duct (CBD) dilatation or stone. It also helps in diagnosis of liver pathology in right upper quadrant pain.
  - *Magnetic resonance cholangiopancreatography (MRCP)*: It is indicated in suspected CBD pathology such as dilatation on USG or elevation of liver enzymes, particularly serum alkaline phosphatase.

OPERATIVE TECHNIQUE 

- Single-dose preoperative antibiotic is given.
- Supine position, GA, and both arms tucked along the side.
- Surgeon should stand on the left side, camera assistant on left, and one more assistant on the right for retraction. Monitor is placed at the head end near right shoulder.
- Procedure is same till the insertion of the first infraumbilical port as described for laparoscopic appendectomy.
- Insert second, third, and fourth ports under vision.
- Insert second port in epigastric region (10 mm), two fingerbreadths below xiphisternum in such a manner that it should come out from the right of falciform ligament.
- Insert third port 5 mm in midclavicular line two fingerbreadths below costal margin.
- Insert fourth port 5 mm in midclavicular line right iliac fossa.
- Pass grasper from third port and catch the fundus of the gallbladder and retract in a cephalad direction.
- Pass the grasper from fourth port to catch the Hartmann's pouch of the gallbladder.

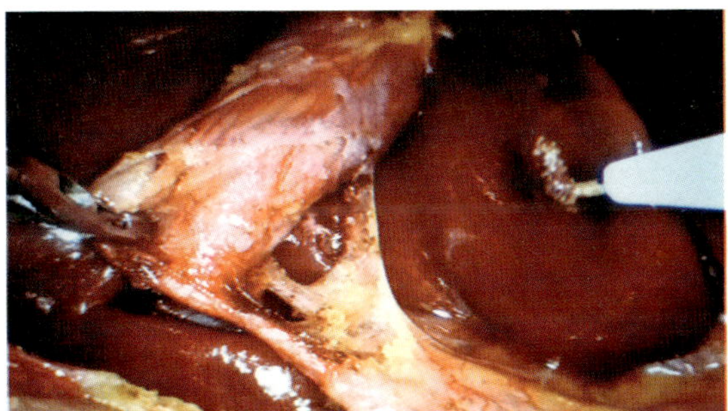

Figure 6.20 The critical view of safety is a 'window' crossed by two structures: The cystic duct and the artery. Visible liver bed between the two structures.

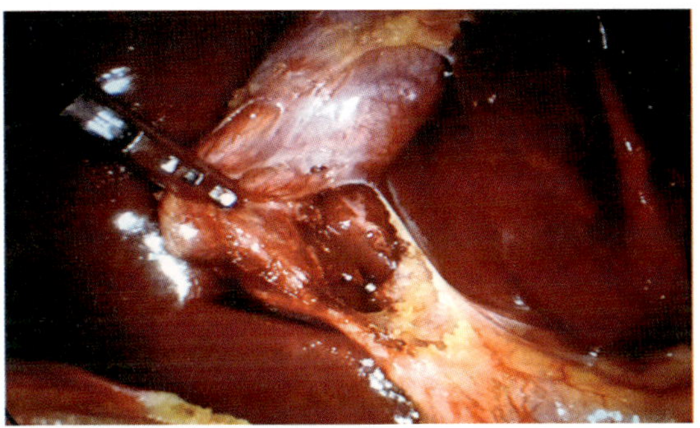

Figure 6.21 Clip on the cystic artery.

- Pass the Maryland forceps from the epigastric port for dissection; identify the cystic duct, cystic artery and CBD.
- While dissecting, stay as close as possible to the gallbladder to avoid injury to bile duct.
- Make a window between cystic duct and cystic artery; expose the Calot's triangle (Fig. 6.20).
- With the help of clip applicator, apply two clips on the cystic artery (Fig. 6.21).
- Now divide artery with either monopolar hook or endoscopic scissor (Fig. 6.22).
- With the help of clip applicator apply clip either 2 or 3 in the cystic duct, 1 or 2 toward the bile duct, and 1 toward the gallbladder (medium-sized Ligaclip) (Fig. 6.23); cut the cystic duct (Fig. 6.24) with the help of endoscopic scissor.
- Dissect the gallbladder from gallbladder fossa (Fig. 6.25).
- Inspect the fossa for bleeding before completely separating gallbladder from its bed.

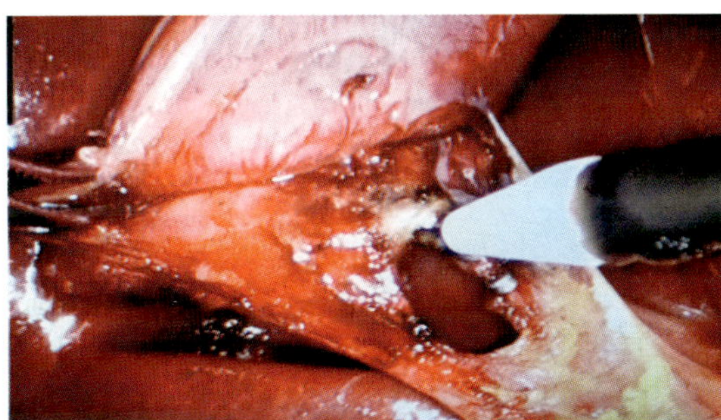

Figure 6.22 Cutting of cystic artery with monopolar hook.

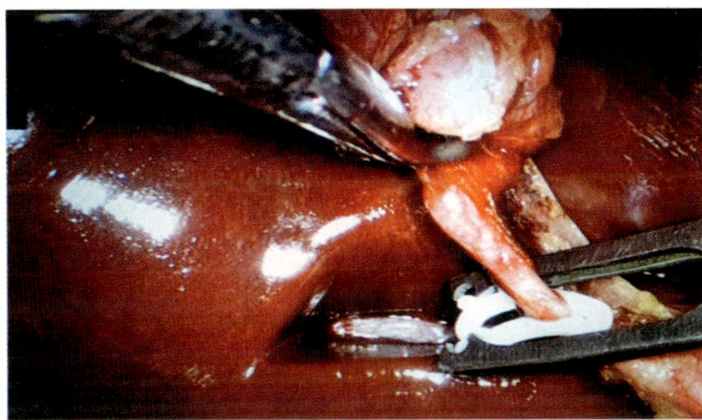

Figure 6.23 Clip applied on the cystic duct with the help of clip applicator.

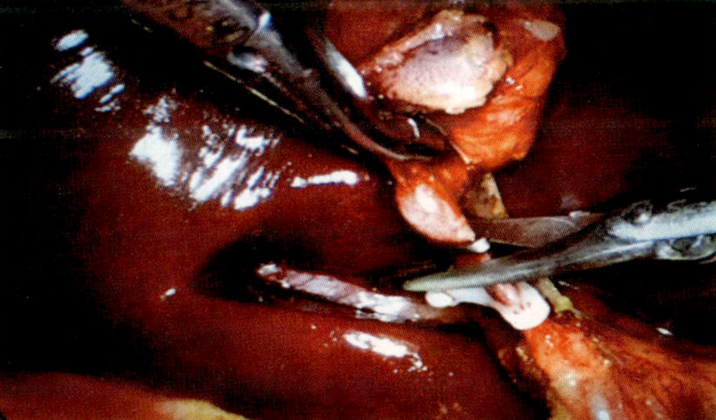

Figure 6.24 Division of the cystic duct with the help of scissor.

- Disconnect gallbladder completely, park over the liver, check for hemostasis, and carry out suction if required.
- Remove cannulas under vision.
- For 10-mm incision, close fascia with polyglactin 910, 1-0 suture.
- Skin is closed with either stapler or nylon 3-0.
- Dressing is applied.

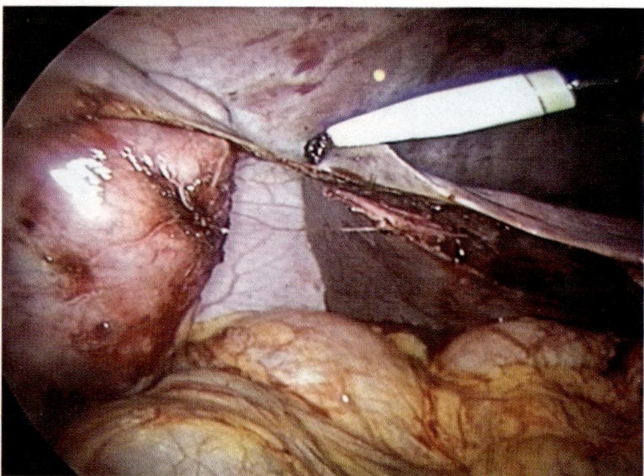

Figure 6.25 Separation of gallbladder from the liver bed.

Conversion to open is indicated in:

- Bleeding
- Abnormal anatomy
- Major bile duct injury
- Bowel perforation
- Failure to progress in a timely manner (45 minutes)
- Operable suspected gallbladder cancer
- CBD stone that was not possible to remove laparoscopically or endoscopically

POSTOPERATIVE CARE

- Nil by mouth (NBM) for 6 hours and liquid diet followed by soft diet
- IV proton pump inhibitor (PPI)
- IV antispasmodic or anti-inflammatory (hyoscine or diclofenac sodium)
- IV fluid

COMPLICATIONS

- Bowel injury
- Vascular injury
- Bile duct injury
- Bile leak due to slipping of clip over cystic duct
- Postcholecystectomy syndrome

Timing of cholecystectomy

- *Acute cholecystitis*: Tokyo guideline for acute cholecystitis (Box 6.2) recommends early laparoscopic cholecystectomy for mild cholecystitis and early or interval cholecystectomy for moderate cholecystitis. Selected patients with severe cholecystitis may require percutaneous cholecystostomy.
- *Gallstone pancreatitis*: Once pain subsides, laparoscopic cholecystectomy at index admission for mild to moderate pancreatitis. In case of severe pancreatitis, because of local and systemic illness, delay in cholecystectomy is advised.
- *Obstructive jaundice*: If CBD stone present, endoscopic retrograde cholangiopancreatography (ERCP) is performed preoperatively followed by elective cholecystectomy; or if an expert is available, single-sitting laparoscopic cholecystectomy with laparoscopic CBD exploration is performed.

Box 6.2 Severity grading (Yokoe et al, 2018)[2]

- *Mild*: Not meeting moderate or severe criteria
- *Moderate*: The presence of one or more criteria—WBC count >18,000/mm^3, palpable lump in right hypochondrium, duration >3 days, and marked inflammation (biliary peritonitis, liver abscess, gangrenous or emphysematous cholecystitis)
- *Severe*: The presence of any organ system failure

COLOSTOMY

DEFINITIONS

- The word stoma is derived from Greek word *stomata*, meaning mouth.
- Gastrointestinal stomas are artificial connections between gut and the skin.
- Colostomy is artificial opening made in the colon to divert feces to the exterior.
- The more general term for the operation is ostomy, which denotes an artificial opening on the abdominal wall through which waste material passes out of the body. In colostomy the opening is from the colon. When the opening is in the left colon, only a pad may be needed to cover the opening, but when the opening is in the right side, an appliance or bag is required.
- A related technique is *ileostomy*, in which the ileum (the last portion of the small intestine) is brought to the abdominal surface. When waste matter reaches the ileum, it is liquid, so an appliance is needed to collect it (Table 6.2).

Table 6.2 Differences Between Ileostomy and Colostomy

Characteristics	Ileostomy	Colostomy
Site	Right iliac fossa	Right upper quadrant or left iliac fossa
Content	Liquid or semisolid	Solid
Electrolyte imbalance	Possible	Absent
Odor	Odorless	Foul smelling
Skin excoriation	More common	Less common
Prolapse or retraction	Less common	More common

Difference between stomy, tomy, and ectomy:
- *Stomy*: Making an opening into a hollow organ and keeping it open, for example, colostomy
- *Tomy*: Making an opening into a hollow organ and closing it, for example, gastrotomy
- *Ectomy*: Removal of a part or whole of an organ, splenectomy

AIMS OF COLOSTOMY

- To decompress the distal colon
- To evacuate when distal colon or rectum is removed
- To protect distal anastomosis
- To divert fecal matter in preparation for resection of inflammatory/traumatic injury to the rectum

CLASSIFICATION

There are various ways of classification of colostomy, but the common classification is based on the type of loop used.

On the Basis of Loop

- Single loop colostomy or end colostomy (permanent)
- Double loop colostomy (temporary)

Anatomical

- Sigmoid
- Transverse
- Descending
- Cecostomy

Functional

- Decompressing
  - *Indications*: Distal obstruction and toxic megacolon, and severe sigmoid diverticulitis with phlegmon
  - *Types*: Blowhole cecostomy or transverse colostomy, tube cecostomy, and transverse colostomy

It is a bridge to definitive operation and patients require subsequent definitive surgery.

- Diverting
  - *Indications*: Known or suspected perforation or obstruction (obstructing cancer, anastomotic leak, or trauma), and completely resected distal bowel (abdominoperineal resection [APR]) and destruction of distal large bowel (failed anal sphincter reconstruction)
  - *Types*: Loop transverse or sigmoid colostomy and end colostomy

INDICATIONS

Colostomy

- End colostomy
  - APR
  - Radiation proctitis
  - Incontinence of anal canal
- Double loop colostomy
  - Distal obstruction
  - Distal anastomosis
  - Trauma to the rectum
  - Sigmoid diverticula perforation
  - Imperforate anus
  - Hirschsprung disease

Ileostomy

- Proctocolectomy for ulcerative colitis
- Crohn disease
- Familial adenomatous polyposis (FAP)
- Multiple perforations or big perforation in typhoid
- Protection of distal anastomosis
- Distal obstruction

CRITERIA FOR IDEAL STOMA

Colostomy

- Visible

- Away from umbilicus, skin crease, scar, bony prominence
- Site marked in all positions such as supine, standing, and sitting
- Located within the rectus
- Surrounding abdominal tissue to be as flat as possible

Ileostomy

- No prolapse or retraction
- No leak
- Allows normal physical and sexual activity
- No skin complication
- Allows regular diet

PREOPERATIVE PREPARATION

- Before major bowel surgery
  - Clear liquid 1 day prior to surgery
  - Mechanical cleansing with polyethylene glycol (PEG) or sodium phosphate
  - Broad-spectrum antibiotics at 1 pm, 2 pm, and 11 pm on the day before surgery
- Preoperative planning
  - Counseling and psychological preparation
  - Stoma site marking

The stoma should lie within ostomy triangle. It is outlined by anterior superior iliac spine, pubic tubercle, and umbilicus. It should overlie the rectus muscle and the site of infraumbilical bulge. It should be 5 cm away from the bony prominence, umbilicus, previous scar, and skin folds. Once site has been selected, patients should be allowed to sit up to ensure any new skin fold should not interfere. The belt line should be avoided.

OPERATIVE TECHNIQUE FOR TRANSVERSE COLOSTOMY

- Anesthesia: SA or GA
- Make a 5-cm transverse incision in right upper quadrant of abdomen between umbilicus and costal margin (Fig. 6.26). Any transverse incision over abdomen follows Langer line and has the following advantages:
  - More intrinsic strength
  - Lower incidence of incisional hernia
  - Better cosmesis
  - Limited accessibility

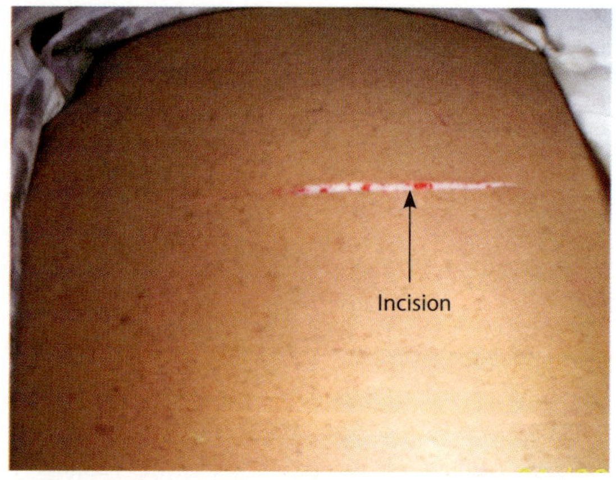

Figure 6.26 Transverse incision in the right upper quadrant.

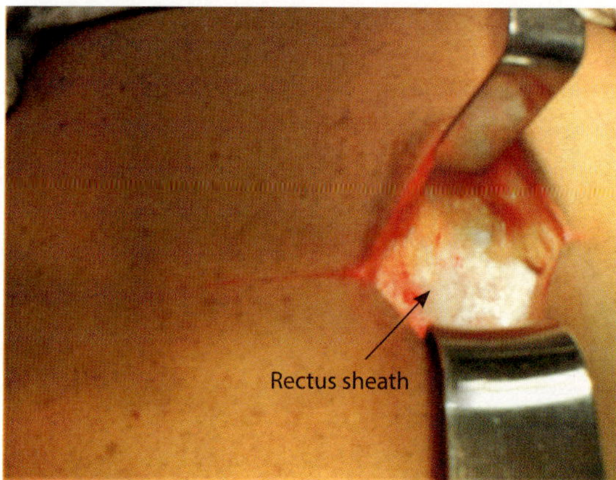

Figure 6.27 Exposed rectus sheath.

- Cut the skin.
- Cut subcutaneous tissue.
- Cut rectus sheath (Fig. 6.27), expose rectus muscle (Fig. 6.28), and divide the muscle (Fig. 6.29) (identify superior epigastric vessel and ligate).
- Open posterior rectus sheath (Fig. 6.30) and peritoneum (Fig. 6.31).
- Identify transverse colon; deliver transverse colon into the wound (Fig. 6.32). Make a window in the transverse mesocolon, and pass a plain rubber catheter (spigot) into it (Fig. 6.33).
- Open the transverse colon longitudinally (Fig. 6.34), along the line of tenia, and then suture the full thickness of bowel to skin with Vicryl 2-0 or 3-0.
- Some surgeons prefer using three-stage maturation by suturing seromuscular layer with

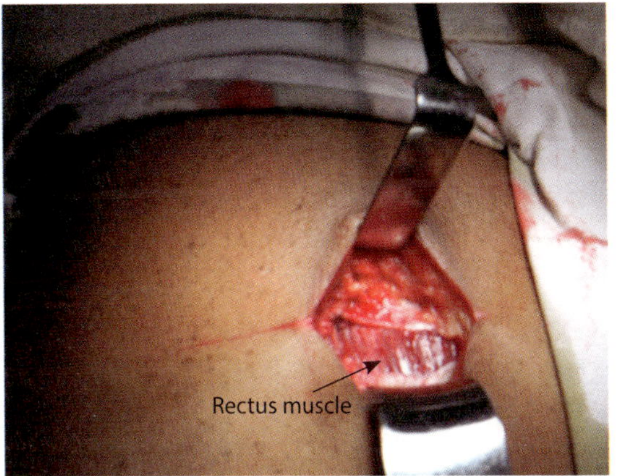

Figure 6.28 Exposed rectus muscle.

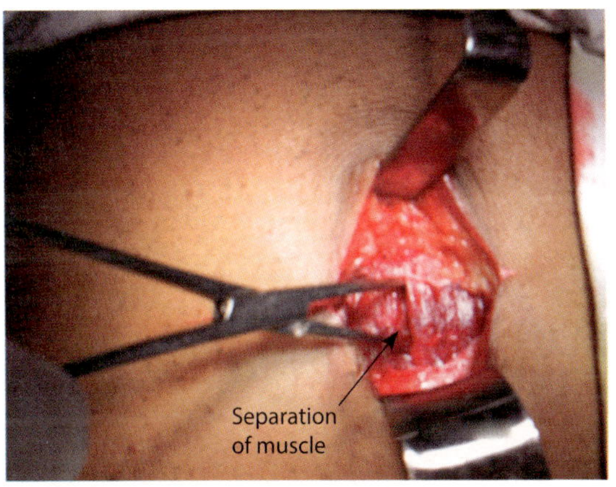

Figure 6.29 Separation of rectus muscle.

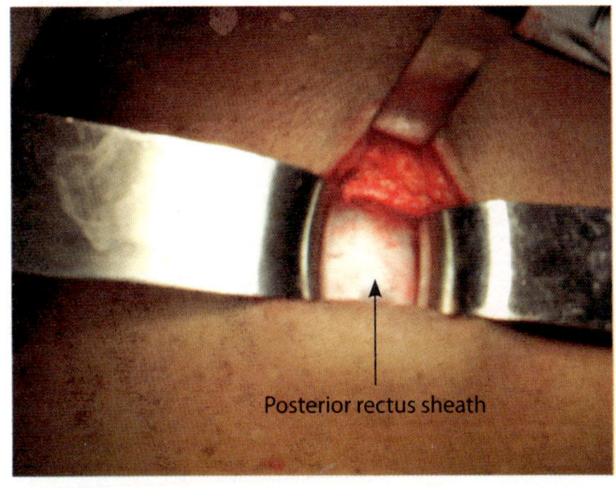

Figure 6.30 Exposed posterior rectus sheath.

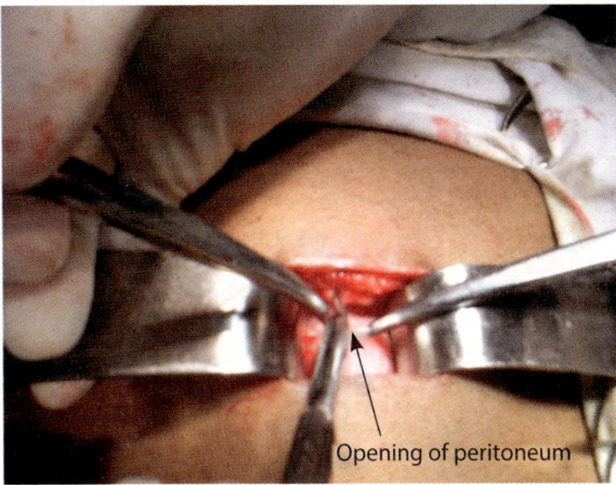

Figure 6.31 Opening of the peritoneum.

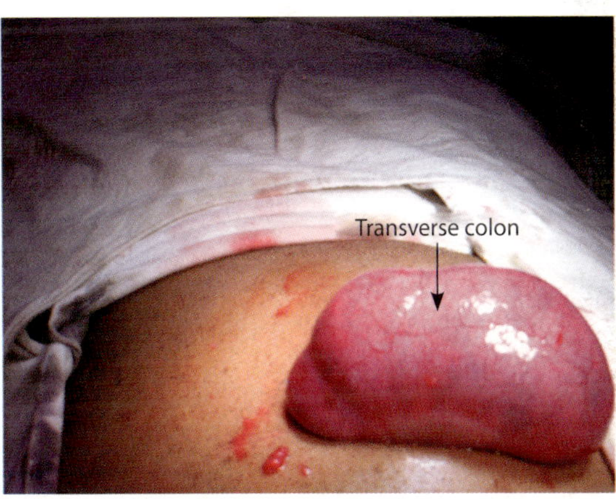

Figure 6.32 Delivery of the transverse colon in the wound.

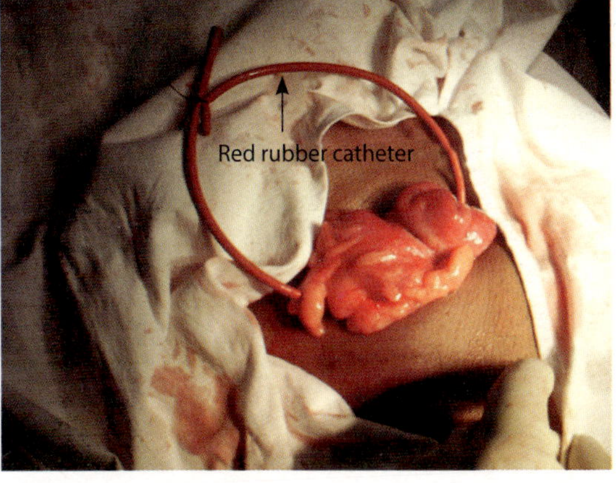

Figure 6.33 Red rubber catheter passed after making window the transverse mesocolon.

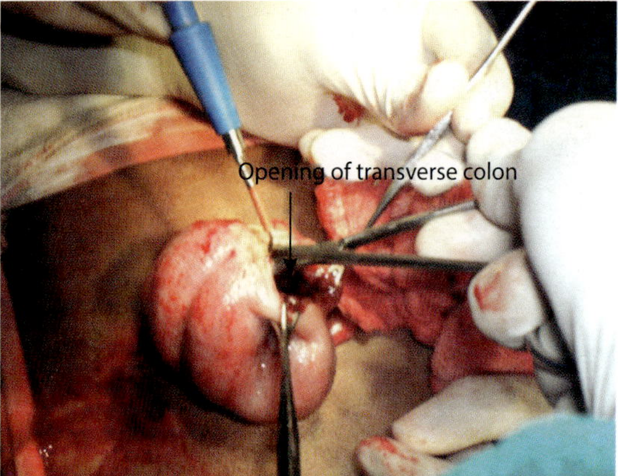

Figure 6.34 Longitudinal opening of the transverse colon.

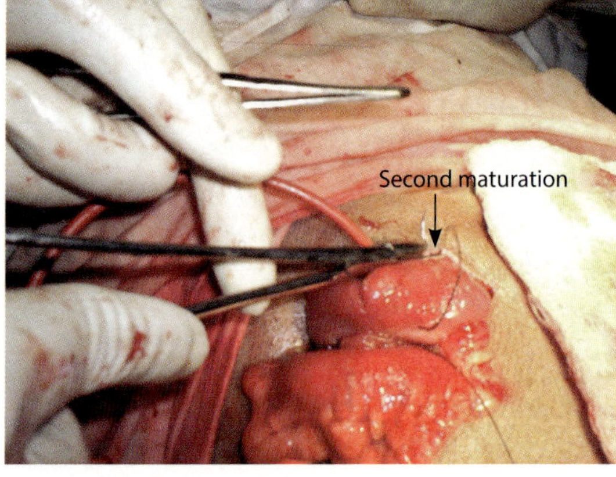

Figure 6.36 Second maturation: suturing of full thickness of the colon with skin.

peritoneum (Fig. 6.35) in the first stage, taking seromuscular layer with anterior rectus sheath in the second-stage maturation and suturing full-thickness bowel with skin in the third-stage maturation. Some surgeons use two-stage maturation, in which second maturation is full thickness of colon with skin (Fig. 6.36).

- Double loop colostomy is constructed and checked for proximal and distal opening (Fig. 6.37)
- Apply Vaseline gauze over the stoma and put a dressing.
- Once the colostomy starts functioning and edema subsides, apply Coloplast (stoma adhesive) or colostomy bag (Fig. 6.38). If colostomy does not start functioning within 4–5 days, irrigate stoma with 250 mL of normal saline to initiate stoma function.

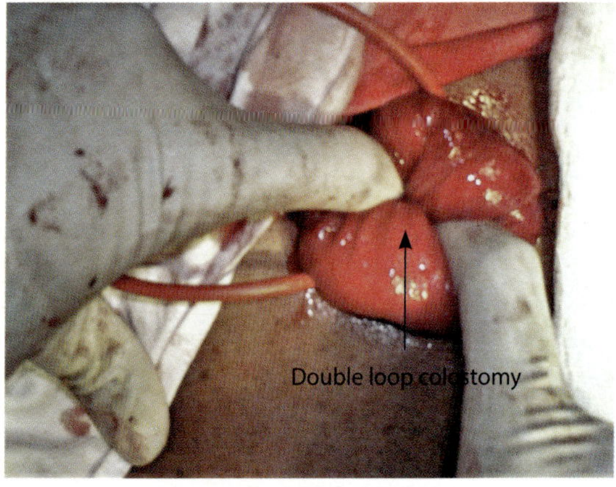

Figure 6.37 Double loop colostomy.

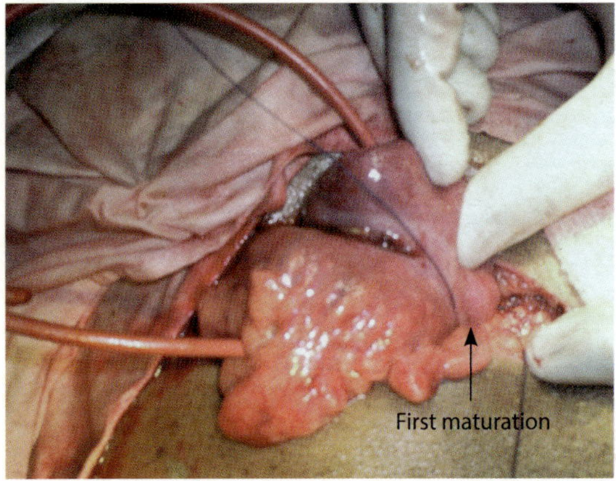

Figure 6.35 First maturation: Seromuscular stitch with peritoneum.

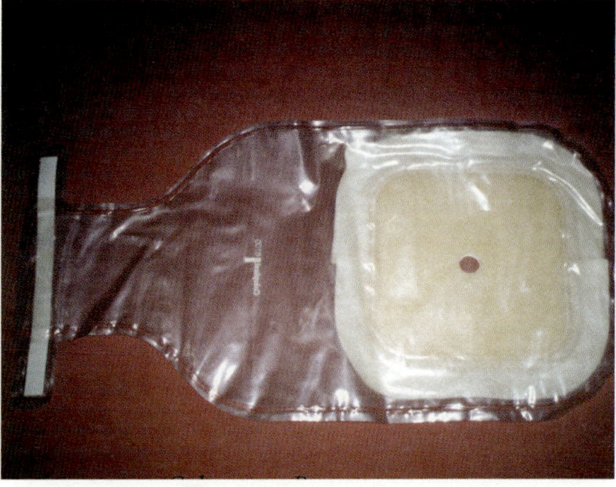

Figure 6.38 Coloplast bag.

- Some surgeons prefer to apply stoma appliance with skin barrier in the operating room itself. No adhesive should be applied.

Specific Techniques

Hartmann colostomy

Proximal loop is brought out as end colostomy and distal loop is closed and left inside the body (pelvic colon is excised).

Double barrel colostomy

If a loop or both ends of the colon are exteriorized, it is known as double barrel colostomy. It completely diverts the fecal matter. Proximal loop acts as a colostomy and distal loop serves as a mucous fistula.

In case of permanent colostomy, sigmoid colon is preferred to transverse colon, because usually stool in the sigmoid colon is solid, only once-a-day evacuation is needed, no appliances are required, and complications such as prolapse and leakage are less common.

POSTOPERATIVE CARE

- The patient should remain NBM for 24 hours.
- Give antibiotic, analgesic and anti-inflammatory drugs.
- Provide intravenous fluids.
- From the next day, start oral feeding.
- Red rubber spigot can be removed after 7 days, once firm adhesion between colostomy and abdominal wall occurs (usually on the seventh postoperative day).
- Colostomy in descending or sigmoid colon can be irrigated.
  - *Advantage*: Control of bowel movements
  - *Disadvantage*: Time consuming (full irrigation will require 45–60 minutes)

Care of colostomy

- Odorous substance a such as onion, asafetida, garlic, and fish should be avoided.
- Odor-proof stomy packs are used if available.
- Simethicone can be used to reduce amount of flatus.
- Toilet training: Constipation should be avoided and food such as oatmeal, whole grains, fruits, and vegetables should be taken. But avoid diarrhea.
- At least six to eight glasses of water should be taken daily.
- Chewing gum and smoking should be avoided.
- Pouch (bag) should be emptied when one-third or one-half full and the bag should be changed every 5–6 days.
- The surrounding skin should be taken care of by skin protectives.
- Colostomy irrigation
  - This option is available for sigmoid or descending colostomy.
  - It is contraindicated in parastomal hernia and prolapse, and in children.
  - It establishes regular bowel movement.
  - It should be performed in the morning with 500–1000 mL water with the use of cone tip which provides a secure seal.
  - Drainage bag is applied after instillation of water and the person can proceed with normal work.
  - Between works, the patient usually wears security pouch which permits passage of flatus through charcoal filter.

COMPLICATIONS OF INTESTINAL STOMA[4]

Early (Within 1 Month)

Skin irritation, pain associated with poor stoma location, leakage, high output and ischemia, partial necrosis

Skin irritation

- Most common early complication
- More common with ileostomy due to high output and its caustic content
- Leads to chemical dermatitis
- Other skin problems include: Candidiasis, allergic dermatitis, and mechanical injury to skin
  - Prevention
    - Preoperative planning of site, careful appliance fitting
    - Avoiding skin ointment or cream that may hamper the adhesion of appliance
    - Downsizing the appliance if needed
  - Treatment
    - Most cases can be treated with conservative measure except those with redundant pannus, surgical scar, or crease with poor

stoma marking site (revision surgery is the option).

High-output stoma

- It is more common with ileostomy.
- Diarrhea and dehydration is common.
- Ileostomy starts functioning on the third day.
- High output can lead to nausea and is associated with hyponatremia.
- Ileostomy output should be maintained at less than 1.5 L/day.
- Gradual adaptation of mucosa will allow the output to decrease within few days.
  - Treatment
    - It mainly involves intravenous fluid and electrolyte correction.
    - Bulk agents and opioids help in maintaining output around 1.5 L/day.

Ischemia or necrosis

- Causes
  - Impaired vascular supply due to skeletonization of distal bowel
  - Tension on mesentery
  - Tight fascial opening
  - Low perfusion
- Treatment
  - If necrosis is limited to the bowel above the fascia: Observation and stoma revision later
  - If necrosis extends below fascia: Exploration and resection of stoma
  - To see extent of necrosis: Scopy through stoma advisable

Parastomal abscess

It can be early or late complication.

- Late complication is usually associated with inflammatory bowel disease (IBD).
- Treatment
  - Incision and drainage (I&D) at the mucocutaneous junction with drain insertion. If abscess is a little distance from the stoma, lateral incision is preferred. Paracolostomy abscess is treated as same.

Paraileostomy fistula

- It is usually the end result of abscess. It may be because of injury to the ileum or deeply placed suture in the ileum or recurrent Crohn disease.
- Treatment
  - Relocation of stoma
  - Paracolostomy fistula treated by laying open the tract in the same manner as for fistula in ano

Late (After 1 Month)

Parastomal hernia, prolapse, obstruction, and stenosis

Parastomal hernia

- Gradual opening or widening of fascia due to increased abdominal pressure
- Relative weakness of posterior rectus sheath in lower abdomen
- Treatment
  - *Asymptomatic hernia*: No treatment, only observation
  - *Symptomatic hernia*: Relocation or repair—suture repair, open mesh repair, and laparoscopic intraperitoneal mesh repair

Prolapse

Normal prolapse up to 2–4 inches is not abnormal. Transverse loop colostomy is notorious for prolapse and is almost always efferent loop prolapse.

- Causes
  - Lack of fixation of transverse mesocolon to the retroperitoneum and size of opening of fascial defect are important factors in prolapse.
  - There is insufficient suturing to the abdominal wall.
  - Stoma should not be placed through rectus muscle.
  - Distended bowel is present.
- Treatment
  - Asymptomatic prolapse: No treatment is required.
  - Treatment of the primary condition and restoring intestinal continuity is the best option.
  - Convert it to end colostomy and mucous fistula.
  - In case of end colostomy: Mucocutaneous junction is discontinued, redundant colon amputated, and the mucocutaneous junction recreated.

Stenosis or stricture

- Causes
  - Serositis because of exposed serosal surface of colon to air before maturation (time taken

for mucosa to completely anneal to the epidermis)
  - Ischemia
  - Retraction
  - Recurrent IBD
  - Excessive tension
- Treatment
  - Mild asymptomatic: No treatment
  - Low-residue diet
  - Stool softeners
  - Local stenosis at skin level: Z-plasty
  - Associated with IBD: Local resection
  - For long stricture: Gentle digital dilatation till acute inflammation subsides and later on definitive revision of stoma through transabdominal approach associated with better results

Stoma retraction

- It may be a stoma retraction or skin retraction.
- Stoma retraction occurs when stoma is at or below the skin level and skin retraction is at the mucocutaneous junction or stoma is protruded 2 cm above the skin level.
- Main problem is skin irritation due to leakage.
- Treatment
  - Adequate appliance seal maintained; convex appliances with skin barrier ring used
  - Ostomy belt
  - Revision surgery if problem persists

Colostomy perforation

- Causes
  - Careless irrigation of stoma and during contrast examination
- Treatment
  - Mild inflammation and only extravasations of air: Antibiotics and localized drainage
  - Gross contamination with fecal matter or barium: Laparotomy, reconstruction of stoma with lavage and drainage

Peristomal varices

- Causes
  - Anastomosis between high-pressure portal system and low-pressure subcutaneous veins of the abdominal wall.
  - Caput medusa in peristomal skin
  - Significant bleeding
  - Associated with portal hypertension and may be seen in liver disease, either metastases or sclerosing cholangitis
- Treatments
  - Very short life expectancy: Disconnection between bowel and skin till fascia
  - Percutaneous coil embolization
  - For more life expectancy, TIPS, liver transplants, or surgical shunts

EXPLORATORY LAPAROTOMY FOR GASTROINTESTINAL PERFORATION

Laparotomy is a surgical operation involving incision through the flank, or through any part of the abdominal wall. This operation is performed to examine the problems associated with the abdominal organs such as stomach, liver, intestines, kidneys, and bladder. In many cases such as *peptic ulcer*, the problem can be treated during the laparotomy; in others, another operation is needed.

Exploratory laparotomy is used to:

- Explore the anterior wall of stomach and posterior wall of stomach (if perforation suspected in the posterior wall).
- Explore the first to fourth parts of duodenum for perforation, malignancy, diverticula, etc.
- Identify junction of duodenum and jejunum.
- Explore ascending colon, transverse colon, and descending colon.
- Explore rectovaginal or rectovesical pouch for collection and malignancy.
- Explore retroperitoneum, if retroperitoneal organ pathology is suspected.

PERFORATION WITH SIGNS OF PERITONITIS

Signs of Peritonitis

- Guarding
- Rigidity
- Tenderness
- Rebound tenderness

Various Stages of Perforation

- Stage of irritation (up to 6 hours)
  - Patient pale and anxious

- Subnormal temperature
- Rigidity all over abdomen
- Tachycardia
- Tender per rectal examination
- Stage of illusion
  - Decreased pain, tenderness, and rigidity
  - Temperature: Normal or higher
  - Tachycardia
  - Bowel sound: Absent
- Stage of diffuse peritonitis
  - Increased abdominal distension
  - Rise in pulse rate
  - Board-like rigidity

IMMEDIATE TREATMENT

It is the same as mentioned for acute pancreatitis till IV fluids (refer Chapter 16, *Frequently Asked Questions*).

OPERATIVE TECHNIQUE FOR LAPAROTOMY

Midline Incision

- Anesthesia: GA is given.
- Technique: It involves midline or right paramedian incision.
- Cut the skin.
- Cut the subcutaneous tissue (Fig. 6.39).
  - No muscle cut
  - Blood less
  - No nerve cut
  - Rapid access to peritoneal cavity
  - Can approach upper abdominal viscera better
  - Bilateral access possible
- Cut the linea alba (Fig. 6.40).
- Hold the posterior rectus sheath with artery forceps.
- Cut the sheath and peritoneum (Fig. 6.41).
- If pus comes out (Fig. 6.42), send it for culture and sensitivity.
- Suction the fluid.
- Retract the liver with Deaver's liver retractor.
- Look for perforation (Fig. 6.43).
- Suture the perforation (Fig. 6.44) with black silk 3-0 or polypropylene or Dexon stitches.
- Intermittent stitches of full thickness of stomach wall and central suture tied last, so that there is less chance of cutting through the edematous wall.

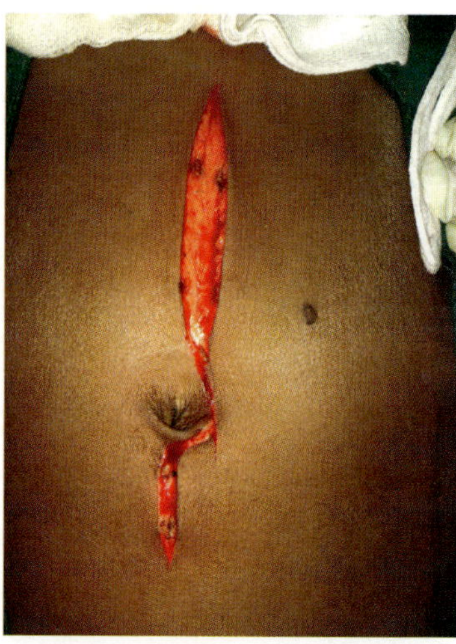

Figure 6.39 Skin and subcutaneous tissue cut.

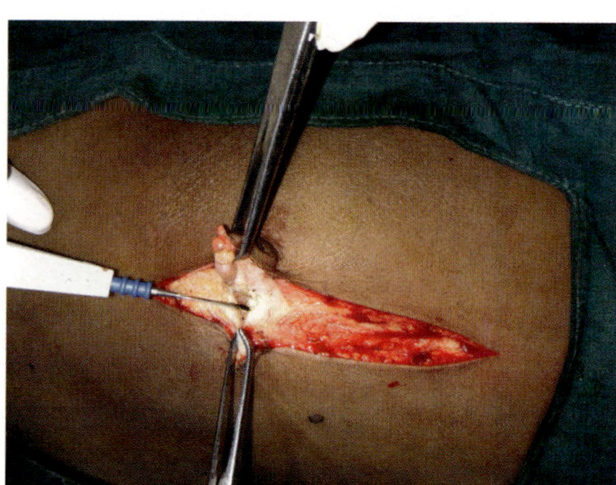

Figure 6.40 Cutting of linea alba.

- Secure the omental tag in place with the same suture (omentopexy) (Figs 6.45 and 6.46).
- Irrigation of peritoneal cavity with warm saline (at least 5–6 L), till the wash becomes relatively clear.

> - Use of povidone-iodine, even in diluted form, may lead to irritation.
> - If peritoneal wash is adequate, perforation closed immediately, and is secure, drainage is not required (drainage is no substitute for good technique).

- Put two drains, one in Morrison's space (right) and one in the pelvis (left).

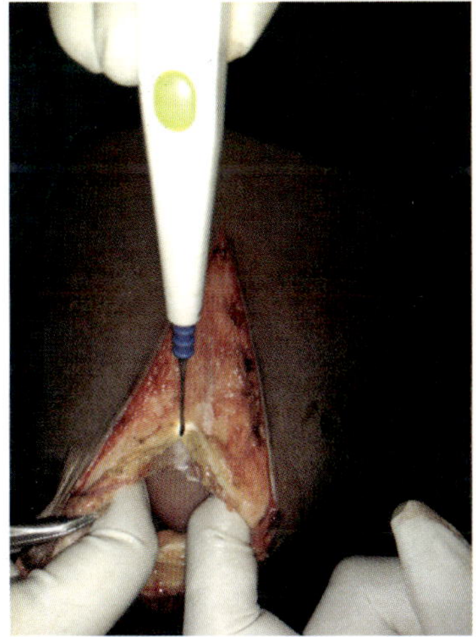

Figure 6.41 Cutting of sheath and peritoneum.

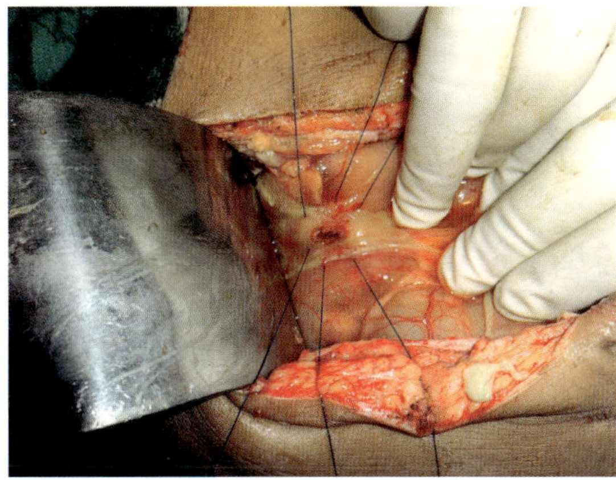

Figure 6.44 Three suture taken at the upper, middle and lower part of perforation.

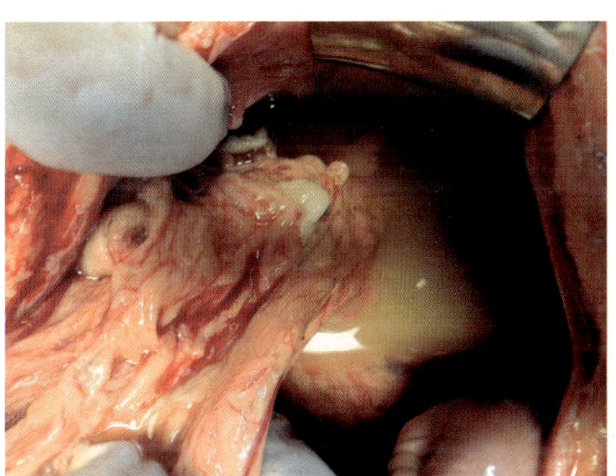

Figure 6.42 Pus in the peritoneal cavity.

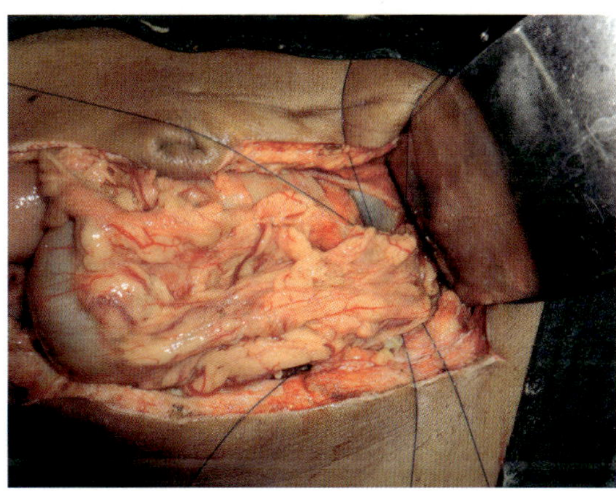

Figure 6.45 Omentum is kept over the perforation.

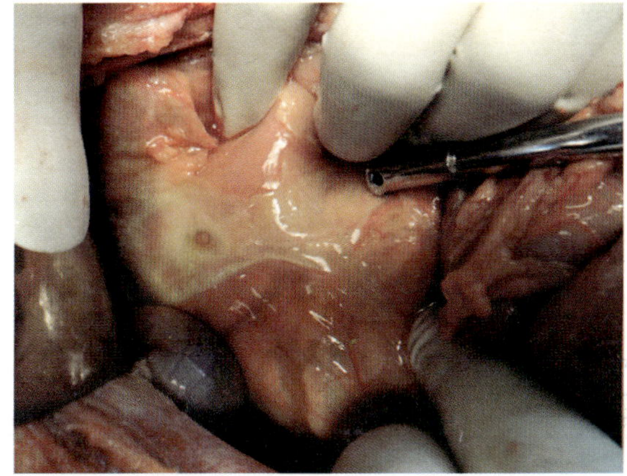

Figure 6.43 Perforation in the first part of duodenum.

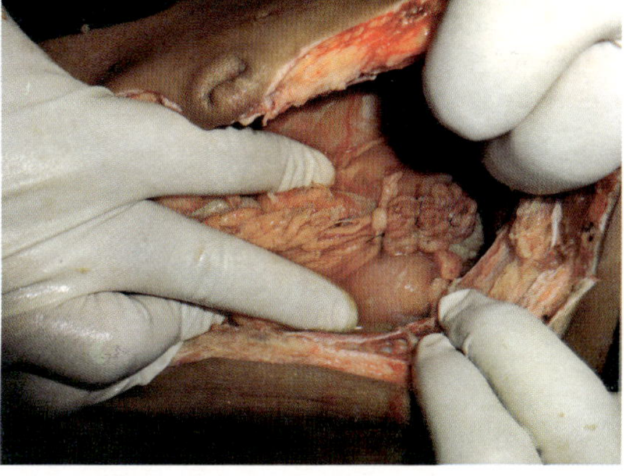

Figure 6.46 Omentum is sutured over the perforation (omentopexy).

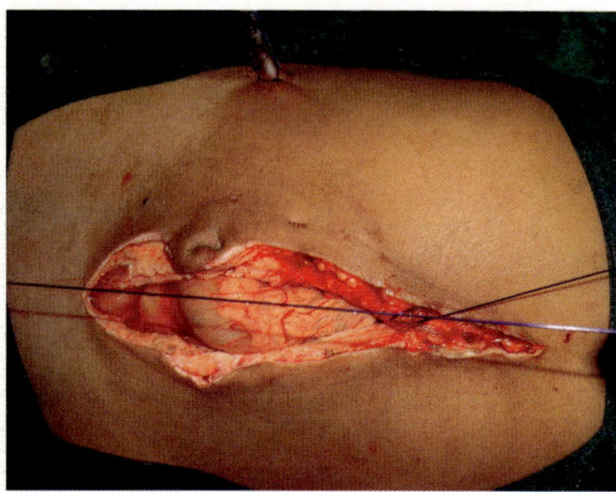

Figure 6.47 Mass closure with PDS.

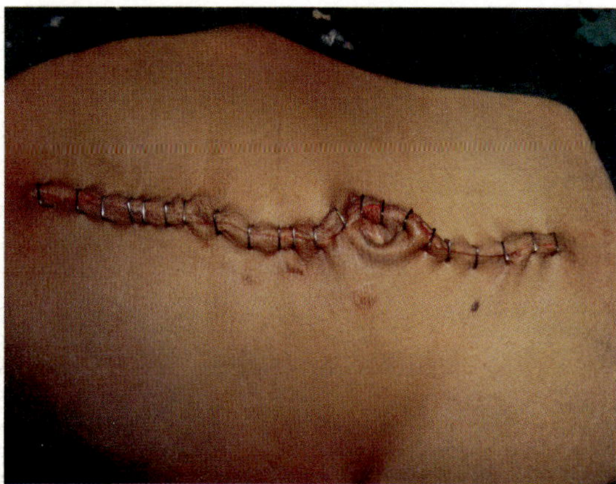

Figure 6.48 Skin closed with skin stapler.

- Perform mass closure with polydioxanone no. 1 continuous locking or running stitch with Aberdeen knot in between at after every four to five run (Fig. 6.47).
- Close skin with either skin stapler (Fig. 6.48) or Ethilon 2-0 or 3-0 vertical mattress intermittent stitches.
- Apply dressing.
- Vagotomy in emergency is not advisable because of:
  - Duration of surgery mostly being more than 6 hours
  - Contamination
  - Pus
  - Patient not being fit

Right Paramedian Incision

- If laparotomy is performed through the right paramedian incision, the layers are:
  - Skin
  - Subcutaneous tissue
  - Anterior rectus sheath
- Retract rectus muscle laterally.
- Hold posterior rectus sheath with artery forceps and cut the peritoneum open.
- Closure
  - Posterior rectus sheath with Vicryl 2-0 continuous locking stitch
  - Anterior rectus sheath with Prolene 1-0 with figure of 8 stitches or continuous locking stitch
  - Skin with either skin stapler (Fig. 6.48) or Ethilon 2-0 or 3-0 vertical mattress intermittent stitches
- Right paramedian incision is 2.5–5 cm from the midline and extends from costal margin to 2 cm below umbilicus. It gives good exposure, but it is time consuming to make and close and bilateral access is difficult.

POSTOPERATIVE CARE

- NBM till further order
- Temperature, pulse, blood pressure, and respiratory rate (TPR) 1 hourly
- Input/output chart
- Antibiotics
- Analgesics
- PPIs/H2 blockers
- IV fluids (5% dextrose for first 24 hours followed by DNS and Iso-M)
- Tincture benzoin steam inhalation and H2O2 gargle
- Active and passive leg exercises
- Chest physiotherapy
- Gradually, oral liquids started when the peristalsis returns and patient passes flatus
- Ryle's tube removed when aspiration is minimal
- Drain (if kept) removed after 5 days and suture removal between 8th and 10th days
- If NBM is to be continued for long, then total parenteral nutrition (TPN) considered

COMPLICATIONS

- Paralytic ileus
- Wound infection

- Retention of urine
- Hiccups
- DVT
- Pulmonary embolism
- Leakage from suture line

Relaparotomy—opening of abdomen again after initial operation is of two types:

- *Planned relaparotomy*: It is usually performed within 48 hours of initial operation; this is decided from the beginning (packing of liver surface in trauma).
- *Relaparotomy on demand*: It is a demand of clinical situation, for example, when the clinical condition of a patient who has been operated upon deteriorates in the postoperative period and it is suspected to be due to some problem within the abdomen.

RIGHT HEMICOLECTOMY

DEFINITION

Right hemicolectomy is an operation designed to remove terminal ileum, entire right colon, and proximal portion of right transverse colon followed by ileotransverse anastomosis.

INDICATIONS

- Carcinoma involving ascending colon, cecum
- Adenocarcinoma of the appendix
- Carcinoid tumor of the appendix >2 cm
- Crohn disease affecting terminal ileum and cecum and causing obstruction
- Ileocecal Koch disease not responding to medical management (quadrucolectomy: resection of terminal ileum, cecum, appendix, and part of ascending colon with ileoascending anastomosis)
- Bleeding from angiodysplastic lesion not controlled with nonoperative treatment
- Diverticular lesion of the right colon

RELEVANT ANATOMY OF LARGE INTESTINE

- Length is 1.5 m from cecum to anus.
- The widest portion is cecum.
- The narrowest portion is sigmoid colon.
- Length of various colonic segments
  - *Cecum*: 6–8 cm
  - *Appendix*: 2–20 cm
  - *Ascending colon*: 15 cm
  - *Transverse colon*: 45 cm (longest segment of large bowel)
  - *Descending colon*: 25 cm
  - *Sigmoid colon*: 35 cm
- The ascending colon and proximal transverse colon embryologically derived from the midgut, and distal transverse colon, descending colon, sigmoid colon, and rectum derived from the hindgut. Rectosigmoid junction is confluence of tenia coli. Rectum is last 12–15 cm from the anal verge. Transverse colon and sigmoid colon are fully intraperitoneal and have a free mesocolon. Both ascending and descending colon with the flexure are partially located in the retroperitoneum.
- Distinguishing features from small intestine
  - It has a large caliber.
  - Most part is in fixed position.
  - Tenia coli: It represents outer longitudinal coat of muscle that traverses the colon from the base of appendix to the rectosigmoid junction. There are three tenia, named anterior (tenia libera), posteromedial (tenia mesocolica), and posterolateral (tenia omentalis).
  - Appendices epiploicae: It is the small appendages of fat that protrudes from the serosal surface of bowel.
  - Sacculation or haustra: It is outpouching of bowel wall between tenia. It is because of relative shortness of tenia (tenia is one-sixth shorter than the length of the bowel). The haustra are separated by the plica semilunaris or crescentic fold of the bowel wall.

Blood Supply

- Arterial supply
  - *Superior mesenteric artery (SMA)*: It supplies cecum, ascending colon, and proximal two-third of transverse colon via ileocolic, right colic, and middle colic arteries. It originates from the aorta behind the superior border of pancreas at the level of L1.
  - *Inferior mesenteric artery (IMA)*: It supplies rest of the bowel via left colic, sigmoidal, and superior rectal arteries. It originates from the

left anterior surface of aorta 3–4 cm beyond the bifurcation at the level of L2–3.
  - *Arc of Riolan*: It constitutes direct communication between superior and inferior mesenteric arteries; parallel and posterior to the middle colic artery in the transverse mesocolon.
  - *Marginal artery of Drummond*: This vessel lies closest to and parallel to the bowel wall and is formed by the main trunks, and the arcade arising from the ileocolic, right colic, and middle and left colic arteries.

The areas prone to development of ischemia are:
- *Griffith's critical point*: At the splenic flexure, marginal artery may be discontinuous or absent.
- *Sudeck's critical point*: At the rectosigmoid junction, there is discontinuous area of marginal artery.

- *Venous drainage*: Venous drainage of the colon parallels the arterial supply.
  - *Ascending and transverse colon*: Superior mesenteric vein
  - *Left and sigmoid colon*: Inferior mesenteric vein
  - *Distal colon and rectum*: Iliac vein

Lymphatic Drainage

The lymphatics flow parallel to the arterial and venous drainage. The right side of colon drains into superior mesenteric nodes or into the portal systems via superior mesenteric vein. The left side of colon drains into inferior mesenteric nodes. The upper third of the rectum follows inferior mesenteric vein while the lower two-third drains into hypogastric nodes and finally into para-aortic nodes. The lower one-third of the rectum also follows pudendal vessels and drains into inguinal nodes.

The groups of lymph nodes are:
- *Epicolic*: Drain the submucosa and are located in the colonic wall. This group of lymph nodes runs along the inner bowel margin between the intestinal wall and the arterial arcades.
- *Paracolic*: Epicolic nodes drain into the paracolic nodes. It follows the route of marginal arteries.
- *Intermediate*: Paracolic nodes drain into the intermediate nodes and follow the main vessels.
- *Central or principal nodes*: Intermediate nodes drain into principal nodes which are located at the origin of SMA and IMA and are continuous with para-aortic nodes.

Nerve Supply

- Right colon
  - *Sympathetic*: Lower six thoracic which synapse within celiac, preaortic, and superior mesenteric ganglia
  - *Parasympathetic*: Right vagus and celiac nerve which synapse with the nerve within the intrinsic autonomic nerve plexus with bowel wall
- Left colon
  - *Sympathetic*: L1, L2, L3
  - *Parasympathetic*: S2, S3, S4 via splanchnic nerve

PREOPERATIVE PREPARATION OF BOWEL

Mechanical Bowel Preparation (MBP)

A few recent studies suggest that MBP does not prevent surgical site infection and should not be used in clinical practice. Still many surgeons including myself routinely perform MBP at least for left side of colonic surgery.

- Undisputed advantages of MBP
  - Empty colon is easy to manipulate.
  - Preanastomotic stool load is avoided.
  - Intraoperative colonoscopy can be performed if required.
  - Traditional belief of MBP associated with low risk of wound infection and anastomotic complications is not supported by evidence.
- Disadvantages of MBP
  - Dehydration and electrolyte imbalance
  - Spillage of residual liquid stool

Method: PEG or sodium phosphate is used. PEG is to be taken with 2 L of water on the night before the surgery. Bloating and nausea are common. Sodium phosphate is well tolerated but it is contraindicated in patients with renal failure. Magnesium citrate is another option but it is associated with electrolyte imbalance.

- Only clear liquid to be taken for 3 days
- Enema or bowel washes twice daily
- Can also use castor oil instead of enema

Chemical

Antibiotics prophylaxis: It should be started within 1 hour of incision and limited to less than 24 hours. It should be broad spectrum to include aerobic as well as anaerobic bacteria. To minimize the antibiotic resistance, it should be adequately dosed and targeted within a short period. Various regimens used are:

- Ertapenem or piperacillin tazobactam
- Co-amoxiclav plus metronidazole plus amikacin
- Cephalosporin (second or third generation) plus metronidazole plus amikacin or gentamicin (oral antibiotics do reduce rate of wound infection if MBP is not used [metronidazole plus neomycin]; combined with MBP, it increases the risk of nosocomial superinfection such as *Clostridium difficile*)

Ureteral stenting

- It is not routinely used but can be helpful in previous history of colorectal procedure or pelvic dissection.
- Lighted ureteral stents are useful in challenging laparoscopic procedures.
- It is placed after induction via cystoscopy.

DVT Prophylaxis

It is discussed in detail in Chapter 1, *Preoperative Preparation*.

Ryle's Tube

It is not used routinely but can be placed in patients presenting with complete or partial obstruction.

OPERATIVE TECHNIQUE

- Anesthesia: GA is performed.
- Position: The patient is in supine position.
- Incision: Midline or right paramedian incision is made.
- Till the opening of the peritoneum, the procedure is the same as that for gastrointestinal perforation.
- Search for metastatic diseases, such as those in the liver, peritoneal surface, omentum, and pelvic organs (primarily in women).
- Apply Doyen's retractor or self-retaining retractor.
- By keeping small bowel to the left, incise white line of Toldt and mobilize the colon.
- Take care that the second and third parts of duodenum, ureter, and gonadal vessels are not injured.
- Clamp, divide, and doubly ligate ileocolic, right colic, and right branch of middle colic arteries near their origins.
- For tumor of the cecum and ascending colon, 10 cm of the ileum is sufficient margin (distal).
- Apply clamp on the ileum and transverse colon (on the portion to be preserved—apply occluding clamp; and on the portion to be removed—apply crushing clamp).
- Divide the intestine in between the occluding and crushing clamps (while dividing, take care to prevent spillage of intestinal contents).
- Remove the portion of the bowel with mesentery.
- Carry out anastomosis between ileum and transverse colon (end to end)—hand sewn or by using a stapler.
- Close the defect in the mesentery with interrupted silk 3-0.
- Put a drain.
- Closure is the same as that for peptic perforation.

Difference between colectomy done in tuberculosis and carcinoma—in case of tuberculosis, before clamping, dividing, and double ligation, mobilization of colon is done. All lymph node removal is not mandatory and instead of ileotransverse anastomosis (done in carcinoma), ileoascending anastomosis is done.

POSTOPERATIVE CARE

- NBM till further order
- Temperature, pulse, and respiratory rate (TPR) 1 hourly
- Input/output chart
- Antibiotics
- Analgesics
- PPIs/H2 blockers
- IV fluids (5% dextrose for first 24 hours followed by DNS and isolyte M)
- Tincture benzoin steam inhalation and H_2O_2 gargle

- Active and passive leg exercises
- Chest physiotherapy
- If hemicolectomy done for malignancy, then using low-molecular-weight heparin considered
- Gradually, oral liquids started when the peristalsis returns and patient passes flatus
- Ryle's tube removed when aspiration is minimal
- Drain (if kept) removed after 5 days and suture removal between 8th and 10th days
- If NBM is to be continued for long, then total parenteral nutrition (TPN) considered.

COMPLICATIONS

- At the time of operation: Injury to the surrounding structures such as duodenum, ureter, and gonadal vessels
- Hemorrhage: Primary, reactionary, or secondary
- Wound infection
- Anastomotic leak/stenosis
- Injury to the duodenum, ureter, gonadal vessels, etc.
- Respiratory complications: Pneumonia, pleural effusion

- Important factors associated with failure of anastomotic technique are:
  - Ischemia
  - Tension on the suture line
  - Obstruction
  - Peritonitis
  - High-dose steroids
  - Radiation
  - Persistence of the disease on the suture line
- Submucosa is the strongest layer of the bowel; it must be included in the suture.
- Traditionally anastomosis is done in two layers:
  - Inner continuous layer—full thickness with Vicryl 3-0
  - Outer interrupted seromuscular layer with black silk 3-0
- Nowadays a single-layer anastomosis is considered to be ideal. Some surgeons believe in single-layer extramucosal anastomosis.
- Two types of stapling devices are available for anastomosis:
  - *Linear*: Side-to-side anastomosis
  - *Circular*: End-to-end anastomosis

INGUINAL HERNIA

DEFINITION

Hernia is abnormal protrusion of viscus or part of viscus through a normal or abnormal opening, from the cavity which contains it. The most common location for a hernia is the abdominal wall, particularly the groin (inguinal hernia). Apart from the inguinal hernia, other types are femoral, umbilical, incisional, and diaphragmatic hernias.

This chapter shall focus on the most common type, that is, inguinal hernia. It will be worthwhile to recapitulate the related anatomical features since no other disease of the human body belonging to the province of surgeon requires in its treatment a better combination of accurate anatomical knowledge and surgical skill than hernia in all its variations.

RELEVANT ANATOMY OF THE INGUINAL REGION

- Groin: It is a part of the anterior abdominal wall, which lies below anterior superior iliac spine.
- Inguinal region: It lies 2 inches above and 2 inches below the inguinal ligament.
- Inguinal canal (house of Bassini): It is an obliquely placed natural hiatus in the tissue of anterior abdominal wall, extending from deep to superficial inguinal ring.
  - Length: 4 cm
  - Contents
    - *In males*: Spermatic cord
    - *In females*: Round ligament of uterus
    - *In both sexes*: Ilioinguinal nerve
- Boundaries of canal
  - Anterior
    - Skin
    - Superficial fascia
    - External oblique aponeurosis
    - Fibers of internal oblique (lateral one-third)
  - Posterior
    - Fascia transversalis
    - Conjoined tendon
  - Superior: Arched fibers of internal oblique and transverse abdominis
  - Inferior: Union of transversalis fascia with inguinal ligament and on medial side lacunar ligament (fascia transversalis is a continuous

layer of endoabdominal fascia that completely encloses the abdominal cavity)

- Superficial inguinal ring: It is a triangular opening in the external oblique aponeurosis, just above and lateral to the pubic tubercle.
  - Apex: It is pointing toward the line of deep fibers of aponeurosis.
  - Base: It lies along the pubic crest. It has lateral (strong and thick) and medial (thin) crura.
  - Ring is smaller in females.
  - Size of ring: It does not admit more than the tip of the little finger.
  - In addition to spermatic cord in male and round ligament in female, ilioinguinal nerve emerges through superficial ring
- Deep inguinal ring: It is a U-shaped defect in fascia transversalis
  - Location: It lies 1.25 cm above the midinguinal point.
  - Spermatic cord in male and round ligament in female emerge through deep ring.
- Inguinal ligament (Poupart ligament): It is a lower thickened portion of external oblique aponeurosis suspended between anterior superior iliac spine and pubic tubercle. It is 10 cm in length and medial part is thick and rounded while lateral part is flat and bent upon itself.
  - Structures passing deep to the inguinal ligament
    - *Muscles*: Psoas major, iliacus, and pectineus
    - *Nerves*: Lateral femoral cutaneous and femoral nerve
    - *Femoral sheath*: Femoral artery, vein, and lymphatics (sheath lies below inguinal ligaments and iliacus and psoas major muscle)
- Lacunar ligament (Gimbernat ligament): It is a thick triangular band of tissue, lying posterior to the medial end of inguinal ligament (2 cm long).
- Cooper ligament (ileopectineal ligament): It lies posterior to the iliopubic tract and is formed by periosteum and fascia along the superior pubic rami. It is a condensation of transversalis fascia and periosteum of superior pubic ramus lateral to the pubic tubercle.
- The femoral vessels run between inguinal and the Cooper ligament and enclosed in a femoral sheath.
- Saphenous opening or fossa ovalis: It lies 4 cm below and lateral to pubic tubercle.
- Conjoined tendon: It refers to the fusion of the lower fibers of internal oblique aponeurosis with similar fibers from the aponeurosis of the transverses abdominis where they insert into the pubic tubercle and superior ramus of pubis.
- Myopectineal orifice of Fruchaud (MPO): It is a funnel-shaped opening, lined in its entirety, by fascia transversalis. According to Fruchaud, all groin hernias occur through this orifice, due to failure of transversalis fascia to retain peritoneum.
  - Boundaries
    - *Superior*: Internal oblique and transverse abdominis
    - *Inferior*: Cooper ligament
    - *Medially*: Rectus abdominis and its sheath
    - *Laterally*: Iliopsoas
- The inguinal ligament and ileopubic tract divide the MPO into two areas:
  - Superior compartment contains inguinal canal. The inferior epigastric artery further divides it into:
    - *Hesselbach's triangle*: All direct hernias occur through this triangle. It is bounded medially by lateral border of rectus muscle, laterally by inferior epigastric vessels, and below by upturned part of inguinal ligament.
    - *Lateral triangle*: Containing internal ring. A defect in this area is an indirect hernia.
  - Inferior compartment contains femoral canal.
- Important nerves in the inguinal region
  - *Iliohypogastric*: L1, pierces the external oblique and innervates the skin above the pubis
  - *Ilioinguinal*: L1, anterior to the spermatic cord, gives sensation to the lateral scrotum, labia (ipsilateral)
  - *Genitofemoral*: L1–L2
- Preperitoneal space: As the name itself suggests, it is internally bounded by peritoneum and its anterior boundary is formed by the fascia transversalis.
  - Contents
    - Transmits blood vessels, lymphatics, and nerves to and from the leg
    - Transmits vas deferens and vessels of spermatic cord to and from scrotum
    - Important nerves: Lateral femoral cutaneous nerve and genitofemoral nerve

- Coverings of the spermatic cord (from outside to inside)
  - External spermatic fascia
  - Cremasteric fascia
  - Internal spermatic fascia
- Coverings of the testis
  - Skin
  - Dartos muscle
  - External spermatic fascia
  - Cremasteric fascia
  - Internal spermatic fascia
  - Tunica vaginalis
  - Tunica albuginea
  - Tunica vasculosa
- Contents of spermatic cord
  - Vas deferens
  - Testicular artery and vein
  - Cremasteric artery
  - Artery to vas
  - Genital branch of genitofemoral nerve
  - Sympathetic nerves
  - Pampiniform plexus of veins
  - Four to eight lymph vessels

MECHANISMS THAT NORMALLY PREVENT HERNIA FORMATION WHEN INTRA-ABDOMINAL PRESSURE RISES

- *Ball valve*: Due to contraction of cremaster, superficial inguinal ring plugged by spermatic cord
- *Shutter*: Arched fibers of internal oblique
- *Flap valve*: Obliquity of inguinal canal
- *Slit valve*: Crura of the superficial ring

CAUSES OF INGUINAL HERNIA

- Congenital: Patent processus vaginalis
- Acquired
  - Increased intra-abdominal pressure
    - Chronic constipation
    - Benign prostatic hyperplasia (BPH)
    - Heavy weightlifting
    - Ascites
    - Chronic obstructive pulmonary disease (COPD; chronic cough increases intra-abdominal pressure)
- Previous surgery (damage to nerve)
- Smoking (acquired collagen deficiency)
- Obesity (fat separates the bundles and layers)

CLASSIFICATION OF INGUINAL HERNIAS

Anatomical Classification

- *Indirect inguinal hernia*: It occurs through deep ring and is of the following types:
  - *Bubonocele*: Hernia is limited to the canal.
  - *Funicular*: Processus vaginalis is closed at its lower end; testis is separately palpable.
  - *Complete*: Processus vaginalis is patent throughout.
- *Direct inguinal hernia*: It occurs through posterior wall through Hesselbach's triangle, medial to inferior epigastric vessels.

Clinical Classification

- *Reducible*: Content can be reduced.
- *Irreducible*: Content cannot be reduced.
- *Obstructed*: Irreducibility + signs of obstruction.
- *Strangulated*: Obstruction + impaired blood supply.
- *Inflamed*: Hernia + signs of inflammation (appendicitis or salpingitis).
- *Incarcerated*: Content is loaded colon (feces). Palpation leads to indentation.

Nyhus Classification

- *Type I*: Indirect inguinal hernia with normal internal ring (pediatric hernia)
- *Type II*: Indirect inguinal hernia with widened inguinal ring, with normal posterior wall
- *Type III*: Posterior wall defect
  - Direct
  - Indirect
  - Femoral
- *Type IV*: Recurrent
  - Direct
  - Indirect
  - Femoral
  - Combined

Gilbert's Classification

- *Type I*: Indirect hernia with snug internal ring
- *Type II*: Indirect hernia with widened inguinal ring, admitting one finger, but not more than two fingers
- *Type III*: Indirect hernia with widened inguinal ring, admitting more than two fingers

- *Type IV*: Large blowout through posterior wall
- *Type V*: Punched-out defect in the posterior wall, with normal internal ring
- Robbin and Rutkow added two more types:
  - *Type VI*: Pantaloon hernia (indirect and direct hernia present simultaneously)
  - *Type VII*: Femoral hernia

Schumpelick Classification

L: Lateral indirect

M: Medial direct

F: Femoral

Type I: Defect size <1.5 cm

Type II: Defect size 1.5–3 cm

Type III: Defect size >3 cm

DIAGNOSIS

- Groin pain
- Inguinal or inguinoscrotal swelling
- Cough impulse and reducibility present
- Right-sided hernia more common
- In adults, 65% hernia—indirect; 12% hernia—bilateral (Table 6.3)

SPECIAL CASES

Recurrent Hernia

The most common site for recurrence of hernia is near the pubic tubercle.

Causes of recurrent hernia

- Persistent predisposing conditions such as chronic constipation, BPH, and persistent cough.
- Improper operation, for example:
  - Patient requiring hernioplasty, but herniorrhaphy done instead
  - During operation, absorbable suture material used
  - Tension on the suture line
  - Pantaloon hernia (one sac missed)
  - Failure to high ligate the sac
  - Imperfect hemostasis leading to hematoma and infection
- Wound infection
- Late recurrence after 2 years due to metabolic problems, such as defect in the collagen metabolism

Sliding Hernia (Hernia en Glissade)

When posterior wall of the sac is formed by viscera, it is called sliding hernia, for example, on right side cecum, on left side sigmoid colon, and bladder on both sides. It is seen usually in males over the age of 40 years and more common on left side. Failure to recognize during surgery leads to injury to bowel or bladder.

Sacless Hernia

It is epigastric hernia of linea alba. It is more common in males and 20% of hernias are multiple. It is located between xiphoid process and umbilicus within 5–6 cm of umbilicus. It is better felt than seen. Epigastric hernia does not have classical signs

Table 6.3 Classification of Groin Hernia[5]

Modified traditional classification of groin hernia		Nyhus–Stoppa	Modified Gilbert	Schumpelick/Aachen (1995)
I	A. Indirect small	I	1	L1
I	B. Indirect medium	II	2	L2
I	C. Indirect large	IIIB	3	L3
II	A. Direct small	IIIA	5	M1
II	B. Direct medium	IIIA	-	M2
II	C. Direct large	-	4	M3
III	Combined	IIIB	6	MC
IV	Femoral	IIIC	7	F
O	Other	-	-	-
R	Recurrent	IV A, B, C, D	-	-

of hernia such as cough impulse and reducibility. Preperitoneal fat is the most common content. Mostly they are asymptomatic and occasionally give rise to pain due to strangulation of fatty content. Smaller hernias are more likely to be symptomatic.

Dual Hernia or Pantaloon Hernia

In this hernia, one sac is medial to inferior epigastric vessel and one sac is lateral to it. It is a common cause for recurrence if you miss the one sac.

Sportsman Hernia

It is characterized by the presence of groin pain, without evidence of obvious inguinal swelling.

Causes of sportsman hernia

- Occult hernia
- Nerve entrapment
- Tendon injury
- Osteitis pubis
- Urinary tract infection (UTI)
- Hip disorders

Treatment of sportsman hernia

- Anti-inflammatory drugs
- Physiotherapy

Named Groin Hernias

- *Richter's hernia*: Content is part of circumference of bowel wall.
- *Littre's hernia*: Content is Meckel's diverticulum.
- *Maydl hernia*: Content is two adjacent loops of bowel.
- *Amyand hernia*: Content is appendix.
- *Beclard hernia*: It is hernia through opening for saphenous vein.
- *Laugier femoral hernia*: It is hernia through gap in lacunar ligament.
- *Narath hernia*: It is seen in congenital dislocation of hip, behind the femoral vessels.
- *Cloquet hernia*: Sac lies under the fascia covering the pectineus muscle.
- *Gibbon hernia*: It is hernia with hydrocele.
- *Berger hernia*: It lies in the pouch of Douglas.
- *Petersen hernia*: After Roux-en-Y gastric bypass, hernia under Roux loop is Peterson hernia.
- *Stammer's hernia*: It is hernia after retrocolic gastrojejunostomy through defect.
- *Ogilvie hernia*: It is a circular rigid defect in conjoined tendon.

MANAGEMENT

Guidelines for the Management of Groin Hernia[7]

The guidelines on inguinal hernia management have been recently changed in February 2018. An expert group of international surgeons (the HerniaSurge Group) and one anesthesiologist pain expert were the part of the team that developed the guidelines on the management of inguinal hernia in an adult. Complete literature searches (including comprehensive search by The Dutch Cochrane database) from January 1, 2015 to July 1, 2015, for level 1 publications were carried out. The summary of recommendation is as follows:

- They identified following risk factors for an inguinal hernia (IH): family history, history of a contralateral hernia, male sex, age, defective collagen metabolism, surgery on prostate, and low BMI. The risk factors for recurrence were also identified and are poor surgical techniques, low surgical volumes, surgical inexperience, and local anesthesia.
- Diagnosis can be confirmed by physical examination alone in the vast majority of patients with appropriate signs and symptoms. Rarely, ultrasound is necessary. Less commonly still, a dynamic MRI or CT scan or herniography may be needed.
- Symptomatic groin hernias should be treated surgically.
- Asymptomatic or minimally symptomatic male IH patients can be managed with 'watchful waiting.' Surgical risks and the watchful waiting strategy should be discussed with patients as most patients eventually require surgery.
- Mesh repair is recommended as the first choice, either by an open procedure or a laparo-endoscopic repair technique.
- Lichtenstein and laparo-endoscopic repair are best evaluated. Many methods need further evaluation.
- Laparo-endoscopy methods have faster recovery time, lower chronic pain risk, and are cost-effective in expert hand.
- After patient's consent, in transabdominal preperitoneal prosthetic (TAPP), the contralateral side should be inspected. This is not suggested

for unilateral total extraperitoneal prosthetic (TEPP) repair.
- In tissue repair, the first choice is the Shouldice technique.
- Mesh selection only on weight alone is not recommended as low weight meshes are associated with short-term benefit of decreased pain and early recovery, but long-term outcomes are not good in term of recurrence and chronic pain.
- Day surgery is recommended for the majority of groin hernia repair provided aftercare is organized. Surgeons should be aware of the intrinsic characteristics of the meshes they use. The incidence of erosion seems higher with plug versus flat mesh.
- Mesh fixation in total extraperitoneal prosthetic (TEPP) repair is not required. In both TEP and TAPP repair, it is advisable to fix mesh in M3 hernias (large medial) to reduce recurrence risk.
- Antibiotic prophylaxis in average-risk patients in low-risk environments is not recommended in open surgery. In laparo-endoscopic repair, it is never recommended.
- Local anesthesia in open repair has many advantages. General anesthesia is preferred over regional anesthesia in patients aged 65 and older as it is associated with fewer cardiac and respiratory complications.
- Perioperative field blocks and subfascial/subcutaneous infiltrations are recommended in all cases of open repair.
- Patients are advised that they can resume normal activities of daily living without restrictions as soon as they feel comfortable. Provided expertise is available, it is suggested that women with groin hernias undergo laparo-endoscopic repair to decrease the risk of chronic pain and avoid missing a femoral hernia.
- Watchful waiting is suggested in pregnant women as groin swelling most often consists of self-limited round ligament varicosities. Timely mesh repair by a laparo-endoscopic approach is suggested for femoral hernias provided expertise is available.
- Chronic pain is managed by a combination of pharmacological and interventional measures and, if this is unsuccessful, followed by, in selected cases (triple) neurectomy and (in selected cases) mesh removal.
- For a recurrent hernia after anterior repair (Lichtenstein), posterior repair (preperitoneal) is recommended. If recurrence occurs after a posterior repair, an anterior repair is recommended. After a failed anterior and posterior approach, management by a specialist hernia surgeon is recommended.
- Probably about 100 supervised laparo-endoscopic repairs are needed to achieve the same results as open mesh surgery like Lichtenstein.

Operative Modalities

Treatment of hernia involves surgical repair of the muscle wall through which hernia protrudes. First, through an incision, the segment of bowel is placed back into the abdominal cavity. Next, the muscles are stitched closed. A plastic mesh is often used to reinforce the defect in the abdominal wall. The operative modalities for treatment of hernia are:
- Herniotomy (done in children and adolescents): Opening of sac, reduction of content, transfixation of sac, and excision of sac
- Herniorrhaphy (done in adults with good muscle tone)
  - *In case of indirect hernia*: Herniotomy and repair of posterior wall of inguinal canal
  - *In case of direct hernia*: Reduction of sac and repair of posterior wall
- Hernioplasty (done in elderly or patients with poor muscle tone)
  - *In case of indirect hernia*: Herniotomy and reinforcement of posterior wall by mesh
  - *In case of direct hernia*: Reduction of sac and reinforcement of posterior wall by mesh

Nowadays treatment modalities are classified in the following manner:
- Pure tissue repair: Its disadvantage is higher recurrence rate. Even in specialized centers, it is around 1–4%.
- Pure prosthetic repair: Various types of mesh are available for the prosthetic repair:
  - Polypropylene mesh
  - Polytetrafluoroethylene (PTFE) mesh
  - Vicryl mesh
  - Combined Vicryl and Prolene mesh (Vypro)
  - Gore-Tex mesh

- Preperitoneal repair
  - Indications
    - Sliding hernia
    - Recurrent hernia
    - Prevascular femoral hernia
    - Obese and elderly patients with hernia
    - Bilateral hernia
    - High-risk patient in whom operation is to be completed fast
    - Patients with collagen vascular disease
    - Incisional hernia
    - Umbilical hernia
- Darn repair: It forms a lattice network and strengthens the posterior wall; Nylon or Prolene no. 1 is used.
- Laparoscopic repair
  - Transabdominal preperitoneal prosthetic (TAPP) repair
  - Total extraperitoneal prosthetic (TEPP) repair

Anesthesia

- For herniorrhaphy and hernioplasty, the ideal choice of anesthesia is LA plus, if required, sedation.
- Either 0.5% lignocaine with adrenaline 1 in 1,000,000 or 0.25% bupivacaine is used.
- Safe dose of lignocaine with adrenaline is 70 mg/kg.
- Advantages of LA
  - Better postoperative analgesia
  - Shorter recovery room stay
  - Better tolerated by patients with underlying cardiac and respiratory problem
  - Negligible postoperative urinary retention

Criteria for ideal mesh

- Permanent
- Inert
- Noncarcinogenic and nonallergic
- Resistant to strain and infection
- No crevices and pore size less than 10 μm
- Pliable
- Should be reactive enough to stimulate the growth of fibroblasts
- Easy to sterilize, cheap, and easily available

Operative Technique

Herniotomy

- Anesthesia: GA is given.
- Carry out painting, draping, and isolation of the part.
- Incision: Make 1-inch transverse incision in the lowest inguinal skin crease. Always start at the site of obvious clinical evidence of hernia.
- Cut subcutaneous tissue.
- Catch, cauterize, and cut superficial epigastric, superficial circumflex iliac, and superficial external pudendal vessels.
- Cut the external oblique aponeurosis.
- By blunt dissection, cremasteric fibers are gently elevated.
- Identify the sac; it is always located anteromedial to the cord. Separate the sac from the cord till the deep ring.
- Open the sac and reduce contents.
- Twist the sac and transfix it at the deep ring (highest point of the canal; identified by preperitoneal fat, and inferior epigastric vessels).
- Always transfix the sac; do not ligate, because, sometimes, it may slip, when intra-abdominal pressure rises, in the immediate postoperative period.
- Close external oblique aponeurosis with Prolene 2-0.
- Subcuticular stitches with Prolene 4-0 or rapid Vicryl 4-0.
- Apply dressing.

In children <2 years, inguinal canal is not formed. Superficial and deep rings are superimposed, so there is no need to open the external oblique aponeurosis. Rest of the procedure is same.

Herniorrhaphy (Modified Bassini Repair)

- Anesthesia: SA or hernia block is given.
- Carry out painting, draping, and isolation of the part.
- Cut skin 1.25 cm above inguinal ligament on medial three-fifth (Fig. 6.49).
- Cut superficial fascia.
- Catch, cauterize, and cut superficial vessels (superficial external pudendal, superficial epigastric, and superficial circumflex iliac).
- Keep nick over the external oblique aponeurosis (Fig. 6.50). Hold the cut ends of the aponeurosis with artery forceps and cut external oblique aponeurosis with scissors (Fig. 6.51).

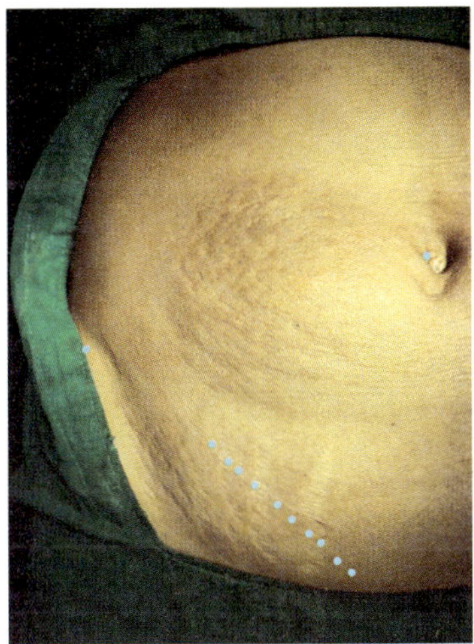

Figure 6.49 Marked skin incision.

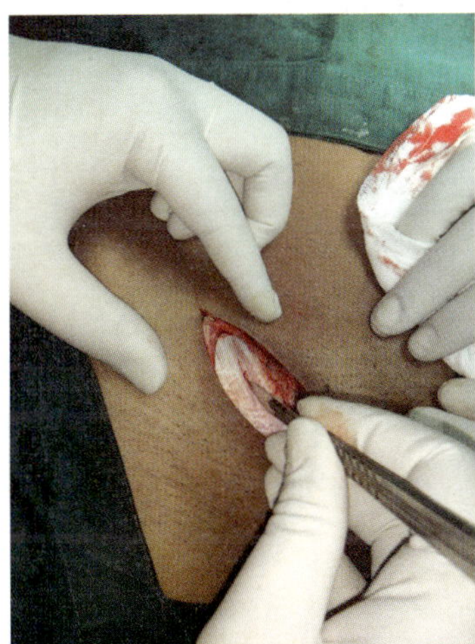

Figure 6.50 Cutting of external oblique aponeurosis.

- Raise the flap on superior aspect, to expose the conjoined tendon, and on inferior aspect, to expose the upturned part of inguinal ligament.
- Palpate pubic tubercle. Put a finger over the pubic tubercle, and then behind the cord and separate the cord and mobilize it.
- Hold the cord with Collingwood–Stewart ring-bladed forceps or gauze (Fig. 6.52).
- Cut cremaster. Identify the sac (pearly white) (Fig. 6.53).
- Skeletonization of cord is done.
- Separate the sac till the internal ring (identified by preperitoneal fat, inferior epigastric vessels, narrowest part of the sac).

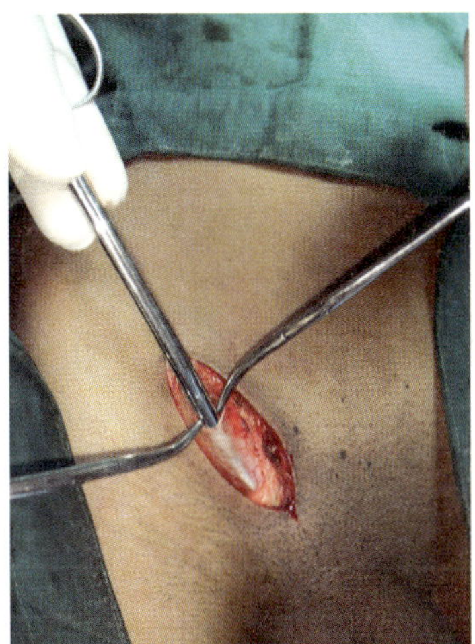

Figure 6.51 Holding of external oblique aponeurosis with artery forceps.

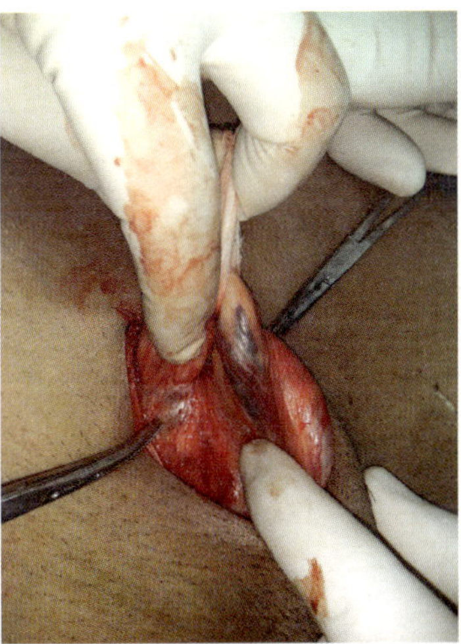

Figure 6.52 Holding of spermatic cord with gauze and visible inferior epigastric vessels at the deep ring.

- Open the sac (Fig. 6.53a). Direct sac requires only reduction without opening (Fig. 6.53b).
- Reduce the content.
- Twist the sac.
- Transfix with Vicryl or polypropylene.
- Excise the sac.
- Repair posterior wall with Prolene 2-0.
- Pass the first stitch through periosteum of pubic tubercle.
- Suture the upturned part of inguinal ligament with conjoined tendon, with intermittent stitches. (Suture should not be under tension; if

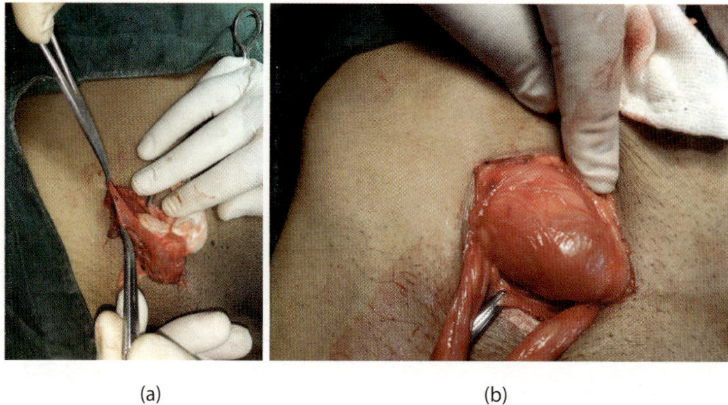

(a) (b)

Figure 6.53 (a) Hernia sac (indirect hernia). (b) Hernial sac direct hernia.

suture is under tension, then relaxing incision should be kept over rectus sheath.)

- If deep ring is wide, then correct it by Lytle's repair, before posterior wall repair.
- Close external oblique aponeurosis with Prolene 2-0 through continuous locking or running stitches.
- Close skin with monofilament 2-0 or 3-0 vertical mattress stitches.

Shouldice repair

- Double breasting of fascia transversalis
- Double breasting of conjoined tendon and upturned part of inguinal ligament
- Double breasting of external oblique aponeurosis or single-layer closure of external oblique aponeurosis

Advantage

Low recurrence rate compared to other pure tissue repairs

Rutledge Cooper ligament repair

Conjoined tendon is sutured with Cooper ligament after Tanner's slide.

There is a possibility of herniation through Tanner's slide, so inlay mesh is placed.

Pure prosthetic repairs

Lichtenstein tension-free hernioplasty

- Procedure is same till excise the sac in *herniorrhaphy* (*modified Bassini repair*)
- Size of mesh (Fig. 6.54): It is kept minimum 15 × 8 cm.

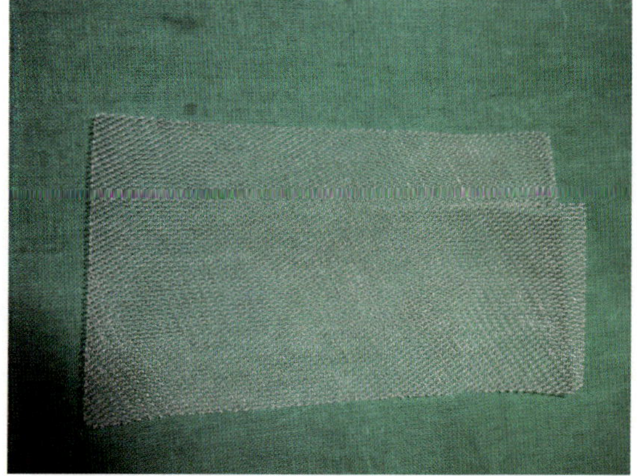

Figure 6.54 Polypropylene mesh with slit at the lateral end to encircle deep ring.

- Cut medial end of mesh in a round fashion to suit the anatomy.
- Slit the mesh on lateral end (upper two-third and lower one-third) for 2–3 cm to encircle the deep ring.
- Keep the medial end 1–2 cm beyond the pubic tubercle and fix with Prolene 2-0. Pass the first stitch through periosteum of pubic tubercle. It is called master stitch (Fig. 6.55).
- Fix the lower border with upturned part of inguinal ligament, with intermittent Prolene 2-0 stitches (Fig. 6.56).
- Take stitch to approximate lateral end, which is divided into two parts—upper two-third and lower one-third—such that lower end of upper part is stitched with lower end of lower part to create shutter–valve at the deep ring (Fig. 6.57).

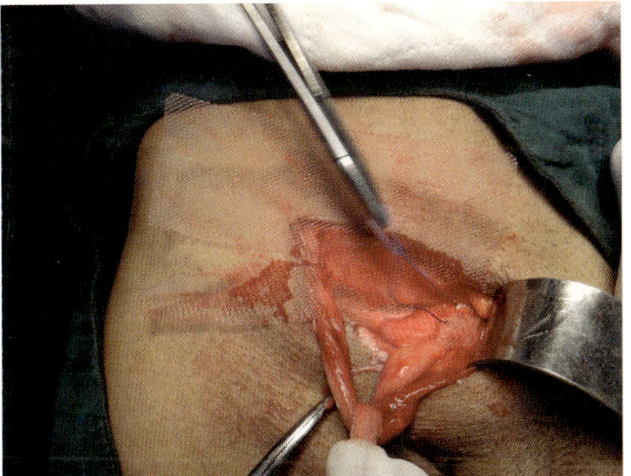

Figure 6.55 Fisrt stitch on the pubic tubercle (Master stitch).

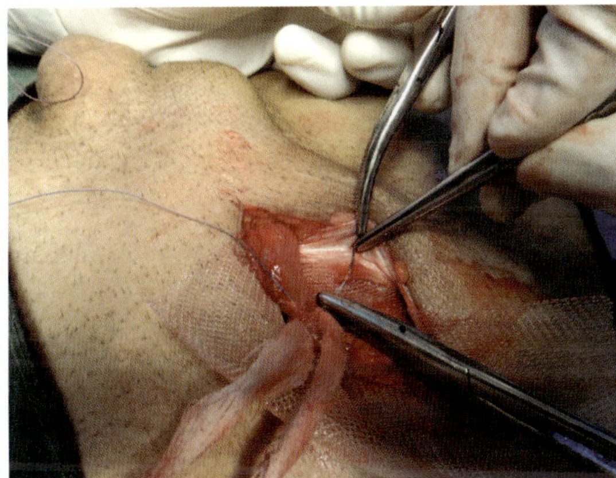

Figure 6.56 Fixing of the mesh with upturned part of the inguinal ligament.

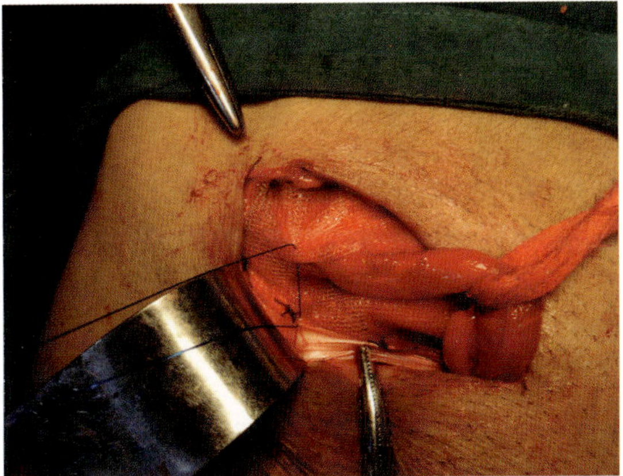

Figure 6.57 Creating shutter valve mechanism.

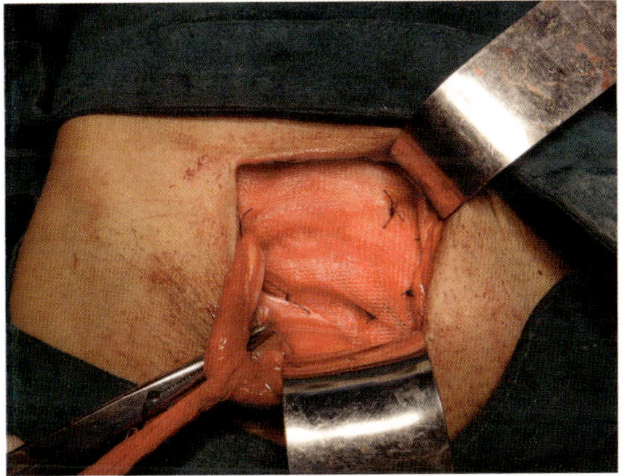

Figure 6.58 Fix mesh in position.

- Use a few interrupted sutures to fix the mesh with conjoined tendon (Fig. 6.58).

- If femoral hernia is present, then posterior surface of the mesh is sutured to Cooper ligament, after lower border has been attached to inguinal ligament.
- Rest of the procedure is same as in herniorrhaphy.

Mesh for repair

- Types of mesh
  - Various meshes available for repair (Table 6.4) are polypropylene, polyester, PTFE, and absorbable synthetic.
  - Most widely used mesh is polypropylene: It is thermoplastic polymer of ethylene with an attached methyl group. It is hydrophobic, resistant to many chemical solvents, acids, and bases. It is thermoplastic (can be remelted and reformed). It is made with semicrystalline polypropylene fiber extruded and woven into monofilaments and multifilaments.
  - Large-pore mesh and standard polypropylene mesh comparison: Only foreign body sensation is less in large-pore mesh.

Table 6.4 Types of Meshes[8]

Polypropylene mesh	Area	Pore size
Heavy weight (Marlex)	>90 g/m^2	0.6 mm
Midweight (Prolene soft)	45 g/m^2	2.4 mm
Lightweight (Ultrapro)	28 g/m^2	4 mm

- Self-fixation mesh: Avoid placement of suture. It leads to reduced operative time, less postoperative pain, and less requirement of postoperative analgesic.
- Absorbable mesh: Vicryl and Dexon
  - It is used in highly contaminated areas.
  - It is absorbed within few weeks so associated with high recurrence rate.
- Biological mesh
  - Is indicated in highly contaminated cases
  - Lower tensile strength and higher rate of rupture
  - Examples of xenograft: Permacol and Surgisis mesh
- Nowadays, a Prolene Hernia System is available, consisting of two layers of Prolene mesh, with a connector. Deeper layer is kept deep to the fascia transversalis and superficial layer remains in the routine plane of mesh. It is associated with lower recurrence rate but learning curve and cost are the disadvantages.

• Properties of mesh
  - Burst strength is expressed in newtons and stiffness is expressed in newtons per centimeter. Stiffness and burst strength is maximum in heavy-weight mesh as compared to in light-weight mesh.
  - Lightweight mesh is associated with less incidence of chronic groin pain and less foreign body sensation.
• Factors influencing the choice of prosthetic mesh in hernia
  - *Size and shape*: All prostheses shrink. Allow minimum overlap of at least 2 cm by the mesh for initial fixation to reduce the recurrence.
  - *Elasticity*: It should be flexible enough to conform to the abdominal wall movement. Heavy-weight meshes are very strong and result in pain and sensation of stiffness as compared to lightweight meshes.
  - *Strength*: It is related to the density of material.
  - *Adhesion*: Dual mesh with one side engendering tissue in growth and the other inhibiting it. It is important for intraperitoneal implantation of mesh.
  - Other factors such as cost and infection also affect the choice of mesh.

Giant prosthesis for reinforcement of the visceral sac (GPRVS)

• Infraumbilical midline incision
• Mesh kept in preperitoneal space, between anterior abdominal wall and peritoneum
• Mesh fixation not required, is kept in position by Pascal's law

Dacron mesh is more pliable and more suitable for this procedure.

Indications

Same as in preperitoneal repair, except:
• Incisional hernia
• Umbilical hernia

Iliopubic tract repair (Nyhus and Condon's repair)

• Incision: It is transverse lower abdominal (two fingerbreadths above the symphysis pubis).
• After dealing with sac, transverse aponeurotic arch is sutured to the iliopubic tract.
• For femoral hernia, iliopubic tract is sutured to Cooper ligament.

Plug and patch repair (Gilbert's repair)

Cone-shaped plug of Prolene mesh is inserted into the internal ring and this plug is sutured to surrounding tissue and held in place by overlying mesh.

Laparoscopic hernia repair

Indications

• Recurrent hernia
• Bilateral hernia
• Presence of inguinal hernia in a patient who requires laparoscopy for some other reason

Contraindications

• Intra-abdominal abscess
• Ascites
• Sliding scrotal hernia
• Previous bladder or prostatic surgery

Open versus laparoscopic hernia repair

Controversy still persists between open and laparoscopic hernia repair.

• Proponents of laparoscopic method
  - Less pain
  - Better visualization of anatomy
  - Can deal with all defects simultaneously
  - Less risk of infection

- Opponents
  - Long learning curve
  - Long operative time
  - GA
  - Large prosthesis
  - Increased cost and technical challenge

The author prefers open hernia repair because:
- Laparoscopic accidents may lead to major complications such as bowel perforation and vascular injury.
- There is a possibility of adhesion where peritoneum has been breached.
- Cost of surgery is more in laparoscopy.
- There may be complications related to trocar placement, pneumoperitoneum, and GA.

Types of laparoscopic hernia repair
- TAPP
  - There is large hernia and lower abdominal incisional hernia.
  - Peritoneal flaps are elevated over the sac.
  - Sac is reduced.
  - Mesh is fixed with suture or ticker.
  - Peritoneum is closed over the mesh to make it preperitoneal.
- TEPP
  - Smaller and simple hernia, 15 × 11 cm mesh is used.
  - Plane of dissection is between posterior surface of rectus muscle and posterior rectus sheath.
  - Balloon dissector is used.
  - Hernial sac is identified and reduced.
  - Mesh is placed

Advantage of TEPP: Peritoneal cavity is not opened.

Disadvantage: Working space is limited and inadvertent damage to the peritoneal cavity cannot be seen.

- *Triangle of Doom*: Between vas deferens laterally and internal spermatic vessels medially (medial triangle). Apex is oriented superiorly at deep ring. This name is given because below this are the external iliac vessels.
- *Triangle of pain (lateral triangle)*: It is lateral to the vas deferens, bounded superolaterally by the iliopubic tract. The name is given because of presence of lateral cutaneous nerve, genital and femoral branches of genitofemoral nerve.
- *Corona mortis (crown of death)*: Over Cooper ligament, anastomotic vessels between obturator and inferior epigastric vessels are present. This point is a threat in preperitoneal and Cooper ligament repair. Significant bleeding can occur during this procedure.

Postoperative care
- NBM till further order (usually for 4–6 hours)
- TPR monitoring
- Input/output charting
- Analgesic
- Antacid
- Drain, if kept, is removed when drain output is <25 cm^3

Complications
- Wound infection (increases risk of recurrence) 1%: Gram-positive organism is the usual cause
- Treatment
  - It consists of antibiotics and opening and drainage of wound.
  - Very rarely mesh removal is required.
- Seroma: Due to foreign body reaction. Aspiration is done only when symptomatic.
- Hematoma
  - Causes
    - It occurs due to bleeding from cremasteric, internal spermatic, and inferior epigastric vessel.
    - Aspirin and clopidogrel should be stopped as per guideline mentioned in Chapter 1.
  - Treatment
    - *If small*: It is self-limiting.
    - *If large*: Open the wound and control the bleeding.
- Osteitis pubis: Pain is caused by suture taken through periosteum. It presents as medial groin or symphyseal pain.
  - Diagnosis: CT or MRI to exclude recurrence. Bone scan confirms the diagnosis.
  - Treatment
    - Anti-inflammatory drugs
    - Physiotherapy
    - Corticosteroid injections
    - Surgical exploration to remove the suture performed as the last option
    - Sometimes bone resection and curettage required

- Pain
  - Types
    - Neuropathic, due to damage to ilioinguinal, iliohypogastric, genitofemoral, lateral cutaneous nerve of thigh and femoral nerve. It is localized sharp burning or tearing sensation. Treatment is NSAIDs or local steroid or LA injection
    - Somatic (nociceptive), due to damage to muscle, tendon, or ligament: It is the most common type of pain. Treatment is rest, NSAIDs, and reassurance.
    - Visceral: It is poorly localized and it is mediated through afferent autonomic fibers.
    - Chronic pain is prevented by meticulous identification of all the three nerves.
    - Postherniorrhaphy inguinodynia: It is caused by combination of neuropathic, somatic, and visceral components.
    - It is a chronic debilitating condition leading to severe pain.
    - Local nerve entrapment: Most common is entrapment of ilioinguinal and iliohypogastric loss in open repair. Acute neuropathic pain is the main symptom in the distribution of nerve.
    - Meralgia paresthetica: It occurs due to injury to lateral cutaneous nerve of thigh.
  - Treatment includes selective neurolysis or neurectomy of either all three or one nerve and removal of mesh or suture material. Treatment for local nerve entrapment and meralgia paresthetica is same as for neuropathic pain.
- Recurrence: 10% of patients with primary inguinal hernia can develop recurrence.
- Bladder injury: In case of sliding hernia, bladder injury can occur.
- Ischemic orchitis: Painful enlargement of testis due to thrombosis of veins draining the testis. It is due to injury to the pampiniform plexus. The testis is painful, enlarged, and indurated.
  - Treatment: Scrotal support, anti-inflammatory drugs
- Secondary hydrocele occurs due to damage to lymphatics.
- Injury to testicular artery leads to testicular atrophy.
- Injury to vas causes infertility or dysejaculation syndrome.
- Complication due to mesh: These include contraction, rejection, infection, erosion, and breakdown.

- Hernia is a clean surgery; antibiotics are usually not recommended.
- Rest is advised for 3 weeks and the patient should be advised not to do heavy work for 6 months.
- Correction of the precipitating condition is a must.

OPERATION FOR HYDROCELE

Hydrocele is the word derived from two Greek words, *hydro* meaning water and *kele* meaning mass.

Hydrocele is abnormal serous fluid collection within the processus vaginalis, especially within tunica vaginalis.

RELEVANT ANATOMY

Small amount of fluid is usually present between tunica vaginalis and tunica albuginea. Approximately 0.5 cm^3 of fluid is continuously secreted and reabsorbed by mesothelial layer every day. The pouch of peritoneum is dragged down during the descent of gubernaculum of testis. This extends from the deep ring to the superficial ring and bottom of the scrotum. The part of the processus vaginalis up to the top of the scrotum disappears and the distal-most part persists as tunica vaginalis.

CHARACTERISTICS OF HYDROCELE FLUID

- Amber or straw color
- Sterile
- Specific gravity 1.022–1.024
- Contains albumin, fibrinogen
- Cholesterol and tyrosine crystals seen in long-standing cases

MECHANISM FOR DEVELOPMENT OF HYDROCELE

- Decreased absorption of fluid (primary)
- Increased secretion of fluid (secondary)
- Lymphatic blockage (filarial)
- Patent processus vaginalis (congenital)

CLASSIFICATION

There are various ways of classification: Anatomical classification, classification depending on connection with peritoneum, and classification depending on etiology.

Anatomical Classification

- *Congenital hydrocele*: Patent processus vaginalis throughout
- *Infantile hydrocele*: Processus vaginalis patent up to internal ring (inguinoscrotal swelling)
- Encysted hydrocele of cord: On traction to the testis, it goes downwards and becomes less mobile.
- TVH (tunica vaginal hydrocele (TVH): It refers to collection of fluid within tunica vaginalis.
- Funicular: It is a type of congenital hydrocele. Processus vaginalis remains patent up to the top of the testis.
- Hydrocele of the spermatic cord: Midportion of processus vaginalis is patent and proximal and distal parts are obliterated. It appears as a localized enlarged swelling in relation to the cord.
- Hydrocele en bisac: Two intercommunicating sacs are seen—one above and one below the neck of the scrotum.
- Hydrocele of canal of Nuck: It is a female counterpart of hydrocele of spermatic cord and seen in relation to round ligament. It is always in the inguinal canal.

- The hydrocele that does not communicate with peritoneal cavity is physiological and mostly resolves by 1 year. Congenital hydroceles that persist after 1 year or those which demonstrate change in size (communicating) should be operated.
- In pediatric patients, processus vaginalis is patent throughout, so operation is performed through inguinal incision, while in adult patients, processus vaginalis is not patent throughout, so procedure is done through scrotal route.
- Tense hydrocele is due to lack of reabsorption of fluid and flaccid due to excessive production of fluid.

Classification Dependent on Etiology

- Primary hydrocele (Table 6.5)
- Secondary hydrocele

Table 6.5 Differences Between the Primary and Secondary Hydrocele

Primary	Secondary
Idiopathic	Etiology known
Old age	Young age
Rugosity over the scrotum is lost and large swelling	Rugosity preserved and small swelling
Testis and epididymis are not separately palpable	Testis and epididymis are separately palpable

Etiology of Secondary Hydrocele

- Tuberculosis
- Trauma
- Tumor
- Epididymo-orchitis (most common cause for secondary hydrocele)
- Postherniorrhaphy, postvaricocelectomy
- Renal transplantation: A common surgical cause for hydrocele due to division of spermatic vessel and vas deferens
- Syphilis
- Filariasis (transillumination test is negative)

5% of inguinal hernias are associated with hydrocele.

Classification Depending on Connection with Peritoneum

- Communicating
- Noncommunicating

COMPLICATIONS

- Infection
- Hematocele
  - Rupture
  - Traumatic
- Spontaneous
- Calcification in long-standing cases
- Hernia of hydrocele sac: In long-standing cases protrusion of hydrocele sac through dartos muscle
- In very large hydrocele, excoriation of the scrotal skin
- Psychological

- Difficulty in performing sexual intercourse in large hydrocele

DIAGNOSIS OF HYDROCELE

- A four-step approach to diagnose hydrocele:
  - Scrotal swelling
  - Soft
  - Fluctuation positive
  - Transillumination positive
- Cardinal sign for hydrocele: Fluctuation and transillumination (transillumination is not reliable in newborn and infant as intestine and fluid transilluminate equally well)
- Cardinal sign for hernia: Cough impulse and reducibility

The hallmark of hydrocele is that one can palpate the normal spermatic cord above the swelling (gets above the swelling).

Differential Diagnosis

Difference between congenital hydrocele and congenital hernia

In congenital hernia, swelling reduces spontaneously, while in congenital hydrocele it reduces gradually (inverted ink bottle phenomenon). Typical history in case of congenital hydrocele is: No swelling in the morning, but it gradually develops as the day passes.

Difference between hematoma and hematocele

Scrotal skin can be lifted up in case of hematocele, but not in hematoma.

OPERATIVE TECHNIQUE

- Anesthesia: Small hydrocele—hydrocele block or spinal. Large hydrocele—spinal.
- Carry out painting, draping, and isolation of the part.
- Make 4 cm vertical and 1–1.5 cm lateral incision over the scrotum (Fig. 6.59).
- Cut the following layers:
  - Skin
  - Dartos muscle (Fig. 6.60)
  - External spermatic fascia
  - Cremasteric fascia
  - Internal spermatic fascia
- Identify parietal layer of tunica from bluish discoloration due to Raman effect.

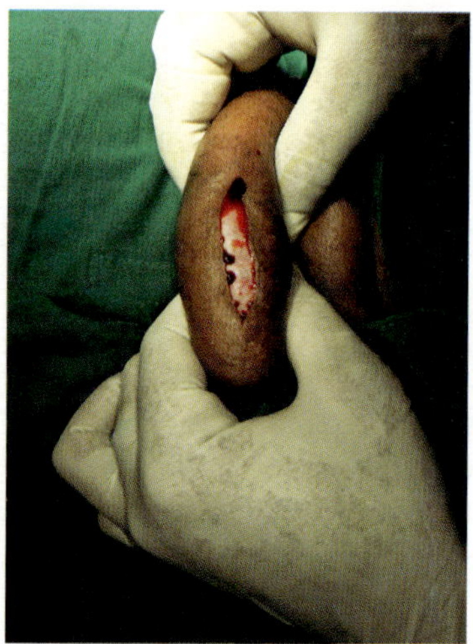

Figure 6.59 Incision over the scrotum (4 cm vertical and 1–1.5 cm lateral from median raphae).

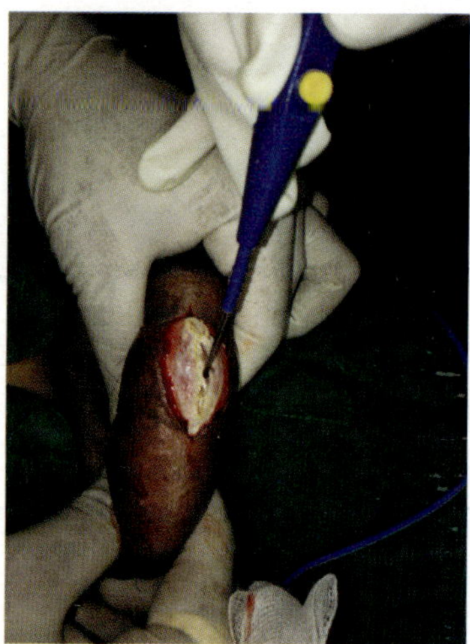

Figure 6.60 Cutting of dartos muscle.

- Puncture the sac with stab knife (Fig. 6.61).
- Apply suction to suck the fluid.
- Cut the sac above and downwards with scissors.
- Evert the sac.

Methods for Removal

- Lord's plication: It is done for small- or medium-sized and thin-walled hydrocele. Make four to five plicating stitches from testis side to the edge with chromic catgut 3-0 or Vicryl 3-0 (Fig. 6.62).
- Jaboulay bottle neck procedure
  - It is done for large, floppy, thin-walled hydrocele.

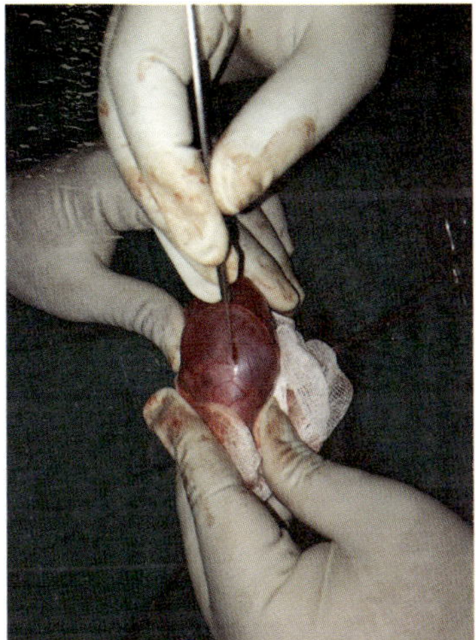

Figure 6.61 Tunica vaginalis being punctured by knife.

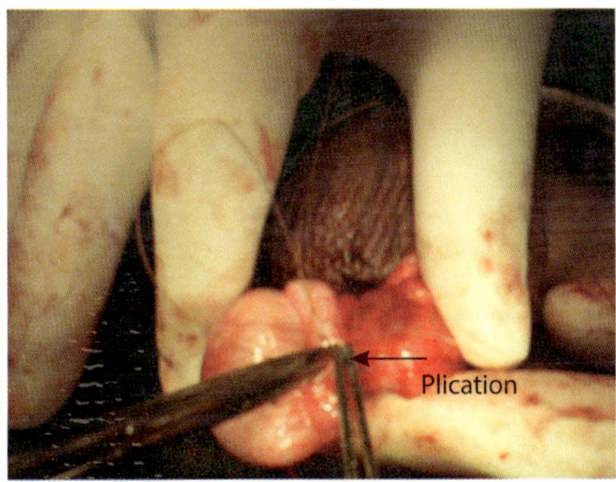

Figure 6.62 Plicating stitches being made from the testis side to the edge.

- Do partial excision of sac and sew edges together behind the testis.
- Margin should be 1 cm to prevent constriction of the cord.

- Subtotal excision of sac
  - It is performed in large, long-standing, loculated, thick-walled sac.
  - Cut edges are known to bleed, so it is sutured all around with continuous locking or running stitch, with chromic 3-0 or Vicryl 3-0.
  - The testis is repositioned back into its anatomical position.
  - Before closing, check for hemostasis.
- Closure
  - Single-layer closure of scrotum with chromic catgut 3-0 intermittent

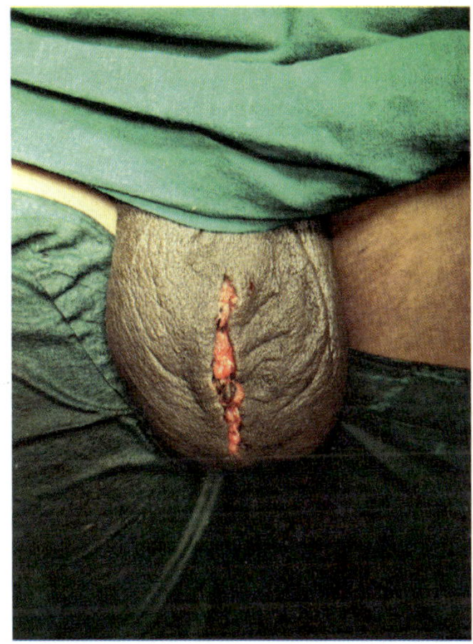

Figure 6.63 Closure of dartos muscle.

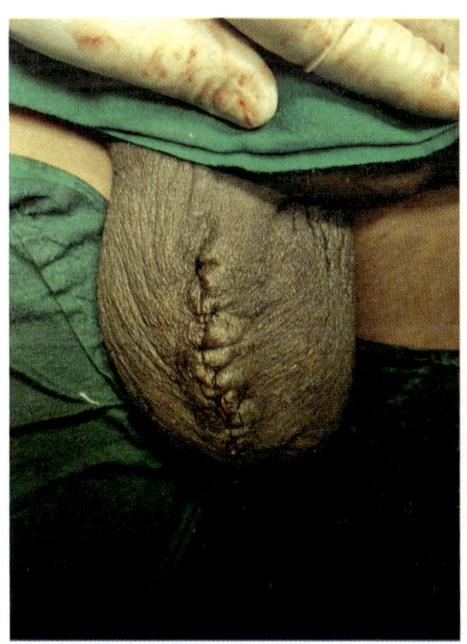

Figure 6.64 Closure of skin.

  - Closure of dartos muscle (Fig. 6.63)
  - Skin with black silk or Ethilon 3-0 vertical mattress suture (Fig. 6.64)
  - Dressing applied
  - Coconut bandage applied

Bandage is to be removed after 48 hours.

POSTOPERATIVE CARE

- Prophylactic antibiotics (three doses)
- Analgesics

COMPLICATIONS OF OPERATION

- Injury to testis, vas, pampiniform plexus, epididymis
- Hematoma (most common complication)
- Infection
- Chronic pain
- Persistent swelling
- Secondary sterility—due to ischemia of testis
- Recurrence—very rare

- *Encysted hydrocele of cord*: Traction test is positive.
- Sign of vas is for differential diagnosis of testicular tumor from inflammation. In case of neoplasm, vas is not thickened and in case of inflammation it is thickened.
- *Prehn sign*: Elevation of testis will relieve the pain in epididymo-orchitis, but not in torsion.
- *Spermatocele*: Unilocular retention cyst is the area of sperm-conducting mechanism in the globus major. It is usually small and nonobstructive and located in the head of epididymis. It is transillumination positive and appears as Chinese lantern pattern, and on aspiration barley water colored fluid comes. Painful swelling-requires excision.
- *Epididymal cyst*: Multilocular cyst in the globus minor. On transillumination, Chinese lantern pattern is seen. Treatment is excision.

CIRCUMCISION

Circumcision is a surgical procedure that involves partial or complete excision of preputial skin.

INDICATIONS

- Religious: In Muslims and Jews
- Phimosis (Fig. 6.65, Box 6.3): American Association of Pediatrics (AAP) does not endorse routine circumcision. Indications in phimosis are:
  - In uncircumcised boys more than 7 years of age
  - Phimosis not responding to local steroid for 4–6 weeks

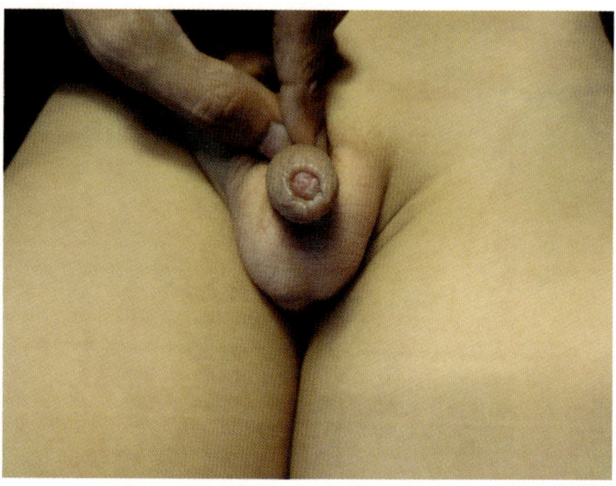

Figure 6.65 Phimosis.

Box 6.3 Phimosis

This condition involves constriction of the orifice of the prepuce so that it cannot be drawn back over the glans. At 1 year of age approximately 50% of boys have nonretractile foreskin; by 4 years it has decreased to 10% and by 16 years only 1% have nonretractile foreskin. Difficulty in micturition is the chief complaint. Ballooning of preputial skin is common. Chronic infection from poor hygiene is the main culprit for this condition.

Grading of phimosis[9]

I: Fully retractile prepuce with stenotic ring in the shaft
II: Partial retractability with partial exposure of the glans
III: Exposure of the meatus only
IV: Nonretractile

Types

It can be of two types:

- *Congenital*: Previously, this term was used for inability to retract preputial skin, but true phimosis means white scarring of foreskin and is rare before 5 years of age.
- *Acquired*: Recurrent balanitis, that is, inflammation of the glans penis, may be due to:
  - Diabetes
  - Balanitis xerotica obliterans

Complications associated with phimosis

- Recurrent UTI
- Recurrent balanoposthitis
- Cystitis
- Bladder stone
- Preputial calculi
- Urinary obstruction
- Interference with sexual activity
- Predisposition to carcinoma
- In the worst case, patient presenting probably with bilateral hydronephrosis and hydroureter

- Ballooning of skin
- Recurrent balanitis
- Paraphimosis
  - Involves inability to revert preputial skin over the glans
  - Initially manual reduction → dorsal slit
  - Elective circumcision once edema subsides (after 8–10 days)
- Recurrent balanoposthitis
  - This condition involves inflammation of the glans penis and prepuce.
  - Single attack can be treated with antibiotics.
- Genital warts
- Recurrent UTI
- Spina bifida: Required to perform clean intermittent catheterization
- Abnormally tight frenulum
- Preputial calculi
- Zip injury to prepuce
- Stage 1 Ca penis involving preputial skin only
- For prevention of HIV: Mucosal surface of foreskin containing Langerhans cells that are highly susceptible to HIV infection

CONTRAINDICATIONS

- Acute infection of glans or prepuce (acute balanoposthitis)
- Hypospadias (preputial skin is used for repair)
- Chordee
- Webbed penis
- Small penis
- Blood dyscrasias

OPERATIVE TECHNIQUE

- Anesthesia
  - For children: GA or penile block with sedation
  - For adults: LA (penile block)
  - For dorsal penile nerve block: 0.5% bupivacaine and 1–2% lidocaine without epinephrine is used (with epinephrine, there is a risk of local tissue ischemia)
- Position: The patient is made to lie in supine position.
- After painting and draping, isolate the part.
- Lubricate probe with xylocaine jelly (lignocaine) and introduce between prepuce and glans; check for any adhesions.
- If present, then rotate the probe circumferentially to break them.
- One can also use mosquito forceps (lubricated with xylocaine jelly)—pass it till coronal sulcus.
- Open the forceps and remove it with blades kept open. This will help to break adhesions.
- Retract prepuce to expose coronal sulcus.
- Clean smegma with povidone–iodine and saline.
- Return the prepuce to its normal position.
- Prepuce is held at 3 and 9 o'clock positions with mosquito forceps and pulled forward with light traction (Fig. 6.66).
- Prepuce is cut at 12 o'clock position after crushing with straight artery forceps (Figs 6.67 and 6.68).
- Outer skin is separated from inner skin; cut parallel to corona all around.

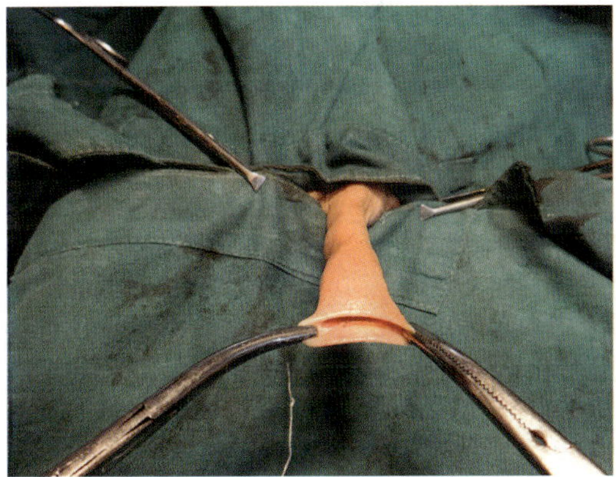

Figure 6.66 Preputial skin is held at the 3 and 9 o'clock positions with light traction.

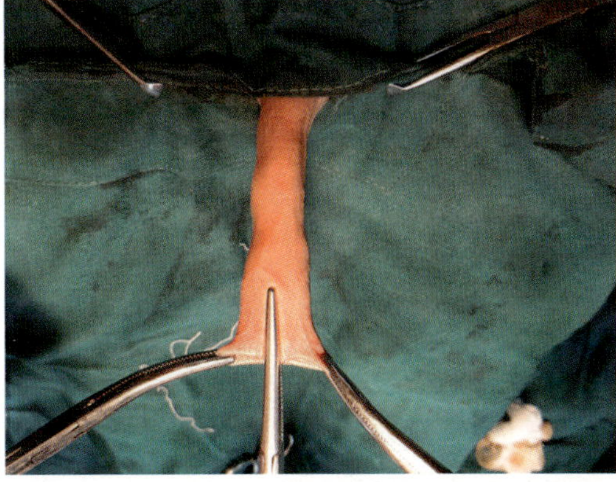

Figure 6.67 Crushing of preputial skin with straight artery forceps.

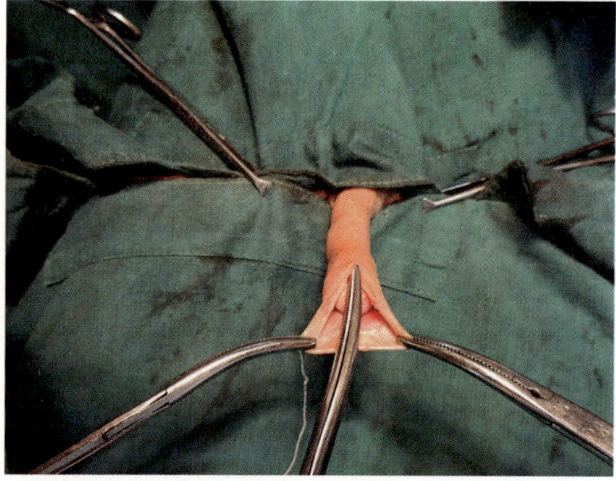

Figure 6.68 Cutting of skin with scissor.

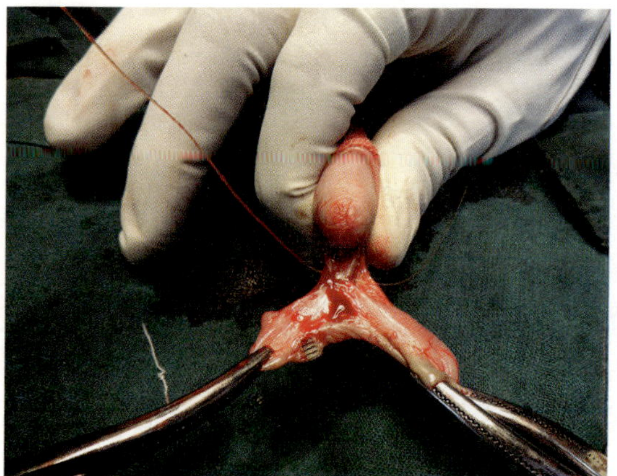

Figure 6.69 Ligation of frenular artery with Plain Catgut 3-0.

- Inner layer (mucosa) is held at 3 and 9 o'clock positions; cut parallel, leaving a cuff approximately 0.3 cm long, which just covers corona of glans.
- Achieve hemostasis by ligation of frenular vessel ventrally (Fig. 6.69) (branch of internal pudendal artery) by any of the following:
  - Figure of 8 stitch
  - Frenal stitch (U stitch)
  - Mattress suture
- Dorsal vein of penis and other bleeders—bipolar cautery can be used to achieve hemostasis, or ligation with plain catgut.
- Outer and inner layers are closed with fine interrupted absorbable (plain Catgut 3'-0) suture (Fig. 6.70).
- Ideal circumcision should look like an 'egg in an eggshell' (Fig. 6.71).

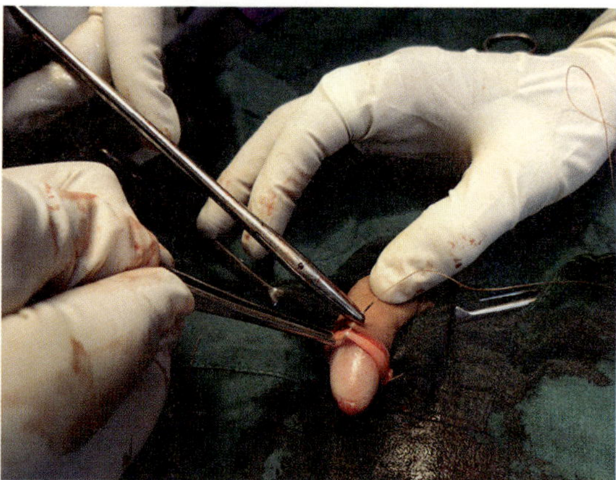

Figure 6.70 Closure of skin with mucosa with Plain Catgut 3-0.

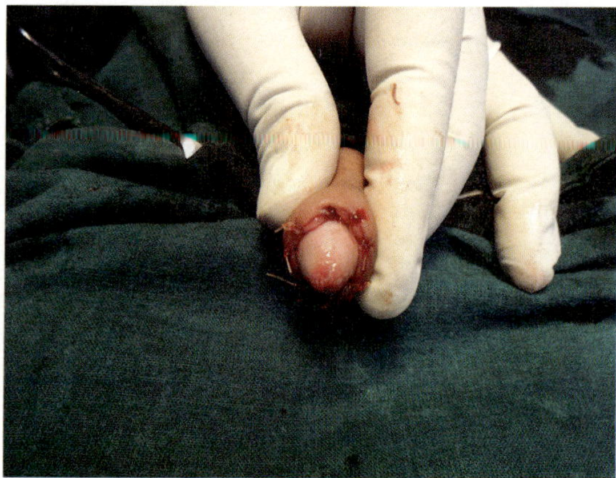

Figure 6.71 Egg in an egg shell appearance at the end of circumcision.

- Do not cut excess preputial skin (to prevent dyspareunia).
- Always examine meatus to exclude stenosis.
- Other techniques for circumcision:
  - Hollister Plastibell technique
  - Guillotine method, in which skin and mucosa are cut simultaneously

Dressing

- Apply emollient dressing.
- Cover it with dry gauze piece.
- Apply micropore dressing.
- From the next day, keep the wound open.
- Clean daily with warm water and apply Neosporin ointment.

POSTOPERATIVE CARE

- NBM for 4 hours if GA was given
- Antibiotics
- Analgesics
- In case of adults, use any of the following:
  - Ethinyl estradiol (0.001 mg) TDS, started 3 days prior to surgery and continued for 1 week
  - Can use chlorpromazine to prevent erection
  - Sedative (diazepam for 1 week)
- Remove dressing after 24 hours.
- Wear loose-fitting briefs.
- Maintain complete sexual abstinence for 4–6 weeks.

COMPLICATIONS

- Bleeding (most common complication)
  - It may be primary or secondary.
  - It is either from the frenulum or occasionally from the large arteries or vein from the shaft
  - For hemostasis, first compress. If not controlled, then cautery with silver nitrate stick or ophthalmic cautery, and if still bleeding is present, suturing is done.
- Infection: Local antibiotic application
- Excessive skin removal with scarring
- Inadequate skin removal
- Monopolar cautery in children, which may lead to penile loss
- Injury to the glans, urethral injury, and injury to penile shaft
- Retention of urine
- Secondary phimosis
- Meatal ulceration, due to loss of protection by preputial skin (very rare)
- Urethrocutaneous fistula and urethral damage (while passing sutures to control bleeding from frenular artery)
- Meatal stenosis: Most common late complication (may be because of disruption of normal adhesion between prepuce and glans and removal of skin, significant inflammatory reaction occurs and leads to cicatrix formation)
- Glandular adhesion and dense skin bridge between glans and shaft of penis

POTENTIAL BENEFITS OF CIRCUMCISION

- Prevention of carcinoma of penis
- Prevention of UTI/STD including HIV
- Decreases the risk of balanitis

SEXUAL EFFECTS OF ADULT CIRCUMCISION[10]

- Worsened erectile function
- Decreased penile sensitivity
- No change in sexual activity and improved satisfaction
- Increase in ejaculatory latency time

ORCHIECTOMY

Orchiectomy is surgical removal of testis either by scrotal or by inguinal route.

RELEVANT ANATOMY OF TESTIS

- Paired organ
- Average size: 4 cm length, 2.5 cm in breadth, and 3.5 cm in anteroposterior diameter
- Weight: 10–15 g
- Left testis lying lower than the right
- Covering of the testis: From outside inward—tunica vaginalis, tunica albuginea, tunica vasculosa

Blood Supply

- Arterial supply
  - Testicular artery (branch of abdominal aorta), cremasteric artery (branch of inferior epigastric), artery to vas deferens
- Venous drainage
  - Testicular vein: Right testicular vein opens into inferior vena cava at an acute angle and the left renal vein opens into left renal vein at right angle.
- Lymphatic drainage: Testicular lymphatics drain into the retroperitoneal lymph nodes—right primarily into interaortocaval node and the left into para-aortic node.

INDICATIONS

- Neglected testicular torsion
- Testicular tumor
- Advanced prostate cancer
- Major testicular injury, where it is not salvageable
- Atrophic testis with hematocele
- In undescended testis, where on operation table it is found to be flabby or atrophic

- Gumma of testis
- In longstanding hernia associated with undescended testis

OPERATIVE TECHNIQUE

- Anesthesia: SA or GA or LA
- Position: Supine
- Incision: Scrotal or inguinal (scrotal incision is same as hydrocele and inguinal incision is same as hernioplasty)

Here, we shall focus on orchiectomy for testicular abscess with gangrene.

- Incision: Scrotal incision is done.
- Operative procedure is same as described under hydrocele till opening of internal spermatic fascia.
- Testis is delivered out.
- Gentle traction is applied to the testicle and the cord structure cleaned to free 4–6 cm of cord (Fig. 6.72).
- Clamp cord with two hemostats at a distance of 0.5–1 cm (Fig. 6.73); transfix with strong absorbable suture (Fig. 6.74) and cut in between the two hemostats (Fig. 6.75). Do not release hemostat before applying the second tie.

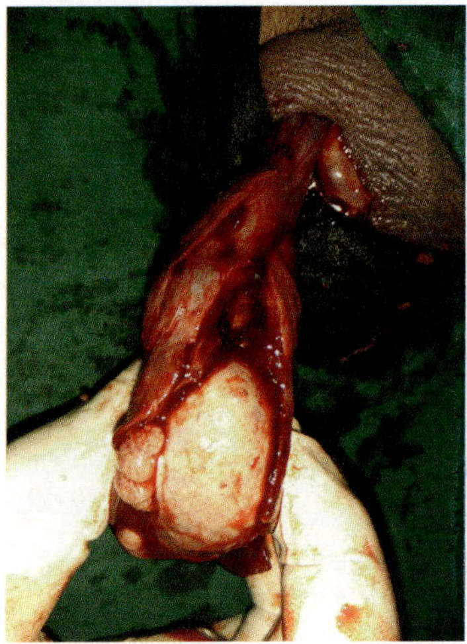

Figure 6.72 Spermatic cord is cleaned 4 cm from the testis.

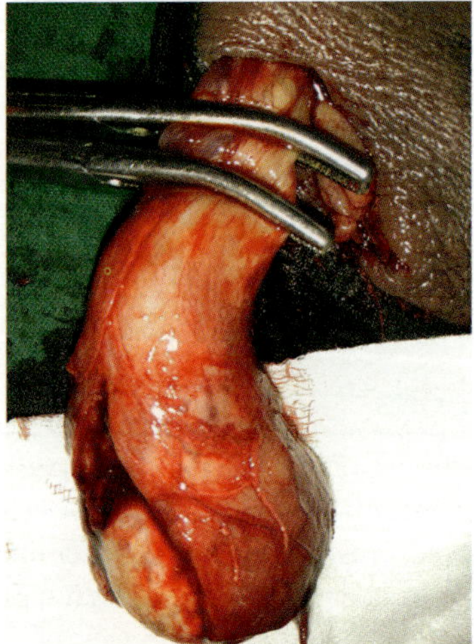

Figure 6.73 Two hemostats applied on the spermatic cord at a distance of 1 cm.

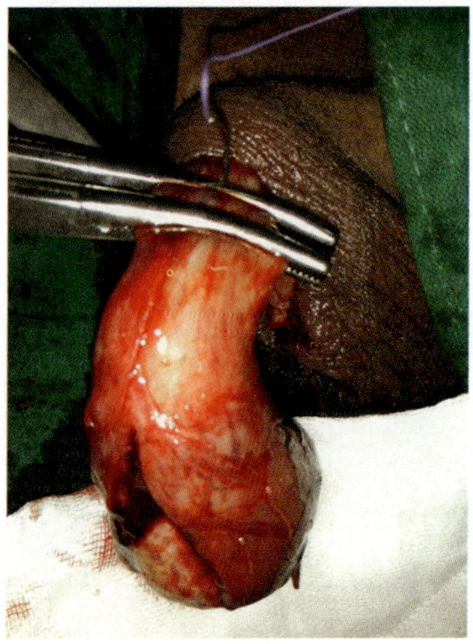

Figure 6.74 Transfixation of the spermatic cord with polyglactin 910 1 number suture.

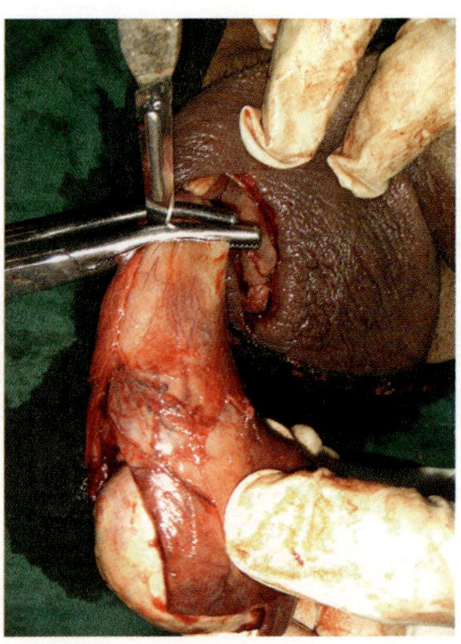

Figure 6.75 Cutting of the cord between two hemostats.

- Check cut end of the spermatic cord for bleeding (Fig. 6.76).
- Leave the scrotal wound unsutured if infection is present. Otherwise, closure is same as described for hydrocele.
- Apply sterile dressing.
- Provide scrotal support.
- In case of testicular torsion, always fix the opposite testis (orchiopexy). Examine the removed testis (Fig. 6.77).

In case of torsion of testis the cord is untwisted and viability of testis is checked. If not viable, orchiectomy is carried out (in case of viable testis, orchiopexy should be done).

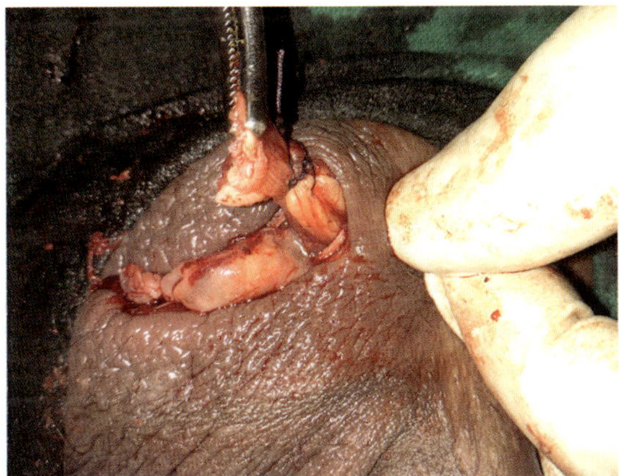

Figure 6.76 Cut end of the spermatic cord with transfixation suture in place.

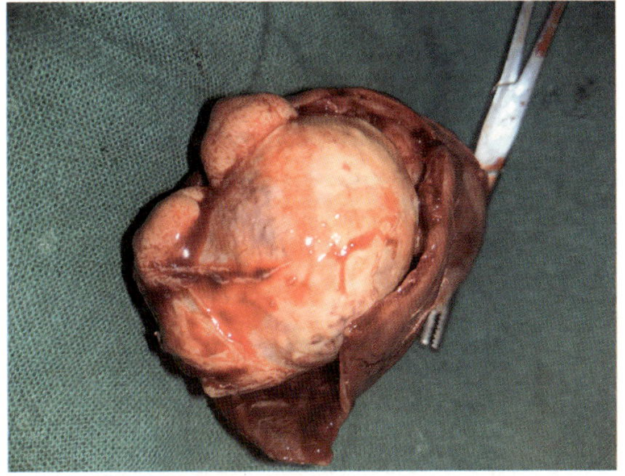

Figure 6.77 Orchiectomy specimen.

POSTOPERATIVE CARE

- NBM till 4–6 hours
- Antibiotics
- Analgesics
- In case of unsutured wound, daily dressing and plan for delayed primary closure

COMPLICATIONS

- Scrotal hematoma: Drainage required if it is large, increasing in size, or infected
- Infection
- Psychiatric upset
- Infertility with bilateral orchiectomy
- Damage to the ilioinguinal nerve (loss of sensation overlying the scrotum)

- In testicular tumor and undescended testis, inguinal incision is made.
- There are four types of orchiectomy:
  - *Simple*: It is performed through scrotal route.
  - *Subcapsular*: Tunica of the testis is incised and seminiferous tubules contained within excised part. This approach is used in patients who want cosmetic effect of testis being present without use of prosthesis.
  - *Subepididymal (epididymis sparing) orchiectomy*: It is for cosmetic benefit. Operating microscope is used and epididymis is cut off from the testis. Clamp and ligate three major groups of epididymal vessels: Superior, middle, and caudal with 2-0 silk. Approximate with the caput and cauda of the epididymis with absorbable suture. Rest of the procedure is same as of simple orchiectomy.
  - *Radical*: It is performed through inguinal route (for testicular tumor).
- Inguinal route is preferred in tumor because of:
  - Ligation of testicular lymphatics as high as possible. It removes any cancer cells that might have started to metastasize along the cord.
  - Clamping of cord before any manipulation prevents dissemination of tumor cells.
  - Scrotal incision leads to dissemination of tumor cell into scrotal lymphatics. This leads to spread of tumor to the scrotal skin and inguinal node.

- Chevassu maneuver: Keep inguinal incision whenever diagnosis is in doubt. Apply vascular clamp or hemostat with rubber tube to the cord. Bisect the testis and look for malignancy. If it is malignant, remove the testis; but if it is not malignant, then suture it and reposition.

VASECTOMY

DEFINITION

Vasectomy is surgical removal of all or part of the vas deferens, usually as a means of permanent sterilization.

INDICATIONS

- Family planning
- Eugenic—to prevent genetically transmitted diseases
- In the past, was done prior to prostatectomy, to prevent retrograde spread of infection

MEDICOLEGAL ASPECTS

- Consent of both partners must be taken.
- Counseling of both partners should be done to explain the possibility of late failure (spontaneous recanalization).
- Selection of patient: The patient should be married with at least two children, one of which should be at least 2 year old.

OPERATIVE TECHNIQUE

Marie Stopes Scalpel Vasectomy

Vasectomy is performed in a warm room with warm preparation solutions to allow scrotal relaxation.

- Anesthesia: LA. GA is required in patients with previous scrotal or inguinal surgery.
- Carry out painting, draping, and isolation of the part.
- Infiltrate 1% lignocaine 2–3 mL.
- Incision: It is 1-cm long, after locating vas (identification: Cord-like structure that slips under palpating finger).
- Cut skin and subcutaneous tissue.
- Hold vas with forceps and pull into the wound, to form an inverted U.
- Apply clamp after stripping off adventitia and cut 1–2 cm piece of the vas.
- Keep the ends of the vas in different tissue planes.
- Check for hemostasis.
- Occlude the testicular and abdominal end of vas with suture ligation, hemoclips, or intraluminal fulguration with electrocautery. Repeat the procedure on the opposite side.
- Apply sterile dressing.

POSTOPERATIVE CARE

- Place ice pack on scrotum intermittently for the first 2 days.
- Avoid strenuous activity for 1 week.
- Look for the local complication.
- Provide analgesics if required.
- American Urological Association (AUA, 2012) guidelines for postoperative follow-up
  - Most patients achieve azoospermia by 3 months and after 20 ejaculations. Perform first postvasectomy semen analysis after 8–16 weeks. If patient is not having azoospermia, periodic semen analysis is advised every 6–12 weeks. Vasectomy should be repeated if any motile sperm are seen in the ejaculate 6 months after the initial vasectomy.
- Contraception should be used till two consecutive samples of semen are negative for sperms.

COMPLICATIONS

- Hemorrhage
- Hematoma (most common)
- Sperm granuloma (treatment is excision)
- Infection
- Traumatic fistula/scrotal sinus
- Fournier gangrene
- Failure (spontaneous reconnection)
- Postvasectomy pain syndrome
  - Various suggested theories
    - Epididymal duct dilatation
    - Increased pressure in the epididymis
    - Extravasation of sperm
  - Treatments
    - Scrotal elevation, ice pack, and NSAIDs
    - If not relieved within 3 months, spermatic block
    - If sperm granuloma present, excision of granuloma

- Epididymectomy: As a last resort—inguinal orchiectomy which is found to be superior in relieving pain as compared to scrotal orchiectomy in studies

- Psychological issues

Previous few studies showed that vasectomy puts patients at an increased risk for prostate cancer and cardiovascular and neurological disease but subsequently it has been disproved by recent studies.

Antibodies seen after vasectomy: Antisperm antibodies (80%), sperm-agglutinating antibodies (60%), and sperm-immobilizing antibodies (30%).

- Some surgeons used midline incision.
- Routinely, vas is not sent for HPE.
- Some surgeons used to send vas for histopathological confirmation because of medicolegal reasons. However, AUA guideline states that removal of segment of vas deferens for histological confirmation is neither required nor recommended.
- Nowadays, vasectomy is done by LI method, also known as non-scalpel vasectomy (NSV). In this method, incision is not required; pointed forceps are used (specially made) to make a puncture. Advantages of this method are less pain, less bleeding, less infection, early return to sexual activity, and quicker wound healing.
- Reversal of vasectomy may not be successful because of autoantibodies developed against sperm. Success rate is 70% if performed within 3 years.

OPERATION FOR URINARY STONE DISEASE

Urinary tract stone disease is also known as urolithiasis and stone located in the kidney is known as nephrolithiasis. Most stones develop in the kidney and may migrate to the ureter. Nephrolithiasis is a common problem in India as well as in the USA. Despite advances in management of urolithiasis, recurrence is common and recurrence rate is 50% at 5–10 years and 75% at 15–20 years. In this section, we will discuss about stones in the kidney, the ureter, and the bladder.

RENAL STONE

Types

- Calcium oxalate
- Brushite
- Uric acid
- Struvite
- Cystine
- Indinavir
- Triamterene
- Silica

Predisposing Factors

- Age: More than 40 years
- Sex: More common in males than in females
- Geography: Common in hot, dry climate
- Obesity
- Low citrate (citrate forms a soluble complex with calcium, so it prevents formation of a complex of calcium with oxalate [stone]
- Hypercalcemia and hypercalciuria
- Deficiency of vitamin A
- Prolonged immobilization
- Low pH (uric acid stone)
- Cystinuria
- Infection (struvite stone—in the presence of urea-splitting organisms, ammonia is produced by breakdown of urea, so alkalinization of urine occurs; under alkaline conditions, crystals of magnesium and ammonium phosphate precipitate)
- Anatomical obstruction: Ureteropelvic junction (UPJ) obstruction, horseshoe kidney, and calyceal diverticula

Clinical Features

- Asymptomatic
- Symptomatic: Loin pain, hematuria, UTI

Diagnosis

- Plain X-ray KUB (radio-opaque stone can be detected [90%])
- USG (95% of renal stones can be detected by ultrasound)
- Intravenous urogram (IVU)
- CT—urography

Treatment

Medical management

Stones smaller than 5 mm are treated conservatively with:

- Plenty of liquids taken orally
- Antibiotics
- Analgesics
- Smooth muscle relaxants (e.g., hyoscine butylbromide [Buscopan])

Nonmedical management of renal stone[2]

- Treatment based on size
  - *Stone of 5–10 mm size*: Extracorporeal shock wave lithotripsy (ESWL) has been the first line of therapy till now but with the advent of flexible ureteroscopic removal of stone (URS), in experienced hands, flexible URS is now the alternative first-line therapy.
  - *Stone of 1–2 cm size*: For stones not in the lower pole, ESWL is favored if stone attenuation <900 HU, skin to stone distance <10 cm, and patient has no history of ESWL-resistant stone (cystine, brushite stone). For rest of the stones, flexible URS or percutaneous nephrolithotomy (PCNL) is the option. Miniperc is preferred over standard PCNL (miniperc: PCNL performed through sheath of 12–20 Fr).
  - *>2 cm size*: PCNL is the first-line therapy.
- Staghorn calculi: PCNL
- Location-wise treatment
  - *Lower pole calculi*: PCNL
  - *Non-lower pole calculi*: ESWL or flexible URS
- Based on stone composition
  - Cystine, brushite, and calcium phosphate stones are relatively resistant to fragmentation by ESWL. Attenuation value >900 HU is associated with poor outcome with ESWL. PCNL is preferred in such conditions.
  - Matrix renal stone (consists of organic proteins, sugars, and glucosamines): PCNL is the preferred treatment option.
- Anatomic abnormality
  - *UPJ obstruction*: PCNL followed by laparoscopic pyeloplasty
  - *Calyceal diverticula*: PCNL the first-line treatment (flexible URS for stone <2 cm size can be an alternative in the experienced hands)
  - Horseshoe kidney
    - *<1.5-cm stone not situated in the lower pole*: ESWL or flexible URS
    - *>1.5-cm stone*: PCNL

UPJ obstruction must be excluded prior to ESWL.

Percutaneous nephrolithotomy

Indications

- Large (>2 cm in diameter) or complex calculi (filling the majority of the intrarenal collecting system, such as Staghorn calculi) or lower pole stone >1 cm
- Failed ESWL or ureteroscopic removal
- Anatomic abnormalities, including horseshoe kidneys or UPJ obstruction or stone in the calyceal diverticula
- Pediatric patients with large stone
- Patient's wish

Contraindications

- Sepsis
- Active urinary infection
- Pregnancy
- Uncorrected coagulopathy

Operative technique VIDEO

- *Position*: The patient is placed in lithotomy for retrograde ureteric catheter placement followed by prone position.
- *Anesthesia*: GA is preferable. However, procedure can also be performed under SA.
- It is done after PDI (painting, draping, and isolation).
- With the patient in a supine position, a retrograde ureteral catheter is placed using a 19-Fr sheath over the cystoscope. Position is confirmed with fluoroscopy. Place per urethral catheter alongside the ureteric catheter and ureteric catheter is fixed with urethral catheter with either thread or micropore tape.
- After turning the patient to a prone position, contrast nephrogram or air nephrogram is taken (Fig. 6.78). After identifying appropriate calyx for puncture, the renal collecting system is accessed via an 18-gauge puncture needle under fluoroscopic guidance. Position of the needle is confirmed within the system if fluid or urine comes from the needle or retrograde injection of saline comes from the needle (Fig. 6.79).

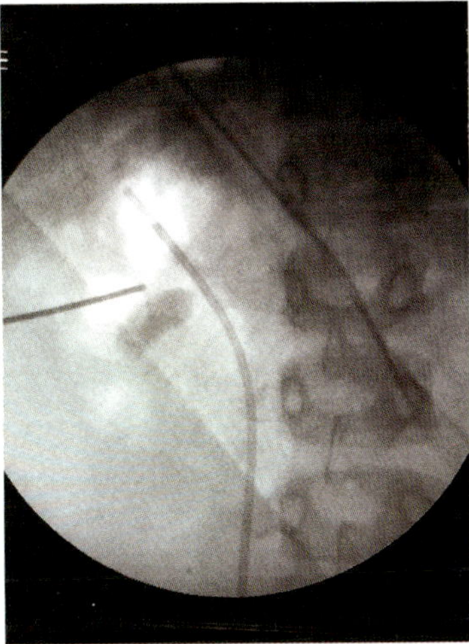

Figure 6.78 Air nephrogram with ureteric catheter in renal collecting system.

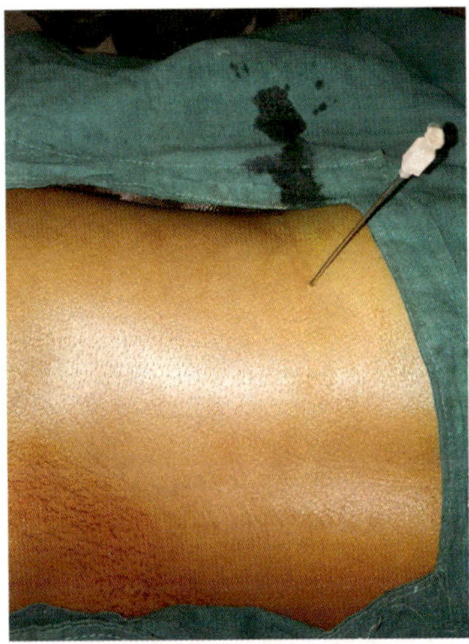

Figure 6.79 18-Gauge puncture needle with saline drop at the outer portion indicates in situ position.

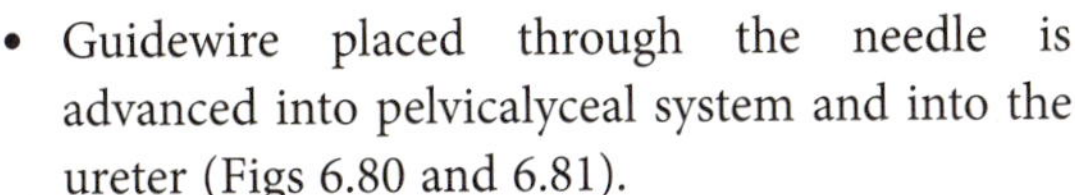

- Guidewire placed through the needle is advanced into pelvicalyceal system and into the ureter (Figs 6.80 and 6.81).
- Serial dilation of the tract is performed over the guidewire to 26 Fr with dilator; a 26-Fr working sheath is placed in the renal collecting system (Figs 6.82–6.85).
- A rigid nephroscope is passed into pelvicalyceal system through the sheath along the wire. Stone is identified (Fig. 6.86).

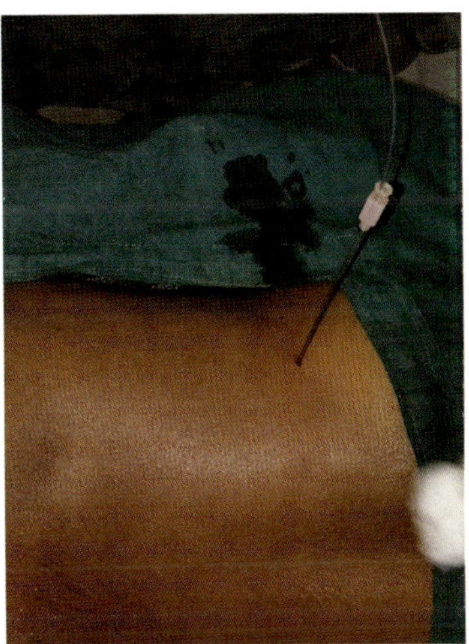

Figure 6.80 Placing guidewire through needle.

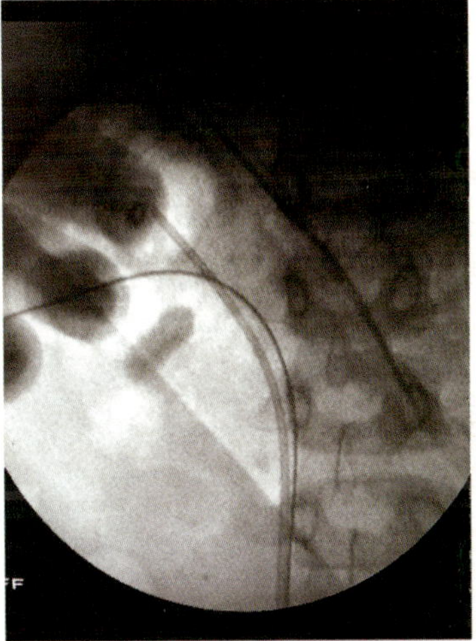

Figure 6.81 Guidewire in the ureter.

- Stone is fragmented using electrohydraulic lithotripsy (Fig. 6.87) (other options for lithotripsy are ultrasonic, laser, or pneumatic).
- Stone fragments are extracted with grasping forceps (Fig. 6.88).
- Check fluoroscopy is performed at the end of the procedure to confirm the stone clearance (Fig. 6.89).
- Double J (DJ) stent is placed down the ureter (Fig. 6.89).
- 24-Fr nephrostomy tube is placed and fixed (Fig. 6.90).

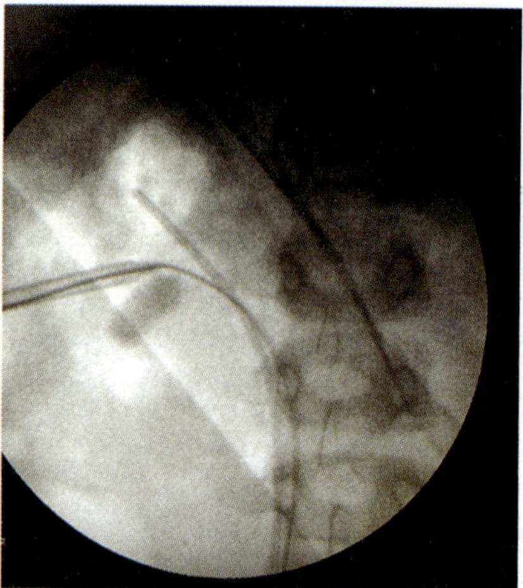

Figure 6.82 Dilator within renal collecting system.

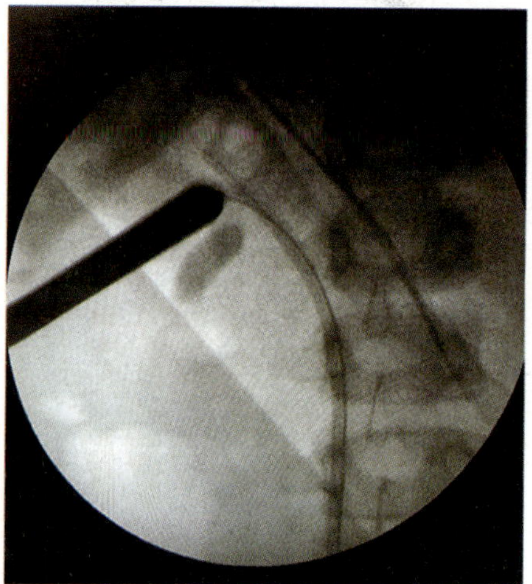

Figure 6.83 Gradual dilation with set of dilator.

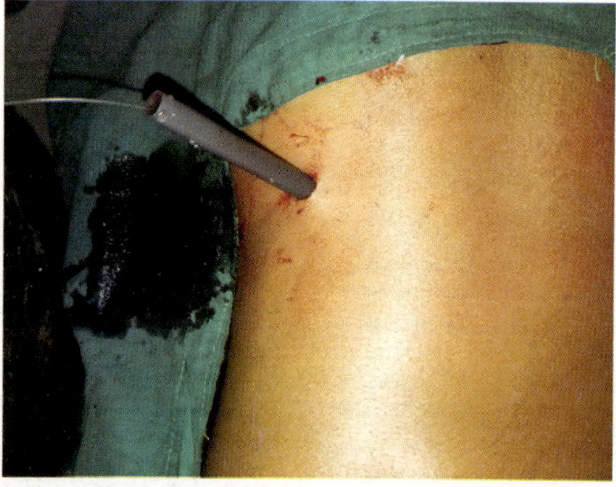

Figure 6.84 26-Fr Amplatz.

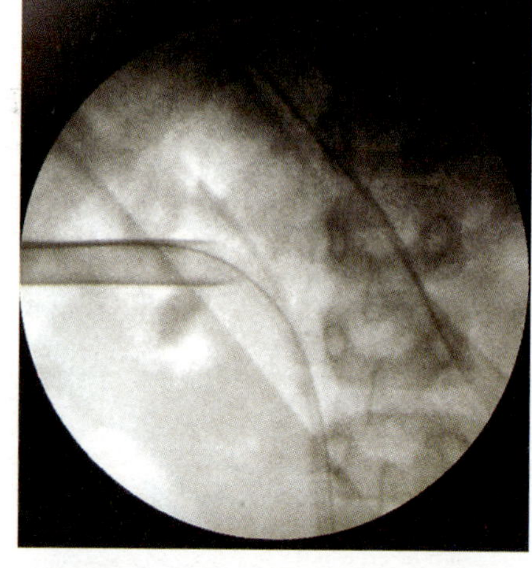

Figure 6.85 26-Fr Amplatz within renal collecting system.

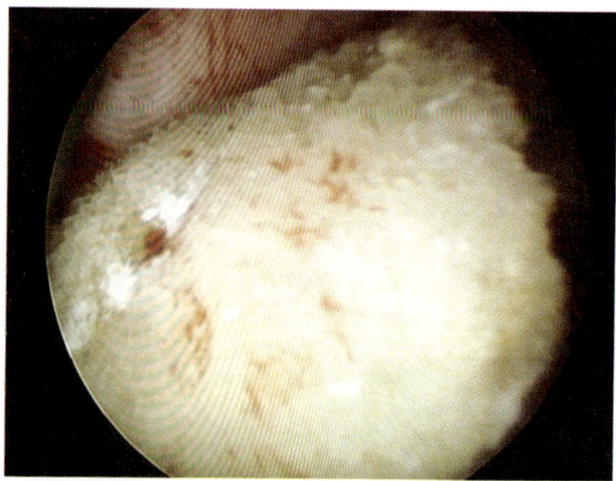

Figure 6.86 Stone in the collecting system.

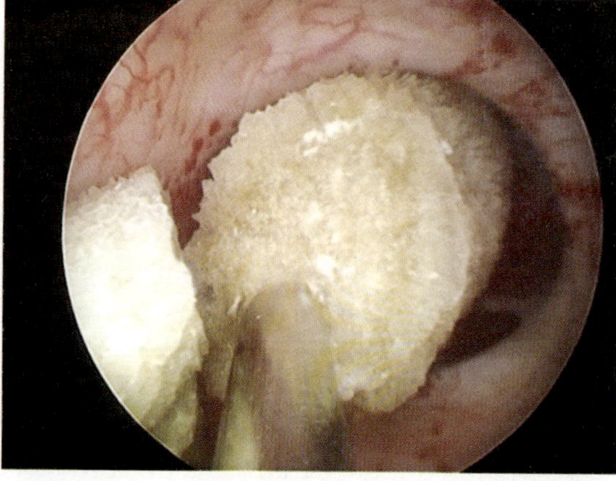

Figure 6.87 Fragmentation of the stone.

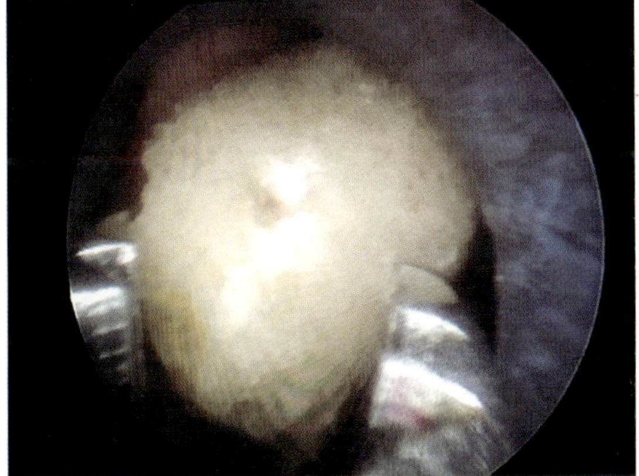

Figure 6.88 Stone extracted using grasping forceps.

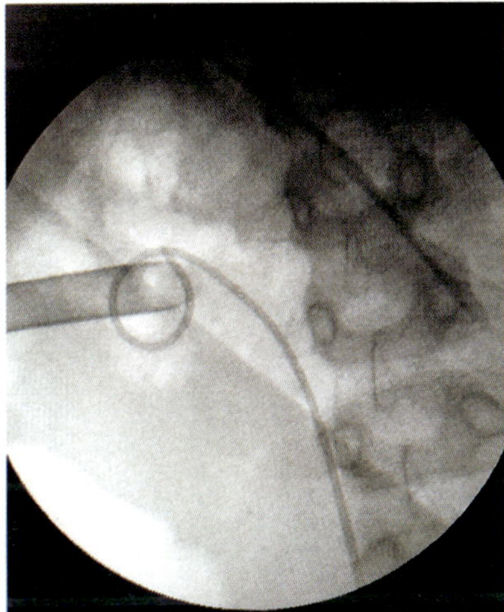

Figure 6.89 Fluoroscopy showed complete clearance of the stone with DJ stent in position.

Postoperative care

- NBM for 6 hours
- Antibiotics
- Analgesics
- PPI
- IV fluid
- Nephrostomy tube removed on the third day and per urethral catheter on the fourth day
- DJ stent removed between second and third weeks. (before removal of DJ stent, check X-ray KUB is taken)

Complications

- Perforation of the renal pelvis
- Vascular injury

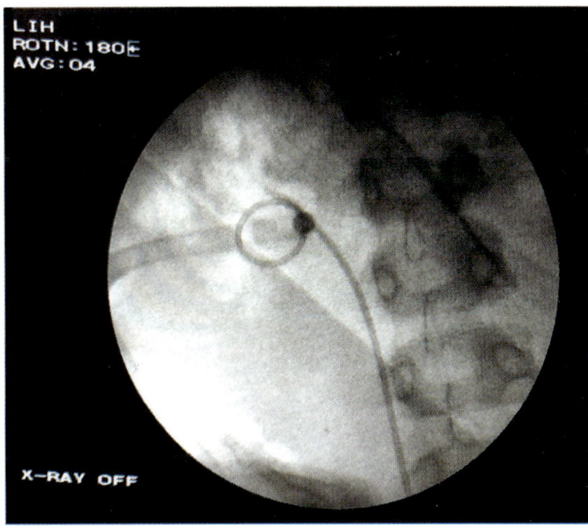

Figure 6.90 Nephrostomy tube within renal collecting system.

- Colon injury
- Splenic injury
- Access failure
- Extravasation
- Sepsis
- Pneumothorax/pleural effusion
- Wound infection
- Retained stone fragments

URETERIC STONE

Relevant Anatomy

- The average length of the ureter is 25 cm and the diameter is up to 4 mm.
- The sites of obstruction in the ureter are as follows:
  - UPJ
  - At the crossing of iliac vessels
  - Vesicoureteric junction (VUJ)
- Blood supply
  - Upper ureter: Renal artery
  - Midureter: Abdominal aorta, common iliac, gonadal artery
  - Lower ureter: Branches from internal iliac

Indications for Intervention in Ureteric Stone

- Acute
  - Patients with ureteric stone with signs and symptoms suggestive of obstructed and infected urinary system should be treated with

either urgent DJ stenting or percutaneous nephrostomy (PCN).
  - Patient with single kidney with anuria and obstruction is also an indication for urgent drainage.
  - Uncontrolled pain is a relative indication for intervention.
- Subacute
  - *<10-mm stone*: Well-controlled pain, no infection, and normal renal function. Medical expulsive therapy is given.
  - *>10 mm stone*: It is less likely to pass by itself and intervention is advised.

Guidelines for Intervention

Joint EUA (European Association of Urology) and AUA Nephrolithiasis Guideline Panel 2007 and 2016 recommendations:[3]

- Proximal ureteric
  - *<10-mm stone*: ESWL has a higher stone-free rate as compared to URS.
  - *>10-mm stone*: URS is a better option.
- Distal ureteric stone (any size): URS has a higher stone-free rate.
- Midureteric calculi (any size): URS has a higher stone-free rate.

- Both ESWL and URS are acceptable options.
- Routine stenting is not recommended as a part of ESWL.
- Stenting following uncomplicated URS is not mandatory.
- Bacteriuria should be treated with appropriate antibiotics.
- Blind basket extraction without endoscopic visualization should not be performed.

Ureteroscopic Removal of Stone

Operative technique

- Position: The patient is placed in lithotomy position.
- Anesthesia: SA is given.
- Antibiotic prophylaxis is provided.
- Cystoscopy is performed. Balloon dilator with guidewire is introduced through the cystoscope. By keeping tip of the balloon dilator at the VUJ, guidewire is positioned in the renal collecting system under fluoroguidance.
- Balloon is passed over the wire in the distal ureter and balloon dilatation performed.
- Introduce 6-Fr or 8-Fr rigid ureteroscope and identify the stone (Fig. 6.91).
- If stone is too small to extract, grasping forceps is used to remove the stone.
- For larger stone, electrohydraulic lithotripsy is performed to fragment the stone (Fig. 6.92).
- Remove fragment with ureteric grasping forceps (Fig. 6.93). Very small fragments can be left as such.
- At the end of the procedure, place a DJ stent (optional).

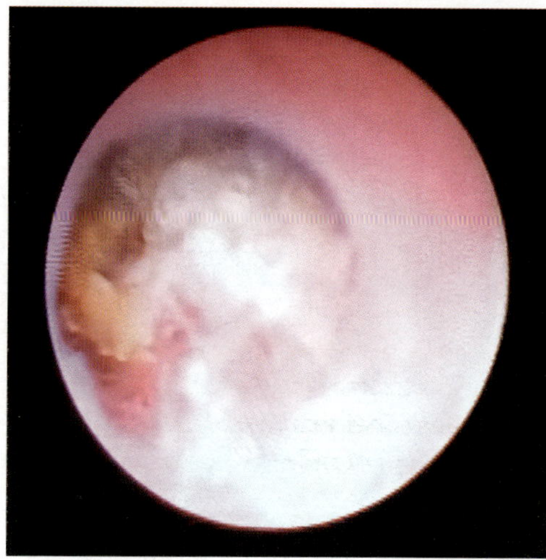

Figure 6.91 Identification of stone within ureter.

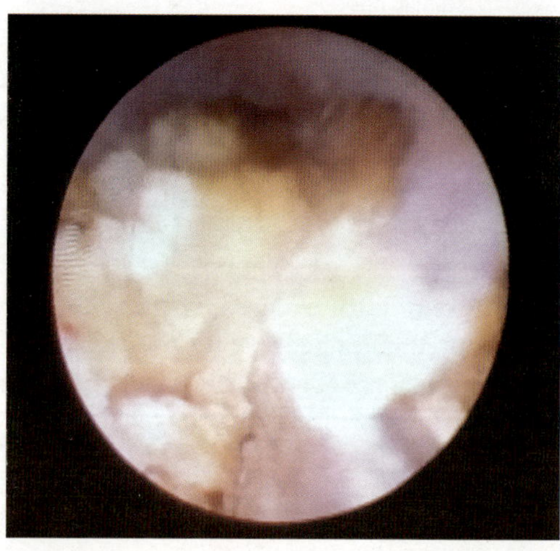

Figure 6.92 Stone fragmentation.

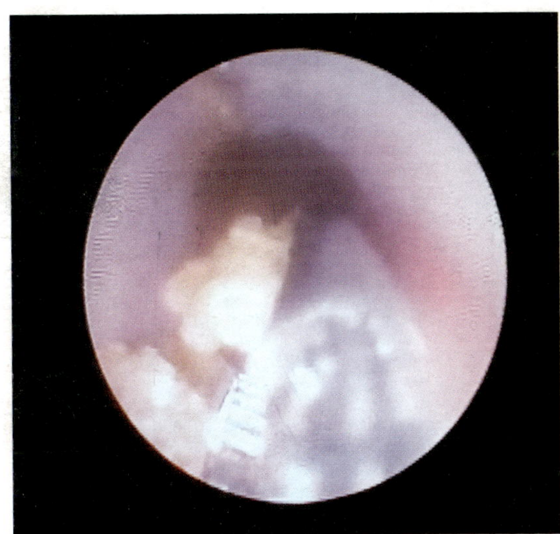

Figure 6.93 Stone removal using grasper.

Postoperative care

- Antibiotics
- Analgesic
- X-ray KUB prior to DJ stent removal is required to confirm stone clearance
- DJ stent removal after 3 weeks

Complications of URS

- Perforation
- Avulsion
- Sepsis
- Stricture
- Steinstrasse

BLADDER STONE

Primary bladder stones are common in children and defined as those without functional, anatomical, or infectious etiology.

Secondary bladder stones are secondary to bladder outlet obstruction (males: BPH, stricture urethra; females: Pelvic prolapse, cystocele) or chronic infection from the neuropathic bladder or augmented bladder.

Clinical History

Typical presentation is intermittent painful micturition, suprapubic pain, and terminal hematuria (most common symptoms). Strangury (painful irritation of the bladder leading to strong desire to micturate, often associated with pulling of penis by young boys) is unusual but said to be pathognomonic of this condition.

Diagnosis

- X-ray KUB: Radio-opacity seen in the pelvis
- USG KUB: Shows stone in the bladder; also shows reason for the stone sometimes, and back pressure changes, if present
- Urine routine and microscopic examination

Management of Bladder Stone

- *For small stone*: Cystoscopic removal of stone
- *For larger stone*: Cystolitholapaxy by using either electrohydraulic energy or holmium laser (holmium laser is now the modality of choice to treat large calculi)

Cystolitholapaxy

Most stones in the bladder are removed through cystoscopy. Small stones can be removed intact while large stones are required to be broken into small pieces for removal via cystoscopy. This procedure is called cystolitholapaxy.

Contraindications for cystoscopic removal or litholapaxy

- Contracted bladder
- Very large stones (>3 cm)
- Patient age <10 years
- Urethral stricture which cannot be dilated sufficiently

Percutaneous suprapubic litholapaxy is the best option if it is not possible to carry out the procedure perurethrally.

Operative technique

- Position: Lithotomy
- Anesthesia: Spinal
- Preoperative antibiotic
  - It is done after PDI (painting, draping, and isolation).
  - Cystoscope with 19-Fr sheath is introduced into the bladder.
  - Irrigation using normal saline is continued to have a better vision.
  - Small stone is removed with grasping forceps or stone-crushing forceps.

  - Large stone requires laser lithotripsy or electrohydraulic lithotripter is used to fragment the stone.
  - Stone fragment is removed through Ellik evacuator.
  - Catheterization is performed.
- Postoperative care
  - Antibiotic
  - Analgesic
  - Per urethral catheter removed on next day
  - X-ray checked to confirm clearance of stone

Complications

- UTI
- Hematuria
- Bladder perforation
- Urethral stricture

TRANSURETHRAL RESECTION OF PROSTATE (TURP)

It is resection of prostate through urethra in a patient with benign enlargement of prostate not responding to medical management or with complications of BPH.

RELEVANT ANATOMY

Prostate is a chestnut-sized organ present only in males. It lies between bladder neck and urogenital diaphragm. Its volume is 20 g. It is 3 cm in length, 4 cm wide, and 2 cm in depth.

Prostate is divided into three zones as described by McNeal:[13]

- *Transitional zone*: It lies in the superior part of the gland, around the urethra and above the ejaculatory duct. It has two lateral lobes and a median lobe. The prostatic urethra extends from the bladder neck to the membranous urethra. BPH develops in this zone. It is the smallest of the three zones and occupies 5% of prostate volume till <30 years of age. In BPH, it can comprise up to 95% of the prostate volume.
- *Central zone*: It lies between the peripheral zone and the ejaculatory duct.
- *Peripheral zone*: It is 1 cm thick and covers the posterior and lateral aspects of prostate. It contains prostatic capsule. Most carcinomas develop in this area.

The main arterial supply is through the inferior vesical artery and the venous drainage is into the deep dorsal veins. The lymphatics drain into the internal iliac and the obturator nodes.

INDICATIONS

- Patients who do not respond to medical management of BPH
- Complications of BPH
  - Recurrent UTI
  - Refractory urinary retention
  - Recurrent gross hematuria
  - Bladder stone
  - Renal failure

CONTRAINDICATIONS

- >100 g prostate
- Uncontrolled coagulopathy
- Sepsis or active UTI

OPERATIVE TECHNIQUE 

- Position: The patient is placed in lithotomy position.
- Anesthesia: SA is given.
- Preoperative antibiotics are provided.
- After PDI, perform cystoscopy to rule out stricture or bladder pathology with 19 Fr sheath and have a look at the ureteric opening in the bladder as well as verumontanum, lateral lobe, and median lobe (Figs 6.94 and 6.95).
- Introduce 26-Fr resectoscope. Resection of median lobe starts at the bladder neck and progresses in downward direction (Fig. 6.96).
- Lateral lobe is also resected in a similar manner to create a satisfactory channel (Fig. 6.97).
- Distal-most boundary of resection is verumontanum.
- Remove prostatic chips using Ellik evacuator.
- Secure hemostasis with cautery (Figs 6.98 and 6.99).
- Place a three-way Foley, 22-Fr catheter for irrigation purpose. Inflate balloon up to 30 cm^3 and apply traction.
- Irrigation is continued throughout the procedure and glycine is used as an irrigating fluid.

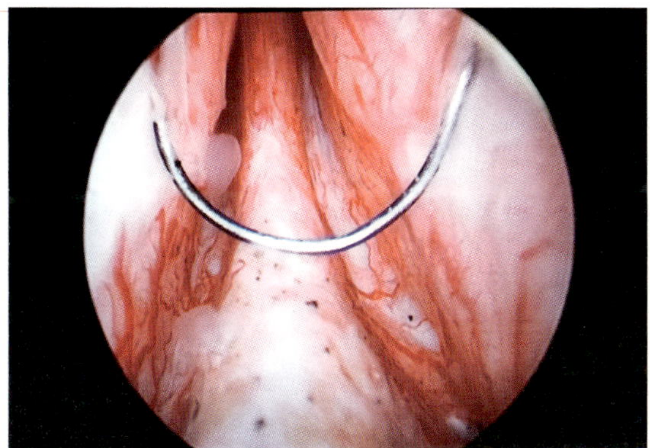

Figure 6.94 Lateral lobe and verumontanum.

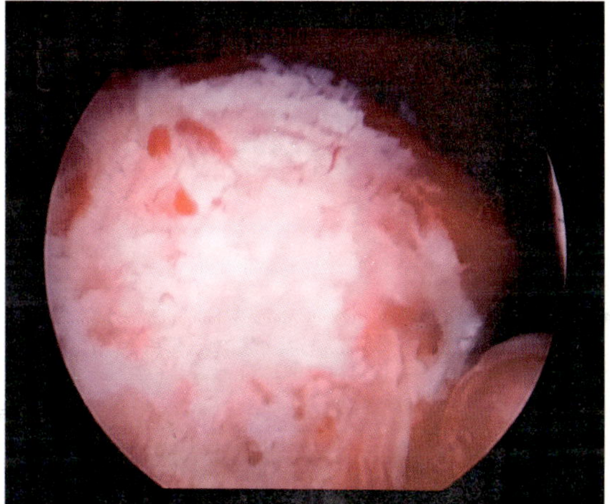

Figure 6.95 Median lobe.

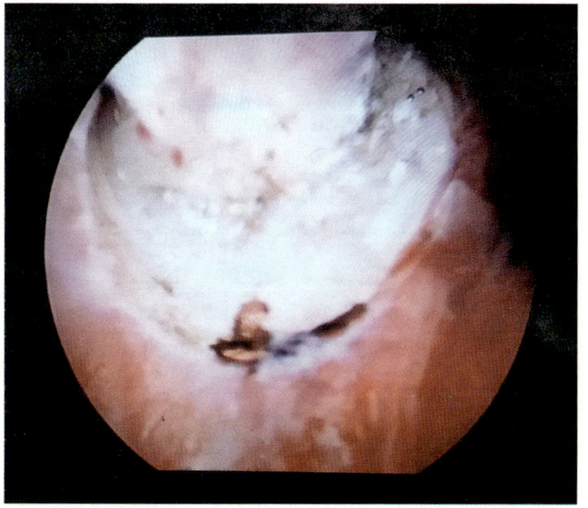

Figure 6.96 Resection of median lobe.

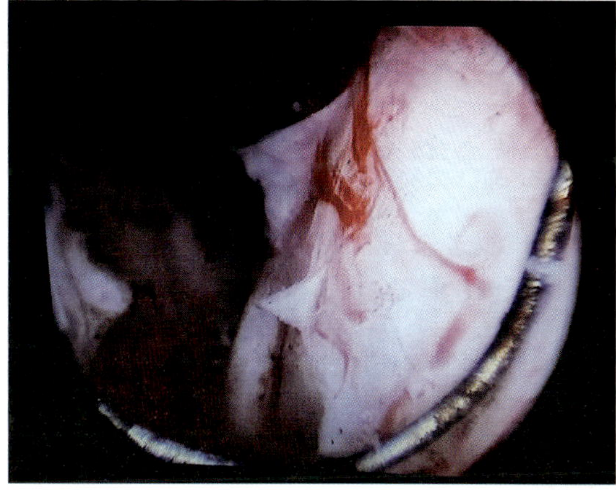

Figure 6.97 Resection of lateral lobe.

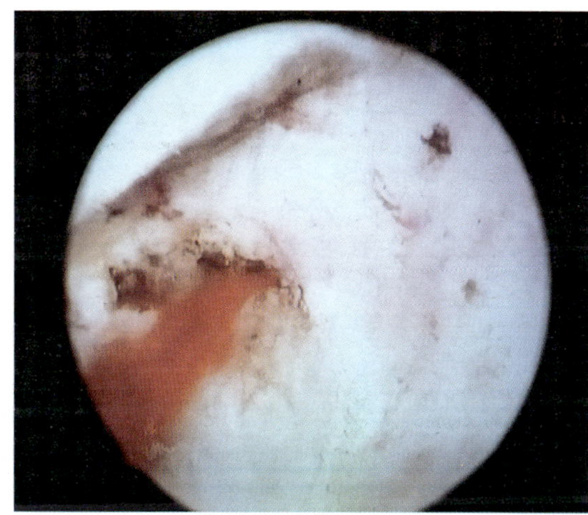

Figure 6.98 Bleeding from the resected lobe.

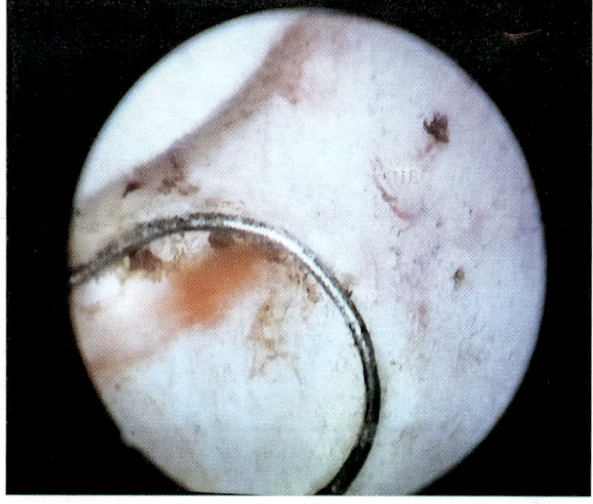

Figure 6.99 Hemostasis with cautery.

POSTOPERATIVE CARE

- Continue irrigation. Normal saline can also be used as a irrigating fluid in postoperative state.
- Deflate 10-cm^3 balloon in the next morning and release traction.
- Watch for signs of TURP syndrome.
- Administer antibiotics and analgesics.
- Remove catheter on 3rd or 4th postoperative day.

COMPLICATIONS

For details refer Chapter 16, *Frequently Asked Questions*.

OPERATION FOR EPIDERMOID CYST (SEBACEOUS CYST OR PILAR CYST)

An epidermoid or sebaceous cyst is a benign tumor formed by invagination and cystic expansion of the epidermis or epithelium forming the hair follicle. It is usually found in face, neck, scalp, or trunk.

CHARACTERISTIC FEATURES

- Commonest site scalp
- Located in the deep dermis but connected to superficial epithelium through the pilosebaceous duct
- Usually results from ruptured pilosebaceous follicle
- Contains keratin and lipid
- Soft, mobile and punctum seen
- Should consider multiple epidermoid cyst and osteomas as a part of Gardner syndrome

OPERATIVE TECHNIQUE

- Carry out painting, draping, and isolation of the part (Fig. 6.100).
- Inject LA (0.5% lignocaine) in the intracutaneous plane over and around the cyst (Fig. 6.101).
- Keep the incision along the Langer's line, or, in case of a large cyst, make an elliptical incision (Fig. 6.102).
- Cut the skin.
- Cut the subcutaneous tissue.
- Achieve hemostasis by identifying small bleeders and apply hemostat and cauterize.

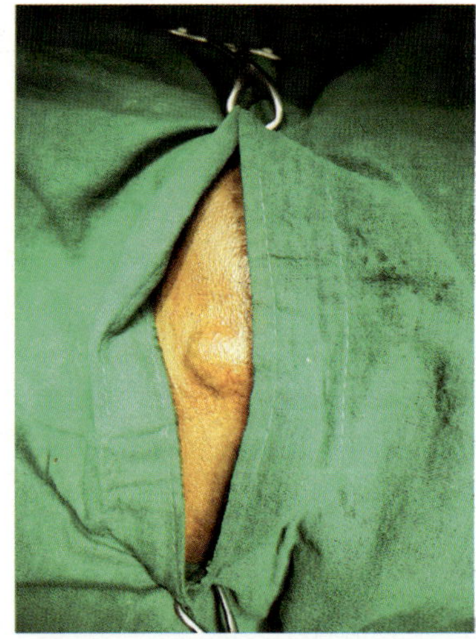

Figure 6.100 Painting, draping, and isolating part with epidermoid cyst.

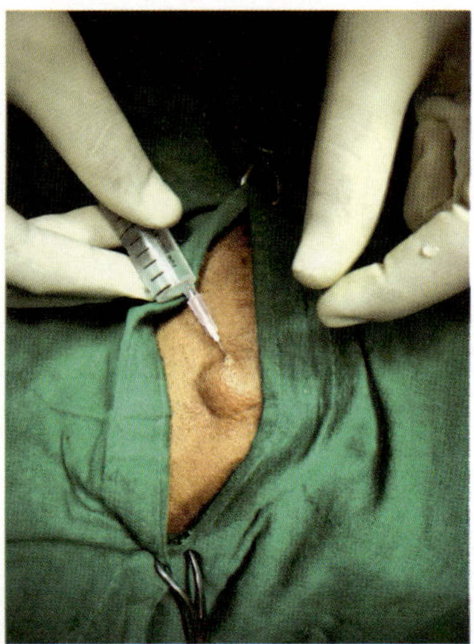

Figure 6.101 Injection of local anesthetics surrounding the epidermoid cyst.

- Identify cyst wall; dissect it free from surrounding tissues (Fig. 6.103) by blunt dissection (LA, infiltrated in the surrounding tissues, will help in separating the cyst).
- The last portion to be freed is punctum.
- Excise the cyst (Fig. 6.104).
- Remove hemostat and check for bleeding. Achieve hemostasis.
- Close skin with Mersilk 3-0 or Ethilon 3-0.
- Apply dressing.

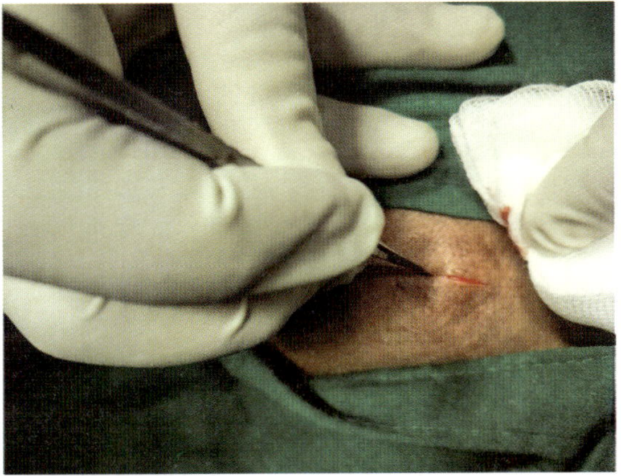

Figure 6.102 Incision parallel to Langer's line.

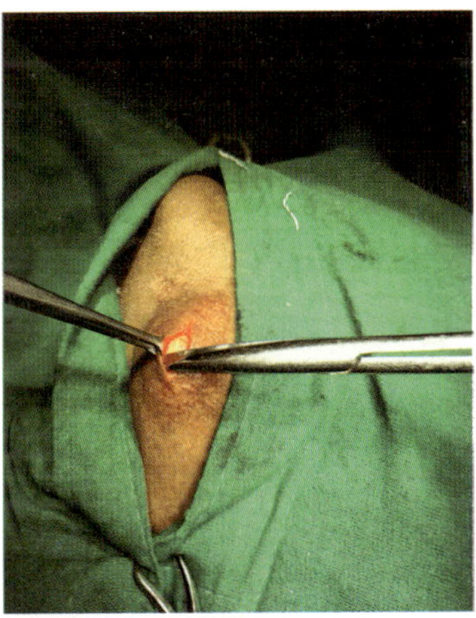

Figure 6.103 Dissecting cyst from the surrounding tissue.

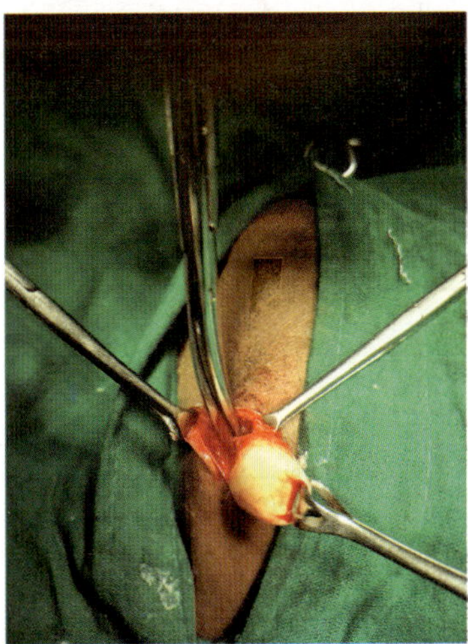

Figure 6.104 Excision of the cyst from the base.

POSTOPERATIVE CARE

- Prophylactic antibiotics
- Analgesic
- Suture removal after 7 days.

COMPLICATIONS

- Wound infection
- Stitch abscess
- Recurrence

- If cyst ruptures during the procedure, carefully remove the whole capsule to prevent recurrence.
- Avoid holding the cyst with forceps, which may unnecessarily damage the wall or lead to rupture. If necessary, use Babcock's forceps.
- Infected sebaceous cyst: Carry out I&D with removal of capsule and daily dressing. If there is only mild inflammation, give antibiotics for 5 days and then do excision.

INCISION AND DRAINAGE OF AN ABSCESS

DEFINITIONS

- *Abscess*: Collection of pus in a cavity, lined by a pyogenic membrane
- *Empyema*: Abscess in an anatomical cavity (gallbladder and pleura)
- *Pus*: Liquefied end product of inflammation; consists of degraded protein, plasma, dead and living neutrophils
- *Systemic inflammatory response syndrome (SIRS)*: It may involve:
  - Hyperthermia ($>38°C$) or hypothermia ($<36°C$)
  - Tachycardia (>90/min, without β-blocker) or tachypnea (>20/min)
  - WBC count $>12,000/mm^3$ or $<4000/mm^3$ or $>10\%$ band cells in peripheral smear

  If two of these conditions are present, it is considered to be SIRS.
- *Sepsis*: Life-threatening organ dysfunction caused by a dysregulated host response to infection (as per the Third International Consensus Definitions for Sepsis and Septic Shock [Sepsis-3], organ dysfunction can be identified as an acute change

in total SOFA score ≥2 points consequent to the infection; SOFA is sequential or sepsis-related organ failure assessment score; It includes PaO_2/FII_2, platelet count, mean arterial pressure [Map], *S. bilirubin*, Glasgow Coma Scale, *S. creatinine*, and urine output)

- *Septic shock*: Sepsis with persisting hypotension requiring vasopressors to maintain MAP ≥65 mmHg and having a serum lactate level >2 mmol/L (18 mg/dL) despite adequate volume resuscitation (the Third International Consensus Definitions for Sepsis and Septic Shock [Sepsis-3])

SUPERFICIAL SURGICAL SITE INFECTION

According to the Centers for Disease Control and Prevention (CDC) definition, it involves:

- Infection within 30 days of surgery
- Only skin and subcutaneous tissue infected
- Purulent discharge, isolation of organism from discharge (one of these two should be present at the incision site)
- Pain or tenderness, localized swelling, redness or heat, deliberately opened by surgeon
  One of these should be present at the incision site.

DEEP SURGICAL SITE INFECTION

In addition to involving skin and subcutaneous tissue, it involves muscles and fascia. Less than 30 days with no implant and <1 year with an implant. One of the following should be present: purulent discharge from the deep space with no involvement of organ space, presence of infection on radiological examination, direct examination, and/or on opening the wound, diagnosis by a surgeon, or fever and tenderness leading to dehiscence.

ORGAN-SPECIFIC SURGICAL SITE INFECTION

Infection involves target organ of the original operation. Less than 30 days with no implant and <1 year with an implant.

ABSCESS

- Visible pus, tenderness, and fluctuation are signs of abscess formation.
- Signs of inflammation are present.
- Increase in vascular permeability secondary to infection or trauma leads to outpouring of macrophages and neutrophils which releases lysosomal enzymes and causes tissue destruction and release of toxins from the bacteria also causes tissue destruction and formation of pus. Pyogenic membrane formation is due to exudation of protein and fibrin formation is due to increase in capillary permeability.
- To start with, it is cellulitis which then becomes localized to form abscess.
- Patients usually present with fever with rigor, throbbing pain (hyperosmolar material within abscess draws fluid leading to increased pressure and pain or pressure on the nerve by pus) and localized swelling or lump.
  - If untreated, leads to bacteremia, septicemia, multiple abscess formation, antibioma (if treated with antibiotic without drainage)

OPERATIVE TECHNIQUE

Anesthesia for Incision and Drainage

- *Superficial abscess*: Ethyl chloride spray or LA (infiltration of local anesthetic into dermal tissue), additional injections of anesthetic in a local field block pattern, IV analgesic agents, or TIVA
- *Deep abscess*: IV analgesic plus TIVA (total intravenous anesthesia)
- *In children*: IV analgesic plus TIVA

pH of the abscess cavity is acidic and that of LA is alkaline; hence, effect will be neutralized; therefore, LA into abscess cavity should be avoided.

Operation Technique

Modified Hilton's method

- Carry out painting, draping, and isolation of the part.
- Keep incision over the most prominent part, with stab knife (no. 11), parallel to Langer's lines (Fig. 6.105).
- As far as possible, keep incision in the most dependent part (if the most prominent part is not dependent, counterincision should be given for better drainage).

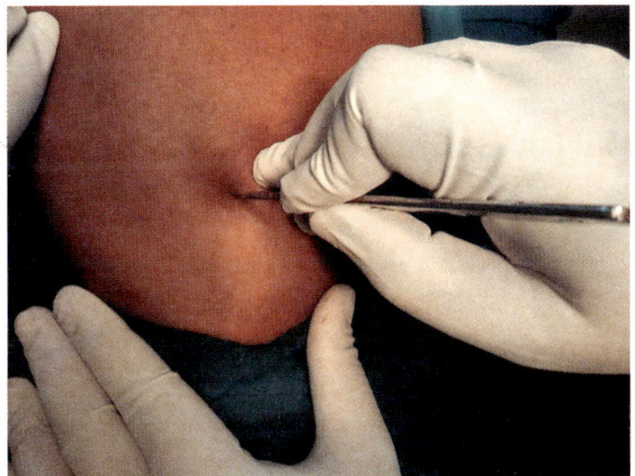

Figure 6.105 Incision over the most prominent part of abscess with stab knife.

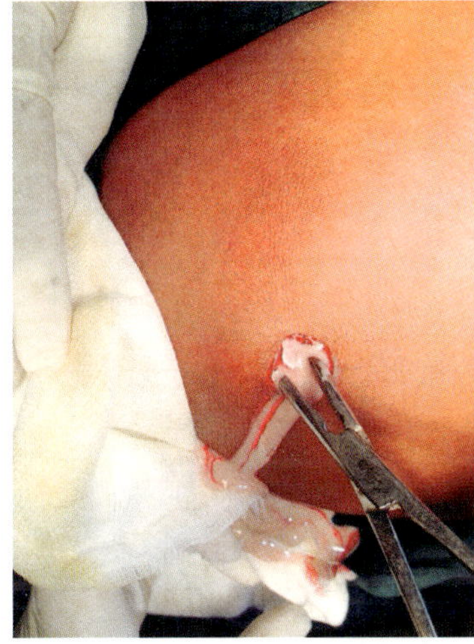

Figure 6.106 Sinus forceps introduced and blade opened.

- Introduce sinus forceps (Fig. 6.106). After introducing, open the blades and rotate to widen the tract and break the septa. If required, gloved finger should be introduced to break the septa (Fig. 6.107).
- Take pus for culture and sensitivity. Culture and sensitivity is not recommended in every case. However, it may be useful in recurrent abscess, immunocompromised individual, suspicion of atypical organism, persistent cellulitis, and exposure to methicillin-resistant *Staphylococcus aureus* (MRSA).
- Irrigate cavity with povidone—iodine and hydrogen peroxide (H_2O_2), followed by irrigation with saline.

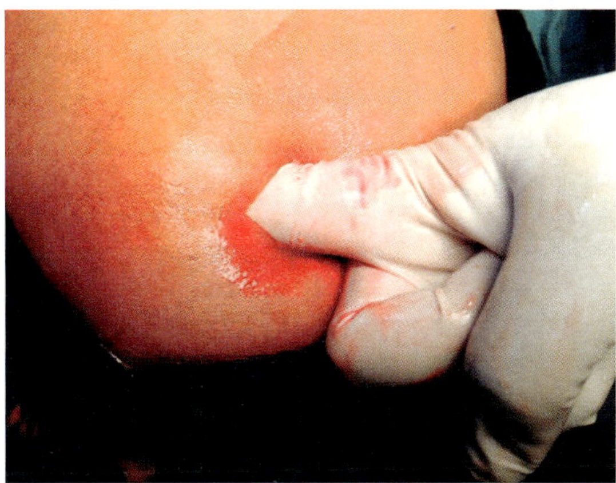

Figure 6.107 Introduce finger to break the loculi and septa.

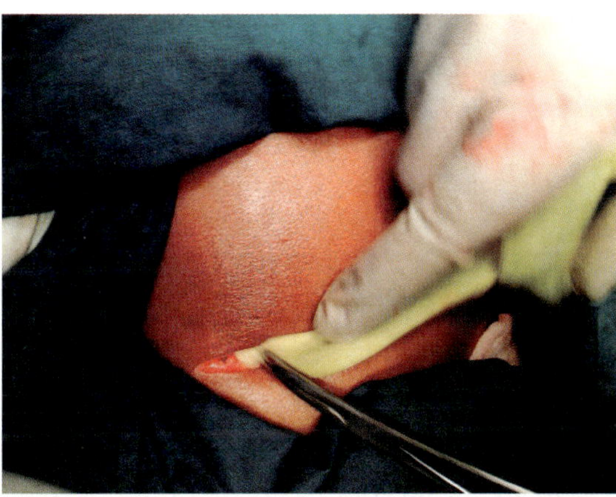

Figure 6.108 Packing of the abscess cavity.

- Pack the cavity with roller gauze (bleeding due to congested vessels and granulation tissue in the wall is controlled by tight packing) (Fig. 6.108). Packing of abscess cavity is indicated in the following situations: Abscess >5 cm in diameter, Pilonidal abscess, and immunocompromised patient.

Avoid overpacking the wound; this may impair the drainage of purulent material and can cause ischemia of the surrounding tissues.

- Apply sterile dressing and secure with adhesive tape (Micropore or Elastoplast).

Postoperative care

- Antibiotics (initially broad spectrum followed by culture specific)
- Analgesics
- Anti-inflammatory

- H_2 blocker or PPIs
- Daily dressing (allow the cavity to heal from the bottom; pack needs to be gradually reduced)

Postoperative antibiotics are suggested in the following conditions:[4] Single abscess ≥2 cm, multiple abscess, extensive surrounding tissue involvement, immunocompromised or other comorbidities, toxemia (e.g., fever >100.5°F/38°C, hypotension, or sustained tachycardia), inadequate response to I&D alone, presence of an indwelling medical device (such as prosthetic joint, vascular graft, or pacemaker), high risk for adverse outcomes with endocarditis, and high risk for transmission of *S. aureus* to others (such as in athletes or military personnel).

Complications

- No drainage
- No effect of the anesthesia (accidental injection of LA into the abscess cavity instead of intradermal infiltration into surrounding tissues results in neutralization of its effect by the acid environment in the pus)
- Bleeding from inadequate hemostasis
- Damage to the adjacent structure

Hilton's method protects the underlying important vital structures such as nerves and vessels. In this method, deep structures are not incised with knife but are opened with sinus forceps instead.

Abscess Over Specific Sites

Breast abscess

- Anesthesia: GA with sedation with TIVA or eutectic mixture of local anesthetics (EMLA) (cream 30 minutes before surgery)
- Incision: Circumareolar or radial incision
- Technique: Same as above (large abscess will require counterincision)

- It is most commonly seen during lactation.
- The most common organism involved is *S. aureus*.
- Fluctuation is a late sign, so incision must not be delayed until it appears.
- If infection does not resolve within 48 hours, it requires I & D.
- Needle aspiration and ultrasound will help in confirming diagnosis. Needle aspiration is the mainstay of treatment for breast abscess. When needle aspiration is not possible or not effective and there is marked skin changes, I&D may be performed.
- In lactational breast abscess, the patient is advised to empty the breast by breast pump or manually, from diseased breast.
- Breast-feeding is continued from normal breast. Feeding from the affected side may also be continued if the patient can manage.[5]
- The patients may notice milk draining from the wound. However, anti-infective property of milk actually accelerates the healing.
- There is no role of suppression of lactation.
- Whenever pus is present, let it drain out. When antibiotics are given in the presence of pus, most of the time, pus does not completely resolve and antibioma is formed. Treatment is excision.

Anorectal abscess

- Anesthesia: Sedation using TIVA is given.
- Cruciate incision is placed over the most prominent part or point of tenderness.
- Rest of the technique is same.
- Skin edges are excised to prevent early sealing of incision and recurrence of abscess.
- Except for temporary hemostasis, wound packing is not required.
- Tight packing will lead to pain and impaired drainage of pus.
- From the next day, loose packing is sufficient.

Parotid abscess

- Anesthesia: GA with sedation with TIVA
- Incision: Vertical
- Fascia opened horizontally to avoid injury to facial nerve

- Fluctuation is a late sign, because parotid gland is covered by tense fascia.
- Delay in drainage may lead to spread of infection into deeper tissue planes of the neck.

VENESECTION

Venesection is open exposure and cannulation of subcutaneous vein by cutdown.

INDICATIONS

Nowadays, because of experience in percutaneous vein puncture and availability of central line, its use is restricted to the following situations:

- Superficial veins are thrombosed and skill of placing central line is not available.
- A larger cannula is required for rapid infusion of fluid (usually in burns cases).

SITE

- Great saphenous vein—2 cm anterior and superior to the medial malleolus
- Basilic vein

OPERATIVE TECHNIQUE

- Anesthesia: LA is given.
- Carry out painting, draping, and isolation of the local part.
- Incision: Make transverse incision above and medial to medial malleolus (Fig. 6.109) with a no. 15 knife.
- Cut skin and subcutaneous tissue.
- Clear superficial fascia by artery forceps.

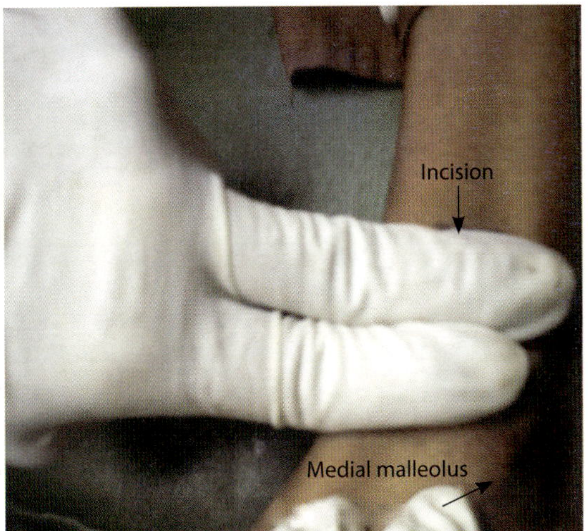

Figure 6.109 Incision above the medial malleolus.

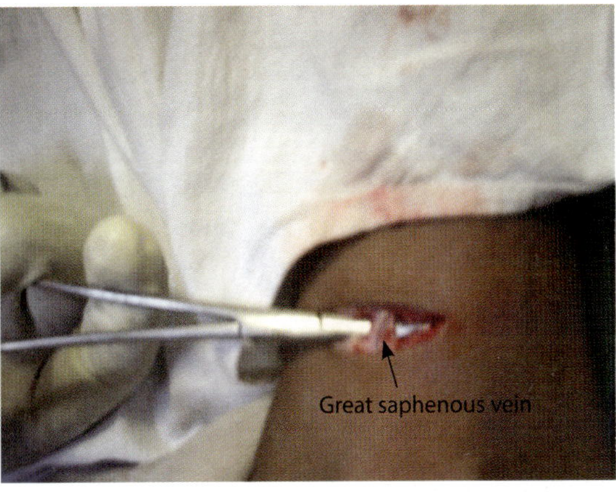

Figure 6.110 Great saphenous vein (GSV) is identified.

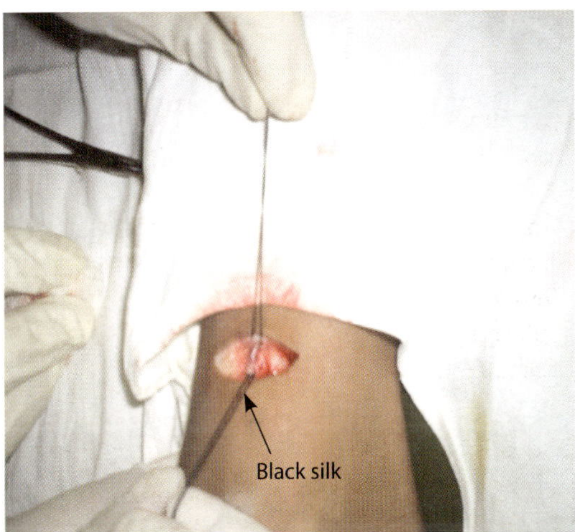

Figure 6.111 Black silk 3-0 is passed below the GSV.

- Identify great saphenous vein (Fig. 6.110) and isolate it.
- After isolation, pass black silk 3'-0 below the vein (two ligatures) (Fig. 6.111).
- Tie distal ligature, and give a slight traction.
- Pass IV needle through the vein (partial circumference) (Fig. 6.112), and cut the vein over the needle (avoid complete transection of vessel).
- Infant feeding tube is brought into the field, through a separate skin incision, through a subcutaneous tunnel.
- Insert infant feeding tube gently (5 or 6 Fr), after cutting the tip in an oblique fashion, while applying traction on the distal ligature (Fig. 6.113).
- Flush the tube with saline.

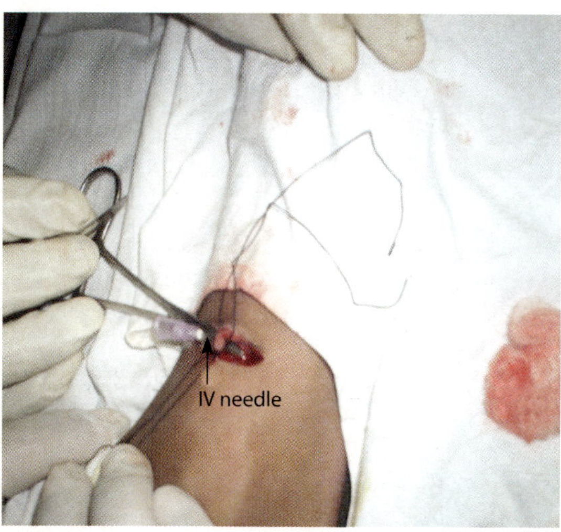

Figure 6.112 IV needle is being passed through the vein.

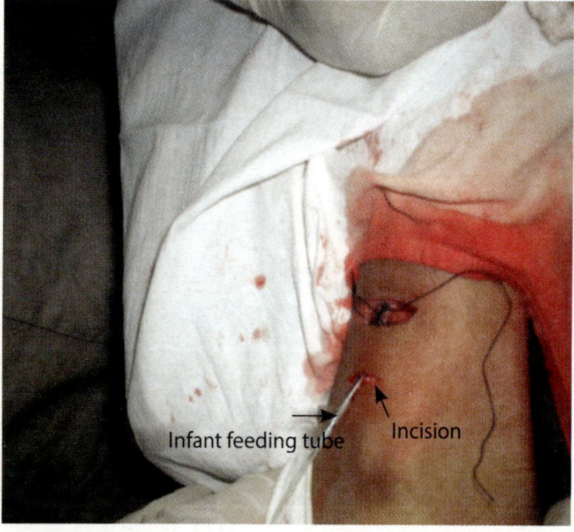

Figure 6.113 Infant feeding tube is being inserted through separate incision.

- Tie the proximal ligature, in order to secure the proximal vessel wall to the tube.
- Fix the tube to skin.
- Close skin with Ethilon 3'-0 vertical mattress stitch.
- Apply sterile dressing.

Fluid may not go freely in case of counterpuncture, blocked cannula, or spasm of vein.

POSTOPERATIVE CARE

- Daily dressing of local wound
- Daily flushing of infant feeding tube with diluted heparin
- Checking for the local complications and DVT

COMPLICATIONS

- Infection
- Bleeding
- Superficial thrombophlebitis
- DVT
- Through and through puncture, leading to perforation of posterior wall

Prevention of Complications

- Thrombophlebitis. It may be prevented by:
  - Changing of IV line every 48–72 hours
  - Daily flush of IV line with diluted heparin
  - Treatment by local application of hirudin ointment
  - Anti-inflammatory drugs
- Blockage
  - Flush with normal saline or diluted heparin
  - Injury to neighboring nerve

Recommended IV cannula in venepuncture is listed in Table 6.6.

Table 6.6 Recommended Cannulae for Different Uses

Size/color of cannulae	Uses
22 G (blue) and 24 G (yellow)	Pediatric patients
20 G (pink)	Adult patients, for IV fluids and drugs
18 G (green)	IV fluids, drugs, and blood transfusion
16 G (gray)	Large amount of IV fluids and blood transfusion

CENTRAL VENOUS ACCESS

Catheter placed in the central venous system, mainly either subclavian or internal jugular veins, terminates in the vena cava. It can be placed by either percutaneous technique or open procedure.

Two veins are commonly used for central venous access: subclavian and internal jugular.

- Subclavian approach

- Site of insertion: 1 cm caudal and 1 cm medial to the midpoint of the clavicle, with needle entering the vein at the junction of middle and medial thirds of the clavicle
- Easier catheter site care
- More comfortable for the patients

- Internal jugular venous access
  - *Site of insertion*: Middle approach (at the apex of triangle formed by two heads of the sternocleidomastoid muscle)
  - *Posterior approach*: Three fingerbreadths above the clavicle at the posterior border of sternocleidomastoid muscle

Other veins used for central venous access are: External jugular and femoral. Subclavian insertion is associated with a lower rate of infection. It has also been associated with a higher rate of pneumothorax and insertion failure. Jugular access is preferable in patients with respiratory compromise. We generally do not prefer femoral cannulation due to higher rate of infectious and thromboembolic complications. In addition, it also limits ambulation (Table 6.7).

Table 6.7 Average Fasting Interval That Has Minimal Deleterious Effect on the Body of Otherwise Healthy Individual According to Age

Age (years)	Fasting interval (days)
<60	12–14
60–80	7–8
>80	5–6

INDICATIONS

- Inadequate peripheral access
- Monitoring of central venous pressure, venous oxyhemoglobin saturation
- Parenteral nutrition: Those patients who are at risk of nutrition-related complications such as serum albumin <3 g/dL in stable patients and weight loss >10% of body weight or a current body weight at <80–85% of the ideal body weight
- Hemodialysis
- Plasmapheresis
- Administration of chemotherapy or vasopressor agent

CONTRAINDICATIONS

- Vascular injury proximal to placement site
- Coagulopathy

TECHNIQUE FOR RIGHT INTERNAL JUGULAR VEIN CANNULATION

- Choose the site and local infiltration at the cannulation site (if possible, identify the vein with ultrasound) (Fig. 6.114).
- Insert the angiocatheter or needle (Fig. 6.115). Confirm venous location with aspiration of blood (Fig. 6.116).
- Introduce the guidewire into the vein through the access needle or angiocatheter (Fig. 6.116).
- Remove the needle or angiocatheter while holding the guidewire.

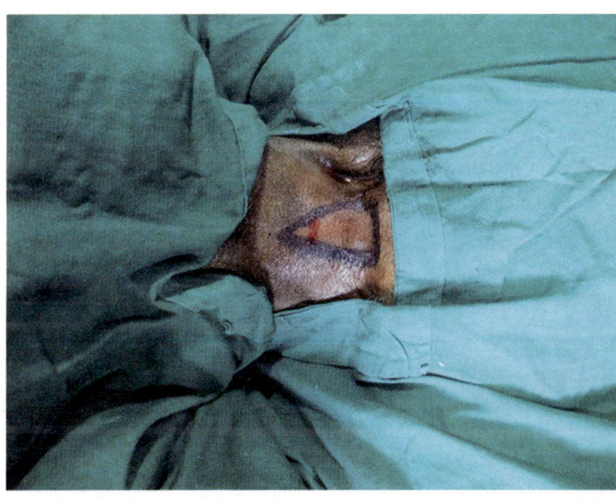

Figure 6.114 Site of insertion at the apex of triangle formed by two heads of the sternocleidomastoid muscle.

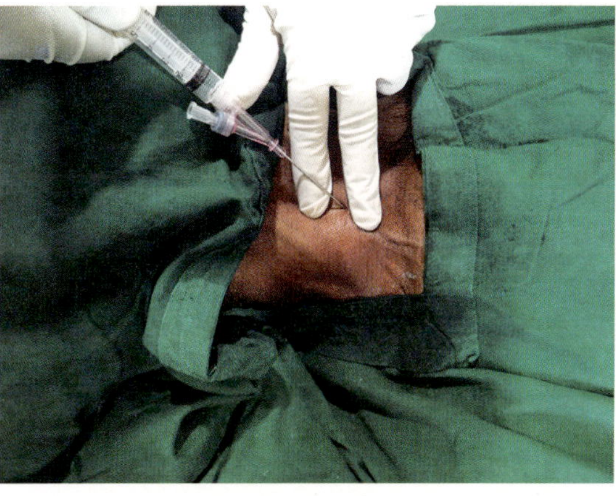

Figure 6.115 Insertion of needle.

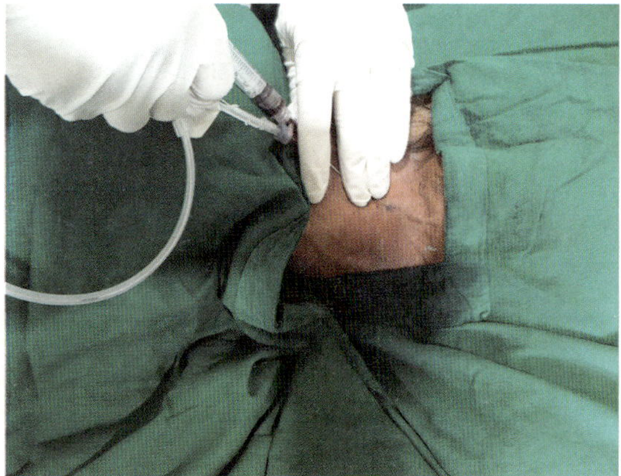

Figure 6.116 Aspiration of blood confirms the location and insertion of the guidewire.

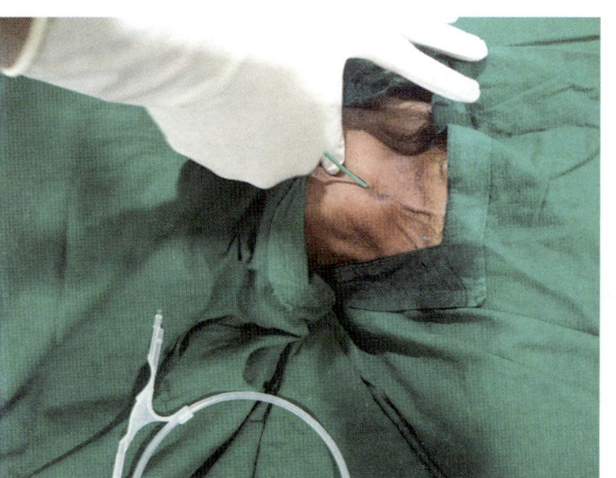

Figure 6.117 Dilatation of the tract over guidewire.

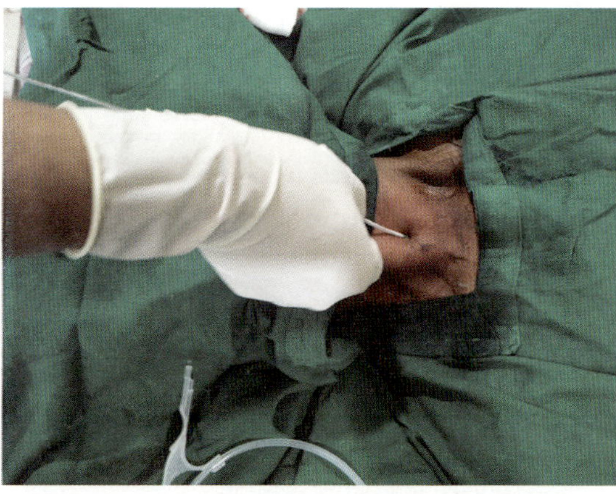

Figure 6.118 Insertion of the catheter over the guidewire.

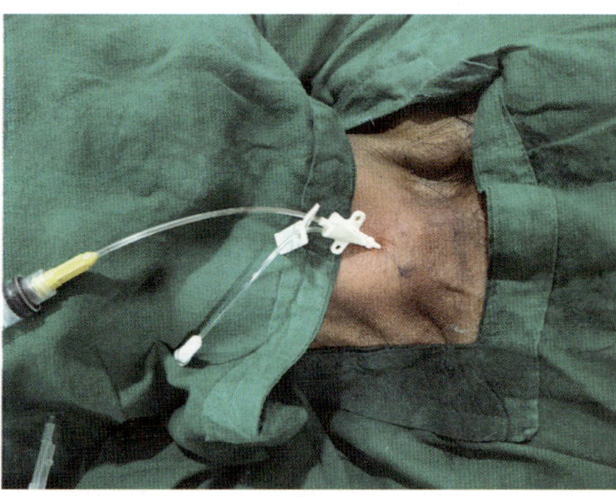

Figure 6.119 Position of central venous catheter after removal of guidewire.

- Small incision is made over the skin with stab knife adjacent to the guidewire.
- Dilate the tract over the guidewire into the vein (Fig. 6.117).
- Insert the catheter over the guidewire (Fig. 6.118).
- Remove the guidewire.
- Confirm the position again with aspiration of blood from each access hub (Fig. 6.119) and flush with saline to check the patency.
- Fix the catheter with stitch.
- Apply sterile dressing.
- Confirm the position of the tip of the catheter with chest X-ray (tip should be in the superior vena cava or at the junction of the vena cava and the subclavian or innominate vein).

POSTOPERATIVE CARE

- Inspect catheter site every other day. Presence of infection or purulent discharge from the catheter site is an indication for changing catheter. Although chances of infection increase after a week of placement, change of catheter is not routinely recommended
- Gauze dressing should be changed every third day and transparent dressing on the seventh day (gauze dressing is associated with less chances of wound infection as compared to transparent dressing).
- Intravenous infusion set is changed on the fourth day.
- Cap all stopcocks when not in use.

- Continuous infusion of normal saline in low dose or flushing with low-dose heparin is used to prevent blockage or thrombosis of the catheter.

COMPLICATIONS

- Immediate (acronym: PATH)
  - **P**neumothorax
  - **A**ccidental puncture of the artery
  - **A**ir embolism
  - **A**rrhythmia
  - **T**horacic duct injury with left side subclavian or internal jugular vein cannulation
  - **H**emorrhage
  - **H**emothorax
- Delayed (acronym: TIME)
  - Central venous catheter (CVC) **t**hrombosis
  - **I**nfection
  - Nerve **i**njury
  - **M**igration of catheter
  - **M**yocardial perforation
  - **E**mbolization of catheter

INTERCOSTAL DRAINAGE (ICD)

An intercostal drain is a flexible plastic tube that is inserted through the chest wall into the pleural space. Drainage of the pleural space by means of an ICD tube is the commonest intervention in thoracic trauma.

INDICATIONS

- Collapse of lung, secondary to pneumothorax, hydropneumothorax, or pleural effusion
- Empyema
- Post-thoracotomy
- Collapse of lung due to blunt thoracic trauma (hemothorax, hemopneumothorax)
- Pleurodesis to facilitate the instillation of sclerosing agents in case of refractory effusion
- Spreading surgical emphysema
- Patients with penetrating chest wall injury who are intubated or about to be intubated
- Chylothorax

CONTRAINDICATIONS

- Absolute: Need for emergency thoracotomy
- Relative
  - Profound coagulopathy
  - Pulmonary bullae
  - Pleural, pulmonary, or thoracic adhesion

Before ICD insertion, X-ray chest (PA and lateral views) should be carefully examined.

OPERATIVE TECHNIQUE

- Anesthesia: LA is given (Fig. 6.120).
- Good anatomical knowledge is required.
- Keep the patient in 45° head-up position on back rest.
- Turn the patient's head to the opposite side.
- Mark the site of incision.
- Paint, drape, and isolate the part.
- Usual site of incision is in the *triangle of safety*.

Triangle of safety: Anterior to midaxillary line, above the level of nipple, and below and lateral to the pectoralis major muscle. Usually, this comes over the fifth or sixth intercostal.

- Cut skin with stab knife (Fig. 6.121).
- Cut subcutaneous tissue.
- Split muscle with artery forceps till the pleura is reached (Fig. 6.122).
- Open pleura on the superior border of underlying rib, to avoid injury to the neurovascular bundle.

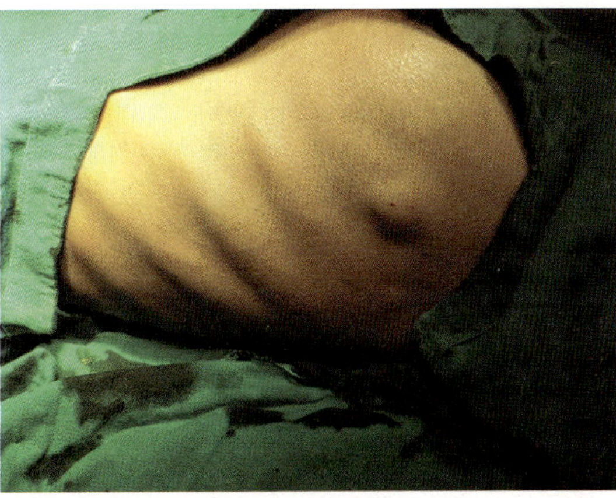

Figure 6.120 Injected local anesthesia at the site of insertion.

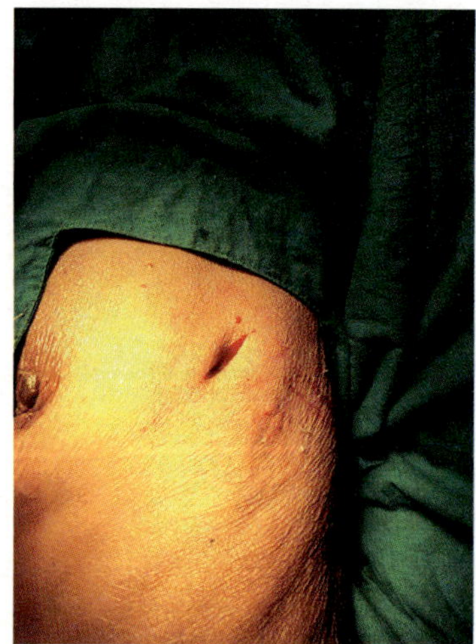

Figure 6.121 Skin cut.

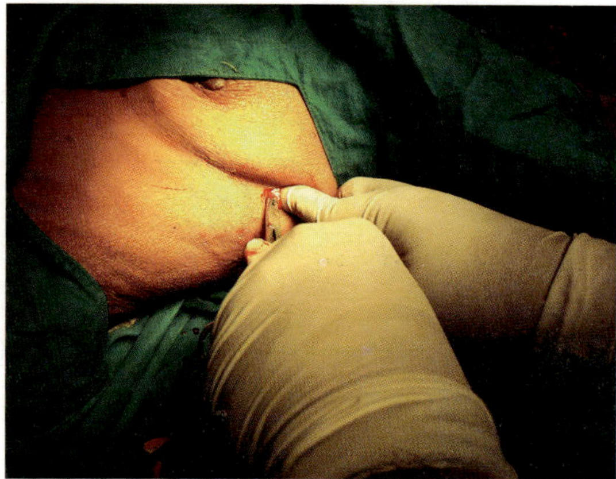

Figure 6.122 Splitting of the muscle.

- When pleura is opened, there is escape of fluid or air.
- ICD tube mounted on another artery forceps is introduced through the same oblique tract, into the pleura (Fig. 6.123). This will decrease the chance of entry of air.
- As the intercostal neurovascular bundle runs in groove on the lower border of each rib, so ICD tube should be passed at the upper border of the ribs.
- Insertion of the ICD tube lower than the sixth rib should be discouraged because during respiration, diaphragm can raise up to the fifth intercostal space.
- This tube is connected to an underwater seal drainage (saline is filled up to the mark on the ICD bag).

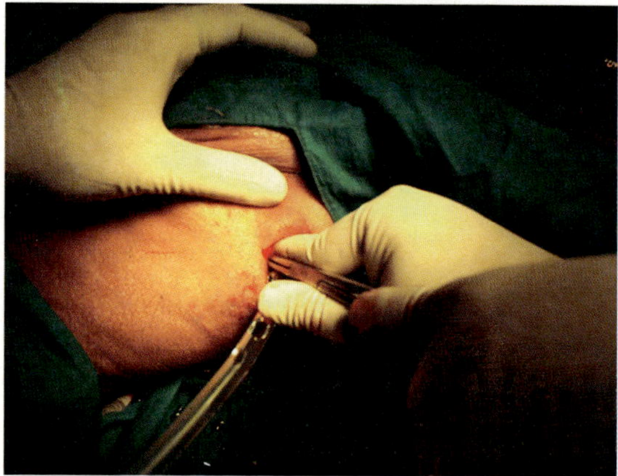

Figure 6.123 Insertion of ICD mounted over artery forceps.

- Drain pneumothorax toward the apex.
- Drain pleural effusion and empyema toward the base.
- All holes of the tubes must be inside the pleural cavity, to avoid surgical emphysema.

- Check:
  - Position of ICD
  - Column movement with respiration
  - Clinical improvement of the patient
  - Subsiding of tachycardia and tachypnea
  - Breathlessness decreased
  - Air entry improved
  - Chest X-ray showing lung expansion
  - Intercostal tube fixed with skin stitch (Fig. 6.124)

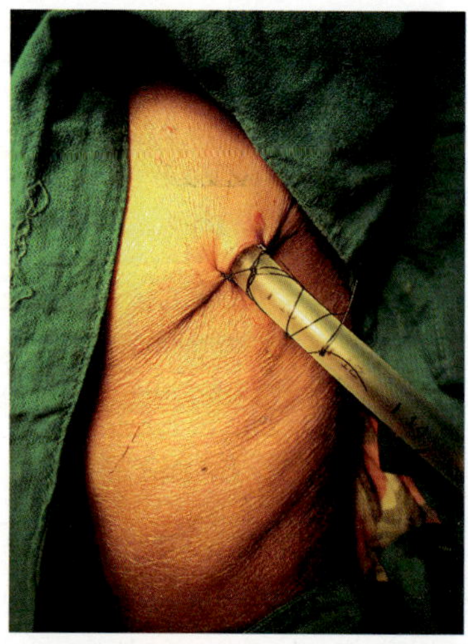

Figure 6.124 Fixing the ICD tube with either silk or nylon.

Figure 6.125 ICD bag kept below the level of chest and checked for contents.

- ICD bag kept below the level of the chest to avoid siphoning of the water seal back into the chest (Fig. 6.125)

POSTOPERATIVE CARE

- ICD care
  - Daily changing of drain fluid: Clean with normal saline; fill ICD bag till the water level mark with normal saline.
  - Milking and stripping of the tube is not recommended unless there is a clot.
  - Daily examine the drainage system for underwater seal, function, and kinking.
  - In the presence of air leak, drain should never be clamped, because of risk of tension pneumothorax.
  - Dressing is changed every third day.
  - Serial CXR: Evaluate progress of drainage and look for the most proximal hole.
- Chest physiotherapy: Remove sputum and maintain expansion (tipping [postural drainage] and incentive spirometry).
- Analgesics: Either NSAIDs or epidural anesthesia is given.
- Prophylactic antibiotics: Before insertion of tube and not more than 24 hours. Some authors found it beneficial but Society of Thoracic Surgeons Workforce on Evidence-Based Medicine found no benefit.
- Dressing is changed every third day.

REMOVAL OF ICD

Indications for Removal of ICD

- Nonfunctioning of ICD (column movement absent)
- Chest X-ray showing full expansion of lung
- Drainage 2 mL/kg/day

Technique of Removal

- Removal of ICD is painful. Give intravenous analgesic 30 minutes before procedure.
- Apply EMLA 3 hours before surgery.
- Cut stitch.
- Pull ICD tube with gauze pad in hand.
  It should be removed at the end of inspiration.
- Carry out immediate strapping with Elastoplast.
- X-ray done immediately and 24 hours later to rule out re accumulation.

Complications

- Infection
  - Risk of infection increased if kept >7 days
  - Nonsterile technique
- Blockage: Small drains more likely to get blocked leading to reaccumulation of blood and air, aggravating the condition
- Injury to surrounding structures
  - In case of insertion below the sixth rib and in traumatic rupture of diaphragm, injury to liver, spleen, or stomach can occur.
  - Bleeding due to intercostal or internal mammary vessel injury and rarely ICD tube entering the heart (usually in patients with cardiomegaly) can occur. Injury to the intercostal nerves may lead to neuritis.
- Failure to drain the pleural cavity: Due to either wrong placement or small drain
- Subcutaneous emphysema
- Local hematoma
- Postexpansion pulmonary edema: Due to rapid drainage of large effusion, so not recommended to drain more than 1 L fluid initially (it is more common in patients with diabetes, tension or large pneumothorax, and gross pleural effusion)
- Sudden increase in capillary permeability

- Pain: Small caliber, less rigid, silastic drain less painful
- Routinely, insert ICD, just anterior to the midaxillary line or in the midaxillary line (insertion posterior to midaxillary line—tube may get compressed while patient is lying on the back).
- Insertion into the second intercostal space is best avoided, because transfixation of the two major accessory respiratory muscles will occur (which help in respiration in case of collapsed lung).
- The first intercostal space, posteriorly, is preferred when apical drain is required.
- In adult patients, the usual number of ICD tube is more than 20 Fr, and in children, it depends on their age and distance between ribs.
- Size of the tube depends on the indications.
  - An uncomplicated spontaneous pneumothorax: 14-Fr chest tube. In patients with large air leak or bronchopleural fistula, 24–28 Fr. Tension pneumothorax, 24–28 Fr.
  - For trauma, one must be able to evacuate accumulations of blood, so a larger tube (32, 34, or 36 Fr) is required.
  - Empyema requires the largest tubes (32, 34, 40 Fr).
  - Malignant effusion: 14- to 18-Fr tube is required.
  - Problem which persists after 3 weeks of insertion of ICD requires surgical intervention in the form of thoracoscopy or thoracotomy.
- Author's preference is to keep ICD in the fifth intercostal space in midaxillary line. The reason for this preference is that air, fluid, and blood will find the tube; as the lung expands, these will follow the path of least resistance.
- Occult pneumothorax: It refers to pneumothorax that is not seen on initial chest radiograph but visible on CT scan.
- Indications for thoracotomy in trauma (refer Chapter 16, *Frequently Asked Questions*, page 430).

LYMPH NODE BIOPSY

A lymph node biopsy involves removal of lymph node tissue to be looked at under a microscope for signs of infection or a disease.

RELEVANT ANATOMY

- Lymph nodes: Lymph nodes are components of the lymphatic system and act as filters that collect and destroy bacteria and viruses. When the body is fighting an infection, lymphocytes multiply rapidly and produce a characteristic swelling of the lymph nodes.
- Lymph nodes are oval or kidney- or bean- shaped structures found along the length of lymphatics. They are 1–25 mm in size. They contain a slight depression on one side which is called hilum. In the hilum, nodal artery enters while efferent lymphatic and nodal veins leave. The lymphatic vessels that enter the lymph node are called afferent lymphatics. Each lymph node is covered by a capsule. Beneath the capsule, there is a subcapsular space. Fibrous connective tissue extends into the node and is called trabeculae. The lymphocytes and other cells make a dense aggregation of tissue called lymphatic nodule. Nodules surround the germinal center that produces lymphocytes.

FUNCTIONS OF LYMPH NODES

- Filtration of bacteria, effete cells, and antigens: Any microorganism or foreign substance in the lymph stimulates germinal center to produce lymphocytes. Lymphocytes are released into lymph and reach the blood and produce antibodies. The macrophages remove dead microorganisms and foreign substances via phagocytosis.
- Lymph nodes regulate protein content of efferent lymph.

SOME GOLDEN RULES FOR LYMPH NODE BIOPSY

- Any swelling in the region of lymph node should be considered to be arising from lymph node unless proved otherwise.
- Up to 1 cm submandibular and up to 2 cm inguinal lymph nodes are normally palpable,

without any pathology. Any other palpable lymph node should be considered pathological.

- Involvement of two or more lymph node regions, without anatomical continuity, is known as generalized lymphadenopathy.
- Order of preference in biopsy in case of generalized lymphadenopathy is: axillary > cervical > inguinal. This is because cervical lymphadenopathy can be nonspecific because of unknown septic focus and inguinal can be due to repeated trauma, caused by the habit of walking barefoot.
- Around 300 lymph nodes are present in the neck out of total 800 in the human body. Mesentery consist of 150 lymph nodes.
- While taking biopsy from lymph nodes, always take two intact lymph nodes, one for pathologist in formalin and one for microbiologist in saline.

RULES FOR BIOPSY IN GENERAL

- In a large lesion, to avoid sampling errors, take multiple biopsies.
- In a fungated or ulcerated lesion, take biopsy from the periphery and not from the center as central portion is most likely to have only necrotic tissue.
- Always take full-thickness biopsy if feasible.
- Avoid handling biopsy with traumatic instrument as it may lead to loss of architecture.
- Orientation of resected specimen is very important.
- Do not use electrocautery, cryoprobe, or laser to obtain biopsy as it may lead to loss of tissue.
- Do not use morcellator to retrieve specimen in minimal access surgery if tissue diagnosis is required.

TYPES OF BIOPSY

- Incisional (core) biopsy: When a part of the suspected lesion is removed, it is called an incisional biopsy.
- Excisional biopsy: When the whole of the suspected lesion is removed, it is called an excisional biopsy.
- Tru-Cut biopsy: The core of the tissue is removed with a Tru-Cut needle.
- Frozen section biopsy: This is indicated on an urgent basis when the patient is under anesthesia, because confirmation of diagnosis (benign or malignant) may change the type of operation that a patient should undergo. It is also helpful in evaluating margin of excised tumor to ascertain that the entire neoplasm has been removed. In this method, the tissue is frozen at about –25°C. Liquid nitrogen is used to freeze the tissue.
- Brush biopsy: It is used for skin or endoscopic biopsy.
- Sentinel lymph node biopsy: Sentinel lymph node is the first node that receives lymph flow from the primary tumor. A radiolabeled tracer or blue dye is used. The method is used in carcinoma breast, melanoma, and colon cancer.
- Fine needle aspiration cytology (FNAC): A fine needle (no. 22, 23) is used to aspirate the tissue.
  - Advantages:
    - OPD procedure
    - No anesthesia
    - Safe and painless
    - Rapid results obtained
  - Disadvantages:
    - Will not distinguish between follicular adenoma and follicular carcinoma in thyroid
    - Not possible to distinguish between in situ and invasive cancer in solid tissue
    - Pathologist cannot study the architecture of the lymph node.

OPERATIVE TECHNIQUE

- Procedure for inguinal lymph node (Fig. 6.126) biopsy.
- Anesthesia: LA is given.
- Carry out painting, draping, and isolation of the part.
- Inject LA along the crease line and into surroundings.
- Make an incision with a knife.
- Cut the skin (Fig. 6.127).
- Cut the subcutaneous tissue.
- If it is superficial, then identify it and hold with a Babcock's forceps.
- Dissect it free from surrounding tissues by blunt dissection (Fig. 6.128).
- Identify the feeding vessel—Catch, cauterize, and cut it (Fig. 6.129).
- Excise the lymph node (Fig. 6.130). Send for HPE.
- Check for hemostasis (Fig. 6.131).
- Close the skin with Mersilk or Ethilon 3-0 vertical mattress suture.
- Apply sterile dressing.

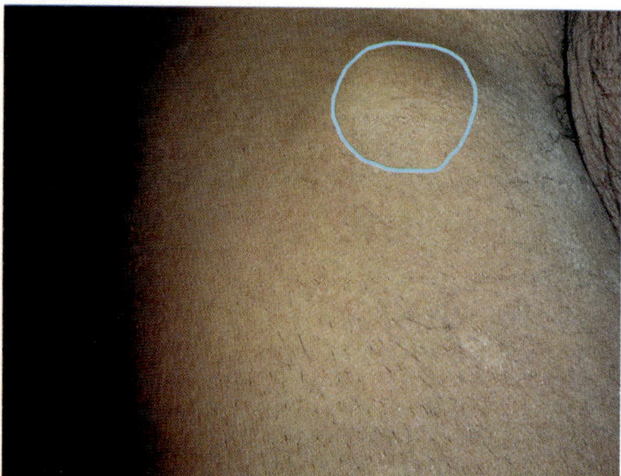

Figure 6.126 Visible swelling in the inguinal region that is confirmed to be inguinal lymph node by clinical examination and ultrasonography.

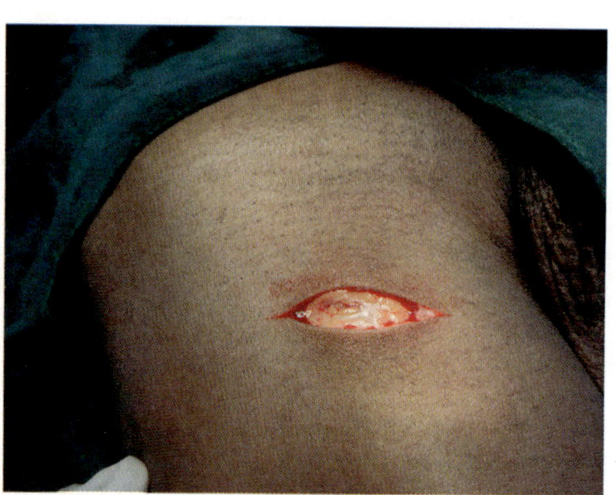

Figure 6.127 Cut skin.

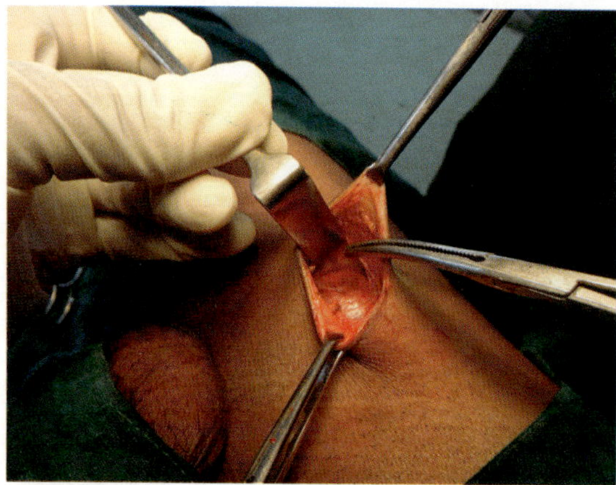

Figure 6.128 Dissecting from the surrounding structure.

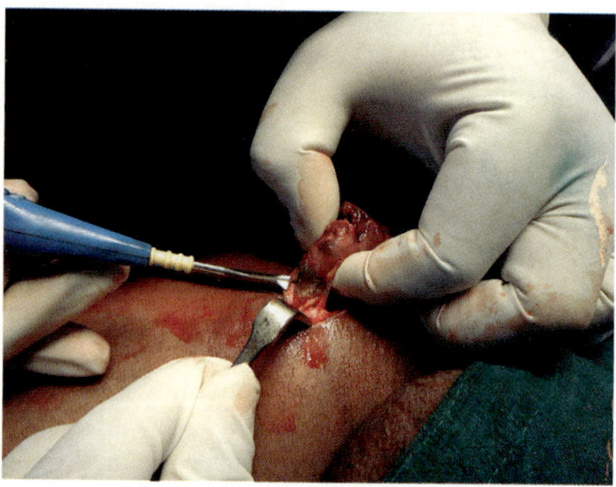

Figure 6.129 Feeding vessel cauterized and dissecting node from the base.

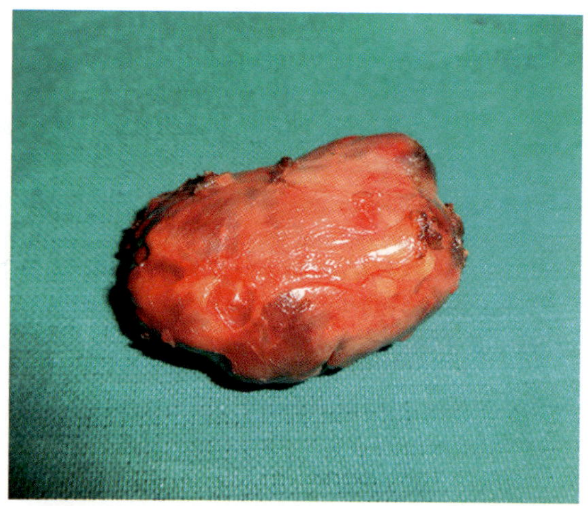

Figure 6.130 Lymph node specimen.

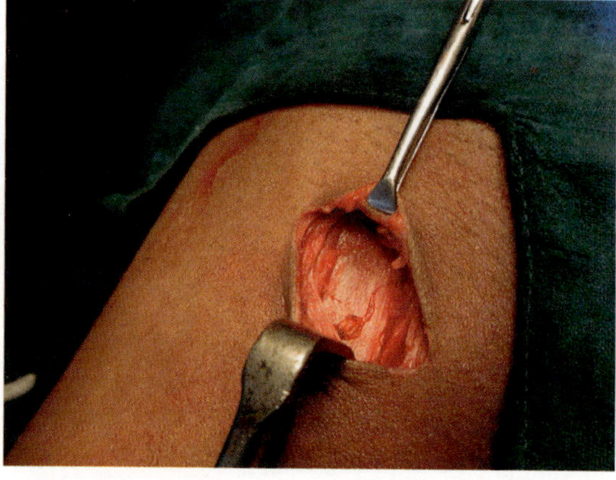

Figure 6.131 Clean area after proper hemostasis.

Postoperative Treatment

- Antibiotics
- Analgesics
- Stitch removal after 7 days

Complications

- Primary hemorrhage
- Injury to surrounding structure
- Damage to spinal accessory nerve (SAN)
- Stitch abscess
- Sinus formation (in TB)

- In case of a cervical lymph node, if it is deep, it requires incising the investing layer of deep cervical fascia.
- In case of lymphadenopathy, first take FNAC. If it is inconclusive, go for Tru-Cut, incision, or excision biopsy.
- Before carrying out lymph node biopsy, the surgeon must have a thorough knowledge of anatomy, because most lymph nodes are in close proximity to major vessels.
- Cut surface of the lymph node gives an idea about diagnosis:
  - Caseation in tuberculosis
  - Diffuse and fleshy in Hodgkin lymphoma
  - Solid lesion in metastasis
- Lymphatic organs in the body: These include tonsil, spleen, thymus gland, and Peyer patches in small intestines.

CLW SUTURING

CLW stands for contused lacerated wound, a combination of contused and lacerated wounds.

In a contused wound, there are injuries to the cellular tissue, but the skin is intact. A lacerated wound is an open wound where the edges of the wound are torn irregularly.

CLASSIFICATION OF WOUNDS

In general, wounds may be classified as:

- Closed: Contused
- Open
  - Incised (caused by sharp cutting instruments; evenly cut edges)
  - Lacerated
  - Punctured (penetrating) (caused by sharp and slender objects, which pass through skin and go into the underlying tissue)
  - Perforated (penetrating wounds that extend into the viscus or body cavity)

OPERATIVE TECHNIQUE

- As most of the CLWs have legal implications, make careful notes; draw a diagram.
- Anesthesia: LA is given for small CLW (Fig. 6.132), and LA plus TIVA and IV analgesics or regional for large or multiple CLWs.
- Carry out painting, draping, and isolation of the part.
- Thoroughly wash the wound with Betadine and hydrogen peroxide.
- Administer anesthesia depending on the site, size, and number of wounds.
- Closure of CLW: Insert the needle approximately 4 mm from the wound edge (Fig. 6.133a). Pass the needle from the opposite wound edge at the exact same distance (Fig. 6.133b).
- Tie the knot (Fig. 6.134).
- Closed CLW (Fig. 6.135)
- In case of superficial wounds: Use subcutaneous stitch with poliglecaprone or chromic catgut 3-0, skin with Mersilk 3-0 or Ethilon 3-0 vertical mattress suture.
- In case of deep wounds: Use muscle approximated with Vicryl 3-0 intermittent stitch.

- CLWs over face should be closed with monofilament 4-0 subcuticular stitch, for cosmetic reasons.
- Hemostasis should always be checked and achieved.
- All patients with CLW should receive prophylaxis against tetanus.
- All patients should receive prophylactic antibiotics, active against Gram-positive organisms.
- If wound is contaminated or dirty, or more than 8 hours old, or wound is due to animal bite, closure should be deferred for delayed primary closure.
- If there is skin loss and it is not possible to close the wound primarily, then do primary grafting if the wound is clean. If the wound is dirty, then defer for delayed primary closure or grafting.

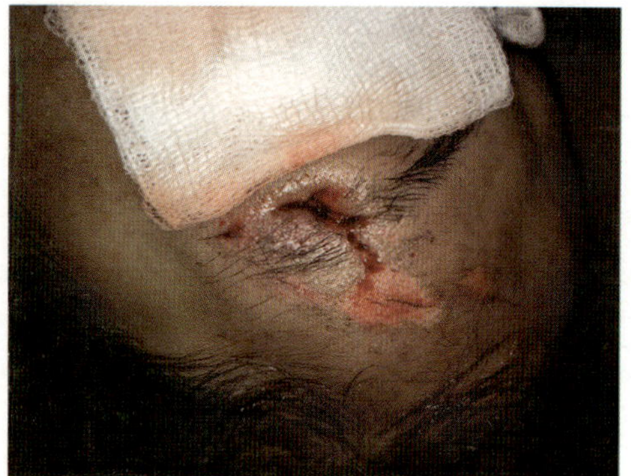

Figure 6.132 CLW.

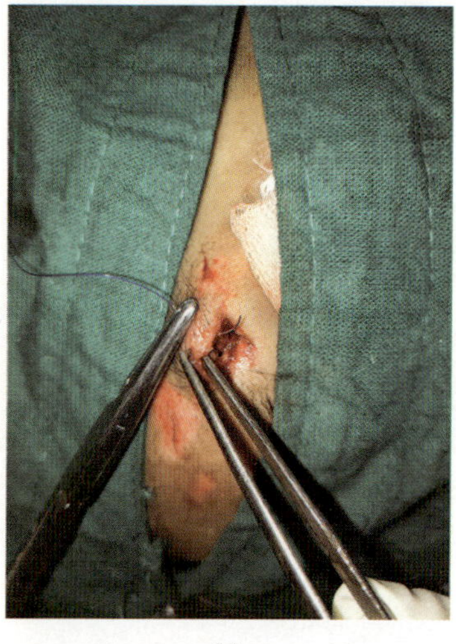

(a)

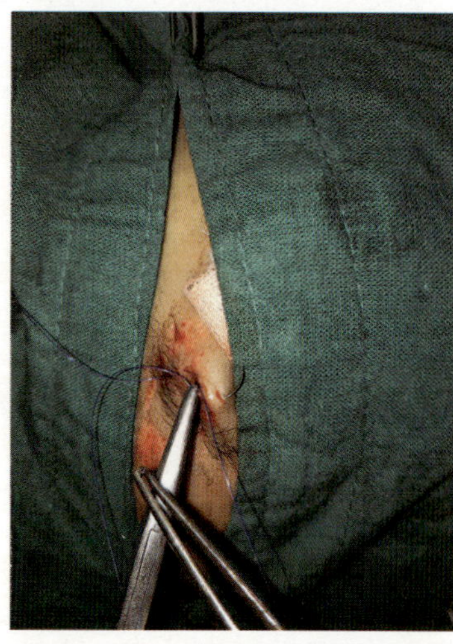

(b)

Figure 6.133 (a) First bite for closure of CLW. (b) Second bite for closure of CLW.

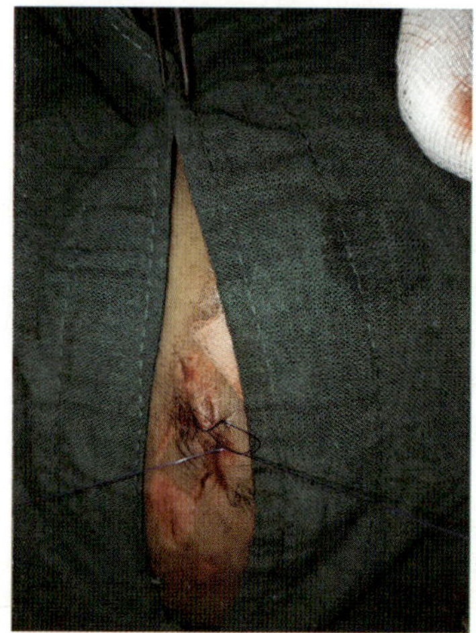

Figure 6.134 Knot tying.

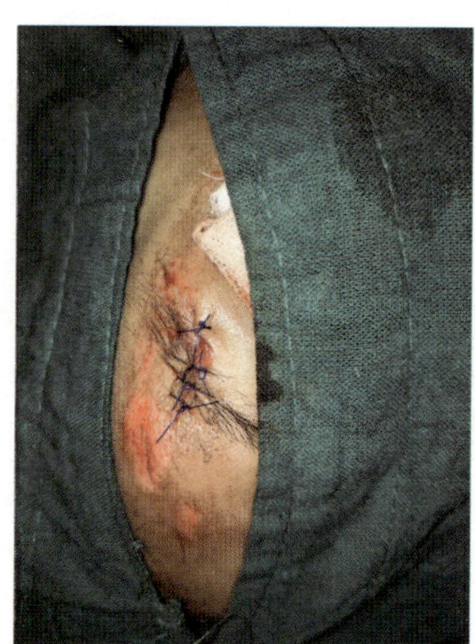

Figure 6.135 Closed CLW.

RECONSTRUCTIVE LADDER

- Direct primary closure
- Delayed primary closure
- Skin grafting
- Local flap
- Pedicle flap
- Free flap or free tissue transfer

VARIOUS METHODS OF SKIN CLOSURE

Following are the commonly used methods for skin closure:

- Vertical mattress (Figs 6.136–6.139): The vertical mattress suture is initiated by inserting the needle

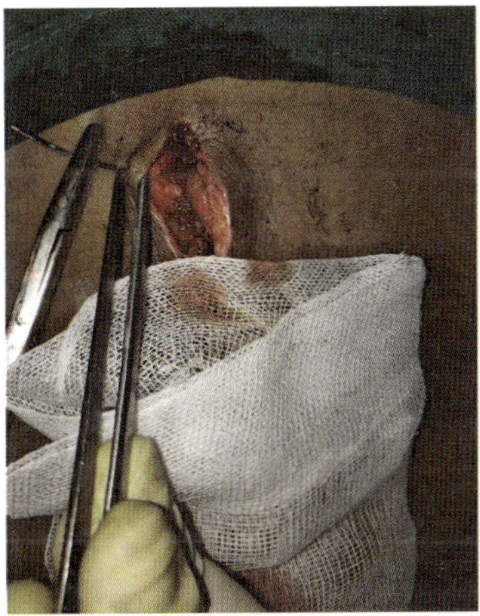

Figure 6.136 The vertical mattress suture is initiated by inserting the needle approximately 4 mm from wound edge (far bite).

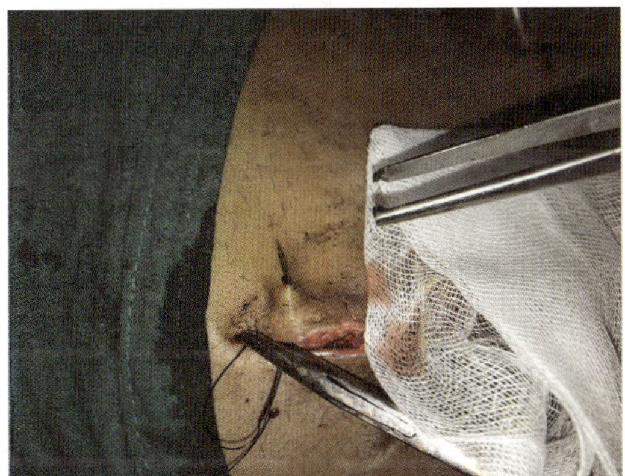

Figure 6.137 The needle passes through to the opposite wound edge, where it exits the skin. Vertical mattress suture is the most commonly used suture. It is used to evert the skin edge.

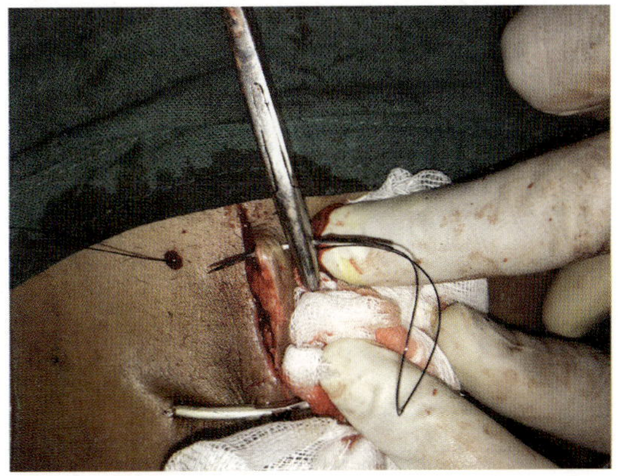

Figure 6.138 First near bite (as close as possible to edge) is taken by reversing the needle on needle holder.

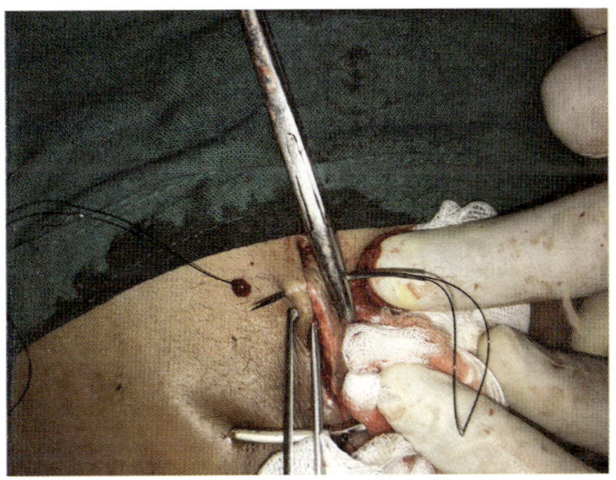

Figure 6.139 Second near bite by passing the needle at same distance (as close as possible to wound edge).

approximately 4 mm from wound edge (far bite). The needle passes through to the opposite wound edge, where it exits the skin. Vertical mattress suture is the most commonly used suture. It is used to evert the skin edge.

- Horizontal mattress: It is sometimes used in scalp and in tension closure of burst abdomen (Figs 6.140–6.144).
- Subcuticular stitch: It is cosmetically better; no stitch marks are left on the skin. Prerequisite—there should be no tension on the skin (Figs 6.145–6.147).
- Skin stapler can also be used.
- Wound closure strips (Steri-Strip™): Before applying it, skin must be perfectly dried; there should not be any oozing and approximation should be good.

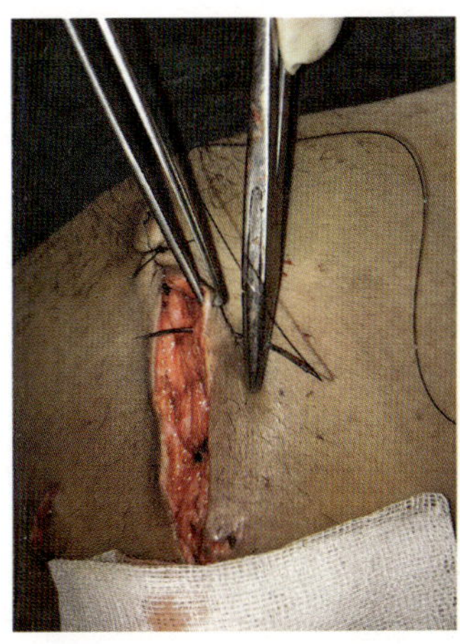

Figure 6.140 The horizontal mattress suture is initiated by inserting the needle approximately 8 mm from wound edge.

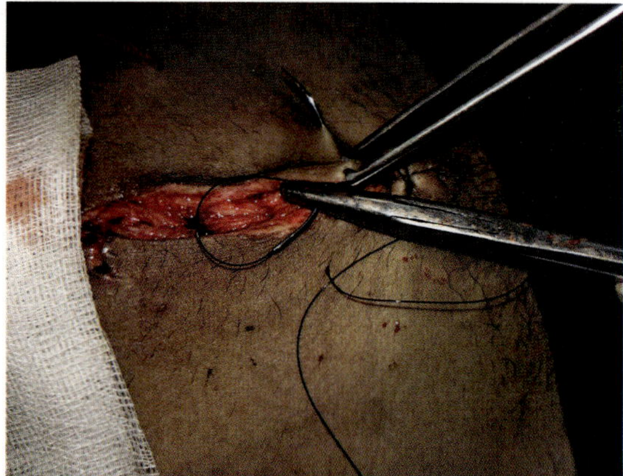

Figure 6.141 The needle passes through the opposite wound edge where it exits the skin.

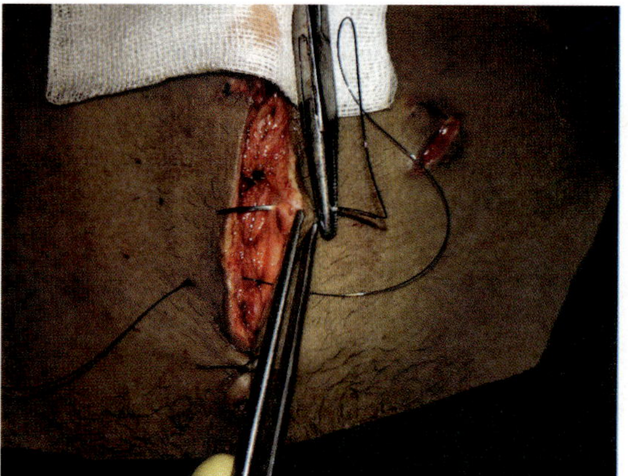

Figure 6.142 The needle is placed backwards in the needle holder, inserted into the skin about 8 mm farther down that edge, and passed from the far side of the wound back to the near side.

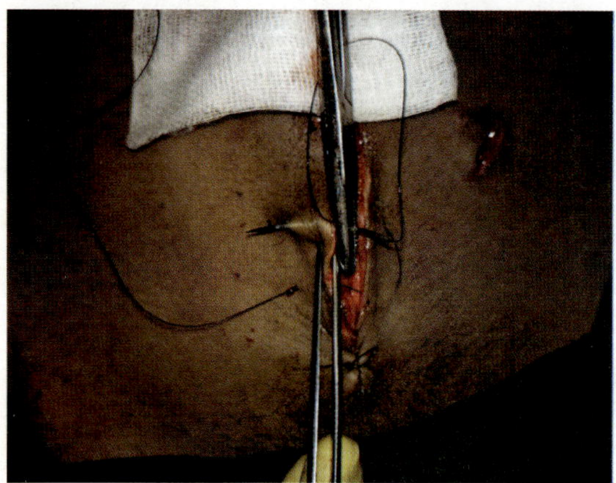

Figure 6.143 The needle exits the skin about 8 mm down the original wound edge from the original insertion site.

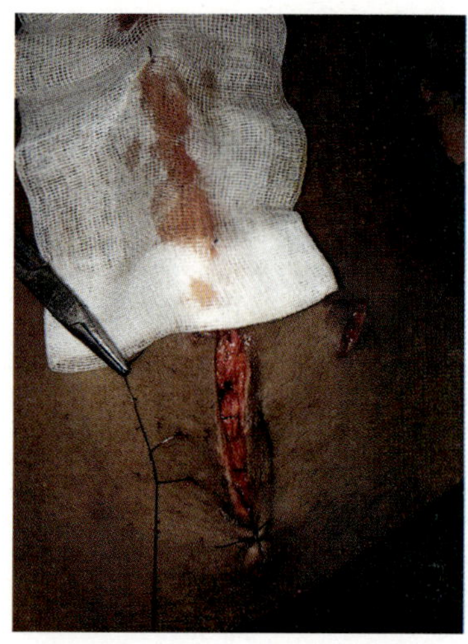

Figure 6.144 Knot tying.

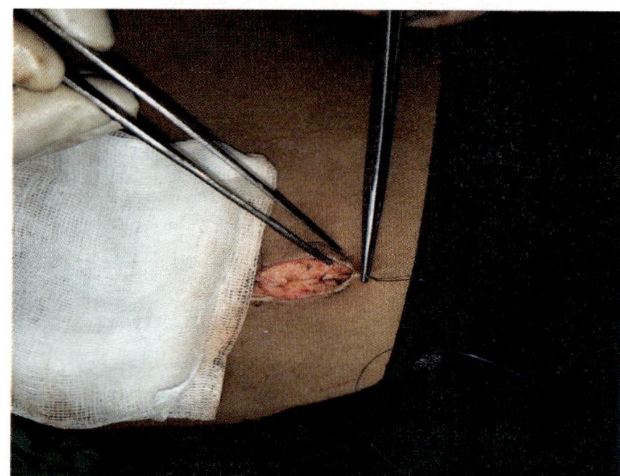

Figure 6.145 Subcuticular stitch is initiated by passing the needle from the corner of the wound.

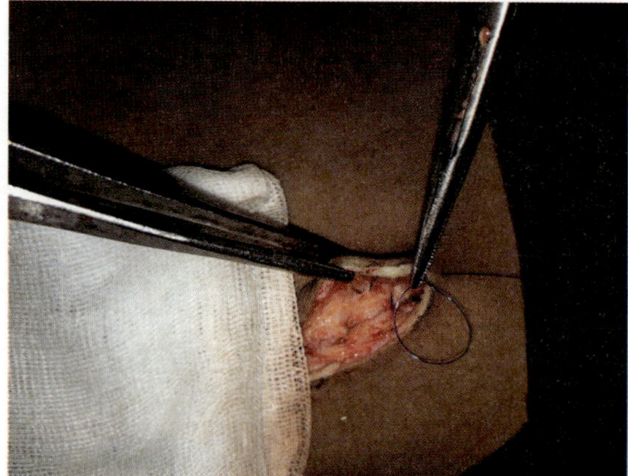

Figure 6.146 Stitch is taken through subcuticular tissue by passing the needle as shown in the figure for approximately 5 mm and exit on the same side.

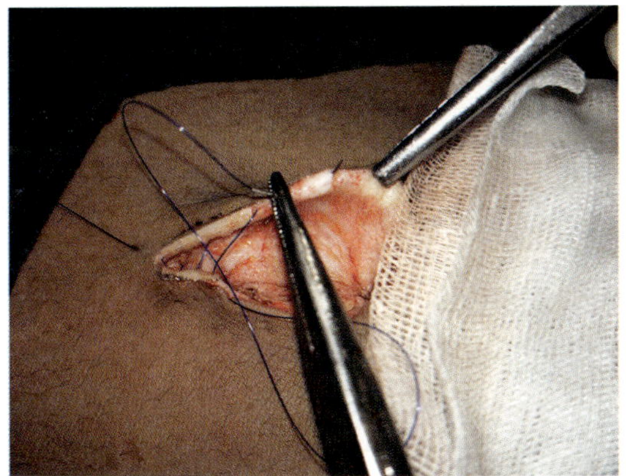

Figure 6.147 Stitch is taken in the same manner as shown in Figure 6.146 on the opposite side.

POSTOPERATIVE

- Analgesic
- Antibiotic

Suggested removal time for interrupted suture at various sites of the body is given in Table 6.8.

Table 6.8 Suggested Removal Time for Interrupted Suture

Body part	Time of removal of suture
Scalp	7–8 days
Face	5–7 days
Neck	7–8 days
Trunk	7–10 days
Upper limb	10–14 days
Lower limb	15–20 days
Exterior surface of hand	14 days

FIBROADENOMA EXCISION

Fibroadenomas are lumps made up of normal fibrous and glandular tissue. These may be due to:

- Aberration of normal lobular development
- Proliferation of both connective tissue and epithelium

CHARACTERISTICS

- Develops from the stroma of lobules of breast
- Age of presentation: 15–25 years (lobular development is most active in this age group)
- Solitary, well capsulated, spherical, discoid
- Cut surface: Firm, gray white, slightly myxoid, with slit-like spaces
- Lump in the breast, which is firm and nontender
- Freely mobile (known as breast mouse)
- Ten percent of cases presenting with multiple fibroadenomas
- <1 cm: normal; 1–3 cm: disorder; >3 cm: disease; multiple fibroadenoma: disease
- Second most common tumor of breast after carcinoma and most common tumor of breast in females younger than 30 years

ETIOLOGY

Hypersensitivity of estrogen within a lobule

TYPES

- *Pericanalicular*: Connective tissue stroma surrounds the duct circumferentially.
- *Intracanalicular*: Connective tissue stroma is compressed adjacent to the duct.

DIAGNOSIS

Fibroadenoma is usually a clinical diagnosis; no other investigation is required.

- USG provides an accurate diagnosis.
- In case of doubt, carry out FNAC and mammography (well-marginated density against radiolucent background). At menopause, fibroadenoma may involute, turning into mass of hyaline fibrous tissue leading to popcorn calcification. In FNAC findings, high number of ductal and stromal cell and bare nuclei in staghorn configuration is characteristic of fibroadenoma.

TREATMENT

- In a woman of age less than 30 years, if the lump is <3 cm, it does not require excision, unless:
  - It is associated with suspected cytology.
  - Patient desires to remove the lump.
  - It is a very large lump.
- Other modes of treatment of fibroadenoma
  - Vacuum-assisted core needle removal
  - Cryoablation
- Fibroadenoma may increase in size from 1 to 3 cm in 5 years; active growth phase is for 12 months. After that, it becomes static or gradually subsides.
- For patients >30 years, it requires excision.

Operative Technique

- Anesthesia: LA or GA is given.
- Position: The patient is made to lie in supine position.
- Carry out painting, draping, and isolation of the part done.
- Incision: It is circumareolar or radial (Fig. 6.148).
- Cut the skin (Fig. 6.148).
- Cut the subcutaneous tissue.
- Blunt dissection with artery forceps till the capsule is identified.
- Use a traction suture over the lump (Fig. 6.149).
- Perform dissection around the fibroadenoma to make it free from the surrounding tissue (Fig. 6.150) and remove it (Fig. 6.151).
- Achieve hemostasis with electrocautery.

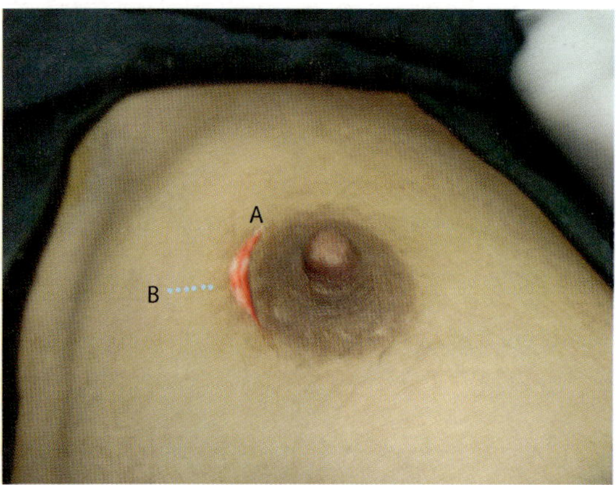

Figure 6.148 Circumareolar incision (A) and radial incision (B).

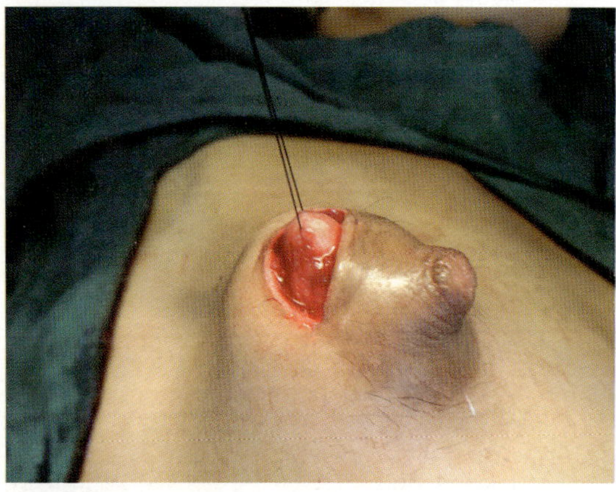

Figure 6.149 Traction suture over the lump.

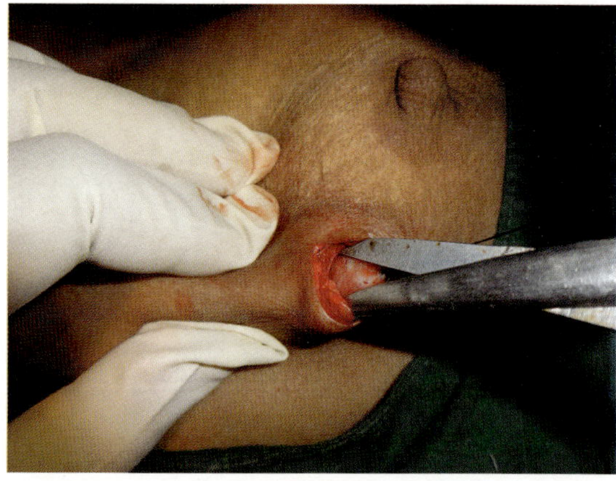

Figure 6.150 Freeing fibroadenoma from the surroundings.

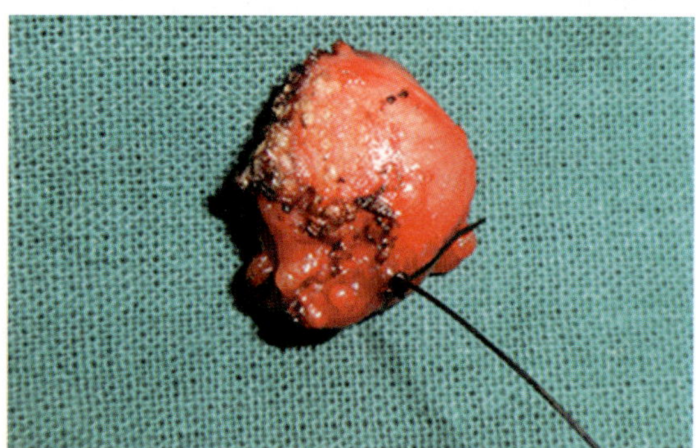

Figure 6.151 Excised fibroadenoma.

- Approximate subcutaneous tissue with rapid Vicryl.
- Close skin with Prolene 4-0 subcuticular stitch.
- Apply dressing.

Postoperative care

- NBM for 4 hours, if operation done under GA
- Analgesics as and when required
- Change of dressing and suture removal after 7 days

Complications

- Wound infection
- Recurrence

SPECIAL CASES

Aberration of Normal Development and Involution (ANDI)

Breast is considered to be a dynamic structure. It undergoes numerous changes throughout the life of a woman, and these changes are so extensive that sometimes we cannot call these normal. Such changes should be regarded as a disorder rather than a disease.

Clinical features

- Breast pain is the most common presentation. It may be:
  - Cyclical
  - Bilateral
  - More just prior to menstruation
  - Waxing and waning
  - In upper and outer quadrant
- Nodularity: Presence of nodularity that might be tender and changes with next cycle
- Lump: Fibroadenoma, cyst, fibroadenosis
- Nipple discharge: Due to duct ectasia or galactorrhea

Various suggested theories

- Excessive estrogen
- Abnormal prolactin secretion
- Inadequate essential fatty acid intake

Investigations

Triple assessment:

- *Clinical*: Examination of the breast
- *Radiological*: Ultrasound and mammography
- *Pathological*: FNAC or biopsy

Treatment

- Reassurance
- Adequate support with bra
- Avoiding caffeine
- Excluding cancer
- Danazol: 200–400 mg/day (inhibitory effect on ovarian estrogen production)
- Tamoxifen: 10 mg/day (antiestrogen)
- Evening primrose oil: 320 mg/day (gamolenic acid: Reverses the imbalance between saturated and unsaturated fats)

Giant Fibroadenoma

- >5 cm
- Intracanalicular fibroadenoma
- Treatment: Excision

Duct Papilloma

- Altered blood-stained nipple discharge (most common cause of bloody nipple discharge)
- Lump in the breast
- Benign, mostly solitary, and <1 cm in size
- Cytology: Ductal cells with papillary formation
- Ductography: Small filling defects
- Treatment: Microdochectomy via tennis racquet incision

Do not express blood prior to surgery as it may then be difficult to identify the duct.

Breast cyst

- It originates from the terminal ductal lobular unit.
- It occurs in the last decade of reproductive life.
- Breast stroma and epithelium undergo repeated integrated involution and cyst originates as a by-product of this process.
- Single or multiple asymptomatic masses or tender, painful masses may be present.
- Treatment
  - Aspiration
  - If fluid is clear and completely resolves, then no further treatment needed
    - Excision is required if cyst recurs more than two times following aspiration, residual lump, blood-stained fluid, or cytology reveals atypia (to rule out cystadenocarcinoma).

MODIFIED RADICAL MASTECTOMY

ANATOMY OF THE FEMALE BREAST

The female breast is a modified sweat gland in the subcutaneous tissue located between the second and the sixth rib. It is loosely attached to the underlying pectoral, axillary, and superficial abdominal fascia. Suspensory ligaments of Cooper run from the deep fascia to the skin and additionally support the breast and are responsible for dimpling of skin in carcinoma of the breast.

- Arterial supply: Internal thoracic or internal mammary via perforating branch
- Venous drainage into axillary vein
- Lymphatic drainage: Axillary (75%) and internal mammary nodes
- Axillary nodes
  - *Lower axillary group (level I)*: Lateral to pectoralis minor

- *Middle axillary group (level II)*: Along the pectoralis minor
- *Upper infraclavicular group (level I)*: Medial to pectoralis minor
- Rotter node: Interpectoral node

- Nerve supply: Lateral and anterior cutaneous branch of second to sixth intercostal nerves (sensory)
- Nerves in the axilla
  - Motor nerve
    - *Long thoracic nerve*: It is also known as nerve to serratus anterior (injury to nerve results in winged scapula).
    - *Thoracodorsal nerve*: It is also known as nerve to latissimus dorsi (injury to nerve results in weakness in arm adduction and medial rotation).
    - *Medial pectoral nerve*: It supplies lateral third of pectoralis major muscle and injury to nerve results in atrophy of lateral third of pectoralis major muscle.
  - Sensory nerve
    - *Intercostobrachial nerve*: Injury to the nerve results in numbness in the posterior and medial aspect of upper arm.

Complete removal of the breast and the underlying pectoralis major fascia along with the axillary lymph node dissection. MRM or Patey's mastectomy: Pectoralis major muscle, pectoralis minor excised. Patey's mastectomy has two modifications:

- *Scanlon*: Pectoralis major muscle preserved, pectoralis minor divided from coracoid process but not excised
- *Auchincloss*: Both pectoralis major and pectoralis minor muscles preserved

INDICATIONS

- Biopsy-proven axillary nodes in case of carcinoma of the breast
- Carcinoma of the breast candidate not suitable for breast conservation surgery:
  - Multicentric disease
  - Diffuse microcalcification on mammography
  - Pregnancy
  - Positive margin after excision
  - Prior radiation exposure to the breast
  - Patient's wish

PREOPERATIVE PREPARATION

- Prophylactic antibiotic with Gram-positive coverage
- DVT prophylaxis
- Anesthesia: GA

OPERATIVE TECHNIQUE

- Do painting, draping, and isolation of part.
- Either transverse elliptical (Stewart incision—for central and subareolar tumor) or oblique elliptical (Orr incision—for upper and outer quadrant tumor) incision is kept (Fig. 6.152).
- Cut skin.
- Cut subcutaneous tissue; raise the upper flap till clavicle (Fig. 6.153) and lower one (Fig. 6.154) depending on the need of surgery or up to the superior aspect of the rectus sheath.
- Divide the pectoral and clavipectoral fascia.

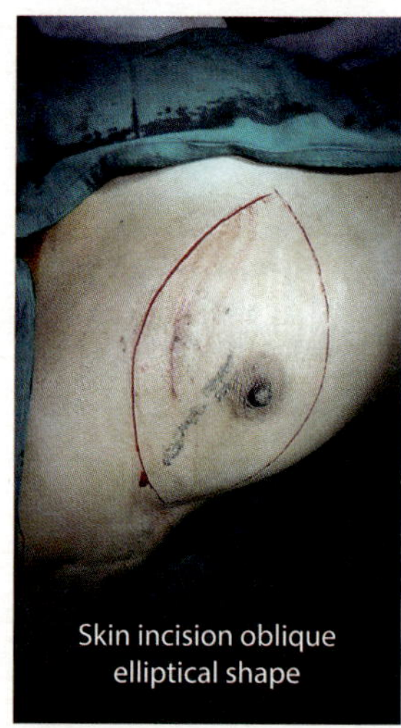

Figure 6.152 Oblique elliptical incision (Orr incision).

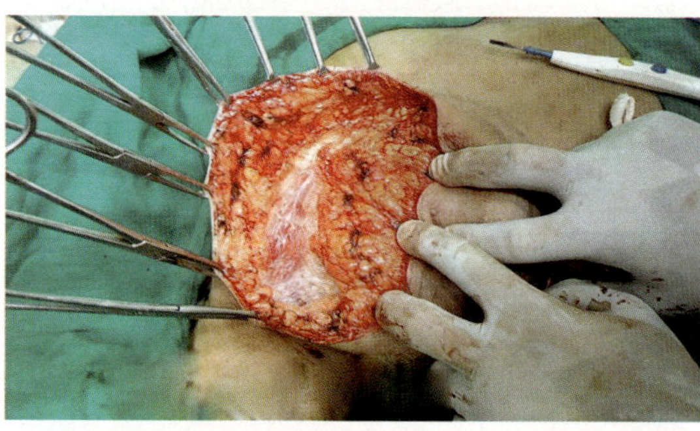

Figure 6.153 Upper skin flap.

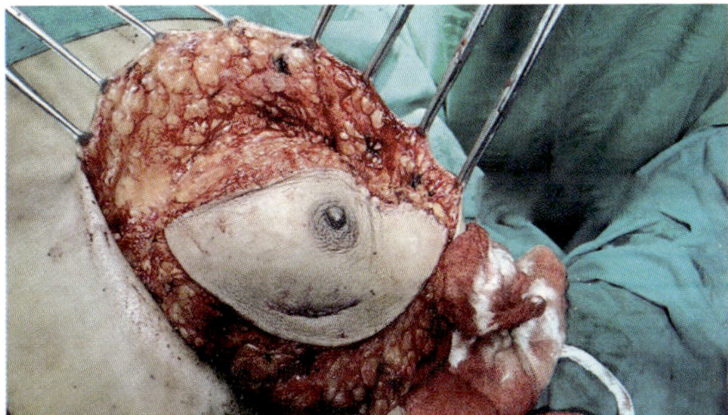

Figure 6.154 Lower skin flap.

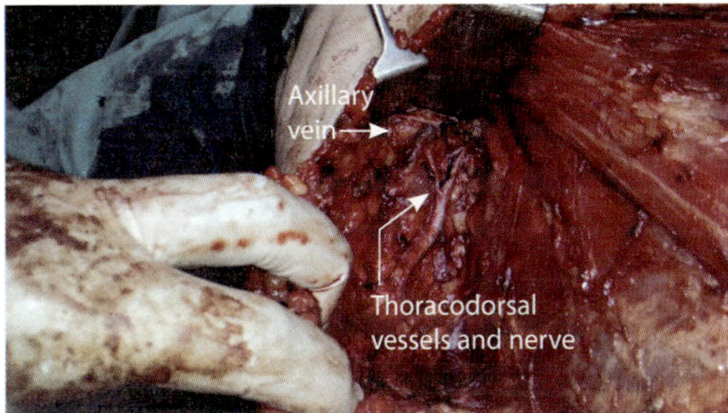

Figure 6.155 View of axillary dissection with axillary vein and thoracodorsal pedicle.

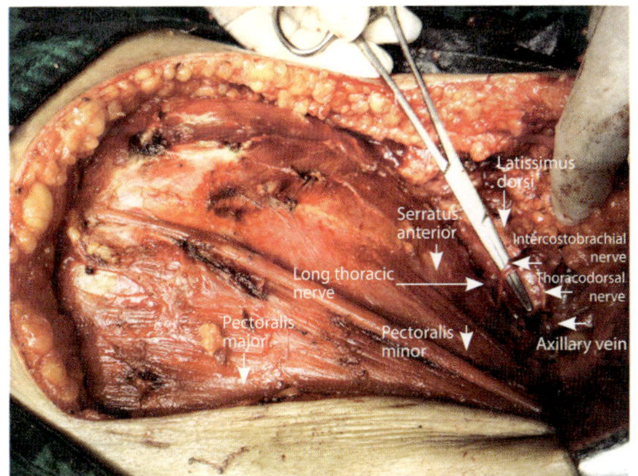

Figure 6.156 Complete view of axillary clearance. *Courtesy*: Dr Nishant Sanghavi, Oncosurgeon, Ahmedabad.

- Retract the pectoralis major muscle and minor muscle (pectoralis minor muscle can be cut from the coracoid process if required).
- Excise all the axillary group of lymph node.
- Dissect the axillary vein along the inferior surface and remove all fibrofatty tissue and the axillary lymph node and divide its tributaries (Figs 6.155 and 6.156).
- Mobilize the breast along with the clavipectoral fascia by ligating and cauterizing the perforating vessels.
- Remove specimen along with the axillary dissection (Fig. 6.157).
- Secure hemostasis.
- Negative suction drain is kept (one end is in the axilla and other end is in the skin flap).
- Close primarily with nylon 3-0 or skin stapler (Fig. 6.158) and if primary closure is not possible, put split-thickness skin graft (STSG).

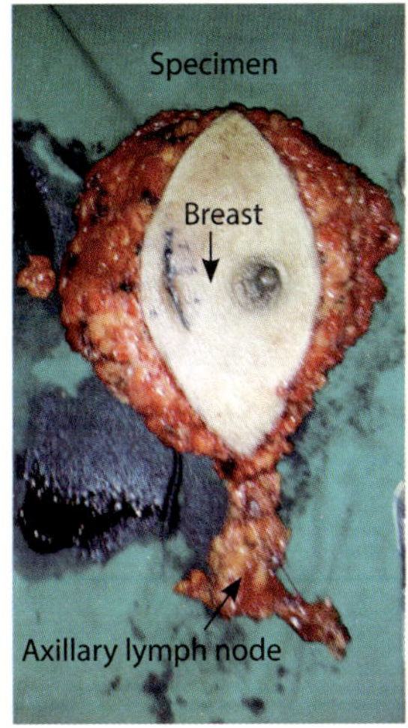

Figure 6.157 Specimen of modified radical mastectomy.

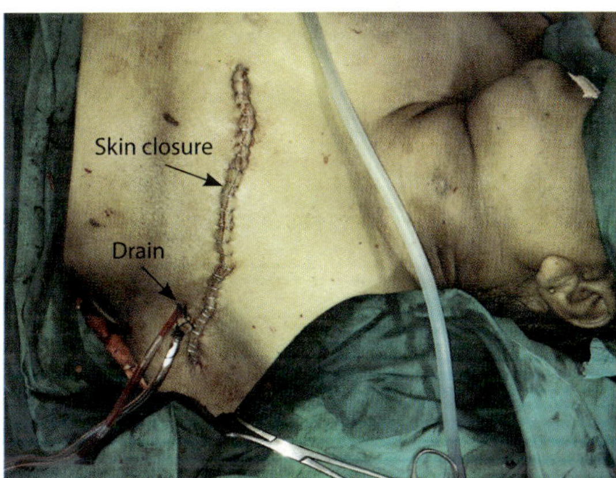

Figure 6.158 Skin closure of transverse elliptical incision (Stewart incision). *Courtesy*: Dr Nishant Sanghavi, Oncosurgeon, Ahmedabad.

- Apply dressing.
- Arm is adducted.

POSTOPERATIVE CARE

- NBM for 6 hours followed by liquid and soft diet
- Analgesic and anti-inflammatory drugs
- Should remove negative suction drain once discharge from the drain is minimal
- Gradual exercise of the shoulder after 48 hours

COMPLICATIONS

- Seroma
- Wound infection
- Pain
- Flap necrosis
- Brachial plexopathy
- Decreased arm mobility

- Management of axilla
  - Clinically positive axillary node
    - Complete axillary lymph node dissection
  - Clinically negative axilla: Perform sentinel lymph node biopsy (blue dye in operating room [lymphazurin or methylene blue] or technetium-labeled sulfur colloid scan used in nuclear medicine department):
    - *If positive*: Complete axillary dissection is preferred if there is no plan to give radiation to axilla and chest; complete dissection is not required if the patient is a candidate for adjuvant radiation.
    - *If negative*: No dissection is required.
- In axillary dissection, preserve the axillary vessels, nerve of Bell, cephalic vein, thoracodorsal nerve.
  - Usually level I and II lymph nodes are removed. Level III clearance is required if grossly involved.
  - Axillary lymph node dissection should yield 10 or more lymph nodes.
  - >4 lymph node-positive patients require adjuvant radiation.
- Prophylactic mastectomy: It is skin-sparing mastectomy with or without nipple areola complex preservation. It is indicated in the following conditions:
  - Hereditary breast and ovarian syndrome
  - Mutations of the breast cancer susceptibility genes (*BRCA1* and *BRCA2*)
- Types of mastectomy
  - Radical mastectomy (Halsted mastectomy): En bloc removal of breast with pectoralis major and minor muscle along with level I, II, III nodes
  - Modified radical mastectomy (discussed above)
  - Total or simple mastectomy
    - *Skin sparing*: Removal of entire breast with preservation of pectoralis major and minor muscle with no axillary dissection
    - *Nipple areola complex sparing* : Nipple and areola along with skin preserved

Skin-sparing mastectomy: Breast parenchyma is removed but skin is preserved.

THYROIDECTOMY

ANATOMY OF THE THYROID GLAND

- Weight 20–25 g, it varies inversely with iodine uptake.
- Location: It is C5 to T1.
- Functioning unit is lobule and consist of follicles which contain colloid in which thyroglobulin is stored.
- It has two lobes joined by isthmus.
- Right lobe is more vascular and often larger as compared to left lobe.
- Isthmus is located in front of second, third, and fourth tracheal rings.
- Blood flow is 4–6 mL/min/g.
- It has two capsules:
  - *True*: Formed by condensation of connective tissue of thyroid
  - *False*: Derived from pretracheal fascia

Blood Supply

- *Superior thyroid artery*: Branch of external carotid artery
- *Inferior thyroid artery*: Branch of thyrocervical trunk of subclavian artery
- *Thyroid ima artery*: Branch of arch of aorta

Venous Drainage

- Superior and middle thyroid veins drain into internal jugular vein.

- Inferior thyroid veins form a plexus and drain into the brachiocephalic vein.

Lymphatic Drainage

- Pretracheal nodes
- Prelaryngeal
- Deep cervical node

Nerve Supply

- Recurrent laryngeal nerve (RLN) runs close to the inferior thyroid artery. It is a branch of vagus nerve and innervates all the muscle of larynx except cricothyroid. On the right side, it runs behind the subclavian artery before entering in to the tracheo-oesophageal groove in close proximity to Berry ligament. On the left side, it runs behind the arch of the aorta before entering into the tracheo-oesophageal groove and has more vertical courses.
- External laryngeal nerve (nerve of Amelita Galli Curci) runs close to the superior thyroid artery. It is a branch of vagus nerve and innervates the cricothyroid muscle.

Types of Thyroidectomy

- Total thyroidectomy: Removal of all thyroid tissue.
- Near-total thyroidectomy: Total lobectomy on one side and 1–2 g thyroid tissue left on other side adjacent to the RLN at the ligament of Berry
- Lobectomy (hemithyroidectomy): Removal of one side of lobe along with isthmus and pyramidal lobe (if present)
- Isthmusectomy: Only isthmus removed
- Subtotal thyroidectomy (4–7 g of thyroid tissue is preserved in tracheoesophageal groove)
  - Bilateral subtotal (leaving 1–2 g thyroid tissue on each thyroid lobe)
  - Hartley–Dunhill procedure (unilateral total lobectomy with contralateral subtotal lobectomy where 4–7 g thyroid tissue is preserved)

INDICATIONS

- Thyroid nodule: Benign or malignant
- Goiter with or without pressure symptoms
- Hyperthyroidism or thyroiditis refractory to medical management

Preoperative Preparation

- Routine blood investigations plus thyroid function test; ideally patient must be euthyroid at the time of operation
- USG neck
- FNAC from suspicious nodule
- CT or MRI if retrosternal extension or suspected malignancy
- Indirect laryngoscopy must be done before any thyroid operation
- Isotope scan: Not an option in case of toxic nodular goiter and total thyroidectomy
- Patient must be euthyroid at the time of surgery: American Thyroid Association guidelines (2016)[16] for preoperative management of hyperthyroid patients
  - Antithyroid medications and/or beta-blockade (avoid thyroid storm)
  - Oral Lugol's solution (potassium iodide, SSKI) to block iodine uptake and the secretion of thyroid hormone (it also decreases vascularity of the thyroid gland)
  - Vitamin D and calcium supplementation: Reduce the risk of symptomatic hypocalcemia postoperatively
- Preoperative antibiotic in patients with high risk of developing infection
- Eight milligrams dexamethasone preoperative to reduce postoperative nausea and vomiting

OPERATIVE TECHNIQUE

The procedure is performed under GA with endotracheal intubation.

- The patient lies supine with pillow under the shoulder to extend the head.
- Head ring or sand bag is used to stabilize head.
- The patient is made to lie in 10–15° head-up position.
- Incision is marked with a thread midway between thyroid cartilage and suprasternal notch (Fig. 6.159).
- Cut the skin from one sternomastoid to other after infiltration with saline and adrenaline (facilitates the dissection and makes the operative field bloodless).
- Cut the platysma and raise the upper flap till superior thyroid notch (Fig. 6.160) and lower flap till suprasternal notch (Fig. 6.161).

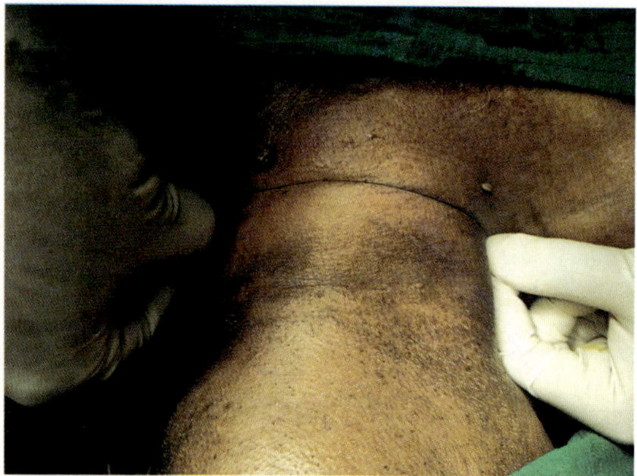

Figure 6.159 Marking of incision with thread.

- Take stay suture or use Joll's self-retaining thyroid retractor.
- Divide deep cervical fascia in midline till the thyroid capsule.

  Retract strap muscle (small nodule) or divide in large goiter (Fig. 6.162).
- Ligate and divide middle thyroid vein with silk 2-0 (Fig. 6.163).
- Ligate the branches of the superior thyroid artery individually (allows downward delivery of upper pole) (Fig. 6.164). Traditional recommendation is to ligate superior thyroid pedicle as close to the thyroid gland as possible.
- Retract upper pole medially.
- Identify RLN.

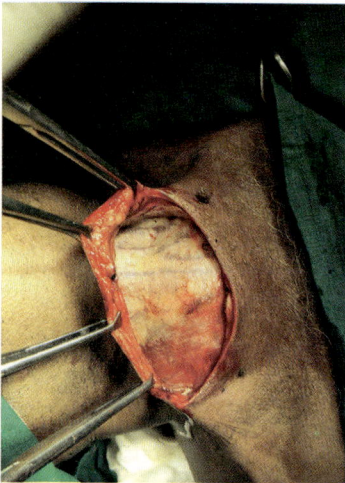

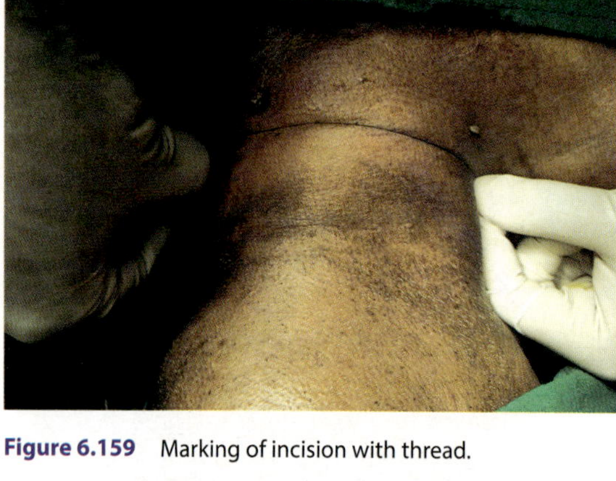

Figure 6.160 Upper flap.

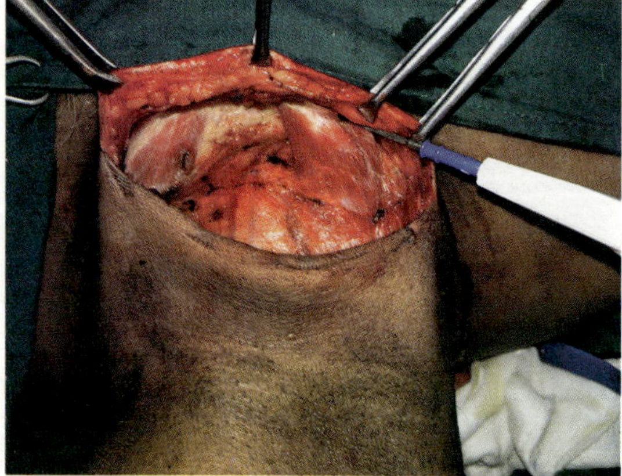

Figure 6.161 Lower flap.

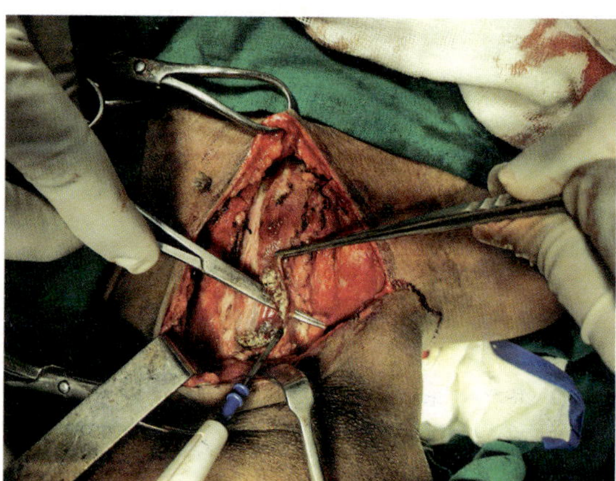

Figure 6.162 Cutting of strap muscle.

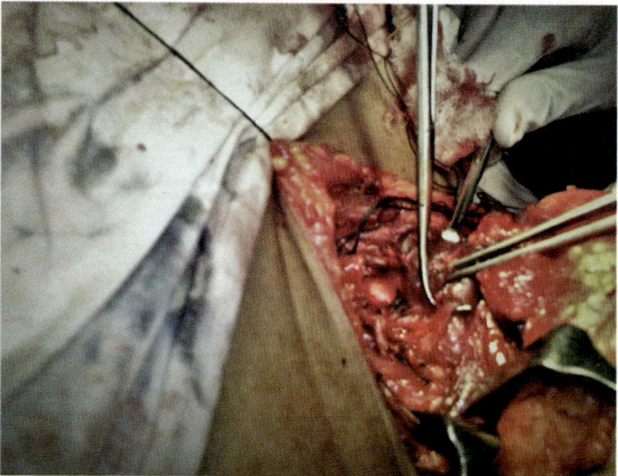

Figure 6.163 Middle thyroid vein pedicle.

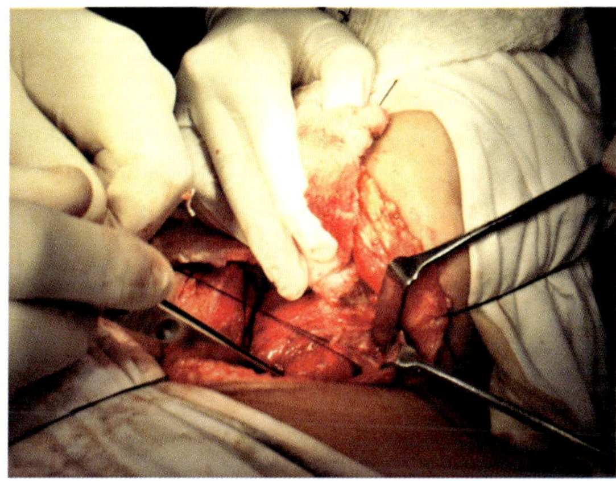

Figure 6.164 Superior thyroid pedicle.

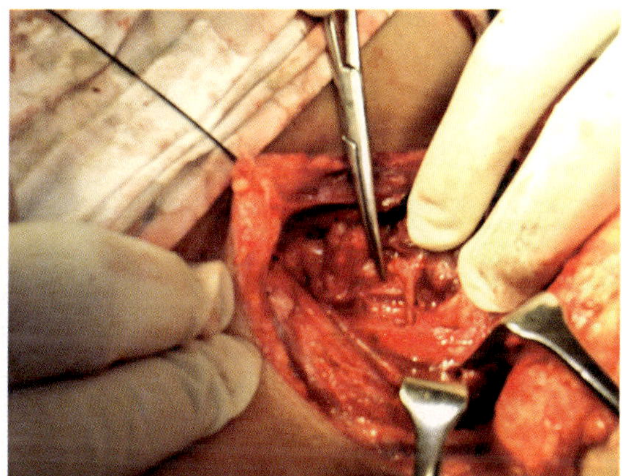

Figure 6.165 Inferior thyroid pedicle with recurrent laryngeal nerve.

- Dissect lower pole under constant supervision with preservation of RLN.
- Small superior branch of inferior thyroid artery isolated underneath the RLN and clipped or ligated and cut (Fig. 6.165).
- Sharp dissection is performed to detach lower pole from Berry's ligament.
- Excise the nodule.
- Check for hemostasis (Fig. 6.166).
- Strap muscle is sutured with polyglactin 910, 3-0 (Fig. 6.167).
- Close platysma with 4-0, polyglactin 910.
- Close skin with 5-0, Rapide polyglactin 910 (Fig. 6.168).
- Dressing is applied.

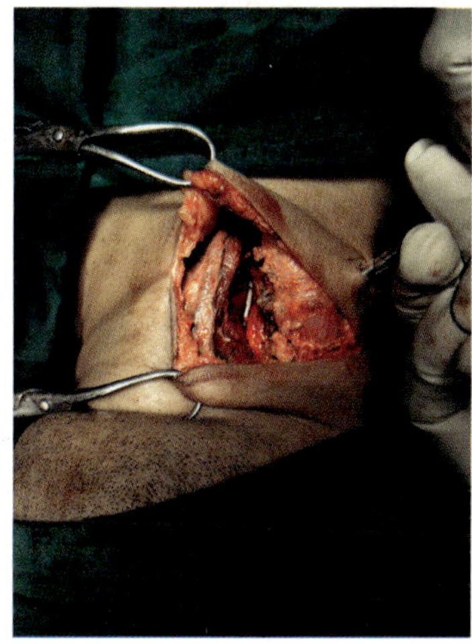

Figure 6.166 Hemostasis checked.

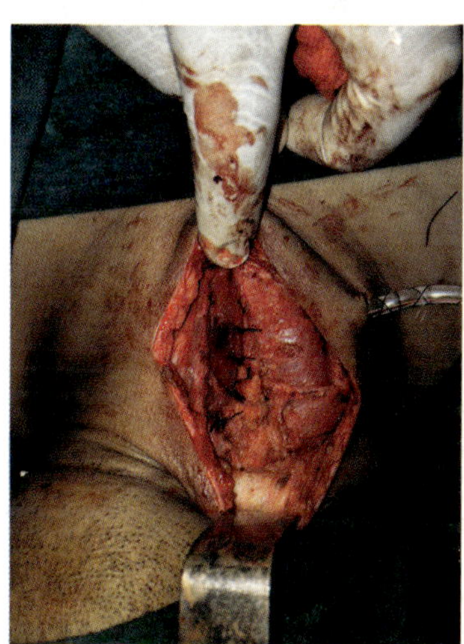

Figure 6.167 Sutured strap muscle.

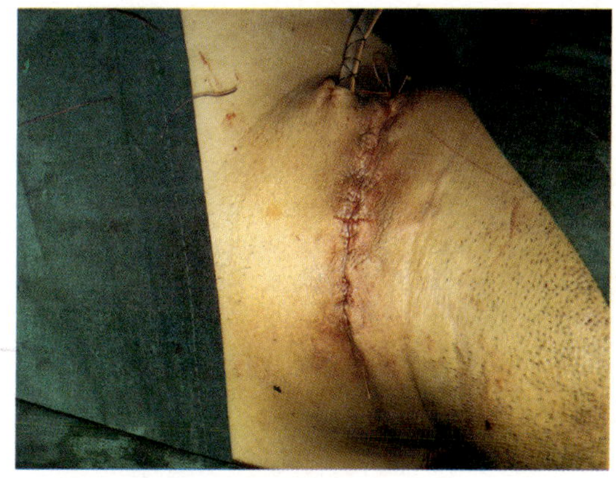

Figure 6.168 Closure of the skin.

POSTOPERATIVE CARE

- Soft collar for 24 hours
- Thirty-degree head-up position
- Watching for local swelling and respiratory problem
- Liquids started after 6 hours followed by soft diet
- Routine use of antibiotics not recommended
- Can manage pain with injectable diclofenac sodium, immediate postoperatively and later on with tablet
- Anti-inflammatory drugs
- Watching for sign of hypocalcemia
- Removal of drain after 24 hours if placed
- Discharge after 48 hours

In case of total thyroidectomy, check serum calcium daily for 48 hours and thyroxine replacement should be started on the first postoperative day.

COMPLICATIONS[17]

General

- Cardiac complications may occur.
- Respiratory complications: Bronchitis and pneumonia may occur.
- Allergic reaction may occur.

Specific

- Wound complications
  - Seroma: Aspiration
  - Infection: Cellulitis which requires antibiotics and abscess which needs to drained
  - Keloid: Scar near sternum which will result in keloid (a well-placed incision such as 1 cm below cricoid cartilage and 2 cm above jugulum and extended laterally and closed by intracutaneous suture heals well and gives best cosmetic results)
- Hemorrhage: Neck hematoma may present with pain, swelling, pressure symptoms such as dysphagia, and respiratory distress. Most bleeding develops within 24 hours of surgery and mostly within first 6 hours. Respiratory distress is because of laryngeal edema secondary to impaired venous return from larynx from hematoma.
  - Risk factors: Age, male gender, extensive dissection, surgery for Grave disease
  - Prevention and management
    - Wound irrigation and meticulous hemostasis is the key to prevent postoperative bleeding.
    - Deep to cervical fascia (tension hematoma): Remove skin stitch and all other layers need to be open to decompress and relieve pressure before shifting the patient to OR to secure bleeding vessels.
    - Subcutaneous: It requires evacuation.
- Edema: Fascial, neck, and tracheal edema is secondary to decreased venous return and lymphatic drainage. It is seen with thyroidectomy with neck dissection. Head and neck elevation in postoperative period will reduce the edema.
- Respiratory tract obstruction: Laryngeal edema is the most common cause. However, trauma to the larynx at the time of intubation and surgical manipulation also contribute to respiratory obstruction. Management is same as for tension hematoma.
- Hoarseness of voice: It may be due to laryngeal irritation or edema, neck hematoma, or RLN injury.
- Nerve injury: Best test to detect injury postoperatively is electromyography (EMG).
  - RLN injury
    - It may be unilateral or bilateral, transient or permanent. Unilateral injury causes hoarseness of voice while bilateral injuries cause inspiratory stridor. If injury is identified on table, it is managed by microsurgical repair with polypropylene 10-0, free nerve graft (ansa cervicalis), and/or neurorrhaphy with vein wrapping.
    - To prevent injury: Stimulation of vagus nerve is done prior to dissection in the tracheoesophageal groove and after complete hemostasis.

      The various methods by which RLN is identified clinically are as follows:
      - It is identified at the lateral border of lower pole of thyroid near inferior thyroid artery where nerve or its branch passes behind, before or in between the branches of the artery.
      - It can be identified where it crosses between medial and cranial nerve of the common carotid artery.

    - It is also identified at the level of Berry ligament, just caudal to its level of entry through the cricothyroid muscle into the larynx.
    - Moreover, it is identified by gently pressing below the level of lower pole (it can be felt as a string).
    - Nerve lies deep and medial to the tubercle of Zuckerkandl if present.
  - Stimulation of RLN is done prior to resecting thyroid and after completely transecting ligament of Berry. Preoperative and postoperative laryngoscopy is recommended in all cases.
- Superior laryngeal nerve: External branch of superior laryngeal nerve injury is very crucial in professional singers and preservation is of utmost importance. Poor voice projection, difficulty with higher-pitch sound, and vocal fatigue on prolonged speech are the clinical problems associated with this injury. Use of nerve stimulator may identify the nerve in such cases. Traction is given to the superior lobe in the downward and outward direction leading to opening up of the space of Reeves, and EBSLN is normally found in the space of Reeves. Ligate the vessel should be done as caudally as possible on the surface of the thyroid and avoid clamp even for small vessels.

- Tracheomalacia and tracheal perforation are rare but seen in patients with large neglected goiter.
- Hypoparathyroidism
  - It may be temporary or permanent. It usually manifests 2–5 days after surgery. It is caused by accidental removal (10%), devascularization (90%), or heat coagulation.
  - Symptoms: Symptoms of hypocalcemia such as tingling and numbness circumorally and around fingertip, carpopedal spasm, and stridor may be seen.
  - Prevention of hypoparathyroidism
    - Identification of gland by color, position, surface mobility, etc.
    - Identification of pedicle by magnifying glass
    - Should not be mobilized extensively, ischemic glands need to be autotransplanted in either sternocleidomastoid muscle or brachioradialis muscle of nondominant hand
- Chyloma and chylous fistula: Thoracic duct on left side and lymphatic duct on right are vulnerable for injury. Initial management is conservative with aspiration, TPN, and somatostatin. Persistent fistula requires surgical correction.
- Thyrotoxic crisis may be present.

AMPUTATION

Amputation is removal of any hanging part of the body/a body extremity by trauma, prolonged constriction, or surgery.

CLASSIFICATION OF AMPUTATIONS

Depending on Location

- *Cone-bearing amputation*: Above knee and below knee (BK)
- *End-bearing amputation*: Gritti–Stokes, through knee, Syme method

Based on Urgency

- Emergency amputation
  - Guillotine—all tissue is divided at the same level.
  - It is done at the site of accident.
  - It is also done in rapidly spreading gas gangrene.
  - Revision is the rule in this type of amputation.
- Elective amputation
  - *Circular*: Skin and muscle are cut circularly, but bone is cut at a higher level.
  - *Flap method*: It is described in the method of BK amputation (Burgess method).
  - *Elliptical*: Scar is not terminal.
  - *Racquet method*: Racquet-shaped incision is kept. It is used for disarticulation of distal joints, such as metatarsophalangeal joint.

INDICATIONS

- Congenital: Polydactyly
- Ischemia: Severe rest pain, gangrene
- Trauma: Crush or blast injury (massive destruction of tissue)
- Infection: Rapidly spreading gas gangrene, chronic osteomyelitis with deformed joints, with multiple discharging sinuses
- Malignancy: Osteosarcoma, soft-tissue sarcoma involving bone

PREOPERATIVE PREPARATION

- The patient's wish is the most important aspect and one should explain to the patient alternatives of painful useless limb or painless useful limb (artificial). The final decision should be left to the patient.
- General condition of the patient should be improved (correction of anemia or pain).
- Preoperative physiotherapy should be performed.
- Antibiotic prophylaxis should be given.

Optimum Levels of Amputation

- *Above knee*: 25 cm from greater trochanter (not less than 20 cm)
- *BK*: 15 cm from tibial tuberosity (not less than 8 cm)
- *Above elbow*: 20 cm from acromion
- *Below elbow*: 20 cm from tip of olecranon

Choice of Amputation Site

Make a choice depending on the pathology:

- *Malignancy*: Amputation should be performed one joint proximal to the involved site.
- *Trauma*: Amputation should be performed as distal as possible.
- *Ischemia*: Amputation should be performed at the level of healthy tissue with good perfusion to the part.

One golden rule is debridement should be as radical as possible and amputation should be as conservative as possible.

Clinical Assessment

- Look for signs of ischemia such as hair loss, shiny skin, muscle wasting, and brittle nails. Skin should be viable. There should not be any demarcation or fixed staining.
- Skin temperature and bleeding from the incision site is not a reliable sign.
- Check for pulsations. Amputation should be performed at a site distal to the proximally palpable pulsation.

Investigations

- Full blood count, blood sugar, lipid profile, serum creatinine, serum urea, and electrolyte
- ECG
- Color Doppler
- Plethysmography
- Transcutaneous oxygen pressure ($TcPO_2$)
- Xenon-133 clearance test

TECHNIQUE FOR BELOW-KNEE AMPUTATION (BURGESS METHOD)

- It is also known as the 'posterior flap method.'
- Blood supply to the posterior flap is usually good, because the sural artery, supplying gastrocnemius and soleus muscles, arises higher in the popliteal artery, which is rarely diseased.
- Length of the flap should be at least 1.5 times the diameter of the leg, at the point of bone section.
- One can also follow a simply rule of anterior two-third and posterior one-third at the level of bone section. So, suppose the diameter at the bone section is 27 cm; then anterior two-third means 18 cm and posterior one-third means 9 cm. So, the length of flap should be 9 cm.
- Anesthesia**:** SA should be given.
- Mark the amputation stump with a marker (Figs 6.169 and 6.170).
- Cut the skin (Fig. 6.171).
- Cut the subcutaneous tissue up to the bone. Then cut the posterior skin, subcutaneous tissue, and muscles.
- Identify blood vessels first, ligate, and cut (Fig. 6.172 and 6.173).
- Identify nerves; pull down gently and transect as high as possible (Fig. 6.174).

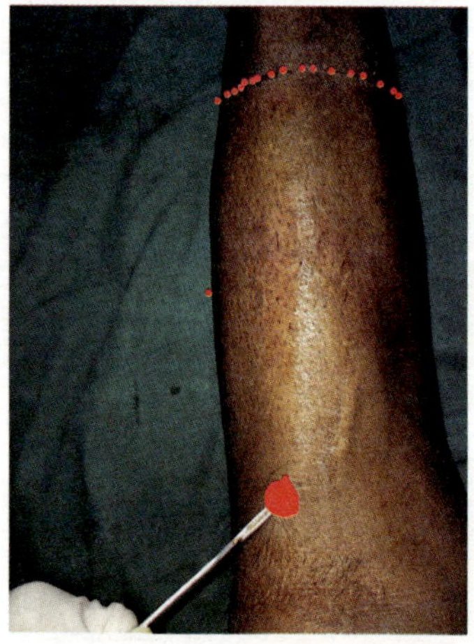

Figure 6.169 Amputation stump marked on anterior two-third.

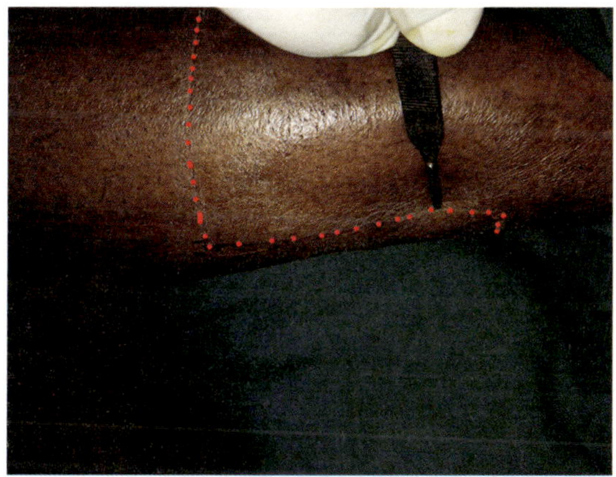

Figure 6.170 Amputation stump marked on posterior one-third.

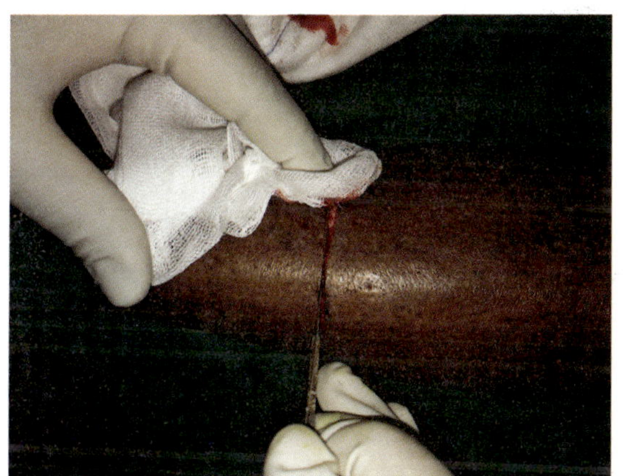

Figure 6.171 Cutting of the skin.

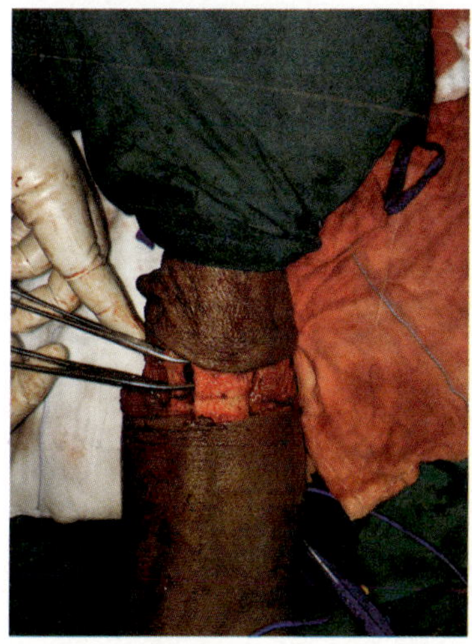

Figure 6.172 Blood vessel identified and clamped.

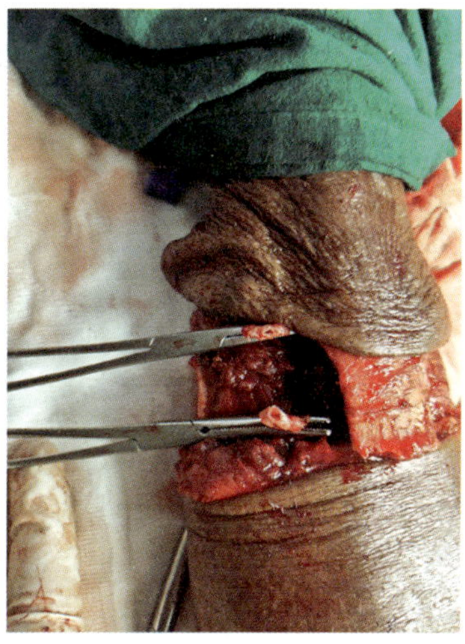

Figure 6.173 Blood vessels cut.

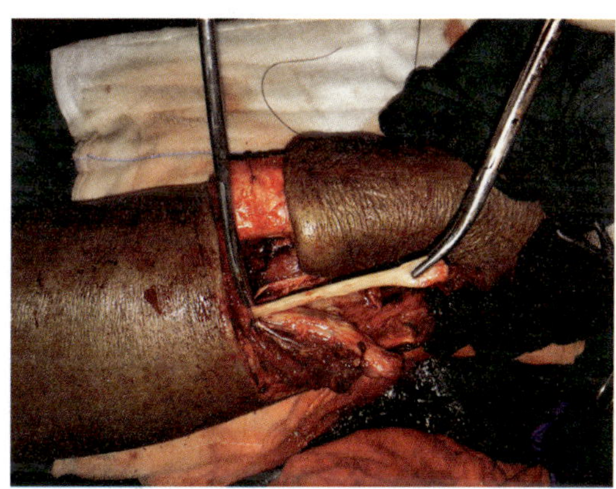

Figure 6.174 Transecting nerve after pulling.

- Cut tibia at the proposed level (for cutting of bone with either bone saw or Gigli saw) and do anterior beveling (Fig. 6.175).
- Divide fibula 2 cm proximal to the level of cutting of tibia (Fig. 6.176).
- Trim the bulk of soleus (Fig. 6.177).
- Suture the muscle to periosteum (myodesis) with Vicryl 2-0 (Fig. 6.178).
- Keep two negative suction drains, one deep to muscle and one in subcutaneous plane.
- Close skin with either Prolene 3-0 or Ethilon 3-0 (Fig. 6.179).
- Apply dressing.
- Apply plaster cast (advantages: Prevents flexion contracture, protects from trauma, controls edema, and improves healing).

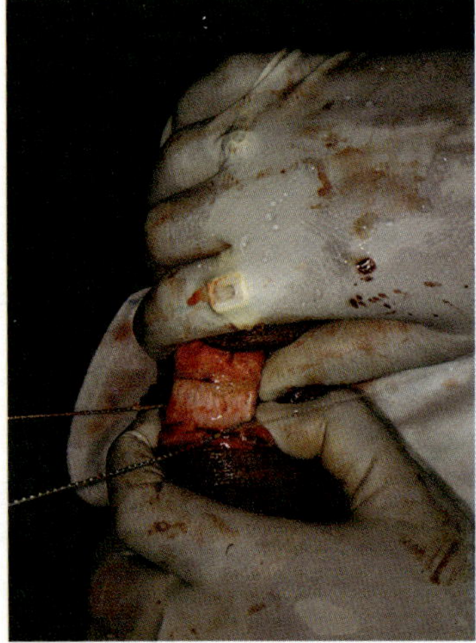

Figure 6.175 Cutting of tibia with Gigli saw.

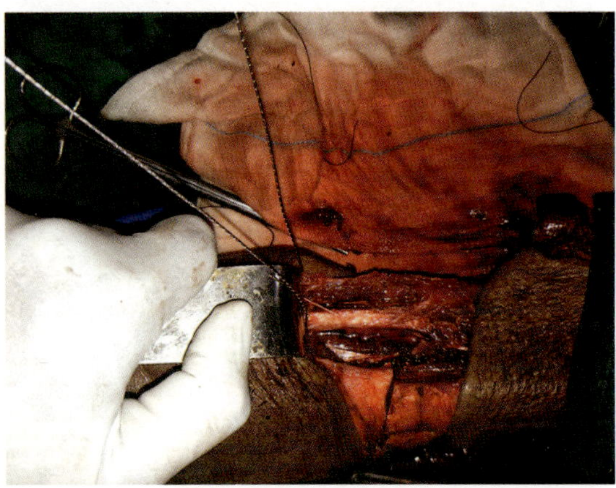

Figure 6.176 Cutting of fibula with Gigli saw.

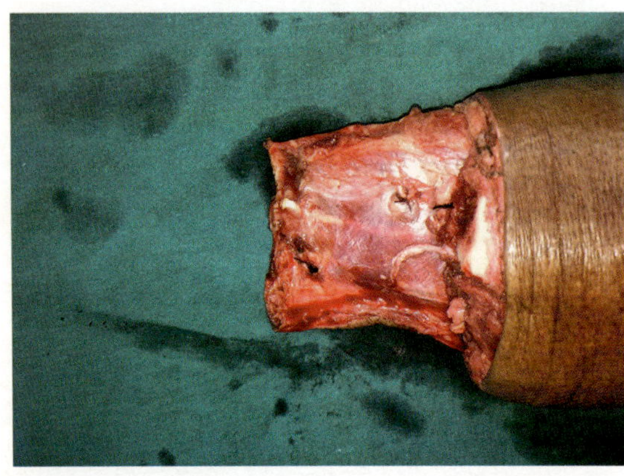

Figure 6.177 Bulk of soleus.

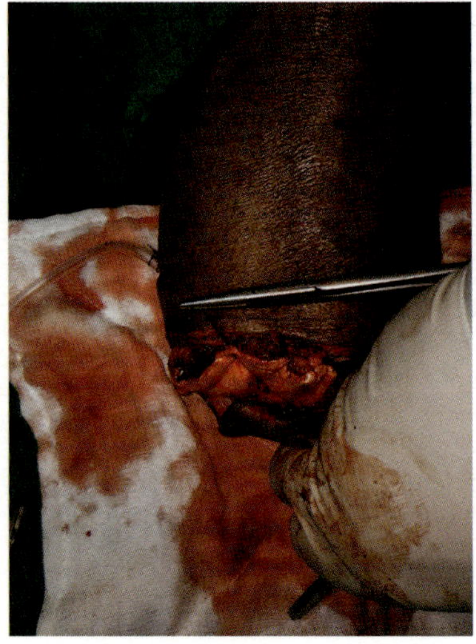

Figure 6.178 Suturing of the muscle with periosteum.

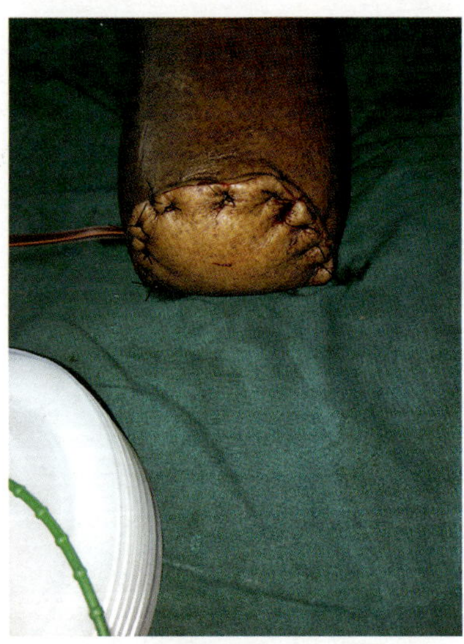

Figure 6.179 Sutured skin.

POSTOPERATIVE CARE

- Antibiotics are given.
- Analgesics are provided.
- If plaster cast is not applied, then use a sand bag to keep the limb straight.
- Early mobilization and physiotherapy after removal of dressing
  - Advantages: Decreases hospital stay, increases rate of rehabilitation, decreases complications associated with prolonged bed rest, and improves psychological outlook

Prosthesis

- There are two types of prostheses available in India: Jaipur foot and solid ankle cushioned heel (SACH).
- Jaipur foot: With this, one can sit cross-legged. It does not get wet after dipping in water; one can walk bare feet, and one can climb a tree.
- SACH: Advantages available with the Jaipur foot are not available with SACH. It is reserved for poor people.

COMPLICATIONS

Early

- Primary hemorrhage
- Reactionary hemorrhage
- Skin necrosis
- Hematoma
- Infection
- Wound dehiscence
- DVT
- Pulmonary embolism

Late

- Pain (sinus, osteitis, sequestrum)
- Bone spur
- Scar adherent to bone
- Stump neuroma (due to outgrowth of nerve fibrils that attach to the scar, muscle, or fibrous tissue)
- Phantom limb (feeling of amputated limb)
- Phantom pain due to nerve endings in residual limb, which represent parts originally innervated by severed nerves or due to psychological effects such as guilt, loss of sensory input, and decreased self-sustaining activity. Treatment includes carbamazepine, amitriptyline, ultrasonic therapy, transcutaneous electrical nerve stimulation (TENS), and psychological support.
- Causalgia: Sympathetic overactivity
- Ring sequestrum
- Jactitation: Intermittent spasm of amputation stump
- Flexion contracture of proximal joint

CRITERIA OF IDEAL AMPUTATION STUMP

- It should be of optimal length.
- It should have smooth, rounded ends.
- It should be firm.
- Scar should be freely mobile.
- Vascularity of flap should be normal.
- Opposing group of muscles should be sutured over the end of stump.
- Scar should not be adherent.
- There should not be any complications, such as painful neuroma and callosity.
- Proximal joint should be normal.

SKIN GRAFTING

Skin grafting is a surgical graft of healthy skin from one part of the body to another or from one individual to another in order to replace damaged or lost skin.

TYPES OF SKIN GRAFTS

- *Split-thickness (Thiersch's) graft (STSG)*: Epidermis + part of dermis
  - *Thin*: 0.01–0.015 inch
  - *Thick*: >0.015 inch
- *Full-thickness graft (FTG; Wolfe graft)*: Epidermis + dermis
- *Reverdin graft*: Epidermis + dermis + subcutaneous tissue
- *Composite graft*: Skin + subcutaneous tissue + cartilage
  - Free graft
  - Commonly used in face to cover defect in alar border of nose

Advantages of STSG

- Donor site heals by epithelialization.
- Larger area is covered.
- No primary closure is required.

Disadvantages of STSG

- Less resistant to trauma
- Pigmentation
- Hair not able to grow
- Can contract by 50%

Aesthetically demanding area and joint are relative contraindications for STSG

Advantages of Full-Thickness Graft

- It is more resistant to trauma.
- It is less likely to undergo contraction.
- Hair can grow and secretion of sebum and sweat occurs.
- Pigmentation is less likely.

Sites from where FTG is taken: Behind the ear, groin crease, neck, and abdomen.

In case of FTG: de fat the graft, cutting in slit, and bolstering improves the graft uptake.

Disadvantages of FTG

- Larger area cannot be covered.
- Primary closure of donor site is must.
- Donor sites are limited (postauricular area, upper eyelid, groin, and flank).
- Scarring occurs at the donor site.

OPERATIVE TECHNIQUE

STSG Procedure

- Anesthesia: LA or SA is given.
- Carry out painting, draping, and isolation of the part.
- Prepare donor and recipient areas.
- Apply normal saline or jelly over the donor area.
- The assistant surgeon and nursing staff stretch the thigh (Fig. 6.180).
- Assistant surgeon will support the thigh from behind and nurse will stretch from above with a sling of gauze piece (Fig. 6.181).
- The surgeon can use wooden block or his/her own hand to flatten the thigh (Fig. 6.181).
- Take graft with a mechanical dermatome (Watson knife; Fig. 6.181).
- Initially, hold knife at 45°; deepen until you see a piece of skin.
- Then, make the knife horizontal and with even movements take a graft (Fig. 6.181). (Size of the graft depends on the area required to be covered at the recipient site.)
- Apply Sofra-Tulle or vaseline gauze over the donor area and apply dressing.
- Prepare the recipient area (Fig. 6.182) by scooping, if hypergranulation is present, or by rubbing with gauze piece.

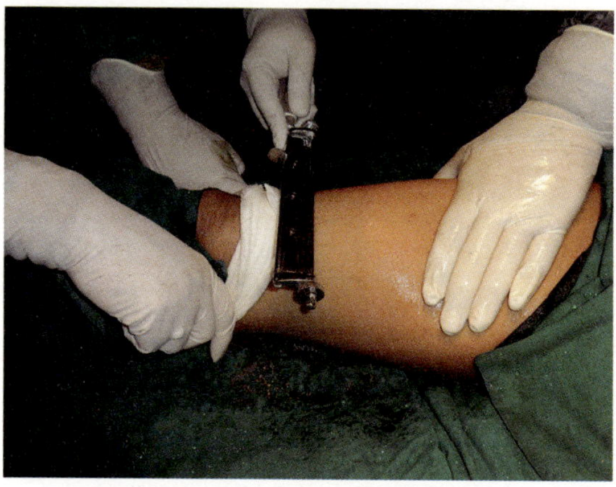

Figure 6.180 Assistant stretching the thigh.

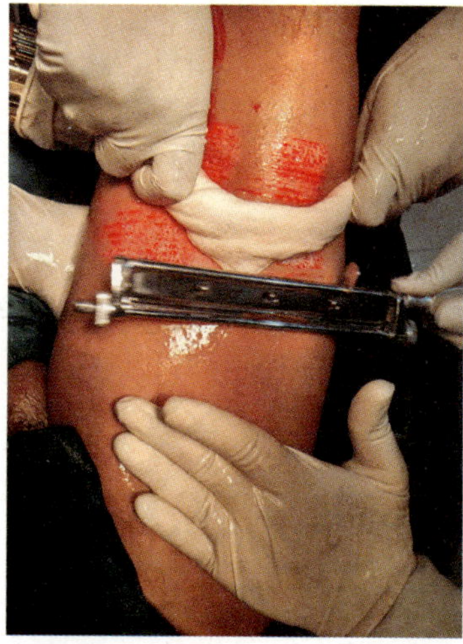

Figure 6.181 Supporting of the thigh from behind and stretching from above by assistant. Surgeon uses his/her hand to flatten the thigh and keep the mechanical dermatome at 45° initially.

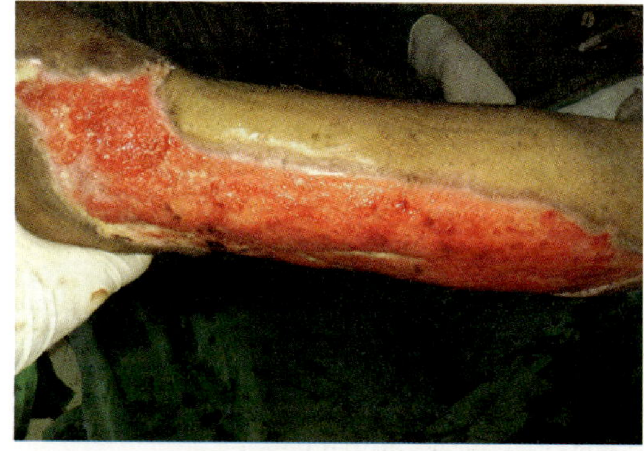

Figure 6.182 Recipient area.

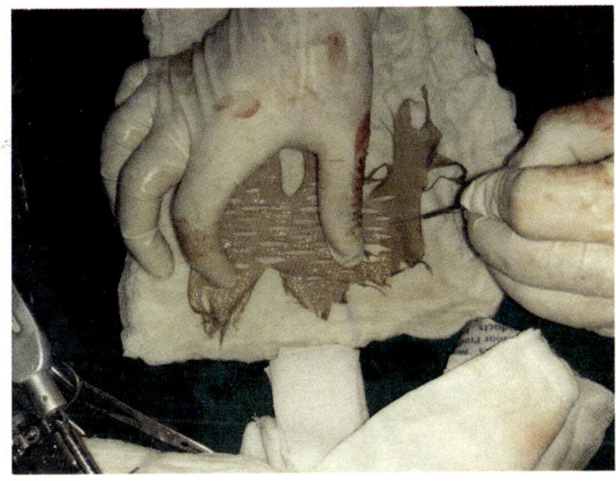

Figure 6.183 Meshing of the graft with stab knife.

Figure 6.184 Meshed graft.

- If there is bleeding, put an adrenaline-soaked gauze piece.
- Mesh the graft with a stab knife (multiple puncture) (Figs 6.183 and 6.184).
- Advantages of meshing: It increases the surface area and allows for drainage (it can increase the surface area from 1:1.5 to 1:6).
- Place the graft over the recipient area and fix with skin stapler (Fig. 6.185); apply vaseline gauze or Sofra-Tulle (Fig. 6.186), and then apply a 'tie over dressing.'
- Apply gauze pad, and then gamgee. After that, apply plaster slab or cast of POP (Plaster of paris) to immobilize the part.

Instruments used for taking graft

- Razor blade
- Skin grafting knife
- Electrical dermatome

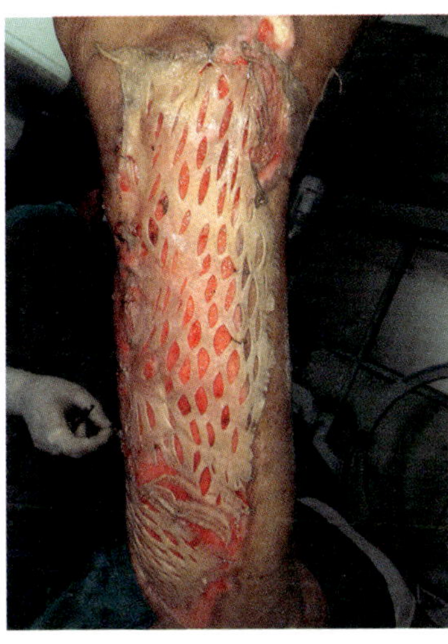

Figure 6.185 Graft in position over the recipient area and fix with skin stapler.

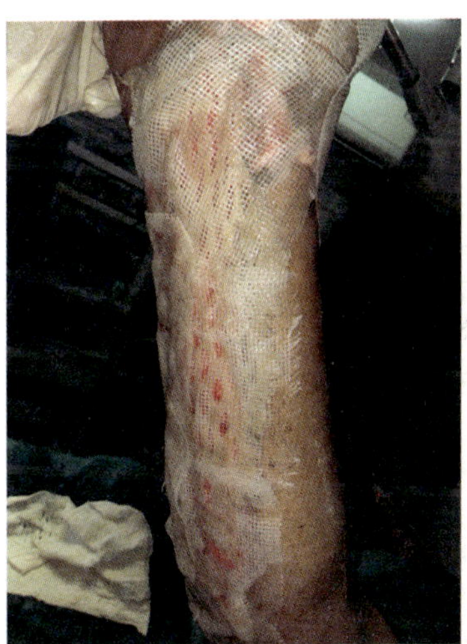

Figure 6.186 Sofra-Tulle dressing.

- Electrical dermatome can be used when larger area is to be covered.
- Some surgeons prefer fixing of graft to surrounding skin with sutures to prevent the shearing effect, but the author does not find any advantage with that. He would like to fix only in case of large graft and graft near the joint area.
- Dressing of donor area can also be done with alginate, which is more comfortable compared to Sofra-Tulle or vaseline gauze, but cost is the limiting factor.

- Any extra graft can be wrapped in saline-soaked gauze piece and at 4°C temperature it can be stored for 3 weeks.

Most used donor site is thigh; in children and cosmetically sensitive individuals, buttock is preferable.

POSTOPERATIVE CARE

- Analgesics
- Antibiotics
- Change dressing on the fifth day in healthy granulation tissue, or on second or third day in infected case. After that, do alternate-day dressing of the recipient area.
- Dressing of the donor site should be done on the 14th day, unless there is evidence of infection or soakage of wound, which requires earlier change of dressing.

MECHANISM OF TAKING UP OF GRAFT

- *Serum imbibition*: It takes place within the first 24 hours. It is characterized by absorption of nutrients from the recipient capillary bed.
- *Inosculation*: It takes place within 24–72 hours. It is characterized by connection between donor and recipient vascular beds.
- *Angiogenesis*: It takes place after 72 hours. It is characterized by ingrowth of recipient vessels into the graft.

Causes of Graft Rejection

- Hematoma
- Pus formation
- Exudates or residual dead tissue beneath the skin
- Shear stress
- Thick graft

Important Factors Helpful in Preventing Graft Rejection

- Clean wound
- Healthy granulation tissue
- Immobilization of graft
- Adequate contact between graft and recipient area
- Adequate blood supply

ABSOLUTE CONTRAINDICATIONS FOR SKIN GRAFTING

- Infection with group A β-hemolytic streptococci, which produces hemolysin and can destroy split graft completely
- Any organism with colony count more than 10^5/g

SPLENECTOMY

Splenectomy is excision of spleen carried out due to certain disorders of spleen. For example, spleen may enlarge and rupture; bleeding may become life-threatening and splenectomy is needed to remove the spleen.

SURGICAL ANATOMY

Spleen is slightly larger than a clenched fist or size of cupped hand (Box 6.4). It is located in left hypochondrium, opposite the left 9th to 11th ribs, and weighs around 150 g in adult. It is 12 cm long, 7 cm broad, and 3 cm thick. Its long axis corresponds to the long axis of the left 10th rib. On ultrasound, 13 cm is considered to be upper limit for normal spleen. Normal spleen is not palpable; it becomes palpable only when it is enlarged more than twice the normal size. Spleen length is length between two poles and measured by a straight line connecting two poles. The variations in spleen length are:

- *Normal*: 7–11 cm
- *Moderate splenomegaly*: 12–20 cm
- *Massive splenomegaly*: 21–30 cm
- Mega spleen: >30 cm

Ligaments of spleen

- Gastrosplenic, splenocolic, splenorenal, and splenophrenic. Except gastrosplenic ligaments which contain short gastric vessels, other ligaments are avascular.
- In case of portal hypertension and myeloproliferative disorder, splenorenal ligament contains pancreatic and splenic vessels.

Blood Supply

Arterial supply

Splenic artery is a branch of celiac trunk. It is different from other two branches of celiac trunk as

Box 6.4 Functions of spleen[18]

- Major functions
  - Filtration
    - Culling: Effete and damaged red cell removal. Normal red cells are biconcave and deform easily. This allows passage of normal red blood cells (RBCs) through microvasculature and allows exchange of oxygen and carbon dioxide. Aged red cells lose osmotic balance and membrane integrity. Red cells with decreased plasticity become trapped and are destroyed within spleen.
    - Pitting: Culling and pitting are functions of red pulp. Nuclear inclusions, Howell–Jolly bodies (nuclear remnant), Heinz bodies (denatured hemoglobin), Pappenheimer bodies (iron or siderotic granules), acanthocytes (spur cells), and codocytes (target cells) are removed by pitting.
    - Erythroclasis: This refers to destruction of abnormal RBCs with liberation into circulation of erythrocyte fragments.
    - Removal of other particulate material (bacteria, colloidal particles) is also done by spleen.
  - Immunological
    - Trapping and processing of antigen
    - Homing of lymphocytes
    - Lymphocyte transformation and proliferation
    - Antibody and lymphokine production
    - Macrophage activation
- Minor functions
  - Storage of RBCs: 8% of red cells are stored in spleen.
  - Cytopoiesis: During intrauterine life, extramedullary erythropoiesis occurs in spleen. It also occurs in myeloproliferative disorders.
  - Reservoir of platelets (pooling): About one-third of the platelet mass is pooled in the spleen and that pool exchanges freely with the circulating platelets.

it has a tortuous course along the superior border of the pancreas. The terminal branching pattern is either distributive or magistral type. Main pattern is distributive type (70%), shorter main trunk and relatively early branching. In magistral type (30%), splenic artery main trunk is long while limited and there are small terminal branches. The splenic artery has pancreatic branch (pancreatica magna artery).

Venous drainage

Venous drainage is via splenic vein which receives inferior mesenteric vein centrally and then joins the superior mesenteric vein to form portal vein.

The spleen has an acidotic, hypoxic, and hypoglycemic environment. The spleen receives 300 mL blood/min. In the spleen, blood takes two paths:

- Closed or fast circulation in which blood directly flow from the arterioles to venules
- Open or slow in which blood circulates through the pulp

SPLENIC DISORDERS

Splenic Rupture

- Most common cause of spontaneous rupture is malarial spleen.
- Most common cause of death due to rupture of spleen is infectious mononucleosis.
  Various presentations of splenic rupture:
- The patient dies immediately due to grade 5 injury.
- Initial shock is followed by recovery and late bleeding.
- Delayed phase—the patient may later present in shock.

Diagnosis

- USG
- Contrast-enhanced CT scan: To assess grade of injury and other associated injuries
- X-ray abdomen (not done routinely)
- Angiography

Treatment

Depends on the grade of injury and condition of the patient. The American Association for the Surgery of Trauma (AAST) grading of splenic injury[19]

- *Grade I*: Hematoma—subcapsular, <10% of surface area
  Laceration: capsular tear <1 cm in depth
- *Grade II*: Hematoma—subcapsular, 10–50% of surface area
  Laceration: Capsular tear, 1–3 cm in depth, but not involving a trabecular vessel
- *Grade III*: Hematoma—subcapsular, >50% of surface area *or* expanding, ruptured subcapsular or parenchymal hematoma *or* intraparenchymal hematoma >5 cm or expanding.
  Laceration: >3 cm in depth or involving a trabecular vessel.
- *Grade IV*: Laceration involving segmental or hilar vessels with major devascularization

- *Grade V*: Hematoma—shattered spleen
  Laceration: Hilar vascular injury which devascularizes spleen
- *Grades I, II, III*: Close observation with serial hematocrit and angioembolization if bleeding risk is substantial (best candidate for angioembolization is pseudoaneurysm on CT)
- *Grades IV and V*: Splenectomy

  Any patient who is hemodynamically unstable at the time of admission or in whom there is failure of nonoperative management (rebleeds after successful nonoperative management) requires splenectomy.

Ectopic Spleen (Wandering Spleen)

Due to long splenic pedicle, spleen is in the lower abdomen or pelvis. Radionuclide scan is diagnostic. It may present as torsion of spleen.

Treatment: Either splenectomy or splenopexy is indicated.

Splenunculi (Accessory Spleen)

Most common site is splenic hilum, followed by the sites along the ligaments of spleen. But it may occur anywhere from mediastinum to scrotum. Its importance lies in that failure to identify these at the time of splenectomy will lead to persistence of the disease.

Splenosis

It is spontaneous regrowth of splenic tissue after splenectomy done for trauma. It helps in preserving the immune function. It may be associated with adhesions. At least 30% of splenic tissue is required to preserve the immune function.

Massive Splenomegaly

In massive splenomegaly (Fig. 6.187), the spleen is more than 1500 g or 10 cm below the costal margin. Diseases associated with massive splenomegaly are:

- Tropical splenomegaly
- Lymphoma
- Hairy cell leukemia
- Lipid storage disease
- Chronic lymphocytic leukemia (CLL)

Hypersplenism

Splenomegaly + cytopenia + bone marrow hyperplasia + condition reverses after splenectomy.

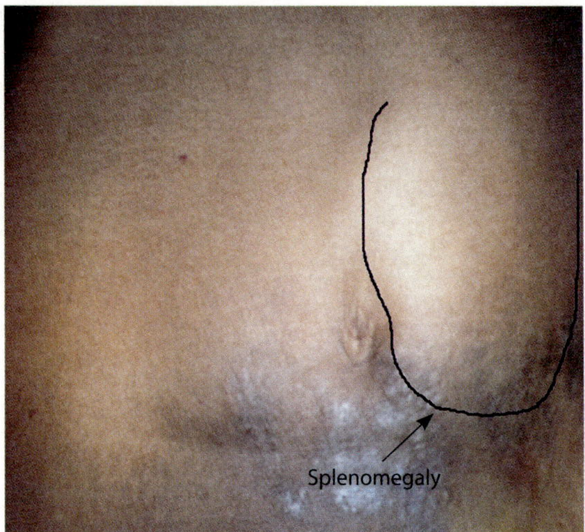

Figure 6.187 Massive splenomegaly.

PREOPERATIVE PREPARATION

- Multidetector spiral CT scan or USG to assess the spleen size, volume, splenic vascular anatomy, presence and size of accessory spleen, and parenchymal lesion. Right upper quadrant USG for those who are at high risk for gallstone such as sickle cell or hemolytic anemia, so, if required, concomitant cholecystectomy can be performed.
- Vaccination against pneumococci (2 weeks prior to surgery with 23-polyvalent pneumococcal polysaccharide vaccine) in all patients. *H. influenzae* (if not vaccinated in infancy) and meningococcal (>2 years old) vaccines are indicated in young patients. The CDC recommends vaccination with all the three vaccines preoperatively. It recommends revaccination with pneumococcal vaccine only once after 5 years.
- Severe thrombocytopenia requires preoperative transfusion of platelets just before induction to reduce the risk of bleeding and laryngeal edema. one unit platelet will raise platelet count by $5000/mm^3$, so if platelet count is $<20,000/mm^3$, at least 6 units should be transfused. Preoperative platelet transfusion should be avoided in patients with immune thrombocytopenic purpura (ITP).
- Preoperative splenic artery embolization is advised in patients with portal hypertension and in massive splenomegaly to reduce the risk of bleeding.

- Those who are on chronic steroid therapy will require preoperative exogenous steroids.
- Preoperative antibiotics are recommended in immunocompromised patients and those conditions where gastrointestinal tract is likely to open.
- Heparin should be considered in high-risk patients for DVT such as myeloproliferative disorder.

INDICATIONS FOR SPLENECTOMY

- Definite
  - Primary splenic malignancy or tumor: Angiosarcoma, malignant fibrous histiocytoma, plasmacytomas, littoral cell angioma, hemangiosarcoma, etc.
  - Primary parasitic cyst
  - Nonsalvagable splenic rupture and rupture of diseased spleen
  - Enblock resection of adjacent proximal gastric neoplasm
- Desirable
  - Chronic ITP: Recurrent thrombocytopenia on steroid withdrawal or tapering, failure of medical therapy such as steroid or immunoglobulin, undesirable side effects with prolonged use of steroids, persistent requirement of prednisolone >10 mg for >3 months, signs of hemorrhage despite maximum medical therapy
  - Hereditary spherocytosis in patients aged more than 5 years. In those less than 5 years, splenectomy should be performed only in transfusion-dependent disease (hemolytic anemia, intractable leg ulcer, and recurrent transfusion requirement are indications for splenectomy)
  - Splenic vein thrombosis: Sinistral portal hypertension secondary to splenic vein thrombosis
  - Primary hypersplenism
  - Splenic abscess
    - *Single abscess*: Percutaneous drainage and antibiotics
    - *Multiple abscess*: Splenectomy
  - AIDS-related thrombotic thrombocytopenic purpura
  - Sickling syndrome
- Sometimes indicated:
  - *Splenic trauma*: Grade IV and V injury
  - *Thrombotic thrombocytopenic purpura (TTP)*: Main treatment is plasma exchange. Indications for splenectomy are relapse on plasma exchange and excessive or multiple plasma exchange requirement
  - Myelofibrosis: Symptomatic splenomegaly
  - Hodgkin disease: Suspicion of lymphoma without peripheral involvement restaging for suspicion of failure after chemotherapy
  - Autoimmune hemolytic anemia: Main treatment being steroids (second-line treatment is anti- CD20 antibody; splenectomy is indicated in case of failure of medical treatment)
  - Nonparasitic primary cyst: Large and symptomatic cysts requiring total or partial splenectomy
- Rarely indicated
  - Lymphoproliferative disorders such as CLL, chronic myeloid leukemia (CML), splenic marginal zone lymphoma, and hairy cell leukemia. Indications for splenectomy:
    - Symptomatic splenomegaly
    - Hypersplenism
    - Tissue diagnosis when only spleen is involved
  - Thalassemia major: It should be delayed up to the age of 4 years. Indications for splenectomy are
    - Excessive transfusion requirement >200 mL/kg/year
    - Symptomatic splenomegaly
    - Painful splenic infarction
  - Splenic artery aneurysm: Operative management is indicated:
    - Large aneurysm >2 cm, in those where pregnancy is anticipated and pseudoaneurysm with inflammation
    - For proximal and middle third aneurysm: Ligation proximal and distal to aneurysm
    - Distal third: Splenectomy
  - Sickle cell anemia: Indications for splenectomy:
    - Chronic hypersplenism characterized by reduced red cell survival, leukopenia, and thrombocytopenia

    - Acute splenic sequestration characterized by sudden splenomegaly with worsening anemia and profound hypotension
  - Pseudocyst: It can be managed with laparoscopic deroofing and marsupialization
  - Felty syndrome: Neutropenia
  - Storage disorder such as Gaucher disease, Niemann–Pick disease, amyloidosis, and sarcoidosis
    - Symptomatic splenomegaly and hyperspl-enism are the indications for splenectomy.
- Incidental splenectomy for distal pancreatic tumor or injury at the time of operation

OPERATIVE TECHNIQUE

- Anesthesia: GA is given.
- Position: The patient is made to lie in supine Position.
- Incision
  - Left subcostal incision (Fig. 6.188) in elective splenectomy (most common)
  - Midline incision in trauma and massive splenomegaly
  - Thoracoabdominal incision in multiple adhesions and massive splenomegaly
- Carry out painting, draping, and isolation of the part.
- Cut the following layers in subcostal incision:
  - Skin, subcutaneous tissue
  - External oblique, internal oblique, and transverse abdominis
  - Anterior rectus sheath—medially
  - Rectus muscle
  - Peritoneum
- Cut the following layers in midline incision:
  - Skin
  - Subcutaneous tissue
  - Linea alba
  - Peritoneum
- In case of elective splenectomy, by passing hand between the spleen (Fig. 6.189) and the diaphragm, do transection of splenocolic (Fig. 6.190), splenorenal, and splenophrenic ligaments (Fig. 6.191). In case of trauma, detach most of the ligaments, because of risk of hematoma. Carry out rapid delivery of the

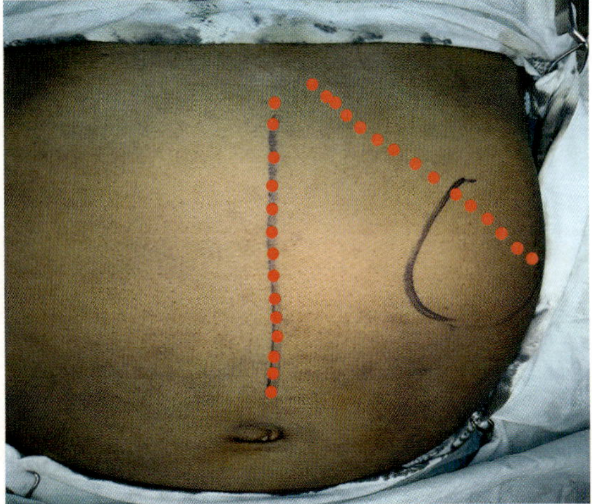

Figure 6.188 Commonly used incisions in splenectomy (midline and left costal incision).

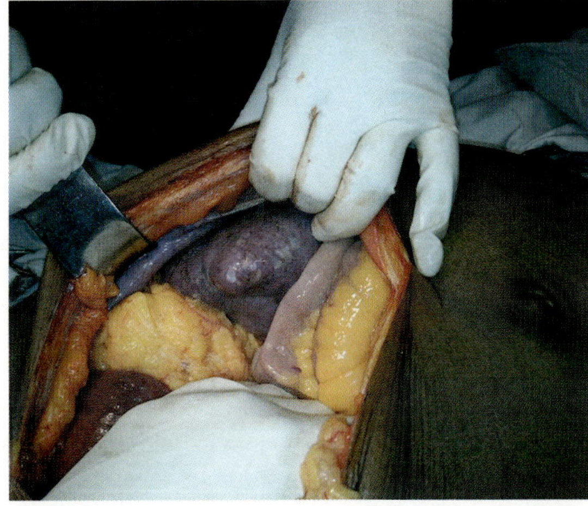

Figure 6.189 Massively enlarged spleen seen on opening the abdomen.

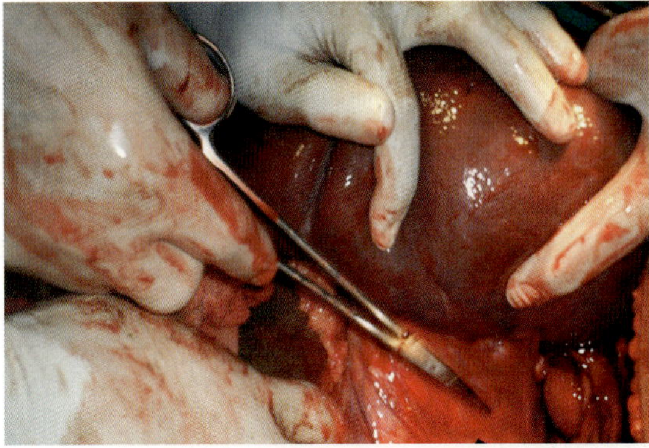

Figure 6.190 Splenocolic ligament.

spleen into wound and achieve control of vascular pedicle by pressing with thumb.

- Ligate gastrosplenic ligament (Fig. 6.192), which contains short gastric vessels, and cut between clamps.
- Take care of pancreatic tail, stomach, and splenic flexure.
- After delivery of spleen into the wound, carry out dissection into the hilum (Fig. 6.193).
- Ligate the artery and vein separately (Fig. 6.194), with double ligation proximally and single ligation distally. Then cut in between. Ligated pedicle is checked for hemostasis (Fig. 6.195).

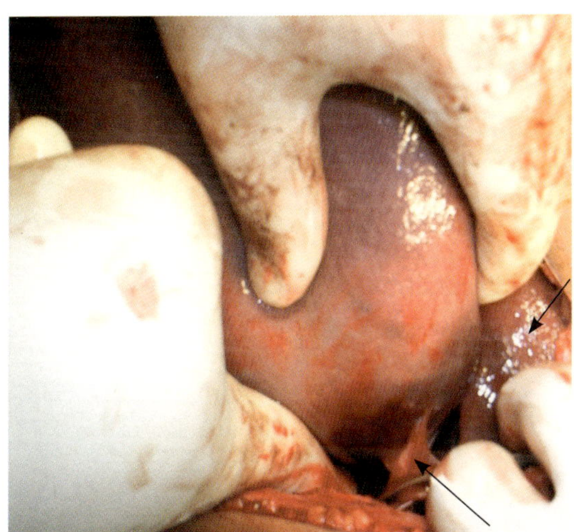

Figure 6.191 Splenophrenic ligament.

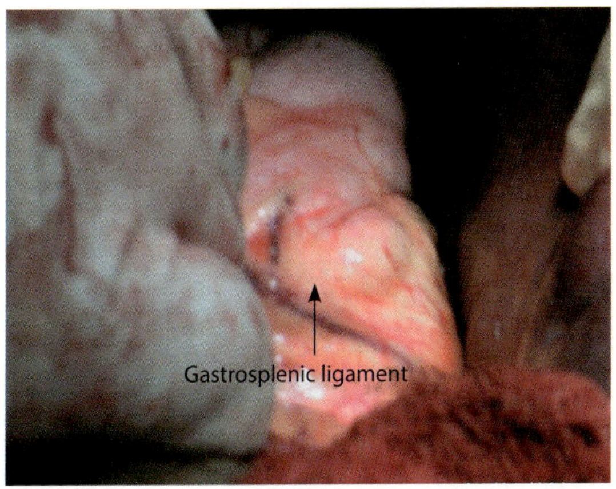

Figure 6.192 Gastrosplenic ligament.

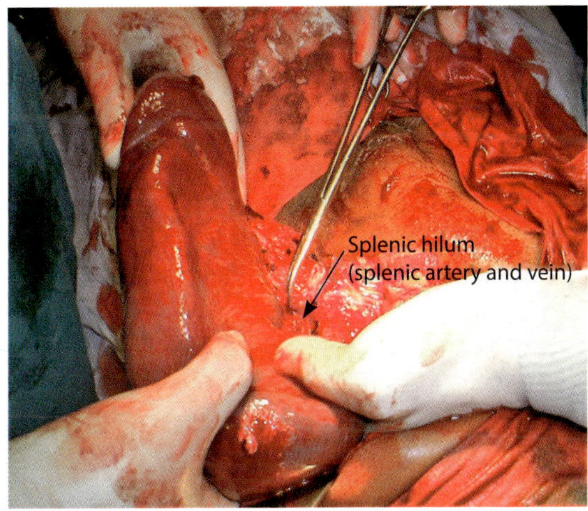

Figure 6.193 Dissection of the splenic hilum.

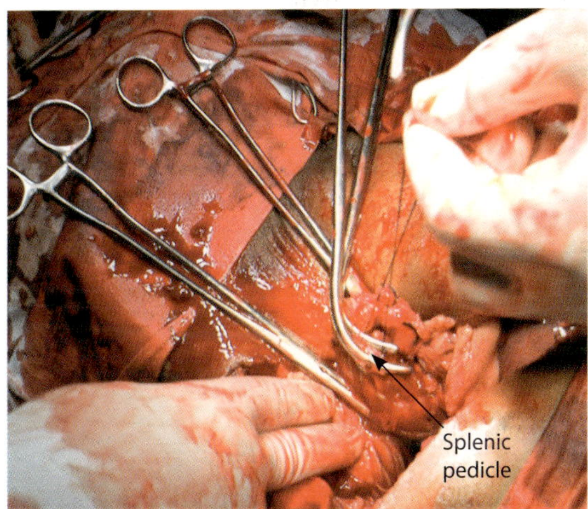

Figure 6.194 Ligation of the splenic artery and vein.

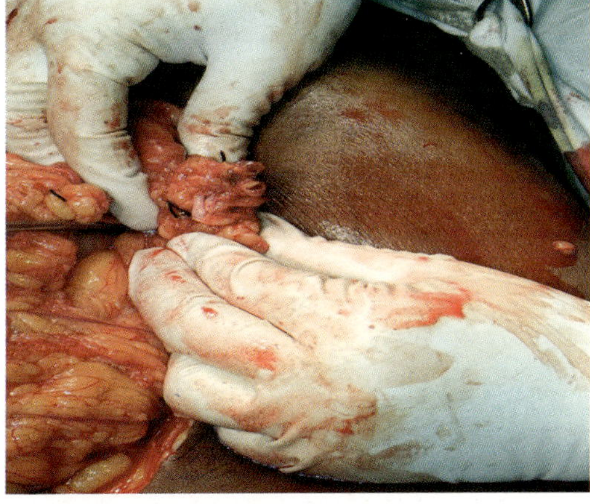

Figure 6.195 Ligated splenic pedicle.

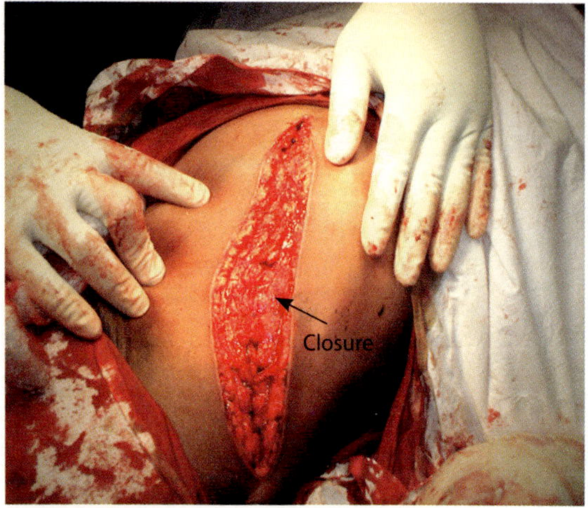

Figure 6.196 Single-layer closure of subcostal incision.

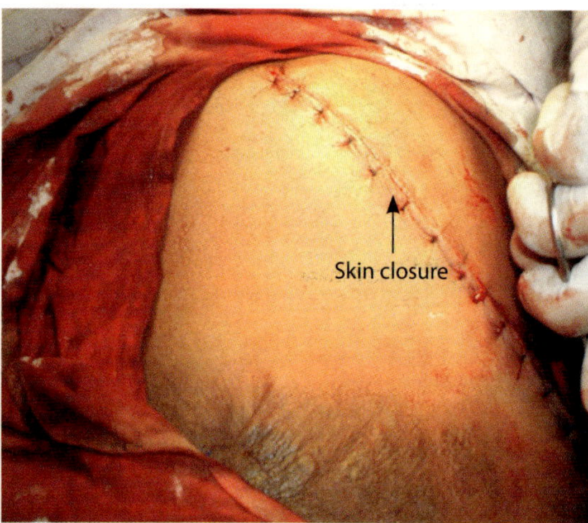

Figure 6.197 Skin closure.

- If splenectomy is done for hematological problem, then search for accessory spleens (splenunculi).
- After removal of spleen, check for hemostasis with three mop tests. Mops are kept on:
  - Inferior surface of diaphragm
  - Hilum
  - Greater curvature of stomach
- Put drain, if there is suspicion of injury to tail pancreas or stomach, or inadequate hemostasis.
- Closure
  - Perform single-layer closure with Prolene no. 1 intermittent stitches (Fig. 6.196).
  - Close skin with Ethilon 3-0 or 2-0, vertical mattress stitches (Fig. 6.197).
- Examine the splenectomy specimen (Fig. 6.198)

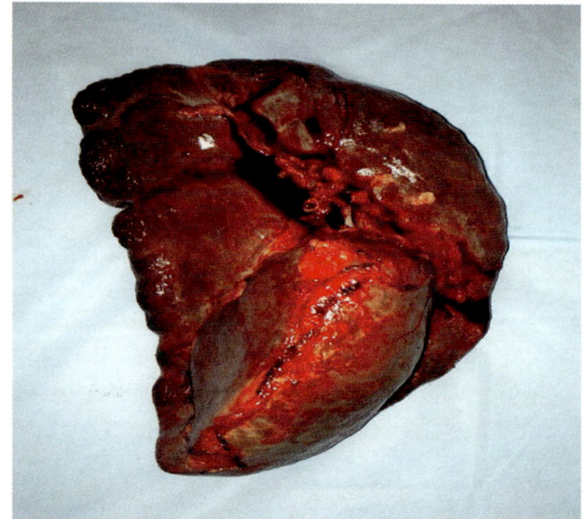

Figure 6.198 Splenectomy specimen.

POSTOPERATIVE CARE

- NBM till further order
- TPR 1 hourly
- Input/output chart
- Ryle's tube aspiration half-hourly
- Antibiotics
- Analgesics
- PPI/H2 blockers
- IV fluids (5% dextrose for the first 24 hours followed by DNS and isolyte M)
- TBSI and H_2O_2 gargle
- Active and passive leg exercises
- Chest physiotherapy
- Gradually, oral liquids started when the peristalsis returns and the patient passes flatus
- Ryle's tube removed when aspiration is minimal
- Drain (if kept) removed after 5 days and suture removal between 8th and 10th days
- Check for complete blood count (CBC); peripheral smear sent for cell morphology
- Prophylaxis considered for DVT

COMPLICATIONS

Early Complications

- Pulmonary: Atelectasis, pneumonia, and pleural effusion. Left lower lobe atelectasis is the most common complication after open splenectomy. Pulmonary complications are less common with laparoscopic approach.

- Hemorrhagic: Hemorrhage can be primary, reactionary, or secondary. It may also present as a subphrenic hematoma.
- Subphrenic abscess: Incidence is more with open splenectomy. Placement of drain in left upper quadrant may be associated with subphrenic abscess and is better avoided. Treatment is percutaneous drainage and antibiotics.
- Wound infection and other wound complications such as seroma and hematoma can occur.
- Thromboembolic and thrombotic complications: These include splenic vein thrombosis, portal vein thrombosis, and mesenteric thrombosis.
  - Portal vein thrombosis is more common in patients with splenomegaly >650 g, myeloproliferative disorders, hemolytic state, and splenic vein diameter >8 mm.
  - Splenic vein and portal vein thrombosis is more common in laparoscopy as compared to open (decreased portal blood flow and hypercoagulable state during laparoscopy surgery).
  - Thrombocytosis: Platelet count is raised after 7–10 days and if it lasts for 3 months and count is more than 100×10^9/L, it is an indication for aspirin prophylaxis.
- Pancreatic complications: Pancreatitis, pancreatic pseudocyst, and pancreatic fistula. These result from trauma to the pancreas while dissecting hilum of spleen.
- Paralytic ileus: It is more common with open splenectomy. One should suspect either subphrenic abscess or portal vein thrombosis if ileus is prolonged.
- Gastric complications: Acute gastric dilatation and gastric fistula; during ligation of short gastric vessels, damage to the greater curvature of stomach can be the cause.

Late complications

- Overwhelming postsplenectomy infection (OPSI)
  - It is an uncommon complication.
  - It develops after years or decades.
  - Lifetime-risk is <1–5%.
  - High index of suspicion is required. Fever should not be ignored and requires aggressive treatment. Even nonspecific flu-like symptoms such as myalgia, malaise, and headache may rapidly progress to fulminant sepsis and septic shock within 48 hours.
  - High-risk factors
    - Age: <5 years (highest incidence <2 years) and >50 years
    - Splenectomy for hematological disease more susceptible than traumatic
    - Splenectomized patients treated with chemotherapy or immunocompromised patients
  - Causes: These include loss of macrophage from the spleen associated with reduced clearance of extracellular (bacteria) or intracellular (malaria) particulate antigen, decreased tuftsin and properdin production, and absence of reticuloendothelial screening from the spleen.
  - Organisms
    - Spleen responsible for clearance of encapsulated organisms, such as *H. influenzae, S. pneumoniae, N. meningitides, and Babesia microti*
    - Encapsulated bacteria: *S. pneumoniae (most common in 50–90%), H. influenzae,* and *N. meningitidis*
    - Protozoa: *B. microti* and *Plasmodium*
    - Other bacteria such as *E. coli, Salmonella, S. aureus*
    - *Capnocytophaga canimorsus* from dog, cat, or other animal bite
  - Prevention
  - Vaccination: As mentioned in Section 'Preoperative preparation, page 148.' In emergency splenectomy, vaccination should be done in immediate postoperative period.
  - Splenic autotransplantation is performed in greater omentum in case of trauma or preservation.
  - Daily prophylactic antibiotics in children until the age of 5 or 2–3 years postsplenectomy in teenagers. Daily use is not recommended in adults due to lower incidence of OPSI.
  - With the onset of fever, patients should take antibiotics such as penicillin. Erythromycin, co-amoxiclav, and levofloxacin are the appropriate oral antibiotic prophylaxis. Cefotaxime, ceftriaxone, or chloramphenicol can be used in patients with allergy to penicillin.
  - 5 days' supply of antibiotics should be provided.

- Antimalarial prophylaxis should be given to those who are going to visit endemic area.
- Patient of splenectomy should have a card showing that splenectomy has been done or he/she should wear a bracelet and carry antibiotics for 5 days.

- Splenosis: Disseminated intra-abdominal splenic tissue which is seen after trauma in some cases. It is not common in laparoscopy surgery but care should be taken at the time of morcellation to avoid spillage of splenic tissue.

HEMATOLOGICAL EFFECTS OF SPLENECTOMY

Red blood cells: Counts normal, but Howell–Jolly bodies, Heinz bodies (exception is infants), and siderocytes, Pappenheimer bodies (iron deposits), and spur cells (acanthocytes) are seen.

WBC series: Initially, granulocytosis is seen. Later lymphocytosis and monocytosis are seen.

Platelets: Transient thrombocytosis occurs.

For chronic hemolytic anemia, a rise in hemoglobin level to >10 g/dL without need for blood transfusion indicates successful response to splenectomy.

TRACHEOSTOMY

Tracheostomy operation consists of making an opening into the trachea and inserting tracheostomy tube to relieve obstruction of the upper air passage to improve respiratory function and in case of respiratory paralysis to allow assisted or positive-pressure ventilation. It is a commonly performed procedure in a patient who has had difficulty weaning off a ventilator.

INDICATIONS

In critically ill patients:

- Predicted prolonged mechanical ventilation due to presence of pathology, inability to protect the airway, or both
- Airway edema and high-risk airway either because of maxillofacial injury or trauma or surgery and cervical immobilization for fracture fixation
- Inability to intubate
- Impacted foreign body in the upper airway
- Bilateral RLN injury during thyroidectomy
- Glottic edema
- Comatose patient
- Barbiturate poisoning
- Poliomyelitis
- Tetanus
- Flail chest
- Ludwig's angina
- Cut throat

Timing of tracheostomy in critically ill patients—in patients predicted to require mechanical ventilation for more than 14 days, early tracheostomy within 48 hours is found to be beneficial in terms of decreased mortality, pneumonia, and accidental extubation as compared with late tracheostomy.

TYPES OF TRACHEOSTOMY

- Percutaneous tracheostomy with special kit
- Open tracheostomy

  Tracheostomy performed above the second ring is known as high tracheostomy and that performed below the fourth ring is known as low tracheostomy.

  Both of these types of tracheostomy should be avoided because high tracheostomy is associated with a high incidence of chondritis and subglottic edema, while low tracheostomy is associated with tracheal trauma and it slips out easily.

OPERATIVE TECHNIQUE FOR OPEN TRACHEOSTOMY (EMERGENCY TRACHEOSTOMY)

- Anesthesia: LA is given.
- Position: The patient is made to lie in supine position with pillow under the shoulder and extended neck.
- Incision: Midline and vertical incisions are used.
- Cut the skin.
- Cut the platysma.
- Cut investing layer of deep fascia.
- Retract strap muscle with L-retractor.

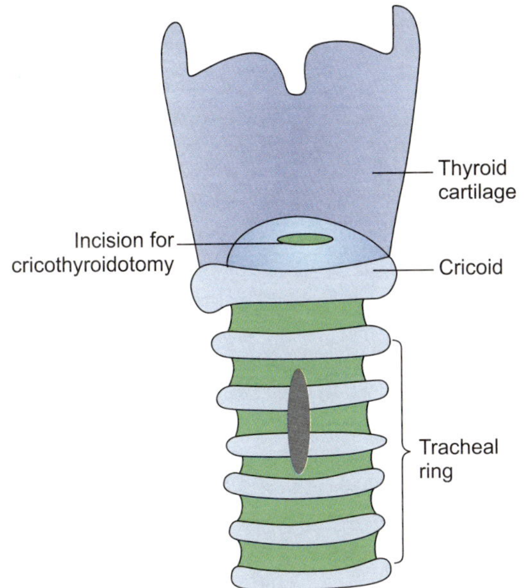

Figure 6.199 Anatomy of trachea. In case of emergency tracheostomy, vertical incision is kept between second and fourth tracheal rings.

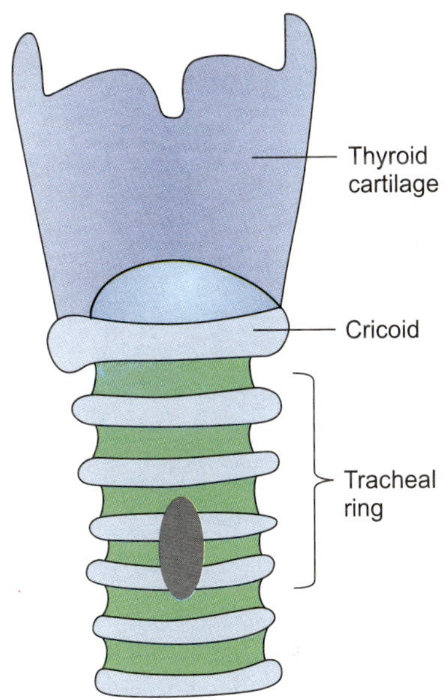

Figure 6.200 Window in open tracheostomy (elective tracheostomy).

- Cut pretracheal fascia.
- Retract or divide isthmus of thyroid.
- Identify trachea by palpating tracheal rings and make stoma over the second, third, or fourth ring.
- Infiltrate LA into the trachea.
- Now make vertical or cruciate incision over trachea with a stab knife (Fig. 6.199).
- With the help of tracheal dilator, dilate stoma and pass tracheostomy tube into the trachea (cuffed Shiley no. 6 or no. 8) and inflate cuff.
- Carry out suction and aspiration of secretion.
- Then fix the tracheostomy tube.
- Apply sterile dressing.
- To verify the position of tube and condition of lung, chest X-ray should be done.

Important structures coming in the way in case of tracheostomy are isthmus of thyroid, thyroid ima artery, and communicating vein between two anterior jugular veins.

In elective tracheostomy, stoma is little wider and oval shaped (Fig. 6.200). In some cases, Bjork flap is used. The advantage of Bjork flap is that it is safe and allows easy reintroduction in case of early accidental decannulation and reducing the risk of extraluminal placement of tube.

POSTOPERATIVE CARE

- Daily examine stoma.
- Keep the wound clean and free of blood.
- Provide warm and humidified air.
- Mechanical humidifier is used (as normal humidifying function of nose has been bypassed).
- Keeping the airway clean of excessive secretion is important. Regular suction is performed (diameter of suction catheter should not exceed half the internal diameter of the tracheostomy tube).
- Remove the inner tube and wash with sodium bicarbonate every 4 hours.
- In case of very thick secretion, administer isotonic saline through a nebulizer.
- Outer tube should be changed once every week.

COMPLICATIONS

- Early
  - Peristomal bleeding: Due to injury to anterior jugular vein or thyroid isthmus
  - Pneumothorax
  - Pneumomediastinum
  - Surgical emphysema
  - Tube displacement: Extraluminal placement of tube by creating false track

  - Block
  - RLN injury
  - Wound infection
- Late
  - Tracheoesophageal fistula
  - Tracheocutaneous fistula
  - Tracheal stenosis
  - Aspiration
  - Air leak
  - In case of accidental decannulation before mature tract (2 weeks), blind attempt to cannulate to immature tract leads to placement into pretracheal space and surgical emphysema may result, either orotracheal intubation or bronchoscopy-guided placement is preferred
  - Failure to close after decannulation

ADVANTAGES AND DISADVANTAGES OF TRACHEOSTOMY

- Advantages
  - Decreased risk of hospital-acquired infection
  - More secure airway
  - Allows patient to speak
  - Allows better oral hygiene
  - Allows oral intake
  - Psychological benefit
  - Allows more rapid weaning from mechanical ventilation
  - Easier airway management in non-ICU setting
- Disadvantages: Scar, stenosis

PERCUTANEOUS TRACHEOSTOMY

- In case of percutaneous tracheostomy, after giving LA, skin is punctured with a needle covered by sheath and inserted into trachea.
- Needle is removed and a guidewire is passed through sheath.
- Now sheath is removed and track is dilated with dilator over the guidewire to a suitable size and tracheostomy tube is advanced over the dilator and dilator and guidewire are removed.
- Decannulation is safe if the patient can tolerate capping of tracheal tube for more than 24 hours.
- Spontaneous closure usually occurs within 2 weeks' period.

BENIGN PERIANAL CONDITIONS

ANATOMY OF THE ANAL CANAL

Anal canal begins at the site where rectal ampulla becomes narrow at the puborectalis part of the levator ani muscle. It is divided into two parts: Upper part extends from the anorectal junction to the pectinate line or dentate line and lower part extends from the dentate line to the anal verge (Table 6.9).

Anatomic anal canal begins at the dentate line and extends up to the anal verge. Surgical anal canal extends from the anorectal ring to the anal verge. It is formed by internal anal sphincter (IAS), external anal sphincter (EAS), and puborectalis (Table 6.10). Surgical anal canal is slightly longer in males as compared to in females (4.4 cm vs. 4 cm). The mucosa in the upper part is seen to be thrown into longitudinal folds known as column of Morgagni. Between columns of Morgagni, there are unevenly distributed anal crypts which are usually

Table 6.9 Difference Between Upper and Lower Parts of the Anal Canal

	Upper part	Lower part
Origin	Endoderm	Ectoderm
Epithelium	Columnar	Stratified squamous
Blood supply: Arterial supply	Superior rectal artery which is a branch of inferior mesenteric artery	Inferior rectal branch of internal pudendal branch of internal iliac
Venous drainage	Superior rectal vein drains into inferior mesenteric vein that drains into portal vein (portal circulation)	Inferior rectal vein drains into internal pudendal that drains into internal iliac, common iliac, and inferior vena cava (systemic circulation)
Nerve supply	Inferior hypogastric plexus (autonomic)	Inferior rectal nerve, pudendal nerve, and sacral plexus (somatic)
Lymphatic	Inferior rectal, inferior mesenteric, and preaortic nodes	Superficial inguinal node, internal iliac, common iliac, and para-aortic nodes

Table 6.10 Difference Between Internal Anal Sphincter and External Anal Sphincter

	Internal anal sphincter	External anal sphincter
Relation	Downward continuation of the circular muscle coat of the rectum	It has a subcutaneous, superficial, and deep part. Deep part fuses with puborectalis part of levator ani muscle
Location	Surrounds upper two-third of anal canal	Surrounds lower two-third of anal canal
Muscle type	Smooth muscle (involuntary)	Skeletal muscle (voluntary)
Innervation	Autonomic innervation	Somatic innervation

connected to anal glands (3–12 in numbers). More than one gland may enter the same crypt or some crypts may not be connected to glands. The ducts proceed inferior and lateral to enter the submucosa where they either enter IAS or intersphincteric space, or through IAS into EAS. The anal valves are semilunar flaps that join the lower ends of columns. This cone-shaped limit is known as *pectinate* or *dentate line* or *mucocutaneous line.*

Anorectal Spaces

- *Perianal space*: It communicates with the intersphincteric space and contains external hemorrhoid cushion, subcutaneous EAS, and deep IAS.[20] Cephalad boundary is dentate line and lateral is subcutaneous fat of the buttocks.
- *Intersphincteric space*: It is the space between IAS and EAS. It communicates with the perianal space. Cryptoglandular infections begin here.
- *Submucous space*: It lies between the medial border of IAS and the anal mucosa proximal to the dentate line. It contains internal hemorrhoid vascular cushion.
- *Ischioanal (ischiorectal) space*: The boundaries of the ischiorectal space are given in Table 6.11. It contains adipose tissue, branches of pudendal nerve, and branches of internal pudendal vessels (Table 6.12).

Table 6.11 Boundaries of Ischiorectal Space

Boundaries	Bounded by (structure)
Medial	Levator ani and EAS
Lateral	Obturator internus muscle and obturator fascia
Caudal	Skin of the perineum
Anterior	Superficial and deep transverse perineal muscle
Posterior	Lower border of gluteus maximus muscle and sacrotuberous ligament

Table 6.12 Boundaries of Supralevator Space

Boundaries	Bounded by (structure)
Upper	Peritoneum
Lower	Levator ani
Medial	Rectum
Lateral	Pelvic wall

HEMORRHOIDS

Anal submucosa is thick and highly vascular, and contains a discontinuous series of three main and constantly sited masses known as anal cushions. The anal cushions contribute to the anal closure. There are three main cushions: Left lateral, right anterior, and right posterior. Each of these cushions contains muscle fibers and blood vessels. Disruption of these muscle fibers and downward displacement of the anal cushions leads to formation of hemorrhoids.

- *External hemorrhoid*: Lies below dentate line
- *Internal hemorrhoid*: Lies above dentate line

Symptoms

Bright red bleeding per rectum, itching, prolapse, and pain with bowel movement are rarely seen in internal hemorrhoid but are common in external hemorrhoid, soiling, and sensation of incomplete evacuation.

Management

The classification and grading of hemorrhoids along with their management are given in Table 6.13.

Table 6.13 Grading of Hemorrhoid and Management

Grade	Description	Management
I	Only bleeding present but no prolapse	High-fiber diet (for males 38 g and for females 25 g fiber) is recommended. increased fluid intake. Polyethylene glycol (hyperosmolar laxative), flavonoids (anti-inflammatory, increased venous tone, increase lymphatic drainage), rubber band ligation, infrared coagulation
II	Spontaneously reducing prolapse	Sitz bath, high-fiber diet, increased fluid, polyethylene glycol, flavonoids (anti-inflammatory, increased venous tone, increase lymphatic drainage), rubber band ligation, infrared coagulation, transanal hemorrhoidal dearterialization
III	Prolapse requiring manual reduction	Sitz bath, high-fiber diet, increased fluid, polyethylene glycol, rubber band ligation, flavonoids (anti-inflammatory, increased venous tone, increased lymphatic drainage), excisional hemorrhoidectomy, stapled hemorrhoidectomy, transanal hemorrhoidal dearterialization
IV	Permanent prolapse	Sitz bath, high-fiber diet, increased fluid, polyethylene glycol, excisional hemorrhoidectomy, stapled hemorrhoidectomy

Rubber band ligation

Indications

Grade I–III hemorrhoid

Principle of banding

Applying band at the apex of internal hemorrhoid will fix the hemorrhoid higher up and correct the prolapse. It also decreases blood supply caudally and helps in shrinking of the piles.

Materials required for rubber band ligation

These include hemorrhoid bander, lidocaine jelly, proctoscope (Fig. 6.201), and elastic band (Fig. 6.202).

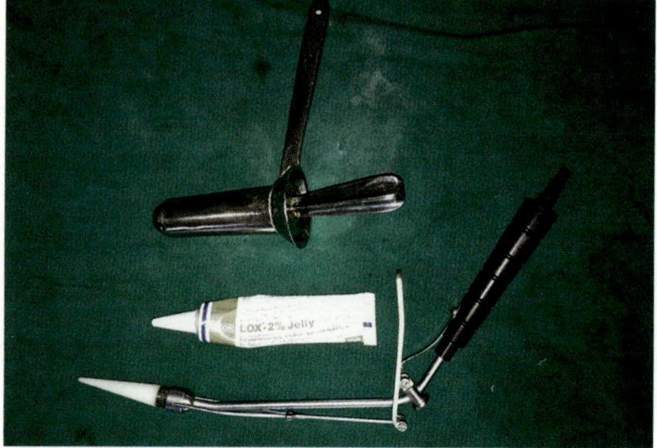

Figure 6.201 Hemorrhoid bander, lidocaine jelly, and proctoscope.

Figure 6.202 Elastic band.

Operative technique

- Anesthesia: LA
- One to three bands, 1–2 cm above dentate line can be applied.
- No special preparation required. Lactulose enema may be given prior to banding. There are two types of bander available; one utilizes the grasp while another uses suction.
- Load the band over hemorrhoid bander (Figs 6.203 and 6.204).
- Apply suction pipe (Fig. 6.205).
- Introduce proctoscope.
- Locate the piles to be banded.
- Apply bander over the hemorrhoid (Fig. 6.206).
- Apply suction to suck the hemorrhoid.
- Deploy the band at the apex of internal hemorrhoid (Figs 6.207–6.209).
- If required, similar technique can be repeated at two more places.

Figure 6.203 Loading of band over bander.

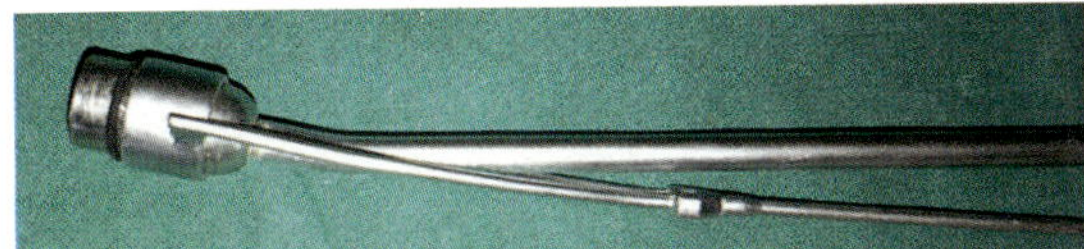

Figure 6.204 Loaded band over the bander.

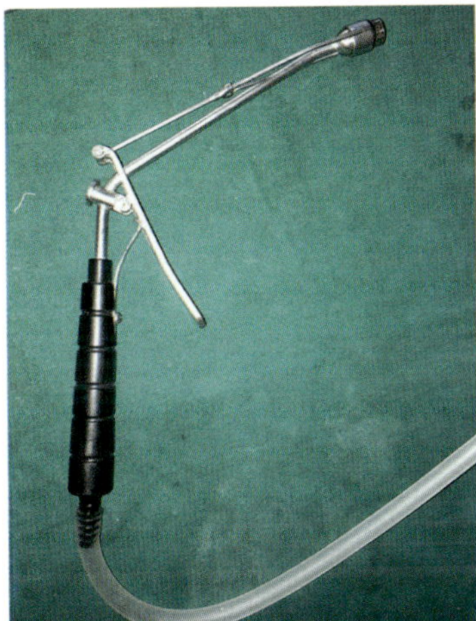

Figure 6.205 Suction pipe at the end of bander.

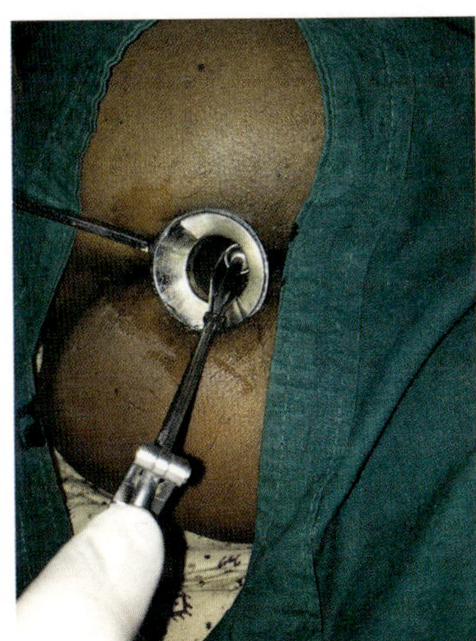

Figure 6.206 Application of bander through proctoscope over the located hemorrhoid.

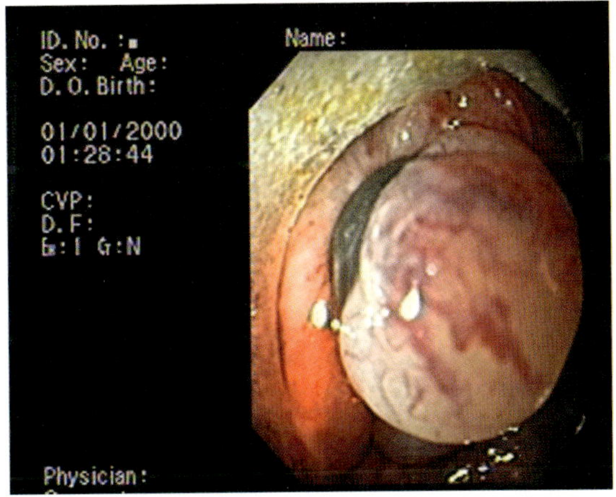

Figure 6.207 Band at 11 o'clock position hemorrhoid.

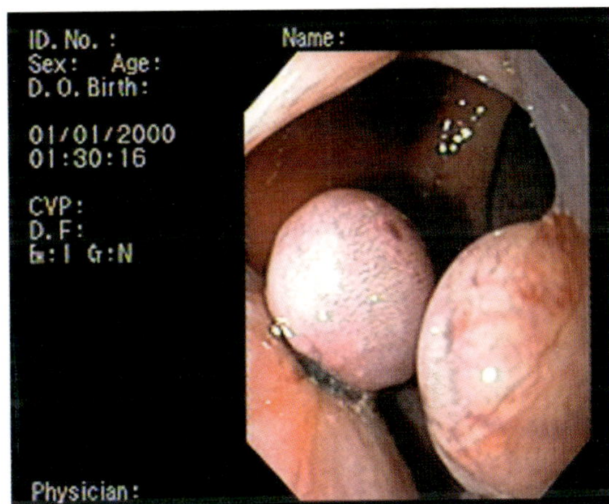

Figure 6.208 Band at 7 o'clock position.

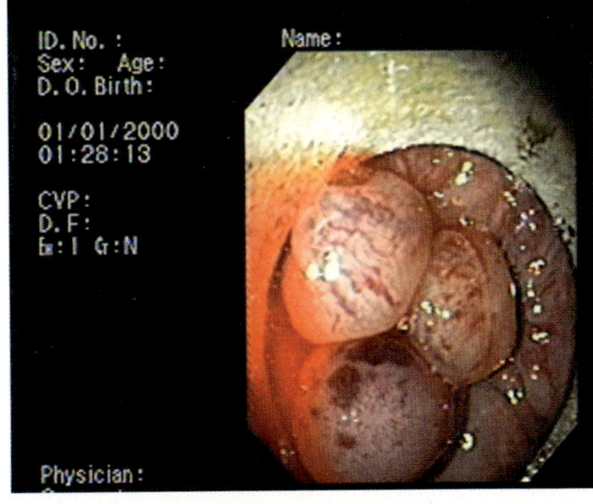

Figure 6.209 All three hemorrhoids banded.

Postoperative care

- Normal diet after few hours
- Laxative
- Analgesic as and when required

Complications[21]

- Thrombosis
- Abscess
- Urinary dysfunction
- Pelvic sepsis: Triad of increasing pain, fever, and urinary retention which indicates pelvic sepsis (early presentation in the milder form can be treated by local debridement with intravenous antibiotics and advanced case may require debridement and laparotomy with diverting colostomy)

Hemorrhoidectomy

Indications

- Grade III or IV hemorrhoids
- Complicated hemorrhoids such as strangulated or associated with fissure or fistula
- Symptomatic external piles
- Failed conservative management

Operative technique
(Milligan Morgan hemorrhoidectomy)

- Anesthesia: LA, regional, or GA is given.
- In lithotomy position, dilate sphincter with two index fingers.
- Put a dry swab in the rectum and withdraw it to make the piles prolapsed.
- A V-shaped cut is kept with either stab knife or scissor with base toward the piles and apex away from the piles; limb of V is extended up to mucocutaneous junction (it should extend beyond the junction) (Figs 6.210 and 6.211).
- Dissect hemorrhoid under the skin and mucous membrane (Fig. 6.212).
- Ligate pedicle with polyglactin 910, 2-0 suture (Fig. 6.213).
- Excise the hemorrhoid with electrocautery, scissor, or ultrasonic shear (Fig. 6.214).
- Inspect raw area after excision for bleeding (Fig. 6.215)
- Other two hemorrhoids are handled in the same manner.

Postoperative care

- Antibiotics: Oral metronidazole three times a day for 5 days

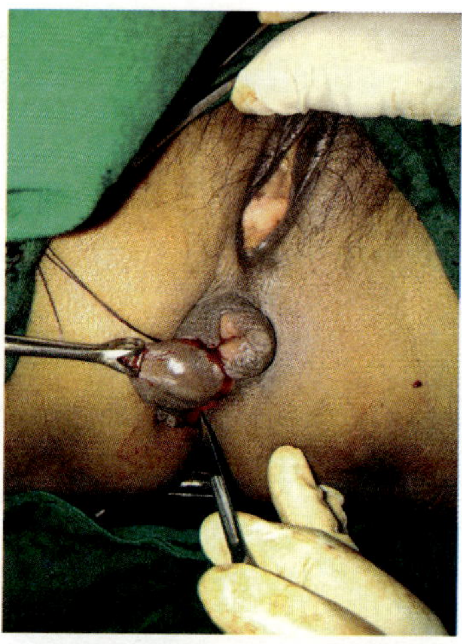

Figure 6.210 Incision with stab knife.

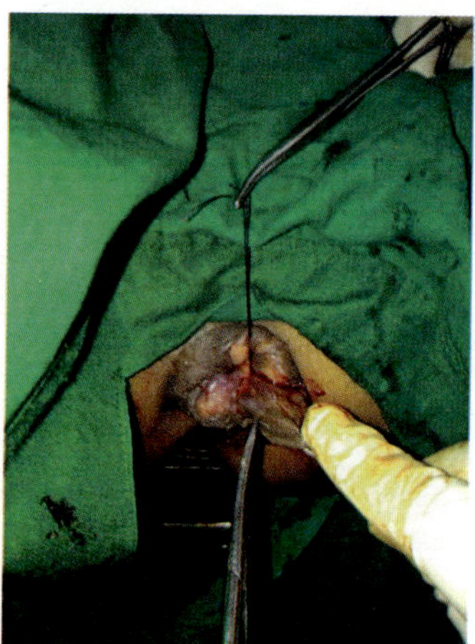

Figure 6.211 Extending cut toward the mucocutaneous junction.

- Analgesics
- Sitz bath
- Local antibiotic ointment application (metronidazole ointment) which reduces the postoperative pain (local diltiazem ointment also reduces postoperative pain)
- Laxative (15 mL lactulose or paraffin at the bedtime)

Complications

- Pain
- Bleeding
- Urinary retention
- Fecal incontinence
- Infection

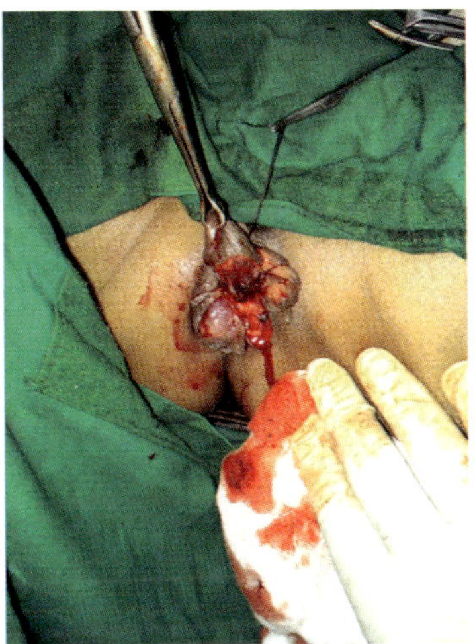

Figure 6.212 Dissected hemorrhoid till pedicle.

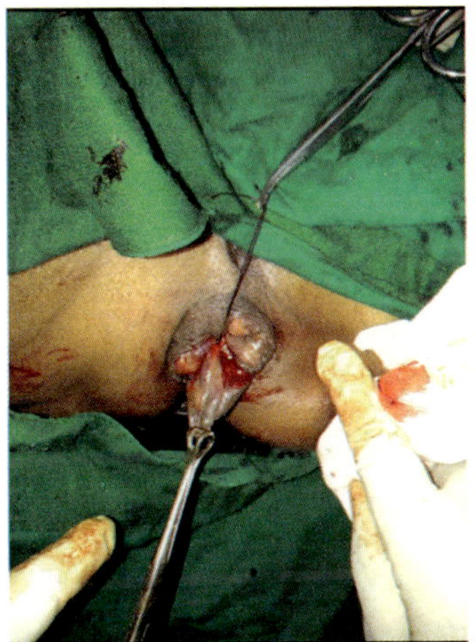

Figure 6.213 Pedicle ligated with polyglactin 910 2-0.

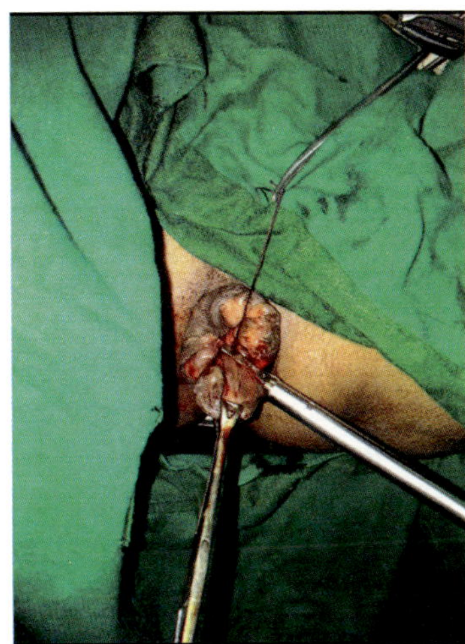

Figure 6.214 Excision of hemorrhoid with ultrasonic shear.

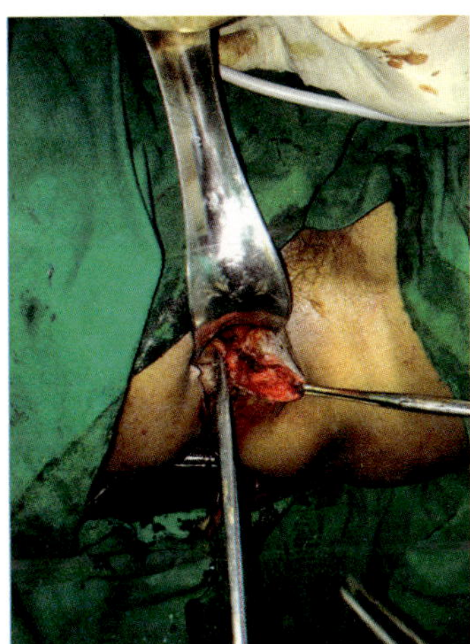

Figure 6.215 Raw area after excision of hemorrhoid.

- Anal stenosis
- Mucosal ectropion

Other methods of hemorrhoidectomy

- Fergusson closed hemorrhoidectomy: It is the same as Milligan Morgan method except wound is closed.
- Harmonic scalpel or ultrasonic hemorrhoidectomy: It is used to remove excess hemorrhoidal tissue with minimal lateral thermal damage.
- Procedure for prolapse and hemorrhoids (PPH)/ stapled hemorrhoidopexy/stapled hemorrhoidectomy (Longo procedure) can be used.
- PPH or stapled hemorrhoidopexy is the preferred terminology over stapled hemorrhoidectomy as procedure does not involve the excision of hemorrhoid, but instead pexes the redundant mucosa above the pectinate or dentate line.
  - Principle: A circular stapling device is used to excise a circumferential column of mucosa and submucosa from the upper anal canal, which reduces the hemorrhoidal tissue back into the anal canal. It also interrupts the blood supply, thereby reducing the vascularity.
  - Indications
    - Grade II–IV hemorrhoid
    - Failed rubber band ligation
  - It is less painful as compared to conventional procedure but has a high recurrence rate.

- Procedure
  - First, reduce piles.
  - Purse string suture is taken 3–4 cm above the dentate line deep up to submucosa. Too closely placed suture near dentate line results in severe and intractable pain while deeply placed suture is associated with formation of fistula.
  - After purse-string suture, stapler is fired. It results in excision of the circumferential mucosa and submucosa of the lower rectum and upper anal canal and pexes the redundant mucosa above the dentate line. Stapler simultaneously repairs the cut mucosa and submucosa by stapling the edges together.

This technique is not useful for external hemorrhoids. In case of combined internal and external hemorrhoids, external component is excised surgically.

FISSURE-IN-ANO

It is a longitudinal ulcer in the distal anal canal.

Classification

- *Acute*: <6 weeks' duration
- *Chronic*: >6 weeks' duration (chronic fissure is characterized by *triad* of a hypertrophied internal sphincter, a hypertrophied anal papilla, and an external skin tag)

  Another way of classification is:
- *Typical (midline)*: Posterior midline fissure is due to passage of large amount of hard stool while anterior midline fissure is much more common in females and is associated with vaginal delivery.
- *Atypical*: Lateral location; it may be due to Crohn disease, tuberculosis, HIV, and malignancy.

Various Theories

Posterior midline is the most common site for fissure. There are two theories that suggest why posterior midline fissure is more common:[22]

- *Mechanical*: Anorectal angle creates the greatest stress at posterior midline.
- *Relative ischemia*: Posterior midline is relatively ischemic as documented by arteriography and laser Doppler flowmetry.

Clinical Features

- Severe perianal pain at the time of defecation
- Bright red bleeding per rectum
- Constipation
- Mucus discharge

Management of Fissure-in-Ano

The management based on the duration of fissure is given in Table 6.14. The various procedures are discussed next.

Lateral internal sphincterotomy

Indication:
- Failed medical management

Position:
- Lithotomy

Anesthesia:
- Local, regional

Operative technique:
- Palpate the intersphincteric groove and cut the skin.
- Do blunt dissection with artery forceps and hook the internal sphincter.
- Expose the internal sphincter completely (Fig. 6.216).
- Divide IAS completely (Fig. 6.217).
- Close skin with nylon 3-0.

Table 6.14 Management of Fissure-in-Ano

Types of fissure	Treatment
Acute (<6 weeks)	• High fiber intake, increased fluid intake, laxative, sitz bath, topical lidocaine • In case of failure, follow guidelines for chronic fissure
Chronic (>6 weeks)	• Medical therapy BD • Nitroglycerin ointment (0.2%) or diltiazem (2%) ointment or nifedipine (0.3%) • Local application of L-arginine (a nitric oxide donor) and/or topical bethanechol (a muscarinic agonist) may also be useful • If above measures fail – Injection botulinum toxin into IAS – Lateral anal sphincterotomy

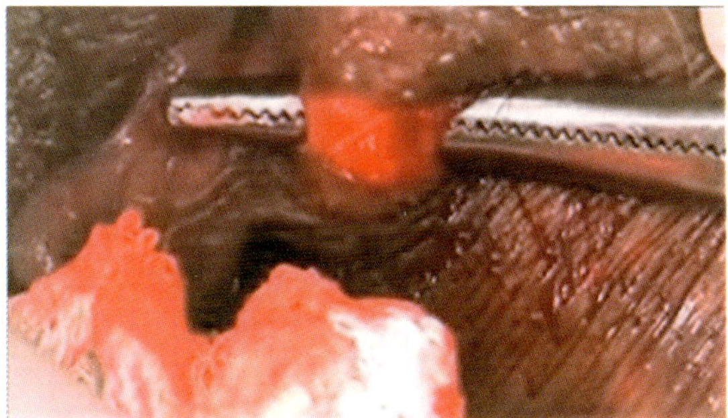

Figure 6.216 Exposed IAS.

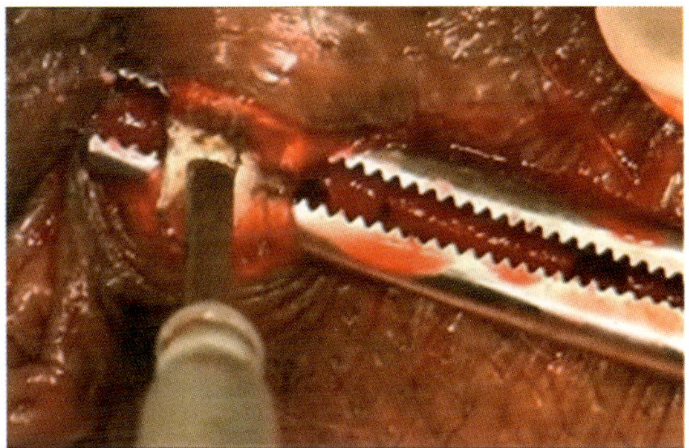

Figure 6.217 Cutting of the IAS.

Postoperative care

- Sitz bath
- Analgesic
- LA infiltration at operated site
- Laxative (bulk fiber or lactulose)

Complications:

- Fecal incontinence
- Keyhole deformity
- Infection
- Persistent drainage from the sphincterotomy site
- Recurrence

The most common cause of complication is incorrect diagnosis and failure to understand the continent mechanism.

Closed internal sphincterotomy

- Insert a blade either directly under the anoderm or into the intersphincteric groove.
- Divide the internal sphincter without incising the anal mucosa.

Other methods to treat anal fissure

- Botulinum toxin type A injection
  - Indication: In includes failed medical treatment.
  - It is a potent inhibitor of the release of acetylcholine at the neuromuscular junction.
  - One hundred units is injected into the internal sphincter on both side with a 27-gauge needle.
- Fissurectomy
  - Excision of the anal fissure
  - Indicated in chronic anal fissure that has a low recurrence rate and a low risk of fecal incontinence
- Anal advancement flap[23]
  - Inverted house-shaped flap of perianal skin is mobilized with its blood supply and advanced over the fissure without tension to cover the fissure. It is closed with interrupted absorbable suture.
  - It is particularly useful in patients with normal or low resting pressure anal fissure.

FISTULA-IN-ANO

- It is an abnormal communication between anal canal epithelium and epidermis of the perianal skin.
- It usually follows cryptoglandular abscess due to liquid stool, tobacco abuse, and poor emptying of the duct due to cystic dilatation. Other causes for fistula are trauma, tuberculosis, IBD, cancer, and radiation.
- Cryptoglandular theory: Anal crypt obstruction by foreign body or perianal debris leads to abscess formation due to stasis.

Types of Fistula

- Parks classification
  - Intersphincteric
  - Trans-sphincteric
  - Suprasphincteric
  - Extrasphincteric
- Another way of classification
  - Simple fistulas
    - Low-lying trans-sphincteric
    - Intersphincteric fistulas
  - Complex fistulas: Associated with high risk of treatment failure
    - External sphincter (>30% involvement)
    - Suprasphincteric fistulas

- Extrasphincteric or high fistulas
- Proximal to the dentate or pectinate line
- Fistula multiple tracts
- Recurrent fistulas
- Fistulas related to IBD
- Rectovaginal fistulas

Goodsall Rule

- Fistulas with external opening anterior to the transverse plane (joining the ischial tuberosity which divides the anal opening into two halves) penetrate toward the dentate line in a straight course, whereas posterior one has a curved course with internal opening in the posterior midline.
- Exception to this rule: Opening is located more than 3 cm from the anal verge.

Indications for Preoperative Imaging

Indications include recurrent fistula, fistula with multiple external openings, and unclear anatomy.

MR fistulography is the best preoperative imaging modality.

Management

Simple fistula: fistulotomy

- Fistula-in-ano (Fig. 6.218)
- Position: Lithotomy
- Anesthesia: Local or general or regional
  - Palpate for the internal opening.
  - If not identified by palpation, inject either povidone–iodine or hydrogen peroxide through external opening with the help of feeding tube and look for the internal opening. Either bubbles of H_2O_2 or povidone-iodine coming out through internal opening would help locate the site (Fig. 6.219).
- The entire tract laid open over the artery forceps (Fig. 6.220)
- The entire tract curetted
- Dressing applied

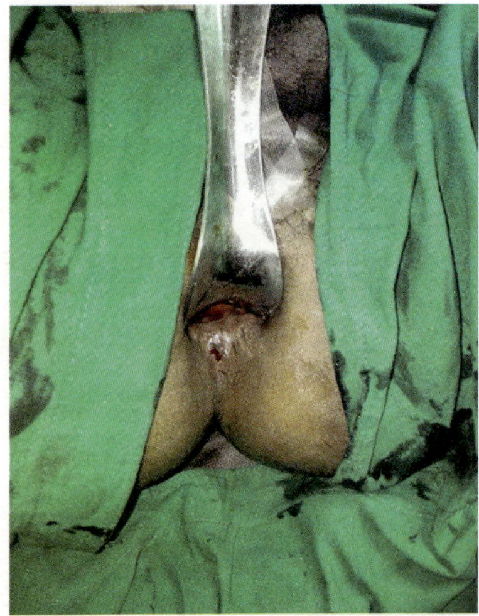

Figure 6.218 Fistula in ano.

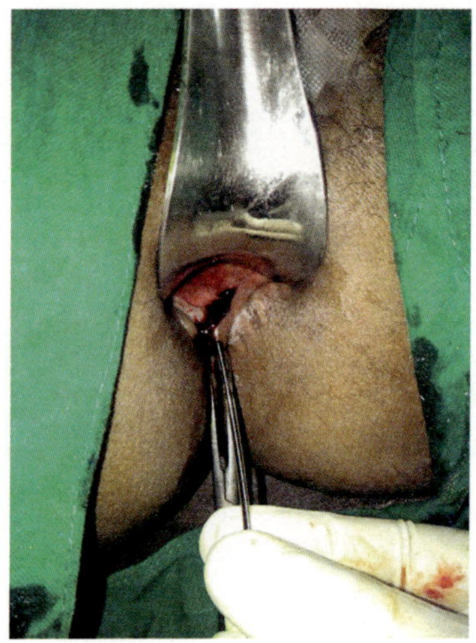

Figure 6.219 Povidone-iodine coming out through internal opening.

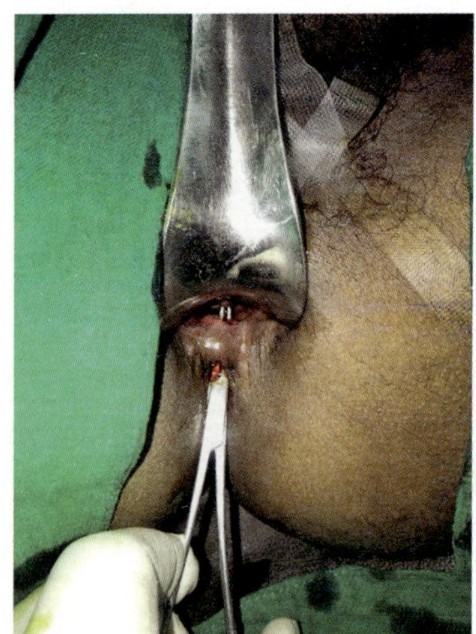

Figure 6.220 Connecting external opening with internal opening.

Complex fistula

- Procedure is fistulotomy with seton. Two types of seton are used: (a) cutting seton is tightened at regular intervals and cuts the tract slowly while (b) draining seton is used for drainage purpose and it does not cut the sphincter.
- Locate the internal opening.
- Insert fistula probe.
- Cut the skin bridge between external and internal sphincters.
- Silk is pulled through the tract and tied properly.

Postoperative care

- High-fiber diet
- Plenty of liquid orally
- Sitz bath
- Laxative
- Analgesics

Other modalities of treatment in fistula-in-ano

- Ligation of intersphincteric fistula tract (LIFT)[24]
  - It is indicated in well-formed fistula tract with high trans-sphincteric fistula.
  - It involves ligation and division of the tract in the intersphincteric groove.
  - Internal part is removed and external part is drained and curetted.
- Fibrin glue
  - The basic principle is collagen formation within the fistula tract. It consists of fibrinogen concentrate and thrombin.
- Anal fistula plug
- Advancement flap: Indicated if there is not too much indurated sphincter complex and adequate drainage of abscess has been obtained
- Laser technique with internal opening closure by anorectal flap
  - Laser destruction of epithelium of fistula tract helps in obliterating the tract.
- Adipose-derived stem cells for complex fistula
- Porcine dermal collagen cross-linked

References

1. Alvarado A. A practical score for the early diagnosis of acute appendicitis. Ann Emerg Med 1986;15:557–64.
2. Yokoe M, Hata J, Takada T, et al. New diagnostic criteria and severity assessment of acute cholecystitis in revised Tokyo guidelines. J Hepatobiliary Pancreat Sci 2018;25:41–54.
3. Podda M, Cillara N, Di Saverio S, Lai A, Feroci F, Luridiana G, Agresta F, Vettoretto N. Antibiotics-first strategy for uncomplicated acute appendicitis in adults is associated with increased rates of peritonitis at surgery. A systematic review with meta-analysis of randomized controlled trials comparing appendectomy and non-operative management with antibiotics. Surgeon 2017;15(5):303.
4. Cataldo P, Hyman N. Ostomy management. In: Yeo CJ, McFadden, Pemberton JH, Peters JH, Matthews JB, eds. Shackelford's Surgery of the Alimentary Tract, 7th edn. Philadelphia, PA: Elsevier, 2013, 2248–61.
5. Natarajan B, Sathyaprasad C, Cemaj BS, Fitzgibbons RJ(Jr). Basic features of groin hernia and its repair. In: Yeo CJ, McFadden, Pemberton JH, Peters JH, Matthews JB, eds. Shackelford's Surgery of the Alimentary Tract, 7th edn. Philadelphia, PA: Elsevier, 2013, 556–82.
6. Zollinger RM. Classification systems for groin hernias. Surg Clin North Am 2003;83:1053–63.
7. HerniaSurge Group. International guidelines for groin hernia management. Hernia 2018;22(1):1–165.
8. Cobb WA, Burn JM, Peindl RD, et al. Textile analysis of heavy weight, mid-weight, and light weight polypropylene mesh in a porcine ventral hernia model. J Surg Res 2006;136(1):1–7.
9. Meuli M, Briner J, Hanimann B, Sacher P. Lichen sclerosus et atrophicus causing phimosis in boys: a prospective study with 5-year followup after complete circumcision. J Urol 1994;152(3):987–9.
10. Fink KS, Carson CC, DeVellis RF. Adult circumcision outcomes study: effect on erectile function, penile sensitivity, sexual activity and satisfaction. J Urol 2002;167(5):2113–6.
11. Leavitt DA, Rosette JJ, Hoening DM. Strategies for nonmedical management of upper urinary tract calculi. In: Wein AJ, Kavoussi LR, Partin AW, Peters CA (editors). Campbell-Walsh Urology, 11th edn. Philadelphia: Elsevier; 2016:1235–59.
12. Goldsmith ZG, Jibara G, Lipkin ME, Preminger GM. Surgical treatment options for ureteric stone. In: Hamdy F, Eardley I (editors). Oxford Textbook of Urological Surgery, 1st edn. Oxford: Oxford University Press; 2017:167–74.
13. McNeal JE. The zonal anatomy of the prostate. Prostate 1981;2(1):35–49.

14. Spelman D, Baddour LM. Cellulitis and Skin Abscess in Adults: Treatment (https:// www.uptodate.com/contents/cellulitis-and-skin-abscess-in-adults-treatment?search=ABSCESS&source=search_result&selectedTitle=1~113&usage_ type=default&display_rank=1).
15. Sainsbury RC. The breast. In: Williams NS, O' Connell PR, McCaskie A (editors). Bailey and Love Short Practice of Surgery, 27th edn. London, UK: CRC Press, Taylor and Francis; 2018, 860–82.
16. Ross DS, Burch HB, Cooper DS, et al. 2016 American Thyroid Association Guidelines for diagnosis and management of hyperthyroidism and other causes of thyrotoxicosis. Thyroid 2016;6(10).
17. Schepers A, Velde CJ, Kievit J. Occurrence and prevention of complications in thyroid surgery. In: Clark OH, Duh Q-Y, Kebebew E, Gosnell JE, Shen WT, eds. Textbook of Endocrine Surgery, 3rd edn. New Delhi: Jaypee brothers, 2016, 437–48.
18. Neiman RS. Pathology of the spleen. In: Hiatt JR, Phillips EH, Morgenstern L (editors). Surgical Disease of the Spleen, 1st edn. Berlin: Springer; 1997:25–52.
19. Tinkoff G, Esposito TJ, Reed J, Kilgo P, Fildes J, Pasquale M, Meredith JW. American Association for the Surgery of Trauma Organ Injury Scale I: Spleen, liver, and kidney, validation based on the National Trauma Data Bank. J Am Coll Surg 2008;207(5):646.
20. Carmichael JC, Mills S. Anatomy and embryology of the colon, rectum, and anus. In: Steele SR, Hull TL, Read TE, Saclarides TJ, Senagore AJ, Whitlow CB (editors). The ASCRS Textbook of Colon and Rectal Surgery, 3rd edn. New York: Springer; 2016:3–26.
21. Luchtefeld M, Hoedema RE. Hemorrhoid. In: Steele SR, Hull TL, Read TE, Saclarides TJ, Senagore AJ, Whitlow CB (editors). The ASCRS Textbook of Colon and Rectal Surgery, 3rd edn. New York: Springer; 2016:183–203.
22. Lu KC, Herzig DO. Anal fissure. In: Steele SR, Hull TL, Read TE, Saclarides TJ, Senagore AJ, Whitlow CB (editors). The ASCRS Textbook of Colon and Rectal Surgery, 3rd edn. New York: Springer; 2016:205–14.
23. Nugent K. The anus and anal canal. In: Bailey and Love's Short Practice of Surgery, 27th edn. London, UK: CRC Press, Taylor and Francis; 2018:1339–73.
24. Davis BR, Kasten KR. Anorectal abscess and fistula. In: Steele SR, Hull TL, Read TE, Saclarides TJ, Senagore AJ, Whitlow CB (editors). The ASCRS Textbook of Colon and Rectal Surgery, 3rd edn. New York: Springer; 2016:215–44.

CHAPTER 7

General Postoperative Complications

Complications are any deviation from the expected postoperative course. Conditions that are expected to occur and are inherent to the procedure such as pain and scar formation are *sequelae.*

The postoperative complications can be divided into two categories: local and systemic complications. The local complications include hemorrhage, wound infection, wound hematoma, and wound dehiscence, while systemic complications include postoperative fever, respiratory complications, urinary complications, cardiac complications, and GI complications.

CLASSIFICATION OF SURGICAL COMPLICATIONS (CLAVIEN–DINDO CLASSIFICATION)

- *Grade I*: It includes complications that can be treated without need for pharmacological treatment or radiological, endoscopic, or surgical intervention. It includes therapeutic regimen such as antipyretic and antiemetic. It also includes bedside opening of wound.
- *Grade II*: It includes complications that require pharmacological treatment with drugs other than those allowed for class I such as blood transfusion and TPN.
- *Grade III*: It includes complications that require surgical, radiological, or endoscopic interventions:
  - Without GA
  - With GA
- *Grade IV*: It includes life-threatening complications requiring ICU admission:
  - Single organ dysfunction
  - Multiorgan dysfunction
- *Grade V*: It includes complications that result in death of patients.

LOCAL COMPLICATIONS

Hemorrhage

- It may be primary or reactionary. Primary hemorrhage is dealt with at the time of operation by various methods of hemostasis as described in Chapter 16, *Frequently Asked Questions.* Reactionary hemorrhage occurs within 48 hours.
- *Presentation*
  - It presents as hypotension and tachycardia.
- *Management*
  - It requires exploration and adequate hemostasis.

Wound Infection (Surgical Site Infection)

Risk factors for wound infection are classified into either of the following:

- *Procedure related*: Type of operation, duration of operation, urgency of operation, and degree of wound contamination
- *Patient related*: Age, smoking, diabetes, steroid use, obesity, chronic illness, preexisting distant infection, malnutrition, and nasal colonization with *Staphylococcus aureus*

  The most common organism involved is coagulase-negative *S. aureus.* Gram-negative infections are commonly seen after GI procedure, and anaerobes may be present after pharyngoesophageal operation.

Dressing done in the operation theater is very sterile dressing. So, unless there is some sign that indicates a problem in the local wound, it should not be opened for 7 days in elective surgery and 5 days in emergency surgery.

Clinical presentation

- Signs indicating problems in the local wound are fever, local tenderness, soakage of dressing, and swelling of wound. For details, refer to superficial surgical site infection in the operative procedure of Incision and Drainage given in section 'Incision and Drainage' in Chapter 6.

- A clean wound has a possibility of developing infection in <3% of cases.
- A dirty wound has a possibility of developing infection in >40% of cases.

Prevention

Measures to reduce surgical site infections such as patient's preparation and antibiotic prophylaxis are discussed in detail in Chapter 1, *Preoperative Preparation*. Other measures are as follows:

- *Preoperative*: Quitting smoking, losing weight, tight glycemic control, and selective use of antibiotics
- *Intraoperative*
  - Tissue respect and careful handling, minimal dissection, meticulous hemostasis, irrigation of wound with saline, removal of foreign body if present, debridement of devitalized tissue, maintaining euthermia, avoiding spillage of GI content, and timing of administration of antibiotics (at the time of induction) play a crucial role in preventing SSI.
  - Compulsive control of luminal content, maintaining strict asepsis, drainage and irrigation of any purulent pocket in the wound or cavity, and closed suction drain in very deep and large cavity may also help to prevent SSI.
- *Postoperative*: Keeping incision covered for at least 72 hours and removing drain as early as possible

Treatment

Regular examination of the incision site, especially in the setting of fever, is critical. Erythema, indurations, and active drainage of pus from the wound are obvious signs of infection. Pain is greater than expected and increases after several days.

- Open the wound; it allows the drainage of pus. If fascia is intact, necrotic tissue is debrided and the wound is irrigated with saline and packed with saline-moistened gauze. The wound should be cultured to permit target antibiotic therapy.
- The wound should be cultured and sent for sensitivity testing. If it is a superficial infection, it does not require antibiotics. Cellulitis requires parenteral antibiotics. Empirical antibiotics should cover MRSA (linezolid, vancomycin, and clindamycin).
- If discharge is deep to the fascia and the fascia is not intact, raise the suspicion of intra-abdominal abscess and required drainage and possibly reoperation.
- Perineal infections after bowel surgery are more likely due to enteric organisms or anaerobes and require emergent operative debridement and broad spectrum antibiotics.
- Most infections are allowed to heal by secondary intention with healing from the base.

Wound Hematoma

- Causes include rough handling of tissue, inadequate hemostasis, bleeding disorders, and liberal use of blood-thinning agents such as aspirin, clopidogrel, and heparin.
- It presents as purplish blue discoloration of the overlying skin with swelling.
- Small hematoma can be observed safely. Large hematoma leading to compromise of the overlying skin may be managed by aspiration with a large-bore needle or evacuation.
- In case of inadequate hemostasis, open the wound and achieve adequate hemostasis.
- In case of bleeding abnormality, correct it along with drainage of hematoma.
- Careful meticulous hemostasis and discontinuation of medicine that prolongs bleeding time will prevent the development of hematoma.

Seroma

- It is quite common.
- It is a collection of serum, lymphatic fluid, and/or liquefied fat.
- Small seroma can be observed safely.
- Large seroma may cause discomfort and cosmetically looks ugly. It may be aspirated once or managed by repeated serial aspirations.
- For large seromas not responding to conventional treatment, percutaneous drain is maintained until drain output is <30 cm^3/day.
- It can also be evacuated and packed with saline-moistened gauze.

Wound Dehiscence (Burst Abdomen or Acute Wound Failure)

Dehiscence is the separation of fascial layer and evisceration is protrusion of the intestine through the fascial layer and out onto the skin surface. This complication is particularly important in abdominal surgery.

Risk factors

- Local factors
  - Wound infection
  - Hematoma
  - Seroma
  - Tension on suture line
  - Use of absorbable suture for single layer closure in laparotomy and inadequate or poor closure of wound (suture too close to the edge, too far apart)
  - Increased intra-abdominal pressure (IAP) due to excessive coughing
- General factors
  - Advanced age
  - Tobacco smoking
  - Low albumin level
  - Renal failure
  - Jaundice
  - Ascites
  - Obesity
  - Cancer
  - COPD
  - Diabetes
  - Inherited connective tissue disorder
  - Hypothermia
  - Low tissue oxygen
  - Steroids
  - Chemotherapeutic drugs
  - Prolonged ileus
  - Emergency operation
  - Operating time >2.5 hours

Clinical features

Serosanguinous discharge from the wound on the fifth day is the first sign of wound dehiscence.

Most commonly it is seen when the wound is at its weakest (fifth and eighth postoperative days). It may occur any time after surgery from 1 to 20 days.

Treatment

- Full-length dehiscence requires tension closure. Another option is daily dressing; put Vaseline gauze over the bowel and allow the wound to granulate. Later on, carry out skin grafting and treat as incisional hernia.
  - Evisceration is an emergency and the bowel should be covered with a moist towel.
  - If fascia is strong, primary closure is preferred and in case of necrotic or infected fascia, debridement followed by retention suture is advised.
  - If there is a tension on suture line, absorbable mesh is used to avoid tension. It prevents evisceration and allows the underlying cause to resolve. Once the wound is granulating, skin grafting is applied.
  - Small and fairly late dehiscence can be managed by debridement of the wound, saline-moistened gauze packing, and abdominal binder.
- Tension suture should be removed on the 21st postoperative day.
- A small defect may require only stay suture.

Stitch Abscess

- It is most commonly seen on the 10th postoperative day.
- It is superficially present as a brown circumscribed blister in the line of incision and deep stitch abscess is present as indurated mass.
- Use of polypropylene as compared to that of delayed absorbable suture is more associated with deep stitch abscess.
- Treatment of superficial abscess: Remove the stitch, incise the overlying skin, and evacuate the content.
- In case of deep stitch abscess, permanent suture must be removed.

Incisional Hernia

- It is the most common long-term complication of abdominal surgery.
- All the factors responsible for wound dehiscence are likely to contribute to the development of incisional hernia.
- Clinical manifestations are same as those for hernia such as reducibility and cough impulse.
- Usually there is a mild attack of colicky pain.
- Sometimes it may present with obstruction.
- Treatment: It is treated through repair, which involves primary suture, open mesh repair, and laparoscopic mesh repair.

SYSTEMIC COMPLICATIONS

Postoperative Fever

- Mild fever is due to tissue breakdown at the time of operation and hematoma.
- Postoperative fever that is caused by infection (SSI, wound infections, pneumonia, UTI) is

associated with increase in temperature >38.5°C and moderate elevation of white blood cell count 3 or more days after surgery.

- Noninfectious causes of fever: These include postoperative inflammatory response, resolving hematoma, and atelectasis.
- In case of persistent fever, check for the following:
  - *P*: Pulmonary infection
  - *U*: UTI
  - *S*: Superficial surgical site infection
  - *D*: Drug fever
  - *V*: Venous thromboembolism
  - *T*: Thrombophlebitis (superficial, due to IV line)

One can remember these checkpoints using the acronyms PUS and DVT.

- Evaluation of postoperative fever
  - Review records for preoperative presentation, operation, and postoperative course. Take careful history of cough, pain, diarrhea, and skin rash. Also carefully inquire about allergic reaction and any significant medical history.
  - Vitals such as temperature, pulse, blood pressure, oxygen saturation, and respiratory rate should be observed.
  - Physical examination includes respiratory, cardiovascular, and abdominal system examination. Catheter entry site and examination of the lower limb should be performed.
  - Patients with persistent fever should be investigated: CBC, CXR, urine routine, microscopy and culture, blood culture, and sputum examination.
  - CT scan abdomen should be performed to rule out intra-abdominal infection.
  - Color Doppler should be performed to rule out DVT.
- Fever
  - *Within first 48 hours*: Usually due to basal atelectasis, other causes being blood products, drug fever, and pre-existing infections
  - *Three to 7 days*: Surgical site infection—superficial or deep—thrombophlebitis, UTI, ventilator-associated pneumonia (VAP) in those who are receiving mechanical ventilation, and respiratory infection
  - *>7 days*: DVT, SSTI, anastomotic leakage, intra-abdominal abscess, central venous catheter infection, antibiotic-associated diarrhea (*Clostridium difficile* infections), VAP, sinusitis, UTI, and thrombophlebitis
- For prevention of basal atelectasis
  - Tincture benzoin steam inhalation (mucolytic)
  - Chest physiotherapy including incentive spirometry
  - Deep breathing and coughing (most valuable approach in resolving atelectasis)
  - Induced sputum culture and sensitivity
  - Broad spectrum IV antibiotics
  - Patient-controlled analgesia and epidural catheter for pain management, which may help in prevention as well as management

Treatment

- Remove potential sources of infections such as drain, catheter, and nasogastric tube.
- Antipyretic should be used.
- Antibiotics are not routinely used except in critically ill and hemodynamically unstable patients.
- Culture-specific antibiotics should be used in patients with a documented source of infection.
- Empirical antibiotic agents should not be used in patients with negative blood culture and nonidentified source.

Pulmonary Complications

- For details, refer to Chapter 1.
- Postoperative pulmonary complications can be prevented by the following:
  - Oxygen
  - Incentive spirometry
  - Bronchodilators
  - Early mobilization

Postoperative hypoxia

It may be due to the following:

- Upper airway obstruction may occur due to residual effect of anesthetic drugs, or secretion, laryngeal edema from traumatic endotracheal intubation, and RLN palsy and collapse of trachea from thyroid operation.
- Hypoventilation, pulmonary edema, and basal atelectasis are other causes of postoperative hypoxia.

Treatment

- Oxygen with nonbreathing mask at 15 L/min

- Head tilt
- Chin lift
- Oral suction for secretion and blood collection
- Oropharyngeal airway
- Endotracheal intubation (if required)

Aspiration and pneumonia can be best prevented by effective pulmonary toilet and treatment for the following:

- Aspiration: Oxygen, general supportive care, and intubation with aggressive suctioning
- Pneumonia
  - Management of hypoxia: Broad spectrum antibiotic is initiated before the causative organism is identified (piperacillin–tazobactam is the initial choice).
  - Culture-specific antibiotics should be given once results are available for culture.
  - When Gram-positive cocci are identified by Gram staining: Vancomycin or linezolid is preferred. Once the organism is identified, antibiotic is tailored according to the organism.
  - Chest physiotherapy is performed.
  - Bronchodilators are also helpful in the treatment.

Pulmonary edema

It can be cardiogenic, noncardiogenic, or mixed.

- It is due to accumulation of fluid in the alveoli.
- Most patients have a history of cardiac problem or recent history of massive fluid administration.

Treatment

Fluid restriction and diuretics

Acute lung injury and ARDS

It occurs due to accumulation of fluid in the alveoli and inflammatory response leading to thickening in the space between capillaries and the alveoli leading to hypoxia. ARDS is a diagnosis of exclusion.

As per Berlin definition of ARDS, all of the following criteria must be fulfilled:[1]

- Respiratory symptoms must have begun within 1 week of a known clinical insult and the patient must have new or worsening symptoms during the past week.
- Bilateral opacities simulating with pulmonary edema must be present on a chest X-ray or CT scan.
- Symptoms must not be fully explained by heart failure or fluid overload.
- Hypoxia must be present on minimal ventilator settings.

Clinical presentation

Tachypnea, dyspnea, and shortness of breath, bilateral alveolar infiltrate, and diffuse crackles

Treatment

- Urgent intubation with invasive monitoring of wedge pressure and right heart pressure with Swan–Ganz catheter
- Ventilatory support
- Careful administration of IV fluids

Pulmonary embolism

Clinical presentation

- These include chest pain, shortness of breath (most common), pleuritic chest pain, hypotension, hypoxemia, pulmonary hypertension, and raised CVP.
- Massive embolism may be associated with syncope and hemoptysis.

Investigation

- ECG, chest X-ray (findings are nonspecific; however, it helps to rule out other causes of chest pain), and arterial blood gas (PaO_2 <70 mmHg indicates pulmonary embolism, hypocapnia, and respiratory alkalosis)
- Plasma D-dimer
- The investigation of choice being CT pulmonary angiography; ventilation–perfusion scan if CT unavailable or contraindicated

Treatment

- ICU admission
- Supplemental oxygen to maintain saturation >90%. Those who are not maintaining saturation on supplemental oxygen, are hemodynamically unstable, and have respiratory failure are candidates for ventilator support.
- Five hundred milliliters to 1 L normal saline infusion is given to correct hypotension. Ionotropic support is given for those not responding to IV fluid.
- Low-molecular-weight heparin or fondaparinux is preferred over unfractionated heparin. Once-a-day dose is preferred over twice a day. Simultaneous oral anticoagulation should be started. LMWH or Fondaparinux should be discontinued once aPTT is 50–80 seconds and

INR is >2.5 for at least 24 hours. It should be continued at least for 48–72 hours and warfarin should be allowed to start its full action. Warfarin should continue for 3–6 months.

- Recent major surgery (<10 days) is the contraindication for thrombolytic therapy.
- IVC filter is used in patients with very high risk for bleeding
- Oral anticoagulation should be continued at least for 3 months.
- Surgical embolectomy or catheter embolectomy is indicated if the patient is having massive PE.

Urinary Tract Complications

Urinary retention

Refer Chapter 8, *Ward Procedures.*

Prophylactic catheterization is performed when surgery is expected to last more than 3 hours or when a large amount of fluid has been administered.

Urinary tract infection

It is one of the most common infections in the postoperative period.

High-risk patients are diabetic, immunocompromised, those with indwelling catheter, and those with a history of retention of urine.

The most important risk factor for UTI in patients with indwelling catheter is the duration of catheter followed by errors in catheter care.

Clinical presentation

It is as follows: Dysuria, burning micturition, pyuria, and fever.

Fever is the most common presentation of catheter-associated UTI.

Treatment

- Proper catheter care should be followed.
- Urine culture and sensitivity. In case of indwelling catheter, catheter should be removed and midstream sample should be collected. If there is an ongoing need for catheter, insertion of new catheter is required.
- Broad spectrum antibiotic is given till the culture report is made available.
- Urinary antibiotics are given according to the sensitivity of microorganisms.
- Plenty of liquid is administered orally.
- Catheter is changed and condom catheter put on if accurate charting of urinary output is mandatory.
- Patients who require extended indwelling catheter should be managed with intermittent catheterization.
- If intermittent catheterization is not feasible, the catheter should be replaced prior to initiation of antibiotic therapy.

Acute Kidney Injury (AKI)/Acute Renal Failure

Nowadays, AKI is the preferred term.

As per the Kidney Disease: Improving Global Outcomes (KDIGO), diagnosis of AKI[2] is made when any of the following is present:

- Increase in serum creatinine by ≥0.3 mg/dL within 48 hours
- Increase in serum creatinine to ≥1.5 times baseline, which is known or presumed to have occurred within the prior 7 days
- Urine volume <0.5 mL/kg/h for 6 hours

Risk factors

Risk factors for postoperative renal failure are the following:

- Preoperative renal insufficiency
- Diabetes
- Nephrotoxic drugs
- Intraoperative hypotension
- Aortic cross-clamping
- Advanced age
- Congestive cardiac failure
- Peripheral vascular disease
- Liver failure
- Sepsis
- Hypovolemia
- Abdominal compartment syndrome

Postoperative renal failure is higher in patients with hypovolemia. The causes are as follows:

- *Prerenal*: Due to hemorrhage, dehydration or third space loss, and insufficient fluid administration
- *Renal*: Due to nephrotoxic drugs, acute tubular necrosis from shock or renal hypoperfusion, and sepsis
- *Postrenal*: Due to BPH, blocked catheter, obstruction of upper urinary tract, and injury to the bladder or ureter

Clinical presentation

The main clinical features are decreased urine output and raised serum creatinine. Fractional excretion of sodium differentiates between prerenal and renal azotemia. Oliguria is defined as urine output <0.5 mL/kg/h.

Treatment

- Maintain hydration.
- Catheterize the patient.
- Maintain accurate urine output charting.
- Treat the underlying cause.
- Patients with normal preoperative blood urea and creatinine and no urine out postoperatively almost always have postrenal dysfunction. First, check Foley catheter for kinking and occlusion, and flushing of the catheter is the next step.
- If urine output is less than 0.5 mL/kg/h for 6 hours, check Foley catheter, correct hypovolemia, and correct metabolic and electrolyte disturbance.
- The best test that differentiates prerenal from renal azotemia is the fractional excretion of sodium.
- IV fluid requirement is tailored according to urine output (urine output + 500 mL).
- In prerenal patients without cardiac problem, iso-osmotic (normal saline) fluid should be administered.
- Avoid nephrotoxic drugs.
- Consider diuretics and CVP monitoring if fluid administration does not result in improvement of oliguria.
- Most urgent management is for severe hyperkalemia and fluid overload. Ten percent, 10 mg calcium gluconate IV over 10–15 minutes, dextrose 0.5 g/kg, and insulin 0.3 unit regular insulin/g of dextrose should be given in infusion. $NAHCO_3$ IV is given over 3–5 minutes and is repeated after 10–15 minutes if ECG changes persist. Inhaled β-agonist should be administered. Fluid overload not responding to diuretics, hyperkalemia >6.5 mEq/L, severe metabolic acidosis (pH <7.1), and sign of uremia (pericarditis, decreased mental status, neuropathy) require urgent dialysis.

Cardiac Complications

Hypotension

Causes

- Inadequate fluid replacement
- Anesthesia: Spinal or epidural (vasodilatation)
- Hemorrhage
- Sepsis
- Cardiac failure
- PE
- Acute MI

Clinical features

Cold, clammy skin; tachycardia; low urine output; and low CVP.

Treatment

- Hypovolemia corrected with either crystalloid or colloid
- Blood transfusion for massive blood loss
- Inotropes or vasoconstrictors

Hypertension

- At least 25% of patients with a preoperative history of hypertension develop postoperative rise in blood pressure. It is particularly important because of risk of stroke and bleeding from the incision.
- Diastolic blood pressure >110 mmHg requires medical management.
- Beta-blockers and alpha-2 agonists are used. Beta-blockers are associated with reduced perioperative myocardial complications. Alpha-2 agonists such as clonidine can reduce perioperative heart complications.
- Nitroglycerine and nitroprusside should be reserved for severe intractable hypertension not responding to conventional medication.
- Antihypertensive medications should be continued till the morning of the surgery.

Acute myocardial infarction

Risk factors

High-risk patients for acute myocardial infarction are the following:

- Recent MI, decompensated CHF, unstable angina, significant arrhythmias, and valvular heart disease are the major risk factors.
- Prior history of MI, diabetes, and renal failure are intermediate risk factors.

- Uncontrolled hypertension, old age, history of stroke, and abnormal rhythm in ECG are the minor risk factors.

Types of surgery and duration of surgery such as thoracic, upper abdominal, neurosurgery, and emergency surgery, long operative time, and high fluid replacement are also important risk factors for cardiac complications.

Postoperative MI usually develops within the first 4 days of surgery.

It is because of increase in myocardial oxygen demand from fluid shift, hypotension, stress, and anesthesia.

Those patients who had a history of MI within 3 months have reinfarction rate ranging from 8% to 15%.

Clinical presentation

Acute onset of chest pain on the left side of the chest with nausea, vomiting, perspiration, anxiety, and shortness of breath

Investigations

ECG shows ST elevation in two continuous leads (usual presentation), new-onset left bundle branch block and/or arrhythmia. Elevated cardiac enzyme (troponin I) in the setting of ECG changes is diagnostic of MI.

> Perioperative beta-blockers started prior to surgery, delivered at the end of surgery, and continued postoperatively for 1 week are associated with significant risk reduction in both cardiac morbidity and mortality.

Treatment

- Treatment of the underlying cause
- Oxygen
- Morphine
- Aspirin
- Sorbitrate
- Beta-blocker
- Percutaneous coronary intervention or thrombolysis (risk of major bleeding), which may be considered by a cardiologist
- ICU admission for hemodynamically unstable patients

> Mainstays of treatment can be remembered by the acronym MOSA, that is, *m*orphine, *o*xygen, *s*orbitrate, and *a*spirin.

Cardiac dysrhythmias

Risk factors

- Underlying cardiac disorders
- Hypoxia, hypercapnia, perioperative stress, electrolyte, and acid–base imbalance

Supraventricular tachycardia

This includes atrial fibrillation and flutter.

Ventricular rate may be controlled with diltiazem. Amiodarone or beta-blockers may be used. When pharmacological method fails, particularly in hypotensive patients, cardioversion is indicated.

Sinus bradycardia

It may be due to beta-blockers, increased IAP (during or after surgery), digoxin therapy, and hypoxia. If heart rate is 40/min or less, glycopyrrolate or atropine is used.

GI Complications

Nausea and vomiting (PONV)

Risks associated with nausea and vomiting include wound dehiscence (increased tension on suture line) and bleeding (dislodgement of blood clot).

Risk factors

- History of PONV
- Women
- Nonsmokers
- Motion sickness
- History of migraine
- General anesthesia and administration of volatile anesthetics
- Preoperative nausea and vomiting
- History of chemotherapy-induced nausea and vomiting
- Cholecystectomy, gynecological surgery, and laparoscopy surgery (have a moderate risk)

It is usually due to the effect of anesthesia or paralytic ileus and intra-abdominal abscess.

Prevention

- Opioids sparing pain control
- Avoidance of general anesthesia and use of total intravenous anesthesia (TIVA)
- Prophylactic antiemetic
- High risk factors according to Apfel scoring (Table 7.1) are women, nonsmoker, previous PONV, postoperative opioid administration—transdermal scopolamine, dexamethasone, and

Table 7.1 Apfel Scoring System to Predict PONV

Sr. no	Risk factors	Score
1	Female gender	1
2	History of motion sickness or PONV	1
3	Postoperative opioids analgesic treatment is planned	1
4	Nonsmoker	1

Probability of PONV according to score: 0: 10%, 1: 21%, 2: 39%, 3: 61%, 4: 78%.

Source: Reference 3.

ondansetron; GA avoided if possible; regional with TIVA preferred

Treatment

- Proper treatment of dehydration, hypotension, and pain
- Proton pump inhibitors
- Antiemetics (ondansetron, dexamethasone, and prochlorperazine)
- Prokinetics (metoclopramide, levosulpiride)
- At least one antiemetic round the clock
- May require multimodal therapy such as like antiemetic, acupuncture, and modification of anesthetic technique

Paralytic ileus and early small bowel obstruction

- Early postoperative obstruction develops within 30 days of surgery.
- It may be functional (ileus) or mechanical.
- Ileus that develops immediately after surgery without a precipitating cause is primary or postoperative ileus. It usually takes 3–4 days to resolve.
- Paralytic ileus develops in the presence of precipitating factors termed as secondary, adynamic, or paralytic ileus and takes time to resolve.
- Mechanical ileus may be due to luminal, mural, or extramural factors, most common being adhesion followed by abscess.
- Paralytic ileus is due to dysfunction of myenteric neural plexus and presents as abdominal distention, nausea, vomiting, not passing of stool or flatus, and absent or tinkly bowel sound. Early ambulation is the mainstay of preventing paralytic ileus.
- Bowel sound usually returns within 6 hours once the effect of anesthesia is over, except in GI surgery.
- Typical average duration of paralytic ileus is 3 days following abdominal surgery.
- Return of bowel sound occurs in the following pattern: Small intestine (within few hours), stomach (24–48 hours), and large intestine (48–72 hours).
- Presentation of obstruction is detailed in Chapter 9, *Radiological Investigations*.

Reasons for prolonged postoperative ileus are the following:

- Intra-abdominal infection
- Hematoma
- Effect of narcotics
- Electrolyte imbalance (hypokalemia and hypomagnesemia)

Diagnosis

- Differentiate early bowel obstruction from ileus. Traditionally X-ray abdomen standing is advised; however, it is misleading due to overlapping of ileus and obstruction.
- Upper GI contrast study and CT using oral contrast are more sensitive and specific.

Preventive measures

- Minimize the injury to bowel and peritoneal surface.
- Handle tissue gently.
- Cover the bowel with moist laparotomy pads and moisten frequently if required.
- Electrolyte must be monitored and balance must be maintained.
- Nasogastric intubation is selectively practiced.
- Routine use of prokinetics does not help.
- Thoracic epidural analgesia with non-narcotics (local anesthetic based) reduces postoperative ileus in elective abdominal surgery. Lumbar epidural has no role in reducing postoperative ileus, indicating that inhibitory reflex arc involving thoracic spinal cord plays a major role.
- Chewing gum: It represents sham feeding. It is safe and well tolerated. It helps in early return of GI motility after surgery.
- Alvimopan: 12 mg BD for 7 days. It is a selective antagonist of the peripheral mu receptor and

confers most significant benefit in early return of GI motility.

Treatment

- Can use nasogastric intubation, continuation of NBM, antibiotics, anti-inflammatory drugs, erythromycin, and COX-2 inhibitors
- Correction of electrolyte imbalance
- TPN considered in case of persistence of ileus >7 days

Indications for laparotomy in obstruction are the following:

- Closed-loop, high-grade, complicated small bowel obstruction
- Internal hernia
- Intussusception
- Peritonitis

Adynamic ileus and partial small bowel obstruction is managed conservatively; if the patient is stable, showing clinical and radiological signs of improvement, it can be managed expectantly up to 2 weeks.

If early bowel obstruction lasts more than 2 weeks, only 10% of the cases resolve spontaneously and the rest require exploration.

Intra-abdominal abscess

- *Sites of abdominal abscess*: These include subphrenic, paracolic, pelvic, and retroperitoneum.
- *Presentation*: It presents as fever, chills, pain, tachycardia, tachypnea, anorexia, focal tenderness, and prolonged ileus.

Diagnosis

This includes neutrophilic leukocytosis and positive blood culture.

- *CT abdomen*: Any collection or subphrenic abscess. Intravenous contrast identifies abscess and oral contrast differentiates fluid-filled bowel loop from abscess cavity.
  - *Disadvantages*: Septation is better visualized on ultrasonography. Occasionally, CT cannot differentiate subphrenic from pulmonic fluid and in the absence of contrast enhancement CT cannot differentiate sterile from septic or infected fluid collection.
  - *Advantage*: CT has a major advantage of detecting retroperitoneal abscess and pancreatic collection.

Treatment

- Resuscitation should be performed.
- Broad spectrum antibiotics that cover Gram-negative organisms with enteric streptococci and anaerobes should be given followed by targeted antibiotics depending on the results of culture.
- Indications for empirical antifungal treatment: These include critically ill patients with upper GI source, presence of yeast on Gram stain, recent history of TPN, and surgically treated necrotizing pancreatitis.
- For adequate source control, duration of antibiotics is 4–5 days, and for inadequate source control, a longer duration may be required.
- Source control
  - CT-guided percutaneous drainage is preferred whenever possible and a small-bore catheter sufficient enough to drain the collection is used. Patients should improve within 48 hours of drainage. Daily flushing of catheter with saline to ensure patency is advised; the catheter should be removed when there is minimal drainage and patients show clinical as well as radiological improvement.
  - Surgical drainage: It is indicated where percutaneous drainage is contraindicated or not possible—diffuse peritonitis, massive intraperitoneal air, difficult access for percutaneous drainage (subphrenic abscess and multiple abscesses), and collection distant from anastomotic site.

Enterocutaneous fistula

- <200 mL: Low-output fistula
- 200–500 mL: Moderate-output fistula
- >500 mL: High-output fistula

Causes

These include obstruction (distal), foreign body, radiation, infection, neoplasm, persistence of the disease at the site, and surgical factors such as emergency surgery, tension on anastomotic line, poor blood supply at the anastomotic site, and technical error in suturing.

Adverse factors for spontaneous fistula closure are the following:

- Distal obstruction to the fistula site
- Persistent disease at operated site (malignancy, Crohn disease)

- Foreign body (mesh, suture)
- Local infection
- Poor nutrition and steroid use
- Fistula characteristics
  - High-output fistula
  - Gastric, duodenal, and jejunal fistula
  - <2 cm fistula tract
  - >1 cm defect
  - Epithelized and short fistula tract
  - Multiple fistula

Diagnosis

It is diagnosed when bilious or fecal matter is seen coming out through the drain or operative site.

Fistulogram: It is used to define the anatomy and characteristics of fistula and has a great sensitivity in localizing origin. Evaluate intestinal continuity and distal obstruction.

CT abdomen: It demonstrates anatomy of the fistula tract, intra-abdominal abscess, and distal obstruction. CT is best to identify infected collection.

Prevention

- Optimization of general condition
- Tension-free anastomosis in healthy, well-perfused intestine
- Reduction in chance of hematoma formation, abscess, as well as enterocutaneous fistula formation by careful hemostasis

Treatment

- Stabilization
  - Resuscitation
    - Rehydration fluid should be isotonic. Small bowel, pancreatic, and biliary losses are isotonic and colonic losses are hypotonic.
    - Strict input, output charting, CVP monitoring, and urinary catheter are essential in managing high-output fistula.
    - Urine output should be more than 0.5 mL/kg/h.
    - Electrolytes and calcium, phosphorus, and magnesium should be corrected.
    - In proximal and high-output fistula, sodium bicarbonate should be given to correct metabolic acidosis.
    - Normal saline and lactated Ringer's are the best fluids for resuscitation and others can be decided by measure of electrolyte and acid–base imbalance.
    - Red blood cells may be transfused depending on the hemodynamic status, oxygen-carrying capacity, and oxygen delivery.
    - Positive nitrogen balance must be achieved and those patients who are in severe catabolic state may require short-term salt-poor albumin.
  - Nutrition
    - Enteral versus parenteral nutrition: Enteral nutrition is preferred whenever possible.
    - Oral rehydration solution is the best for proximal fistula.
    - Enteral feeding tube should be passed beyond ligament of Treitz and at least 4 ft of functional bowel should exist between fistula and tube. In case of proximal fistula, if intestine beyond the fistula can be intubated, enteral feeding can be given (fistuloclysis).
    - Parenteral nutrition is suitable for long-term management of fistula or patients with small bowel fistula where enteral nutrition is not possible due to increase in fistula output.
    - Main *complications* are catheter-related sepsis and subclavian thrombosis. New-onset hyperglycemia indicates intra-abdominal abscess, surgical site infections, line sepsis, and pneumonia.
  - Control of sepsis
    - Percutaneous drainage of intra-abdominal abscess along with antibiotics according to culture and sensitivity is performed.
    - Fistula drainage must be controlled and skin must be protected: Fistula can be controlled with an indwelling tube or adjacent drain.
    - Disposable ileostomy bag can be fitted to the fistula site.
    - Surrounding skin can be protected by Stomahesive paste, karaya gum, aluminum paste, tincture of benzoin, and zinc oxide cream.
  - Pharmacological support
    - Octreotide, H_2 blocker, and proton pump inhibitor can be employed.

  - Octreotide reduces gastric, biliary, and pancreatic secretion. PPI and H_2 blocker reduce gastric acid production. They also reduce gastric secretion and slow transit.
  - Infliximab, cyclosporine, and azathioprine may be helpful in patients with Crohn disease.
- Decision
  - Those fistulas that do not heal by 4–6 weeks of conservative management are unlikely to close and require surgery.
  - Wait till stabilization of infection, nutrition, and fluid balance, and till abdomen is soft and without significant tenderness.
- Definitive therapy
  - Favorable operative time is within 10 weeks of diagnosis or after 4 months.
  - Perform circular excision of the fistula tract and mobilization of intestine from the fistula site. It should never be closed locally.
  - Locally resect the segment of the bowel containing fistula and hand-sewn anastomosis is preferred because chronically dysfunctional bowel is atrophic, line walled, and stiff. In this situation, staplers are unable to accommodate the pathological nature of this bowel.
  - Anastomosis should not be performed in presence of persistent abdominal sepsis and hypoalbuminemia (<32 g/dL)
- Postsurgical care
  - Longer hospital stay, ICU admission, and complications such as infections of either surgical site or abdomen or line-related infections are likely to develop and patients may require prolonged hospital stay and repeated radiological and surgical interventions.
  - Physical rehabilitation and emotional support are essential.

Postoperative GI bleed

Causes of GI bleed are discussed in Chapter 16.

GI bleed is a well-recognized complication of surgery and trauma.

Stress ulceration is a common cause in critically ill patients.

Mucosal ischemia due to loss of gastric mucosal protective function and back diffusion of hydrogen ion leads to erosion formation by gastric acid. Once the protective mechanism is lost, gastric acid also causes bleeding and perforation.

Risk factors for stress ulceration are as follows: major trauma, sepsis, MI, major abdominal surgery, and CNS injury.

H/O recent surgery (bleeding from suture line), portal hypertension (variceal bleed), antecedent history of vigorous vomiting (Mallory–Weiss tear), and aortic aneurysm repair (aortoduodenal fistula) increase the risk of GI bleeding.

H/o NSAIDs, anticoagulants, and antiplatelets is an increased risk factor of GI bleeding.

Melanotic stool indicates upper GI source; bright red stool indicates colonic or distal small intestinal source. However, massive bleeding from upper GI source can also lead to bright red stool.

Signs indicating massive blood loss are as follows: Tachycardia, hypotension, and decreased hematocrit.

- Prevention
  - Fluid resuscitation: Aggressive fluid resuscitation to improve tissue oxygenation
  - Neutralization of gastric acid by H_2 blockers and PPI
- Principles of GI bleed management
  - Identify and treat the source.
  - Restore intravascular blood volume by fluid resuscitation.
  - Transfuse blood products.
  - Identify and treat the aggravating factor.
  - Correct coagulopathy.
  - NG tube is placed if drainage is required. Non-blood bilious vomiting may rule out upper GI source. If blood is present, saline lavage at room temperature is performed.
  - Endoscopy, angiography, and sometimes laparotomy may be performed.
- Indications of blood transfusion
  - Tachycardia and hypotension refractory to volume expansion in patients with hemoglobin concentration 6–10 g/dL
  - Hemoglobin <6 g/dL
  - Those who are at a high risk of ischemia
  - Rapid blood loss >30%

Clostridium difficile colitis

It is associated with overgrowth of *C. difficile* after depletion of normal flora of the gut with the use of antibiotics. It is due to production of two toxins—toxin A (enterotoxin) and toxin B (cytotoxin).

Although risk is more with prolonged use of antibiotics, even single dose may also cause the disease. In some patients, the disease may develop after 10 weeks of completion of therapy.

Any antibiotic can cause the disease.

Risk factors

People with immunosuppression (medicine, HIV chemotherapy), prolonged hospitalization, medical comorbidities, and advanced age are at risk of developing the disease.

Clinical features

- It can range from mild disease to severe fulminant disease.
- Pseudomembranous colitis develops in 40% of individuals who are significantly symptomatic.

Diagnosis

Diagnosis is usually made with stool culture or sigmoidoscopy.

Treatment

Treatment according to severity is provided in Table 7.2.

Table 7.2 Grading of *Clostridium difficile* Colitis

Severity	Clinical features	Treatment
Mild case	Watery diarrhea is the most common symptom	These are treated with oral metronidazole for 10 days
Severe cases	Watery diarrhea with fever, abdominal pain, and dehydration are present	These are treated with bowel rest, intravenous hydration, and oral metronidazole or vancomycin. Proctosigmoiditis may be treated with vancomycin enema
Fulminant	Septicemia, tachycardia, raised leukocyte (>20,000/cmm) count and bandemia (>30%), hypotension, frank peritoneal sign, toxic megacolon, shock, and multiple organ dysfunction are present	Treatment of this involves emergency laparotomy with total colectomy with end ileostomy

Recurrent infection[4]

Recurrence is defined as return of symptoms within 60 days after completion of adequate course plus either toxin positive stool or pseudomembranes on colonoscopy. Recurrent infection involves treatment with pulsed vancomycin therapy, combination of rifampicin and vancomycin, *Lactobacillus acidophilus*, and *Saccharomyces cerevisiae*.

Refractory CD

It is defined as persistent symptoms despite 6 days of adequate treatment. Total abdominal colectomy is required.[4]

Anastomotic leak

Factors associated with increased leak rate are the following:

- Esophageal, pancreaticoenteric, and colorectal anastomoses are at risk of leak due to lack of serosa in esophagus and in pancreatic surgery; texture of gland, size of duct, and experience of surgeon are the contributing factors. Small bowel and ileocolic anastomosis are safe.
- Inadequate microcirculation at resection margin: Factors that impair microcirculations are smoking, hypertension, perianastomotic hematoma, and presence of vascular disease.
- Leak rate may increase due to inadequate mechanical strength because of poor construction of anastomosis (it should be watertight and airtight).
- Intra-abdominal drain more than 24 hours may increase chances of infection. Local sepsis reduces collagen synthesis, increases collagenase activity, and causes increased lysis of collagen at the anastomosis.
- Leak rate may increase due to emergency bowel surgery.
- Blood transfusion: It should be used judiciously as it may impair cell-mediated immunity on one hand and increases oxygen-carrying capacity in patients with anemia and improves healing on the other hand.

- Anemia, steroid, obesity, malignancy, malnutrition, and vitamin deficiency may increase leak rate.
- Use of bevacizumab may increase leak rate.

Clinical features

- Diffuse peritonitis or localized abscess
- Leak from the wound or drain site
- SSI or wound dehiscence
- Bowel obstruction, rectal bleeding, and suprapubic pain

Prevention

- Nutritional support in malnourished patients
- Bowel preparation in colorectal surgeries
- Four- to 8-week interval between bevacizumab therapy and anastomosis
- Best to avoid anastomosis in emergency and immunocompromised patients or in sepsis

Precautions while constructing anastomosis are the following:

- Aseptic technique should be employed with gentle handling of tissue.
- Anastomosis should be tension free and well vascular.
- Lumina of two organs should be matched.
- Correct technical placement of suture or staple should be ensured.
- Avoid risk to mesenteric vessel by clamps or suture.
- Single layer continuous or interrupted suture is safe.
- In case of large size discrepancy, side-to-side or end-to-side anastomosis is preferred. Small discrepancy in size can be managed by Cheatle slit (cut on the antimesenteric border), which is used to allow safe end-to-end anastomosis.

In case of anastomotic leak, the following are helpful:

- Resuscitation
- NG tube
- Abscess open and drained
- Proximal fistula such as jejunal and duodenal: Transgastric placement of jejunal tube and feeding jejunostomy and drain by the side of fistula
- Ileal and colonic leakage
  - Anastomosis taken down and proximal end brought as stoma
  - In colon, either colostomy or ileostomy with either distal end closed or brought out as mucus fistula

Abdominal compartment syndrome (ACS)

It refers to persistent IAP higher than 20 mmHg at three consecutive times at least 6 hours apart at the end of expiration in a relaxed state that is associated with new onset of organ dysfunction or failure.

Intra-abdominal hypertension refers to a sustained IAP ≥ 12 mmHg. Grading of intra-abdominal hypertension (IAH) is given in Box 7.1.

Box 7.1 Grading of IAH[5]

- *Grade I:* IAP 12–15 mmHg
- *Grade II:* IAP 16–20 mmHg
- *Grade III:* IAP 21–25 mmHg
- *Grade IV:* IAP >25 mmHg

Risk factors for ACS are the following:

- >5000 mL crystalloid resuscitation in 24 hours
- Massive blood transfusion
- BMI >30
- Acidosis
- Hypothermia
- Liver transplantation
- Intra-abdominal bleeding
- Pelvic fracture with hemorrhage, pancreatitis, and ruptured aortic aneurysm
- Sepsis
- Severe sepsis and septic shock
- Major burns

Abrupt increase in pressure leads to hypotension, respiratory compromise, mesenteric and liver ischemia, and AKI.

Renal perfusion correlates well with severity of injury (decreased renal blood flow due to venous compression along with cortical compression and aortic and renal artery compression):

- >15 mmHg, oliguria; and >30 mmHg, anuria
- Primary ACS: Pathology within the abdomen (ruptured aneurysm, trauma)
- Secondary: Pathology or injury outside the abdomen (massive resuscitation)
- Recurrent ACS: Develops after decompression in open abdomen

Diagnosis

- Effect on various systems (Table 7.3)
- Clinical and measurement of bladder pressure

Table 7.3 Effect of ACS on Various Systems

Systems	Effects
Pulmonary	Hypoxia, hypercapnia, decreased compliance, and increased pulmonary artery pressure
Renal	Oliguria
CNS	Neurological manifestation due to raised intracranial pressure in the absence of head injury
GIT	Abdominal distension
Cardiac	Decreased cardiac index

Prevention

Keep abdomen open in very high-risk patients and use Bogota bag, biomesh, or vacuum-assisted closure.

Treatment

Nonsurgical

- Positive fluid balance avoided
- Nasogastric and rectal decompression
- Sedation
- Neuromuscular blockade
- Paracentesis
- Prokinetic agents
- Diuretics
- Diuretic plus (25% human albumin)
- Treatment of the cause
- Ventilatory support: Severe hypoxia and hypercapnia required

Surgical

- Abdominal decompression
  - Temporary abdominal closure (laparostomy) using mesh or saline socked dressing
  - Negative pressure system (towel and sponge-based), and silo closure
  - Patch technique: Interposition of Wittmann patch or PTFE patch between the fascial edges
- Vacuum-assisted closure
- Only skin closure

Hepatobiliary complications are discussed in detail in Chapter 5, *Fundamentals of Minimal Access Surgery*, in sections 'Bleeding from the Gallbladder Bed' and 'Perforation of the Gallbladder' (page 48); in Chapter 6, *Operative Procedures* in section 'Complications' (page 64) and in Chapter 16, *Frequently Asked Questions*, Question no. 68 (page 364). Stomal complications are discussed in detail in Chapter 6 (page 69), section 'Complications of Intestinal Stoma'.

Endocrine complications such as adrenal insufficiency, hyperthyroidism, and hypothyroidism are discussed in Chapter 16.

Complications specific to minimal access surgery are discussed in Chapter 5.

References

1. Ferguson ND, Fan E, Camporota L, et al. The Berlin definition of ARDS: an expanded rationale, justification, and supplementary material. Intensive Care Med 2012;38(10):1573–82.
2. KDIGO. Clinical practice guideline for acute kidney injury. Kidney Int Suppl 2012;2(Suppl 1):8.
3. Apfel CC, Laara E, Koivuranta M, Greim CA, Roewer N. A simplified risk score for predicting postoperative nausea and vomiting: conclusions from cross validations between two centers. Anesthesiology 1999;91:693–700.
4. Hudson JL,Turnbull IR. Common postoperative problems. In: Klingensmith ME, Vemuri C, Fayanju OM, et al, eds. The Washington Manual of Surgery, 7th edn. Philadelphia: Wolters Kluwer, 2016, 15–41.
5. Malbrain ML, Cheatham ML, Kirkpatrick A, et al. Results from the International Conference of Experts on Intra-abdominal Hypertension and Abdominal Compartment Syndrome. I. Definitions. Intensive Care Med 2006;32(11):1722.

CHAPTER 8

Ward Procedures

CATHETERIZATION

- The word *catheter* is derived from the Greek *kathiénai*, which means 'to thrust into' or 'to send down.'
- Catheterization is a therapeutic method used in case of patients suffering from acute urinary retention.
- A urinary catheter is any tube system placed in the body to drain and collect urine from the bladder.
- In general, catheters may be used as diagnostic and treatment tools, to drain fluid as well as to inject it.
- There are several types of catheters available, which are useful in a variety of conditions. Catheters come in a large variety of sizes (12–30 Fr, where 1 Fr = 1/3 mm), materials (latex, silicone, Teflon, etc.), and types (Foley catheter, straight catheter, coude tip catheter, etc.).
- The term 'Foley catheter' is derived from the name of American urologist, Frederic Foley.
- The average length of the male urethra is 20 cm. It is divided into anterior (penile) and posterior urethra (prostatic and membranous). The normal adult healthy external meatus allows 24 Fr catheter to pass and prostatic urethra has largest caliber of 32 Fr.
- The normal adult female urethra is 4-cm long with downward inclination in supine position and allows 22 Fr catheter to pass easily.

Types of Catheter

The choice of catheter depends upon indication and expected duration of catheterization. The various types of urinary catheters are as follows:

- Non–self-retaining such as red rubber
- Self-retaining: Foley, Malecot, and Gibbon

Types of Catheterization

- External: Condom catheter for men or urinary pouch for male and female
- Internal urethral
  - Indwelling: Foley, flower tip, Malecot
  - Intermittent: Coude, straight
- Suprapubic: Foley, Rutner, and Malecot

Foley Self-Retaining Catheter (Fig. 8.1)

- Made up of latex
- Available as two- or three-way catheter
- Size 8–24 Fr

Indications

- To relieve retention of urine (most common)
- To act as a traction for controlling bleeding after prostate surgery
- To monitor urine output in critically ill patients
- To monitor urine output in postoperative patients after operations on kidney, ureter, and prostate
- To give bladder wash in cystitis
- Can be kept as a gastrostomy, jejunostomy, or suprapubic cystostomy
- In neurogenic bladder [advise the patient about clean intermittent self-catheterization (CISC)]
- To obtain sterile urine sample in female patients
- To undertake urodynamic study
- For diagnostic purposes, for example, RGU and VCUG

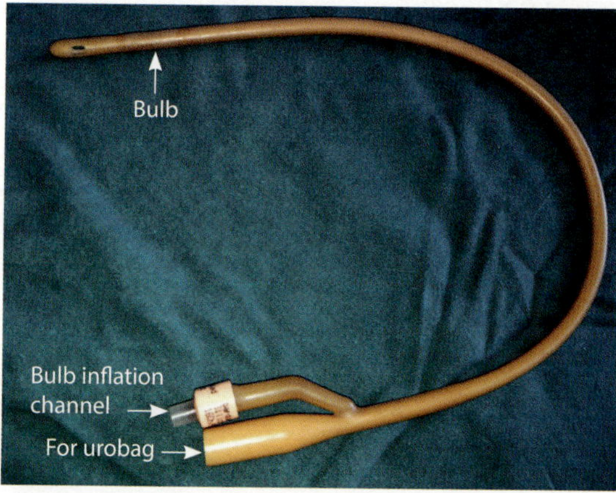

Figure 8.1 Foley self-retaining catheter.

- For giving chemotherapy drugs in carcinoma bladder
- In epistaxis for hemostasis
- As a tourniquet
- To hold urethral skin graft in place after urethral stricture repair

Contraindications

- Allergy to material used such as latex and silicon
- Blood at the meatus, which indicates partial or total rupture of urethra in case of trauma (attempting to pass Foley will convert partial into total rupture)

Size of catheter

- *Pediatric*: 8–12 Fr
- *Adult male*: 16–18 Fr
- <5 years: 5–8 Fr
- 5–10 years: 8–10 Fr
- 10–14 years: 10–12 Fr
- >14 years: 10–16 Fr

The optimal catheter in an adult patient is a 16 Fr latex catheter. Larger-caliber catheters such as 20 or 22 Fr are used to evacuate hematoma or bleeding from upper urinary tract.

Technique

Male

- Position: Supine
- Keep the sterile tray and material required for inserting Foley catheter ready.
- Put on gloves, and clean the glans and urethra with povidone-iodine (Fig. 8.2a).
- Hold the penis straight.
- Under strict aseptic precautions, push 10–20 mL 2% lidocaine jelly with disposable syringe into the urethra and wait for 10 minutes to allow for the action of jelly to start (lubrication and anesthesia) (Fig. 8.2b).
- Insert Foley catheter gently and allow urine to flow (Fig. 8.2c).
- Insert till 'Y' junction.
- Before inflation, ensure that catheter is in the bladder (Fig. 8.2d).
- Inflate bulb with 10 mL normal saline or distilled water (Fig. 8.2e).

Inflation of bulb with normal saline may lead to clogging due to crystal formation and bulb will not deflate if kept for >2 days. So, it is advisable to use distilled water.

- After inflation, withdraw the catheter till resistance is felt.
- Replace the skin over the glans to avoid the possibility of paraphimosis.

Female

- Position: Frog leg
- Keep the sterile tray and material required for inserting Foley catheter ready
- Put on gloves and clean the glans and urethra with Betadine
- Separate the labia to expose urethral opening
- Under strict aseptic precautions, push 10–20 cm^3 2% lidocaine jelly with disposable syringe into the urethra and wait for 10 minutes to allow for the action of jelly to start (lubrication and anesthesia)
- Insert Foley catheter gently and allow urine to flow
- Before inflation, ensure that catheter is in the bladder (Fig. 8.2d)
- Inflate bulb with 10 mL normal saline or distilled water (Fig. 8.2e)
- After inflation, withdraw the catheter till resistance is felt

Solutions to some practical problems

- *No urine flow in tubing*: Applying gentle pressure in the suprapubic region may initiate urine flow. In women, check catheter site, as vaginal catheterization may have occurred. If urine does not appear even after suprapubic pressure, push 10–20 mL sterile saline. This should result in return of saline mixed with urine.
- *Stricture found*: Try a smaller-Fr catheter.
- *Catheter is in the bladder but not draining*: Usually it is due to jelly blocking the catheter. Flush with sterile water or normal saline and aspirate.

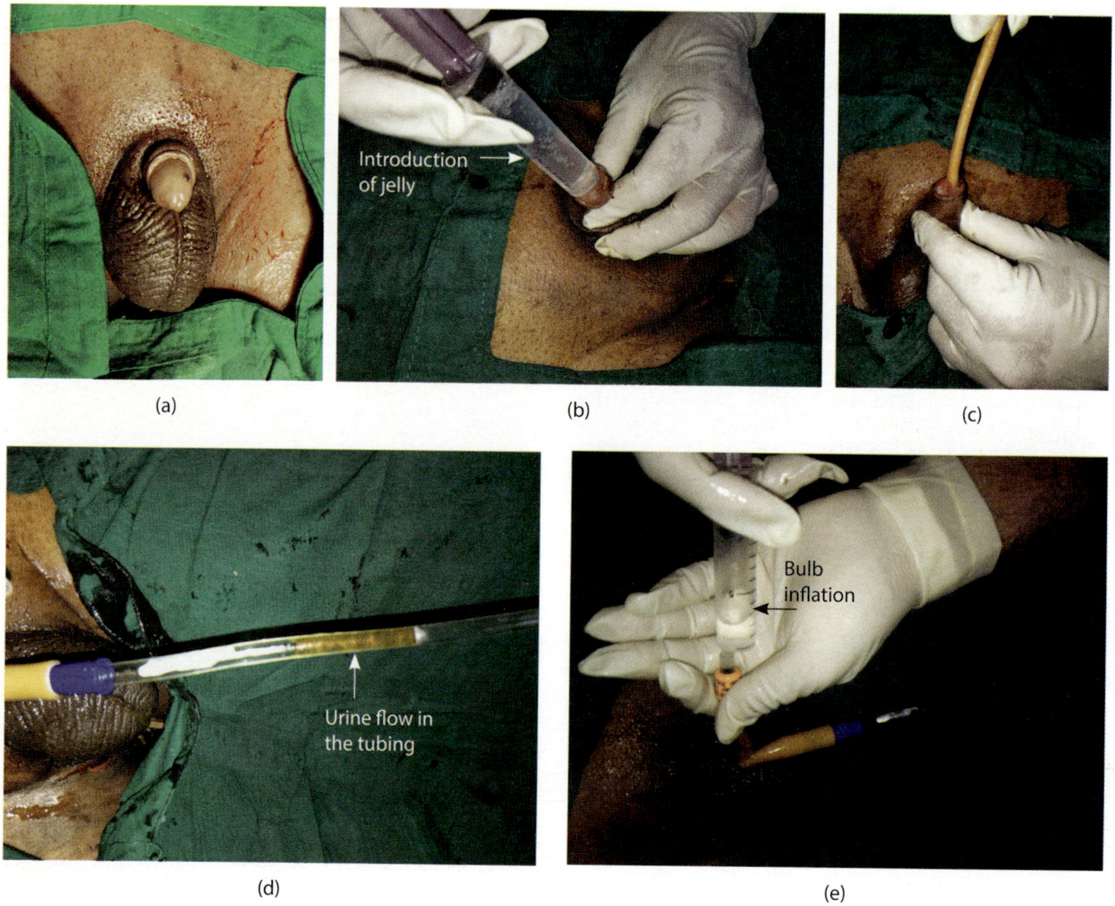

(a) (b) (c) (d) (e)

Introduction of jelly

Urine flow in the tubing

Bulb inflation

Figure 8.2 Technique of catheterization. (a) Cleaned penis with povidone-iodine and draping and isolation of part. (b) Introduction of jelly with syringe. (c) Insertion of Foley catheter. (d) Urine flow in the tube. (e) Inflation of bulb with normal saline.

- *Failed catheterization*: No more than two attempts should be made, and the second attempt should be with a smaller-Fr catheter. If the second attempt fails, consider placement of suprapubic catheter or help from an expert.
- *While inserting catheter, there is bleeding per urethra*: Abandon the procedure. Consider RGU and placement of suprapubic catheter.
- *BPH*: Try a larger-number catheter (18–20 Fr), which will provide more stiffness, or a coude tip catheter.

Catheter care

- Clean the urethral area and catheter daily with soap and water.
- Increase fluid intake.
- Keep the drainage bag below the level of bladder.
- Empty the drainage bag every 8 hours or when full.

Removal of catheter

- Catheter should be removed as early as possible after its purpose is served. In the case of indwelling catheters, removal times for various types of catheters are listed in Table 8.1.

Table 8.1 Removal Times for Various Catheters

Type of catheter	Time of removal
Latex	3–4 weeks
Silicon coated	3 months
Hydrogel coated	3 months
Teflon coated	1 month

- Deflate the balloon and remove the catheter. Failure to deflate balloon is either due to faulty valve mechanism or obstructed balloon channel.
- If balloon does not deflate, then:
  - Instill an extra 1 or 2 ml of fluid and aspirate
  - Cut the channel proximally and aspirate
  - Insert ureteric stylet or guidewire through the inflation channel to dislodge the obstruction
  - Employ USG-guided puncture with spinal needle

- Prophylactic antibiotics should not be used in patients who do not have proven UTI in either short- or long-term catheterization.
- In case of acute urinary retention, once the initiating event such as infection, cystitis, and BPH has been treated, it is possible to void spontaneously.
- Catheter-free trial can be given by performing fill and pull method: Bladder is filled with 450 cm^3 of sterile water or saline via catheter and then catheter is removed and patients are asked to void. If PVR is >200 cm^3, the patient may be at risk of recurrent urinary retention.
- If the patient is not able to void: Recatheterize with possible explanation of all complications associated with indwelling catheter.
- Latex catheters are the most commonly used. These are associated with urethral inflammation due to protein and salt encrustation on the surface of the catheter. Urethral inflammation from prolonged latex catheterization can lead to formation of urethral stricture. So latex catheters are not preferred for long-term use. Silicone-coated catheter may be suitable for long-term use.
- Use of feeding tube as catheter is associated with complications such as strictures, ulcer, and knotting within the bladder. Therefore, its use should be discouraged.

Three-Way Foley Catheter (Fig. 8.3)

- Used mainly in prostatectomy for irrigation purposes
- Used in carcinoma of bladder, where sometimes irrigation is required for prevention of clot retention

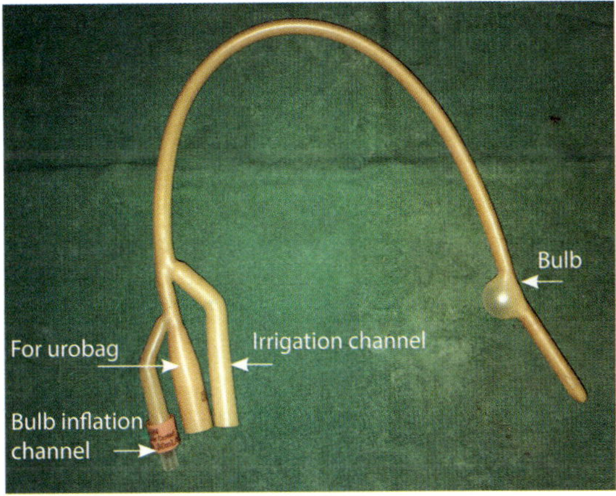

Figure 8.3 Foley three-way catheter.

- Available as presterilized by gamma radiation or ethylene oxide (EO)

Complications

- There can be trauma to the urethra while introducing the catheter.
- Trauma to the prostatic urethra can be present due to inflation of bulb in the urethra.
- False passage: Remove catheter, and evaluate by cystoscopy.
- Infection: Urethritis and cystitis. Clinical signs indicating UTI are fever, cloudy urine, blockage of catheter, and spasm
- Pericatheteric leak due to spasm of bladder: Use of a larger-number catheter will not correct it. It requires use of anticholinergic drugs (flavoxate, oxybutynin)
- Urethral stricture
- Stone formation
- Pyelonephritis may occur
- Catheter may get stuck
- There can be hematuria following sudden decompression (small mucosal disruption)
- Hypotension: Usually, it occurs as a vasovagal response to sudden relief of distended bladder
- Inability to deflate the balloon may result

Clean Intermittent Self-Catheterization

Nowadays, clean intermittent catheterization is the method of choice for bladder evacuation or emptying when neurological or non-neurological causes lead to retention or incomplete emptying.

Indications
- Neurogenic voiding dysfunction
- Postoperative: Optical internal urethrotomy, urethroplasty, and partial amputation of penis
- Spinal cord injury
- Underactive detrusor
- Bladder outlet obstruction unfit for surgery
- Augmentation cystoplasty with catheterization via urethra or continent stoma
- Can also be used for short term in postoperative retention, bladder suspension procedure, hemorrhoidectomy cases, and postpartum

Relative contraindications
- False passage or stricture urethra
- Mentally unsound
- Morbid obesity
- Flexion deformity

Patients should wash their hands with soap and water before and after catheterization. Antibacterial soap or povidone–iodine is recommended for cleaning catheter. Catheter should be thoroughly rinsed with running tap water after soaking in cleaning solution. It must dry before reuse and is kept in a plastic bag.

Advantages
- The risk of UTI minimized when there is normal bladder function allowing to fill and empty periodically
- Done with Nelaton urethral catheter or straight urethral catheter (Fig. 8.4)

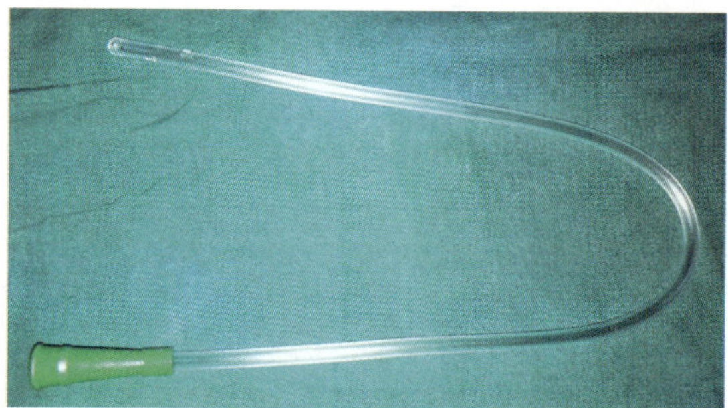

Figure 8.4 Urethral catheter.

Red Rubber Catheter (Fig. 8.5)

The red rubber catheter is used:
- For providing relief in retention of urine as a temporary measure
- To measure postvoid residual urine
- As a tourniquet
- For throat suction
- To give oxygen

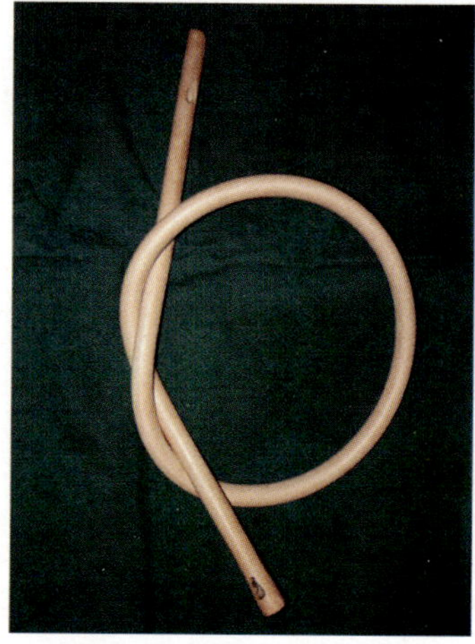

Figure 8.5 Red rubber catheter.

Specific Conditions

Postoperative urinary retention (POUR)

It refers to the inability to void at bladder volume of 600 mL. Two main causes of POUR are:
- Mechanical obstruction to the outflow
- Altered neural control of bladder and detrusor muscle

Risk factors for postoperative retention are as follows:
- Age and sex: POUR increases with increasing age. It is more common in males.
- There is high incidence in pelvic surgery (anorectal surgery, hernia, penile, and urological surgery) and joint orthopedic surgery.
- Neurological disease may predispose to retention.
- Medications commonly used such as anticholinergic (atropine and glycopyrrolate), prazosin, clonidine, and beta-blockers increase the rate of POUR.
- Excessive administration of fluid during perioperative period increases the risk.
- Longer duration of surgery increases the risk.
- Spinal anesthesia or epidural anesthesia with a longer-acting agent such as bupivacaine, tetracaine, and ropivacaine increases the rate of POUR.
- Use of neuraxial opioid with local anesthesia increases the risk.

- In postoperative period: Large bladder volume in recovery room >300 mL, sedative use, and postoperative analgesia such as patient-controlled analgesia also increase the risk.
  Management is as follows:
- Reassurance
- Analgesics
- Hot-water bag application over suprapubic region
- Privacy
- Sound of running tap water (psychological reasons)
- Inj. carbachol
- Foley catheter

Managing difficulty in negotiating urethra

- Seldinger technique can be used. Catheter can be passed over the guidewire.
- With the help of cystoscopy, direct visualization of the difficult portion is possible and once the obstruction is visualized, guidewire can be passed into the bladder and catheter is passed over the guidewire.

Immediate postcatheter management in acute urinary retention

- Watch for postobstructive diuresis; it is usually self-limiting and due to accumulation of urea and hormonal alteration. Persistent urine output is 150–200 mL/hour; electrolyte monitoring and fluid replacement are required.
- Watch for hematuria. Hematuria may be due to damage to mucosal blood vessels due to sudden and rapid decompression of significantly distended bladder. Catheter should be intermittently clamped and gradual decompression allowed over half an hour.

RYLE'S TUBE INSERTION (Fig. 8.6)

- Ryle's tube (RT) is routinely inserted via nasogastric route for nutrition and aspiration of intestinal secretions.
- It is made up of PVC or Portex.
- It is available presterilized with EO.
- It is marked at 50 cm (at the level of body of the stomach), 60 cm (at the pylorus), and 70 cm (duodenum) from the tip.
- It has lateral hole for effective aspiration.
- It has corrosion-less stainless steel beads, which allow smooth introduction of RT due to the effect of gravity.

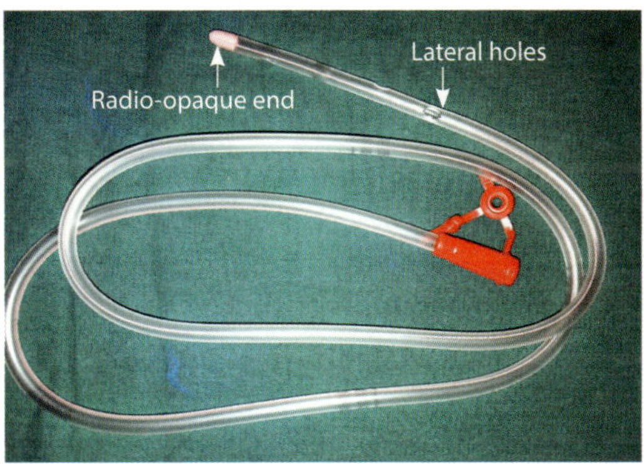

Figure 8.6 Ryle's tube.

There are mainly two types of nasogastric tube:

- *Large-bore RT*: Used for decompression of stomach and removal of its content
- *Fine-bore RT*: Used for feeding

Indications

- Intestinal obstruction
- Peptic perforation
- Acute cholecystitis and acute pancreatitis (to aspirate the stomach contents and give rest to the inflamed organs)
- In emergency upper GI endoscopy (to empty the stomach)
- Acute gastric dilatation
- Paralytic ileus
- Blunt abdominal trauma (hemoperitoneum)
- RT feeding in comatose patients
- Cold saline lavage in patients with hematemesis

Contraindications

- Corrosive poisoning
- Kerosene poisoning
- Aortic aneurysm and nonbleeding esophageal varices
- Basal skull fracture
- Patient's refusal

Complications

- Gastritis and ulceration
- Reflux esophagitis
- Aspiration pneumonia
- Epistaxis, sinusitis, and rhinitis
- Esophageal perforation
- Bleeding from unruptured varices
- Pulmonary abscess (rare)

Complications are more common in unconscious patients and patients with poor cough reflex.

Technique

- Position: Propped-up/supine position is the appropriate choice for the procedure.
- Slightly flex the neck. Choose nostril.
- Lubricate tube with lignocaine jelly (Fig. 8.7a). Pass it gently along the big nostril (Fig. 8.7b).
- Ask the patient to swallow when the tube reaches the posterior pharyngeal wall.
- Keep on pushing till the RT is in between second and third markings.
- Confirm that the RT is in the stomach.

Check length required to reach the stomach or intestine: Calculate distance between tip of nose and ear lobe plus distance between ear lobe and xiphoid process. Add 15 cm for nasogastric placement and 20–25 cm for nasointestinal placement.

Checking whether Ryle's tube is in the stomach or not

- Push air through the syringe into the tube and auscultate over the epigastrium, when a sound of gush of air will be heard (Fig. 8.7c).
- Aspiration reveals gastric content or bilious material (Fig. 8.7d).

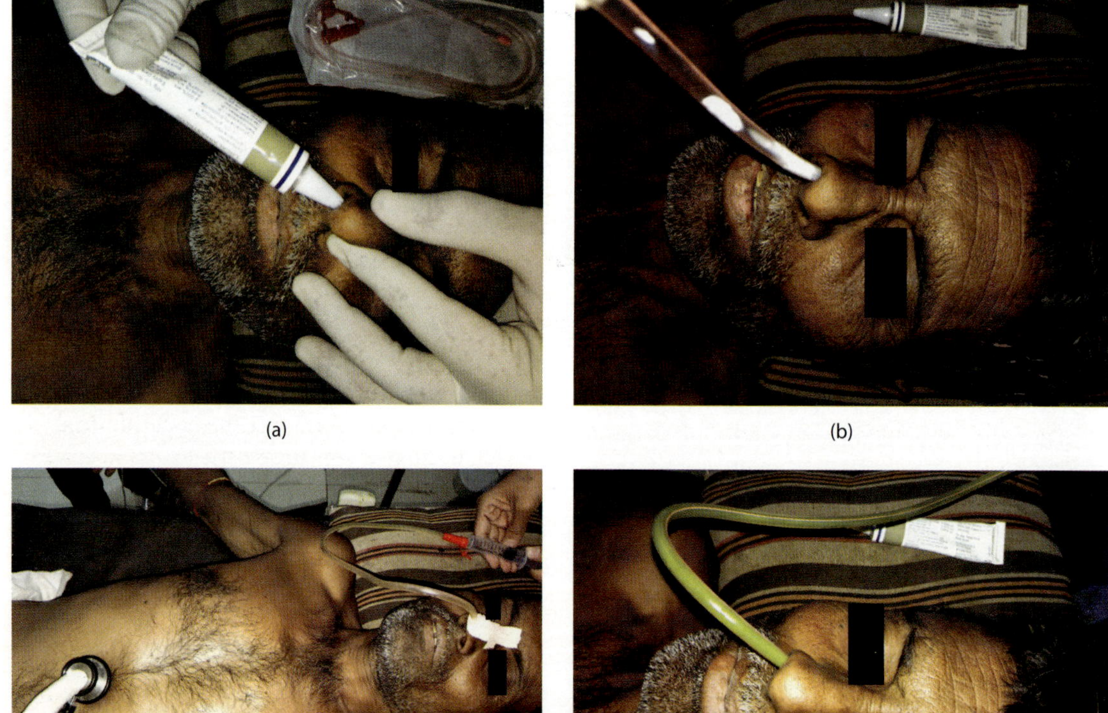

(a) (b) (c) (d)

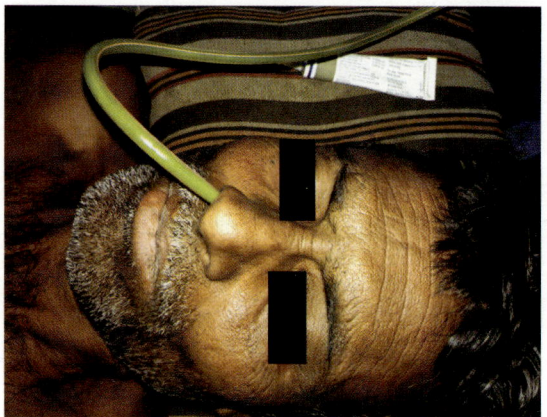

Figure 8.7 Ryle tube insertion. (a) Lubrication of the nostril with jelly. (b) Passing of tube through nostril. (c) Auscultation over the epigastric region to check the position. (d) The presence of bile in the tube confirms the position within stomach.

- Put tube in water; if air bubbles come, it suggests that the tube is in the respiratory tract.
- Capnography is used for verifying Ryle tube position in mechanically ventilated patients.
- The final way of checking is by X-ray.
  - No single method is reliable except X-ray but it is not possible to get the X-ray done routinely for obvious reasons. Metheny and Mcsweeney et al.[1] in 1990 stated that auscultatory method is not absolutely accurate in determining the position of the tube within stomach, respiratory tract, or intestine.

A combination of methods is reliable:

- Tube length measurement: Increased length of the exposed tube indicates dislodgement.
- pH of the aspirate:
  - *Gastric*: Acidic (1–5)
  - *Intestinal*: Alkali (>7)
- Color of the aspirate:
  - *Gastric*: Green, blood, and off-white
  - *Intestinal*: Clear, yellow to bile
  - *Tracheobronchial secretion*: Off-white, mucus

Care of Ryle's Tube

- Withdraw the RT a few centimeters daily and clean it with normal saline and antiseptic solution.
- Inhale tincture benzoin steam (mucolytic, possibility of sinusitis and rhinitis can be decreased).

If it is used postoperatively:

- Perform RT aspiration every 1 hour.
- Keep RT on drain (no aspiration or blocked) if operated for GI surgery before planning removal.
- If there is no increase in abdominal girth, pain, nausea, or vomiting within 6 hours, remove it.

If used for feeding purpose:

- RT feeding is done in a propped-up position.
- Start with clear liquid (50 mL/2 hours).
- There should be a minimum of 2-hour interval between feeds.
- Aspiration should be less than half of the previous feed on subsequent feed.
- After feed, flush RT with normal saline.
- Block the RT and change RT every week.

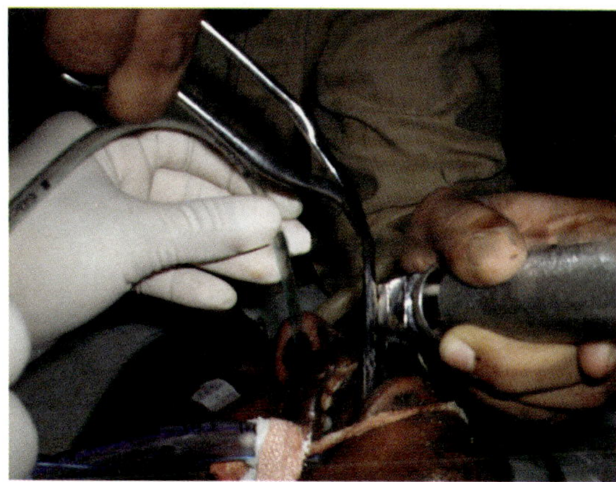

Figure 8.8 Ryle's tube insertion with the help of laryngoscope and Magill's forceps.

- If gag reflex is poor, then a laryngoscope and Magill forceps (Fig. 8.8) can be used to direct the tube into the esophagus.
- In uncooperative patients, fix the tube with columella.

DRAINAGE OF VARIOUS BODY FLUIDS

Fluids or purulent materials are routinely removed from a cavity, wound, or infected area using various types of drains. A drain is a device by which a channel is established for the exit of fluids or purulent material from a cavity, wound, or infected area. Use of drain must be weighed against risk of infection, pain and discomfort, and damage to anastomosis or vital structure.

Types of Drain

- *Open drain*: It utilizes the principle of gravity. Examples are corrugated drain and Penrose drain (increases the chances of infection).
- *Semiopen drain*: Wick; it acts on the principle of capillary action.
- *Closed drain*: It utilizes suction. The types of closed drain are tube drain, sump drain, and suction drain (infection risk is less as compared to that with open drain mostly used in abdominal cavity and chest drain).

The above-mentioned drains could be either active or passive.

- *Active drain*: Rely upon negative pressure suction, e.g., open (Salem sump) or closed systems (Jackson-Pratt)
- *Passive drain*: Rely upon gravity, e.g. the Penrose drain, Foley catheter, tube drain

Aims

- Drain will remove blood, bile, and pus from the cavity, and will not allow collection of harmful fluids.
- When drain is kept in the subcutaneous plane or below muscles by clearing secretions, it will decrease dead space and help in preventing wound gaping.
- It prevents the potential accumulation of various fluids such as blood and serous collection.

Useful Guidelines

- Use a soft and less irritant material for drains.
- Drainage should be gravity dependent.
- Bring drain on the surface through a separate stab wound.
  - It should be brought through the shortest route to prevent kinking in abdominal procedures.
  - Inner end should not be placed close to suture line or anastomotic site.
- Closed suction drain will be a better drain because it is less liable to produce infection.
  - Drain must be checked for volume and types of fluid drained.
  - It should be inspected for blockage, kinking, or leaking or loosening.

Proponents and Opponents of Use of Drain

Proponents

- Decreases the risk of infection
- Prevents accumulation of pus, blood, bile, or lymphatic fluid
- Allows early identification of anastomotic leakage or hemorrhage
- Provides a track for later drainage

Opponents

- It acts a foreign body and increases the risk of infection.
- Much of fluid can be produced in response to a foreign body.
- It may damage the suture line and induce anastomotic leakage.
- Postoperative pain is more.
- Most of the time drain is blocked before serving its purpose.
- It increases hospital stay.
- It decreases pulmonary function.

Table 8.2 Removal Time of Various Drains

Purpose of drain	Removal time
To cover perioperative hemorrhage	1 day (thyroidectomy)
To drain serous collection	5 days (mastectomy)
Localized abscess or infection	Infection subsides or minimal drainage
Colorectal anastomosis	5–7 days
T-tube	10th day

Precautions

- Use of drain must be weighed against risk of infection, pain and discomfort, and damage to anastomosis or vital structure. Drain should be removed as soon as its purpose is over.
- It should be brought through a separate incision to prevent surgical site infection and incisional hernia.
- It should be fixed with skin and stitched properly.
- Removal of drain (Table 8.2): It should be removed as soon as its purpose is over. By the seventh postoperative day, only 20% of drains are functioning. It should be removed once drain has stopped or the output becomes 25–50 mL/day. It can be shortened by withdrawing approximately 2 cm/day and gradual healing allowed.

General Complications of Drain Placement

Complications of drain placement at the time of placement are:

- Damage to surrounding structure
- Hemorrhage

Complications of drain placement during its residence are:

- Pain: Larger-bore tube and stiff tube associated with pain or discomfort
- Infection: Ascending bacterial infection and foreign body reaction
- Decreased mobility

- Peridrain leakage
- Excoriation
- Accidental removal or displacement of drain
- Damage to the anastomosis
- Blockage

Complications of drain placement after removal are:

- Drain site herniation
- Scar formation

Commonly Used Drains

Corrugated drain (Fig. 8.9)

- Made up of red or India rubber or Portex
- Used mainly for drainage of subcutaneous tissue, cavity in abscess, and large wound in delayed primary closure

Glove drain (Fig. 8.10)

- It is a strip of glove rubber.
- It is softer than corrugated rubber drain.
- Uses are similar to those of corrugated drain.

Penrose drain (Fig. 8.10)

- It is made by cutting a glove finger.
- Both ends are cut.
- It is used as a simple drain instead of the corrugated drain, for example, drainage in pancreatic abscess.

Figure 8.9 Corrugated drain.

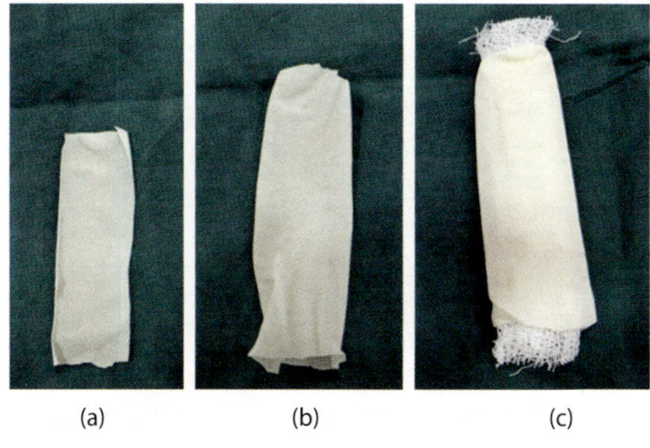

(a) (b) (c)

Figure 8.10 (a) Glove drain, (b) Penrose drain, and (c) cigarette drain.

Cigarette drain (Fig. 8.10)

- It is a Penrose drain with gauze within.
- Its uses are similar to those of Penrose drain.
- With all of the above-mentioned drains, output measurement is difficult. There are chances of contamination and infection and there may be skin irritation.

Tube drain

- Various types of tube drains are as follows:
  - Malecot catheter (made up of red rubber) (Fig. 8.11)
  - Portex drain (Fig. 8.12)
  - RT
- These drains are connected with disposable urobags.
- All the holes should be in the cavity (peritoneal, pleural).
- Drain is fixed to skin with suture.
- Drainage bag should be kept below the level of wound.
- Collection will be drained by gravity and vis a tergo.

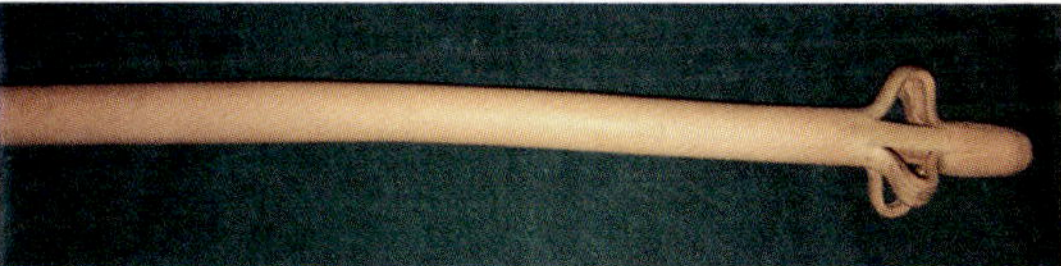

Figure 8.11 Malecot's catheter.

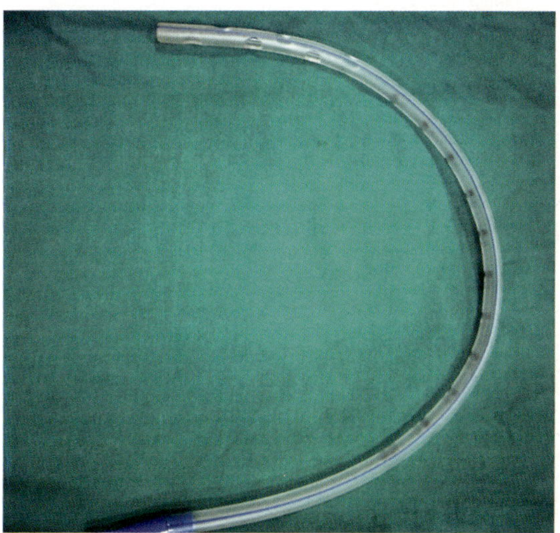

Figure 8.12 Portex drain.

- Drain can be removed when output is minimal or nil.
- Intraperitoneal drain can be removed after 48 hours.
- Malecot catheter can be used:
  - To drain the peritoneal cavity after laparotomy
  - As an ICD
  - As suprapubic drain after prostatectomy
  - As perinephric drain after kidney procedures
- After release of Portex drains in the market, use of Malecot catheter has decreased. Malecot catheter is called self-retaining catheter, but it has to be fixed with skin, because it is not truly self-retaining.

Romo Vac negative suction drain (Fig. 8.13)

- This type of drain is kept in the subcutaneous tissue or beneath the muscle.
- This type of drain is not made for deep cavities.
- It has a plastic disposable receptacle with a connecting tube with blocker.
- Secretions are drained because of negative pressure.
- It can be removed when output is <20 mL in 24 hours.
- Uses:
  - Modified radical mastectomy
  - Thyroid surgeries
  - Parotid surgeries
  - Large subcutaneous swelling excisions
  - Amputations

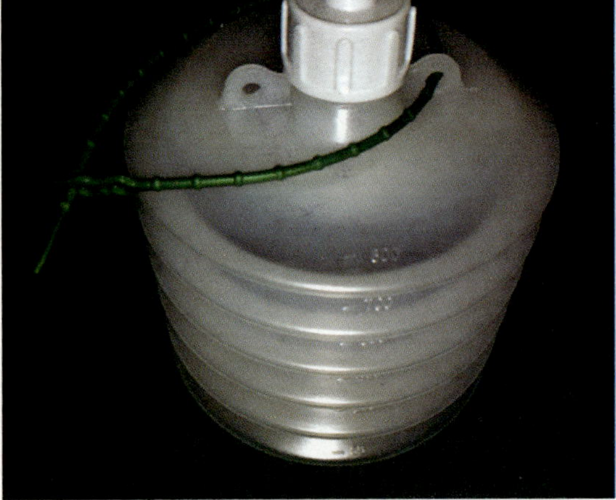

Figure 8.13 Receptacle of Romovac drain.

T-tube (Fig. 8.14)

This tube is used in the drainage and examination of bile. T-tube allows bile to drain out of a patient's body into a small pouch, known as a bile bag. The amount of bile can be measured and its color, etc., can be examined.

- It is made up of Portex.
- Length is 80 × 16 cm.
- It is used for biliary drainage after choledochotomy.

Why biliary drainage?

Careful dissection or handling of common bile duct leads to slowing of motility of CBD and spasm of sphincter of Oddi and causes back pressure leading to disruption of suture line. T-tube will help and prevent disruption of suture line.

Indications

- CBD exploration
- Palpable stone in the CBD
- Obstructive jaundice
- Dilated CBD
- Ultrasonographic evidence of stone in the CBD

Nowadays, exploration of CBD is rare because of the availability of ERCP procedure.

Monitoring

- For the first few days, output through the drain will be more because of edema. As edema subsides, output will gradually decrease.
- Bile should be examined daily for its color.

Figure 8.14 T-tube.

- Watch for color of stool daily.
- On the 10th day, drain is clamped. Watch for pain and distension of abdomen.
- Then take cholangiogram. If there is no distal obstruction, it can be removed.

Why T-tube cholangiogram?
- For residual stone
- To detect small lesion and stricture
- For investigation of bile duct system

Findings in cholangiogram

- Normal cholangiogram should show free flow of dye into the duodenum without filling defect and dilated IHBR.
- Unexpected CBD calculi after cholecystectomy or routine intraoperative cholangiogram: This should be managed by laparoscopic CBD exploration or postoperative ERCP
- Missed, retained, or residual stone
  - If T-tube in situ:
    - Flushing with heparinized solution
    - Methyl tert-butyl ether dissolution therapy
    - Burhenne technique: Percutaneous removal of stone via mature tract of T-tube after 6 weeks
  - If T-tube has been removed: ERCP and stone removal

Removal of T tube

- Clamp T-tube for 6 hours on the first day, 12 hours on the second day, and 24 hours on the third day.
- Watch for jaundice, pain, and fever.
- If there are no signs of complications, then T-tube can be safely removed.
- In diabetic and immunocompromised patients, remove T-tube at 2 weeks.
- Ideally it should be removed in the morning.
- Gentle traction should be applied; care should be taken to completely remove horizontal limb of the T-tube.
- Perioperative antibiotics should be given for 24 hours. Watch for signs of abdominal sepsis if no oral antibiotic can be started.
- If T-tube is not easily removable, then apply hemostat and ask the patient to walk. It will gradually dislodge and external biliary fistula will form, which will resolve within a week.

Some practical problems associated with the use of T-tube

- *Blocked tube*: Irrigate with saline.
- *Retained stone*: Irrigate with saline, or after maturation of track, remove stone with basket.
- *Dislodgement from the tract*: Accidental pulling out of tube from the tract is usually not diagnosed early, till peritonitis develops. If it is not completely pulled from the tract, exploration of abdomen is required in early postoperative period.

Complications of T-tube

- Dislodgement
- Retention
- Fluid and electrolyte imbalance
- Sepsis
- After removal:
  - Bile leak
  - Peritonitis
  - Sepsis

BLOOD TRANSFUSION

Blood transfusion is the transfer of blood or blood products from one person to another as a lifesaving measure. It is usually performed in cases of massive blood loss due to trauma, or to replace blood lost during surgery. Blood transfusion may also be needed in cases of severe anemia, thrombocytopenia, hemophilia, or sickle-cell disease. For blood transfusion to be successful, it has to be ensured by cross-matching of the blood groups so that the recipient's immune system does not reject the donor's blood.

Blood Grouping

- Karl Landsteiner introduced the ABO blood grouping system. Levin and Stetson introduced the Rh systems. Other less commonly used blood grouping systems are the Lewis, Kell, Duffy, and Bombay Blood Grouping systems.
- O negative blood group (ABO blood grouping system) is the universal donor.
- AB positive blood group is the universal recipient.

Components of Blood and Their Storage

- Blood is composed of plasma, water, and cellular components (red blood cells, white blood cells, and platelets).

- Red blood cells can be stored for up to 42 days. Platelets can be stored for only 5 days. Frozen plasma can be stored for as long as 1 year.
- Preservatives used for storing blood are as follows:
  - *ACD*: Acid citrate and dextrose
  - *CPD*: Citrate phosphate and dextrose
  - *CPD2A*: Citrate phosphate, double dextrose, and adenine (this blood can be stored up to 6–8 weeks)
  - *Saline–adenine–glucose–mannitol (SAG-M)*: Stored up to 5 weeks

Whole blood

- It is the blood drawn from the body from which no constituent has been removed. It contains RBCs, plasma, clotting factors, nonfunctional platelets, and granulocytes. Nowadays, it is not routinely used for transfusion.
- *Storage*: CPDA can be stored up to 35 days.

Indication

Massive acute blood loss, open heart surgery, and neonatal exchange transfusion

Fresh whole blood

- Fresh whole blood is blood transfused within 24 hours of collection. This is the least time that is for testing for infections; therefore, this blood is given untested, so it is not recommended for transfusion.
- One unit of platelet concentrate (see the subsequent text) will provide more platelets than 1 unit of fresh blood.

Packed cell volume

- Packed cell volume (PCV) is the fraction of whole blood volume that consists of red blood cells.
- It contains RBCs and most clotting factors except V and VIII.
- After centrifugation of whole blood for 15–20 minutes at 2000–2300 *g*, supernatant plasma is removed.
- *Storage*:
  - It is stored up to 42 days in CPD2A.
  - It is stored at 2–6°C.
  - SAG-M can be used as a storage solution (5 weeks).

Effect of storage on RBCs

- There is decrease in intracellular ADP and 2,3-diphosphoglycerate (DPG), which leads to alteration of oxygen dissociation curve of hemoglobin resulting in decrease in oxygen transport.
- There is decrease in O_2 offloading, loss of cation pumping, loss of cell membrane, and loss of phospholipid asymmetry. Oxidative damage leads to increase in lipid peroxidation. It may also lead to increased cell debris and increased RBC microparticles.
- Stored RBCs gradually become acidotic, with increased level of lactate, potassium, and ammonia.

Indications

- In patients with chronic anemia
- In children and elderly people
- In patients who are likely to end up in cardiac failure if a large amount of fluid is given

Initially, the convention of transfusing blood at Hb around 10 mg% and hematocrit less than 30% was routinely followed. A hemoglobin level of 6 g/dL is acceptable if the patient is not going for major surgery or is asymptomatic (see Table 1.1).

Washed RBCs

- A total of 99.9% of WBCs are removed by filtration and addition of saline wash.
- This fraction contains washed RBCs, minimal plasma, and nonfunctional WBCs.
- RBCs can be stored up to 24 hours at 1–6°C.

Indication

Patients allergic to PCV

Platelet concentrate

- It is obtained by centrifugation of platelet-rich plasma at 1500–2000 *g* for 15–20 minutes.
- Platelet concentrate contains 250×10^9/L; it is used in patients with thrombocytopenia.
- It is stored at room temperature for 5 days.
- Threshold for prophylactic transfusion is 10,000/cmm:
  - *Invasive procedures*: 50,000/cmm
  - *Surgeries*: 1,00,000/cmm
- One unit platelet concentrate will increase platelet by 5000–10,000/cmm.

- Those who are on antiplatelet medicines such as aspirin and clopidogrel suffer from cardiovascular risk. Aspirin is usually not a major risk but those who are on clopidogrel and are actively bleeding in major surgery need continuous platelet infusion throughout the procedure.

Fresh frozen plasma

- Plasma is removed from fresh blood and frozen by immersing in solid carbon dioxide and ethyl alcohol mixture.
- It is a rich source of vitamin K-dependent coagulation factors and albumin. It also contains other coagulation factors, fibrinogen, antithrombin III, protein C, and protein S.
- It is the only source of factor V.
- The most stable coagulation factor is VII.
- Most labile coagulation factors are V and VIII.
- Only male donors are used to reduce the risk of transfusion-related acute lung injury (TRALI).
- Plasma component of same ABO group should be transfused whenever possible.
- No RhD testing is required as it does not contain red cells.
- It can be stored up to 24 months at –40 to –50°C and 36 months at –30°C.
- The recommended dose is 12–15 mL/kg (minimum of 4 units for an adult weighing 70 kg). It should not be used as plasma volume expander and carries a significant risk of allergic reaction.
- One unit FFP increases 400 mg fibrinogen and 1 unit activity of each of the coagulation factors.

Indications

- Coagulopathy of liver disease
- Warfarin overdose
- Massive transfusion
- DIC
- Inherited clotting factor deficiency such as factor V deficiency

Cryoprecipitate

- It is a rich source of factor VIII and fibrinogen.
- It is the precipitate obtained after thawing FFP at 4°C.
- It is stored at –30°C for 24 months and can be stored up to 36 months at <–25°C.
- It should be used within 4 hours of thawing and should not be refrigerated.
- It is used in correction of hypofibrinogenemia and DIC.
- Adult therapeutic dose is two pools of 5 units (or 1 unit/5–10 kg body weight), which will typically raise the plasma fibrinogen level by about 1 g/L.

Prothrombin complex concentrate

- Purified concentrate prepared from pooled plasma
- Rich source of II, IX, and X coagulation factors; may include factor VII
- Used in emergency reversal of warfarin therapy in uncontrolled bleeding

Transfusion Guidelines

- Basic tests required include CBC, PT with INR, fibrinogen, pH, and base deficit
- In case of emergency, O-negative uncross-matched blood can be given (type specific, uncross-matched blood will take 5–10 minutes and full cross-matched blood will take around 45 minutes).
- Send blood sample to blood bank for typing and cross-matching.
- Prior to transfusion, blood must be checked for the patient's identity on the prescription and on cross-match and must be identical.
- For transfusion where cross-match is must, the patient's blood group (on cross-match report) and on the blood bag should be the same.
- The donation number on cross-match report and blood bag should be identical.
- Check for the date of expiry on blood bag.
- Check for sign of leaking.
- Monitoring of the transfusion is required: Temperature, pulse, blood pressure, and oxygen saturation just before the starting of transfusion and initially every 15 minutes for 1 hour, and then half hourly till the transfusion is over.
- Watch for any transfusion reaction (details of the transfusion reactions are provided in Chapter 16, *Frequently Asked Questions*).
- Prophylactic injection frusemide after 2 units of packed red cell and calcium gluconate after 3 units of packed red cell are given in case of symptomatic anemia. Citrate intoxication can cause myocardial dysfunction and arrhythmias. Calcium gluconate helps in stabilizing the myocardium and prevent such toxicities.

- Unstable patients not improving with 2 units of RBCs need to be massively transfused. Massive transfusion is >10 units of RBCs in 24 hours.
- Recently it has been shown in a study that ratio of plasma, platelets, and RBCs should be 1:1:1 as it reduces the incidence and severity of dilutional coagulopathy.
- Once massive transfusion policy is in the place, blood bank should have at least six RBCs, six FFPs, and six platelets ready for emergency supply.
- Underlying coagulopathy should be treated simultaneously. Thromboelastometry and other parameters like fibronogen and clotting time should be monitored at timely intervals.
- A patient with normal preoperative laboratory parameter: Up to 20% of blood loss can be corrected with crystalloid or colloid. More than 20% of blood loss needs transfusion of blood or blood products.
- Crystalloid is given in 3:1 ratio for every unit of red blood cells in case of shock.
- If possible, patients undergoing elective surgery should predonate their own blood if hemoglobin >11 g/dL and hematocrit >34%. The first procurement is 3–5 weeks before surgery and the last 3 days before surgery. Up to 5 units of blood can be collected (autologous transfusion).

INTRAVENOUS INFUSION

Intravenous therapy is based on the intravenous infusion of fluids (with or without drugs) directly into a vein. It may be needed during surgery or in the postoperative period. The blood transfusion set (Fig. 8.15a) contains a filter inside Murphy's chamber, while an intravenous infusion set (Fig. 8.15b) does not contain it.

Compositions of Some Commonly used Intravenous Fluids

- Normal saline (0.9% sodium chloride):
  - *Sodium*: 154 mEq/L
  - *Chloride*: 154 mEq/L
- Hypertonic saline (3% sodium chloride):
  - *Sodium*: 513 mEq/L
  - *Chloride*: 513 mEq/L
- Ringer's lactate solution:
  - *Sodium*: 130 mEq/L
  - *Chloride*: 109 mEq/L
  - *Bicarbonate*: 28 mEq/L
  - *Potassium*: 4 mEq/L
  - *Calcium*: 2.7 mEq/L
- Five percent dextrose:
  - *Glucose*: 50 g/L
- Ten percent dextrose:
  - *Glucose*: 100 g/L

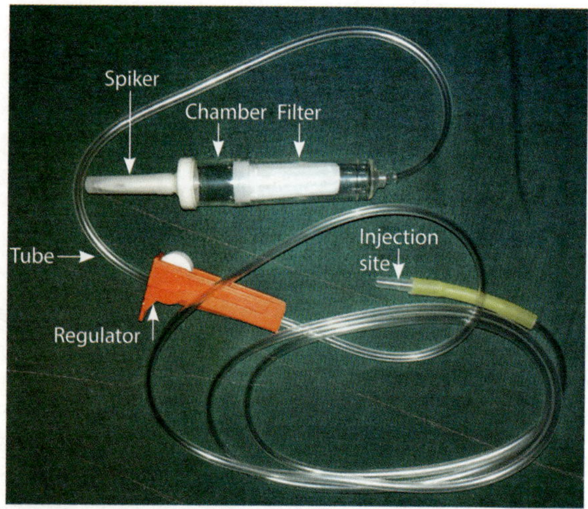

(a)

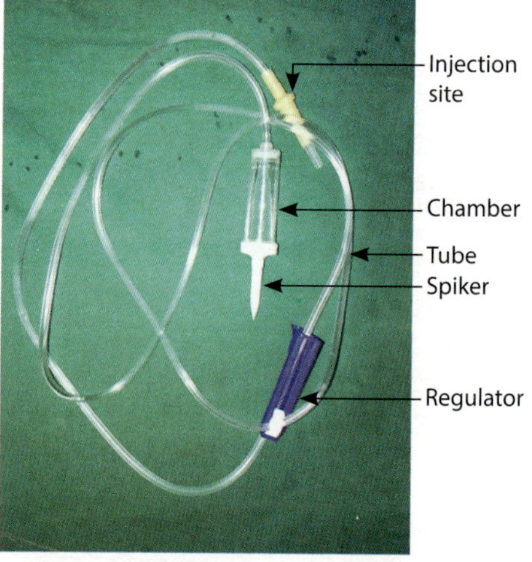

(b)

Figure 8.15 (a) Blood transfusion set. (b) Intravenous infusion set.

Solutions

- *Isotonic*: 0.9% NaCl and RL
- *Hypertonic*: 5% dextrose in half-normal saline, 5% dextrose in normal saline, 10% dextrose in water, and 3% NaCl
- *Hypotonic*: 0.45% NaCl and 5% dextrose

Some Important Points in Intravenous Infusion

- The preferred fluid in case of head injury and burns is Ringer's lactate, because it is the most physiological fluid.
- Postoperative period: For the first 24 hours, fluid to be given is 5% dextrose, because surgery causes stress. The stress hormones cause retention of water and sodium; therefore, fluids containing electrolytes should be avoided.
- Whenever gastric aspirate is more, Isolyte-G should be used (gastric replacement solution).
- In pediatric patients, Isolyte-P should be used.
- In patients with chronic liver disease, the preferred fluid is 10% dextrose.
- Normal saline is the preferred fluid for resuscitation in shock.
- In case of liver disease, Ringer's lactate and Isolyte-G are contraindicated.
- In case of renal failure, Isolyte-M, Isolyte-E, and Ringer's lactate should be avoided.
- Among potassium-containing fluids, Isolyte-M has the highest potassium and Ringer's lactate has the lowest.
- In diabetic patients, preferred fluids are Ringer's lactate and normal saline as they do not contain glucose.
- Ringer's lactate and normal saline are considered isotonic and useful in correcting GI losses and correcting extracellular fluid (ECF) deficit.
- RL is slightly hypotonic and it contains 130 mEq of lactate. Lactate is more stable and is converted into bicarbonate after infusion.
- Sodium chloride is slightly hypertonic and is ideal for correction of volume deficit associated with hyponatremia, hypochloremia, and metabolic alkalosis.
- Golden hour or critical window of opportunity: This concept was initially used for traumatic injury but it can be applied to all the causes of shock. If the patient's duration of shock exceeds 1 hour, mortality increases progressively due to development of refractory shock.
- Normal saline contains 154 mmol/L chloride, which is significantly higher than that in plasma (105 mmol/L). It causes hyperchloremic metabolic acidosis. Hyperchloremia is associated with renal vasoconstriction and decreased glomerular filtration rate and causes renal failure. There are few studies that indicate association of normal saline with increased postoperative infection and bleeding. Thirty-day postoperative mortality is higher in patients with hyperchloremia. Chloride-restrictive fluid has been associated with less acute kidney injury.
- Indications for 0.9% saline are hypochloremia, alkalosis, and neurosurgical patients.
- Six percent hydroxyethyl starch (HES) is associated with more septic complications in an ICU setup.

Perioperative Fluid Management

Preoperative

Fluid requirement based on weight

- *For the first 10 kg*: 100 mL/kg/day
- *10–20 kg*: Additional 50 mL/kg/day
- *>20 kg*: Additional 20 mL/kg/day

Another way to calculate fluid requirement is based on urine output, stool, and insensible losses. Fluid replacement is done with hypotonic saline solution, usually 5% dextrose in 0.45% sodium chloride at 100 mL/hour

- Correct acute volume deficit from diarrhea and vomiting by isotonic fluid 1–2 L followed by infusion
- Monitor urine output (0.5–1 mL/kg/hour)
- Preoperative hypovolemia avoided by avoidance of routine bowel preparation, a preoperative carbohydrate drink, and tolerance of clear fluid until 2 hours before surgery

Intraoperative

- Preoperative condition should be optimized (correcting fluid deficit, optimizing cardiorespiratory status).
- Intraoperative 500–1000/mL RL solution is used. Losses to be considered during surgeries are as follows: Blood loss, ECF loss, and third space loss.
- Intraoperative flow-guided fluid therapy has been associated with reduced postoperative

complications and early discharge from the hospital in major and high-risk surgery but is of limited value in low-risk patients. It improves stroke volume, cardiac index, splanchnic perfusion, and overall outcome. The most commonly used method is transesophageal Doppler; it measures stroke volume–corrected flow time in descending aorta.

Postoperative

- Aim is to preserve fluid and electrolyte balance.
- A total of 35–40 mL/kg/day is the amount of fluid to maintain physiological balance with isotonic crystalloid solution.
- Input and output charting is very important (bleeding, third space loss, profuse sweating, evaporative loss, and GI, urine, and other fluid loss should be considered).
- Fluid therapy choice:
  - *Blood loss severe*: Isotonic fluid or blood
  - *Hypernatremia*: Hypotonic fluid (5% dextrose if only water loss and dextrose with 0.45% normal saline if salt and water loss)
  - *Hyponatremia*: Isotonic or hypertonic saline
- Achieve state of zero fluid balance and avoid fluid overload and dehydration (fluid retention of 2.5 L and >2.5 kg weight gain has been associated with prolonged ileus). Anastomotic dehiscence has been associated with cumulative fluid accumulation of 10.5 L in the first 3 days.

INTRAVENOUS CANNULATION

Indications

- Administration of IV fluids or blood
- Administration of medications (antibiotics, analgesics)
- Collection of blood sample from a newly inserted cannula

Selection of Cannula

- Selection of cannula depends on factors such as purpose of cannulation and the needed rate of infusion.
- Purpose: If purpose is to give IV fluids or antibiotics, a small-bore (no. 20, 22) cannula should be selected, while a larger-bore cannula should be selected for giving blood (no. 18).
- Rate of infusion: If a large amount of fluid is required to be given in a short time (patient in shock), then a large-bore cannula is selected.
- Site of cannulation: It should not be over a joint.
- Size of cannula: Various sizes of cannula and their main uses are described in the operative procedure of venesection in section 'Venesection' of Chapter 6.

Procedure

- Explain the purpose of the procedure to the patient if the patient is conscious.
- Identify the vein to be cannulated.
- Swab the skin with spirit (spirit is antiseptic as well as vasodilator, so vein becomes more prominent) (Fig. 8.16a).
- Stretch the hand of the patient.
- Enter the needle at 15–20° angle (Fig. 8.16b).
- When needle punctures the vein, blood will come (Fig. 8.16c).
- Withdraw the needle gradually and advance the cannula.
- Apply micropore dressing or elastic adhesive tape (Easy fix) (Fig. 8.16d).

Complications

These are the same as described under the operative procedure of venesection in section 'Venesection' of Chapter 6, except nerve injury.

OXYGEN THERAPY (O_2 THERAPY)

Oxygen is essential for life. It is required by each human cell for its survival; the act of exchange of oxygen and carbon dioxide is known as respiration.

Indication

Hypoxia: When oxygen saturation goes below 90% (SPO_2 <90%)

Various Methods of Oxygen Delivery

- Invasive and noninvasive:
  - Invasive: Nasal catheter, endotracheal tube, and tracheostomy tube
  - Noninvasive: Facemask, mask with reservoir bag, nasal cannulae, O_2 hood/head box; best FIO_2 achieved with O_2 hood (6 L/minute and FIO_2 90–95%) followed by mask with reservoir bag (FIO_2 60–80% with 6–12 L/min)

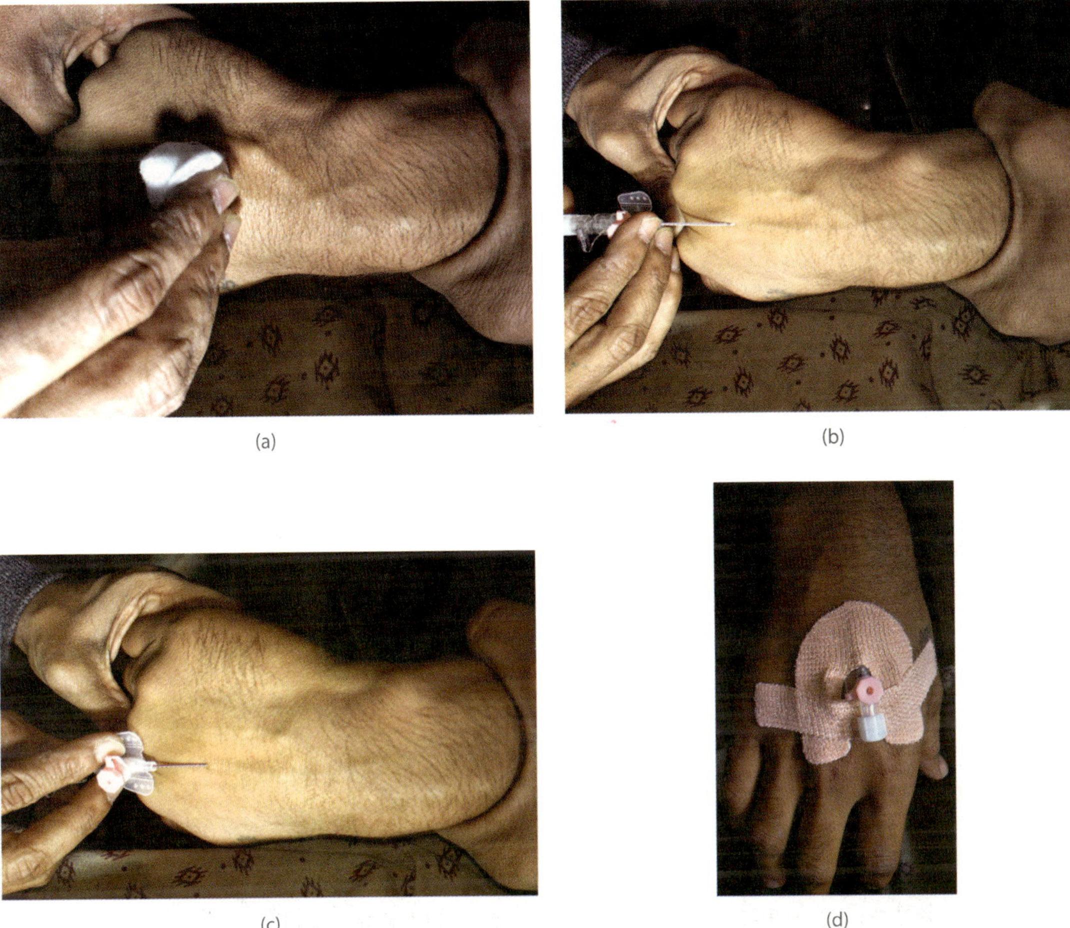

(a) (b) (c) (d)

Figure 8.16 (a) Swab the skin with spirit. (b) Entry of cannula. (c) Appearance of blood in cannula. (d) Securing the cannula by dressing.

- High flow and low flow are the other methods of oxygen delivery.
- Oxygen can be delivered in two ways: Central supply or directly from the cylinder.
- Cylinders are black with white shoulder.
- They are made up of molybdenum and contain O_2 under high pressure (1900–2000 lb/inch^2).
- Main areas where damage can take place in cylinders are as follows: Bottom and junction of the cylinder and valve.
- Periodic checkup of cylinder for corrosion, pitting dents, cracks, and any other damage is essential; to check for tensile strength, internal hydrostatic pressure is measured.
- Humidification of oxygen is essential to prevent drying of respiratory mucous membrane.

Side Effects of Oxygen Therapy

- *Paul Bert effect*: Acute O_2 poisoning leads to convulsion. CNS toxicity due to oxygen poisoning is Bert effect. Twitching of perioral and small muscle of hand, vertigo, nausea, altered behaviors, and convulsion are the manifestations.
- *Lorrain Smith effect*: Dr. J. Lorrain Smith first described the toxic effect of oxygen on the lungs in 1899. Chronic O_2 poisoning occurs due to chronic or prolonged administration of high concentration, around 60%, of O_2 due to inactivation of surfactant and damage to pulmonary epithelium. Manifestations are the following: Chest tightness, difficulty in breathing, shortness of breath, and death due to lack of O_2 if continued for a prolonged period.

- *Retrolental fibroplasia*: Liberal administration of high concentration (40%) of oxygen for 1–2 days following birth leads to retrolental fibroplasias.

ENEMA AND SUPPOSITORY

Enema

It is the rectal administration of drugs. They may be introduced into the rectum to stimulate contraction by distension or chemical action, soften stool, or both.

Types of enema are as follows:

- *Evacuant enema*: It is given to evacuate colon for the treatment of chronic constipation or evacuate large bowel for preparation of sigmoidoscopy or radiographic procedure, for example, phosphate enema, saline, tap water, and glycerin.
- *Retention enema*: Drugs may be retained in the rectum or absorbed systemically, for example, steroid enema in ulcerative colitis.

Phosphate enema (Fig. 8.17a)

It is hypertonic.

- *Mechanism of action*: It includes distention and stimulation of rectum.
- *Technique*: As anterior rectal mucosa is most vulnerable to injury from the tip of catheter introduced through anal canal, nozzle should be directed posteriorly after its introduction in the canal.
- *Complications*: Hyperphosphatemia, hypocalcemic tetany, and coma. This particularly happens in those patients who are unable to evacuate properly.
- *Contraindications*: These include elderly and debilitated patients, impaired renal function, advanced malignancy, colitis, proctitis, and inflammatory bowel disease (IBD).

Saline (Isotonic) and tap water (Hypotonic) enema

- *Mechanism of action*: Distension and softening of feces
- Saline and water enema do not damage rectal mucosa and are safe.
- Large volume of water enema can cause water intoxication if retained.

Soapsuds enema

- *Mechanism of action*: Same as saline and tap water
- Stool evacuation is performed 2–5 minutes after administration.
- It may cause rectal mucosal damage and necrosis.

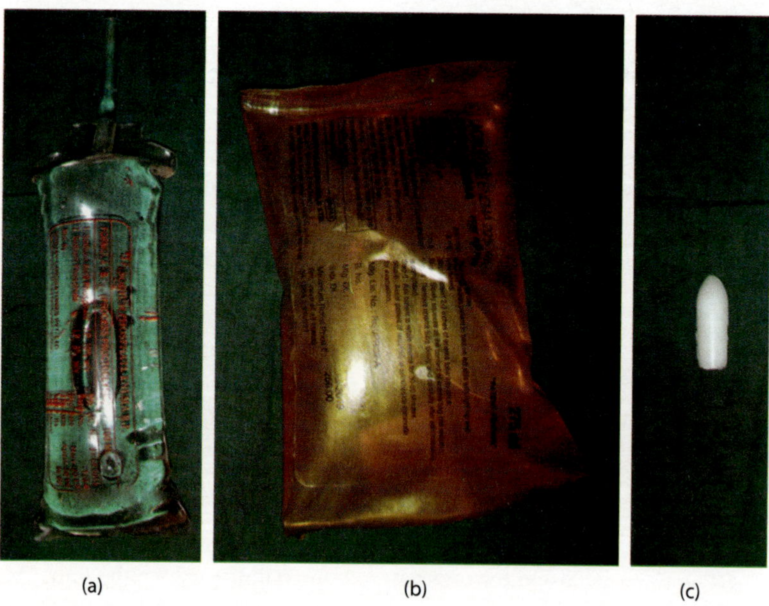

(a) (b) (c)

Figure 8.17 (a) Phosphate enema, (b) lactulose enema, and (c) suppository.

- Large volume causes water intoxication, hyperphosphatemia, and electrolyte disturbances.

Bisacodyl enema

It consists of 19 mg of bisacodyl in 200–250 mL water. It stimulates enteric neuron.

Lactulose enema (Fig. 8.17b)

- *Mechanism of action*: Inhibits intestinal ammonia production
- Three hundred milliliter lactulose and 700 mL water are used as a retention enema (15–30 minutes) and repeated every 4 hours in case of hepatic encephalopathy; lactulose enema is especially useful in comatose patients and those who are not able to take medications orally.

Suppositories

A suppository is a bullet-shaped, wax-like mass that is inserted into the body cavity for the purpose of administering drugs or to lubricate the area. There are rectal and vaginal suppositories.

A suppository dissolves after insertion and releases drugs.

Glycerin

- *Mechanism of action*: Rectum stimulated by osmotic effect
- *Effect on the rectal mucosa*: Unknown

Bisacodyl (Fig. 8.17c)

- *Mechanism of action*: Stimulates enteric neuron
- *Effect on rectal mucosa*: Surface epithelium altered in 25% of cases; regular use not recommended

Procedure

- Examination of perianal region is performed for determining whether any abnormality is present.
- Digital rectal examination is performed to determine whether fecal loading, blood, pus, pain, and obstruction are present.
- Explain the procedure.
- Place the patient in left lateral position (Sims).
- Insert the lubricated suppository 4 cm up in the rectum.
- In case of enema, lubricate the full length of the tube. Air must be removed and use gravity, not force, to administer water-based enema. Full length of the tube is introduced; after entry into the anal canal, direct the nozzle posteriorly.

Reference

1. Metheny N, McSweeney M, Wehrle MA, et al. Effectiveness of the auscultatory method in predicting feeding tube location. Nurs Res 1990;39:262–7.

CHAPTER 9

Radiological Investigations

In radiological investigations, X-rays are used to study the configuration of anatomical structures or the function of body organs. X-rays pass more easily through less dense objects such as skin, fat, muscle, and other tissues, compared to denser materials such as bones, tumors, and lungs affected by severe pneumonia. The latter absorb the X-rays more strongly. The radiation after passing through a patient is focused on an X-ray film. The net result is that areas of the film where more radiation falls (after passing through the body of the patient) appear black compared to the areas where less radiation falls.

The X-rays used for diagnostic purposes can be divided into two types:

1. Plain X-rays
2. Special X-rays

The special X-ray procedure uses fluoroscopy. The objects that are white in plain X-rays are presented as dark or black objects in this procedure and vice versa. The special X-ray procedure uses a contrast medium.

Female patients of reproductive age must be asked about last menstrual period (LMP) before exposing them to X-ray abdomen.

PLAIN X-RAYS

X-Ray Abdomen

- X-rays are passed from the front (AP view).
- Radiation dose = 50 chest X-ray PA views or 6 months of standard background radiation.
- Five basic densities seen in X-rays
  - Natural
    - *Black*: Gas
    - *White*: Calcification
    - *Gray*: Soft tissue
    - *Dark gray*: Fat
  - Artificial
    - *White*: Metal
- Optimum investigations for acute abdomen
  - Erect chest (PA view)
  - Erect abdomen (AP view)
  - Supine abdomen
- In persons with limited mobility or bed-ridden patients
  - Chest (semiupright or AP)
  - Supine abdomen
  - Left lateral decubitus of abdomen (a 'right decubitus' means the patient is lying with his/her right side down; a 'left decubitus' means the patient is lying with his/her left side down)

Indications

X-ray abdomen needs to be recorded in acute abdominal conditions such as the following:

- Peptic perforation
- Intestinal obstruction
- Blunt abdominal trauma

How to read X-ray abdomen

The normal X-ray abdomen is shown in Figure 9.1. Following aspects need to be checked while interpreting an X-ray abdomen of a patient:

- *Diaphragm*
  - Shape: Dome-like convexity of leaflet
  - Position: Higher or lower

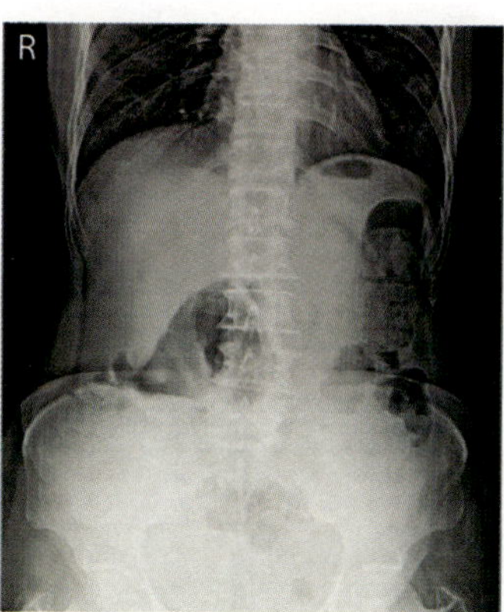

Figure 9.1 Normal X-ray abdomen.

- Free air or gas under diaphragm
- Gastric bubble under diaphragm
- *GIT*
  - Normal gas distribution (stomach, small intestine, and large intestine)
  - Any distended loops or air–fluid levels
  - Displacement of bowel loops
  - Normal colonic haustrations
- *Liver and splenic shadow*
  - Shape
  - Size
  - Position
  - Calcification
  - Air, etc.
- *Kidney and bladder*
  - Shape
  - Size
  - Position
  - Calculi
- *Soft-tissue shadow*
  - Any soft-tissue shadow
  - Any calcification
  - Foreign bodies
  - Gas in any solid organ
- *Skeleton*
  - Any fractures
  - Osteophytes
  - Scoliosis or kyphosis

How to describe X-ray abdomen?

Following aspects should be listed in the description:

- R marker: Check whether the R marker is compatible with visible anatomy on the X-rays:
  - Heart on the left
  - Spleen on the left
  - Stomach on the left
  - Liver on the right
  - Left kidney higher than the right
- Technical quality of the X-ray (Is everything included from hemidiaphragms to symphysis pubis? Is exposure adequate? Underexposed X-ray does not receive sufficient radiation and appears white while overexposed X-ray receives more radiation and appears dark/black)
- Type of the X-ray (plain or special X-ray; abdomen in erect or supine or left lateral decubitus view, etc.)
- Lesion
- Free gas under dome of diaphragm
- Air–fluid level
- Soft-tissue shadow
- Dilatation of any hollow organ
- Enlargement of liver, spleen, or kidney

Important conditions diagnosed on plain X-ray abdomen

Pneumoperitoneum

The presence of free gas under dome of diaphragm almost always indicates perforation of hollow viscus, most likely peptic ulcer. About 70% of perforated ulcers will demonstrate free gas and as little as 10–20 mL of gas is required for free gas to be demonstrated radiographically, on either erect chest or left lateral decubitus X-ray. Absence of gas under dome of diaphragm does not exclude perforation in conditions such as sealed perforation and perforation in the posterior wall of stomach.

Technique The patient should be kept in an erect or sitting position for 5–10 minutes before taking the X-ray, to ensure that the free gas present has sufficient time to rise to the highest position. In small and large pneumoperitoneum (1000 mL free air), the minimum amount of gas is detected with left lateral decubitus radiograph. CT scan detects as little as 1 mL air; large amount of gas is usually indicative of colonic perforation while moderate amount is seen in gastric perforation. Small bowel perforation is usually associated with a limited amount or no gas because small bowel usually does not contain gas. Retroperitoneal perforation such as duodenal loop beyond bulbar segments, appendix, posterior aspect of ascending and descending colon, and rectum beyond the peritoneal reflection does not have free gas. Retroperitoneal gas has a mottled appearance and extends along the psoas shadow. CT scan is more sensitive and advised when results of conventional radiograph are equivocal. The erect X-ray chest is the first ideal investigation if hollow viscous perforation is suspected.

Causes of pneumoperitoneum

- Perforated peptic ulcer (Fig. 9.2a)
- Perforation of any other part of the intestine, such as ileal perforation (typhoid), colonic perforation (due to carcinoma or amoebic ulcer), or appendicular perforation:
  - Gastroduodenal perforation may also be seen with endoscopic instrumentation.

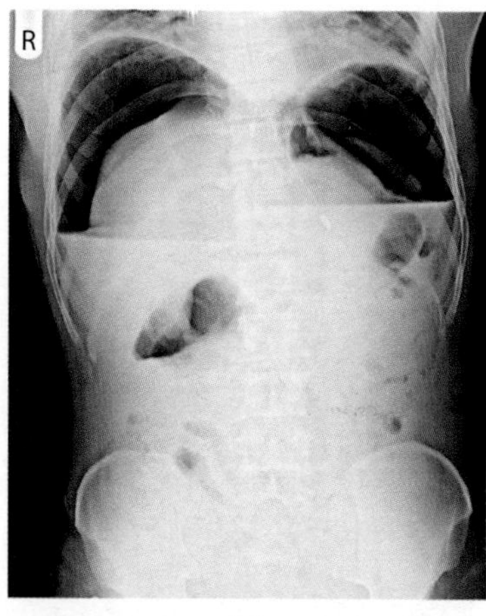

(a)

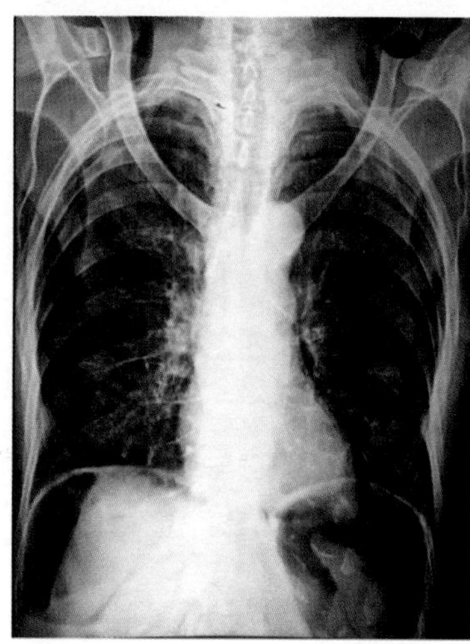

(b)

Figure 9.2 (a) Plain X-ray abdomen (erect) pneumoperitoneum (showing collection of gas between diaphragm and liver). (b) Plain X-ray chest (erect) pneumoperitoneum.

 - Small bowel perforation may be secondary to foreign body, diverticulitis, and/or trauma.
 - Colonic perforation may be due to markedly dilated colon proximal to obstructing lesion, friable secondary to ischemia or UC, and fiber-optic colonoscopy with or without biopsy.
- Gunshot/stab-knife wound
- Postlaparoscopy
- Postlaparotomy
- Pneumatosis coli
- Vaginal inflation (Rubin test done to check tubal patency)
- Peritoneal dialysis
- Nonacute: Without abdominal pain (Chilaiditi syndrome—pocket of gas behind right diaphragm). Usually transverse colon comes into the view; it is seen in conditions such as cirrhosis and COPD

Signs of pneumoperitoneum

- Erect position
  - Cupola sign: Free gas collected under the dome of diaphragm (Fig. 9.2b)
- Supine position
  - Double wall sign of Rigler (outer wall of intestine is lined by gas)
  - Umbilical ligament sign
  - Falciform ligament sign
  - Urachus sign
  - Morison pouch sign
  - Scrotal air sign (in male child)
  - Football sign (in infants) (gas outlines the lateral limit of peritoneal cavity)
  - Triangle sign (triangular collection of gas between intestinal loops)

Gastric and colonic perforation usually produce large amounts of gas under the dome of diaphragm.

Check for abnormal extraluminal gas: (i) under dome of diaphragm (perforated viscus), (ii) in the biliary system (sphincterotomy or biliary surgery, and fistula between bowel and biliary tree), and (iii) within the bowel wall (toxic megacolon).

Small bowel obstruction (Figs 9.3 and 9.4a)

If the stomach contains air/gas, it is visible in the left upper abdomen. The lowermost part crosses the midline. Small intestine is in the central position, having valvulae conniventes—mucosal folds that cross the full width of the bowel. Large bowel and/or colon is in peripheral position in the abdomen, having haustra, and contains feces. The upper limit of normal diameter of the intestine is generally accepted as 3 cm for the small bowel, 6 cm for the large bowel, and 9 cm for the cecum (3/6/9 rule).

Criteria for small bowel obstruction

- Normally on erect abdominal radiograph, three air–fluid levels are seen. These are of gastric fundus, duodenal cap, and ileocecal junction. Presence of more than three air–fluid levels is abnormal.

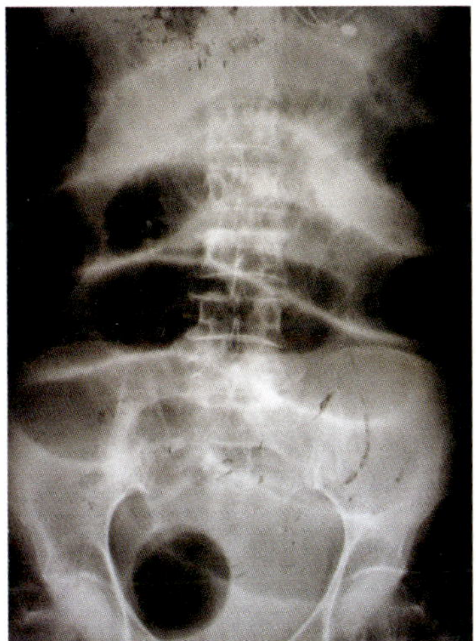

Figure 9.3 Plain X-ray abdomen—supine. Small bowel obstruction (multiple dilated small bowel loops).

- The width of a normal air–fluid level does not exceed 3 cm. So, an air–fluid level with width >3 cm is suggestive of small bowel obstruction.

Localizing the site of obstruction

- In high or proximal obstruction: Few air–fluid levels are seen.
- In low or distal small bowel obstruction: Multiple air–fluid levels with multiple dilated loops are seen.
- The characteristic appearance of the dilated proximal bowel loops can help in determining the site of obstruction.
- Jejunal loops: Classical 'concertina' appearance due to valvulae conniventes, small pockets of gas trapped within the valvulae conniventes create a string of beads sign.
- Ileal loops: Dilated loops are present with a smooth characterless pattern.
- Dilated colonic loops show haustrations.
- String of beads sign: Multiple small collections of gas above fluid level (small bowel obstructions) are present (Fig. 9.4b).

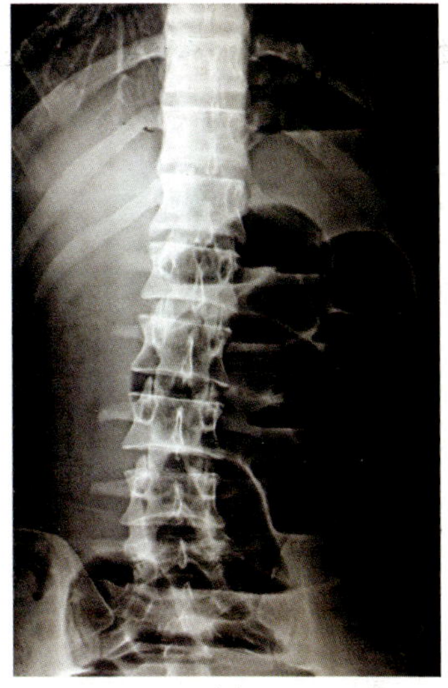

(a)

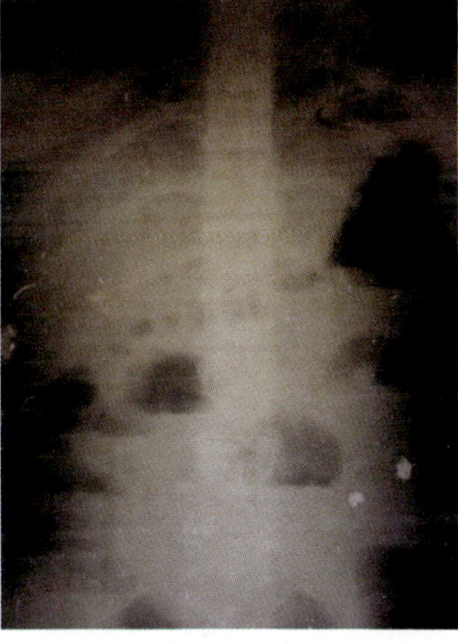

(b)

Figure 9.4 Plain X-ray abdomen (erect). (a) Small bowel obstruction (multiple air fluid level). (b) String of beads sign and valvulae conniventes.

Clinical features indicating the level of obstruction are listed in Table 9.1.

Table 9.1 Clinical Features Indicating Level of Obstruction

Level of obstruction	Pain	Vomiting	Distension	Constipation
High	Intermittent Not classical	Frequent	No	Present
Middle	Intermittent Classical	Moderate	Moderate	Present
Low	Variable	Late feature	Moderate	Present

- Usually, dilated loops are seen on the left side in jejunal obstruction and on the right side in ileal obstruction. Colonic shadows are seen along the periphery of the abdomen.
- It must be remembered that although multiple air–fluid levels are not a characteristic of paralytic ileus, they may be seen in this condition (classically known as stepladder pattern).
- However, in this condition multiple air–fluid levels are at the same place, whereas in dynamic obstruction they are at different levels.
- Localized ileus due to intraperitoneal inflammation may develop in one or two adjacent loops of small intestine called sentinel loops, for example, acute appendicitis, acute cholecystitis, and acute pancreatitis.
- Sometimes, it may be difficult to distinguish between adynamic and dynamic obstruction from plain radiographs. A contrast study (water-soluble) may be needed to establish the diagnosis.
- Gas in the lumen of duodenal loop, jejunum, or ileum is abnormal.
- Air–fluid level in above-mentioned locations or colon is abnormal.

Advantages of CT over conventional radiograph in case of bowel obstruction are as follows:

- Identifies the site, level, and cause of obstruction
- Determines presence or absence of associated bowel ischemia
- Differentiates between simple and closed loop obstruction
- Differentiates mechanical small bowel obstruction from paralytic ileus and large bowel obstruction

If in any CT scan, no obvious cause is found, then adhesion is the most likely cause.

Oral contrast is not advisable in small bowel obstruction because it is not going to reach the site of obstruction by the time scan is completed and fluid acts as a natural contrast.

Classical triad

- Dilated small bowel >3 cm
- Air–fluid levels on standard film (ladder-like pattern, which is due to fixation of the mesentery)
- Paucity of air in the colon

Other methods of diagnosis

- CT abdomen is a useful method of diagnosis.
- Enteroclysis: This is more useful in chronic small bowel obstruction. After placing nasojejunal tube, barium is administered via a tube.

Causes of small bowel obstruction

- Adhesion (most common cause)
- Hernia—external or internal
- Neoplasm—primary or secondary
- Meckel diverticulum
- Foreign body
- Gallstone ileus
- Intussusception
- Volvulus
- CD

Sigmoid volvulus

Classical volvulus is seen in the elderly and in psychiatrically disturbed and mentally retarded people (Fig. 9.5).

Wide fluid levels are seen in both the limbs of the loop in erect/standing radiograph, usually at different levels (pair of scales).

Signs of sigmoid volvulus

- Liver overlap sign
- Left flank overlap sign
- Lack of haustrations
- Apex under left dome of diaphragm
- Apex above the 10th thoracic vertebra
- Air–fluid ratio greater than 2:1

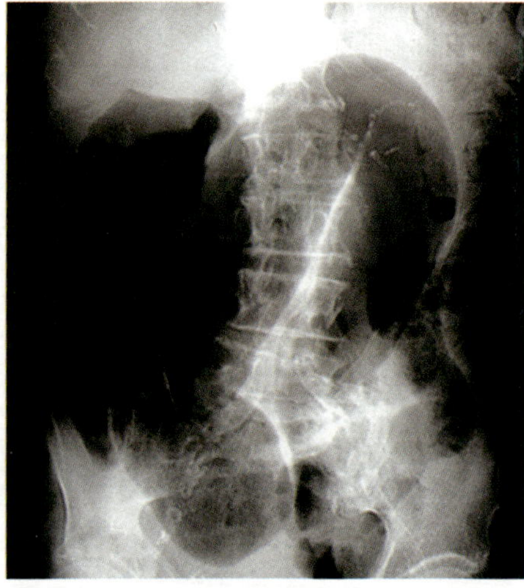

Figure 9.5 Sigmoid volvulus (grossly dilated sigmoid colon with gas; inverted U-shaped interposed between hepatic and splenic flexure) (pair of scales).

- Pelvic overlap sign
- Coffee bean sign: Dilated loop of intestine with convexity of the loop lying in the right upper quadrant (Fig. 9.6)
- Frimann-Dahl sign: Three dense lines converge toward the site of obstruction
- Gastrograffin enema: Narrowing at the sight of volvulus

Volvulus is more common in sigmoid due to the following:

- Loaded colon
- Long pelvic mesocolon
- Band of adhesion

Intussusception

On plain X-ray, it is characterized by the following:

- Mass
- Dilated bowel loop
- Air–fluid level

Ulcerative colitis

- On plain X-ray, it is characterized by the following:
  - Toxic megacolon (>6 cm of large bowel)
  - Excessive gas
  - Pneumoperitoneum
- For details of intussusception and ulcerative colitis, refer to the Section 'Special procedures', page 209.

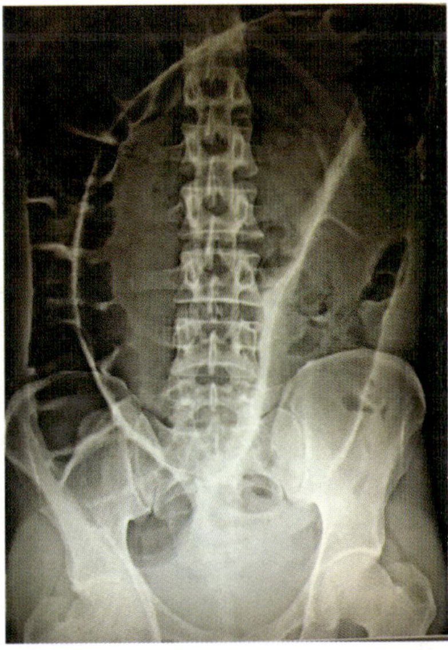

Figure 9.6 Coffee bean sign.

X-Ray Kidney, Ureter, and Bladder (KUB) (Fig. 9.7)

Indications

- The patient presents with signs and symptoms suggestive of pathology of urinary tract, such as stone.
- Postoperative: Check for DJ stent or residual stone.
- Plain X-ray is usually advised with the following preparations:
  - NBM for 6 hours
  - Tablet Dulcolax 2 HS
  - Tablet Diovol 4 HS to be chewed

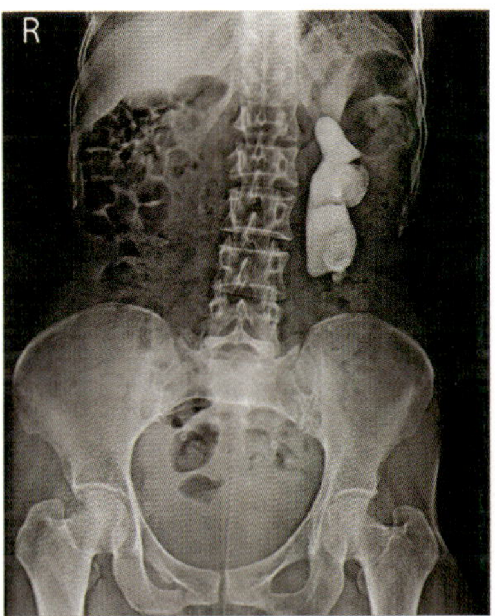

(a)

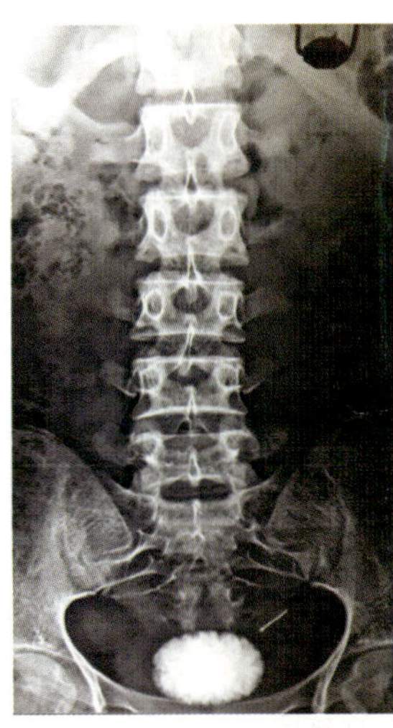

(b)

Figure 9.7 Plain X-ray KUB. (a) Renal stone. (b) Bladder stone.

How to read the X-ray KUB?

Check the following aspects:

- Kidney and bladder shadow
- Liver and spleen shadow
- GIT gas pattern
- Soft tissue
- Skeleton
- Psoas shadow

How to describe X-ray KUB?

- Name the X-ray (plain X-ray KUB).
- Lesion: Calculus is present.
- Obliteration of psoas shadow suggests retroperitoneal fluid or pus.

The differences between X-ray abdomen and KUB are listed in Table 9.2.

Renal stone

Differential diagnosis of radio-opacity includes the following:

- Renal stone
- Calcified mesenteric lymph nodes
- Phlebolith
- Gallstone
- Fecolith
- Calcified tuberculous lesion of kidney
- Foreign body in the bowel
- Calcified adrenal gland
- Ossified tip of the 12th rib
- Radio-opacity in symptomatic patients: Not necessarily obstructing calculus. To rule out this condition, options are as follows:
  - Plain CT scan
  - Excretory urography
  - Looking for the pelvicaliceal system and ureteric jet on ultrasonography

Table 9.2 Differences Between X-Ray Abdomen and KUB

Abdomen	KUB
Erect or supine	Supine
Diaphragm included	Diaphragm not included
Most of the times obtained in emergency	Routine radiograph
No bowel preparation	Bowel preparation required

KUB, kidney, ureter, and bladder.

X-Ray Chest

How to read X-ray chest?

Following details should be checked:

- *Age*: Rough age of the patient—Whether child or adult?
- *Sex*: In adult patients, presence or absence of breast shadow is a useful guide. Also, the pattern of calcification of costal cartilage is quite typical. In males, it is cupped and called 'vaginal' type; in females, it is linear and called 'penile' type.
- *Side marker:* To check for the side. To decide the side on the X-ray, look for the following:
  - Heart: Two-third on the left side
  - Fundal gas shadow on the left side
  - Diaphragm (lower on left side)
  - Dextrocardia and situs inversus
- *Exposure*: If the X-ray is well exposed, spinous processes of the first four thoracic vertebrae will be seen and the rest will be hidden behind the heart shadow. In overexposed films, more than four spinous processes will be seen, and in underexposed films, lesser number will be seen.
- *Centralization*: An X-ray is considered well centralized if the medial ends of both clavicles are equidistant from the spinous process of the vertebra between them. This is very important, because no comment can be made regarding mediastinal shift or comparative lucency of both lungs if the patient is rotated.
- *Degree of inspiration*: At least six rib interspaces are seen anteriorly above the diaphragm.
- Is the film taken in the erect position? Presence of horizontal air–fluid levels, either in the gastric fundus or at any other site in the chest, suggests that the X-ray was taken in the erect position.
- Lung fields
  - *Upper zone*: Upper two ribs
  - *Middle zone*: Two to four ribs (anterior ends)
  - *Lower zone*: Four to 10 ribs (anterior ends)
- Other things that should be noted in X-ray chest are the following:
  - Cardiothoracic ratio
  - Diaphragm
  - Bony skeleton
  - Soft tissue
  - Visualized abdomen

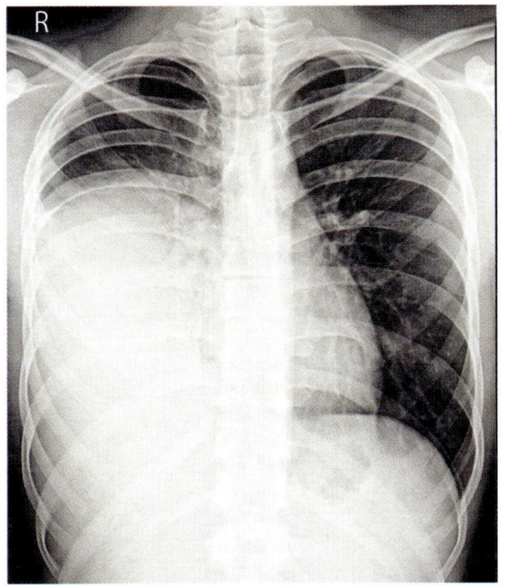

Figure 9.8 X-ray pleural effusion (homogenous opacity in the right hemithorax with shifting of mediastinum).

Important conditions diagnosed on X-ray chest

Pleural effusion (Fig. 9.8)

On X-ray chest, the following are noted:

- Blunting of costophrenic angle
- Homogenous opacity in the hemithorax
- Meniscus sign

Types of pleural effusion

- Free pleural effusion
- Encysted pleural effusion
- Subpulmonic pleural effusion
- Lamellar pleural effusion
- Phantom tumor

Pneumothorax (Fig. 9.9)

- Hypertranslucent area
- Razor sharp border of the collapsed lung
- Absence of bronchovascular marking, which is the hallmark of pneumothorax

How to calculate area of pneumothorax If a is the distance of collapsed lung from the apex (cm), b is the distance of collapsed lung from midway (cm), and c is the distance of collapsed lung from the base (cm), then we have

$$\frac{a + b + c}{3} = d$$

where $d \times 10$ = percentage of pneumothorax.

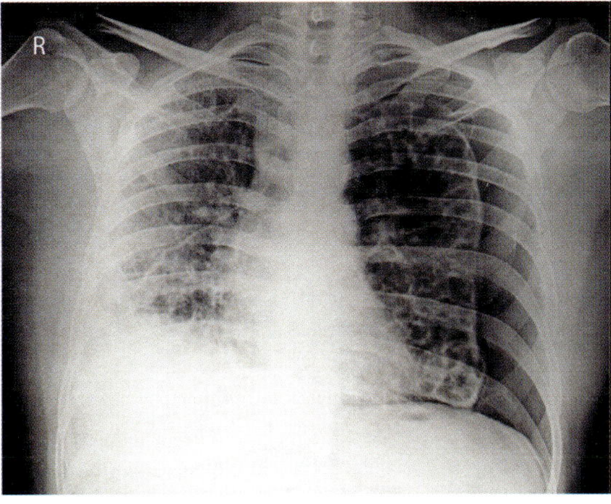

(a)

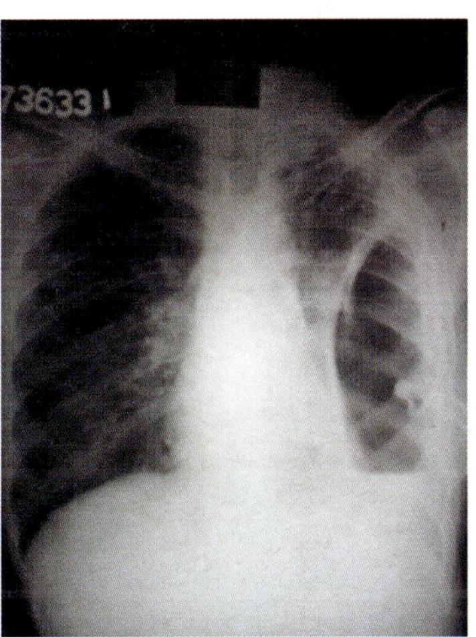

(b)

Figure 9.9 X-rays of (a) pneumothorax (left-sided pneumothorax) and (b) hydropneumothorax (left-sided hydropneumothorax with ICD tube in situ).

Treatment options

- Observation (<20%)
- Aspiration
- Drainage
  - Complete pneumothorax
  - Increased pneumothorax in patients kept under observation or after aspiration

SPECIAL PROCEDURES

Special procedures use contrast agents to improve the visibility of internal bodily structures in an X-ray image. Contrast agents can be of two types:

Positive and negative. A positive contrast agent is a medium that absorbs X-rays more strongly than the body tissues, while a negative contrast agent is a medium that absorbs them less strongly. A common contrast agent is based on barium sulfate, which is mixed with water to form an opaque white mixture. It is usually swallowed or administered as an enema. After the examination, it leaves the body with the feces. The other type of contrast agent is based on iodine, which may be bound in either an organic (nonionic) compound or an ionic compound.

Barium Study: General Information

- Preparation of contrast medium: This includes *barium sulfate*—concentration 250% (w/v); amount 100 mL. It may be used as a thin (thin barium: 1 part barium sulfate and 1 part water [1:1]) or thick barium (thick barium: 3 or 4 part barium sulfate and 1 part water [3 or 4:1]). Thick barium is associated with better coating of mucosal lining of the esophagus and stomach. It is preferred for barium swallow and barium meal examination except suspected gastrointestinal perforation.
- Advantages of barium over water-soluble contrasts are as follows:
  - Cost-effectiveness
  - Better mucosal pattern demonstration
- Disadvantage is barium peritonitis, which is associated with high morbidity.
- Satisfactory clearance of barium takes place within 2 weeks. So, subsequent CT or USG should be performed after 2 weeks. Therefore, it is advisable to do CT before this study.
- Double-contrast barium study is useful in evaluating mucosal pattern in a better way. After barium, air or CO_2 is used as a contrast.
- Iopamidol is a water soluble nonionic contrast useful in case of suspected perforation or meconium ileus (water-soluble contrast absorbed by the body tissue), tracheoesophageal fistula, and anastomotic leak.
- Water-soluble ionic contrast agents should not be used in patients with a risk for aspiration. Aspiration of high-osmolarity agents has been associated with massive pulmonary edema. A low-osmolarity agent like iopamidol may be used in this setting. Iopamidol should always be used first in suspected gastrointestinal perforation, followed by thin barium if there is no obvious leak.

The widespread use of contrast-enhanced computed tomography scan, esophagogastroduodenoscopy, and ileocolonoscopy have significantly diminished the role of plain and contrast X-ray study of the gastrointestinal tact. In nonacute abdominal conditions, plain and contrast X-ray study offers little information and is now almost obsolete.

Barium Swallow

This technique is used to examine esophagus, including the mouth and stomach as needed. After the patient has drunk a suspension of barium sulfate, X-rays are taken. The suspension appears white on the X-rays and outlines the internal lining of the GI tract; pharynx, esophagus, and gastroesophageal junction can be seen. Upper GI endoscopy largely replaces the barium swallow examination for the various upper gastrointestinal pathologies. Main advantages of upper GI endoscopy are as follows: color, contrast, and three dimensions. Simultaneously biopsy can be taken and therapeutic procedure can be performed if pathology is amenable to endoscopic treatment.

Indications

- Dysphagia
- Odynophagia
  - Suspected motility disorder
  - Symptomatic or suspected GERD
  - Assessment of hiatus hernia
  - Inability to pass the endoscope during UGIE
- Assessment of tracheoesophageal fistula
- Assessment of site of perforation
  - Assessments of postoperative status
  - Atypical chest pain unrelated to cardiac or pulmonary disease

Contraindications

- *Absolute*: None
- *Relative*: Regurgitation of barium

Technique

- Keep the patient in erect position.
- Take scout film to rule out foreign body.

- Give an ample mouthful of barium.
- Ask the patient to hold barium in the mouth and then ask him/her to swallow it fast.
- Take spot film of upper and lower esophagus in AP and lateral views.
- The patient is asked to drink low-density barium and kept in right anterior oblique (RAO) position to assess the motility of the esophagus and lower esophageal rings, and stricture.
- GE junction is then observed fluoroscopically as the patient slowly turns to right, looking for elicited gastroesophageal reflux.
- Straight leg rising, Valsalva maneuver, or drinking water can also elicit GERD.
- Extra views such as mucosal relief views are useful in suspected tumors, varices, or esophagitis.

Complications

- Leakage of barium from unsuspected perforation
- Aspiration

Important conditions diagnosed on barium swallow

Carcinoma esophagus (Figs 9.10 and 9.11)

- *Plain film finding*: A soft-tissue mass may be seen, especially if the tumor is large; it extends its shadow over lung fields.
- *Findings on barium swallow*
  - Short-segment stricture is present.
  - Mucosal destruction is seen in the affected segment.

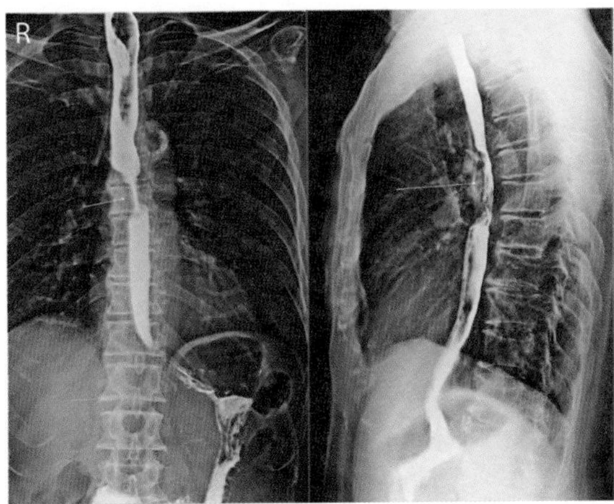

Figure 9.10 X-ray carcinoma esophagus.

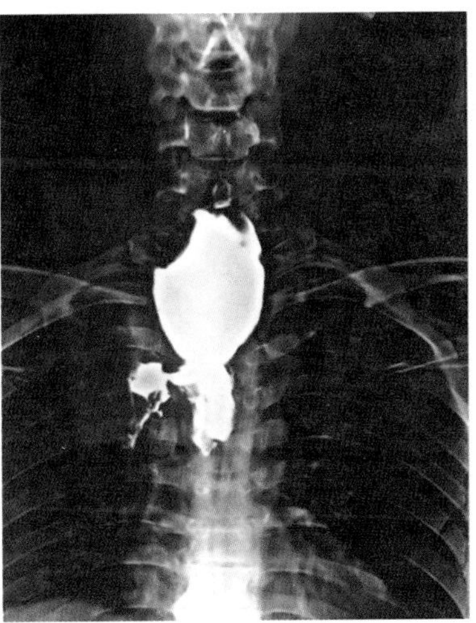

Figure 9.11 Postcricoid cancer with fistula.

  - 'Shouldering' is the hallmark of malignancy.
  - The above-mentioned three features constitute 'apple-core appearance,' which is typical of malignancy.
  - Proximal dilatation is absent or minimal.

How to differentiate between malignant and benign strictures on barium swallow? Benign stricture is smooth and tapering with typical concentric narrowing while malignant stricture is abrupt and asymmetric with eccentric narrowing. Because barium is not reliable in differentiating benign from malignant stricture, endoscopy with biopsy is ideal.

Common causes of esophageal stricture are as follows:

- Caustic ingestion
- Barrett esophagus
- GERD
- Radiation
- Postsurgery (partial or total gastrectomy)
- Prolonged nasogastric intubation
- Web
- Schatzki ring
- Congenital stenosis

Other modalities of diagnosis

- Upper GI endoscopy and biopsy
- For upper one-third and middle one-third—bronchoscopy

- Chest X-ray
  - Pneumonitis
  - Pleural effusion
  - Pulmonary nodule
- CT scan chest and abdomen
  - Liver metastases
  - Mediastinal nodes
  - Celiac nodes
- Endoscopic ultrasound: For locoregional staging

Types

- Upper two-third—squamous cell carcinoma
- Lower one-third—adenocarcinoma

Achalasia cardia

Plain film findings

- Fundal gas shadow is absent.
- The dilated esophagus appears as a mediastinal soft-tissue shadow, with air–fluid level within it. This is usually seen on the right side in the frontal view and lies in the posterior mediastinum in the lateral view.
- In some cases, aspiration pneumonitis is present.

Barium swallow findings

- There is failure of esophageal peristalsis to clear the esophagus of barium when the patient is in the recumbent position, with no primary waves identified. In standing position, barium column is high enough; the hydrostatic pressure can overcome the LES pressure allowing passage of esophageal content (Hurst phenomenon).
- There is failure of relaxation of the lower esophageal sphincter.
- Lower end of esophagus shows abrupt narrowing, with no evidence of mucosal destruction or shouldering (bird's beak [Fig. 9.12] or rat tail appearance).
- Esophageal dilatation: As the disease progresses, dilatation worsens. A sigmoid esophagus is defined as dilation of the distal esophagus to more than 10 cm in diameter and/or one that takes a tortuous course through the chest toward the GEJ.
- Erect film shows air–fluid level.

Radiological findings must be confirmed by upper gastrointestinal endoscopy and esophageal manometry.

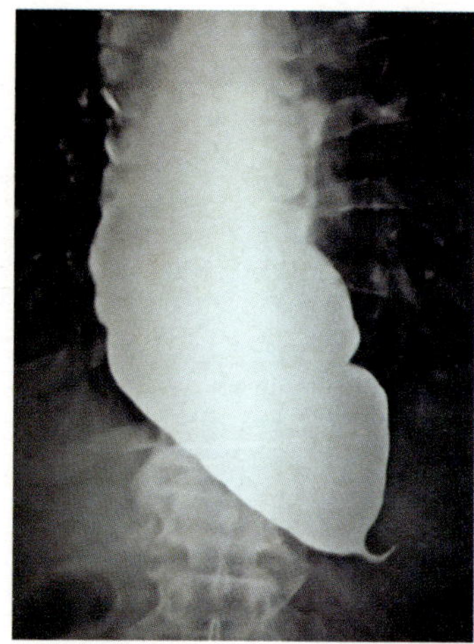

Figure 9.12 Bird's beak appearance with grossly dilated esophagus suggests achalasia cardia.

Pseudoachalasia

It shows similar radiological findings with normal manometry (Table 9.3).

Table 9.3 Differences Between Primary and Secondary Achalasia (Pseudoachalasia)

	Primary	Secondary
Dilatation	Marked	Mild
Peristalsis	Absent	Decreased or absent
Narrowing	Bird's beak deformity, smooth symmetric tapering	Eccentric
Length of involved segment	Less than one vertebral body height	More than one vertebral body height

Esophageal varices (Fig. 9.13)

- Barium swallow shows a moth-eaten appearance.
- For details, refer Chapter 16, *Frequently Asked Questions*.

Barrett esophagus

Barium swallow findings

- Ulceration
- Hiatus hernia
- Stricture
- Intestinal metaplasia of lower esophagus

Diagnosis

- Upper GI endoscopy with biopsy
- Biopsy showing goblet cells

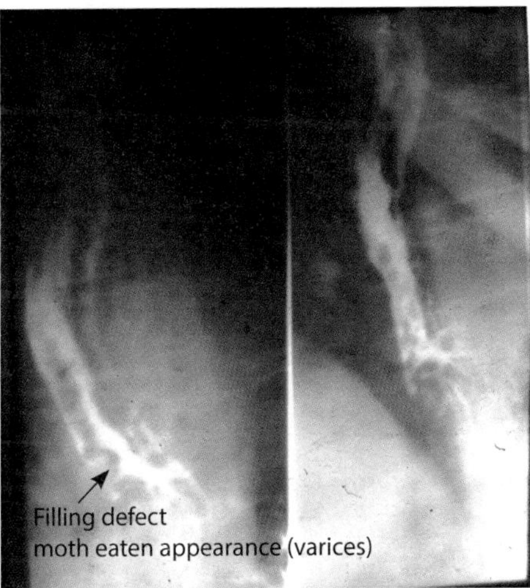

Figure 9.13 X-ray esophageal varices.

Barium meal (Fig. 9.14)

- A total of 135 mL of 250% (w/v) barium sulfate is used.
- In this study, we can identify up to the duodenum.
- Preparation of the patient is the same as for upper GI endoscopy.
- Smoking is to be avoided, as it increases the motility of the stomach.
- Conditions diagnosed are as follows:
  - Gastric outlet obstruction either due to malignancy, pyloric stenosis of any cause like secondary to corrosive ingestion or infantile hypertrophic pyloric stenosis (Fig. 9.15)
  - Gastric ulcer
  - Duodenal ulcer
  - Gastric carcinoma
  - Hourglass stomach
  - Tea pot deformity
  - Gastric volvulus
  - Duodenal diverticula
  - Stricture in the duodenum
  - Postoperative assessment of gastric surgery

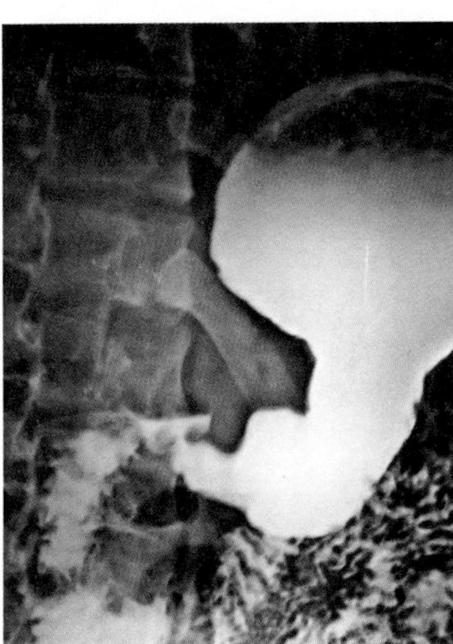

Figure 9.14 X-ray barium meal—stomach (normal).

Technique

- Give an ample mouthful of barium.
- The patient lies supine with left side up and head low (15°) to induce reflux.
- Give injection Buscopan.
- Then take series of films under IITV or under fluoroscopic guidance.

Typical film series

- *Supine RAO*: Antrum and greater curve
- *Supine*: Antrum and body
- *Supine left anterior oblique (LAO)*: Lesser curve
- *Supine left lateral*: Fundus
- *Prone*: Duodenal loop
- *Prone, RAO, supine, and LAO*: Duodenal cup series

Contraindications

- Large bowel obstruction
- Intestinal surgery in near future

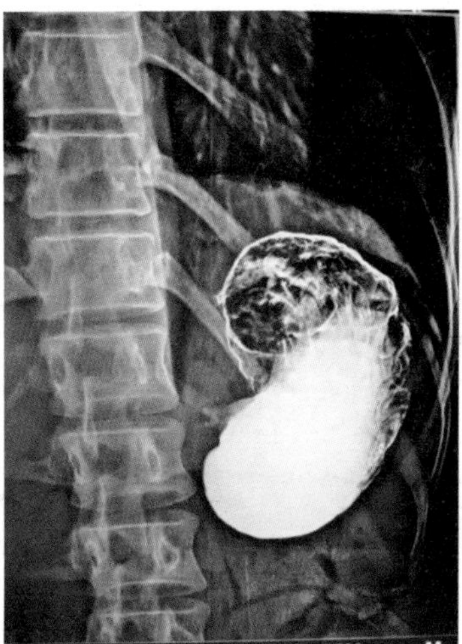

Figure 9.15 X-ray barium meal—infantile pyloric stenosis (barium has not entered the duodenum after 4 hr of the procedure).

Complications

- Aspiration
- Impaction of barium
- Leakage of barium into the peritoneum

Findings

- Hypertrophic pyloric stenosis: Persistent narrowing and elongation of pyloric canal
- Gastric and duodenal ulcer
  - Ulcer crater filled with barium
  - Rugal convergence
  - Complications of ulcer, such as hourglass deformity or pyloric stenosis
- Findings on barium suggestive of malignant ulcer
  - Size more than 2 cm
  - Penetration not beyond the gastric wall
  - Asymmetric mucosal folds
  - Rim of radiolucency surrounding ulcer (Carman meniscus sign)

Upper GI endoscopy has the advantage of being able to take biopsy simultaneously; hence, it is preferred to barium study.

Barium Meal Follow-Through (Fig. 9.16)

In this process, after barium meal, the first X-ray is taken after 15 minutes (supine), and then after every 30 minutes till contrast reaches cecum (prone) (Fig. 9.17).

- Barium sulfate: A total of 300 mL of 60–100% (w/v) of barium sulfate is given.
- Prokinetic drugs should be given 20 minutes before the study.
- Region up to the ileocecal valve can be traced.

Important indications

- Partial obstruction (due to mass or stricture or ileocecal Koch's)
- Anemia and GI bleeding
- Malabsorption
- Diverticula
- Crohn disease

Important findings

- IC Koch's: Refer specimens.
- Crohn
  - String sign and ulcer

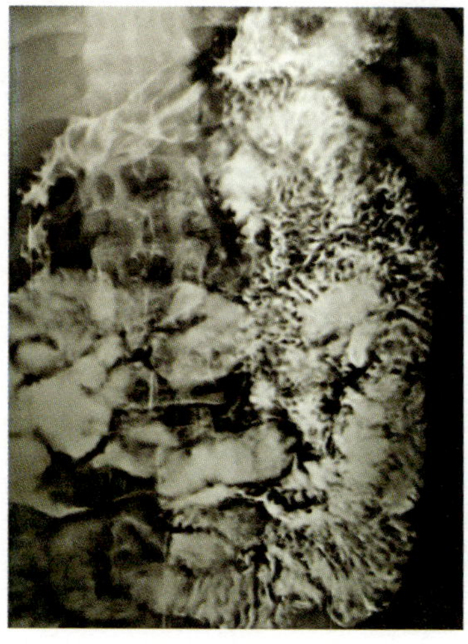

(a)

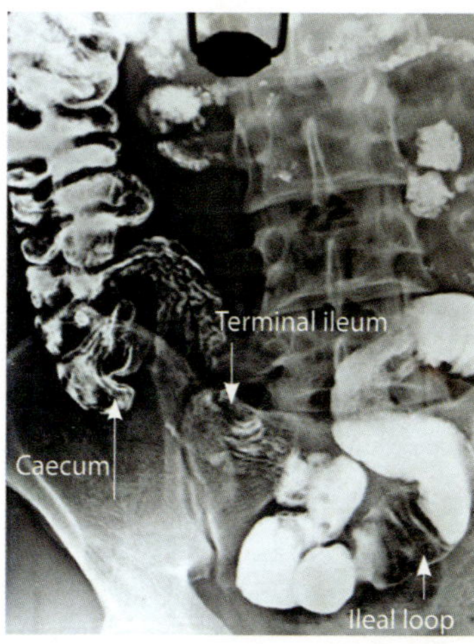

(b)

Figure 9.16 X-ray barium meal follow-through. (a) Jejunal loop. (b) Terminal ileum.

Barium Enema (Fig. 9.18)

- Introduction of barium suspension is done with the help of a simple rubber or balloon catheter through per-rectal route.
- Single contrast: Only barium is issued.
- Double contrast: Air or CO_2 is used as a second contrast (mucosal lining problems are better assessed).
- Instant enema: No bowel preparation is required. It is done in patients with ulcerative colitis (no residue because of inflamed bowels).
- A total of 500 mL of 115% (w/v) barium is used.

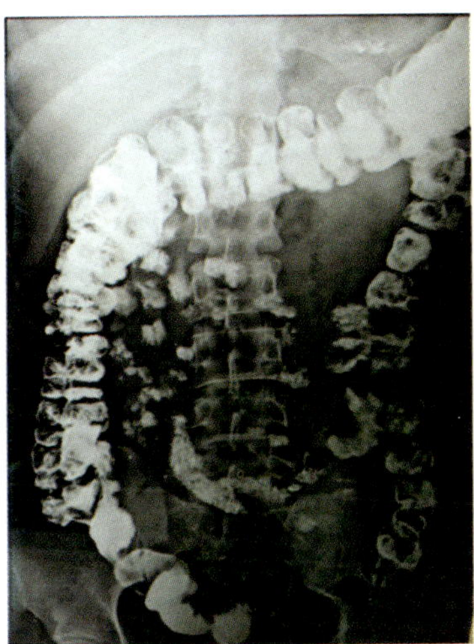

Figure 9.17 X-ray barium meal follow through—colon.

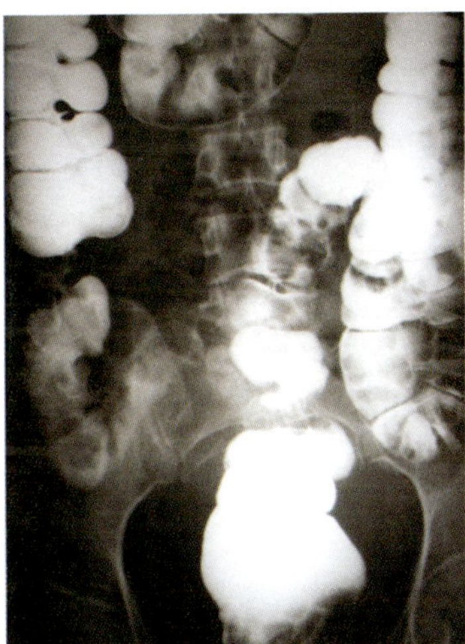

Figure 9.18 Barium enema (pulled up cecum; widening of angle between ileum and cecum) suggests ileocecal tuberculosis.

- Preparation of the patient the same as that for major resection of bowel (to prevent nondiagnostic examination due to retained stool).

Indications

- Large bowel mass
- Change in bowel habits
- Obstruction

Contraindications

- Toxic megacolon
- Pseudomembranous enterocolitis
- Recent barium meal
- Rectal biopsy within 1 week
- Intestinal surgery in near future

Complications

- Allergic reaction
- Barium granuloma
- Sepsis
- Impaction of barium proximal to obstruction
- Intravasation: Pulmonary embolism and liver abscess

Conditions diagnosed on barium enema

Carcinoma of the colon (Figs 9.19 and 9.20)

Findings on enema

- *In left-sided lesion*: Apple-core appearance (constant irregular filling defect)
- *In right-sided lesion*: Constriction or mass

Ulcerative colitis (Fig. 9.21)

Signs on barium enema

- Fine mucosal granularity (earliest sign)
- Loss of haustrations (lead pipe sign)
- Pseudopolyps (filling defect)
- Superficial ulcer
- Deep ulcer (collar button)
- Irregularity due to stricture (malignancy)

Nowadays, colonoscopy is the better option to diagnose ulcerative colitis.

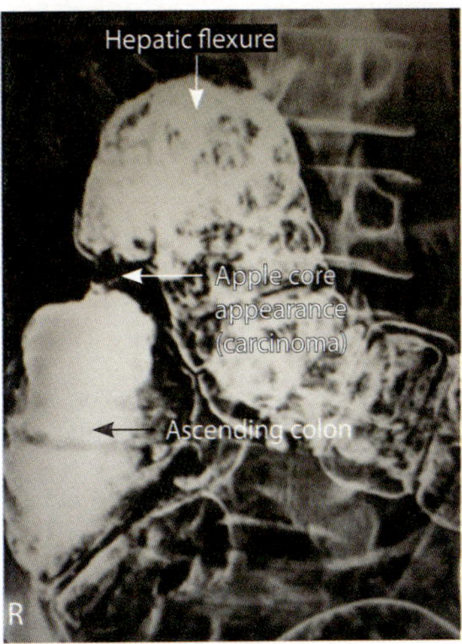

Figure 9.19 Barium enema—carcinoma ascending colon (apple core appearance).

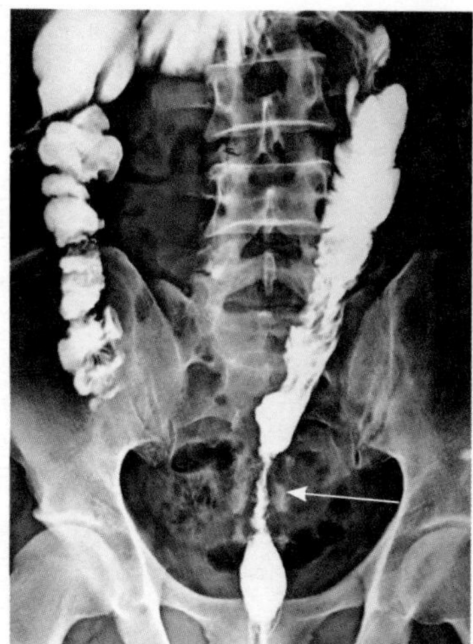

Figure 9.20 Stricture in the distal colon (rectosigmoid junction).

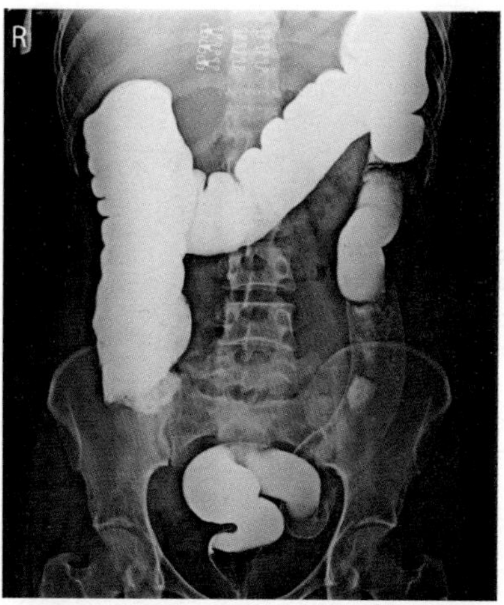

Figure 9.21 Barium enema—X-ray ulcerative colitis (loss of haustration [lead pipe sign] in the distal or left-sided colon suggests ulcerative colitis).

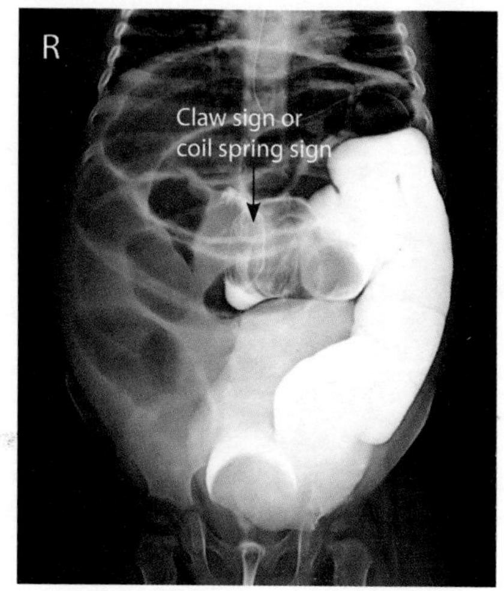

(a)

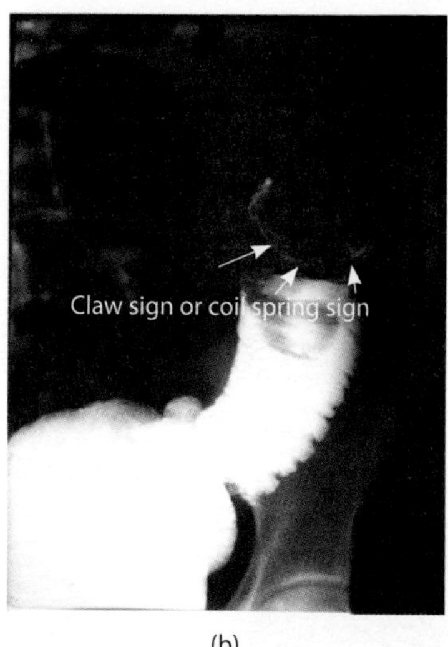

(b)

Figure 9.22 X-ray intussusception. (a) Ileocolic type. (b) Colo-colic type.

Intussusception (Fig. 9.22)

Claw sign or coil spring sign: On water-soluble contrast enema (in the presence of competent ileocecal valve; in ileoileal variety, this examination will be negative) (ileocolic or colocolic)

Excretory Urography (EU, IVP, IVU) (Figs 9.23–9.27)

It gives anatomical as well as functional details of the genitourinary tract. The technique is used to evaluate the kidneys, ureter, and bladder. A medicine, given intravenously, moves through the body, ultimately reaching the kidneys and excreted through them. A series of X-rays are taken to evaluate the kidneys, ureter, and bladder.

Preparation

- Overnight fasting. Laxative would be of great help.
- Inquire about history of allergy.
- Take scout film prior to the procedure.
- Serum creatinine test should be done prior to injecting contrast.
- Metformin has to be stopped 48 hours prior to the procedure and can be continued after 48 hours of the procedure.

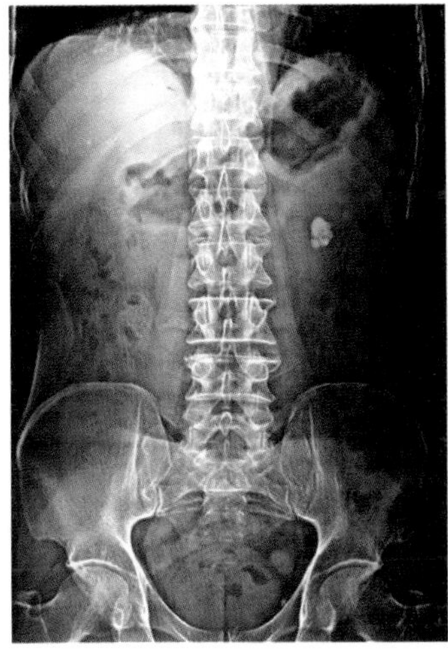

Figure 9.23 Scout film (plain X-ray KUB): first film to be taken for excretory urography (EU).

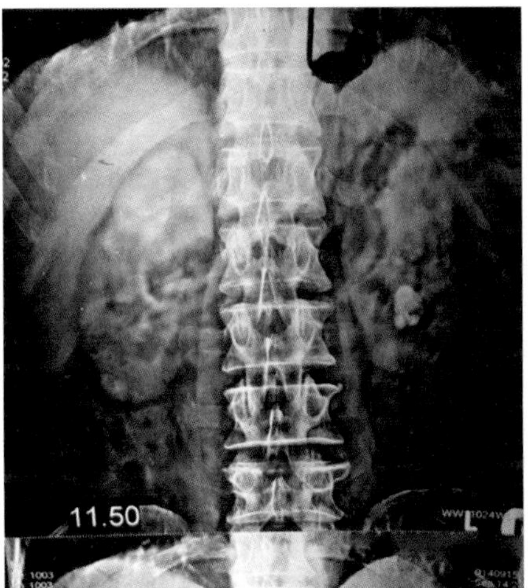

Figure 9.24 Nephrogram.

Contrast media—ionic and nonionic

- *High osmolar contrast media (HOCM; ionic)*
  - Renografin
  - Hypaque
  - Conray
- *Low osmolar contrast media (LOCM; nonionic)*
  - Iohexol
  - Iopamidol
  - Ioversol

LOCM is associated with less drug reactions and has lesser propensity to cause fluid overload and heart failure in patients with cardiac problems.

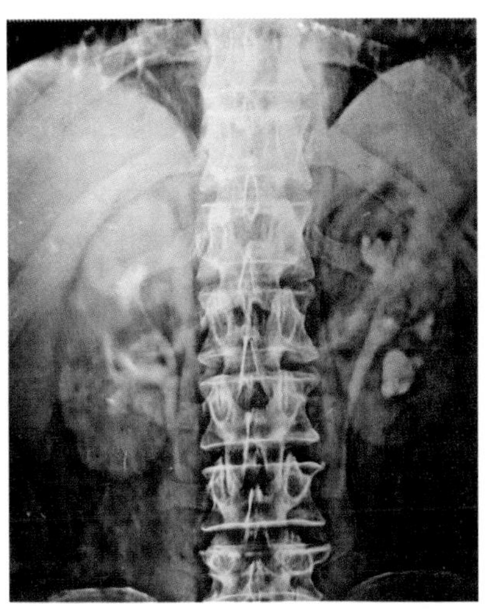

Figure 9.25 Pyelogram.

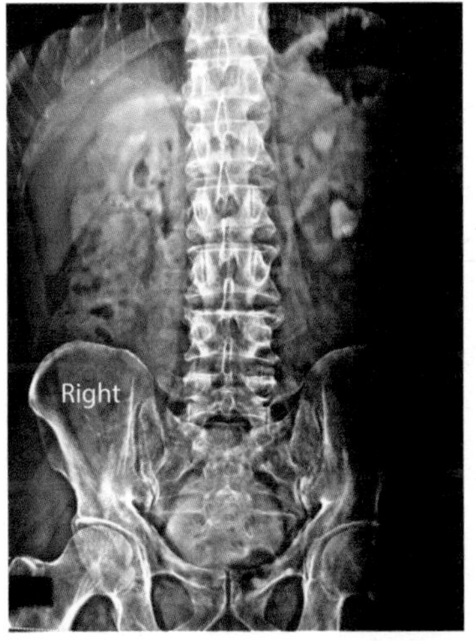

Figure 9.26 Fifteen minutes with compression film.

Film sequence

- Scout film (plain X-ray) (Fig. 9.23)
- IV contrast: After negative test dose, full dose administered—1.5 mL/kg bodyweight
- Immediate nephrogram (10–14 seconds after injection [arm to kidney time]) (Fig. 9.24)
- 5-Minute film—to see the excretion (pyelogram) (Fig. 9.25)
- 10-Minute film with abdominal compression (for better visualization of calices and ureter) (contraindications for compressions are as follows: obstruction seen at the 5-minute film,

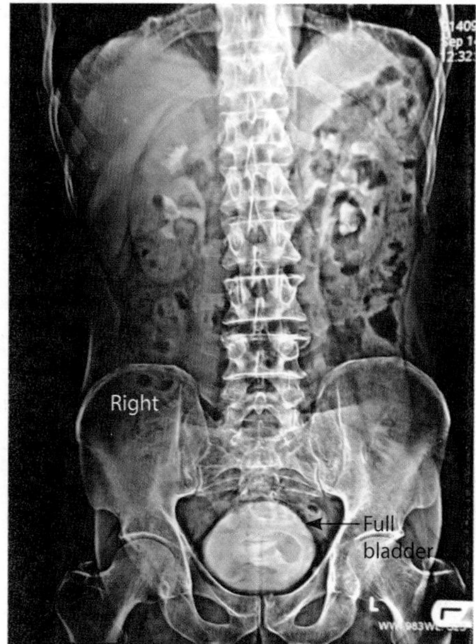

Figure 9.27 Full bladder.

recent abdominal surgery, aortic aneurysm, suspected trauma to the genitourinary tract, presence of urinary diversion, severe abdominal pain, presence of renal transplant)

- 15-Minute prone film—compression released if satisfactory film of the pelvicaliceal system is obtained (Fig. 9.26)
- Twenty-five to 30 minutes—full bladder (Fig. 9.27) and postvoid film
- In case of nonfunctioning kidney, film taken at regular intervals till 24 hours (1, 2, 4, 8, 12, and 24 hours)

- From EU, one can determine the position of the renal pelvis (extrarenal or intrarenal).
- The following are the functions of same as well as opposite kidney:
  - Normally excreting
  - Delayed excreting
  - Nonexcreting
- Pathologies such as hydronephrosis, horseshoe kidney, tumor, and stone can be diagnosed.

Indications

Nowadays, CT scan has become an indispensable tool for the diagnosis of various intra-abdominal pathologies including genitourinary pathologies. The American College of Radiology has recommended the following indications for EU:

- To evaluate the presence or continuing presence of suspected or known ureteric obstruction such as stone disease and to assess the urinary tract for lesions that may explain hematuria or infection (in particular, EU may be used to evaluate for an underlying tumor of renal parenchyma or may be used to evaluate for a lesion of the urothelial tract [when CT is unavailable or inappropriate])
- Abnormal anatomy of the genitourinary tract (when CT is unavailable or inappropriate)
- Assessment of the integrity of urinary tract following trauma or therapeutic interventions, especially when CT is inappropriate or unavailable
- Follow-up of patients with recurrent renal/ureteral calculi, with a limited number of images obtained precontrast and postcontrast administration

Contraindications

- Allergy to contrast media
- Atopy
- Eczema
- Multiple myeloma
- Toxic thyroid
- Pregnancy
- Impaired renal function
- Neonates and young infants

- Normally, ureter should not be filled along its whole length, but if it appears to be so, it may raise the possibility of urethrospasm or ureteric obstruction.
- Always ask for plain X-ray before interpreting contrast film of EU (there is possibility of missing radio-opaque stone).

Complications

- Allergic reactions
  - *Mild*: Nausea, vomiting, and urticaria
  - *Severe*: Anaphylactic shock
- Acute renal toxicity (contrast-induced nephropathy)
  - Patients with renal insufficiency are more prone.
  - Two milligram percent serum creatinine—it is better to avoid EU.
  - Patients should be well hydrated.
  - LOCM is better as it has fewer complications.
  - Avoid large dose.

- Cardiac complications: ECG changes include arrhythmia, myocardial ischemia, and myocardial depression.

Limitations of EU

- It depends on renal function and does not provide exact percentage of renal function. It requires contrast media.
- It does not differentiate between solid and cystic lesions.

Retrograde Pyelography (RGP) (Ascending Pyelography) (Fig. 9.28)

Indications

Patients with renal insufficiency, contrast medium sensitivity, or suboptimal EU imaging are good candidates for an RGP. RGP allows superb visualization of upper urinary tract.

It is used where excretory urogram gives inadequate visualization of upper urinary tract:

- To assess the filling defect such as stone or tumor
- To evaluate ureteric obstruction
- To evaluate a case of trauma and hematuria
- To assist in percutaneous assess by delineating collecting system and for making puncture in PCNL
- Stent placement
- To confirm the diagnosis of ureteropelvic junction (UPJ) obstruction and to determine its exact location

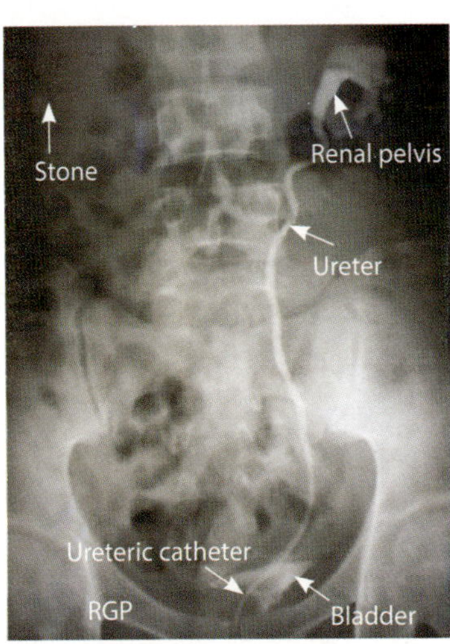

Figure 9.28 X-ray retrograde pyelography.

As this is an invasive procedure, prophylactic antibiotics are given.

Contraindications

- Urine culture and sensitivity positive
- Pregnancy
- Allergy to dye

Procedure

- American urology association (AUA) recommends prophylactic antibiotics for any patient going for RGP.
- Preoperative ureteric catheterization is to be done.
- Procedure is to be carried out under fluoroscopic guidance.
- Three to 5 mL of contrast is injected slowly.

Complications

- Ureteral perforation may occur.
- Pyelovenous backflow: When contrast is injected under increased pressure, the following can occur (i) bacteria are introduced into the bloodstream and (ii) anaphylactic reaction occurs from the contrast. To prevent this complication, the physician should inject contrast gently and under low pressure and appropriate preoperative antibiotic helps in prevention of bacterial infection. Forniceal rupture of calyces, which leads to bleeding, infection, and extravasations of contrast/rupture, will heal spontaneously.

Differences Between EXU and RGP

	EXU	RGP
Nephrogram	Seen	Not seen
Contrast	Bilateral	Unilateral
Ureteric catheter	Not seen	Seen

EXU, excretory urography; *RGP*, retrograde pyelography.

Retrograde Urethrography (RGU) (Ascending Urethrogram) (Figs 9.29 and 9.30)

In this technique, contrast is retrogradely injected with urethral orifice occluded to prevent leakage of contrast.

Indications

- Urethral and pelvic trauma
  - Floating prostate on digital rectal examination following trauma

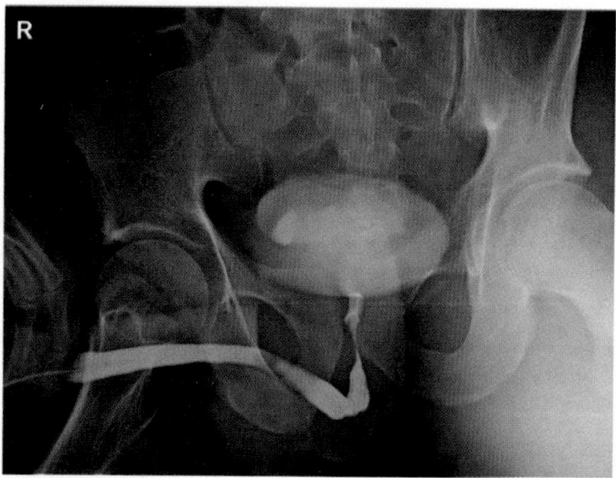

Figure 9.29 X-ray retrograde urethrography normal.

- Strictures
  - History of urethral stricture with lower urinary tract symptoms
  - Postoperative evaluation of urethra after urethroplasty

Contraindications

- UTI
- Recent cystoscopy or instrumentations

Procedure

- Forty-five-degree oblique position with dependent hip acutely flexed
- 14 Fr. Foley's catheter inserted up to 1–2 cm (red rubber catheter or infant feeding tube can be used instead)
- Balloon inflated with 1–2 mL of water
- Thirty to 60% solution of water-soluble contrast slowly injected
- Film taken while the last 10 mL of the material is being injected

Interpretation

- Anterior urethra is better visualized in RGU.
- Posterior urethra is not well visualized.
- Normal retrograde urethrogram: The entire anterior and posterior urethra should be filled with contrast. The verumontanum is seen as an ovoid filling defect in the posterior urethra. The distal end of the verumontanum marks the proximal boundary of the membranous urethra and makes the 1 cm of urethra that passes through the urogenital diaphragm.

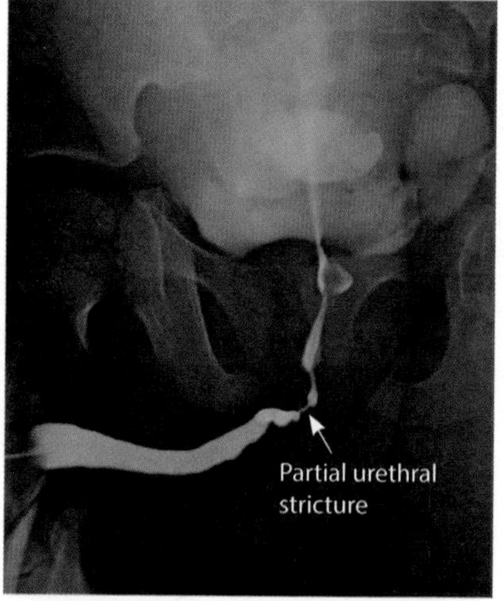

(a)

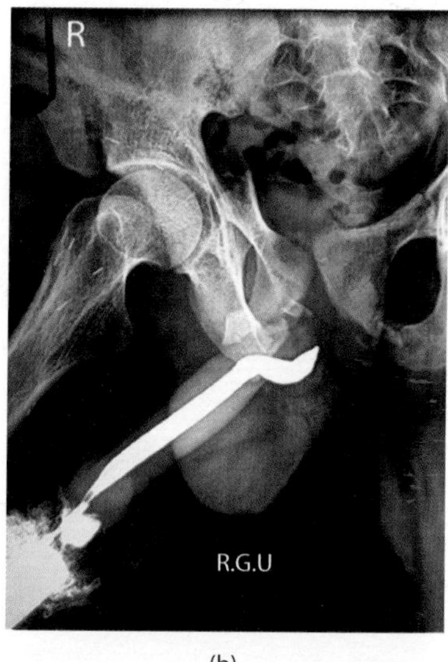

(b)

Figure 9.30 Stricture seen on retrograde urethrography. (a) Partial urethral stricture, (b) complete urethral stricture.

- Conditions diagnosed by RGU are as follows:
  - Stricture
  - False passage
  - Intravasation
  - Extravasation

Complications

- Ascending infection
- Contrast extravasation: Can be prevented by gentle administration of contrast sufficient to visualize the urethra

Voiding Cystourethrogram (VCUG; Descending Urethrogram) (Fig. 9.31)

- VCG X-ray is taken for evaluation of bladder and urethra during the act of micturition.
- Posterior urethra is better visualized.
- Bladder is filled with contrast via suprapubic or retrograde catheterization.
- Once bladder is full, the patient is asked to void in upright position.
- The patient is advised to micturate once before the procedure.

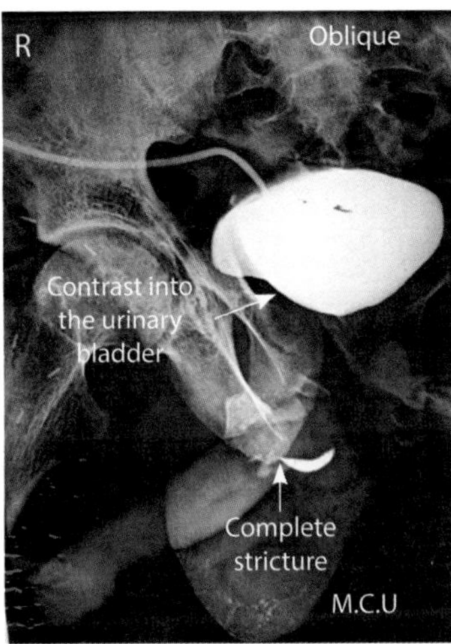

(a)

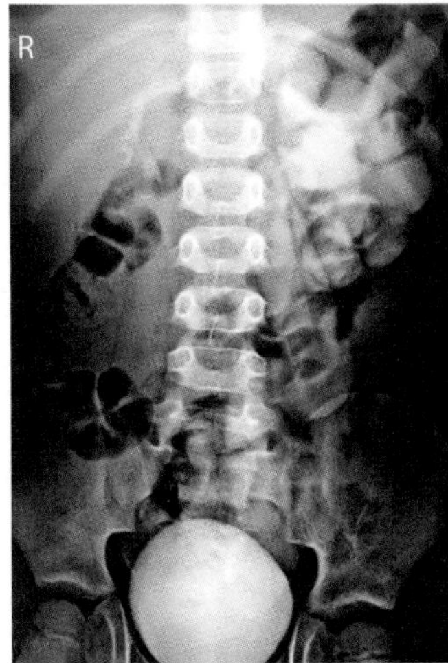

(b)

Figure 9.31 X-ray voiding cystourethrogram. (a) Complete stricture in posterior urethra. (b) Hydronephrosis and hydroureter on left side suggest vesicoureteric reflux.

- X-rays taken during VCUG are the following:
  - *AP with full bladder*: Vesicoureteric reflux (VUR)
  - *Both oblique*: Bilateral vesicoureteric jet
  - *Postvoid*: Ureterocele
- This procedure is more commonly performed in pediatric patients as compared to in adult populations.

Indications

- Evaluation of recurrent urinary tract infection is the most common indication.
- VUR
- Hydronephrosis and/or hydroureter
- Hematuria
- Trauma
- Incontinence
- Neurogenic dysfunction of the bladder, for example, spinal dysraphism
- Congenital anomalies of the genitourinary tract
- Bladder and its outlet pathology (e.g., bladder diverticulum, bladder outlet obstruction)
- Stress incontinence
- Posterior urethral stricture, valve, and fistula
  - Dysfunctional voiding
  - Postoperative evaluation of the urinary tract

Contraindications

- Recent history of urethral instrumentation
- Acute UTI
- Pregnancy
- Allergy or sensitivity to contrast medium
- Labial adhesions (relative contraindication, can be performed after releasing the adhesion)

Grading of VUR

- *Grade I*: Contrast enters the ureter.
- *Grade II*: Contrast enters the renal pelvis.
- *Grade III*: There is slight dilation of the calices or ureter.
- *Grade IV*: There is tortuous ureter with moderate dilatation with forniceal blunting and preserved papillary impression.
- *Grade V*: There is tortuous ureter with gross dilatation with loss of fornices and papillary impression.

Complication

Ascending infection

Nephrotomography

It is performed after placing nephrostomy tube.

Indications

- Postsurgical ureteric leak
- To evaluate residual stone after surgery
- Ureteral fistula

Mammography (Fig. 9.32)

- It is a method of using low-dose X-ray to examine human breast.
- It delivers approximately 0.1 cGy radiation.
- Low-dose, high-contrast, high-resolution film is obtained.

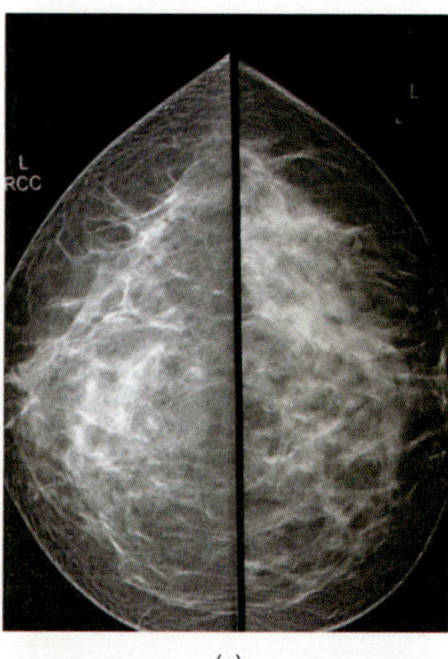

(a)

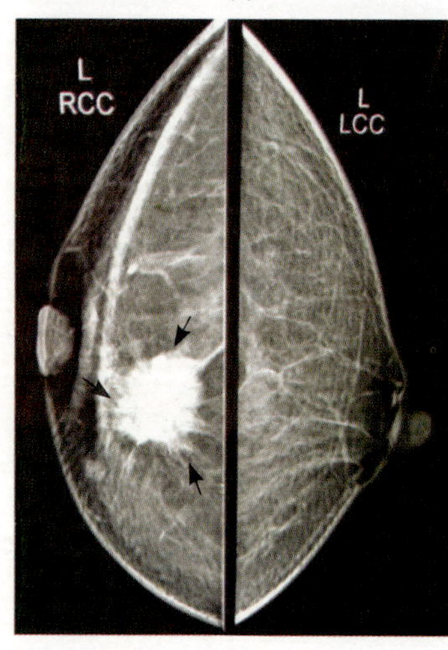

(b)

Figure 9.32 Mammography. (a) Normal. (b) Carcinoma of breast.

There are two types of mammography examinations: Screening and diagnostic. Screening mammography is performed in asymptomatic women. Early detection of small breast mass lesion is possible by screening mammography. Craniocaudal (CC) and mediolateral oblique (MLO) views are taken in screening.

It is recommended for every woman and started at the age of 45 years and performed yearly. After 55 years, it is performed every 2 years.[1] It can be started as early as 25 years in very high-risk women.

Diagnostic mammography is performed in symptomatic women, such as when a breast lump or nipple discharge is found, during breast self-examination, or when an abnormal screening mammograph is obtained. Diagnostic mammography may have additional views that can include lateromedial (LM), mediolateral (ML), exaggerated CC, magnification, and spot compression.

Indications

- Contralateral breast monitoring in a patient operated for carcinoma breast
- Same breast as well as contralateral breast monitoring in a patient treated with breast conservation therapy
- As a screening procedure in women of age more than 35 years
- To search for occult primary in patients with metastatic axillary node
- Mammographic localization of biopsy in suspected lesion

View

CC and MLO

BREAST IMAGING REPORTING AND DATA SYSTEM (BI-RADS) INTERPRETATION

- *0*: Incomplete, further imaging required
- *I*: Normal
- *II*: Benign
- *III*: Probably benign, short-term follow-up
- *IV*: Suspected malignancy
  - Low level of suspicion
  - Intermediate suspicion
  - Moderate suspicion
- *V*: Highly suggestive of malignancy
- *VI*: Biopsy-proven malignancy

- Sensitivity increases with age (breast becomes less dense).
- A lump can be detected before it is clinically apparent.
- Mammography should be done before biopsy (it is not a substitute for biopsy).

ULTRASONOGRAPHY (US)

Basics of Ultrasonography

Audible sound wave frequency is between 20 and 20,000 Hz. US uses frequency that is far greater (i.e., medical US uses between 3 and 20 MHz). Sound wave propagation is worse in gases while it is better in liquids and best in solids. Gas-filled bowel and air-filled lungs conduct sound so poorly that they cannot be imaged properly and structures beneath these cannot be seen. Transducer containing piezoelectric material generates a high-frequency sound wave. The sound wave propagates through the tissue. The generated sound waves are reflected by the tissue interface. The echoes arising from the structure are reflected back to crystal, which in turn vibrates, generating electrical impulse, and it forms the image. The higher the frequency of the wave, the greater is the resolution of the image, but less is the depth of view from the skin. Abdominal sonography uses frequency of 3–7 MHz, while a higher frequency is used for soft and superficial tissue structures. Dedicated transducers are also developed for various cavities such as transvaginal, transrectal, as well as endosonography. Reflection of an ultrasound wave from moving structures such as blood flow in vessels causes changes in the frequency of the ultrasound wave. The velocity of the moving object can be calculated from this frequency shift. This forms the basis of Doppler ultrasound.

Advantages of US[2]

- It is cheap.
- It is easily available.
- It is the first-line investigation in many surgical areas such as hepatobiliary and renal tract. High-frequency probe can be used to evaluate the lesion in the thyroid as well as testes.
- Soft-tissue injury such as ligaments and tendons is initially evaluated by US and later on can be evaluated in detail by further investigation modalities such as magnetic resonance imaging (MRI).
- US can pick up most foreign bodies in soft-tissue region that cannot be picked up by even X-rays.
- Ultrasound-guided interventional procedures such as cytology, core needle biopsy, and injection can be performed. FNA of the thyroid and parathyroid can be performed.

FOCUSED ASSESSMENT WITH SONOGRAPHY IN TRAUMA (FAST) SCAN

Indications

These include blunt abdominal trauma, stable penetrating trauma, and assessment of the free fluid within peritoneal cavity.

FAST includes peritoneal, pleural, and pericardial cavity (subxiphoid window) examination. Extended version (E-FAST) includes examination of hemithoraces for hemothorax and upper anterior chest wall for pneumothorax.

Examination

Blood tends to collects in the most dependent part. Morison pouch is most dependent in supramesocolic compartment and Douglas pouch is most dependent in inframesocolic compartment. FAST includes examination of Morison space, suprapubic or Douglas pouch, perisplenic view, and subxiphoid window.

Advantages

- Noninvasive
- Cheap
- Easily available
- Rapid
- Accurate diagnosis and assessment of the degree of hemoperitoneum
- Serial examination possible, safe in pregnancy, and avoids invasiveness of diagnostic peritoneal lavage

Limitations

- Bowel gas or surgical emphysema may obscure the fluid.
- Organized hematoma may be difficult to locate or visualize.

Sonographic images of common surgical conditions are given in Figures 9.33–9.41.

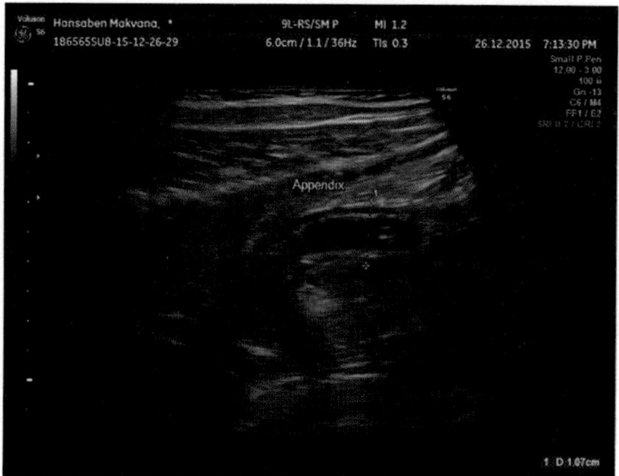

Figure 9.33 Acute appendicitis.

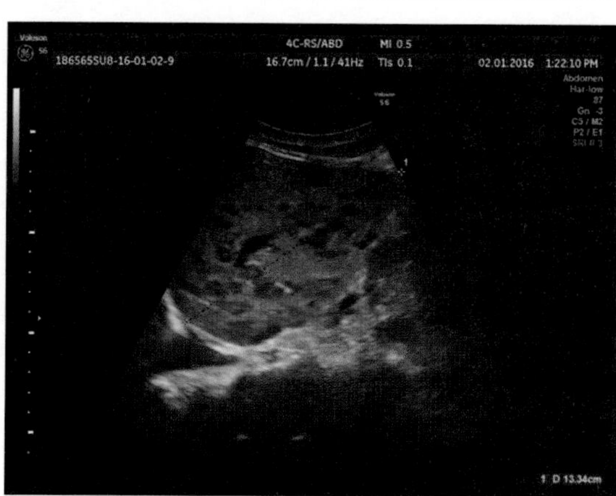

Figure 9.36 Liver metastases.

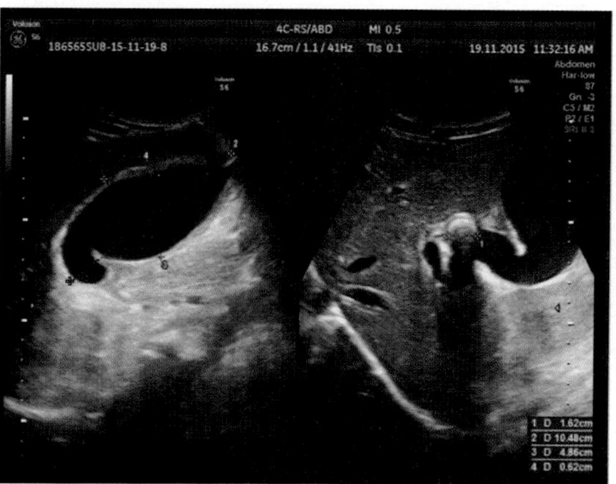

Figure 9.34 Gallbladder stone.

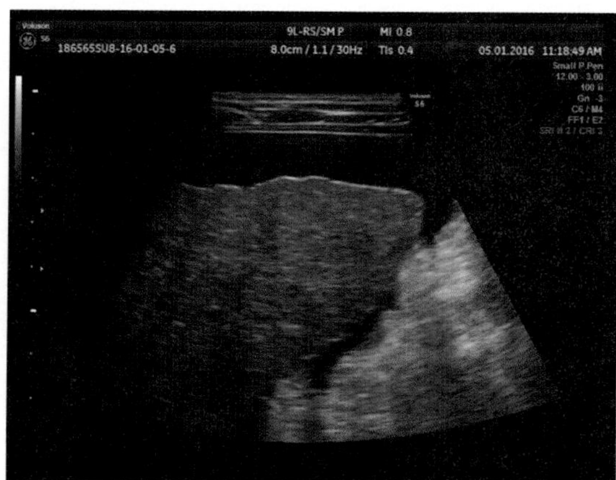

Figure 9.37 Cirrhosis of liver.

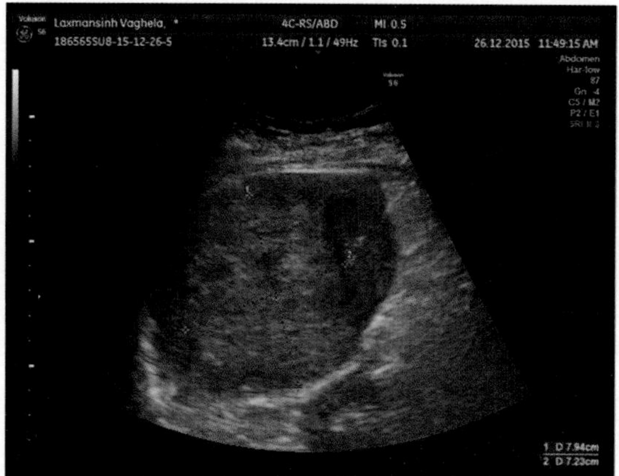

Figure 9.35 Liver mass.

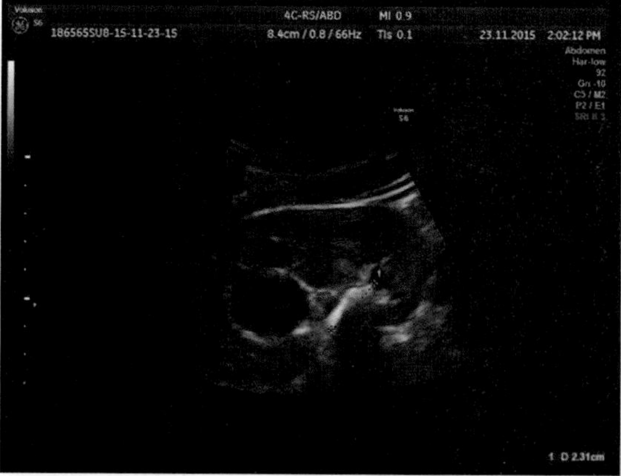

Figure 9.38 Renal stone.

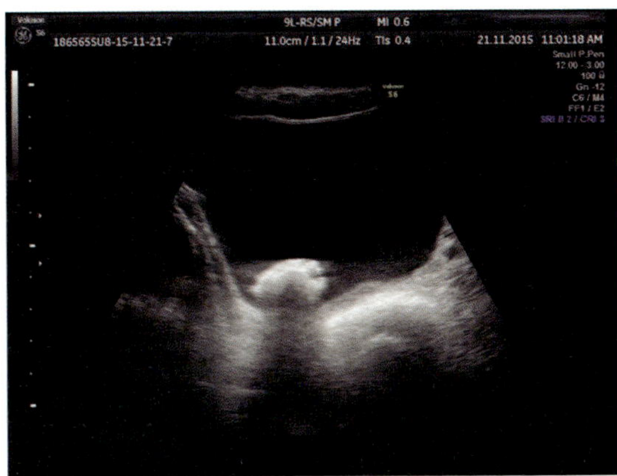

Figure 9.39 Urinary bladder stone.

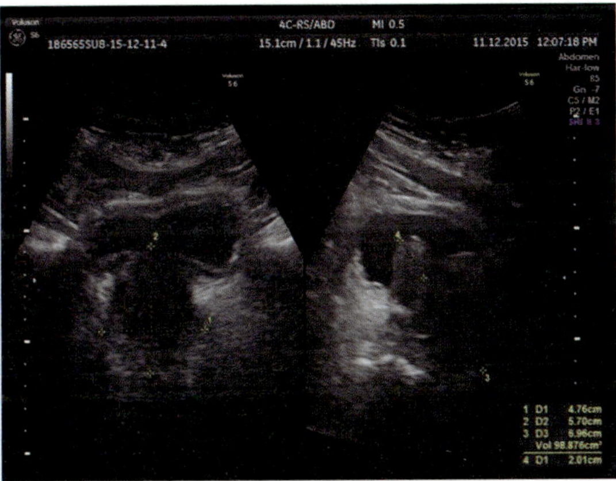

Figure 9.40 Benign enlargement of prostate.

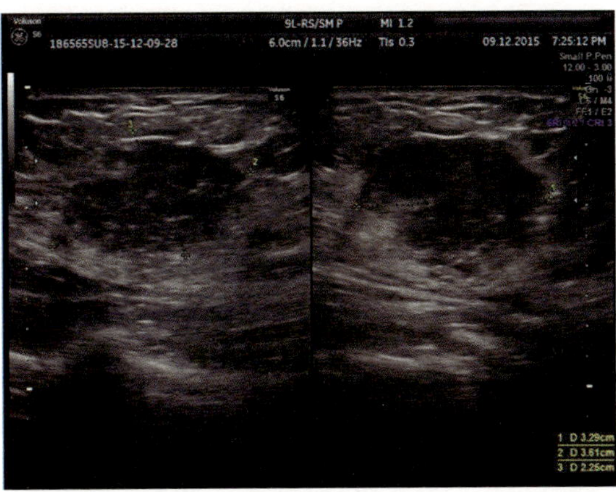

Figure 9.41 Malignant breast lump.

COMPUTED TOMOGRAPHY

The word tomography has been derived from the Greek words 'tomos' (slice) and 'graphia' (describing).

Principle

CT scanners consist of a gantry containing X-ray tube and collimator, tube controller, high-frequency generator, onboard computer, and stationary computer. Gantry revolves around the patient and acquires information at different angles and projections. This information is then reconstructed to produce a 2D grayscale image of a slice through the body.

This technique overcomes the problems associated with conventional radiography such as superimposition, insufficient X-ray absorption, and poor resolution.

- *First-generation CT scan*: Has a narrow pencil beam, single detector per slice, and design mainly for brain (scan time 5 minutes)
- *Second-generation CT scan*: Has a narrow fan beam and multiple detectors (scan time 20 seconds)
- *Third-generation CT scan*: Has a wide fan beam, multiple detectors (600–800), tube–detector translator movement completely avoided, detectors perfectly aligned with X-ray tube (scan time 5 seconds)
- *Fourth-generation CT scan*: Has a continuous wide fan beam, tube rotating in a circle inside the fixed detector (>2000 detectors) ring, scan time <2 seconds

Indications

CT has been widely used.

- *CT chest*: Evaluates abnormalities found on chest X-ray; can help in diagnosis of infection, lung cancer, embolism, and aneurysm
- *CT abdomen*: Upper GI and lower GI malignancy such as stomach, small bowel, and colorectal:
  - Pancreatic pathology such as pancreatitis and pancreatic malignancy
  - Infection or inflammation such as appendicitis and diverticulitis
  - Liver pathologies such as tumor and hemangioma
  - Spleen: Tumor, cyst, and abscess
- *CT KUB or urogram*: To detect stone, obstruction, and or malignancy; CT urography used to detect

stone, obstruction, and function of the same as well as opposite kidney

- *CT pelvis*: In women for uterus, ovary, and fallopian tube and in males for prostate and seminal vesical

In addition, CT can also be used to take the biopsy and perform interventional radiological procedures such as putting drain and proper placement of needle to drain the abscess.

CT scan abdomen can also be performed in trauma to the abdomen in hemodynamically stable patients.

Contraindications

- Allergy to iodine
- Toxic goiter
- Planned radioiodine in patients with thyroid cancer

Advantages of Multislice CT

- Better resolution
- Larger coverage
- Faster scan time
- Less radiation dose
- Less motion artifact
- Better utilization of contrast (8-, 16-, 32-, 64-, 256-slice CT available)

Disadvantages of CT

- High cost
- Higher radiation dose

Dose for CT abdomen is almost equal to 500 chest X-rays.

CT images of common surgical condition are given in Figures 9.42–9.55.

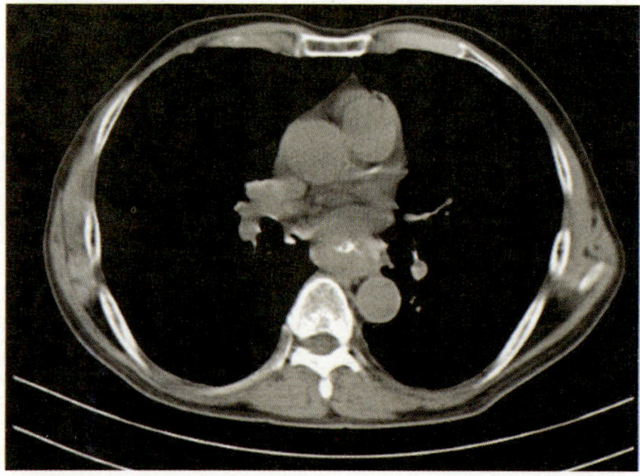

Figure 9.42 Carcinoma esophagus.

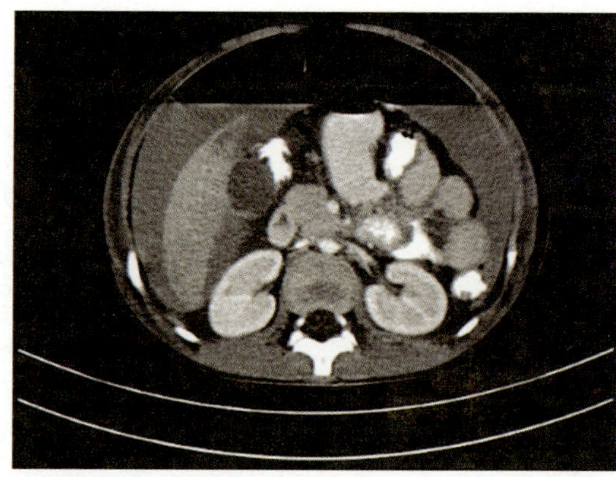

Figure 9.43 Pneumoperitoneum.

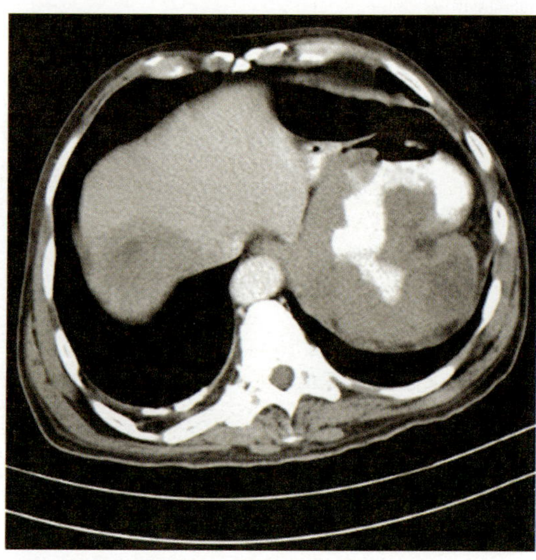

Figure 9.44 Gastric cancer with liver metastases.

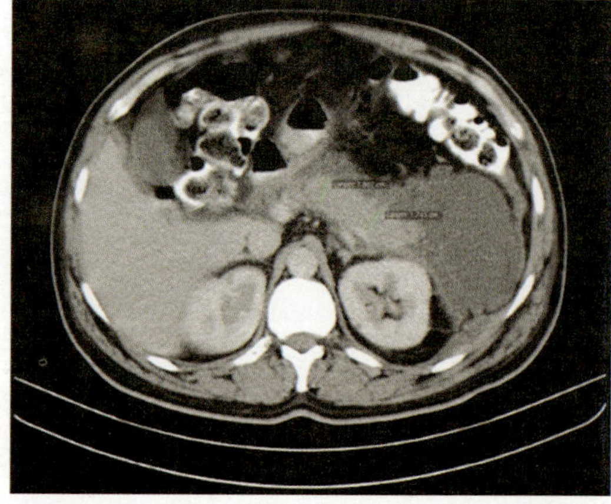

Figure 9.45 Acute pancreatitis with peripancreatic fluid collection.

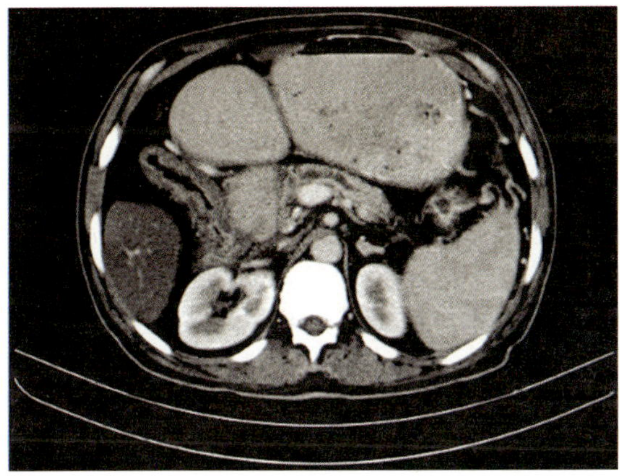

Figure 9.46 Chronic pancreatitis: main pancreatic duct dilated with atrophic pancreas.

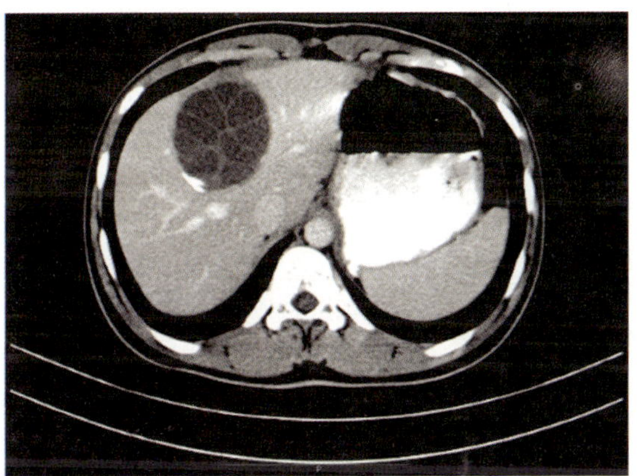

Figure 9.47 Hydatid cyst of liver.

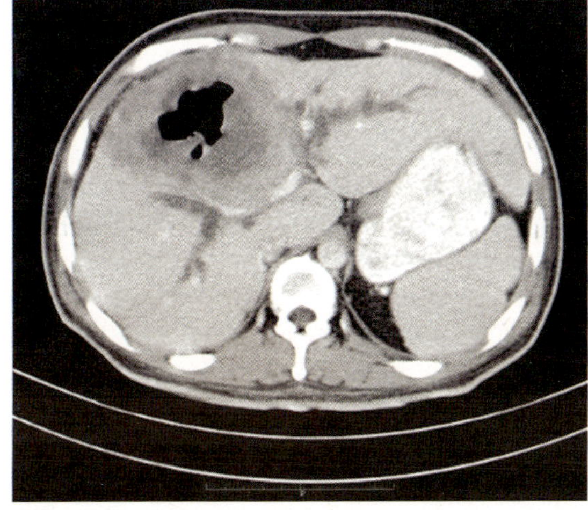

Figure 9.48 Necrotic liver mass.

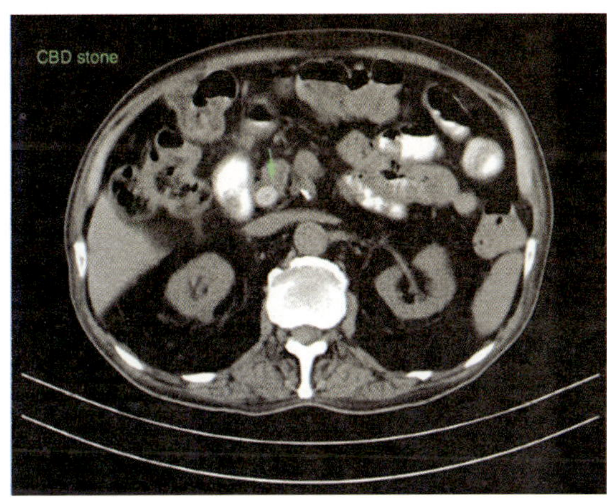

Figure 9.49 Common bile duct stone.

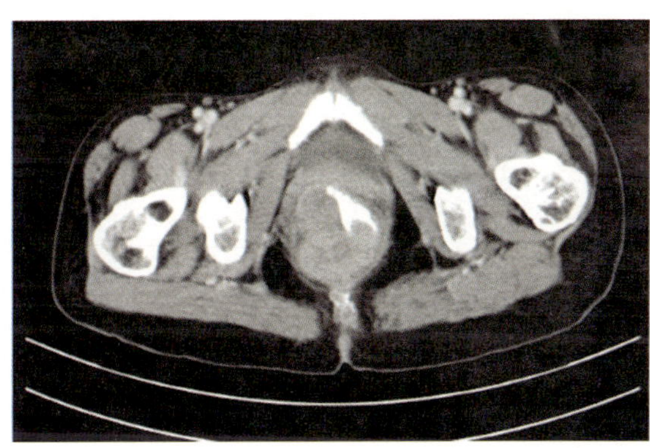

Figure 9.50 Rectal mass.

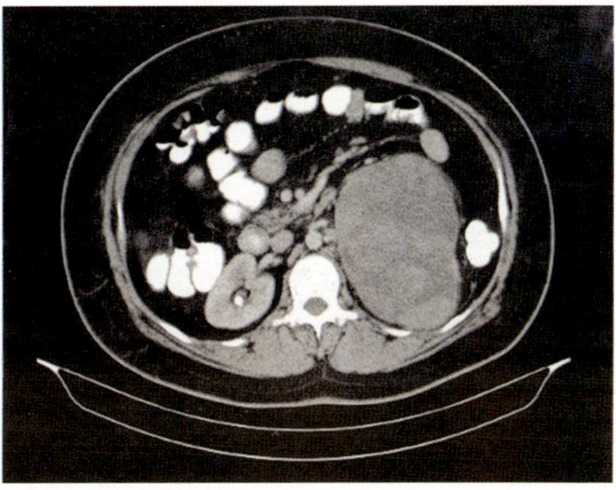

Figure 9.51 Left renal mass.

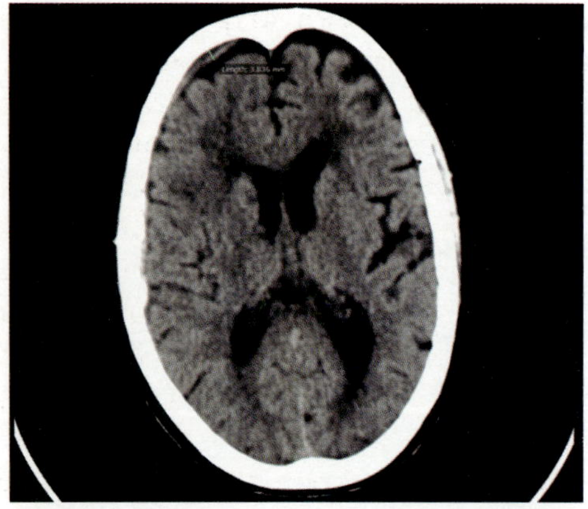

Figure 9.52 Extradural hematoma (EDH).

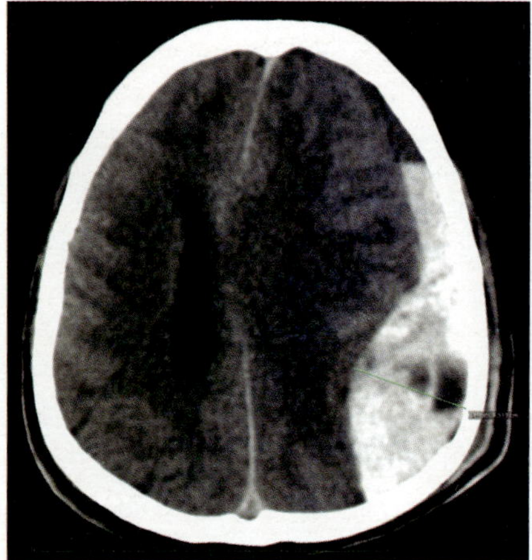

Figure 9.53 Subdural hematoma (SDH).

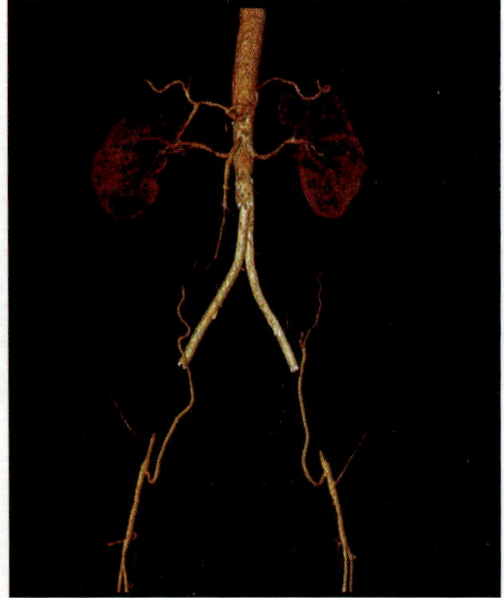

Figure 9.54 CT angiography: complete occlusion of bilateral common iliac artery with collateral and stent in situ.

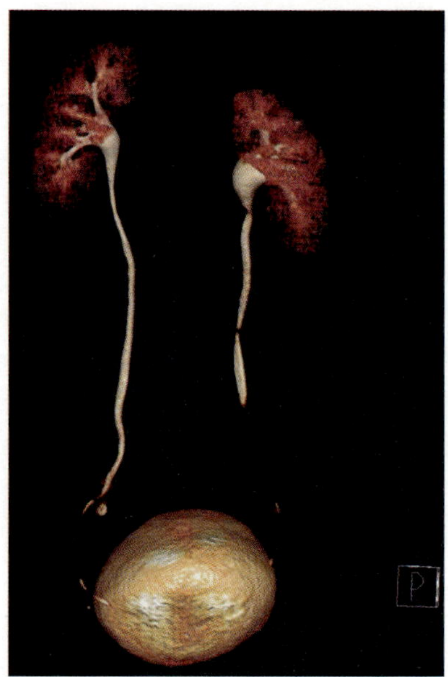

Figure 9.55 Normal CT urography.

MAGNETIC RESONANCE IMAGING

MRI is based on the principle of nuclear magnetic resonance.[2] Nuclei of atom containing an odd number of proton or neutron have characteristic spin, and moving electrical charge, whether it is positive or negative, produces a magnetic field; MRI utilizes magnetic property of proton of hydrogen as hydrogen not only is positively charged but also has magnetic spin. In natural state in our body, hydrogen ions in the body are moving in a haphazard fashion. In MRI, nuclei align themselves with the main magnetic field and produce net magnetic movement. A brief radiofrequency wave is applied to alter the motion of nuclei. RF waves perturb magnetization in a different axis and only transverse magnetization produces signal. When radiofrequency wave is removed, the nuclei realign themselves with the main magnetic field (relaxation). The process produces radiofrequency signal that can be recorded, encoded, and used to construct a grayscale image. Hydrogen nuclei relax by two mechanisms. Different tissues have different relaxation times and these are used to generate image contrast.

- *T1 bright*: Fat, methemoglobin and mucinous fluid, melanin, and slowly flowing blood are bright on T1.

- *T2 bright*: Water and thus most pathological processes in which tissue water content is increased, tumor, infection, and subdural collection are bright on T2.

In general, T1 images are superior for delineating anatomy while T2 images tend to highlight pathology.

Intravenous contrast with gadolinium is beneficial to detect and characterize many intra-abdominal neoplasms, vascular malformations and abnormalities, and inflammatory pathology. However, the use of gadolinium may be omitted when images without contrast are sufficiently diagnostic.

Commonly used MRI machines nowadays are 1.5 and 3 T.

Indications

- Intracranial, spinal, and musculoskeletal pathology
- Pancreatic pathology such as evaluation of pancreatic neoplasm, pancreatic duct problem such as anomalies, obstruction, fistula, chronic pancreatitis, and acute pancreatitis and its complications
- Detection of gallbladder and bile duct cancer, bile duct obstruction (Fig. 9.56), postoperative bile leak, and detection of congenital anomalies of bile duct
- Evaluation of splenic tumor or accessory spleen
- Detection and characterization of renal tumor, vascular invasion in renal neoplasm, urinary tract anatomy and physiology, evaluation of retroperitoneal fibrosis, evaluation of complex congenital anomalies, and detection of adrenal gland pathology such as pheochromocytoma and other adrenal gland neoplasms
- Preoperative assessment of gastric, small bowel, colonic, and rectal neoplasm, peritoneal adhesive disease, and evaluation of lymphadenopathy
- Can also be used as an alternative to CT in case of pregnant women, pediatric patients, and patients with allergy to iodinated contrast media
- Assessment of abdominal wall abnormalities and traumatic injury of the abdomen (where CT is contraindicated)
- Angiography of peripheral and cranial circulation
- Cardiac imaging
- Breast pathology: Can differentiate scar from recurrence in a previously operated case, assesses multifocality and multicentricity in case of lobular cancer, is used as a screening tool in high-risk patients, and is the best imaging modality for breast of women with implants

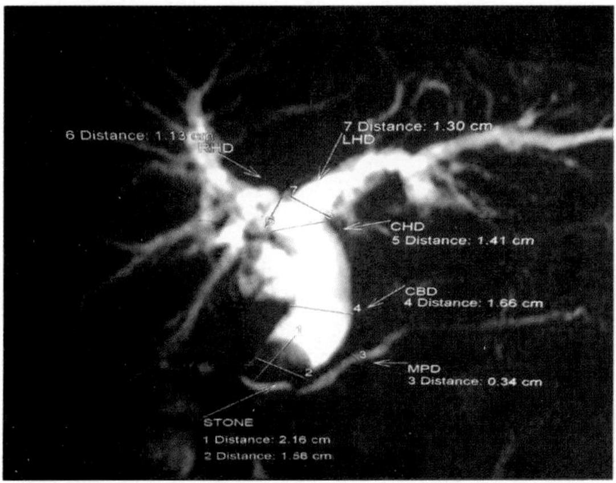

Figure 9.56 Lower CBD stone.

Advantages

- Excellent soft-tissue contrast resolution
- Lack of ionizing radiation
- Multiplanar images

Limitations

- Not able to scan patients with metal implants due to high-strength magnetic field
- Limited availability
- Cost
- Possible degradation of the images due to respiratory, cardiac (respiratory and cardiac gating can help), and bowel movement
- Longer duration (difficult in patients with pain and claustrophobic patients)

NUCLEAR MEDICINE

Basic Principle

Radioactive element or radionuclide such as I-131 and Tc-99m is administered to patients as a part of radiopharmaceutical agent, and gamma camera is then used to record and localize the emission from the patient, thus forming the image.

Radiopharmaceutical → patients → gamma camera → image

Indications

- Renal perfusion and function and to evaluate renal transplant patients
- Thyroid and parathyroid problems such as parathyroid adenoma, hyperthyroidism, thyroid cancer, localization of ectopic thyroid tissue, and parathyroid cancer
- Detection of acute GI bleed
- Detection of testicular torsion
- Detection of pulmonary emboli
- Tumor localization, staging, and bone pain due to metastases
- Ischemic heart disease
- Bone trauma and osteomyelitis

Most radiology procedures delineate anatomical and morphological structures with little or no information on function.

PET is a coalition of physics, physiology, chemistry, and medicine, united in an effort to measure physiological parameters noninvasively.

PET-CT provides functional as well as anatomical information.

In PET, a positron-emitting substance such as ^{18}F is tagged and used to assess tissue metabolic characteristics.

Most commonly used tracer is ^{18}F-2-fluoro-2-deoxy-D-glucose (FDG).

It helps in the assessment of metabolic functions such as oxygen and glucose consumption, and blood flow.

Contraindications for PET

- Use of caffeine, alcohol, or tobacco in the past 24 hours
- Pregnancy
- Sedative use
- Use of insulin (changes the metabolism)

Advantages of Nuclear Medicine

- Functional
- Sensitive
- Quantitative
- Safe
- Minimal invasive
- Low radiation exposure
- Whole-body functional imaging
- Valuable and highly sensitive for detecting metastatic diseases

Disadvantages

- Limited availability
- Nonspecific
- Requires NM instruments and radiopharmaceuticals
- High cost
- Specific agents required for specific organ
- Poor spatial resolution

References

1. American cancer society recommendation. Available at: https://www.cancer.org/cancer/breast-cancer/screening-tests-and-early-detection/american-cancer-society-recommendations-for-the-early-detection-of-breast-cancer.html
2. Matson M, Ahmad M, Power N. In: Williams NS, O'Connell PR, McCaskie A, eds. Bailey and Love Short Practice of Surgery, 27th edn. Florida: CRC Press, Taylor and Francis, 2018, 190–215.

CHAPTER 10

Sterilization

Maintenance of surgical asepsis is of paramount importance. Sterilization of instruments, dressings, hands of the surgeon and his/her assistants, or anything else likely to come in contact with the wound and prevention of wound suppuration is a prerequisite in any surgical procedure. In this section, we shall look at different methods of achieving asepsis. Some important definitions are given in Box 10.1.

Box 10.1 Important definitions

- *Cleaning*: Removal of foreign material (e.g., soil and organic material) from objects; commonly performed by water with detergents or enzymatic products
- *Disinfection*: Process of killing of microorganisms, with the exception of spores
- *Sterilization*: Process of destroying of all forms of microorganisms, including bacteria, virus, spores, and fungi
- *Antiseptics*: Agents that inhibit or kill the organisms when used on living objects (in contrast, disinfectants are used on inanimate objects)
- *Contamination*: Presence of microorganisms without multiplication
- *Colonization*: Presence of microorganisms with multiplication, without host response
- *Infection*: Presence of microorganisms with multiplication, with host response
- *Bioburden*: Number and types of viable microorganisms with which an item is contaminated; also called bioload or microbial load
- *Biofilm*: Presence of bacteria and extracellular material that is tightly adhered to a surface and cannot be easily removed
- *Spore*: Relatively water-poor round or elliptical resting cell consisting of condensed cytoplasm and nucleus surrounded by an impervious cell wall or coat
- *Necrosis*: Rapid pathological microscopic cell death, in the midst of living tissue
- *Gangrene*: Macroscopic cell death (massive necrosis) with superadded putrefaction
- *Granulation tissue*: A highly vascular connective tissue and consists of newly formed fibroblasts, inflammatory cells, collagen, glycosaminoglycan, and in-growing blood vessels
- *Healthy granulation tissue*: Red, fine granulation, which bleeds on touch, with minimal or no serous discharge
- *Unhealthy granulation tissue*: Any deviation from healthy granulation tissue
- *Slough*: Dead soft tissue within living tissue, in the process of separation
- *Apoptosis*: Programmed cell death
- *Necrobiosis*: Physiological cell death
- *Cellulitis*: A nonlocalized, spreading inflammation of subcutaneous tissue, caused by β-hemolytic streptococci
- *Carbuncle*: Infective gangrene of subcutaneous tissue, commonly seen in diabetics, over the nape of the neck; is an abscess with multiple draining sinuses
- *Boils*: Infection of hair follicle with perifolliculitis, caused by *Staphylococcus aureus*
- *Bacteremia*: Presence of viable bacteria in the blood that do not multiply rapidly
- *Septicemia*: Presence of rapidly multiplying bacteria in the blood with clinical manifestations such as sepsis, septic shock, and multiple organ dysfunction syndrome (MODS)
- *Pyemia*: Effect of septic foci at the site of its lodge from the blood (commonly, portal pyemia leads to liver abscess)
- *Signs of inflammation*: *Rubor* (redness), *calor* (heat), *tumor* (swelling), *dolor* (pain), and *functio lesia* (loss of function)

CLASSIFICATION OF SURGICAL ITEMS

Spaulding classified surgical items or equipment as follows:[1]

- *Critical*: These are those items that are high risk for transmitting infection if contaminated with microorganisms. Examples include instruments that come in contact with tissue and vascular space, surgical instruments, urinary catheters, and implants such as joint and mesh. Most of these items are sterilized by steam sterilizer. Heat- or moisture-sensitive materials are sterilized by ethylene oxide (ETO) or hydrogen peroxide gas plasma.
- *Semicritical*: These are those items that come in contact with mucous membrane or nonintact skin. Examples include anesthesia equipment, endoscopes, laryngoscope blades, esophageal manometry probes, cystoscopes, and anorectal

manometry catheters. These items require at least high-level disinfection. FDA recommends glutaraldehyde, hydrogen peroxide, *ortho*-phthalaldehyde (OPA), and peracetic acid with hydrogen peroxide for high-level disinfection.

- *Noncritical*: These are those items that come in contact with intact skin. Examples include bedpans, blood pressure cuffs, bed rails, some food utensils, and bedside tables.

FACTORS AFFECTING STERILIZATION OR DISINFECTION[2]

- *Number and location of microorganisms*: Larger number of microorganisms will take more time to be destroyed. Microorganisms in difficult locations such as crevices and pits of instrument are difficult to sterilize so instruments must be dismantled and there should be no air pocket in between. Only the surface that is in contact with disinfectant will be disinfected.
- *Innate resistance of microorganisms*: Outer cell of Gram-negative bacteria and waxy cell wall of mycobacteria prevent the entry of disinfectant. HIV, *Pseudomonas*, and HCV also have a significant resistance to disinfectants. All of these require high-level disinfectants with at least 10-minute duration.
- *Organic and inorganic matter*: Organic matter in the form of blood and pus also interferes with disinfectants in two ways—it acts as a physical barrier and forms a chemical reaction resulting in complex formation that is less germicidal.
- *Duration of exposure*: Items must be exposed to the germicide for the appropriate minimum contact time. The exact times for disinfecting medical items are somewhat elusive but, in general, longer contact times are more effective than shorter contact times.
- *Biofilms*: Bacteria within biofilms are up to 1000 times more resistant to antimicrobials than the same bacteria in suspension. Chlorine and monochloramines are the best disinfectants for biofilms.
- *Physical and chemical factors*: Increase in temperature, increase in pH, and decrease in water hardness will increase the efficacy of disinfectants.
- *Lumen length and diameter*: Increasing length and decreasing diameter of the lumen impair the penetration of a sterilant.
- *Device design*: Screws, hinges, and joints in the instrument may also affect the sterilization efficacy.

VARIOUS METHODS OF STERILIZATION

Autoclave

- Principle: Autoclave (Fig. 10.1) involves heating water to generate steam, producing a moist heat that rapidly kills microorganisms. Moist heat causes irreversible coagulation and denaturation of enzymes and structural proteins.

  Autoclave destroys microorganisms through the action of steam under pressure. The time taken for sterilization varies with the temperature and pressure of steam as summarized in Table 10.1.
- Autoclaving is the most common method of sterilization used in operation theater. Two types of autoclave are available:
  - *Gravity displacement autoclave*: Steam is from the side or the top of chamber and as steam is

Table 10.1 Variation in Time Taken for Sterilization

Temperature (°C)	Pressure (lb/inch)	Time (minutes)
121	15	15
134	30	3

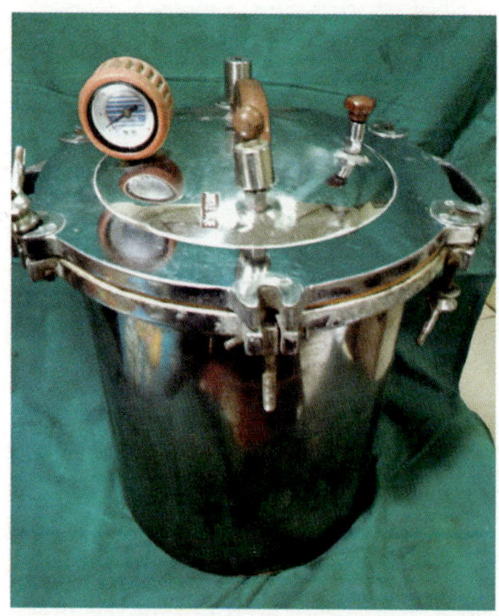

Figure 10.1 Autoclave.

lighter than air, it forces air out the bottom of the chamber through drain vent.
  - *High-speed prevacuum sterilizer*: It is fitted with vacuum pump to ensure the air removal from the chamber and load before steam is admitted.
- Portable steam sterilizers are used in outpatients and rural clinics.
- This method kills most of the bacteria including *Mycobacterium tuberculosis*, viruses including HBV, HCV, and HIV, and spores including *Clostridium tetani* and *Clostridium perfringens*.
- The process is monitored by a chemical indicator. To check for sterilization, a specific gelatin protein is used, which precipitates only in steam under pressure.
- Methods used to check the efficiency of autoclave are as follows:
  - Spores of *Geobacillus stearothermophilus* (formerly *Bacillus stearothermophilus*)
  - Automatic monitoring system
- Autoclaving is used to sterilize the following:
  - Dressing materials
  - Surgical instruments
  - Culture media
  - Pharmaceutical materials
- Disadvantage of autoclave is that moisture may cause corrosion of some instruments. It is advisable to use distilled water instead of tap water to minimize the corrosion.
- This method is not used to sterilize endoscopes and rubber goods, because of the potential of damage to the cementing substance of endoscope and damage to the rubber material of rubber goods.
- Safeguards during the sterilization procedure are the following:
  - Thorough cleaning
  - Packing
  - All the surfaces to be directly exposed to the agent
- Autoclaves are usually located in the central sterile supply department (CSSD), to cater to the needs of the entire hospital.

Gamma Radiation

It is used for sterilization of large quantities of similar products such as syringes, catheters, and IV cannulas.

Ethylene Oxide[2]

- ETO is colorless, flammable, and explosive. The four essential parameters are—gas concentration (450–1200 mg/L), temperature (37–63°C), relative humidity (40–80%), and exposure time (1–6 hours).
- Two types of ETO sterilizers are available: mixed (12% ETO with 88% chlorofluorocarbon [CFC]) and 100% ETO.
- ETO is a highly penetrative, noncorrosive agent with broad-spectrum action against bacteria, viruses, and spores. But it is toxic, irritant, mutagenic, and costly, and requires a longer cycle time.
- It is used for sterilization of heat- or moisture-sensitive materials that cannot be sterilized by steam sterilizer.
- It is suitable for all disposable instruments, insulated laparoscopic hand instruments, and plastic tubes used for gas, suction, and irrigation tubing.
- Sterilization time for ETO is given in Table 10.2.
- ETO is absorbed by many materials; for this reason, items must undergo aeration following sterilization to remove residual gas.
- Side effects
  - *Acute*: Skin and mucus membrane irritation and CNS depression.
  - *Chronic*: Cataracts, cognitive impairment, neurologic dysfunction, and disabling polyneuropathies, hematologic changes, carcinogenic

Hot Air Oven

- The instruments that cannot withstand temperature of autoclave and are poorly penetrated by steam are sterilized by this method.
- Glassware, powder, and liquids are sterilized by this method.

Table 10.2 Sterilization Time for ETO

ETO gas	Temperature (°C)	Contact time (hours)	Aeration (hours)
Cold	85	4.30	12
Warm	145	2.30	8

ETO, ethylene oxide.

- Keeping the hot air oven at 160°C for 1 hour is the standard procedure.

Low Temperature

- This method is used in pasteurization of milk.
- Sterilization of Lowenstein–Jensen and Loeffler serum is achieved at 80–85°C.

ANTISEPTICS

Criteria for ideal antiseptic solution are the following:

- Broad spectrum
- Fast action
- Nonirritant
- Nontoxic
- Should have residual effect
- Should not have been inactivated by organic material such as blood
- Should be inexpensive
- Water soluble
- Good surface compatibility
- Should have a good cleaning property and should be environment friendly

Peracetic Acid

- It is a high-level disinfectant.
- It is an oxidizing agent. It denatures the protein and disrupts cell wall.
- Its special advantage is that it lacks harmful decomposition, enhances removal of organic material, and leaves no residue.
- It is effective in the presence of organic matter and sporicidal even at low temperature.
- It will inactivate Gram-positive and Gram-negative bacteria, fungi, and yeasts in less than 5 minutes at <100 ppm. Presence of organic matter requires 200–500 ppm.
- It is used for endoscopes and cystoscopes.

Formaldehyde

It kills microorganisms by alkylating the amino and sulfhydryl groups of proteins and ring nitrogen atoms of purine bases.

It is available in liquid as well as gaseous states.

- It is mostly available as a water-based solution called formalin (37%, w/w, formaldehyde). It is a broad-spectrum agent (bactericide, tuberculocide, fungicide, virucide, and sporicide).
- It is used for fumigation of operation theater.
- It is used to prepare viral vaccine, to preserve anatomic specimen.
- Efficiency increases with humidity.

Potential disadvantages are the following: Irritant, pungent odor, and carcinogenic.

Povidone–Iodine (Polyvinylpyrrolidone with Iodine) (Fig. 10.2)

- It is a soluble complex of iodine with a large molecular weight.
- It is a broadspectrum (bactericidal, virucidal, fungicidal, and sporicidal) agent.
- It releases free iodine slowly.
- It does not have residual effect.
- It is inactivated by blood.
- It is available as 5% solution, 5% ointment, 7.5% scrub, and 1% mouthwash.
- Mechanism of action: It is an oxidizing agent, which irreversibly oxidizes and inactivates protein, with sulfhydryl group, which is an essential component of microorganisms. Free iodine is responsible for bactericidal activity. Dilution of solution might weaken iodine linkage and results in increase in free iodine concentration.
- Uses: It is the most commonly used solution. It is used for the following:
  - Preoperative skin preparation

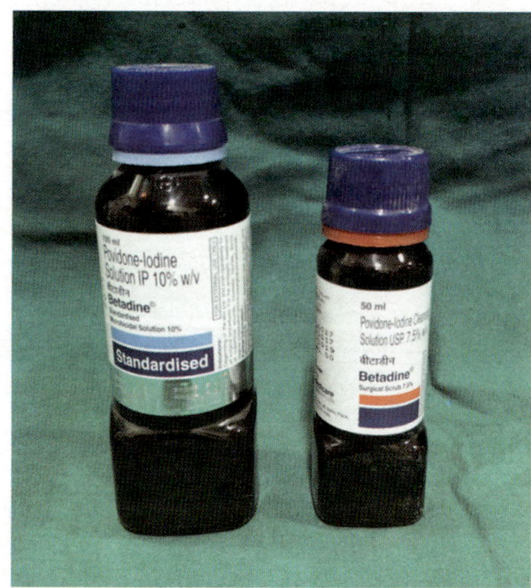

Figure 10.2 Povidone iodine 10% solution and surgical scrub 7.5%.

- Treatment and prevention of infection in wounds, ulcers, and cuts
- Dressing of ulcer
- Mouth gargle (1%)
- Through cystoscopy, intravesical instillation in chyluria
- Povidone–iodine enema as a preoperative preparation in colorectal surgery
- In pleurodesis in malignant pleural effusion (is as effective as talc)
- Vaginitis associated with mixed infection
- Disinfecting blood culture bottles and medical equipment, such as thermometers and endoscopes

- Advantages over tincture iodine: It is nonirritant, nontoxic, and nonstaining.

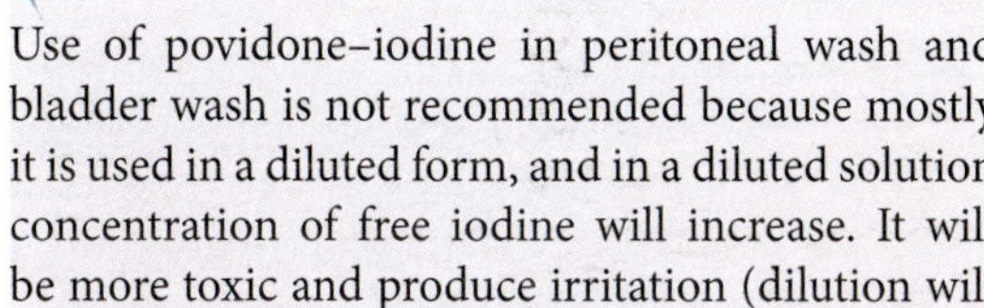

Use of povidone–iodine in peritoneal wash and bladder wash is not recommended because mostly it is used in a diluted form, and in a diluted solution concentration of free iodine will increase. It will be more toxic and produce irritation (dilution will not affect the bactericidal property of Betadine).

It should not be used on silicone catheters because they can adversely affect the silicone tubing.

Other preparations of iodine

- Lugol's iodine (5% I in 10% KI)
- Saturated solution of potassium iodide (SSKI) (one drop of SSKI = six drops of Lugol's iodine)
- Tincture iodine: Solution of iodine in ethyl alcohol; used as topical antiseptic, but should not be used over face and external genitalia

Other uses of iodine

- It is used in preoperative preparation of thyrotoxic patients (Lugol's iodine and SSKI).
- Iodide is used as an expectorant.
- Iodinated hydroxyquinolone is used in the treatment of amoebiasis.

Hydrogen Peroxide (H_2O_2) (Fig. 10.3)

- It is available as 6% (w/v) and 20% (v/v) preparations.
- It produces destructive hydroxyl free radicals that can attack membrane lipids, DNA, and other essential components of cell.
- It is colorless and odorless.

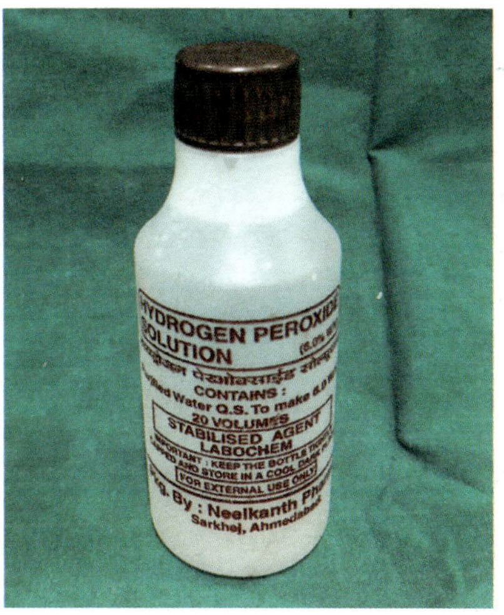

Figure 10.3 Hydrogen peroxide solution.

- A total of 30% of solution produces 10 volumes of oxygen.
- Uses
  - As a desloughing agent
  - Irrigation of dirty wounds (prior to CLW suturing)
  - Irrigation of abscess cavity
  - Mouth gargles
  - As ear drops, to remove earwax
  - Removes blood stains from the clothes
  - Sterilization of various surfaces including surgical tools
  - Used for room sterilization as a vapor
  - Instilled into urinary bag to decrease the incidence of bladder infection and environmental contamination
    - By releasing heat, it coagulates protein and helps in hemostasis.
    - It produces vasoconstriction, so it is not used in ischemic and diabetic ulcers.
    - It should not be used in deep cavities, because after using H_2O_2, it must be cleaned with normal saline. If not properly cleaned, residual solution can promote the growth of aerobic organisms by releasing nascent oxygen.
    - It is more active against Gram-positive than against Gram-negative bacteria.
    - Concern about material compatibility and serious eye damage with contact are the main disadvantages with hydrogen peroxide.

Eusol (Edinburgh University Solution of Lime)

- Releases nascent chlorine and acts as a desloughing agent
- Components: 1.25 g boric acid + 1.25 g bleaching powder in 100 mL of water
- Uses: As a desloughing agent, especially recommended for diabetic and ischemic ulcers

Always use a freshly prepared solution of Eusol.

Turpentine (Fig. 10.4)

- Obtained by distilling *Pinus* oleoresin
- Characteristics: Boot polish–like smell
- Uses
  - For removal of maggots from wound (by causing irritation it produces suffocation and maggots come onto the surface and can be removed with forceps)
  - Removal of stain of zinc oxide and Dynaplast
  - As an irritant in myalgia and arthralgia

As it is an oil-based solution, after using it, always remove it with Savlon (detergent).

Spirit

- It is methylated alcohol (70% surgical spirit).
- Characteristics
  - Aromatic smell
  - Cooling effect

Figure 10.4 Turpentine oil.

  - Evaporation
- It is an antiseptic and cleansing agent.
- It is a poor disinfectant for instruments; it promotes rusting of instruments.
- Mechanism of action
  - Denaturation of proteins
  - Solvent for lipids; damages lipid complex of cell wall
- Uses
  - Application before injections on skin
  - Painting of parts, after Betadine
  - Cleaning of the stitch-line of the wound
  - Cleaning of skin surrounding the ulcer/wound (cleaning of skin surrounding the wound/ulcer is as important as dressing of wound, because infection from surroundings can delay the healing)
  - Prevention of bed sore (as it is an astringent, precipitation of proteins makes the superficial layer of skin to become hard)

- Not used on mucous membrane and scrotum (irritant)
- Not used on open wounds or raw areas (burning sensation, injury to the raw surface)

Savlon (Hospital Concentrate) (Fig. 10.5)

- It contains 7.5% chlorhexidine gluconate (antiseptic) + 15% cetrimide (detergent).
- Characteristics: It is of lemon yellow color, which on shaking produces excessive foam.
- Mechanism of action: It lowers the surface tension and disrupts the bacterial cell wall.
- It is an antiseptic, detergent, and bactericidal agent.
- Uses
  - Sitz bath in perianal conditions; however, some surgeons prefer not to add any chemical in water for Sitz bath
  - Cleaning of skin surrounding a wound/ulcer
  - Removal of turpentine after cleaning of the skin
  - Savlon bath in burn patients
  - As a scolicidal agent (3–5% solution) in hydatid cyst
  - For keeping Cheatle forceps and thermometer
  - Cleaning of the catheter for clean intermittent self-catheterization (CISC; for neurogenic bladder)

Figure 10.5 Savlon.

Figure 10.6 CIDEX (2% Glutaraldehyde).

- Cleaning of stitch-line and surrounding skin after completion of operation
- Cleaning of hands after examination of the patient

- Savlon must be removed with normal saline, because the layer of Savlon acts as a good culture medium for *Pseudomonas.*
- Do not use on external genitalia, as it may cause burns.
- Always prefer a freshly prepared solution.
- Uses
  - 1:30 dilution in operation theater
  - 1:100 dilution in dressing
  - 1:200 dilution in washing hands

CIDEX (2% Glutaraldehyde) (Figs 10.6 and 10.7)

Aqueous solutions available are acidic and are generally not sporicidal; they become sporicidal only when alkalinating agent of pH 7.5–8.5 is added. They have a shelf life of 14 days and need to be changed every 14 days. Glutaraldehyde 2.45% is also available that can also be used up to 28 days (Fig. 10.7).

Glutaraldehyde–phenol–sodium phenate-like novel formulations have a shelf life of 28 days.

- Characteristics
  - It is of olive green color.
  - It is the strongest antiseptic available in the market.

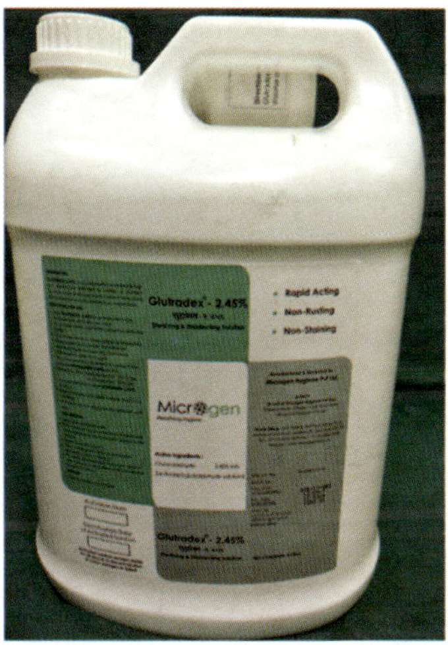

Figure 10.7 Glutaraldehyde 2.45%.

  - It is bactericidal, virucidal (including HIV and HBV), fungicidal, and sporicidal.
- Sterilization time: It is 10 minutes.
- For complete sterilization, it requires 10 hours.
- Maximum allowable exposure limit is 0.2 ppm.
- Uses
  - It is used as a high-level disinfectant for medical instruments such as endoscope and fiber-optic light cord, and laparoscope needs to be soaked at least for 10 minutes (not more than 20 minutes), spirometry tubing, etc.
  - Other metallic instruments such as trocar and hand instruments are allowed to soak for

  60 minutes mainly to avoid infection from atypical mycobacterial infection.
  - It is used to sterilize sharp instruments (instruments in the ward are kept in CIDEX).
- Advantages
  - Noncorrosive to metal
  - Does not damage lensed instruments, rubber tube, or plastics
- Disadvantages
  - Toxic, irritant, and allergenic; so instruments kept in CIDEX should always be cleaned first with saline and then used
  - Has a pungent odor, coagulates blood, and has a relatively slow mycobactericidal activity

ortho-Phthalaldehyde

- It is a high-level disinfectant and contains 0.55% 1,2-benzenedicarboxaldehyde.
- OPA interacts with amino acids, proteins, and microorganisms.
- It is a broad-spectrum bactericidal, sporicidal, and virucidal agent.
- It is clear.
- It is a pale blue liquid (pH of 7.5).

Advantages of OPA are the following:

- Excellent stability
- Requires no activation
- Does not cause irritation to eye and nose

Disadvantages are the following:

- It stains proteins gray (including uncovered skin) and thus must be handled with caution. Meticulous cleaning and copious rinsing with at least 250 mL water per channel helps to avoid the problem of staining.
- Allergic reaction had been reported with OPA. Proper cleaning is a must.
- It needs to be changed every 14 days.
- FDA recommends contact time of 5 minutes at 25°C temperature.

Mercurochrome

- It is used as a 1–2% solution.
- It is bright red in color.
- It is an astringent, bacteriostatic, and weak antiseptic.
- It was traditionally used for treating abrasions, bed sores, and hypergranulation tissue.
- Nowadays, its use is limited because of availability of other good solutions.

It should not be used in patients with nonhealing ulcers and tuberculous ulcers, because it creates a false sense of security (due to the red color it imparts, giving the wrong impression of healthy granulation tissue).

OTHER ANTIMICROBIAL SOLUTIONS USED FOR DRESSING

Silver Nitrate

- Astringent and cauterizing agent
- Used to remove hypergranulation tissue

Glycerin (Fig. 10.8)

- Characteristics
  - Clear, sweetish taste, and viscous
  - On shaking, hanging drop–like appearance on the wall of the bottle
- Uses
  - It has hygroscopic property (adsorbs water), so it is used to reduce edema in cellulitis, prolapsed piles, edema over colostomy site, and edema of the surrounding skin of the ulcer or wound.
  - Because of its hygroscopic action, it produces a warm sensation and irritates the mucosa, so it can be used as glycerin enema for evacuation of bowel.
  - It can be used as an emollient.
  - It can also be used to reduce intraocular and intracranial tension (orally, per rectally, or IV).

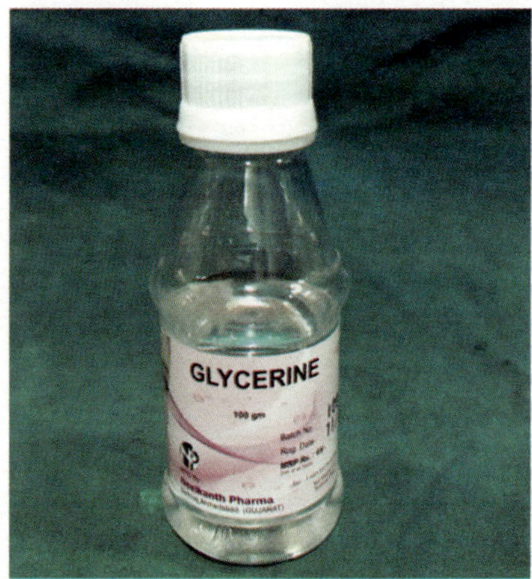

Figure 10.8 Glycerin.

Liquid Paraffin

- It is a mixture of petroleum hydrocarbons.
- Characteristics
  - It is clear and viscous.
  - Unlike glycerin, it has no hanging drop-like appearance and is not sweetish.
- Uses
  - As an emollient in dressing
  - As a laxative

NEWER METHOD OF STERILIZATION

Hydrogen Peroxide Gas Plasma (STERRAD Sterilizer)[2]

- *Mechanism of action*: Gas plasmas are generated in an enclosed chamber using radio-frequency or microwave energy to stimulate the gas molecules and produce free radicals. Free radicals during the plasma phase of cycle along with hydrogen peroxide gas are capable of interacting with enzymes and nucleic acids, and thereby disrupt the metabolism of microorganisms and inactivate them.
- *Process*: Inside the chamber, deep vacuum is drawn, and hydrogen peroxide solution (59% aqueous) is injected and is vaporized. The hydrogen peroxide vapor diffuses through the chamber (50 minutes), exposes all surfaces of the load to the sterilant, and initiates the inactivation of microorganisms. Following the diffusion, chamber pressure is reduced, allowing the generation of low-temperature gas plasma radio-frequency energy that is applied to the chamber; microbicidal free radicals are generated in the plasma. The excess gas is removed and the chamber is returned to atmospheric pressure. The by-products such as water vapor and oxygen are nontoxic and eliminate the need for aeration. Sterilization time is 75 minutes at a temperature of 37–44°C.
- *Uses*: This system is very useful in hospital with high workload where rapid turnaround time is required. Instruments can be utilized immediately and can be stored for the next OT list after drying. It is broad spectrum and inactivates a wide range of organisms including resistant spores. It is suitable for devices that cannot tolerate high temperatures and humidity, such as some plastics, electrical devices, and corrosion-susceptible metal instruments. Endoscopes with length more than 40 cm and diameter <3 mm cannot be processed.

Pearls

- For an ulcer in the healing stage, do dressing with only normal saline to prevent hypergranulation and damage to the granulation tissue caused by antiseptic solution. (Antiseptic solutions impair capillary permeability and are toxic to the granulation tissue.)
- Apply emollient dressing over healthy granulation tissue to prevent bleeding from the ulcer and damage to the epithelialization when dressing is removed.
- Hypergranulation tissue is also known as proud flesh.
- Methods to remove hypergranulation tissue are as follows:
  - Scooping
  - Hypertonic saline
  - $AgNO_3$ (silver nitrate)
  - $CuSO_4$ (copper sulfate)
  - Mercurochrome
  - Carbolic acid
- Skin preparation for major surgery includes 10% povidone–iodine, 1:5000 chlorhexidine, or 1% cetrimide.
- Most resistant to sterilization and/or disinfection are prions followed by bacterial spores and least resistant are lipids or medium-sized viruses (HIV, hepatitis B) preceded by vegetative bacteria (*S. aureus*, *P. aeruginosa*).
- Fumigation of operation theater is achieved by 40% formalin. Humidity (70% relative humidity) and temperature (30–40°C) play an important role. Before starting fumigation, all the doors and windows must be closed and the fans and AC unit should be turned off in the operation theatre. For every 1000 cubic feet (28.3 m^3) of room volume, 280 mL of formalin and 150 g of $KMnO_4$ should be mixed. This would generate formaldehyde gas. Heat-resistant vessels should be used as this reaction produces considerable heat. When formalin vapors are generated, doors should be sealed and the operation room should be closed for at

least 48 hours. Before entering into the OT next morning, 300 mL of 10% ammonia solution should be kept at the center of the room for at least 3 hours to neutralize formalin vapors.[3] Fumigation is recommended at least once weekly.

Another option used for fumigation is bacillocid which contains glutaral (100 mg/g), benzyl-C-12-18-alkyldimethylammonium chloride (60 mg/g), and didecyl-dimethylammonium chloride (60 mg/g). It is used as 2% solution (100 mL in 5 L of water). The room must be kept closed for 6 hours before use by housekeeping personnel.[4]

Other options for fogging include 8–10% H_2O_2, 4–6% H_2O_2 with silver nitrate, peracetic acid with silver nitrate, and D-125 (contains alkyl dimethylbenzyl and dimethyl ethylbenzyl ammonium chloride) (Fig. 10.9). Fogger machine (Fig. 10.10) is required. Fifteen milliliters of D-125 is mixed with 1000 mL of tap water for every 1000 cu.ft. space. This mixture is poured into the fogger machine and the machine is kept on for 15–30 minutes. Operation theater is closed for 30 minutes. There is no irritation and toxicity like that with formalin.

Bacillol (Fig. 10.11) contains ethanol, 2-propanol, 1-propanol.

It is available as a spray for surface disinfection. It does not act on spores. Instant disinfection is achieved with spray.

- Ideal temperature for operation theater is 20–23°C, with relative humidity of 40–60%, and air movement should be from more clean area to less clean area. The use of laminar flow system is advised in certain operation theaters.
- Fungi such as *Aspergillus, Rhizopus, Fusarium,* and *Penicillium* are capable of proliferating in AC units. The filters in the AC unit can act as suitable nidus for growth and proliferation of these opportunistic fungi. Presence of fungi in AC units and subsequent dispersal could be a potential hazard, especially for the immunocompromised patients. AC units in the operation theater and clinic should be meticulously maintained and frequently monitored to minimize the chances of infection. Split AC units are preferable and a safer option than the window AC units.[5]
- Hand washing is the most effective, simple, and cost-effective method to reduce the chance of hospital-acquired infections. There are two ways of hand washing: (a) Casual hand rub: It is recommended after examination of every patient. Soap and water is commonly used. Other products recommended for hand rub are as follows: 60–95% alcohol or 50–95% alcohol in combination with a quaternary ammonium compound or hexachlorophene or chlorhexidine gluconate. (b) Surgical hand scrub: Watches and ornaments such as ring and bracelet should always be removed first. Details of technique are described in Chapter 1, *Preoperative Preparation.*

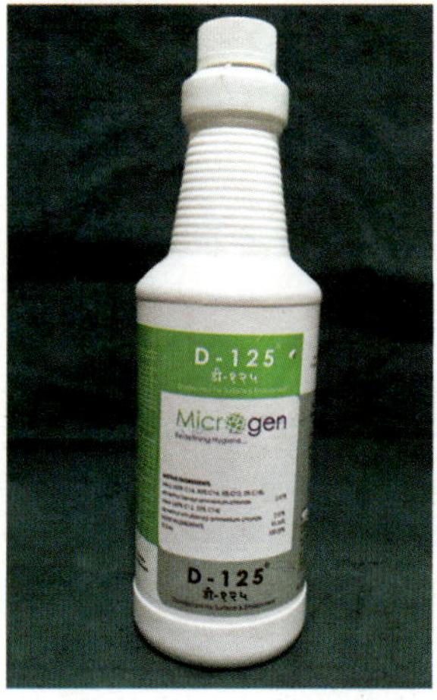

Figure 10.9 D-125 (contains alkyl dimethylbenzyl and dimethyl ethylbenzyl ammonium chloride).

Figure 10.10 Fogger machine.

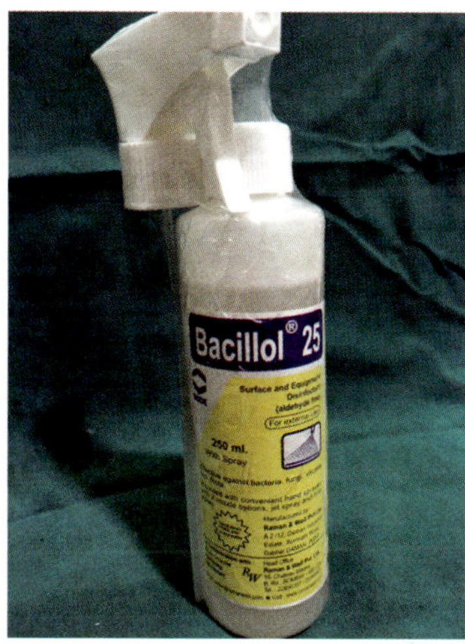

Figure 10.11 Bacillol spray.

References

1. Spaulding EH. Chemical disinfection of medical and surgical materials. In: Disinfection, Sterilization, and Preservation. Lawrence C, Block SS, eds. Philadelphia: Lea & Febiger, 1968, 517–31.
2. Rutala WA, Weber D, HICPAC. Guideline for disinfection and sterilization in healthcare facilities, 2008. Available at: https://www.cdc.gov/infectioncontrol/guidelines/disinfection/
3. Kabbin JS, Shwetha JV, Sathyanarayan MS, Nagarathnamma, T. Disinfection and sterilization techniques of operation theatre: a review. Int J Curr Res 2014;6(5):6622–6.
4. Http://www.nabh.co/Images/PDF/HIC_Guidebook.pdf.
5. Kelkar U, Bal AM, Kulkarni S. Fungal contamination of air conditioning units in operating theaters in India. J Hosp Infect 2005;60:81–4.

CHAPTER 11

Instruments

Surgical instruments are special tools or devices that are used to perform specific functions during surgery such as cutting, dissecting, clamping, grasping, holding, retracting, suctioning, or suturing. A surgeon must be thorough in understanding the functions, quality, and proper preparation of different surgical instruments. The surgical instruments may be broadly categorized according to the above-mentioned functions.

PREPARATION AND CARE OF INSTRUMENTS

- Proper preparation and care of surgical instruments are vital to the success of surgical operations. The instruments are sterilized prior to use. The manufacturers usually provide instructions for cleaning and these must be followed. The institutional and professional protocols for the preparation and maintenance of surgical instruments must be strictly followed. Any laxity may contribute to postoperative infections or mortality.

  Surgical instruments are made from stainless steel. It is a combination of carbon, chromium, iron, and other metals (alloy). SS is resistant to wear and corrosion and this combination makes it very strong.

  There are three types of finishes on the SS instruments: (i) mirror—highly polished, produces glare, highly resistant to corrosion; (ii) satin or matte—most preferred finish, reduces glare as compared to mirror finish; and (iii) ebony—completely eliminates glare, preferred during laser surgery.

  Gold plating indicates tungsten carbide coating, which is an extremely hard metal. The scissor blade is laminated to increase the sharpness and jaw of the needle holder is also coated sometimes to increase the strength and grip of the instruments.
- During a procedure, the instruments are kept clean by wiping them with a moist sponge and rinsing them frequently in sterile water. Blood and other tissues are prevented from hardening and becoming trapped on their surface. One must carefully check the number of instruments used during the operation and guard against the risk of surgical instruments being left inside a person after an operation.
- After a surgical procedure also, the instruments are rinsed, cleaned, and sterilized. Ultrasonic cleaning and automatic washing often follow the manual cleaning and, finally, these may be autoclaved.
- Autoclave is the most commonly used method of sterilization of instruments. Adequate sterilization is checked by either a color change indicator or a biological sterilization indicator. Color change indicators change color from white to black when appropriate conditions are met. A biological sterilization indicator is the best way to confirm adequate sterilization. The indicator contains spores that are supplied in a closed container and kept in a drum containing the instrument to be autoclaved. Inability to culture the spore after autoclaving confirms adequate sterilization.

FORCEPS

Hemostat/Artery Forceps

Parts are as follows:

- Jaws
- Blade
- Joint
- Handle (shaft)
- Ratchet
- Finger bow

Kelly's modification of Spencer Wells hemostatic forceps (Fig. 11.1)

Hemostatic forceps were originally devised by the great French surgeon Ambroise Paré and

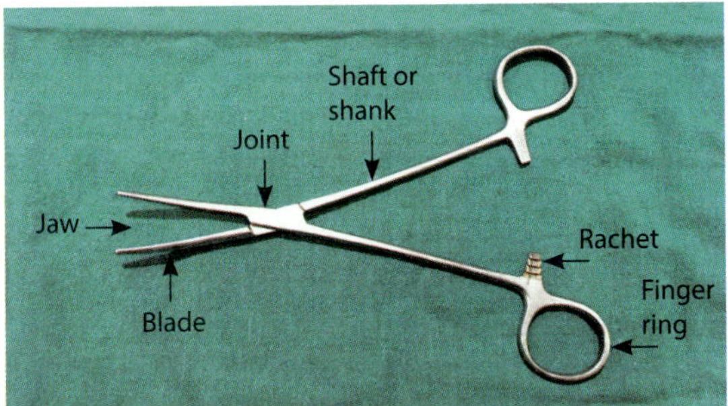

Figure 11.1 Kelly modification of Spencer Wells medium sized curved haemostatic forceps. Used to catch, clamp or crush vessels and achieve haemostasis Checking the quality of the instrument: First see the apposition of blades; there should not be any gap between blades.

later on improved by Sir Thomas Spencer Wells. Kelly later on modified the design and nowadays most hemostats used are Kelly's modification. The differences between Kelly hemostat and Sir Spencer Wells hemostat are given in Table 11.1.

Table 11.1 Differences Between Sir Spencer Wells and Kelly Hemostats

	Kelly hemostat	**Sir Spencer Wells hemostat**
Tip	Pointed but blunt	Broad and blunt
Blade	Blade:shaft ratio is greater	Diamond shaped or fusiform and blade; blade:shaft ratio is smaller
Ratchet	By the side of shaft	On shaft
Joint	Box joint	Screw joint
Shape	Straight or curved	Straight

The hemostat may be small, medium, or large; straight or curved; toothed or nontoothed; and half serrated or full serrated. So, to differentiate among different instruments, which have different functions, one has to be specific and use the full name of the instrument, for example, Kelly medium-sized straight hemostatic forceps. In an examination, students must be able to name an instrument correctly.

The tips of the hemostat have a serration with or without teeth. Because of locking device, bleeding vessel can be held in position while dealing with the other issues. Rings on the handles allow accommodation of fingers. All hemostats have short jaws and narrow tips.

- *Uses*: As the name suggests, it is used for the following:
  - Catching, clamping, or crushing the vessel and achieving hemostasis
  - Various types of dressing
  - Doing blunt dissection in various surgeries
  - Making a window in the mesoappendix, during appendicectomy
  - Opening the abscess cavity, instead of using a sinus forceps
  - Catching the peritoneum during opening and closure
  - Holding the cut edge of external oblique aponeurosis, in appendicectomy
  - Splitting the muscle in appendicectomy
  - Holding one end of the suture material while taking continuous suture
  - Dividing the mesentery in resection and anastomosis
  - Clamping catheter, intercostal tube, etc. (tube should be clamped in between shaft)
  - Holding the needle in absence of needle holder
  - As a pedicle clamp
  - Stepping on knot
  - Holding a mesenteric vessel in resection and anastomosis
  - Holding and passing the per urethral catheter by nontouch technique

- Hemostasis is achieved by separation of tunica intima and media from tunica adventitia. Tunica adventitia contracts and media and intima curl in and form a plug.
- Shaft has ratchets:
  - *First ratchet*: Catch
  - *Second ratchet*: Clamp
  - *Third ratchet*: Crush
- These forceps can be applied and left in place so shaft should be sufficiently so long that handle remains outside the wound.
- To grasp the bleeding vessel, tip of the artery forceps should protrude and should be applied with supinated hand with convexity of curved forceps facing down.
- Pick only the essential tissue as ligature is applied around extra tissue along with blood vessel; attachment will anchor the ligature and allow the vessel to withdraw from it and rebleed if it retracts.

- Hemostatic forceps are lighter than needle holder; their blades are longer and have transverse serration throughout the blade portion.

Allis Tissue Holding Forceps (Fig. 11.2)

- *Identification*: It has a curved tip with interlocking teeth. Blades meet at their ends.
- It is a traumatic instrument and cannot be used to hold soft and delicate structures.
- *Uses*
  - To hold tough structures such as tendons, aponeuroses, and anterior rectus sheath
  - To hold any fibrous capsule of a structure
  - To hold lipoma, neurofibroma, or fibroadenoma, during excision
  - To hold the bladder wall
  - To hold the wound drape in place
  - To hold breast tissue
  - For providing traction of the skin, applied just beneath the skin

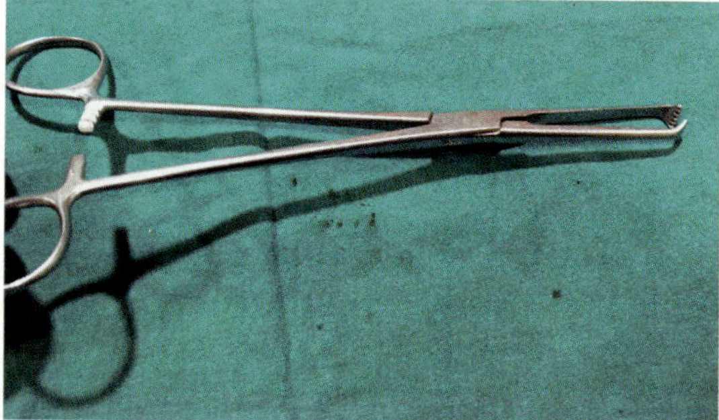

Figure 11.2 Allis tissue holding forceps. Used to hold tough structures like fascia, tendons.

Babcock Tissue Holding Forceps (Fig. 11.3)

- *Identification*
  - Lightweight instrument with curved and fenestrated jaw
  - No serrations
  - Horizontal groove at the end
- *Uses*
  - To hold tubular structures such as appendix and fallopian tube
  - To hold stomach, and small and large bowel in various surgeries
  - To hold lymph node during biopsy
  - To hold lipoma and fibroadenoma during excision
  - To hold the bladder in SPCL and prostatectomy
- *Advantages*: It has no teeth, so trauma is minimal. It is used to hold soft and delicate structures.

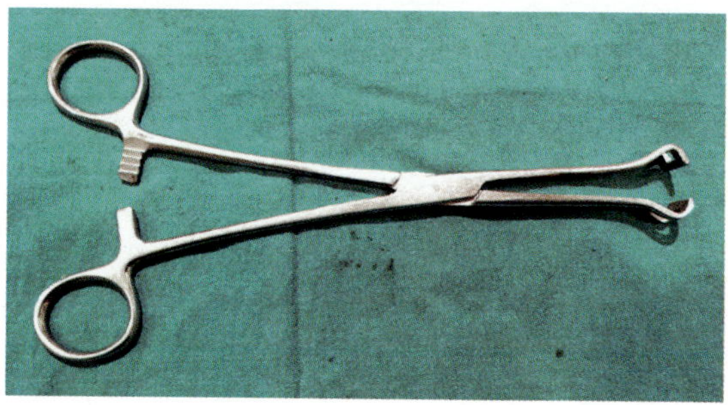

Figure 11.3 Babcock tissue holding forceps used to hold soft and delicate structures.

Lane Tissue Holding Forceps (Fig. 11.4)

- It is a strong, tough, and heavy instrument. It has a short and stout distal blade.
- It has a fenestrated jaw with single tooth (tissue can bulge through fenestra and that prevents slippage of tissue).
- *Uses*
  - To hold tough structures such as fascia and aponeuroses
  - To catch subperiosteal bleeders
  - To hold the lymph node
  - As towel clip and/or sponge holding forceps
  - In case of emergency, in unconscious patients, to hold the tongue and prevent it from falling back

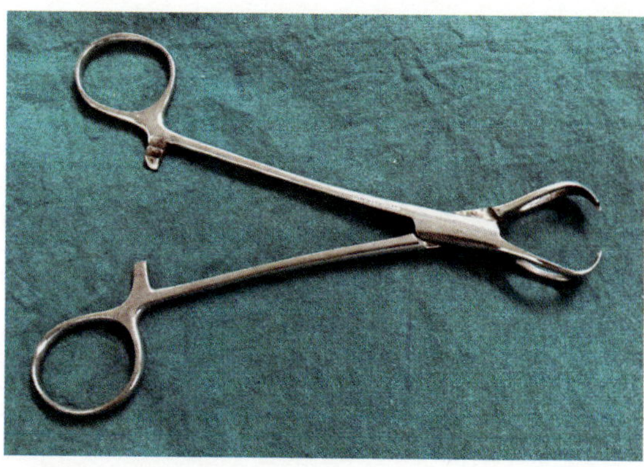

Figure 11.4 Lane tissue holding forceps. Used to hold tough structures like fascia and aponeuroses.

- *Disadvantage*: It causes more trauma.
- Nowadays, use of this instrument is very rare.

Halstead Mosquito Forceps (Fig. 11.5)

- *Identification*
  - Small, lightweight instrument
  - Straight or curved fine tip
  - Other identification points similar to those of Kelly hemostat
- *Uses*
  - To catch small bleeders (hemostasis)
  - In circumcision—to break the adhesions, instead of probe
  - At 3 and 9 o'clock catch in circumcision
  - In fine blunt dissection
  - Plastic surgery
  - In all pediatric surgeries
  - Poking the mesoappendix in avascular plane for making window and ligating appendicular artery
- It is known as mosquito forceps because:
  - Bite of the instrument is like a mosquito bite.
  - It can hold one limb of a mosquito.
  - It resembles the shape of a World War II plane named Mosquito.

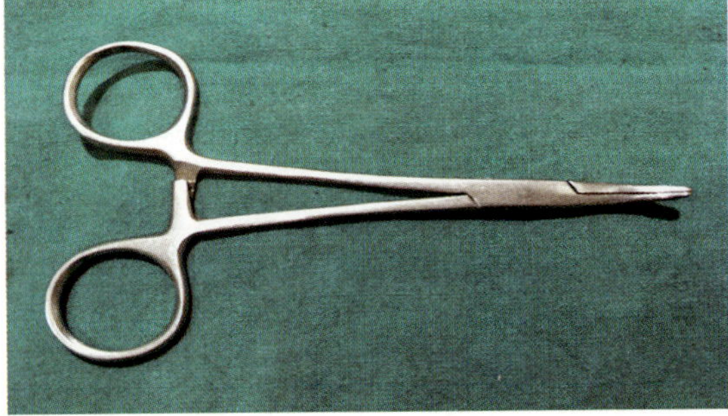

Figure 11.5 Halstead mosquito forceps. Used to catch small bleeders.

Kocher Clamp (Fig. 11.6)

- *Identification*
  - Narrow, with longer blades than those of Kelly forceps
  - Has teeth at the end
  - Transverse serrations
- *Uses*
  - To divide the strap muscles in thyroid surgery
  - To achieve hemostasis in tough and fibrous background (palm, sole, scalp)
  - To divide the pectoralis minor in MRM or radical mastectomy
  - To hold the perforating vessel in MRM
  - To hold the pedicle of piles
  - To hold large pedicle, like those of kidney or spleen

- There are three instruments that come under the category of pedicle clamps: Kocher, Maingot, and Robert clamps.
- Grip on the tissue in Kocher clamp is slightly inferior as compared to that in Maingot clamp, but due to teeth at the end, it can securely catch and hold bleeders and minimal amount of tissue is caught.
- Other contributions of Kocher to surgery are as follows:
  - Kocher's test for scabbard trachea
  - Kocher's maneuver done in anterior dislocation of shoulder
  - Kocher's vein: Fourth thyroid vein
  - Kocherization of duodenum
  - Kocher's subcostal incision for cholecystectomy
  - Kocher's reflex on compressing testicle, contraction of abdominal muscles occurs
  - Kocher–Debré–Semelaigne syndrome: Muscular atrophy and thyroid problem

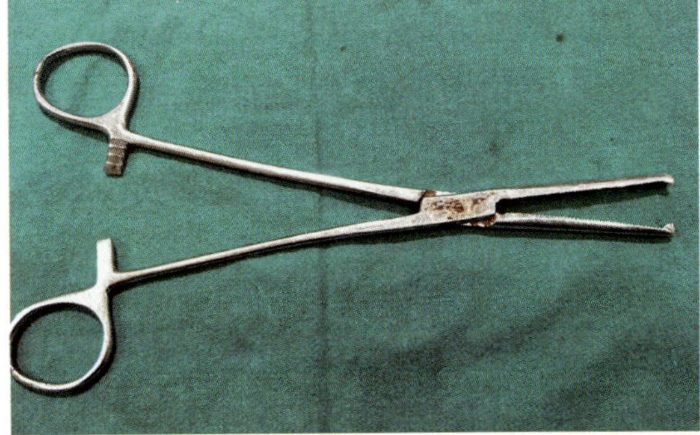

Figure 11.6 Kocher clamp. Used to divide strap muscle in thyroid surgery.

Rampley Sponge Holding Forceps (Fig. 11.7)

- *Identification*: It has fenestrated jaw with horizontal serrations over the jaw.

- *Uses*
  - Is the most commonly used instrument in surgery
  - Painting of part prior to surgery (because of the fenestrations and transverse serrations, there is good grip, and bulk of swab can be taken)
  - To mop in deep cavities
  - To hold the fundus of the gallbladder in cholecystectomy
  - Can be used as a tongue holding forceps
  - Can be used as an ovum holding forceps
  - To hold the bladder in prostatectomy
  - For retraction of peritoneum in surgeries such as pyelolithotomy
  - For pressure hemostasis in the prostatic fossa during prostatectomy
  - For three swab test in appendicectomy, to check hemostasis
  - For removing laminated membrane and daughter cyst in hydatid surgery
  - As a pile holding forceps in piles surgery

It is approximately 7–9.5 inches long. Because of its length, the unsterile part that is to be painted will not come in contact with sterile gloved hand of the surgeon.

Principle of applying antiseptic is as follows: Apply first at the incision site and then move circularly to the peripheral area. Apply at the umbilicus and groin in the last.

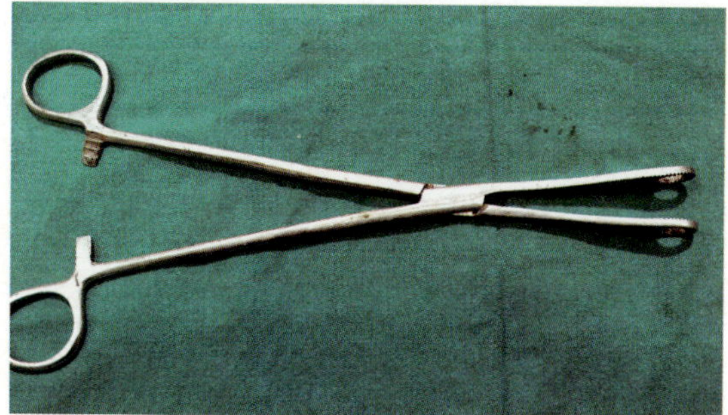

Figure 11.7 Rampleys sponge holding forceps. Used for painting of part before surgery.

Dissecting Forceps (Thumb Forceps, Pickups) (Figs 11.8–11.10)

- The main types are plain or nontoothed, toothed, and Adson forceps (plain and toothed).

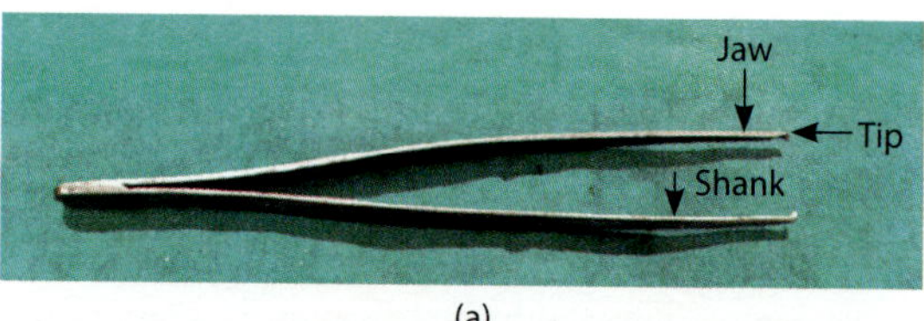

(a)

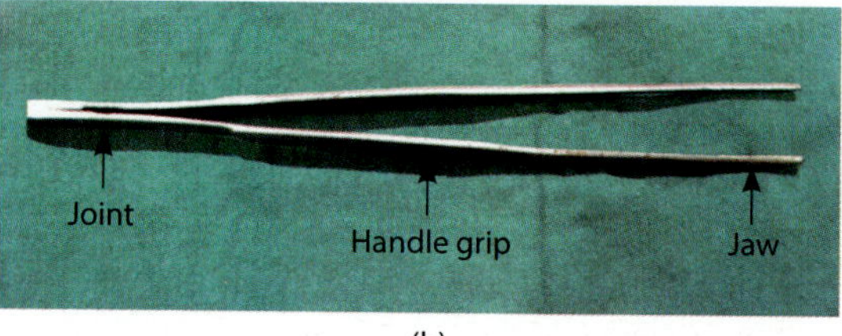

(b)

Figure 11.8 Dissecting forceps. (a) Toothed: used to hold tough tissue (better grip). (b) Plain: used to hold soft and friable tissue.

Figure 11.9 Plain Adson forceps. To hold soft tissue while suturing.

Figure 11.10 Toothed Adson forceps, for better grip.

- There are two shafts and no joint. There are no catch and spring. Outer surface of the shaft is rough to provide a better grip.
- The forceps are available in various sizes, small, medium, and large.
- Plain forceps are nontraumatic, and, therefore, used to hold soft and friable tissue.
- Plain forceps are used for packing of wound.
- Toothed forceps provide a better grip. Possibility of slipping of tissue is less.
- They are used to grasp vessels for electrocautery.
- They are used to hold the tissue during dissection.
- They are used to retract tissues for exposure.
- Toothed forceps are used to hold the needle while suturing.
- Forceps are used to hold the tissues during cutting and suturing.

- They are used to pack sponges and gauze strips in the case of bleeding and packing of abscess cavity.
- They are used to extract foreign bodies.
- They are also known as thumb forceps, because the shaft is closed by the thumb of the surgeon.
- These forceps have a characteristic spring-like action.
- There are transverse serrations or teeth that help in holding the needle while taking sutures.
- Toothed forceps are used to grasp the skin, fascia, and fibrocartilage.
- These forceps do not have locking mechanism as they are intended to provide temporary grip only.
- They should be held like a pen in the nondominant hand.

Plain forceps is an excellent instrument to open up a longitudinal tissue plane, around the nose. Gently insert the forceps as a wedge, and allow their springiness to open up and create a space in between the blade. This is most useful to display longitudinal structures such as blood vessels.

Debakey Vascular Tissue Forceps (Fig. 11.11)

- *Identification*: Parallel fine serrations on one side of the jaw with center raw of serration on the opposite side.
- *Use*: Although popularly known as vascular forceps, they are used in all specialty because of their ability to hold the tissue securely without causing damage to the tissue. They are mainly used in cardiac, vascular, and GI surgery.

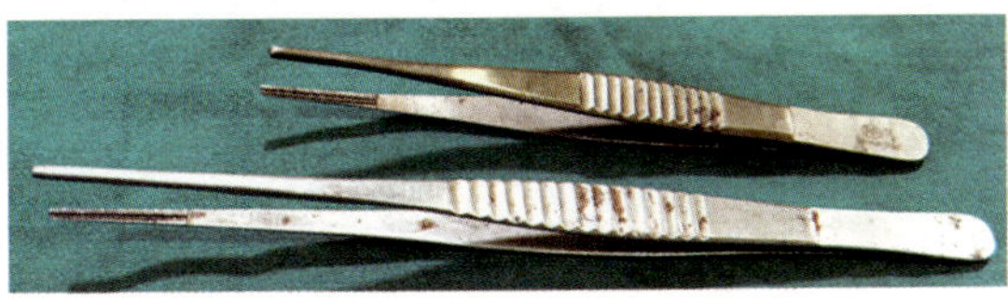

Figure 11.11 Debakey vascular tissue forceps.

Lister Sinus Forceps (Fig. 11.12)

It is called sinus forceps because it was initially used to pack the sinus cavities.

- *Identification*
  - Transverse serrations on the tip
  - Long handle, but no catch
  - Blunt end
- *Uses*
  - Drainage of abscess cavity, to widen the tract in I and D
  - Packing of abscess cavity
  - Removing foreign body from the sinus or packing of sinus cavity
  - Placing dressing in the nasal cavity and ear packing

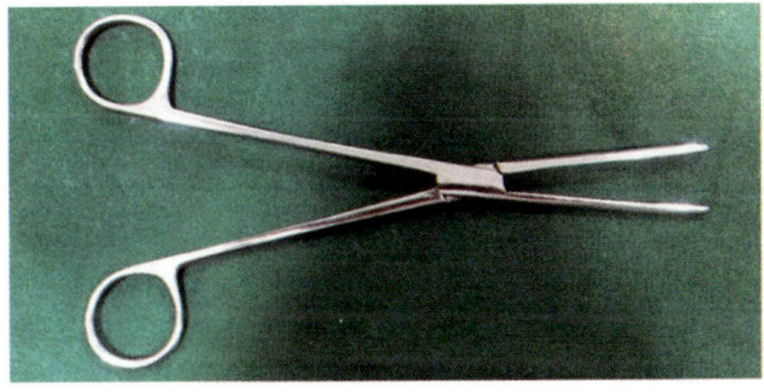

Figure 11.12 Lister sinus forceps—used for drainage of abscess cavity in I and D.

Cheatle Forceps (Fig. 11.13)

- *Identification*
  - Curved blade
  - No catch
  - Serrations on the blade
  - One handle having a complete ring and the other handle having U-shaped end for fingers
- *Use*: To hold sterile objects with unsterile hand

It is kept in vertical position in a bottle containing antiseptic solution such as Savlon, with cotton or gauze pad at the bottom, to prevent damage to both the instrument and the bottle.

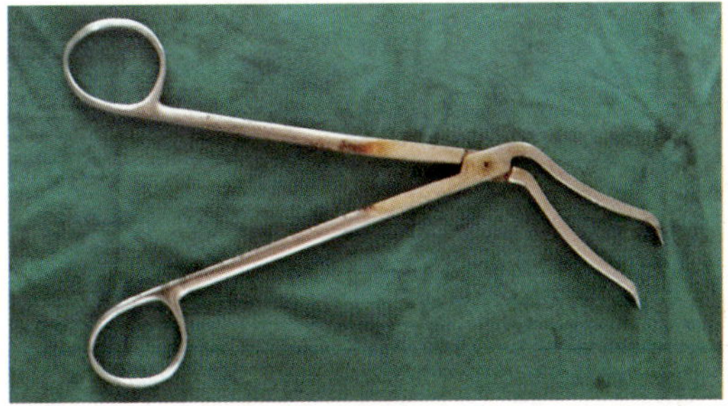

Figure 11.13 Cheatle forceps used to hold sterile objects.

Mixter (Right Angle Forceps) (Fig. 11.14)

- *Identification*: Ends of the blades are curved at 90° and tips are blunt.
- *Uses*
  - To hook the ureter in surgeries for kidney and ureter
  - To hook the cystic artery and duct in cholecystectomy
  - In thyroid surgery (to hook various pedicles)
  - Can be used for blunt dissection in deep cavities

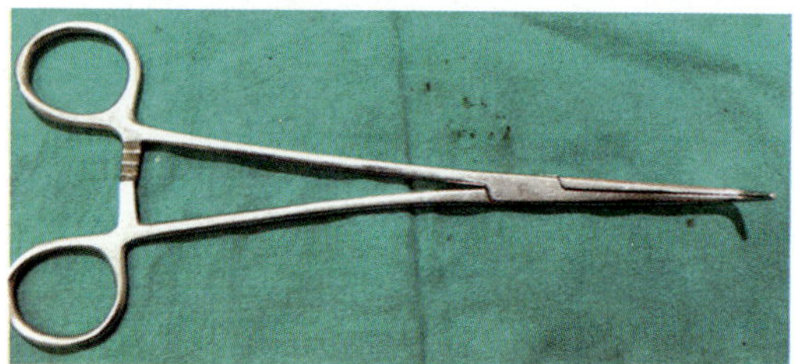

Figure 11.14 Mixter (right angled forceps) used to hook ureter in surgery on kidney and ureter.

Sargent Scalp Hemostatic Forceps

- *Use*: To control bleeding in the scalp
- *Advantage*: More tissue can be held, but possibility of pressure necrosis present

Collingwood Stewart Double-Bladed Cord Holding Forceps (Fig. 11.15)

- *Identification*
  - Has finger bow and catch on the handle
  - Has two semicircular blades, which close to form a ring

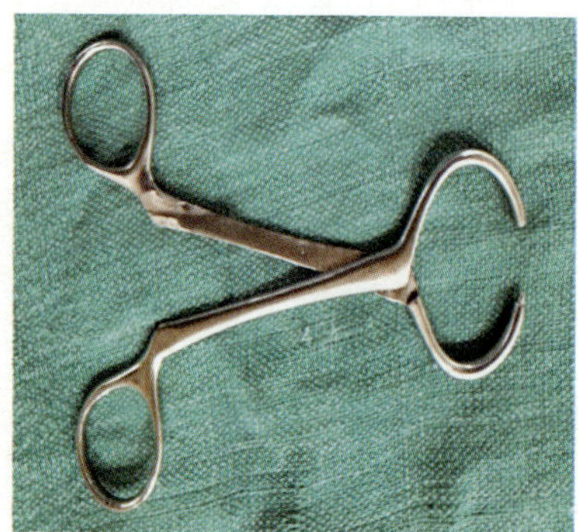

Figure 11.15 Collingwood stewart double bladed cord holding forceps used to hold cord in hernia surgery.

- *Uses*: To hold the cord in hernia surgery and keep it separate from the sac. Other materials used to hold cord in hernia surgery are gauze piece, red rubber catheter, vascular sling, and blunt hook.

Randall Kidney Stone Forceps (Fig. 11.16)

- *Identification*
  - There are fenestrations and serrations on the blades.
  - The instrument is angulated from the blade.
  - There is no catch (to prevent crushing of the stone).
- *Uses*
  - It is used in stone removal from kidney in various operations, such as pyelolithotomy and nephrolithotomy.
  - This instrument is long, so it can work in deep cavities and has serrations for a better grip.

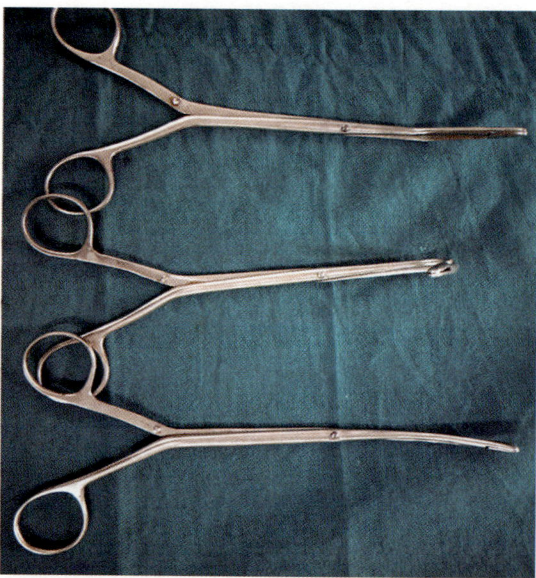

Figure 11.16 Randall kidney stone forceps. Stone removal from the kidney in various operation.

Thomson-Walker SPCL Forceps (Fig. 11.17)

As the name suggests, it is used for stone removal from bladder.

- *Identification*
  - Spoon-shaped blade
  - One closed ring handle for thumb and another U-shaped for fingers
  - No ratchet

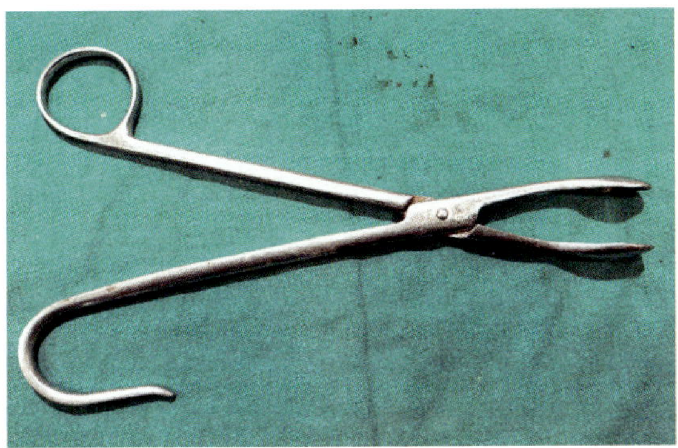

Figure 11.17 Thomson-Walker SPCL forceps used for stone removal from bladder.

Satinsky Vascular Clamp (Fig. 11.18)

- *Identification*
  - C-shaped blade
  - Fine teeth inside the blade
  - Rest of the characteristics same as those of hemostatic forceps
- *Uses*: In vascular surgery (it is available in various sizes for various vessels)

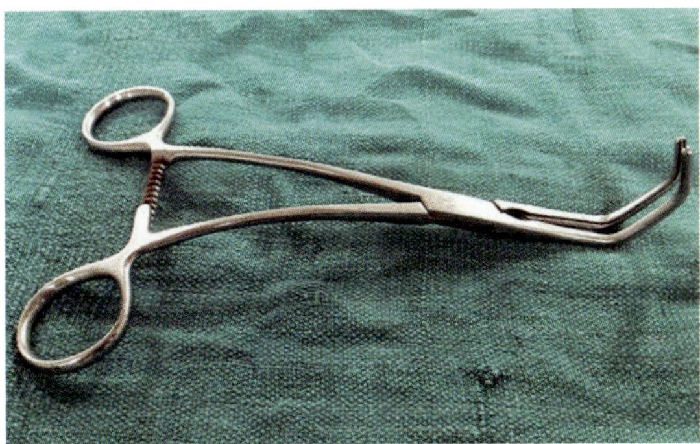

Figure 11.18 Satinsky vascular clamp, used for vascular pedicle.

DeBakey Vascular (Aortic) Clamp (Fig. 11.19)

- *Identification*: Instead of the C-shaped blade, here blades are straight and angulated.
- *Uses*: It is also a vascular clamp, used mainly for vascular surgery, especially to control bleeding in a deep cavity.

Ideally vascular clamp should occlude the vessel lumen without damaging intima and vessel wall.

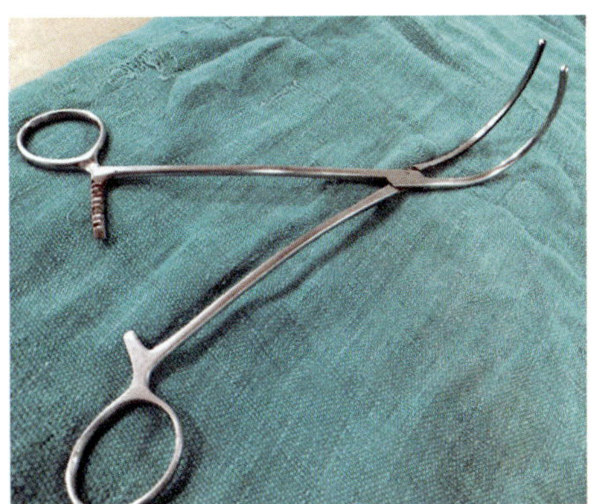

Figure 11.19 Debakey vascular (Aortic) clamp control used to bleeding in deep cavity.

Arbuthnot Lane's (Twin) Gastrojejunostomy Clamp (Fig. 11.20)

- *Identification*
  - It has two pairs of blades and two handles.
  - It has a total of four blades and four finger bows.
  - It has a lock.
- *Uses*
  - One pair of blades occludes the stomach and the other pair occludes jejunum while the lock helps in maintaining the position while suturing.
  - Ideal gastrojejunostomy is isoperistaltic, retrocolic, and vertical; there is no loop and no tension posterior gastrojejunostomy.

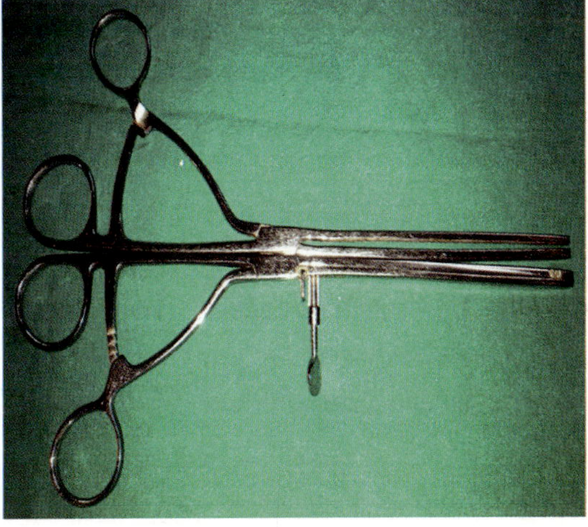

Figure 11.20 Arbuthnot lane (Twin) gastrojejunostomy clamp.

SCISSORS

- There are various types of scissors available, which may be small, medium, or large in size; straight or curved; and sharp pointed or blunt pointed.
- They have a blade, shaft, pivot type of joint, and finger bow.
- *Uses*
  - They are used to cut the tissue, suture, and dressing.
  - Small scissors are useful in cutting.
  - Medium/large scissors are used for dissection in deep cavities.
  - Sharp-pointed scissors are used where there is no risk of damaging a vital structure.
  - Blunt-pointed scissors are used where there is a possibility of damaging a vital structure.
  - Curved scissors are preferred for dissection, because the surgeon can see the structure being cut on both sides of the tip.
  - Straight scissors are used to work on the surface while curved scissors are used in the deep cavity.
- Mostly tip is used for cutting but the tough structure is cut with the back portion of the blade.
- It should never be closed unless tips of blades are clearly seen while cutting the suture (to avoid damage to the vital structure).
- Short scissors are useful for cutting while long scissors are good for dissection.
- Popular scissors
  - Mayo: Suture cutting scissors, available as straight or curved scissor, used to cut the tough tissues such as linea alba and external oblique aponeurosis (Fig. 11.21)

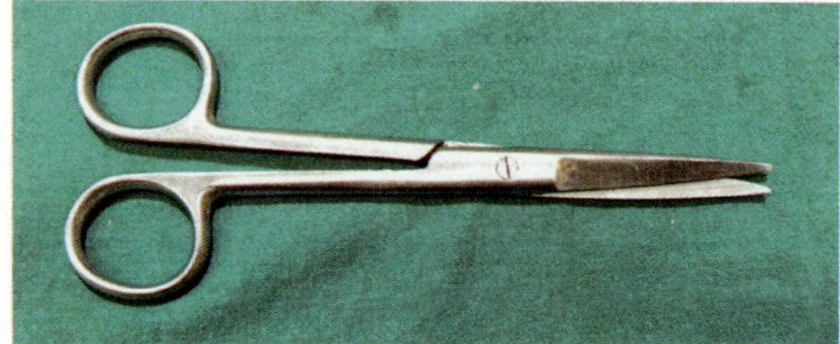

Figure 11.21 Mayo scissor (thread cutting or suture cutting)—cut suture during surgery.

  - McIndoe: Delicate and smaller blade as compared to Mayo and thinner as compared to Metzenbaum scissors (Fig. 11.22).

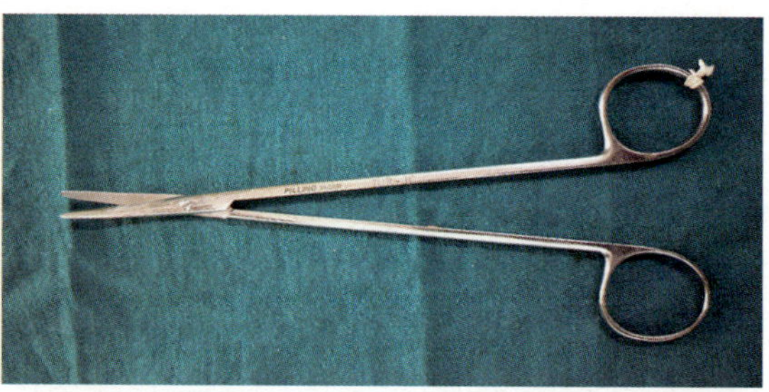

Figure 11.22 McIndoe scissor—for tissue dissection and cutting delicate structure.

  - Metzenbaum—longer handle to blade ratio: (i) For fine tissue dissection; (ii) to open the peritoneum during abdominal operations; (iii) to raise the fine skin flap in thyroid surgery, incisional hernia, and mastectomy; (iv) in cholecystectomy, to cut cystic artery and duct after ligation; (v) to cut the bowel in resection and anastomosis; and (vi) to create a plane between tissues during dissection of lipoma, sebaceous cyst, and/or lymph node (Fig. 11.23)

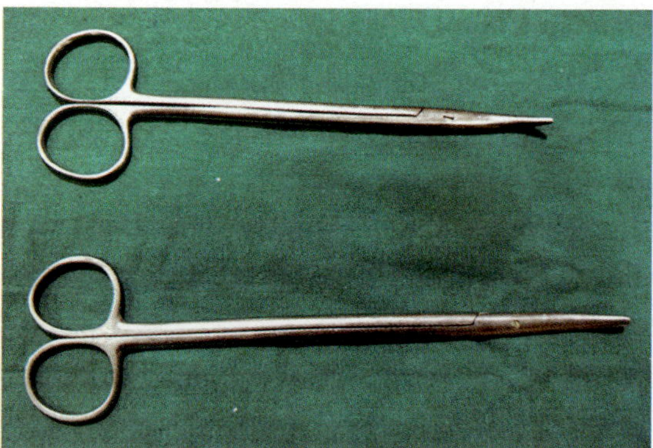

Figure 11.23 Metzenbaum tissue cutting scissor—cut soft tissue during surgery.

  - Heath suture cutting scissor: Fine, curved on angle type scissor. It has small and sharp blade with serration at the tip. Serration helps in gripping the suture well (Fig. 11.24).
  - Pott-Smith vascular scissor: Has short and very sharp pointed tip and is available in 25, 45, and 60 degree angle. It is used for trimming delicate tissues and blood vessels, and opening blood vessels and tubular structure (Fig. 11.25)

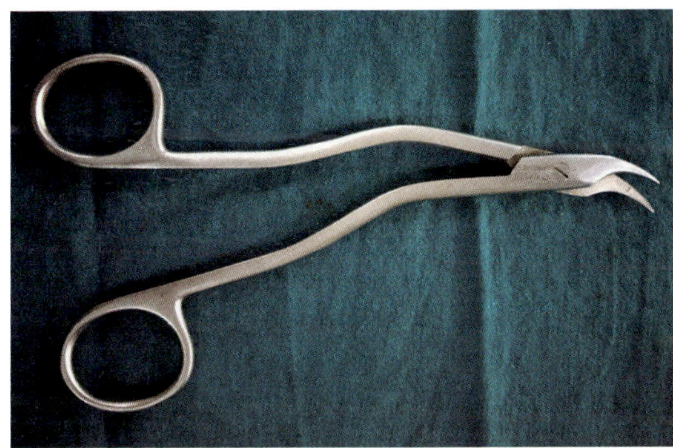

Figure 11.24 Health suture cutting scissor—cut the suture on the skin or mucosal surface.

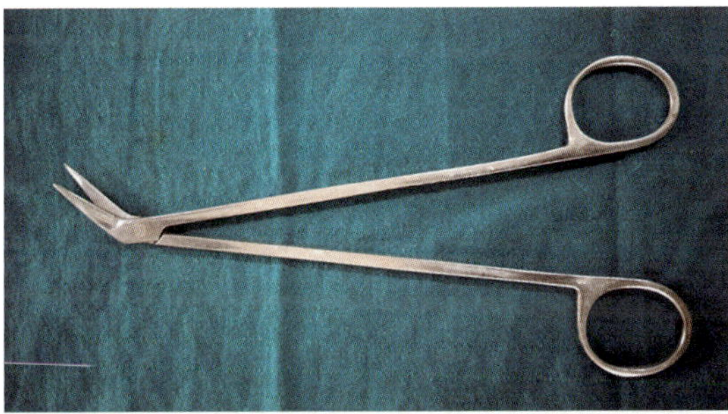

Figure 11.25 Pott-Smith vascular scissor—opening of blood vessels and tubular structure.

Always check the screw to ensure that it is fully tightened to prevent it from drooping into the wound.

Scissors are delicate and each type of scissors should be used for its intended purpose, e.g., suture cutting scissor should not be used in tissue cutting and vice versa. They need to be sharpen to retain their sharpness for cutting.

RETRACTORS

They are very useful for carrying out procedure on a deeply placed organ.

There are two types of retractors—handheld and self-retaining.

Criteria for an Ideal Retractor

- It should retract the tissues without obstructing the field.
- It should not damage the tissues (should be smooth and rounded).

Advantages of a Self-Retaining Retractor

- As the name suggests, it will remain in position by counterpressure of the blade.
- Uniform traction will be maintained.
- Traction can be adjusted.
- Assistant will not be needed to hold it and he/she can help the surgeon in other tasks.

Over-retraction can damage retracted as well as underlying structure. Ask the assistant to provide minimum traction and relaxing in between as and when required.

Sometimes change in position may allow sufficient retraction and retraction by a hand placed over a pack is less damaging.

Deaver Retractor (Fig. 11.26)

- During retraction, the blade should be covered with a mop.
- *Uses*
  - To retract the liver in upper abdominal surgeries, such as cholecystectomy and perforation closure
  - To retract the kidney in surgeries on kidney or ureter
  - To retract the spleen in surgery of adrenal
  - To retract peritoneum in surgery of prostate and bladder

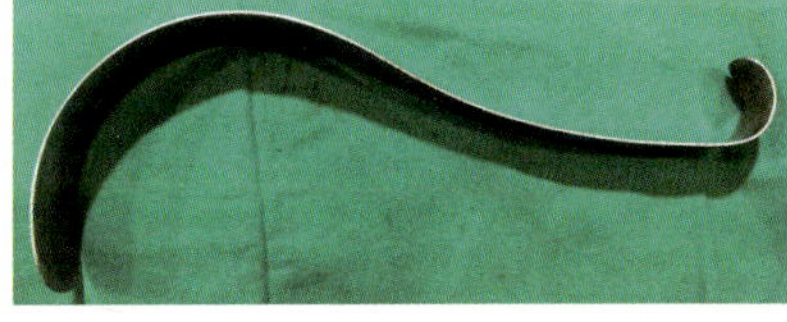

Figure 11.26 Deaver retractor used to retract liver in upper abdominal surgery.

Langenbeck Retractor (Fig. 11.27)

Used for retraction of superficial parts such as skin, subcutaneous tissue, and muscle

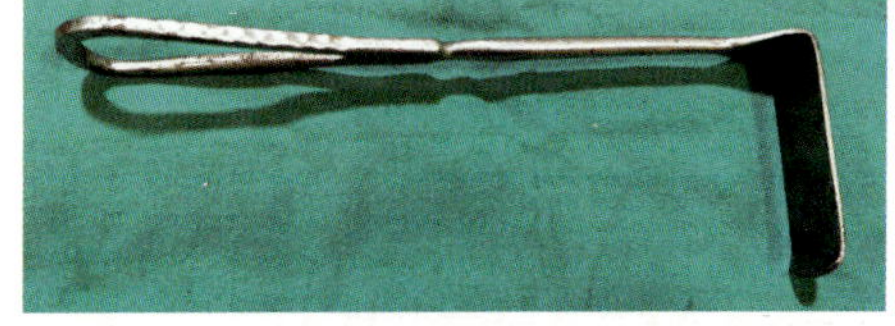

Figure 11.27 Langenbeck retractor. Retraction of superficial part like skin, subcutaneous tissue, and muscle.

Roux C-Retractor (Fig. 11.28)

- It is used for retraction of the abdominal wall in various operations (retracts sides of the abdominal incision).
- It is available in small, medium, and large sizes.

Figure 11.28 Roux C-retractor used for retraction of abdominal wall in various surgeries.

Doyen Abdominal Wall Retractor (Fig. 11.29)

- It is used for retraction of the abdominal wall in various surgeries.
- It is for upward retraction of the abdominal wall.
- It is most commonly used in laparotomy.

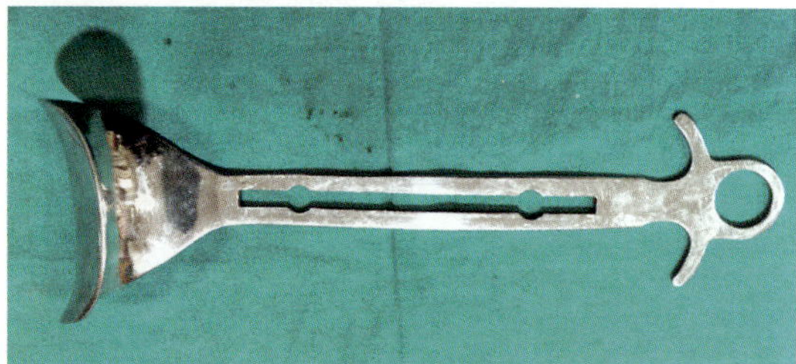

Figure 11.29 Doyen abdominal wall retractor used for retraction of abdominal walls in various surgeries.

Gillies Skin Hook (Fig. 11.30)

It is used to retract skin, especially in mastectomy.

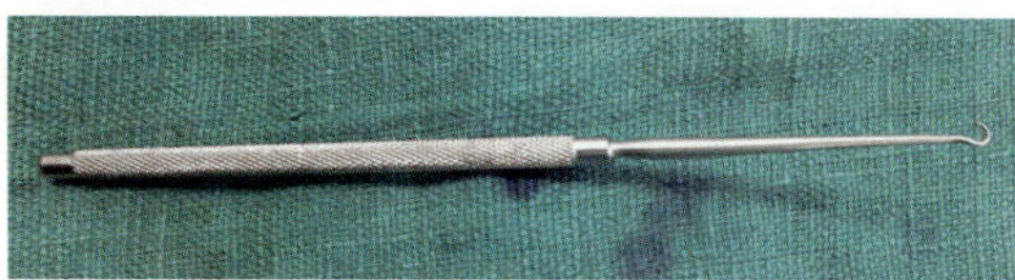

Figure 11.30 Gillies skin hook used for retraction of skin.

Morris Retractor (Fig. 11.31)

It is like a large Langenbeck retractor.

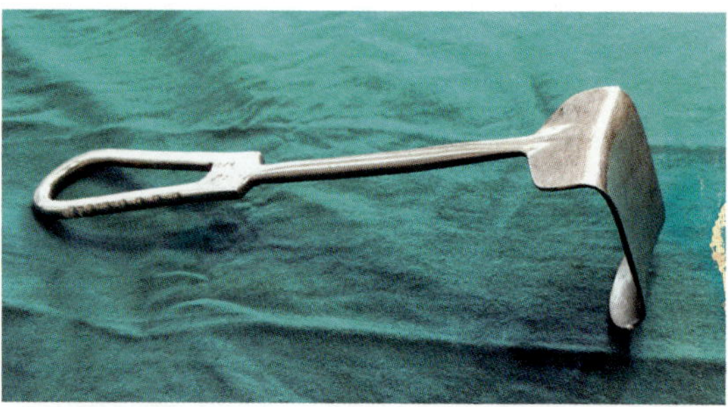

Figure 11.31 Morris retractor like a large Lagenbeck retractor.

Allison Lung Retractor (Fig. 11.32)

- It is used for retraction of lung in thoracotomy.
- Because of its special design, it does not damage the lung, and the lung can expand in between the wires.

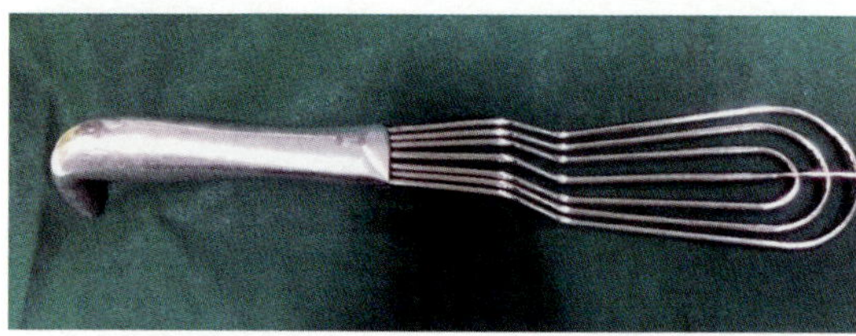

Figure 11.32 Allison lung retractor to retraction of lung in thoracotomy.

Senn Retractor (Fig. 11.33)

It has a handle and two ends. One end has multiple hooks with sharp edges and other end looks like langebach's retractor.

- *Uses*
  - To retract skin during excision of superficial benign skin lesion like lipoma and sebaceous cyst
  - To retract tough structure like fascia of palm and sole

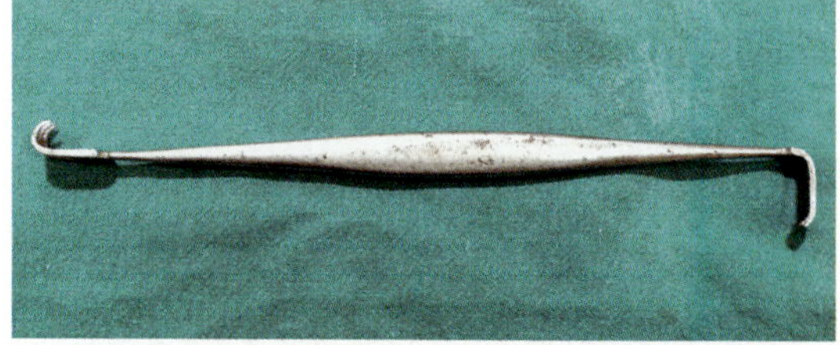

Figure 11.33 Senn retractor.

Self-Retaining Retractors

- Balfour abdominal self-retaining retractor (Fig. 11.34)
  - Used for retraction of the abdominal wall in laparotomy

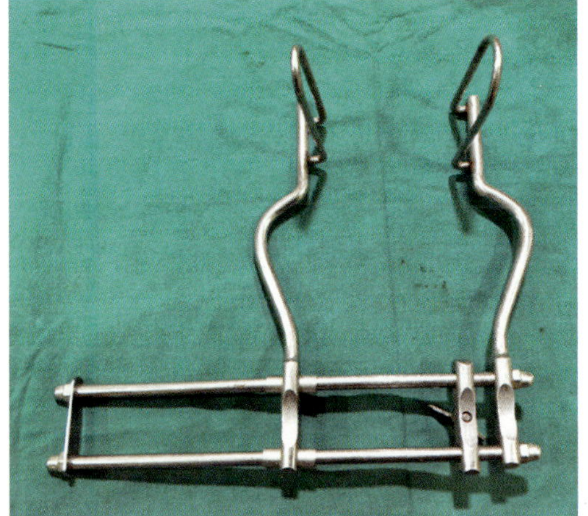

Figure 11.34 Balfour's abdominal self-retaining retractor to retraction of the abdominal wall in laparotomy.

- Cerebellar retractor (Fig. 11.35)
  - It is used to retract shallow incision

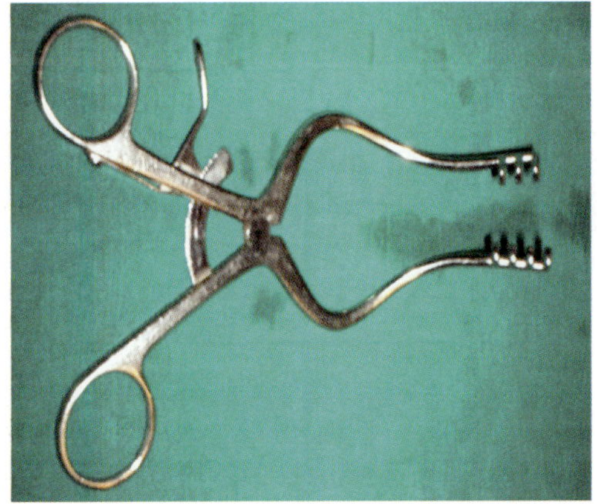

Figure 11.35 Cerebellar retractor for retracting shallow incision.

  - Shank differentiates various retractors of this type:
    - Cerebellar has angled shank
    - Weitlaner has straight shank
    - Beckman has hinged shank (Fig. 11.36)

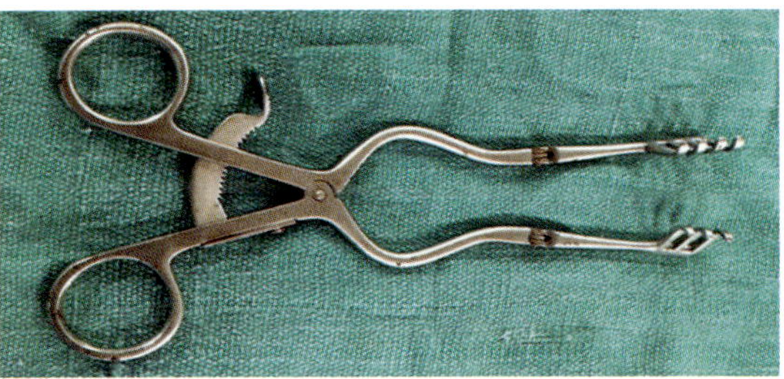

Figure 11.36 Beckman retractor.

- Finochietto rib spreader (Fig. 11.37)
  - It is used to retract ribs in thoracotomy.
  - It can also be used in ministernotomy to retract sternum.

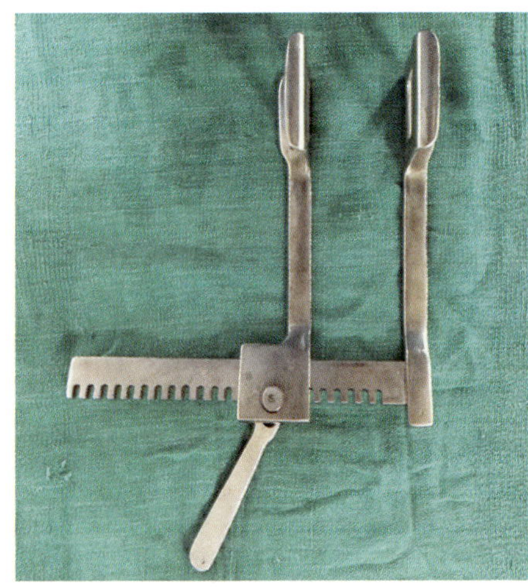

Figure 11.37 Finochietto rib spreader used to retract ribs in thoracotomy.

INTESTINAL CLAMPS

These are of two types—crushing clamps and occluding clamps.

Crushing Clamps

- The aim of using crushing clamp is to crush the muscle.
- It occludes bowel lumen and crushes vessels.
- It is applied on the portion of bowel to be removed.
- It has heavy blades.
- There is close apposition of blades.
- Lever arrangement is such that with minimum pressure, maximum effect can be achieved.
- Pressure is uniform throughout.

Noncrushing Clamps (Occluding Clamps) (Fig. 11.38)

- These have light blades.
- The blades are not in close apposition.
- They occlude only bowel lumen and blood vessels. They do not crush the vessels.
- Pressure is the maximum at the tip.
- These clamps are applied on the portion of bowel to be preserved.
- In resection and anastomosis, they help in preventing spillage.
- They keep the field clear by occluding vessels.

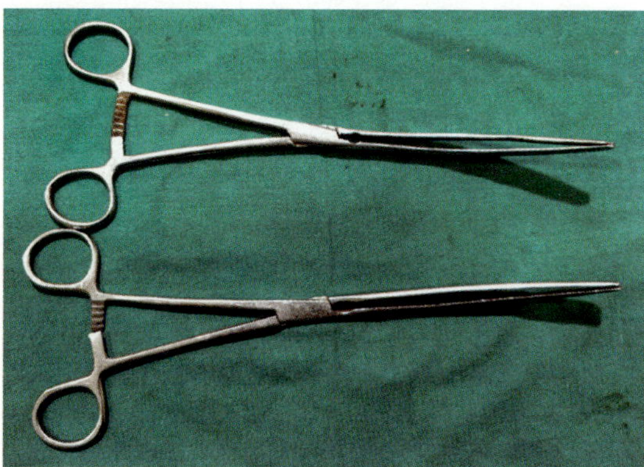

Figure 11.38 Intestinal occluding clamp.

Doyen intestinal occluding clamp (Fig. 11.39)

- *Identification*
  - It has a long, straight, elastic blade.
  - There are longitudinal serrations.
  - It prevents leakage from bowel without crushing, keeps the intestine steady during the procedure, and arrests bleeding.
  - If not applied properly, it can slip and excessive pressure can cause trauma to the bowel.

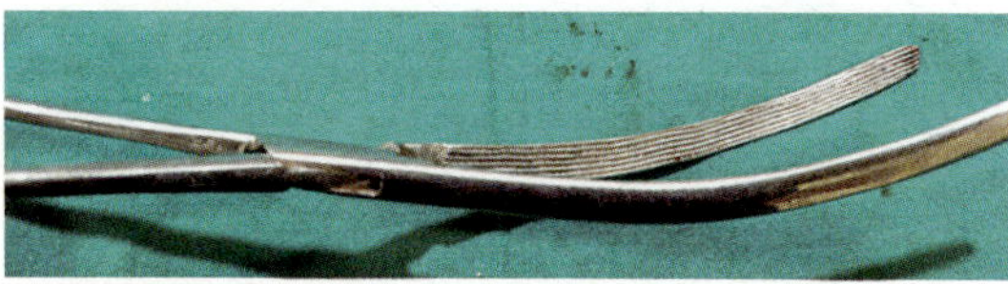

Figure 11.39 Doyen occluding clamp. It is used to occlude intestine in resection and anastomosis and to prevent spillage. It keeps the field clear by occluding vessel.

Moynihan clamp (Fig. 11.40)

It has a transverse serration on the blade.

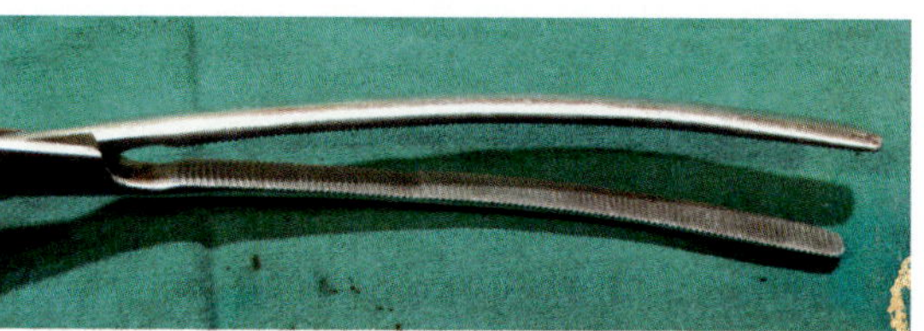

Figure 11.40 Moynihan clamp—used in resection and anastomosis as occluding clamp.

MISCELLANEOUS

Rib Shear (Fig. 11.41)

- *Identification*
  - Sharp edge
  - Fulcrum
- *Uses*
  - To cut the rib
  - To cut the rough edge of large bone
- There are two types of rib resection:
  - Subperiosteal
  - Extraperiosteal (e.g., cervical rib)
- Indications for rib resection
  - Kidney exposure through flank incision
  - Operation on lung
  - Bone grafting

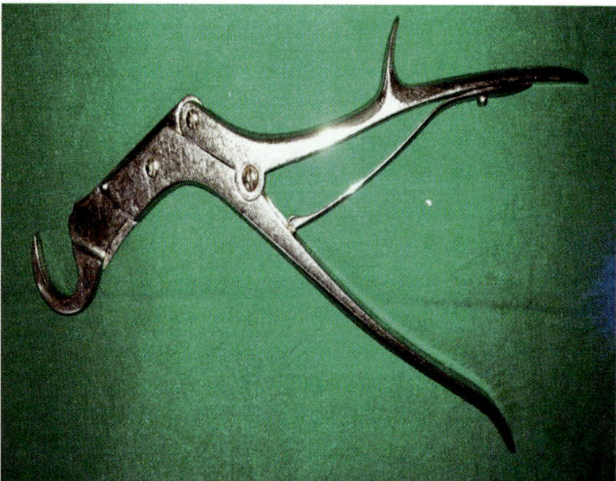

Figure 11.41 Rib shear used to cut the rib.

Horsley-Liston Bone Cutting Forceps (Fig. 11.42)

- It has two sharp edges with one or two fulcrum for double action.
- *Uses*: Cut the small bone (ribs) or rough edges of cut large bone

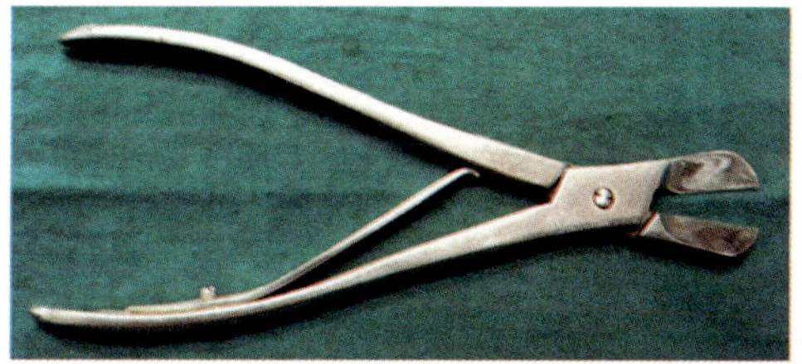

Figure 11.42 Horsley-Liston bone cutting forceps.

Farabeuf Periosteal Elevator (Fig. 11.43)

- *Identification*: The tip is beveled and the shaft has a thumb rest.
- It is used to elevate the periosteum before cutting the bone.
- By elevating the periosteum, it will help in bone healing and regeneration.
- Excessive cutting will lead to formation of ring sequestrum.

Figure 11.43 Periosteum elevator used to elevate periosteum.

Doyen Raspatory (Fig. 11.44)

- *Identification*: It has a polygonal handle with a curved hook-like end. To identify its side (right- or left-sided), keep curvature of the blade pointing upwards and the handle outwards.
- *Uses*: To separate periosteum from the rib, from the medial side. It will help in protecting the pleura and preventing damage to the neurovascular bundle while cutting the rib.

Figure 11.44 Doyen rasparatory used to separate periosteum from rib.

Fergusson Amputation Saw (Fig. 11.45)

- It is used to cut bone. It has two parts—handle and blade. Blade may be fixed or detachable.
- Other use: To cut plaster cast

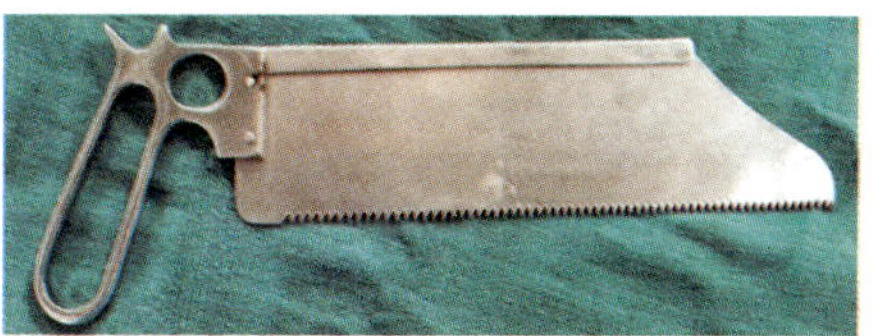

Figure 11.45 Fergusson amputations used to saw to cut bone.

Killearn Bone Nibbler (Fig. 11.46)

- *Identification*
  - It has a long handle and a small blade.
- *Blade*: It is cup shaped; top jaw is for cutting, while the lower jaw holds the tissue firmly to prevent injury to the underlined structure.
- *Uses*
  - To make cut end of bone smooth after amputation, rib cutting
  - To enlarge burr hole

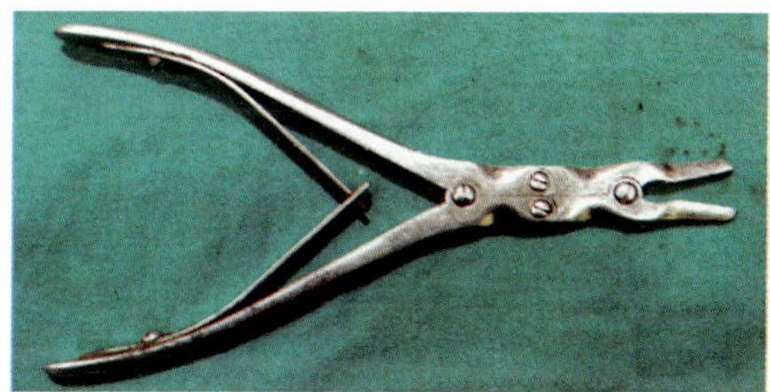

Figure 11.46 Killearn bone nibbler to make cut end of bone smooth after amputation, rib cutting.

Rib Approximator (Fig. 11.47)

- *Identification*: It has two blades (distal fixed and proximal mobile).
- The proximal blade moves with the help of a screw.
- It is used to approximate ribs while closing thoracotomy wound.

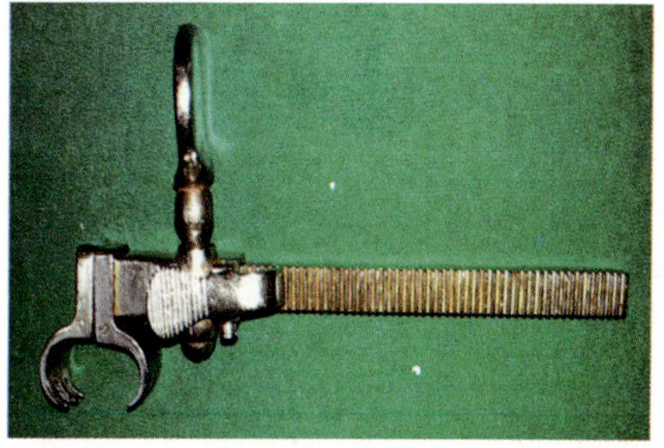

Figure 11.47 Rib approximator used to approximate rib while closing thoractomy wound.

Watson Skin Grafting Knife Handle (Fig. 11.48)

- *Identification*: It has a flat handle with two screws for adjustment and three to five keyhole-shaped slots for holding the knife in position.
- It is used in skin grafting.
- Skin grafting knife is placed in the handle, and after proper adjustment, graft is taken.

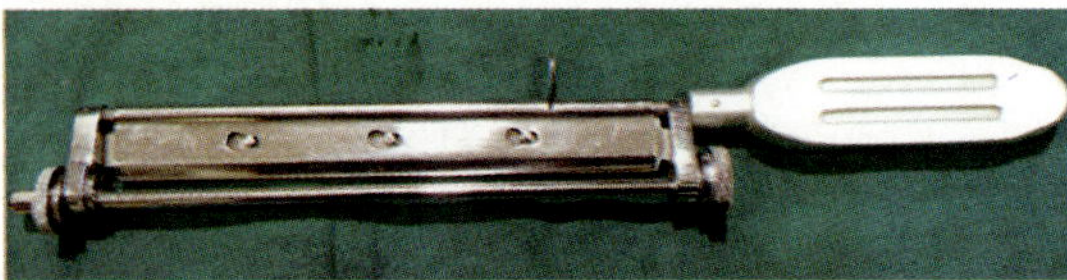

Figure 11.48 Watson skin grafting knife handle used in skin grafting.

Wooden Block (Fig. 11.49)

It is used in skin grafting to stretch/flatten the skin of the thigh.

Figure 11.49 Wooden block used to stretch/flatten the skin of thigh in skin grafting.

Suction Cannula (Tip)

It is mainly used either as Yankauer suction cannula or Poole suction tip.

Yankauer suction cannula (Fig. 11.50)

- *Identification*
  - It is a metal cannula with an expanded tip.
  - On the tip, there is a large central hole surrounding a small hole.
- *Uses*: It is used for suction in various operations such as laparotomy, SPCL, and hydrocele.

It has a strong suction effect at the tip and may suck the structures such as intestine and omentum; so direct suction should be avoided and the tip should be covered with a mop or a rubber tube to protect the tissue.

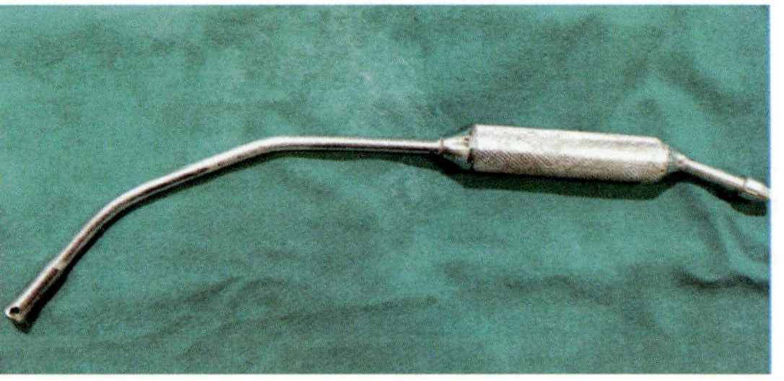

Figure 11.50 Yankauer suction cannula used to suction in various surgeries.

Poole suction (multiperforated suction tip) (Fig. 11.51)

- It has two straight tubes, one inside the other
- Outer tube has multiple holes and a blunt closed end to allow effective suction without trauma even when few holes are blocked
- Inner tube has two holes, one at the proximal end and the other at the terminal end
- Negative pressure can be generated through the application of thumb over holes on the outer tube
- *Use*: For suction in peritoneal cavity

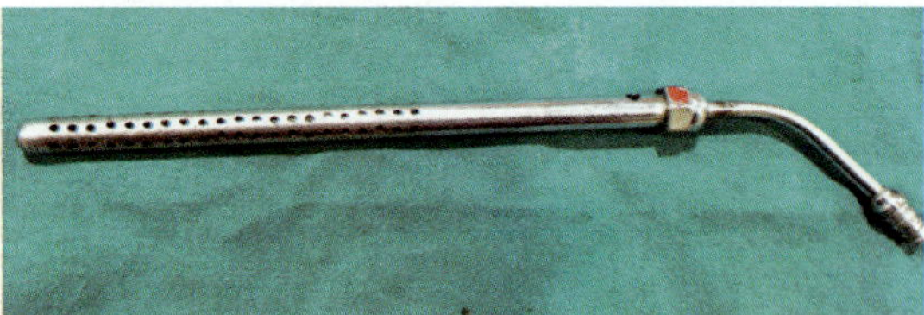

Figure 11.51 Poole suction tip.

Sargent Intestinal Repository

- *Identification*: It is like a long concave blade.
- *Uses*: It helps in repositioning the intestine during closure in laparotomy.

Mayo-Hegar Needle Holder (Fig. 11.52)

- *Identification*
  - It has a small blade.

- It has a groove inside the blade (which makes the grip stronger).
- It has a serration inside the blade.
- Handle to blade ratio is 4:1 (mechanical advantage).

- Two varieties are available:
  - *Straight*: Used on the surface
  - *Curved*: Used in cavities
- Some needle holders are tungsten carbide coated, which reduces the wear and tear of blades and allows them to last longer.
- *Uses*
  - As the name suggests, it is used to hold the needle.
  - Needle should be held at the junction of the anterior two-third and the posterior one-third.
  - If it is held more anteriorly, there is mechanical disadvantage due to sweeping movement. If it is held more posteriorly, there may be damage to the needle (part near the eye is the weakest).

Other contributions of Mayo to surgery are as follows:

- Mayo's double breasting for paraumbilical hernia
- Mayo needle (is strong and has a square eye; mainly used in gynecology)
- Mayo thread-cutting scissor
- Prepyloric vein of Mayo

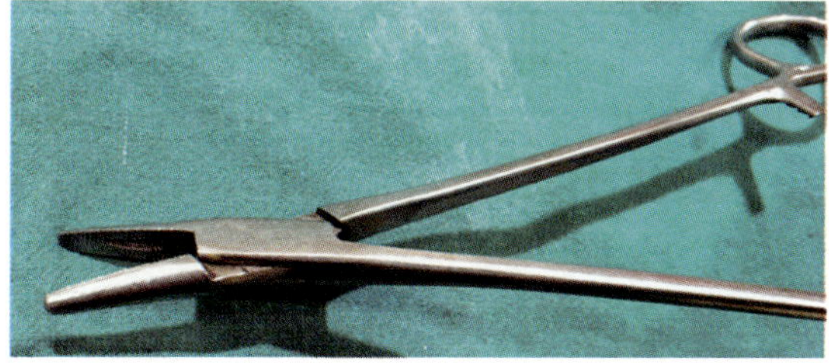

Figure 11.52 Mayo-Hegar needle holder used to hold the needle (also known as needle driver).

Kilner Needle Holder (Fig. 11.53)

- *Identification*: It is a curved instrument
- *Uses*: Used to work in depth shallow cavity where curve gives better views of the tip of the instruments without obstructing the operative field.

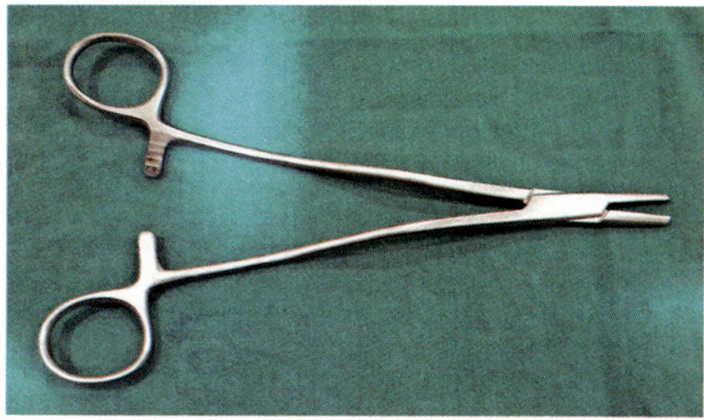

Fugure 11.53 Kilner needle holder—used to work in depth.

Collier Needle Holder (Fig. 11.54)

It has a serration and fenestrated jaw.

Uses: For delicate suturing specifically suited for 3-0, 4-0, and 5-0 sutures

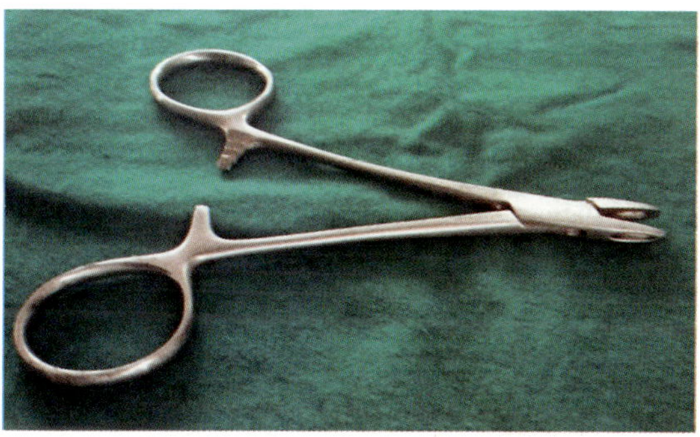

Figure 11.54 Collier needle holder—for delicate suturing.

Towel Clips

Doyen towel clip (Fig. 11.55)

- It is a cross-acting towel clip.
- It opens up on pressing and works by spring action.
- It is used in draping in all types of operations. It retains the towel in position. Blades are curved and sharply pointed for firm gripping of full-thickness towel.
- It can be used to fix suction tubing.
- It can be used to fix the light source wire as well as CO_2 insufflation tubing in laparoscopy.
- It can be used as a tongue holding forceps. Its advantage over routine tongue holding forceps is that it does not produce pressure necrosis if applied for a long time.

- Some surgeons do not recommend this clip for draping in abdominal surgery, because of the possibility of losing it in the abdominal cavity.
- Other instruments that open on pressing are tracheal dilator, mastoid retractor, Cusco speculum, and Bulldog clamp.

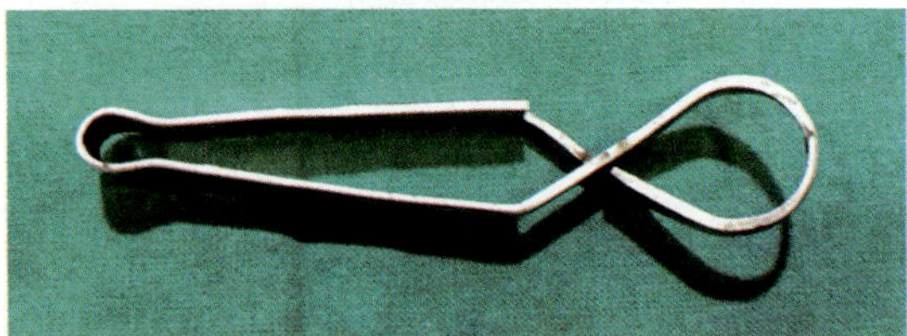

Figure 11.55 Doyen towel clip for draping in all types of operations.

Backhaus towel clip (Fig. 11.56)

- *Uses*
  - It is used for draping before operation.
  - Other uses are the same as those for Doyen towel clip. Preference is given to this clip. Angle at the end of the blade allows towel clip to lie flush to the skin surface.
  - It is used to hold the elevated rib in position in flail chest.
  - It can be used as cord holding forceps.

- When clipping towel together, do not penetrate the skin.
- Sharp tip can easily compromise the integrity of gloves and skin.

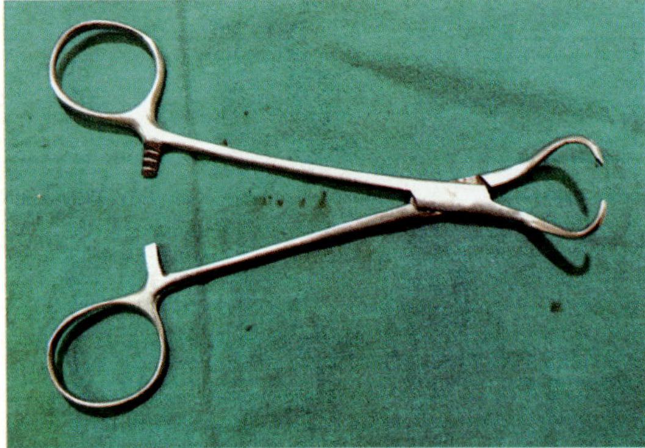

Figure 11.56 Backhaus towel clip for draping in all types of operations.

Hudson Brace (Fig. 11.57)

- *Identification*: Has hand rest, handle, and burr; used as a handle for trephine or burr (Fig. 11.58) to make a hole in the cranium
- *Uses*
  - Burr hole surgeries
  - Craniotomy
  - Craniectomy

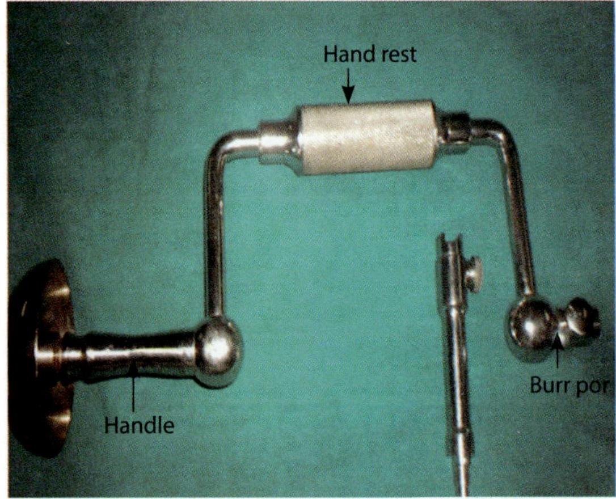

Figure 11.57 Hudson brace in craniotomy.

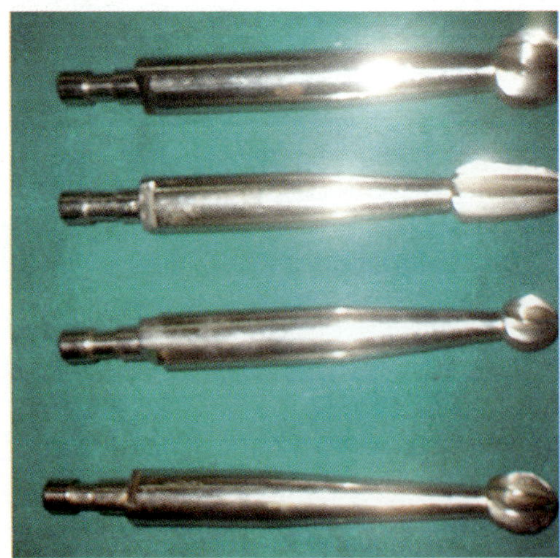

Figure 11.58 Burr.

Lister Bougie (Fig. 11.59)

- Parts: It has tip, shaft, and head (round).
- Bougie: It is used to dilate the narrow portion of natural hollow organ, for example, urethra, biliary tract, and esophagus.

- There is a numbering on the head in French scale. The numerator indicates diameter at the tip while the denominator indicates diameter at the head (6/10 to 28/32).
- One French (1F) unit = 0.33 mm, one English (1E) unit = 0.5 mm, and one American (1A) unit = 0.5 mm. The English scale is 2 numbers less than the American scale, so 5 mm = 15F = 10A = 8E.
- Lister bougie is used to dilate urethra.

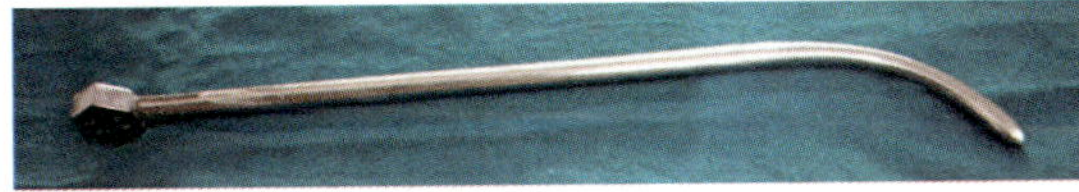

Figure 11.59 Lister's Bougie used as a urethral dilater.

Bakes Common Bile Duct Dilator (Fig. 11.60)

It is a long and narrow instrument with bulbous tip. The tip varies from 3 mm to 11 mm tip and the length of the instrument is 9 cm. This instrument is used to dilate CBD.

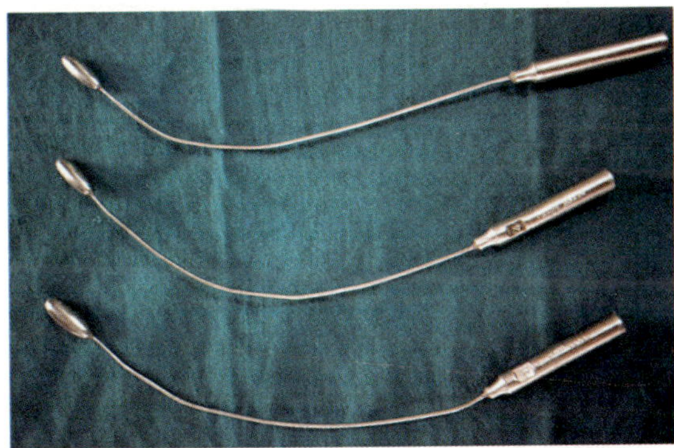

Figure 11.60 Bakes CBD dilator.

Diethrich Bulldog Clamp (Fig. 11.61)

- Straight or curved
- Opens on pressing
- Used for surgery on small vessels, especially AV fistula

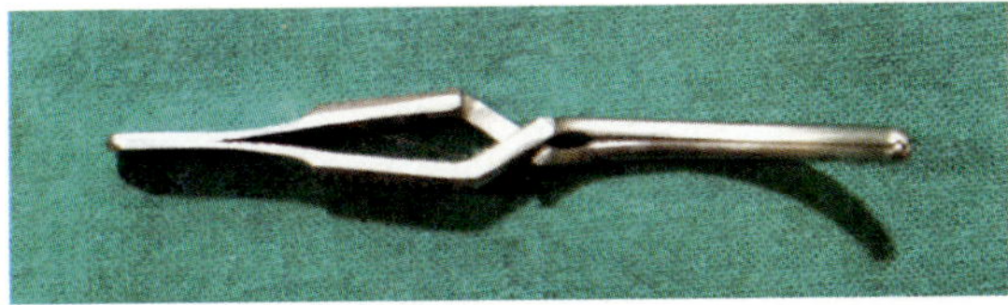

Figure 11.61 Diethrich Bulldog clamp—a vascular clamp.

Surgical Needles (Fig. 11.62)

- Surgical needles are made up of nickel + stainless steel.
- Needle selection depends on its sharpness and its resistance to breaking and bending while passing through the tissue.
- Classification
  - Eyeless and with eye
  - Atraumatic and traumatic
  - Round body and cutting (conventional cutting, reverse cutting, taper cut)
  - Straight or curved (curved needle passes through with a circular movement and allows working in depth) (a straight needle can be used without instruments while a curved needle should be handled with needle holder and forceps)

Eyeless needle

- Atraumatic

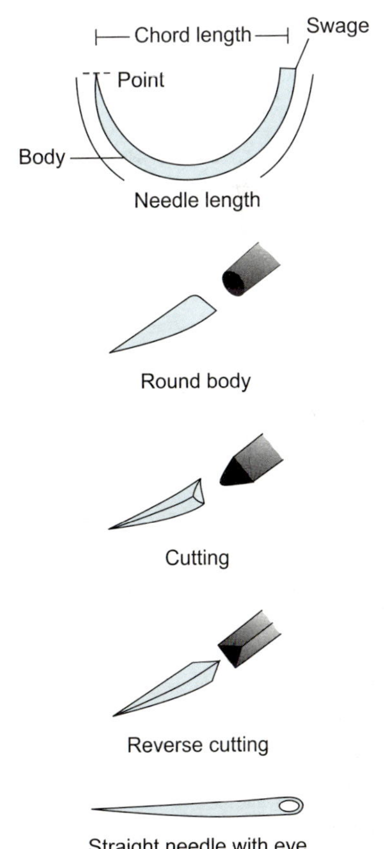

Figure 11.62 Surgical needles.

- Not reusable
- If dropped accidentally, can be recovered easily due to the thread

Needle with eye

- Traumatic
- Reusable
- Can be easily unthreaded

Uses of various needles

- *Round body*: It has a sharp tip with smooth edges and is less traumatic to the surrounding tissue. It is used to close peritoneum, intestine, myocardium, and muscle. It is not good for skin closure because it is difficult to pass the round body needle through the skin.
- *Cutting*: It is used to close skin and fascia.
- *Reverse cutting*: It is used to close skin, buccal mucosa, and periosteum. It is also used in plastic surgery and ophthalmic surgery because of less trauma and minimal scar formation.
- *Taper cut*: It is a combination of reverse cutting and round body. It is used for suturing of heart and liver.
- *Straight needle*: It may be cutting or round body:
  - *Cutting*: For skin closure
  - *Round body*: For intestine

Bard-Parker Knife Handle (Fig. 11.63)

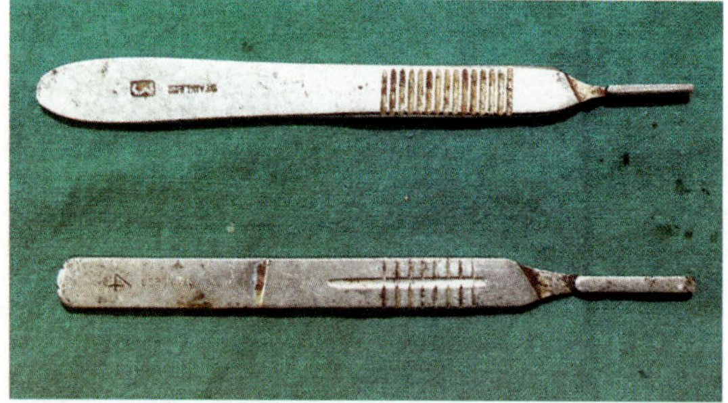

Figure 11.63 Bard-Parker knife handle.

- It is available in various sizes.
- Bard-Parker is the company that manufactured the handle first time.
- It is used for razor sharp cutting of the tissue.
- Various types of blades (Fig. 11.64) can be fitted over different-number handles (Table 11.2).

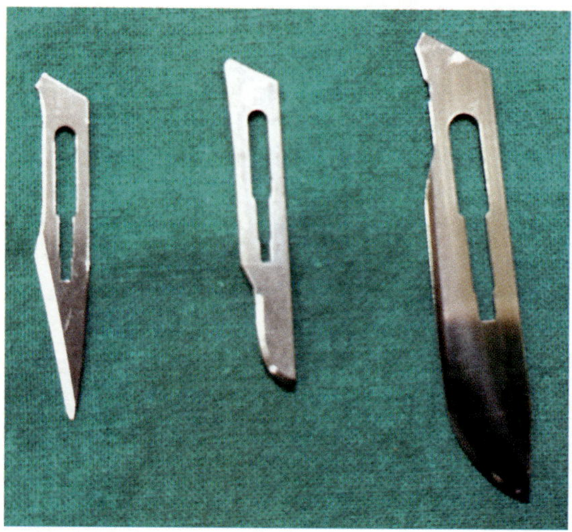

Figure 11.64 Surgical blade—from right to left: number 11, 15, and 22.

Table 11.2 Surgical Blades and Handles

Blade no.	Uses	Handle no.
11 (stab or bayonet)	Stab incision (drains abscess, removing suture)	3 or 5
12 (bistoury)	Tonsillectomy knife (also drains infection of middle ear)	3 or 5
15	Pediatric or plastic surgery	3 or 5
20	Skin incision	4
21 and 22	Skin incision	4

- The Bard-Parker knife handle should be lightweight, with a good grip, and different types of blades should be able to fit into the same blade.
- For short and fine incision, it should be held like a pencil while for long incision fiddle bow position is used to hold the handle. The handle is gripped horizontally between the middle finger and the thumb while the index finger is above the handle. The ring and little fingers are holding the end of the handle.
- Sterilization: The handle is sterilized by autoclaving. Blades are presterilized with gamma radiation and available in an aluminum foil pack.
- Never retrieve the scalpel from the surgeon's hand. Never use finger to load and unload the knife blade.

Pencil Electrode (Fig. 11.65)

The pencil electrode is an active electrode that is used to cut and coagulate the tissue. Tip is inserted into the pencil and types of tip differ according to the type of surgery.

Dispersive or grounding pad or plate is must as it uses monpolar current. Area should be kept clean and dry and the area with large muscle mass is preferable. Upper thigh is the preferred area.

- Flat tip is most commonly used
- Needle tip is for small and delicate structure
- Long tip either needle or flat is used while working in the deep cavity like pelvis

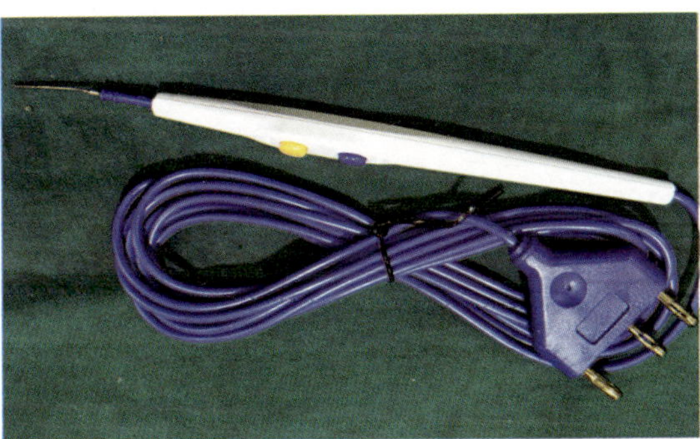

Figure 11.65 Pencil electrode.

Gerald Bipolar Forceps (Fig. 11.66)

For basic principle, refer Section 'Energy Sources for Laparoscopic Surgery' (page 40) in Chapter 5, *Fundamentals of Minimal Access Surgery.*

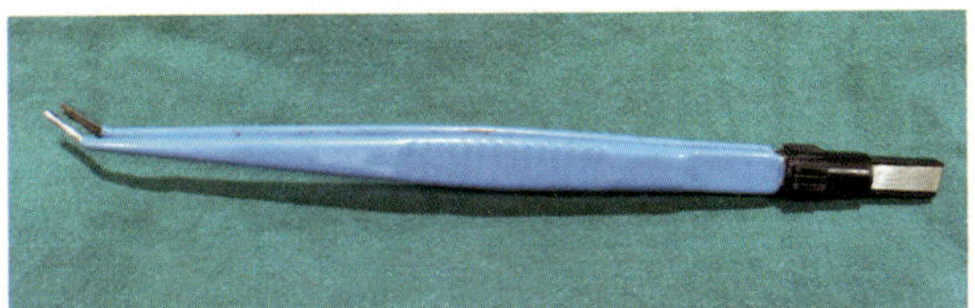

Figure 11.66 Gerald bipolar forceps.

Skin Stapler (Fig. 11.67)

- Principle is same as paper stapler
- Two cut edge of the incision brought together and clip applied
- Good hemostasis is must prior to application of clip
- Clip remover (Fig. 11.68) is available to remove the clip

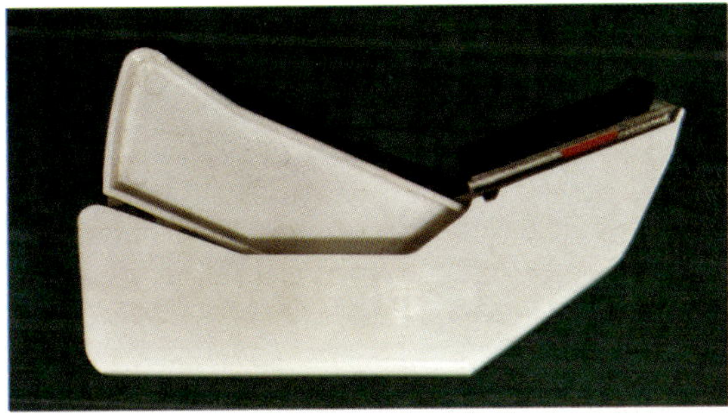

Figure 11.67 Skin stapler.

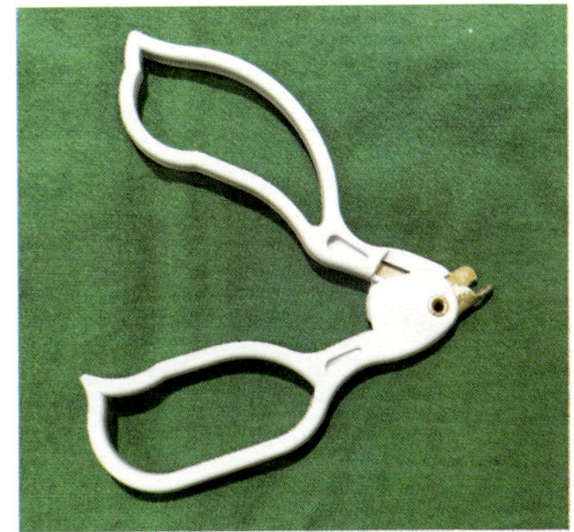

Figure 11.68 Clip remover.

Volkmann Scoop (Fig. 11.69)

It is used to remove hypergranulation tissue in dressing.

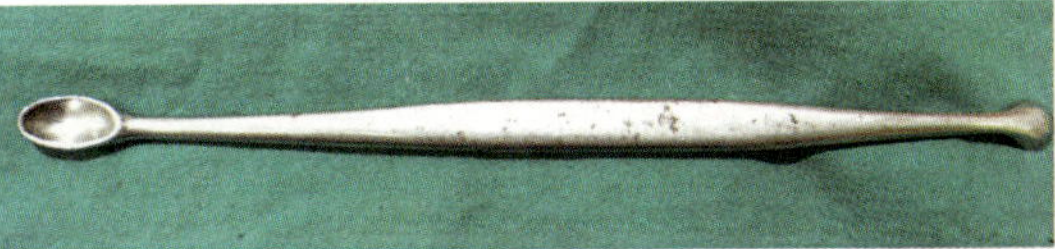

Figure 11.69 Volkmann scoop.

INSTRUMENTS USED FOR LAPAROSCOPY

Veress Needle (Fig. 11.70)

- It was first described by chest physician for pleural tapping in 1938.
- It is available as reusable or disposable.

- Size: These are 80, 100, and 120 mm.
- It consists of outer cannula with beveled needle and inner stylet.
- Stylet is attached with spring and has a lateral hole (for CO_2 delivery).
- It is used for creating pneumoperitoneum and reduces the chance of major internal injury.
- Two distinct pops are felt as the surgeon passes the needle through fascia and peritoneum.
- A major complication of Veress needle insertion is bleeding. The trajectory of the needle should not be angled toward major vessels such as aorta and iliac.
- Before insertion, it must be checked for patency and spring action.
- After insertion, aspiration test should be performed to exclude injury to the bowel or vessels and drop test (drops of saline flow easily if it is within abdominal cavity) to check whether the proper placement is performed.

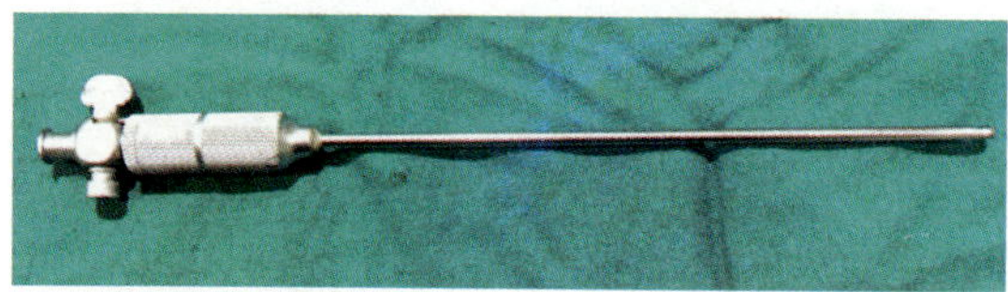

Figure 11.70 Veress needle—used to create pneumoperitoneum.

Trocars (Fig. 11.71)

- They are available in different sizes but the most commonly used trocars are 5 and 10 mm.
- Cannula may be of metal or plastic and may be smooth or threaded.
- The trocar may be disposable or reusable.
- The trocar functions as a portal for the placement of telescope and other instruments, such as graspers, scissors, clip applicators, and staplers.
- Tip of the trocars can be pyramidal, flat double-edged blade, and/or conical tip.
- Conical tip is less traumatic and has advantages of reducing patient discomfort and recovery time.
- A gas-tight valve is located at the top of the trocars.
- Careful inspection of the trocar is mandatory to ensure that all valves move smoothly and that insufflation valve is closed.
- Types of valve: These can be spring-loaded or magnetic trap-door valves and trumpet valves.
- Valveless trocars are available that reduce the leakage of CO_2 gas and smudging of telescope lens.
- Optical trocars are available that allow visualization of tip of the trocar as it passes through layers of abdominal wall.

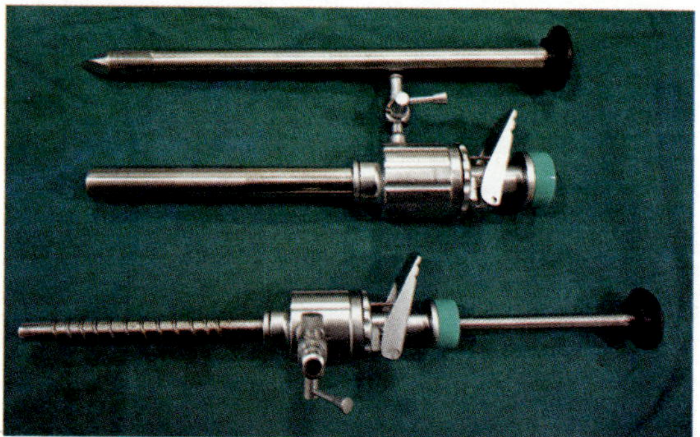

Figure 11.71 5- and 10-mm trocar.

Reducer (Reducing Sleeve) (Fig. 11.72)

It is used to reduce the size of port. Surgeons can change the instrument of larger diameter to that of smaller diameter without losing pneumoperitoneum. Size of the port can be reduced from 10 to 5 mm and from 5 to 3 mm.

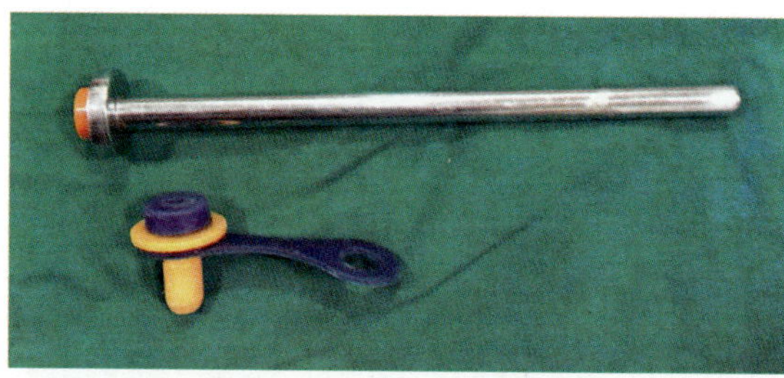

Figure 11.72 Reducer. Through reducer small caliber instruments can be passed through larger trocar.

Insufflators (Fig. 11.73)

- Insufflators deliver gas from high-pressure cylinder to the peritoneal cavity at a high rate and low and accurately controlled pressure.
- Ideal maximum pressure is 14–15 mmHg. Insufflators activate and deliver gas automatically when pressure falls due to leakage of gas.
- It is essential to observe the pressure on the monitor to confirm the intraperitoneal location of the Veress needle. The initial expected

pressure is <6 mmHg. Abnormally high pressure indicates that something is wrong. More than 15 mmHg pressure suggests that the patient is not anesthetized adequately.

- Indicators on the insufflators are as follows: Preset pressure, actual pressure, flow rate, and total gas used.
- An insufflator should be placed within the view of the surgeon so that he/she can monitor the pressure and flow.

Figure 11.73 CO_2 insufflator.

Suction Irrigation Cannula (Fig. 11.74)

- It is available as 5- and 10-mm reusable devices.
- It is very helpful during laparoscopy to maintain a clear field of vision.
- Irrigation solution used is mostly normal saline.
- The handpiece is connected to the pressurized reservoir of saline and suction. They are controlled by the buttons on the handpiece.

(a)

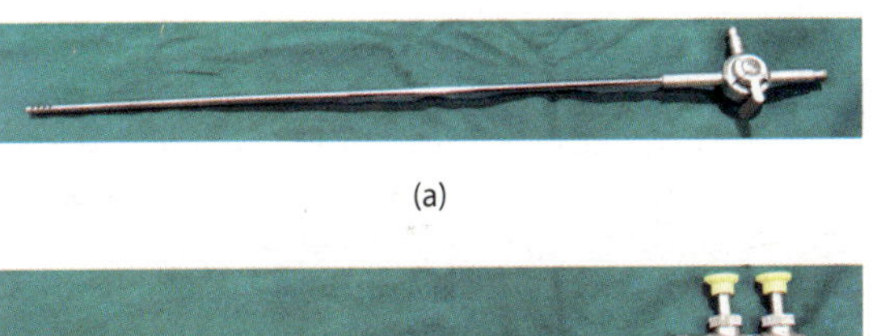

(b)

Figure 11.74 Suction irrigation cannula. (a) Push type, (b) plunger or press type.

Telescope (Fig. 11.75)

- It is either rigid or fiber-optic. Standard length is 24 cm.
- It contains a series of quartz rods and focusing lenses that conduct the image to the eyepiece.
- It is available as straight (0) and angled (30°, 45°). Diameter of the scope can be 3, 5, and 10 mm.
- The 30° angled scope can provide much better field view (152°) as compared to 0° (76°).
- The scope is attached with fiber-optic light cable.
- More than 25% of fiber damage will significantly obscure the field view and the scope needs to be replaced.
- Most commonly used scope is 10 mm, 30°.

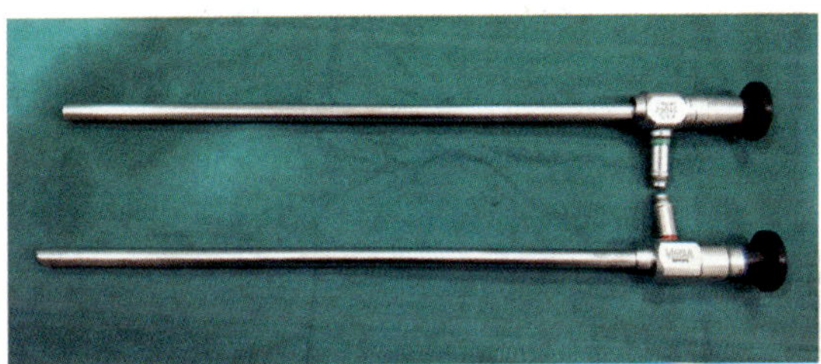

(a)

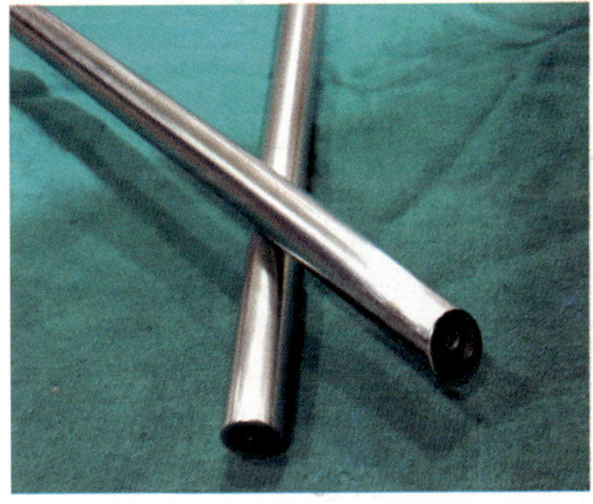

(b)

Figure 11.75 (a) Telescopes, (b) straight lens tip is 0 degree, oblique tip is 30 degrees.

Light Source (Fig. 11.76)

- Xenon, mercury, or halogen bulb is used to create high-intensity light.
- The bulbs are available in different wattages—150, 250, and 300 W.
- Xenon bulb can give better clarity as compared to halogen.

- Light is absorbed by blood so in any procedure where more bleeding is encountered, light will become dull quickly and require more light.
- Nowadays, LED light source is also available.

Figure 11.76 LED light source.

Fiber-Optic Light Cable (Fig. 11.77)

- Diameter of the fiber bundle should always be larger than lens system.
- Cable should not have a crack or sharp bend in the plastic sheath.
- These cables are highly inefficient, losing almost more than 90% of the light delivered from the light source, so for good illumination bright light is necessary.
- When not in use, it must be on standby or turned off. Intense heat light may cause patient drapes or any inflammable to ignite.
- It should never be placed under a heavy object and it should not be kinked or twisted.

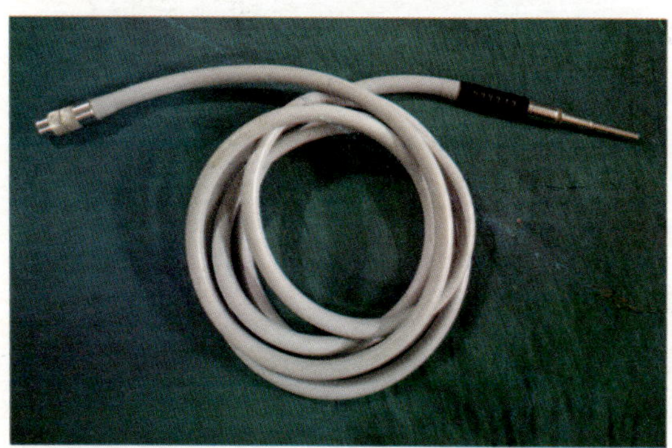

Figure 11.77 Fiber optic cable.

Monitors (Fig. 11.78)

- Large monitors with high-resolution screen are ideal. More than 20-inch monitors are preferred.
- Nonflickering monitors with resolution equal to or greater than that of camera are preferred.
- HD monitors deliver up to eight times more resolution than standard monitors.

Figure 11.78 HD monitor.

Cameras (Fig. 11.79)

- Three types of cameras are available: Single-chip, three-chip, and HD.
- Single-chip has a resolution point of 480, three-chip has more than 750, and HD has 1080 lines.
- Clarity is best with HD followed by three-chip and single-chip.
- To enjoy HD clarity, monitors have to be HD.
- Most important for imaging is illumination followed by resolution followed by color.

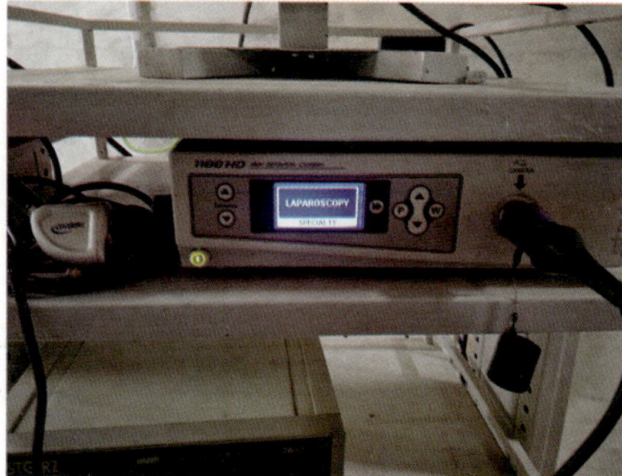

Figure 11.79 HD camera.

Hand Instruments in Laparoscopy (Fig. 11.80)

- Standard length is 30 cm. Forty-five-centimeter instruments are also available that are useful in bariatric surgery.
- They are available as reusable and disposable.
- In India, it is a trend to use reusable instruments more as compared to in the USA and Europe where trend is toward using disposable ones.
- Reusable instruments initially seem to be costly but in the long run are cost-effective.
- For convenience and better ergonomics, half of the instrument should be in and half should be out of the abdominal cavity to allow it to act like a class I lever and stabilize port very nicely.
- Most of the instruments are dismountable so they can be cleaned and washed properly.
- Handles come in many varieties and have a locking or unlocking mechanism depending on the need.
- Most instruments have three separate parts:
    1. *Handle*: It may have a lock that helps to grasp the tissue firmly for a longer period of time without fatigue to the surgeon. It may have a ratchet and attachment for monopolar electrosurgical lead.
    2. *Outer tube with insulating sheath*: It may be made up of silicon or plastic. Utmost care should be taken while cleaning so that insulating sheath should not be damaged or breached. Very small breach in the continuity may be dangerous. Always inspect the sheath prior to surgery.
    3. *Insert*: Insert of the instrument varies only at the tip.

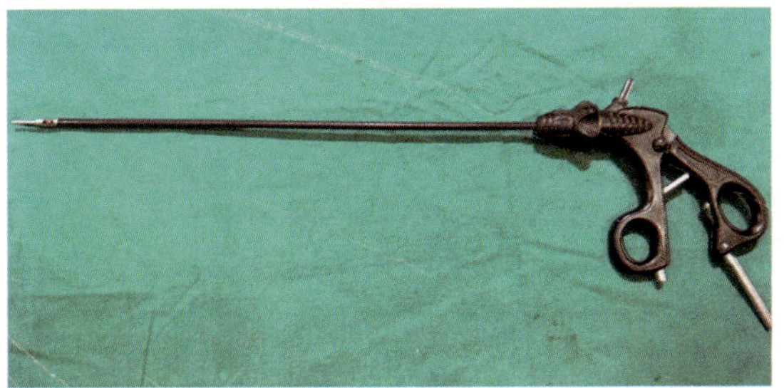

Figure 11.80 Hand instrument for laparoscopy.

Maryland dissector (Fig. 11.81)

- It is useful for dissecting small ductal structures in Calot triangle such as cystic duct and small blood vessels, and for dissection in hernias.
- Grasp and cauterize the bleeding vessel as it has an attachment for monopolar electrosurgical lead.
- As too much pressure is given to the small area by this instrument, it should not be used to grasp very delicate tissues.

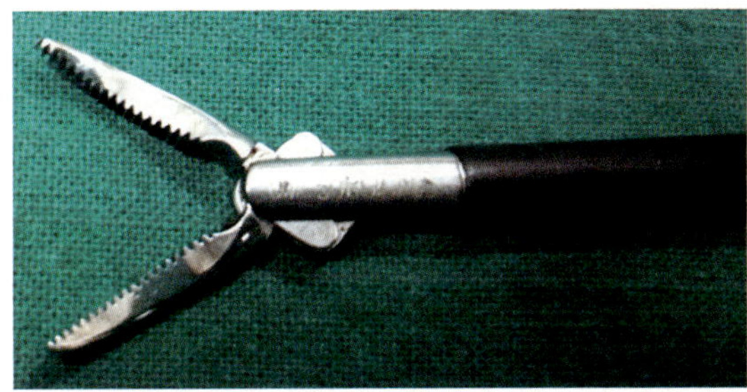

Figure 11.81 Maryland dissector.

Atraumatic grasper (Fig. 11.82)

- It is used to grasp the bowel.
- Blunt tip is very safe and not prone to causing tissue trauma.

Figure 11.82 Atraumatic grasper.

Allis clamp (Fig. 11.83)

Used to grasp the structure that is going to be removed such as gallbladder and thick-walled structures such as stomach

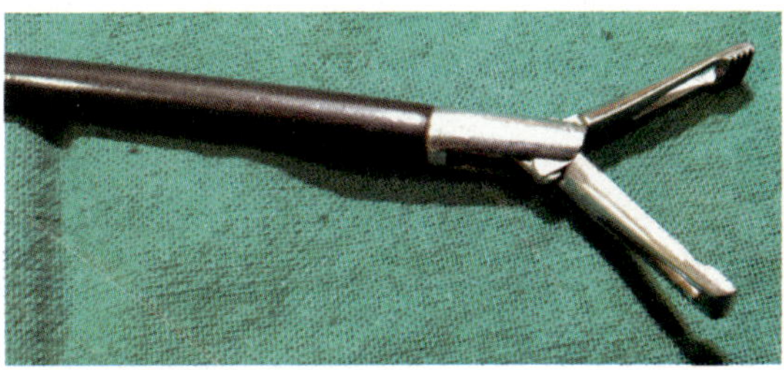

Figure 11.83 Allis clamp.

Scissors (Fig. 11.84)

- Reusable or disposable
- Curved
- Straight
- Micro
- Hook

  Double action curved scissor is commonly used.
- It is used for dissection and division of cystic duct and vessel after ligation.
- Blade must be sharp so it must be checked regularly for sharpness.
- Microhook type is used for cyst or common bile duct incision during CBD exploration.
- Straight type is used for cutting the suture.

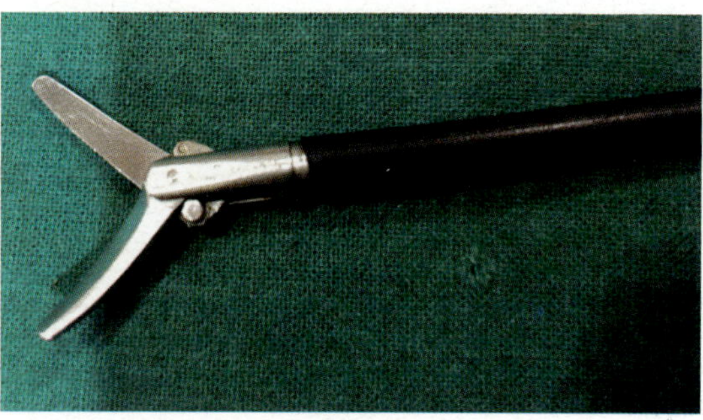

Figure 11.84 Laparoscopic scissor.

Clip applicator (Fig. 11.85)

- It can be reusable or disposable.
- Disposable comes with preloaded 20–30 clips per unit.
- It is available as large (11 mm), medium large (9 mm), and medium (7 mm).
- Medium large is used to clip the cystic duct while medium is for cystic artery.
- Clip size varies from LT 200 to 400.

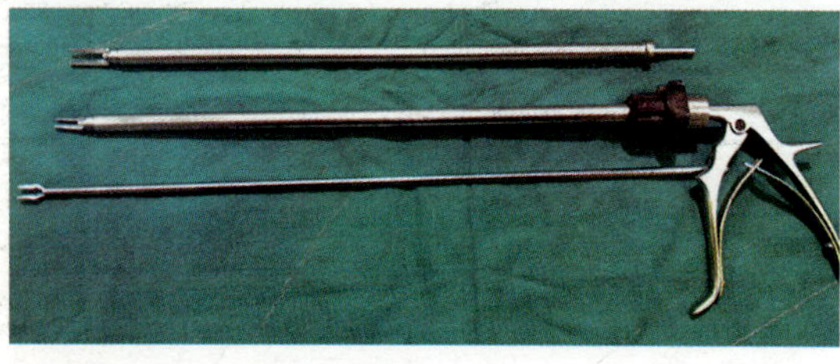

Figure 11.85 Clip applicator.

Hook or spatula (Fig. 11.86)

It is used for dissecting gallbladder from the liver bed.

Figure 11.86 Hook.

Knot pusher (Fig. 11.87)

It is used for extracorporeal knotting of either cystic duct in gall bladder surgery or for appendix in appendectomy.

Prettied loop is available in the market.

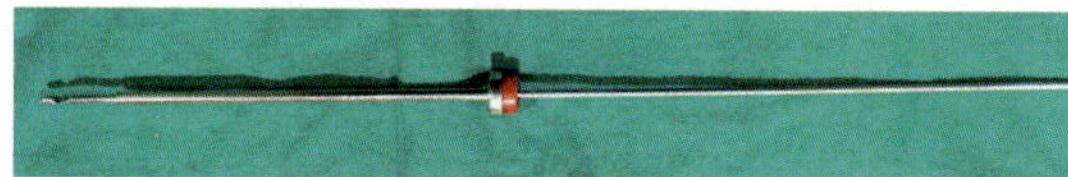

Figure 11.87 Knot pusher.

Needle holder (Fig. 11.88)

- It has a different types of jaw—flat jaw, curved jaw, platypus jaw.
- It is used to grasp the needle for intracorporeal suturing.

Figure 11.88 Needle holder.

HOW TO HOLD COMMON SURGICAL INSTRUMENTS

The proper technique of holding hemostat, scissors, and needle holder is similar.

- Hemostat: The ring finger and thumb are placed through the ring and the index finger is placed on the shaft and together with the middle finger it stabilize the instruments (Fig. 11.89). To apply hemostat on bleeding vessels, tip of the artery forceps should protrude and should be applied with supinated hand with convexity of the curved forceps facing down (Fig. 11.90).

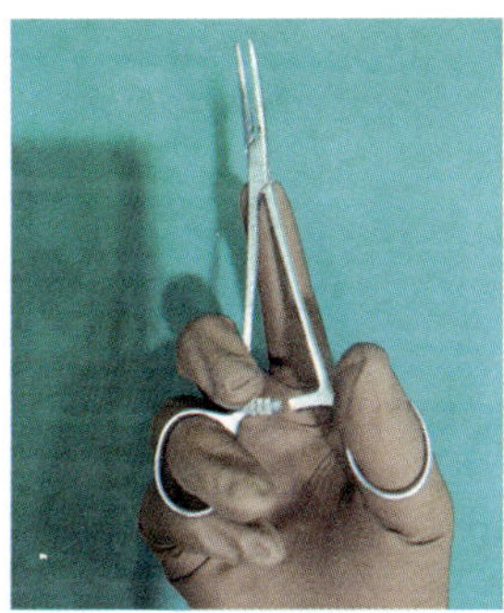

Figure 11.89 Proper technique for holding artery forceps.

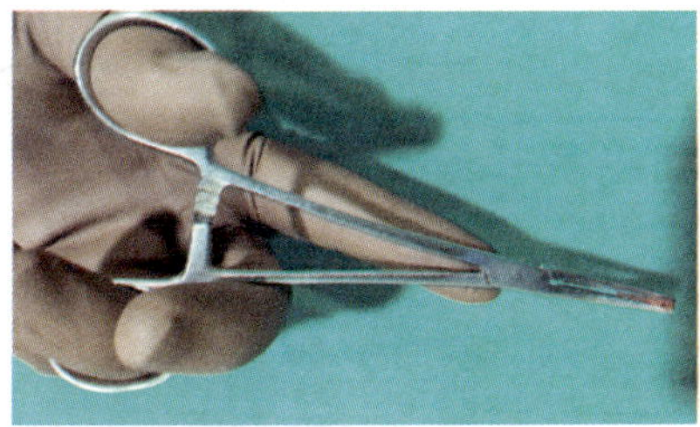

Figure 11.90 Catch the bleeder with artery forceps.

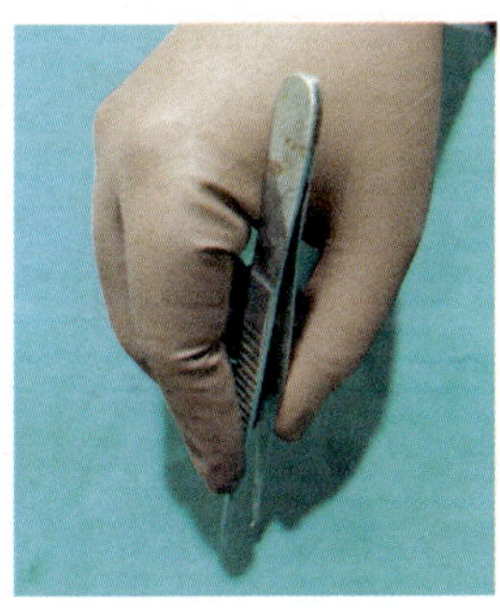

Figure 11.91 Holding of dissecting forceps with jaw in open position.

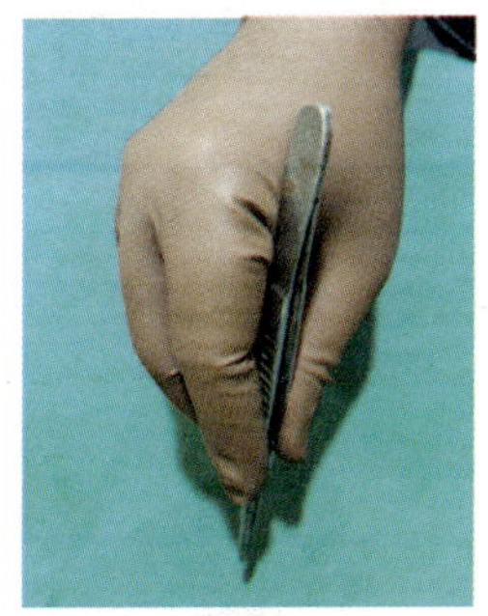

Figure 11.92 Holding of dissecting forceps with jaw in closed position.

- Dissecting forceps: It should be held like a pencil (Figs 11.91 and 11.92).
- Scalpel: The scalpel is held between thumb and middle finger and index finger supports the blade from above (number 22, 10) (Fig. 11.93). Scalpel with number 15 blade should be held like a pencil for finer precise incision (Fig. 11.94).

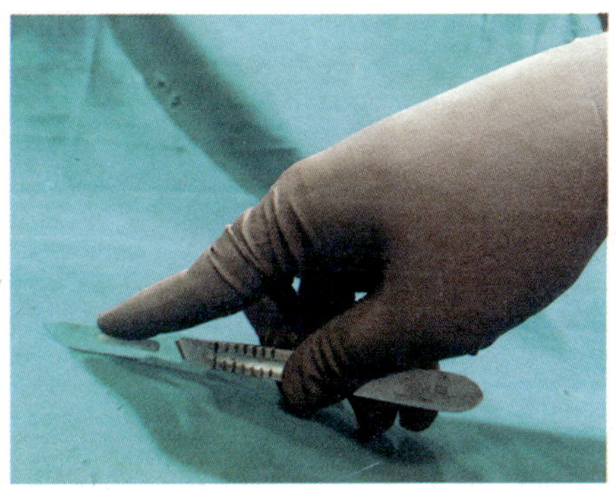

Figure 11.93 Scalpel for incision with 22 number blade.

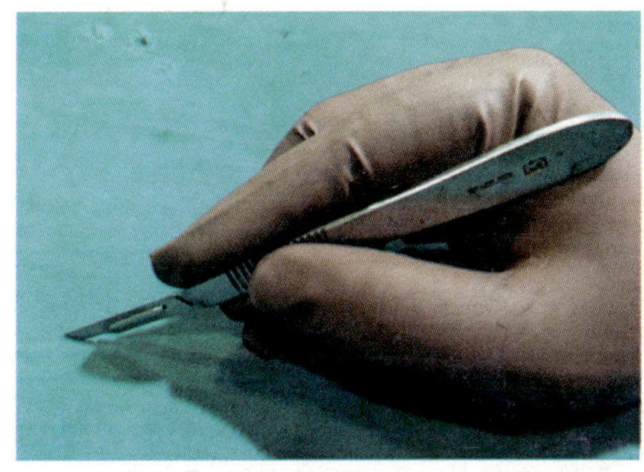

Figure 11.94 Scalpel for incision with 15 number blade.

- Needle holder: It should be held like a hemostat and needle is held at the junction of anterior 2/3rd and posterior 1/3rd (Fig. 11.95).

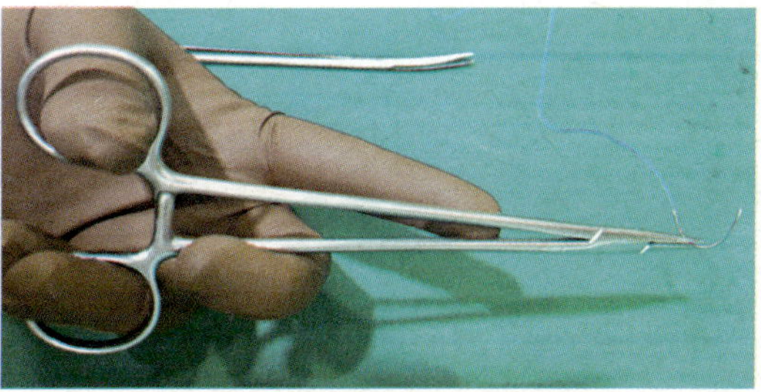

Figure 11.95 Needle is held at the tip of needle holder at the junction of anterior 2/3rd and posterior 1/3 rd of the needle.

To take the stitch, tissue is held with tooth forceps and the needle is passed at the right angle (Fig. 11.96).

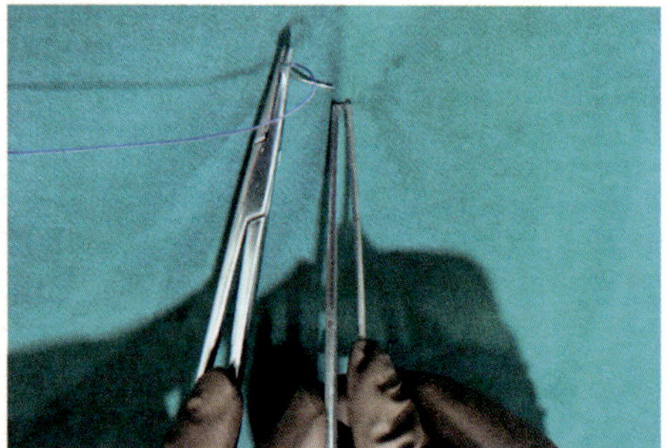

Figure 11.96 Holding of tissue with the tooth forceps and taking stitch.

Other method of holding needle holder is palmer method (Fig. 11.97). Upper ring should rest on the thenar eminence and lower ring is supported by little, ring, and middle fingers while index finger is on the shaft.

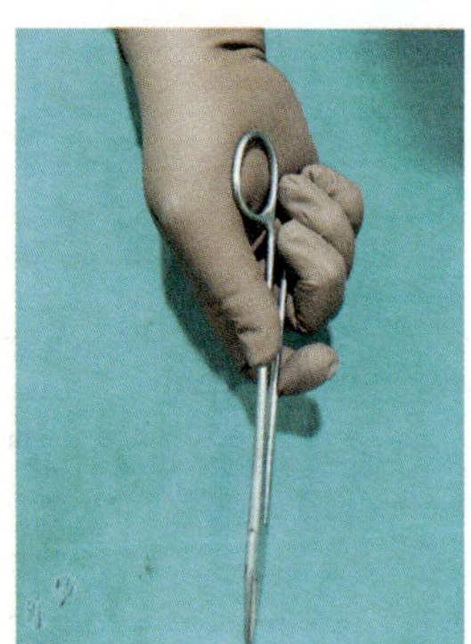

Figure 11.97 Palmer method for holding needle holder.

- Reverse cutting (Fig. 11.98): Cut from the left to right while holding the scissors in right hand.

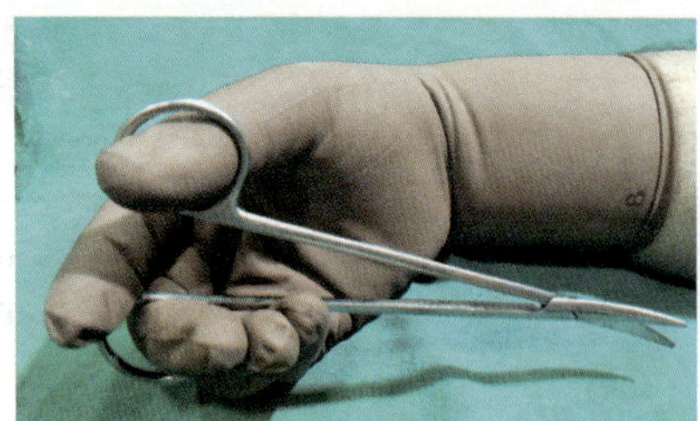

Figure 11.98 Cutting of tissue from left to right.

- Removal of artery forceps with nondominant hand (Fig. 11.99): Hold one ring of artery forceps with thumb and index finger. Insert first phalanx of ring finger into the other ring. Keep the forceps in a steady state with pressure exerted from outside by the little and ring fingers. Gently compress the rings simultaneously and lever the handles in opposite directions to the right angle to the joint which will open up the forceps.

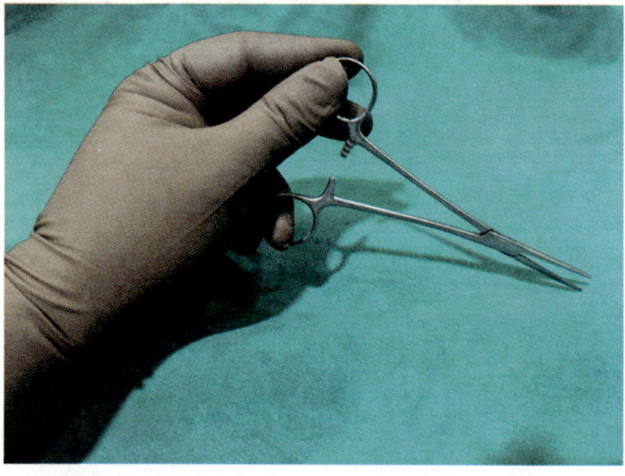

Figure 11.99 Removal of artery forceps with nondominant hand.

- Cutting of suture after application of knot (Fig. 11.100): After holding the scissor properly, tip of the scissor should protrude slightly and knot should be clearly visible while cutting.

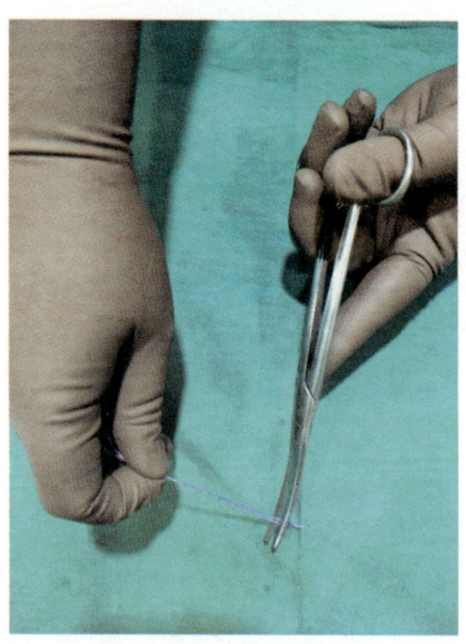

Figure 11.100 Cutting of suture after application of knot.

CHAPTER 12

Suture Materials

CLASSIFICATION

A great variety of suture materials are available for use in surgical operations (Box 12.1). These differ with regard to the nature of their material, tensile strength, absorbability, etc., and may be used according to needs of particular operations.

Absorbability

Various suture materials may be classified on the basis of absorbability as shown in Table 12.1.

Box 12.1 Definitions

- *Ligation*: It refers to occlusion of vessel to prevent bleeding or close off a structure to prevent leakage. There are two types of ligature:
  1. *Free tie:* It is a single strand of suture without needle. After application of hemostat or similar clamp around structures such as blood vessels or ductal structures, suture is tied around the structure under the tip of the hemostat and is removed after first throw and the surgeon tightens the knot using his or her fingers.
  2. *Stick tie (transfixation suture)*: It is a single strand of suture with needle. This technique is used for ligation of deep structure where placement of hemostat is difficult.
- *Suture*: It is the material used to approximate two tissues or surfaces.
- *Memory*: It is the tendency of suture material to return to a given shape.
- *Absorbable sutures*: These are sutures that undergo rapid degradation in tissues, losing their tensile strength within 60 days.
- *Nonabsorbable sutures*: These are sutures that maintain their tensile strength for longer than 60 days.
- *Tensile strength:* It is measured by force (in pounds) that the suture can withstand before it breaks when knotted.
- *Knot strength:* It is a measure of the amount of force required to cause a knot to slip.
- *Elasticity:* It is a suture's intrinsic ability to hold its original form and length after being stretched.
- *Plasticity:* It refers to a material that, when stretched, does not return to its original length.
- *Memory:* It is the inherent ability of a material to return to its former shape after being stretched; polypropylene has a high level of memory.

Table 12.1 Classification on the Basis of Absorbability

Natural	Synthetic
Absorbable	
Plain catgut	Polydioxanone
Chromic catgut	Polyglycolic acid
Fascia lata	Polyglactin 910
	Polyglyconate
	Poliglecaprone
Nonabsorbable	
Silk	Polypropylene
Cotton	Linen
	Polyamide
	Polybutester
	Hexafluoropropylene-VDF
	Polyester

Monofilaments Versus Multifilaments

The suture materials may also be differentiated on the basis of their being monofilaments or multifilaments as shown in the subsequent text. As multifilaments have multiple filaments and crevices in between, chances of infection and sinus formation are more in their case, but knot security is better as compared to that in monofilaments. Multifilaments are preferred when tensile strength and knot security are of prime importance such as ligation and transfixation in plastic surgeries; for suturing of fine and delicate structures, monofilaments are preferred. Tumor cell can adhere to braided suture and can be easily transported to the healthy tissue so in such conditions monofilaments are preferred. Multifilaments may be braided (polyester, polyamide, and polyglactin) and twisted (cotton and linen). In addition to tensile strength and knot security, multifilaments afford pliability and flexibility (Table 12.2).

Monofilaments have a smooth surface, less friction, and less tissue resistance, and are

Table 12.2 Monofilaments Versus Multifilaments

Monofilaments	Multifilaments
Polypropylene	Silk
PDS	Polyglycolic acid
Poliglecaprone	Linen
Nylon	Nylon
Polyglyconate	Polyester
Polybutester	

less traumatic, so extreme care should be taken when handling or tying these sutures. Crushing or crimping can create a weak spot, resulting in suture breakage. They are well suited for vascular surgery.

Monofilaments are more difficult to handle and make a knot. They are stiff and brittle and have a strong memory.

CHARACTERISTICS OF AN IDEAL SUTURE MATERIAL

- Should be pliable for the ability to adjust and secure knot and easy handling
- Should have uniform diameter
- Should have optimal tensile strength
- Should have good knot security
- Should not fray at the ends
- Should be nonallergic and noncapillary
- Should be noncarcinogenic
- Should be cheap and easily available
- Should evoke minimal inflammatory response
- Should have favorable absorption profile
- Should be resistant to infection
- Should be easy to sterilize
- Should not produce any magnetic field around it like steel wire

NAMING OF SUTURE SIZES

- According to the *US Pharmacopeia*, suture size is based on its strength and diameter.
- Size denotes the diameter of the suture material.
- The naming system uses 0 as the baseline.
- As the diameter decreases, more 0s are added or numbers are followed by 0, such as 2-0 and 3-0 (000). More the number of zero, thinner is the suture (Table 12.3).

Table 12.3 Sutures and Their Diameters

USP nomenclature	Diameter (mm)
11-0	0.01
10-0	0.02
9-0	0.03
8-0	0.04
7-0	0.05
6-0	0.06
5-0	0.1
0000	0.15
000	0.2
00	0.3
0	0.35
1	0.4
2	0.5
3	0.6
4	0.6
5	0.7
6	0.8
7	0.9

- So, no .1 will be thicker than 1-0, 2-0, etc., and 2-0 will be thicker than 3-0, etc. The thinnest suture material is 11-0 (used in ophthalmic surgery) and the thickest is 7.
- The tensile strength of suture should not exceed the tensile strength of tissue. The suture should be at least as strong as the tissue from which it is going to pass. The smaller the size, less is the tensile strength suture will have.
- Major suturing materials may be divided into two broad categories: Natural materials and synthetic materials.
- In Europe, metric system is also accepted; it is compatible with SI system. It determines the thickness of the sutures in 1/10 mm.

NATURAL SUTURING MATERIALS

They have good handling and good knotting property. They contain natural protein and absorption is by enzymatic ways. The proteolytic enzymes released from the macrophages and neutrophils digest the tissue substance and cause severe inflammatory reaction.

Absorbable Materials

Catgut

- Its name is derived from the word 'kitgut' (kit: Three-string violin).
- It is prepared from a strip of submucosa of sheep or cow's intestine.
- Knot configuration: 2+1.

Plain catgut (Fig. 12.1)

- Composition: 98% collagen.
- It is absorbed by inflammatory reaction (phagocytosis).
- Absorption time: 70 days. Tensile strength is maintained for 7–10 days (wound support—1 week).
- It is used for tissue that heals rapidly and requires minimal support.
- It is yellowish tan colored.
- Uses
  - In circumcision
  - Subcutaneous tissue closure
  - Ligation of superficial vessels
  - In Lord's plication and plication of hydrocele sac
  - In subtotal excision of hydrocele sac, for continuous locking stitch of the sac
- Advantages
  - Cheap
  - Easily available
  - Presterile
  - Pliable
- Disadvantages
  - It has a gross inflammatory reaction.
  - As it is absorbed by phagocytosis, it cannot be used in the presence of infection.
- Availability: 6-0 to 1 with needle and 4-0 to 3 without needle.

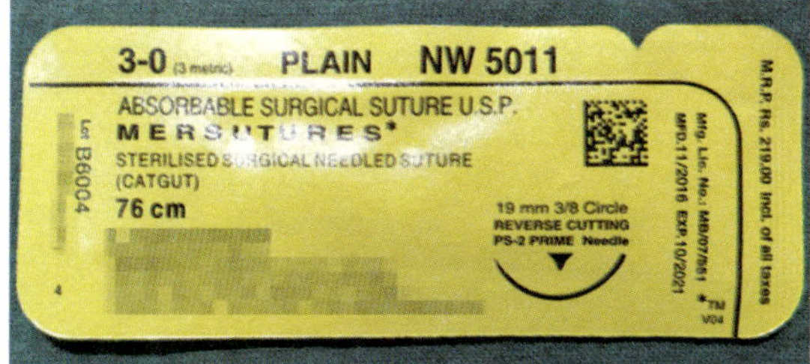

Figure 12.1 Plain catgut.

- Contraindication: It should not be used in the tissue that heals slowly and requires prolonged support.

Chromic catgut (Fig. 12.2)

- It is absorbed by phagocytosis.
- Plain catgut is denatured with chromic acid to make chromic catgut.
- Chromic acid provides resistance to absorption.
- It is of brown color.
- Thirty percent of its strength is retained by the end of 2 weeks.
- Absorption time: 90 days (wound support—2 weeks).

Because of processing with chromic acid, absorption is delayed.

- Uses: These are the same as those of plain catgut.
- Its main use is to close the oral mucosal laceration.
- It is also used to close the skin laceration over fingertip with or without nail bed injury.
- It is used to ligate the base of appendix in open as well as laparoscopic operations.
- Initially it was used for approximation of muscle in laparotomy, appendectomy, and resection and anastomosis, but nowadays, because of the availability of better materials, it is rarely used for this purpose.
- Advantages: These are the same as those of plain catgut. Difference is less tissue reaction as compared to that in plain catgut.
- Sterilization: It is available in preservative fluid (Ethicon fluid: 2.5% formaldehyde and 87.5% denatured absolute alcohol).

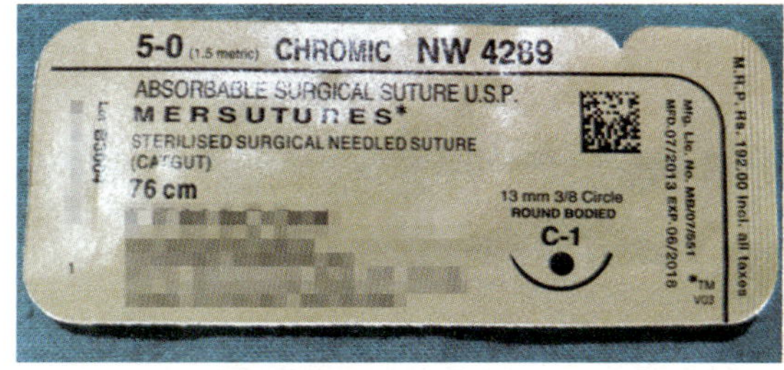

Figure 12.2 Chromic catgut.

Nonabsorbable Materials

Silk (Fig. 12.3)

- It is nonabsorbable.
- It is available in coated or uncoated forms.

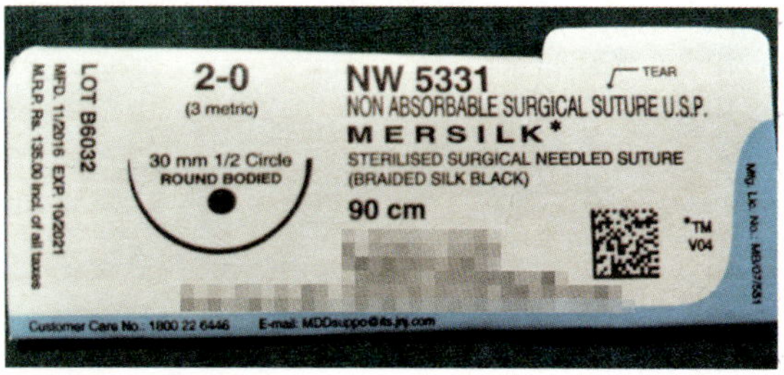

Figure 12.3 Silk.

- Raw silk is obtained from the silkworm cocoon.
- Knot configuration: 2+1.
- Uses
  - Skin closure in various operations
  - Ligation of bleeders
  - Fixation of central lines, chest tubes, and other drainage tubes
  - Resection and anastomosis of bowel for seromuscular layer closure (rarely used nowadays)
  - Closure of perforation of bowel (rarely used nowadays)

Never use silk in kidney, gallbladder, and urinary bladder, as it provides a nidus for stone formation.

- Advantages: It has good knot security and tensile strength.
- Disadvantages
  - Moderate to high tissue reaction
  - Stitch granuloma
  - Infection
  - Least tensile strength among nonabsorbable sutures
- Availability: 10-0 to 2 with needle, and 4-0 to 1 without needle.

Linen

- It is obtained from flax fiber.
- Advantages and disadvantages are the same as in the case of silk.
- Availability: 100–40; 100, thinnest; and 40, thickest.

SYNTHETIC SUTURING MATERIALS

Synthetic suture materials are inert and absorbed by hydrolysis. Proteolytic enzymes are not required. Synthetic suture materials disintegrate when H_2O is released. They produce minimal tissue reaction as compared to natural sutures.

Absorbable Materials

Polydioxanone (PDS) (Fig. 12.4)

- It is a polymer made from polyester poly(*p*-dioxanone).
- It is absorbed by hydrolysis. It is a monofilament.
- Approximately 70% of the tensile strength remains at 2 weeks, 50% at 4 weeks, and 25% at 6 weeks. There is minimal absorption until about the 90th day postoperatively and it essentially completes within 6 months.
- Absorption time: 3–6 months (wound support—45 days).
- Knot configuration: 2+1+1+1.
- Uses
  - Bowel anastomosis
  - Vascular ligature
  - Biliary anastomosis
  - Muscle closure in appendectomy, laparotomy, bladder, and prostate surgery
  - Muscle closure in thoracotomy
  - Bladder closure
- Advantages
  - Soft and pliable
  - Nonallergic
  - Nonpyrogenic
  - Less tissue reaction
  - Lower potential for infection and better knot security than polyglactin 910
  - Can be used in the presence of infection
  - Noncapillary
- Disadvantages
  - Knot security not good (requires more knots)
  - More difficult to use than the braided synthetics because of intrinsic stiffness
  - Cost
- Availability: 10/0 to 2 with needle.

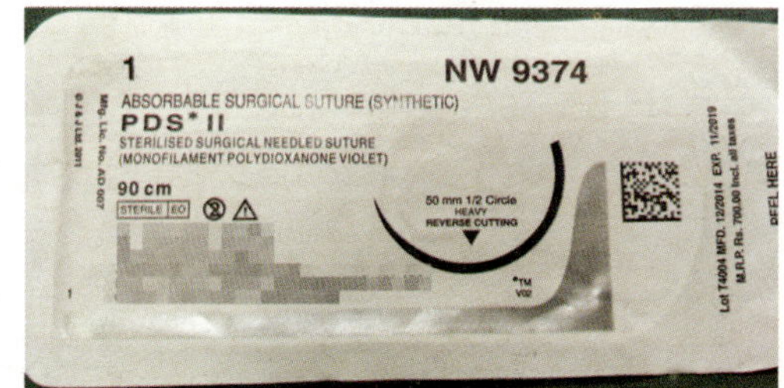

Figure 12.4 Polydioxanone.

Polyglycolic acid (Dexon)

- It is a polymer of glycolic acid.
- It is coated with poloxamer 188.
- Poloxamer acts as a surfactant that enhances surface smoothness.
- It is multifilament, braided, and white or dyed green.
- Absorption: Hydrolysis.
- Absorption time: 90 days.
- Approximately 50% of the tensile strength remains after 21 days.
- Knot configuration: 2+1+1+1.
- Uses: These are the same as those of PDS. It is mainly used where support to the wound is required for a longer time.
- Advantage
  - Excellent knot security
- Disadvantage
  - Binding and snagging in wet suture

Rapid polyglycolic acid

- It is braided and coated multifilament.
- It is coated with polycaprolactone and calcium stearate (1%).
- Absorption time: 42 days.
- Approximately 50% of the tensile strength remains after 7 days.
- Uses
  - Superficial soft-tissue repair of skin and mucosa
  - Circumcision
  - Episiotomy repair
  - Plastic surgery
- It is contraindicated in cardiovascular and neurosurgery and should not be used where wound support is required for more than 7 days.

Polyglactin 910 (Vicryl) (Fig. 12.5)

- It is a copolymer of lactide and glycolide (polyglactin 370).
- It is braided.
- It is absorbed by hydrolysis.
- Seventy-five percent of the tensile strength is retained at 2 weeks.
- Absorption time: 90 days (wound support—21 days).
- Knot configuration: 2+1+1.
- Uses
  - Same as those of PDS
  - Preferable for subcutaneous closure

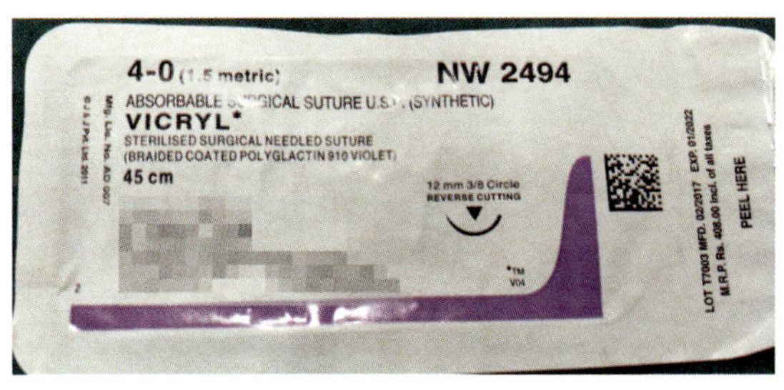

Figure 12.5 Polyglactin 910 (Vicryl®).

- Contraindications
  - Cardiovascular surgery
  - Neurosurgery
  - Should not be used when extended tissue support is required
- Advantages
  - Minimal tissue reaction
  - Less edema
  - Less fraying
  - Knot security
  - Predictable absorption rate
  - Excellent tissue support
  - High flexibility
  - High tensile strength
  - Soft passage through tissue
- Availability: 8-0 to 2 with needle and 5-0 to 2 without needle.

Rapide Vicryl

- Advantage: Initial tensile strength is more, but it loses its tensile strength by the 14th day.
- Absorption time: 6 weeks.
- It is available undyed.
- It is preferable for skin closure where removal of suture is difficult and for suturing of laceration under plaster cast.

Coated Vicryl Plus

- It is Vicryl coated with calcium stearate and polyglactin. The suture becomes smoother on coating.
- It contains triclosan (broad-spectrum antibiotic).
- It is effective against *Staphylococcus aureus*, methicillin-resistant *S. aureus* (MRSA), and methicillin-resistant *Staphylococcus epidermidis* (most often cause surgical site infection) without any adverse effect on normal healing.
- It is available in dyed and undyed forms.
- Absorption: 50–70 days.

Polyglyconate or polytrimethylene carbonate (Maxon)

- It is a copolymer of glycolic acid and trimethylene carbonate.
- Remaining characteristics are same as those of Vicryl.
- It has minimal tissue reactivity, excellent first-throw holding capacity, and smoother knot tie-down than polyglactin 910.
- Uses: It is used for soft-tissue suturing and ligation, and vascular surgery.
- Absorption time: 180 days (wound support—45 days).
- It is absorbed by nonenzymatic hydrolysis. It breaks down into beta-hydroxybutyric acid, glycolic acid, and carbon dioxide. Beta-hydroxybutyric acid and glycolic acid are excreted in urine.
- Availability: 7-0 to 2.

Poliglecaprone 25 (Monocryl) (Fig. 12.6)

- It is a copolymer of glycolide (75%) and epsilon-caprolactone (25%).
- Absorption time: 90–120 days. It is the most pliable, synthetic absorbable suture.
- It is used where high tensile strength is required initially. Sixty to 70% of the tensile strength remains at the 7th day and 30–40% at the 14th day. All tensile strength is lost by 28 days.
- Uses
  - Specially used for subcuticular stitch
  - Can be used as a ligature
  - Used in gastrointestinal and muscle surgery
- Availability: 8-0 to 2 with needle.

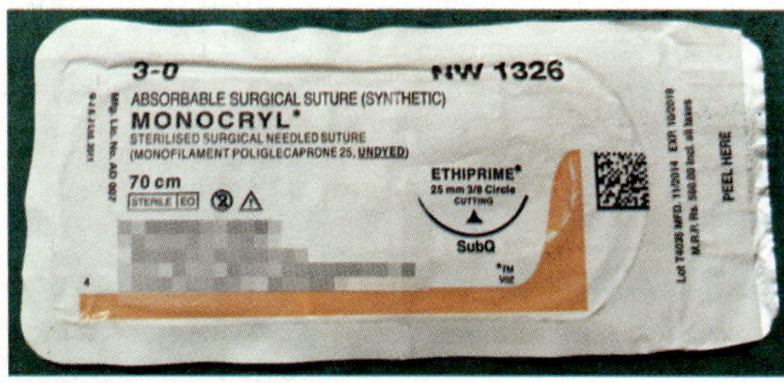

Figure 12.6 Poliglecaprone 25 (Monocryl®).

Polyglytone

- It is a compound of glycolide + caprolactone + trimethylene carbonate + lactide.
- It is a monofilament.
- Absorption: 60 days (wound support—10 days).
- Its main use is in skin closure.
- Advantages: It has good tensile strength, less tissue reaction, and good knot security.
- Disadvantage: Wound dehiscence is present.

Nonabsorbable Materials

Polypropylene (Prolene) (Fig. 12.7)

- It is a polymer of propylene.
- It has monofilaments.
- Its tensile strength >1 year (infinite).
- Knot configuration: 2+1+1+1.
- Knot security is best among all monofilaments.
- It is the best suitable suture for contaminated and infected wounds to minimize lateral sinus formation and suture extrusion.
- Scalp and dark-skinned individuals: It is easily identified due to its color.
- Uses
  - Cardiovascular surgery
  - Plastic surgery
  - Hernia repair
  - Hernioplasty
  - Subcuticular stitch
  - Ophthalmic surgery
  - Mass closure in laparotomy and kidney exposure
- Advantages and disadvantages are the same as for other monofilaments.
- Availability: 10-0 to 1.

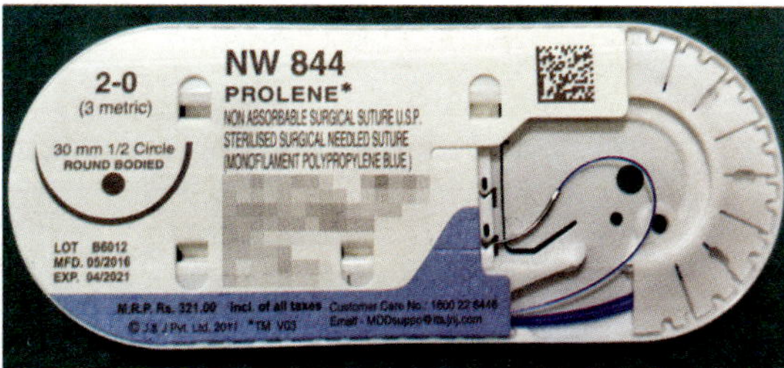

Figure 12.7 Polypropylene (Prolene®).

Hexafluoropropylene-VDF

It is a polymer of poly(vinylidene fluoride) and poly(vinylidene fluoride-co-hexafluoropropylene).

Rest of the things are the same as for polypropylene.

Polyamide (Ethilon) (Fig. 12.8)

- It is monofilament polyamide.
- Knot configuration: 2+1+1+1.

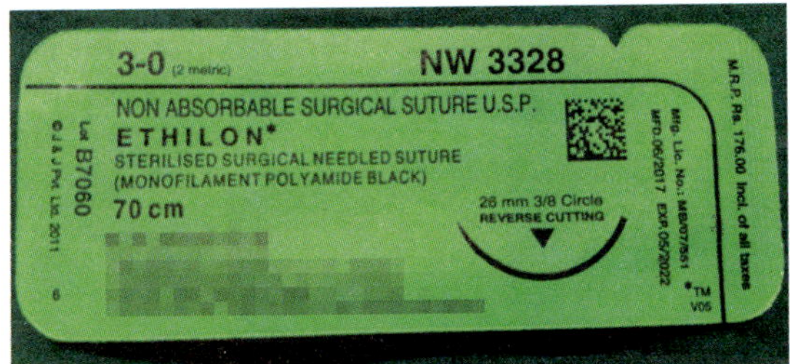

Figure 12.8 Polyamide (Ethilon).

- Because of its elasticity, it is suitable for retention and skin closure.
- Uses
  - Single layer closure in laparotomy (no. 1)
  - Tension closure in burst abdomen (no. 1)
  - Skin closure in various surgeries
  - Fine suture in microsurgery

Nylon (undyed Ethilon)

- It is a polyamide polymer.
- Knot configuration: 2+1+1+1.
- Uses: These are the same as those of Prolene, except vascular procedure.
- Availability: 10-0 to 2 with needle and 4-0 to 2 without needle.

It was discovered at the same time in New York and London; hence, it is known as nylon.

Polybutester (Vascufil)

- It is made up of polytetramethylene, ether, glycol, and polybutylene terephthalate.
- It is a monofilament.
- Its tensile strength >1 year (infinite).
- Uses: These are the same as those of other monofilaments. It is particularly preferred in plastic surgery and cardiothoracic surgery because of its pliability. It has a decreased potential for suture marks as it expands if wound edema develops.
- It is the strongest nonmetallic suture.

Polyester (Ethibond Excel)[1] (Fig. 12.9)

- It is composed of polyester uniformly coated with polybutilate.
- It is braided polyester fiber strand.
- Polybutilate acts as a surgical suture lubricant. It allows easy passage of the braided strands through the tissues and provides excellent pliability, handling qualities, and smooth tie-down with each throw of the knot.
- It is used primarily in cardiovascular surgery, for vessel anastomosis, and placement of prosthetic materials.

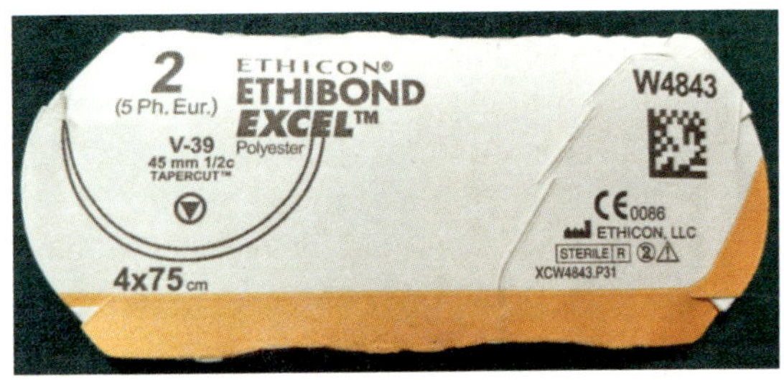

Figure 12.9 Polyester (Ethibond Excel®).

SUTURE CHOICE

- Vascular surgery: Polyester fiber, Ethibond, and polypropylene are used.
- Skin: Polyamide, polypropylene, and black silk-coated polyglactin 910 are used.
- Subcutaneous tissue: Either polypropylene or poliglecaprone is used.
- Fascia regains approximately half of its original strength in 2 months. It may take up to a year to regain maximum strength: Nonabsorbable suture such as polypropylene or absorbable suture with longer duration of wound support such as PDS is used.
- Tendon repair: Polyester and stainless steel are used.
- Gallbladder and biliary tract: Absorbable suture of finest size is preferred such as PDS.
- Stomach: Polyglactin 910 or polypropylene is used.
- Small intestine: Absorbable suture such as polyglactin 910 is preferred.
- Colon: Leakage from the colonic anastomosis is more serious as compared to that from other site in the gastrointestinal tract. Absorbable suture is used. Suture is passed through the submucosa and taking mucosa is avoided because of high microbial contamination.
- Rectum: Large bite of muscle is taken and tied carefully to avoid cut-through as rectum below the pelvic peritoneum does not contain serosa. Monofilament suture is preferred.

- Solid organ within the abdominal cavity such as spleen, liver, and kidney is closed with polyglactin 910.
- Peritoneum does not require to be closed.
- Subcutaneous fat and muscle usually do not hold the suture well; if required, loose polyglactin 910 suture may be placed.
- Nail bed: Chromic catgut or polyglactin 910 is used.
- Lacerations underneath casts or splints: Polyglactin 910, Rapide, or chromic catgut is used.
- Tongue or oral mucosa lacerations: Chromic catgut or polyglactin is used.
- Dermal closure of deep facial lacerations: poliglecaprone 910 or polyglecaprone 25 is used.

STERILIZATION OF SUTURES

- Ethylene oxide
  - PDS
  - Polyglactin 910
  - Polypropylene
  - Polyglycolic acid
  - Silk
  - Linen
- Gamma radiation
  - Catgut
  - Polyamide
  - Polyester fiber (Mersilene)

Pearls

- Barbour thread is linen.
- Sutupack is a polyamide.
- Tissue reaction of sutures in descending order is as follows: Chromic catgut and catgut (strong); linen, silk, and polyamide (average); and polypropylene, polyglycolic acid, and polydioxanone (minimal).
- It is best to use a smaller suture such as 5-0 and 6-0 on face. It is associated with less scarring and produces better cosmetic results. On areas where cosmetic concerns are not of much importance, 3-0 and 4-0 are the best sutures. Use a smaller suture on children due to their delicate skin.
- Loss of tensile strength and rate of absorption are different. It is possible that a suture can lose tensile strength rapidly and yet be absorbed slowly—or it can retain adequate tensile strength throughout wound healing, followed by rapid absorption.
- Selection of suture material
  - Tissue that heals rapidly such as stomach and bladder requires an absorbable suture.
  - Tissue that heals slowly such as skin, tendon, and fascia is usually closed with a nonabsorbable suture.
  - In biliary and urinary tract, use a rapidly absorbable suture because foreign material in the presence of a fluid high in crystalloids acts as a nidus for stone formation.
  - Where cosmetic results are important, use small, fine, inert monofilament, subcuticular stitch, and topical skin adhesive.
  - For closing subcutaneous blood vessels, an absorbable suture is used (it can also be cauterized with electrocautery).
  - In gastrointestinal tract, single-layer or double-layer closure is performed. Second layer is interrupted and inner layer is continuous. For inner layer, an absorbable suture such as polyglactin 910 (Vicryl) is used. For outer layer, polypropylene, polydioxanone, or silk is used.
- What is the difference between hydrolysis and enzymatic absorption?
  - *Enzymatic absorption*: It is active and done by cellular elements. It is seen with natural suture materials that contain proteins. It produces severe tissue reaction, acute inflammatory reaction, formation of the microabscesses, and pathological scar tissue.
  - *Hydrolysis*: It is passive and done without participation of the cellular elements. It is seen with the synthetic suture material. During the process, the chemical and physical bonds located between the molecules of the suture material become loose and the thread is disintegrated to such substances that are similar to the natural metabolites of the body and are lost from the body.

Reference

1. https://www.sutureonline.com/wound-closure-manual. Accessed on 26th march 2018.

CHAPTER 13

Specimens

DESCRIPTION OF SPECIMENS IN THE EXAMINATION

- Identify the organ in the question.
- Identify the pathology.
- List the identification points of the organ and describe the disease.
- Sometimes, an examiner may ask in viva questions whether the specimen is antemortem or postmortem; if the specimen is consistent with the standard surgical procedures, then it is antemortem.

  Some of the examples of specimen are as follows:
- Specimen inside the jar is a pear-shaped hollow organ with a tubular end.
- Probably, it is a cystic duct with a thickened wall of the organ and stone.
- The likely pathology is gallstone leading to chronic cholecystitis.

Figure 13.1 Carcinoma stomach.

GASTROINTESTINAL TRACT

CARCINOMA STOMACH (Fig. 13.1)

- *Identification*
  - Shape, rugosity, lesser curvature, and greater curvature

VIVA QUESTIONS

1. How do patients with carcinoma stomach present?

A Clinical features

- Anorexia and weight loss (most common presentation)
- Abdominal pain
- Acute GI bleeding
- Anemia
- Dysphagia (common in proximal tumor)
- Abdominal lump
- Gastric outlet obstruction (distal tumor)
- Advanced disease
  - Left supraclavicular node enlargement (Virchow node)/(Troisier sign)
  - Sister Joseph nodule (periumbilical nodule)
  - Blumer shelf (on per rectal examination—hard nodule anteriorly)
  - Left axillary node (Irish node)
  - Ascites
  - Pleural effusion
  - Migrating thrombophlebitis (Trousseau syndrome)
  - Enlarged ovary (Krukenberg tumor)

Symptoms of carcinoma stomach can be divided into five groups:

- *Dyspepsia*: New onset of dyspepsia after 40 years
- *Silent*: Cancer of body of the stomach
- *Onset*: Insidious with anemia, anorexia, and asthenia

- *Obstruction*: Usually with pyloric tumor
- *Lump*: In the epigastric region

One can remember the symptoms as the acronym SOLD.

2. How does carcinoma of stomach spread?

A
- *Direct*: To adjacent organs such as pancreas, colon, and liver
- *Lymphatic*
  - Left gastric
  - Right gastric
  - Splenic
  - Gastroepiploic
  - Subpyloric node
    - *N1*: Nodes within 3 cm of the tumor
    - *N2*: Along with the hepatic and splenic artery
    - *N3*: Hepatoduodenal, retropancreatic, and root of mesentery
    - *N4*: Para-aortic
- *Blood*: Liver and other organs
- *Transcoelomic*
  - Blumer shelf
  - Krukenberg tumor
  - Sister Joseph nodule

3. How will you diagnose carcinoma stomach?

A Clinical presentation plus the following:

- *Upper GI endoscopy*: Growth is seen, and simultaneous biopsy can be taken. Magnifying endoscopy with narrow band imaging (NBI) is accurate and reliable for diagnosis of early gastric cancer. Endocytoscopy and virtual endoscopy will be available in near future for screening of the stomach.
- *Chest X-ray*: It is used to rule out metastases.
- *Barium meal*: Nowadays, it is less preferred (compared to endoscopy).
- *Stool*: It helps in the diagnosis of melena.
- CT abdomen
  - Extent of the tumor
  - Ascites
  - Nodal status
  - Liver metastases
- *Endoscopic ultrasound* (EUS): It is most accurate in distinguishing early gastric cancer from advanced cancer. Depth of tumor invasion can be assessed and guided FNA of lymph node can be taken (depth of invasion and LN status are the best prognostic factors).
- *CT scan chest*: It is preferred over chest radiograph to rule out metastases.
- *Diagnostic laparoscopy*: It helps to decide resectability. It is particularly helpful in detection of small liver and peritoneal metastases. It is most useful in proximal tumors or with adenopathy on spiral CT.
- *PET scan*: It helps to diagnose distant metastases. It should be considered before major surgery, in high-risk tumor surgery, and in patients with multiple comorbidities.

4. How will you treat carcinoma stomach?

A Criteria for inoperability

- Invasion of a major vascular structure (aorta, hepatic artery, or celiac axis/proximal splenic artery)
- Left supraclavicular lymph node
- Ascites
- Liver metastases

Treatment in operable cases

- NCCN guidelines:
  - Tis or T1a: Surgery alone or endoscopic mucosal resection (EMR) (carcinoma in situ, invasion of lamina propria and muscularis mucosae).
  - T1b: Surgery alone (invasion of submucosa)
  - T2: Surgery or neoadjuvant chemotherapy or neoadjuvant chemoradiation (invasion of muscularis propria)
  - Indications for adjuvant treatment
    - T3N0
    - Positive lymph nodes, regardless of T stage
- Early gastric cancer (carcinoma limited to the gastric mucosa or submucosa, regardless of involvement of the regional lymph nodes) can be treated with EMR. ESD is preferred over EMR because ESD permits en bloc resection and also permits deeper resection margin in a patient with submucosal involvement.
- The Japanese group follows the following indications for EMR *or* endoscopic submucosal dissection (ESD): Differentiated adenocarcinoma without ulceration, intestinal type, absence of lymphovascular invasion, intramucosal cancer, size of the lesion less than 20 mm, without any endoscopic findings

of ulceration, and no LN involvement or metastasis by computed tomography

- Gastrectomy indicated in case of tumor >30 mm size, differentiated malignancy with ulceration, difficult en bloc resection, lymphovascular invasion and positive margin after EMR or ESD
- For distal carcinoma (distal two-third): Nowadays, most surgeons are doing radical subtotal gastrectomy or distal gastrectomy with D2 dissection and reconstruction with Billroth II gastrojejunostomy.
- Total gastrectomy is performed in case of proximal (upper third) carcinoma of the stomach.
- Frozen section confirmation of negative margin is a must (R0 resection). There is no microscopic or macroscopic margin residue. R1 is microscopic, and R2 is macroscopic.
- Roux-en-y is considered for small gastric remnants.
- Total gastrectomy with D2 dissection with jejunal pouch/esophageal anastomosis is done for fundus and proximal gastric carcinoma.
- Tumor in the distal esophagus, cardia, or gastroesophageal junction: Transthoracic or transhiatal esophagogastrectomy with D2 dissection is done.
- D1 gastrectomy: Removal of N1 group of lymph node is done.
- D2 gastrectomy: Removal of N2 group of lymph node

Treatment in inoperable cases

- Palliative anterior gastrojejunostomy can be performed.
- Linitis plastica: Feeding jejunostomy is done.
- NCCN recommends preoperative chemoradiation therapy for localized GEJ adenocarcinoma and perioperative chemotherapy or postoperative chemoradiation therapy for localized gastric adenocarcinoma.
- Chemotherapy: Most commonly used regimen is Cunningham's Royal Marsden regime—ECF (combination of epirubicin, cisplatin, and 5-FU).
- Adjuvant chemotherapies and radiotherapies in stages II and III of the disease (combination of epirubicin, cisplatin, and 5-FU or 5-FU, doxorubicin, and mitomycin) are given.
- Another regimen is the following: Oral fluoropyrimidine, ftorafur (tegafur), gimeracil, and oteracil.

5. What is the difference between partial gastrectomy, subtotal gastrectomy, and antrectomy?

A
- *Partial gastrectomy*: 60–75% of the stomach is removed
- *Subtotal gastrectomy*: 80% of the stomach is removed
- *Antrectomy*: 35% of the distal stomach is removed

6. What are the paraneoplastic manifestations in gastric cancer?

A
- Migrating thrombophlebitis (Trousseau syndrome)
- Nephrotic syndrome
- Acanthosis nigricans (axilla and groin)
- DIC
- Deep vein thrombosis
- Peripheral neuropathies
- Polyarteritis nodosa
- Microangiopathic hemolytic anemia
- Diffuse seborrheic keratoses (sign of Leser-Trélat)

BEZOAR

Bezoar is concretion of ingested material. It has the following varieties:

- Trichobezoar—hairball
- Phytobezoar—vegetables
- Lactobezoar—milk
- Antacid bezoar

Trichobezoar (Fig. 13.2)

- *Identification*
  - Hairball is present.
  - On examination, a palpable abdominal lump is seen.
  - Involvement of entire small bowel with hairball is known as Rapunzel syndrome.
  - On plain X-ray abdomen, a mottled appearance is shown.
  - It is diagnosed on endoscopy.

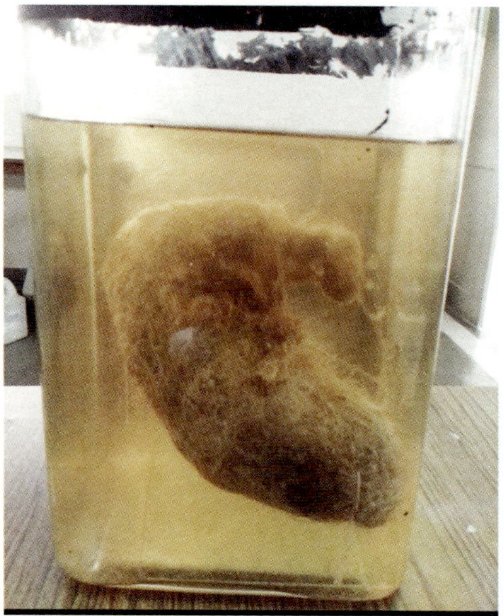

Figure 13.2 Trichobezoar.

VIVA QUESTIONS

1. What are the predisposing conditions for bezoar?

A
- These include pre-existing gastroduodenal pathology, gastric surgery, vagotomy, pyloroplasty, and gastroparesis.
- Predisposing factors, especially for pharmacobezoars, are gastric outlet obstruction, dehydration, and anticholinergic medications and opiates.

2. Describe clinical presentation of a patient with trichobezoar.

A
- Young psychiatric females, h/o trichophagia (eating hair), halitosis, alopecia
- Nausea, vomiting, anorexia, and weight loss
- Pain presents as a late feature
- Large, firm, freely mobile, nontender lump in the epigastric region

3. How will you investigate a case of trichobezoar?

A
- Ultrasonography (USG): Mass in the stomach
- Upper GI endoscopy
- Barium meal: Filling defect in the stomach with penetration of barium into mass

4. What is the treatment for bezoar?

A Chemical dissolution
- It is recommended for mild symptoms due to bezoar.
- It is not recommended for trichobezoar, moderate to severe symptoms, and pharmacobezoars.
- Coca-Cola, papain, acetyl cysteine, and cellulose are used for chemical dissolution.

Endoscopic therapy
- Fragmentation through water jet, Nd:YAG laser, monopolar diathermy knife, extracorporeal lithotripsy, and injection of enzyme solutions or Coca-Cola
- Adjuvant prokinetic drugs can be given along with chemical dissolution and endoscopic therapy

Surgery

Indicated in patients with failed chemical and endoscopic methods, complicated bezoar with obstruction, perforation, and major bleeding
- Removal through open surgical technique—gastrotomy
- For Rapunzel syndrome—enterotomy + gastrotomy

For prevention of recurrence, antipsychiatric medication and dietary advice given

MECKEL DIVERTICULUM (Fig. 13.3)

- *Identification*
  - Blind pouch on the antimesenteric border of small bowel (transverse mucosal fold on inner side and on outer surface no features suggestive of colon)

VIVA QUESTIONS

1. What is Meckel diverticulum?

A Meckel diverticulum is a true diverticulum arising from the antimesenteric border of small intestine and contains all coats of intestine.

2. What is embryological origin of Meckel diverticulum?

A Persistence of vitelline duct remnant on the ileal border

3. What is Littre hernia?

A When hernia content is Meckel diverticulum, it is known as Littre hernia.

4. Which is the investigation of choice for diagnosis of Meckel diverticulum?

A Technetium-99m pertechnetate scan

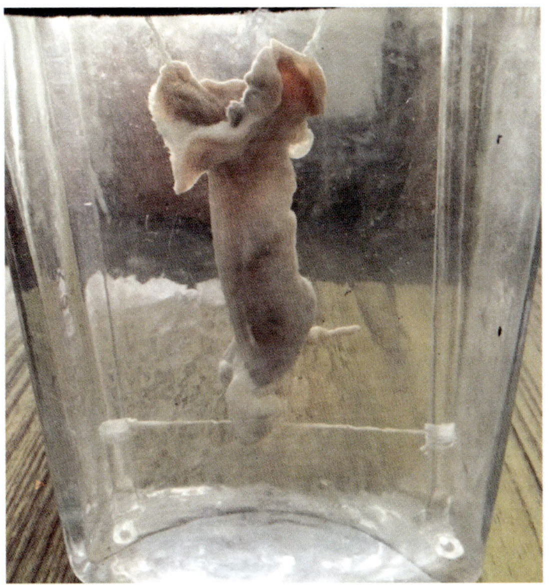

Figure 13.3 Meckel diverticulum.

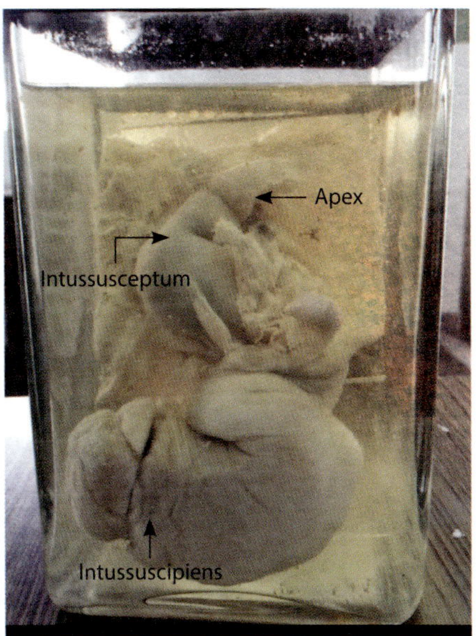

Figure 13.4 Intussusception.

5. What are the causes of bleeding in case of Meckel diverticulum?

A
- Ileal ulceration
- Intussusception
- Chronic peptic ulcer
- Littre hernia

6. What are the causes of obstruction in Meckel diverticulum?

A
- Intussusception
- Volvulus
- Torsion
- Abdominal wall hernia
- Meckel diverticulitis

For further details, see Chapter 16, *Frequently Asked Questions*.

INTUSSUSCEPTION (Fig. 13.4)

- *Identification*
  - Intussusception is invagination of one portion of bowel into another portion of bowel (usually proximal portion into the distal one).

VIVA QUESTIONS

1. What is the clinical presentation of a patient with intussusception?

A
- Age: It is 6–9 months.
- Intermittent cramp-like pain in abdomen is present. Between attacks, the child may be listless and during attack he/she appears pale.
- Red currant jelly stool (late sign) is present.
- Sausage-shaped lump is present in the right upper quadrant with concavity toward the umbilicus.
- Absence of bowel in right lower quadrant leads to feeling of emptiness in the right iliac fossa (Dance sign).
- Per-rectal examination: Apex of the intussusception is palpable or even protruding from the anal canal or blood on gloved finger.
- Failure to relieve in time may lead to dehydration, abdominal distention from small bowel obstruction, and peritonitis from gangrene of the bowel. Rarely, it may reduce spontaneously due to sloughing of intussusception.

2. What are the causes of intussusception?

A
- Idiopathic: Bacterial or viral infection (frequently associated with recent upper respiratory tract infection) and inflamed Peyer patches are the initiating events.
- Secondary to lead point
  - Anatomic (Meckel diverticulum, appendix)
  - Genetic (Peutz–Jeghers syndrome)
  - Tumor (lipoma, lymphoma)
  - Vascular (HSP)

- Infection (bacterial, pseudomembranous enterocolitis)
- Traumatic
- Secondary to foreign body
- Postsurgical

3. What are the different types of intussusception?

A
- Ileocolic (most common)
- Ileoileocolic
- Ileoileal
- Colocolic (most common in adults)

4. What is sonographic appearance of intussusception?

A Pseudokidney or target sign

CT scan is currently the most sensitive investigation showing target or sausage-shaped soft tissue mass.

5. What is retrograde intussusception?

A When the distal bowel invaginates into proximal one, it is known as retrograde intussusception (postsurgery gastrojejunostomy).

6. How will you treat intussusception?

A
- Perform resuscitation with IV fluids and administration of IV antibiotics.
- Assess for the suitability for the radiological reduction. Absence of peritonitis, shock, and pathological lead point makes the patient suitable for radiographic procedure.
- Premedicate the patient with papaveretum and scopolamine.
- First, pneumatic reduction should be tried; if this reduction fails, then hydrostatic reduction should be done.
- Reduction is accomplished by free reflux of air or fluid into the small bowel.

Indications of surgery

- When radiological reduction fails
- Evidence of peritonitis or perforation
- Shock
- Known pathological lead point
- Recurrent intussusception more than three times

Laparoscopy or laparotomy is done. Steps in performing laparotomy:

- Make right lower quadrant incision.
- Perform gentle reduction by distal pressure and milking. Do not try to pull the bowel.
- Inspect bowel for viability (dark color becoming light on reduction, visible mesenteric pulsation, shiny appearance, and visible peristalsis indicate viable bowel).
- Perform appendectomy.

In case of nonviable bowel, do resection and anastomosis.

ILEAL KOCH'S (Fig. 13.5)

- *Identification*
  - The yellow color is due to caseation and breakdown.
  - Transverse ulcer is present along the long axis of the bowel. Serosa may be studded with tubercles and with thickened bowel wall.
  - Small bowel is present.
  - Types of IC Koch's: These are hyperplastic and ulcerative.
  - Tuberculosis is common in IC region because of abundance of lymphoid tissue and prolonged stasis.

VIVA QUESTIONS

1. Describe the clinical features of ileocecal Koch's.

A
- Abdominal pain (most common)
- Diarrhea
- Weight loss
- Lump in RIF
- Constitutional symptoms

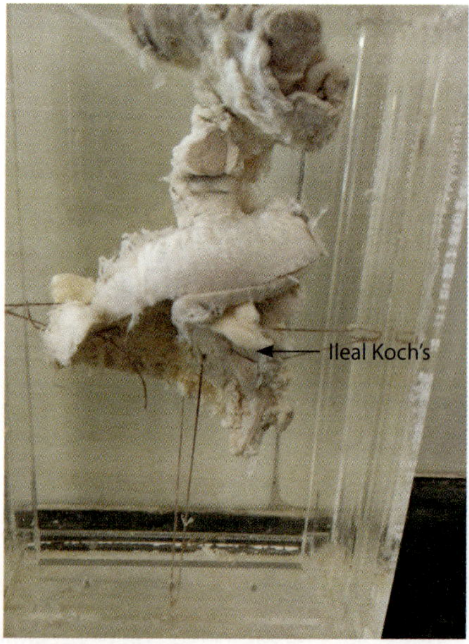

Figure 13.5 Ileal Koch's.

- Small bowel obstruction
- Fistula-in-ano: Multiple with undermined edges and watery discharge
- On examination: Doughy feel due to areas of localized ascites (cocoons)

2. What are the types of intestinal tuberculosis?

A Two types

- *Ulcerative*: Virulence of organism is more as compared to host defense; swallowing of sputum from the pulmonary tuberculosis leads to colonization of the terminal ileal lymphatics with acid fast bacilli.
  - Macroscopically, ulcer is transverse with undermined edges and serosa is studded with tubercles.
  - Microscopically, caseating granuloma with giant cell is present.
- *Hyperplastic*: This occurs when host defense is more as compared to virulence of organism and it is caused by the drinking of contaminated or infected milk.
  - Macroscopically, narrowing of the lumen, stricture, and mesenteric lymphadenopathy are present.
  - Microscopically, hyperplasia and thickening of terminal ileum are present.

3. What are the complications of ileocecal Koch's?

A
- Bleeding P/R
- Obstruction
- Perforation
- Malabsorption
- Ascites (most common)

4. How will you diagnose ileocecal Koch's?

A
- USG abdomen
  - Thickened bowel wall in IC region (alternate echogenic and echo-free areas with interbowel fluid collection—*club sandwich appearance*)
  - Ascites
  - Mesenteric lymphadenopathy
- Plain X-ray abdomen: Calcification of lymph nodes and calcified foci in liver or spleen
- Plain X-ray chest: Pulmonary Koch's
- CT scan abdomen: Findings same as in USG
- Barium meal follow-through
  - *Sterling sign*: Terminal ileal fibrosis; terminal ileum opening into the cecum; contracted cecum
  - *Fleischner sign*: Wide open and thickened IC valve with narrowing of terminal ileum
  - Terminal ileal stricture with pulled-up cecum in the subhepatic region present
- CBC: Lymphocytosis
- Erythrocyte sedimentation rate (ESR): Raised
- Mantoux test: Positive
- Ascitic fluid
  - Routine and microscopic examination
  - Culture and sensitivity
  - AFB staining
  - Albumin (>2.5 g/dL)
  - Serum ascites albumin gradient (SAAG) (<1.1)
  - ADA: Highly sensitive in diagnosis of tuberculosis
- Diagnostic scopy and biopsy: Lower GI endoscopy showing stricture, ulcer, and IC valve deformity
- A cartridge-based nucleic acid amplification test (CBNAAT) performed to rule out rifampicin resistance and categorized as microbiologically confirmed drug-sensitive TB or RIF-resistant TB[1]

5. How will you differentiate between tubercular ulcer and typhoid ulcer?

A

	Tuberculous ulcer	**Typhoid ulcer**
Site	IC region or ileum	Ileum
Shape	Horizontal	Vertical
Floor	Caseous material	Clear
Serosa	Tubercle may be seen	Thinned, no tubercle
Depth	Shallow	Deep
Perforation	Rare	Common in third week

6. What is the treatment of ileocecal Koch's?

A
- New revised guidelines for extrapulmonary tuberculosis (2017)[1] are followed.
  - For new TB cases:
    - Two-month intensive phase consists of administration of four drugs,

such as INH (H), pyrazinamide (Z), rifampicin®, and ethambutol (E) (2HREZ).
    - Four-month continuous phase consists of INH (H), rifampicin (R), and ethambutol (E) (4HRE).
    - Daily treatment is given.
  - For previously treated cases:
    - Three-month intensive phase consists of HREZ plus streptomycin (S). Streptomycin will be stopped after 2 months; 5-month continuous phase consists of HRE (2[HREZS] + 1[HERZ] + 5(HRE]).
    - Drugs should be given as a fixed-dose combination as a daily dose.
  - For multidrug-resistant (MDR) TB:
    - Intensive phase: 6–9 months—kanamycin, levofloxacin, ethambutol, pyrazinamide, ethionamide, and cycloserine
    - Continuous phase: 18 months—levofloxacin, ethambutol, ethionamide, and cycloserine

Changes made in the recent guidelines:
- Daily treatment
- Ethambutol in continuous phase
- Fixed-dose combination as per weight band
- Follow-up of clinical and laboratory investigation
- Long-term follow-up for 2 years

- Surgery is indicated in patients with stricture, adhesion, abscess in mesentery, perforation, and intra-abdominal abscess. It consists of strictureplasty, quadrucolectomy, or hemicolectomy. In case of terminal ileal stricture, if general condition does not permit (extremely ill patients with malnutrition, anemia, and active pulmonary TB), perform only side-to-side ileotransverse anastomosis. In case of perforation, if gross contamination and widespread disease are present, perform exteriorization and resection.

APPENDICITIS (Fig. 13.6)

- *Identification*
  - Long tubular structure, blind-ended
  - Mesoappendix with congested vessel

Figure 13.6 Acute appendicitis.

For details, refer appendicectomy in Chapter 6, *Operative Procedures.*

VIVA QUESTIONS

1. What is the function of human appendix?

A Secretion of immunoglobulins (IgA)

2. What is Sherren triangle?

A It is an imaginary triangle formed by joining the points representing umbilicus, symphysis pubis, and anterior superior iliac spine.

3. What are the anatomical predisposing conditions for appendicitis?

A
- Too long or too short appendix
- Kinked appendix
- External band of adhesion

4. What is the fate of acute appendicitis?

A
- Resolution
- Appendicular lump
- Suppurative appendicitis
- Gangrenous appendicitis
- Perforation—localized or generalized

5. How will you diagnose acute appendicitis?

A Refer section 'Appendicectomy' in Chapter 6.

6. What is appendicular lump?

A When diagnosis is delayed, the body tries to localize the inflammatory process by walling off the pus around the inflamed appendix with adjacent viscera (small bowel, colon), anterior abdominal wall, and omentum.

7. What is 'how do you do' or 'good morning' appendix?

A On cutting peritoneum, if appendix immediately pops out, this condition is known as 'good morning' appendix.

8. What is retrograde appendicectomy?

A When appendicectomy is done from base to tip, it is known as retrograde appendicectomy. This is done when the tip of appendix is not identified (like in subhepatic or retrocolic appendix).

CARCINOMA COLON (Fig. 13.7)

- *Identification*
  - It is growth projecting from inner surface of the colon.
  - Identification of colon is done through teniae coli and appendices epiploicae.

VIVA QUESTIONS

1. Describe the precancerous conditions in carcinoma colon.

A
- Adenoma
- Villous adenoma of the rectum
- Familial adenomatous polyposis
- Ulcerative colitis
- Hereditary nonpolyposis colorectal cancer

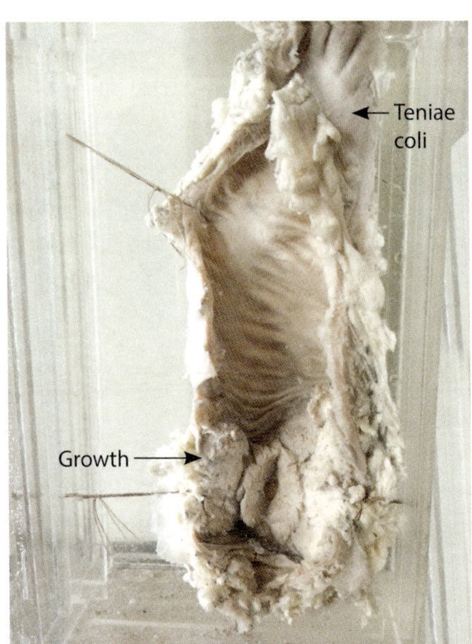

Figure 13.7 Carcinoma colon.

2. When should screening be done for carcinoma colon?

A
- For average-risk population (asymptomatic, no family or personal history of colorectal malignancy, no personal history of polyps or familiar syndrome), start at the age of 50. Perform fecal occult blood testing (FOBT) yearly, flexible sigmoidoscopy every 5 years, both in combination, double contrast or air contrast enema every 5 years, or colonoscopy every 10 years.
- If family history is positive for HNPCC, start screening at the age of 30.
- For FAP, if parents are positive, start flexible sigmoidoscopy at the age of 12 years.

3. What is the difference between right-sided and left-sided colon cancer?

A Right-sided colon cancer presents with anemia and presents late as compared to the left-sided colon cancer, because ulcerative lesions are more common on the right side, while obstructive lesions are more common on the left side. So, left-sided lesions present with alteration in bowel habits or obstruction. Right-sided colon is more capacious and contents are in fluid or semisolid state.

4. What are the macroscopic varieties of colon cancer? Which are the most common microscopic variety and the most common site for colon cancer?

A Macroscopic types
- Annular
- Tubular
- Ulcerative
- Cauliflower

Microscopic variety
- Adenocarcinoma

Most common site is rectum, followed by sigmoid colon followed by cecum.

5. How does colon cancer spread?

A Spread
- *Local*: It invades the surrounding structure.
- *Lymphatic spread*: It is the most common form of spread. It involves epicolic (immediate vicinity of bowel wall), paracolic (along blood vessels proceeding into bowel wall),

intermediate (along branches of superior and inferior mesenteric arteries), and principal (at origin of SMA and IMA) nodes.
- *Blood*: It spreads to liver (most common distant site) and lung.

6. How will you diagnose and treat colon cancer?

A Diagnosis
- CBC: Anemia
- Liver function tests
- USG abdomen: Mass, liver metastases, and ascites
- Stool: Occult blood positive
- Colonoscopy: Advantage over barium enema being that biopsy can be taken simultaneously, and identifies synchronous lesion that is present in up to 5% of cases
- Double contrast barium enema: Good anatomic and topographic details obtained
- Contrast-enhanced CT scan: Details obtained about tumor infiltration locally, lymph node status, and distant metastases
- Plain X-ray abdomen erect: May show obstruction or perforation in acute abdomen
- Chest X-ray: To rule out pulmonary metastases
- PET scan
  - Suspected malignancy but not proven (patients with high tumor marker)
  - Also useful to differentiate scar from recurrence, helps in evaluating liver metastases (single vs. multiple), and also used to evaluate extrahepatic metastatic diseases
- Tumor marker: CEA

Treatment

The aim is to remove tumor en bloc along with its lymphovascular supply.

Indications for total or subtotal colectomy are as follows: Synchronous cancer, presence of adenoma, and/or strong family history of colorectal malignancy (it indicates that entire large bowel is at the risk of cancer and is often referred to as *field defect*).

Metachronous malignancy is also treated similarly.

Stage-wise management
- *Stage 0*: Polyp containing carcinoma in situ—polypectomy.
- *Stage I*—malignant polyp: In the head of polyp with no stalk involvement in pedunculated polyp, polypectomy is performed. However, closed margin with 1-mm poorly differentiated malignancy, lymphovascular invasion, and invasive malignancy in sessile polyp is an indication for segmental colon resection.
- *Stages I and II (localized colon cancer)*: Resection; adjuvant chemotherapy for high-risk young patients in Stage II cancer
- *Stage III (lymph node metastases)*: Adjuvant chemotherapy
- *Stage IV (distant metastases)*
  - If metastases of low volume such as isolated or potentially resectable hepatic lesion, perform resection.
  - High-volume diseases such as carcinomatosis close the abdomen and initiate early chemotherapy

In case of operable tumor, see Table 13.1.

Table 13.1 Treatment Option Depending on Location of Tumor

Location	Treatment
Cecum/ascending colon	Right hemicolectomy
Hepatic flexure/proximal transverse colon	Extended right hemicolectomy
Distal transverse/splenic flexure	Left hemicolectomy
Descending colon	Left hemicolectomy
Sigmoid colon	Sigmoidectomy/left hemicolectomy
Rectum	Refer Chapter 16, *Frequently Asked Questions*

7. What is no-touch technique of Turnbull?

A Early division of feeding vessel supplying the diseased colon before resection can improve the prognosis.

HEPATOBILIARY SYSTEM

GALLBLADDER STONE (Fig. 13.8)

- *Identification*
  - Shape of the gallbladder
  - Cystic duct
  - Stone
  - Thickened wall (suggests chronic cholecystitis)

VIVA QUESTIONS

1. Describe clinical features of chronic cholecystitis.

- There is recurrent attack of steady or colicky epigastric or right upper quadrant pain; it may last up to 1–5 hours.
- It is associated with nausea and vomiting.
- Bloating and belching may be present.
- There may be complications of gallstones (see the subsequent text).
- On examination, tenderness over right hypochondrium is present.

When pain lasts >24 hours, it is a sign of acute cholecystitis.

2. Which factors are essential for the formation of gallstones?

- Cholesterol supersaturation
- Nucleation
- Hypomotility of gallbladder
- Mucus hypersecretion

Figure 13.8 Chronic cholecystitis secondary to GB stone.

3. What are the types of gallstone?

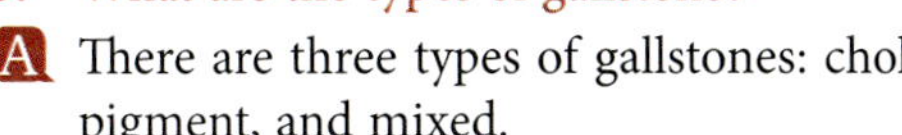

There are three types of gallstones: cholesterol, pigment, and mixed.

In the USA, cholesterol or mixed stones are common while in Asia, pigment stones are common.

- *Cholesterol stones*: Pure cholesterol stone is rare. It invariably contains calcium salts, bile acids, bile pigments, and phospholipids. However, it contains more than 70% cholesterol (w/w). Cholesterol stones are multiple and may be hard or soft, irregular, and mulberry shaped. Primary event is supersaturation of bile with cholesterol.
- *Pigment stones*: They contain <30% cholesterol. Dark color is because of the presence of calcium bilirubinate.
  - *Black pigment stones*: They are usually due to supersaturation of calcium bilirubinate, carbonate, and phosphate. They are seen in patients with hereditary spherocytosis, sickle cell anemia, and cirrhosis. In cirrhosis, there is increased secretion of unconjugated bilirubin.
  - *Brown pigment stones*: They are <1 cm in diameter, soft, and brownish yellow. They contain calcium bilirubinate, palmitate, and calcium stearate plus cholesterol. They are usually formed secondary to bacterial infection in bile stasis. They may be formed in the gallbladder or in the bile duct. They may also be formed in the presence of foreign body such as stent or parasite (*Clonorchis sinensis*, *Ascaris lumbricoides*).

4. Which is the investigation of choice for gallbladder stone?

The investigation of choice for gallbladder pathology, including stones, is USG. X-ray will not help much as 90% of gallstones are radiolucent (90% of renal stones are radiopaque). Gold standard for diagnosis of acute cholecystitis is HIDA scan.

5. **Enumerate the risk factors as well as protective factors for gallstone formation.**

A Risk factors

Age > 40 years, female sex, pregnancy, oral contraceptive pills, obesity, rapid weight loss, family history, serum bilirubin, cirrhosis, hemolytic disease, and Crohn disease

Protective factors

Vegetables high in protein, polysaturated and monounsaturated fats, statins, ascorbic acid, and coffee.

6. **What are the complications of gallstones?**

A
- Chronic cholecystitis
- Acute cholecystitis
- Empyema
- Suppurative cholecystitis
- Gangrenous gallbladder
- Perforation (subhepatic abscess, cholecystoenteric fistula, generalized peritonitis)
- Emphysematous cholecystitis
- Mucocele
- Carcinoma (single stone, >3 cm)
- Gallstone ileus
- Secondary CBD stone (obstructive jaundice, cholangitis, acute pancreatitis)

7. **Describe in brief about cholangitis.**

- Presentation being Charcot triad (see Chapter 16, *Frequently Asked Questions*)
- The 2018 Tokyo guidelines for the diagnosis (Box 13.1) of acute cholangitis[2]

Box 13.1 TG18/TG13 guidelines for diagnosis of acute cholangitis

- Systemic inflammation
  - Fever and/or shaking chills
  - Laboratory findings: An inflammatory response (white blood cell count: <4 or >10 × 1000/μL; increased serum C-reactive protein: >1 mg/dL)
- Cholestasis
  - Jaundice (total bilirubin ≥2 mg/dL)
  - Liver chemistries (elevated alkaline phosphatase [>1.5 × the standard upper limit {STD}], gamma-glutamyl transpeptidase [>1.5 × STD], alanine aminotransferase [>1.5 × STD], aspartate aminotransferase [1.5 × STD])
- Radiological imaging
  - Biliary dilation on imaging
  - Evidence of an etiology on imaging (e.g., a stricture, stone, or stent)

- Suspected cholangitis: One criterion from systemic inflammation plus one from either cholestasis or radiological imaging
- Definite diagnosis: One from each

- *E. coli*, *Streptococcus*, *Klebsiella*, and *B. fragilis* are the common organisms (*Pseudomonas*, skin, and oral flora may be found in patients with biliary tract intervention; anaerobes may be introduced into elderly after biliary surgery)
- USG and CT are the best imaging modalities. CT will better delineate the level of obstruction.

Management

- Fluid resuscitation, correction of electrolytes and coagulopathy, and administration of analgesics are carried out.
- Blood culture and bile culture are performed in all patients to guide antibiotic therapy. Culture should also be obtained from the stent removed.
- Monitoring: Carefully observe for sign of sepsis and septic shock. If the patient develops hypotension, oliguria, and metabolic acidosis, in addition to primary treatment, correct physiological abnormality with supportive measures such as ionotropic support, correction of acidosis, and, if required, ventilator support.
- Broad-spectrum antibiotics should be started followed by culture-specific antibiotic.
  - *Mild*: Piperacillin/tazobactam or ampicillin/sulbactam are given.
  - *Moderate to severe*: Piperacillin/tazobactam plus metronidazole, fluoroquinolones, or carbapenems along with fluconazole may be considered if first line fails to work.
- Drainage of the obstructed system: Obstructed bile duct must be drained as soon as patients stabilize. Emergency decompression may be indicated in patients who did not improve with conservative management for 24 hours.
  - Endoscopic retrograde cholangiopancreatography (ERCP): Endoscopic sphincterotomy with stone extraction and/or stent insertion (depending on the cause of the obstruction)
  - Percutaneous transhepatic bilious drainage (PTC): In case of failed ERCP
  - Open drainage: In case of failed ERCP or PTC or where facilities are not available

8. Describe in brief about diagnosis and management of gallstone disease.

A National Institute for Health and Care Excellence (NICE) guidance for diagnosis and management[3]:

Diagnosis

- USG of the abdomen and liver function tests are performed.
- Magnetic resonance cholangiopancreatography (MRCP): It is indicated in case of ultrasound being negative for common bile duct stone and either or both of the following:
  - Bile duct is dilated.
  - Liver function test results are abnormal.
- EUS is performed in case of negative MRCP.

Management

- Asymptomatic gallbladder stones: Reassurance
- Symptomatic gallbladder stone
  - Laparoscopic cholecystectomy (in case of acute cholecystitis, follow Tokyo guidelines described in section 'Cholecystectomy' in Chapter 6
  - Either bile duct clearance in case of symptomatic or asymptomatic common bile duct stone at the time of surgery (open or laparoscopic common bile duct exploration) or ERCP before or at the time of laparoscopic procedure
- In patients with gallstone disease in whom surgery or ductal clearance is inappropriate:
  - Consider laparoscopic surgery in patients once treated with percutaneous cholecystostomy and fit for surgery.
  - If duct is difficult to clear by ERCP, perform stenting.

9. What is the treatment of acalculous cholecystitis?

A For acalculous cholecystitis (in critically ill patients) due to stasis, sepsis, and ischemia (blood supply is diverted toward vital organs), treatment is cholecystostomy followed by cholecystectomy.

SECONDARIES IN LIVER (Fig. 13.9)

- *Identification*
  - Multiple spherical discrete nodules
  - Central umbilication due to necrosis in larger lesions

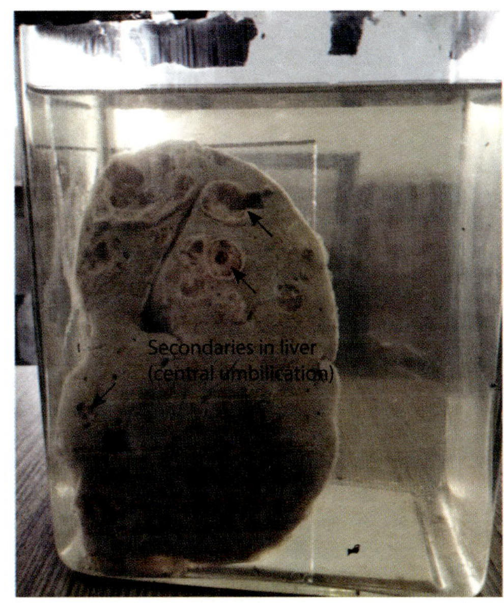

Figure 13.9 Secondaries in liver.

  - Identification of liver by its typical appearance on cut surface—intrahepatic biliary radicles

VIVA QUESTIONS

1. List common primaries.

A Following are the common primaries in descending order of frequency of occurrence:

- Colon
- Pancreas
- Breast
- Ovary
- Rectum

2. How do metastases reach the liver?

A
- Portal vein
- Lymphatics
- Hepatic artery
- Direct (GI, gallbladder)

3. What are the types of liver metastases?

A
- *Nodular*: This is possible with all malignancies.
- *Diffuse*
  - Small cell lung carcinoma
  - Breast
  - Poorly differentiated GI malignancy

4. Describe the clinical presentation of patients with secondaries in liver.

A Symptoms

- Pain
- Ascites

- Jaundice
- Anorexia
- Weight loss
- Fever without demonstrable infection

Signs

- Hepatomegaly
- Palpable abdominal lump
- Portal hypertension
- Rarely friction rub

5. How will you assess patients with secondaries in liver?

A
- Search performed for the primary
- Colonoscopy and CEA for colorectal malignancy
- CA 19-9 pancreatic pathology
- For breast, clinical examination and mammography
- USG abdomen
- Liver function tests
- CT abdomen and pelvis for resectability
- CT chest
- FDG-PET scan to exclude extrahepatic diseases, and baseline PET CT prior to chemotherapy
- MRI: Best for patients who received chemotherapy

6. What are the prognostic factors in case of metastasis from colorectal cancer?

A Fong et al.[4] described clinicopathological factors that give prognostic information:

- Node-positive primary tumor
- Disease-free interval from primary to metastasis <12 months
- More than one hepatic metastasis
- Largest metastases >5 cm
- CEA level more than 200 ng/mL

Each factor is assigned one point.

7. Describe treatment of patients with secondaries in liver.

A In a patient with colorectal primary, surgical management of primaries is required first.

Criteria for resectability

- Criteria for resectability in colorectal liver metastasis
  - R0 resection of both the primary and any extrahepatic site must be present.
  - Two contiguous liver segments must be spared.
  - Future liver remnant (FLR) must be adequate (it is 20–30% for normal liver, 30–40% for steatosis or steatohepatitis, 40–50% for cirrhosis).
  - Vascular inflow and outflow and biliary outflow must be preserved.

Unresectable metastases

In case of unresectable metastases, patients should undergo downstaging with FOLFOX (5-FU, leucovorin, folinic acid, oxaliplatin), FOLFIRI (5-FU, leucovorin, folinic acid, irinotecan), or preoperative portal vein embolization. Then resection should be planned.

For those who are not fit for resection

- Systemic chemotherapy
- Interstitial laser hyperthermia
- Radiofrequency ablation
- Microwave therapy
- Hepatic artery ligation or embolization (particularly useful in neuroendocrine tumor)

8. What are the contraindications for resectability?

A
- Bilobar metastasis or involvement of hilar structure
- Periportal or celiac nodal involvement

9. How will you intraoperatively assess the patients for liver resection?

A
- Search for the local recurrent disease, peritoneal deposits, and regional lymph node involvement.
- Look for periportal and porta hepatis node.
- Perform bimanual and bidigital palpation of liver.
- Perform intraoperative ultrasound. Most sensitive modalities are currently available to detect occult liver metastasis. Patients with multiple unresectable metastases may be saved from major hepatic resection while improving survival by detecting, excising, and abating the residual disease.

GENITOURINARY SYSTEM

WILMS TUMOR (Fig. 13.10)

- *Identification*
  - Uniform pinkish white kidney traversed by fibrous septa; well-defined capsule

Figure 13.10 Wilm's tumor.

VIVA QUESTIONS

1. What is Wilms tumor?

A It is a tumor of kidney containing epithelial and connective tissue elements such as abortive tubules, glomeruli, smooth and skeletal muscle fiber, cartilage, and bone.

2. What is the clinical presentation of patients with Wilms tumor?

A
- Age: 2–5 years
- Left kidney more commonly affected
- Asymptomatic abdominal mass but does not cross the midline (differentiating point from neuroblastoma)
- Abdominal distention
- Pain
- Malaise, weakness, and weight loss
- Hematuria being a late presentation
- Pyrexia
- Hypertension
- Less common symptoms: Hypotension, anemia (from bleeding into tumor), and respiratory symptoms due to lung metastases in advanced cases

3. How does Wilms tumor spread?

A
- *Local*: Adjacent structure
- *Lymphatic*: Para-aortic and paracaval
- *Hematogenous*: Lung, liver, bone, and brain (common)

4. How will you investigate Wilms tumor?

- CBC, renal function tests, urine routine and microscopy, coagulation profile, and cytogenetic study (1p and 16q deletion)
- USG abdomen to see venous invasion
- Contrast-enhanced CT scan abdomen and chest: To see the function of opposite kidney and its involvement, distant metastases, and invasion into IVC
- MRI: Is most sensitive to see caval patency

5. How will you stage Wilms tumor?

- *Stage I*: Tumor limited to the kidney and can be completely excised
- *Stage II*: Tumor extending through the renal capsule but can be completely excised
- *Stage III*: Residual tumor confined to the abdomen (nonhematogenous)
- *Stage IV*: Hematogenous spread
- *Stage V*: Bilateral involvement

6. How will you treat Wilms tumor?

 For favorable histology

- Current standard of care for Wilms tumor is nephrectomy followed by chemotherapy with or without radiation. Those with loss of heterozygosity (1p and 16q) require more aggressive chemotherapy.
  - *Stage I or II without LOH*: Nephrectomy with vincristine and dactinomycin
  - *Stage I or II with LOH*: Nephrectomy with vincristine plus dactinomycin, and doxorubicin
  - *Stage III or IV without LOH*: Nephrectomy with vincristine plus dactinomycin, and doxorubicin with radiation
  - *Stage III or IV with LOH*: Nephrectomy with vincristine, dactinomycin, doxorubicin, cyclophosphamide, and etoposide with radiation

For unfavorable histology (tumor with anaplastic change)

- Stages I–III: Nephrectomy followed by vincristine, actinomycin D, and doxorubicin in addition to local radiotherapy
- Stage IV: Nephrectomy followed by vincristine, actinomycin D, doxorubicin, cyclophosphamide, etoposide, and carboplatin with radiation
- In case of bilateral tumor, partial nephrectomy (nephron-sparing surgery)

- In case of very large tumor, preoperative chemoradiation followed by surgery
- Prognosis better in a small-sized tumor, and in a younger child without hematuria, fever, and metastasis

RENAL CELL CARCINOMA (RCC) (Fig. 13.11)

(*Synonyms*: Grawitz tumor, adenocarcinoma of kidney, and hypernephroma)

- *Identification*
  - Yellow-gray appearance
  - Upper pole involvement
  - Areas of hemorrhage, necrosis, calcification, and cystic changes leading to variegated appearance
  - Identification of kidney by shape and renal pelvis

VIVA QUESTIONS

1. What is the clinical presentation of patients with RCC?

A
- Asymptomatic (50%)
- The triad being flank pain, hematuria, and abdominal lump, but is a late manifestation
- Constitutional symptoms
- Scrotal varicocele (left sided) (varicocele fails to empty on lying- down position)
- Edema feet, ascites, and liver dysfunction (Budd–Chiari syndrome): Due to involvement of IVC
- Paraneoplastic manifestations such as:
  - Elevated ESR
  - Fever
  - Hypercalcemia
  - Cachexia
  - Anemia
  - Amyloidosis
  - Polycythemia
  - Polymyalgia rheumatica
  - Abnormal liver function

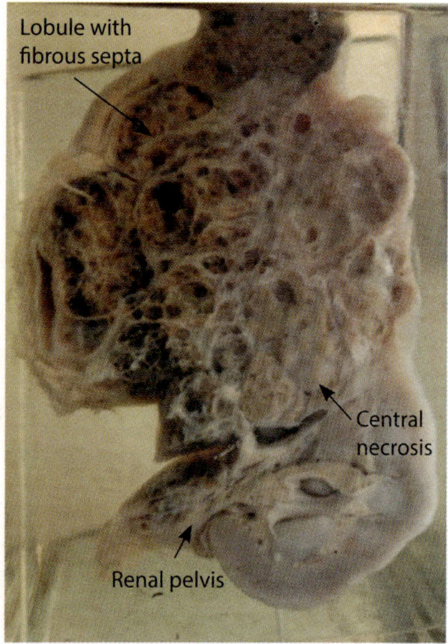

Figure 13.11 Renal cell carcinoma.

2. What are the modes of spread of RCC?

A
- Lung and bone (hematogenous)
- Hilar and para-aortic nodes

3. How will you investigate RCC?

A
- USG abdomen: It is usually the first test that helps to diagnose renal mass.
- Contrast-enhanced CT abdomen: Thick and irregular wall and postcontrast enhancement suggest malignant lesion.
- MRI
  - Indications
    - Nondiagnostic CT or USG
    - Contraindications for contrast administration
    - To look for involvement of collecting system and/or IVC
- X-ray chest or CT chest: It helps to reveal cannon ball metastasis.

4. What is Stauffer syndrome?

A Hepatomegaly without metastases in RCC is known as Stauffer syndrome.

5. What are the indications of renal biopsy in case of renal mass?

A
- In case of suspected renal lymphoma, metastases, and abscess
- Prior to chemotherapy
- Prior to nonsurgical options such as cryoablation and radiofrequency ablation

6. How will you stage and treat RCC?

A
- Staging of RCC (AJCC, 2017[5])
  - *T1*: Tumor ≤7 cm in greatest dimension, limited to the kidney
  - *T2*: Tumor >7 cm in greatest dimension, limited to the kidney

- *T3*: Tumor extending into major veins or perinephric tissues, but not into the ipsilateral adrenal gland and not beyond Gerota's fascia
- *T4*: Tumor invading beyond Gerota's fascia
- *N0*: No lymph node metastases
- *N1*: Lymph node metastases
- *M0*: No distant metastases
- *M1*: Distant metastases

- Stage:
  - *I*: T1N0M0
  - *II*: T2N0M0
  - *III*: T1N1, T2N1, T3N0, T3N1
  - *IV*: M1 with any T and any N, T4 with any T, M0

Treatment

- T1
  - Partial nephrectomy: Open, laparoscopic, or robotic
  - Indications: T1 tumors with normal contralateral kidney; RCC in a single functioning kidney, bilateral synchronous RCC, and patients with Von Hippel-Lindau syndrome[6]
- T2: Radical nephrectomy
- T3
  - Radical nephrectomy is performed with complete excision of all venous thrombus in the renal vein, inferior vena cava, and right atrium.
  - Excision of ipsilateral adrenal gland is recommended in patients with upper pole tumor and radiologically detectable adrenal gland lesion.
  - Resection of regional lymph node is an integral part of radical dissection while nonregional node does not confer any therapeutic advantage and is used for staging purpose.
- In metastatic diseases:
  - *Potentially resectable primary with solitary metastases or multiple resectable lung metastases*: Nephrectomy and resection of the metastatic lesion/s
  - *Potentially resectable primary tumor and multiple unresectable metastases*: Nephrectomy if in good performance status followed by systemic therapy
  - *Clear cell cancer with good performance status*: Systemic therapy with either sunitinib, bevacizumab, and interferon α-2a or pazopanib and high-dose interleukin-2
  - *Clear cell cancer with poor risk*: Temsirolimus and sunitinib
  - *Nonclear cell cancer*: Temsirolimus (EL-2), sunitinib (EL-2), or sorafenib medullary and collecting duct carcinoma treated with platinum-based chemotherapy
  - *Recurrent disease postprimary nephrectomy*: Treatment depending on whether it is resectable or not
    - *Resectable solitary metastases*: Surgical resection should be attempted.
    - *Nonresectable recurrence*: Systemic therapy should be attempted.

- Cryotherapy and radiofrequency ablation are performed for patients who are medically unfit and have a limited life expectancy.
- Average duration of disease control with targeted therapy with temsirolimus, sunitinib, sorafenib, bevacizumab, interferon α-2a or pazopanib, and high-dose interleukin-2 is 8–9 months.

HYDRONEPHROSIS (Fig. 13.12)

- *Identification*
  - Enlarged kidney
  - Dilated pelvicalyceal system
  - Thin parenchyma (bag of water)

VIVA QUESTIONS

1. Define hydronephrosis.

A It is aseptic dilatation of pelvicalyceal system due to intermittent but complete obstruction to the outflow of urine.

2. Enumerate causes of hydronephrosis.

A
- *Unilateral*
  - *Pelviureteric junction obstruction*: Functional and mechanical
  - *Ureteric obstruction*: Stone and transitional cell carcinoma

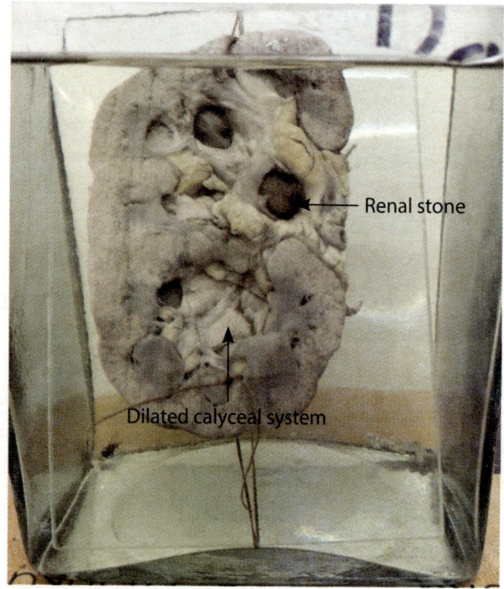

Figure 13.12 Renal stone with hydronephrosis.

- *Bilateral*
  - Bladder outlet obstruction (BOO), BPH, carcinoma prostate, posterior urethral valve, and urethral stricture
  - Bladder pathology
  - Bilateral vesicoureteric junction obstruction due to advanced malignancy
  - Ileal conduits
  - Phimosis

3. How will you differentiate between polycystic kidney and hydronephrosis?

A To differentiate from polycystic kidney—pelvicalyceal system is directly connected to enlarged cystic spaces in case of hydronephrosis.

4. What is the mechanism of development of hydronephrosis?

A
- Increase in pyelovenous backflow
- Increase in pyelolymphatic backflow
- Loss in dynamic equilibrium of urine
- Vascular congestion

5. What are the causes of functional PUJ obstruction?

A Functional PUJ obstruction may be due to abnormality in the musculature of pelvis or aberrant renal vessels.

6. How will you investigate a case of hydronephrosis?

A
- X-ray KUB: Stone in genitourinary tract
- Urine routine and microscopic examination
- USG KUB: Stone, hydronephrosis, hydroureter, assessment of parenchymal thickness, corticomedullary differentiation, tumor, and BPH (paper-thin parenchyma indicates long-standing obstruction)
- IVU: Grade of hydronephrosis, tumor (filling defect), radiolucent stone, and function of the same as well as of the opposite kidney
- Noncontrast CT (particularly helpful in suspected stone disease): Useful in the following conditions: (a) the kidneys cannot be adequately visualized by USG, and (b) to determine cause when the USG documents ureteral obstruction
- CT/MR urography: Helps in differentiating intrinsic causes (stone, stricture, malignancy, UPJ obstruction) from extrinsic causes (retroperitoneal fibrosis, pregnancy, mass, and crossing vessels)
- Renal scan (isotope renography):
  - To know function of kidney; if >15%, possibility of preservation of kidney (diethylenetriaminepentaacetic acid [DTPA] scan, dimercaptosuccinic acid [DMSA], mercaptoacetyltriglycine [MAG-3])
  - Best test to confirm obstructive dilatation in the collecting system
- Whitaker test: Abnormal increase in intrapelvic pressure when fluid is infused via percutaneous puncture of the kidney indicating obstruction (it is rarely performed)
- Retrograde pyelography: Just prior to corrective surgery, to confirm the site of obstruction

7. Describe treatment for hydronephrosis.

A Short-term management

DJ stenting or percutaneous nephrostomy to relieve obstruction

Indications for operation

- On and off renal pain

- Increasing grade of hydronephrosis
- Infection
- Evidence of renal parenchymal damage

For functional PUJ obstruction:

- Dismembered pyeloplasty can be done for any type of ureteral insertion, and anterior or posterior transposition of ureter can be done
  - Foley Y-V plasty: For high ureteral insertion
  - Culp-DeWeerd pyeloplasty: Large and readily accessible extrarenal pelvis
- Other methods: Endoscopic pyelotomy
- Laparoscopic technique for pyeloplasty becoming more popular nowadays

Treatment of the cause

- Similar to that for stone, either extracorporeal shock wave lithotripsy (ESWL) or percutaneous nephrolithotomy (PCNL)

For bilateral hydronephrosis: Treatment of cause such as:

- *BPH*: Transurethral resection of prostate (TURP)
- *Stricture*: Optical internal urethrotomy (most common cause for stricture is instrumentation)
- *Phimosis*: Circumcision

PYONEPHROSIS (Fig. 13.13)

- *Identification*
  - Same as for hydronephrosis, except that parenchyma is thick

VIVA QUESTIONS

1. Define pyonephrosis.

A It is an infected hydronephrosis in which there is total or near-total loss of renal function. It occurs most commonly due to renal calculus disease.

2. Describe clinical presentation of a patient with pyonephrosis.

A
- High-grade fever
- Anemia
- Swelling in the loin
- Tenderness over flank

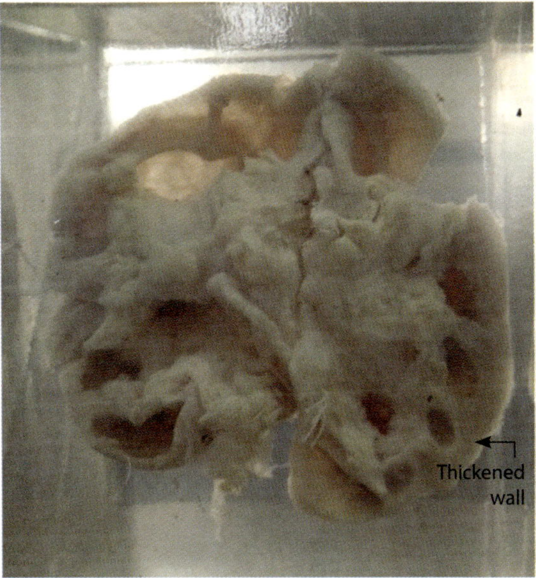

Figure 13.13 Pyonephrosis.

3. How will you investigate the case?

A
- *USG*: Dilated pelvicalyceal system and internal echoes within fluid collection
- *Plain X-ray KUB*: Calculus
- *Intravenous urography*: Hydronephrosis; dilated or nonfunctioning kidney
- *RGP*: Ureteric obstruction with irregular filling defect in the pelvis

4. How will you treat pyonephrosis?

A
- Pyonephrosis is a surgical emergency, and requires immediate drainage, through either percutaneous nephrostomy or DJ stenting (in case pus is too thick); sequelae of pyonephrosis: permanent renal damage and lethal septicemia
- IV antibiotics
- After 10 days: IVU; if kidney functioning, then definitive management of the cause
- In case of nonfunctioning kidney, renal scan should be done. If more than 15% function present, kidney should be preserved and pathology treated. If <15% function, nephrectomy should be done if the other kidney is normal.

TESTICULAR TUMOR

Seminoma Testis (Fig. 13.14)

- *Identification*
  - Testis is enlarged with homogenous gray-white appearance. It is identified by its shape and cord structure.

Teratoma Testis (Fig. 13.15)

- *Identification*
  - Gray-white solid areas with variegated appearance
  - Areas of cartilage and bone
  - Testis identified by shape and cord structure

VIVA QUESTIONS

1. What are the risk factors of testicular tumor?

- Cryptorchidism
- Carcinoma in situ
- Testicular feminization and Klinefelter syndrome
- History of contralateral testicular tumor
- HIV (likely to develop seminoma)
- Genetic abnormality involving chromosome 12

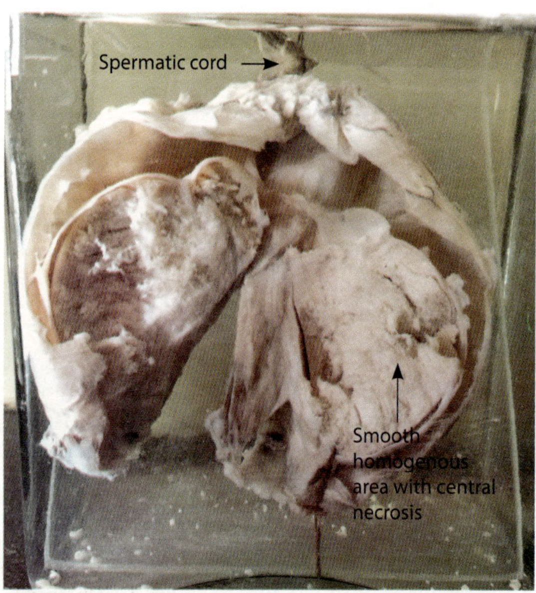

Figure 13.14 Seminoma testis.

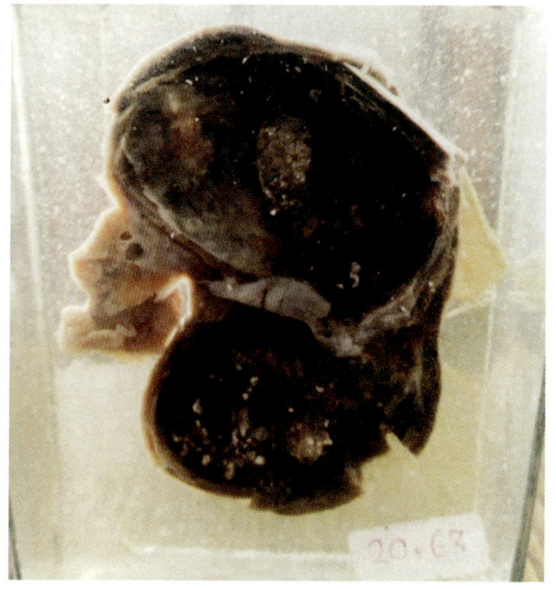

Figure 13.15 Testicular teratoma containing solid and cystic area.

- Race (more common in Whites)
- Maternal estrogen ingestion during pregnancy

2. Describe the clinical presentation of a patient with testicular carcinoma.

A
- Painless, hard, nontender, irregular mass
- Secondary hydrocele
- Acute scrotal pain (due to intratumor hemorrhage)
- Weight loss, supraclavicular lymph node enlargement (left), respiratory problems, and bone pain
- Gynecomastia
- Palpable retroperitoneal nodes

3. How will you classify testicular tumors? What are the features that distinguish seminoma from teratoma?

A Classification
- *I—Germ cell tumors*: Seminoma, teratoma, yolk sac tumor, choriocarcinoma, and embryonal carcinoma
- *II—Nongerm cell tumors*: Sertoli cell tumor and Leydig cell tumor
- *III—Others*: Lymphoma and gonadoblastoma

The differences between seminoma and teratoma are given in Table 13.2.

Table 13.2 Differences Between Seminoma and Teratoma

	Seminoma	Teratoma
Age (years)	35–45	20–30
Origin	Seminiferous tubule	Totipotent cell of rete testis
Spread	Lymphatic spread	Hematogenous
Macroscopic	Testis is enlarged with homogenous gray-white appearance. It is identified by its shape and cord structure	Gray-white solid areas with variegated appearance, areas of cartilage and bone, testis identified by shape and cord structure
Radiosensitive	More	Less

4. What are the different types of seminoma and teratoma?

A
- *Seminoma*: Classic and spermatocytic
- *Teratoma*: Teratoma differentiated, malignant teratoma intermediate, malignant teratoma anaplastic, and malignant teratoma trophoblastic

5. Which are the common tumor markers?

A
- *Alpha-fetoprotein (AFP)*: Nonseminomatous germ cell tumor (NSGCT)
- *Beta-hCG*: Pure seminoma, pure choriocarcinoma, embryonal cell carcinoma, and teratoma
- *LDH*: Seminoma

6. How will you stage the testicular tumor?

A
- *Stage I*: Confined to the testis
- *Stage II*: Nodes below diaphragm
- *Stage III*: Nodes above diaphragm
- *Stage IV*: Distant metastasis

7. What is the incidence of bilateral testicular tumor?

A One to 2%

8. Comment on the prognosis of testicular tumor.

A
- *Seminoma*: Good
- *NSGCT*: Pure choriocarcinoma—worst

9. What is cannon ball metastasis?

A
- Multiple, small, variable sized nodules in the lungs visible on X-ray chest; it suggests lung metastasis.
- Common primary sites are breasts, colorectal area, kidney, prostate, and testis.

10. How will you investigate and treat testicular tumor?

A Refer Chapter 16, *Frequently Asked Questions*.

BREAST

FIBROADENOMA (Fig. 13.16)

- *Identification*
  - Gray-white homogeneous mass and tends to bulge out of its well-formed capsule

CARCINOMA BREAST (Fig. 13.17)

- *Identification*
  - Gray-white to yellowish mass with chalky streak
  - Irregular
  - Extends into surrounding normal fat
  - Identification of breast by nipple and areola

VIVA QUESTIONS

1. What are the risk factors for carcinoma breast?

A Nonreproductive risk factors[7]
- Age: Risk increased after 50 years of age
- Sex: Female sex
- Anthropometric factors
  - Body mass index (obese postmenopausal women are at a higher risk)
  - Tall stature
- Family history and history of cancer in opposite breast
- No relation of diet with breast cancer
- Alcohol (women who drink are at a higher risk)

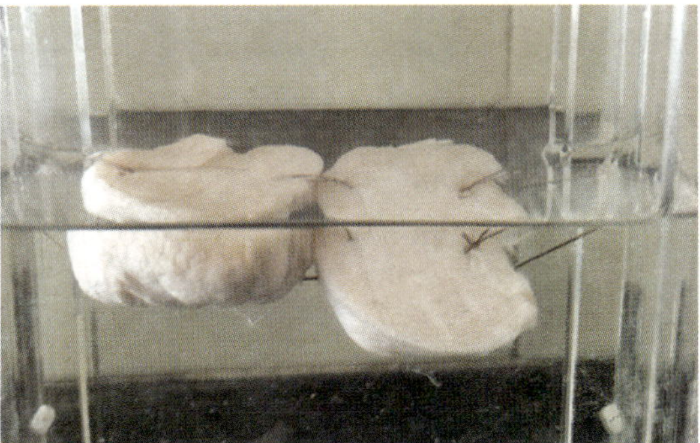

Figure 13.16 Fibroadenoma.

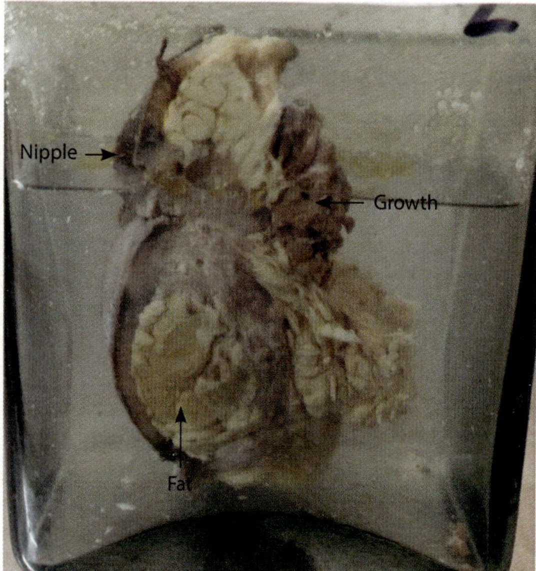

Figure 13.17 Carcinoma breast.

- Race: Western population more commonly affected followed by Asians and Africans.
- Genetics: Mutation in p53 tumor suppressor gene
  - BRCA-1 on chromosome number 17
  - BRCA-2 on chromosome number 13

Reproductive risk factors

- Early menarche
- Late menopause
- Unmarried nulliparous woman
- First pregnancy over 35 years of age
- Hormone replacement therapy (HRT) in postmenopausal women
- Ovarian tumor (functioning)
- Male patient treated with estrogens for carcinoma prostate
- Fibrocystic disease of breast with atypical hyperplasia (moderate or high)

2. Describe the classification of carcinoma breast.

- Carcinoma in situ
  - *Ductal carcinoma in situ*: High grade (comedo, solid), low grade (cribriform, papillary, micropapillary). The most common presentation is calcification on mammography.
  - Paget disease of nipple
- Invasive carcinoma
  - Ductal carcinoma
  - Lobular carcinoma
  - Papillary carcinoma
  - Tubular carcinoma
  - Colloid carcinoma
  - Medullary carcinoma
  - Signet ring cell carcinoma
  - Inflammatory carcinoma

3. What are the clinical features of carcinoma breast?

- Most common site being upper and outer quadrant of breast
- Painless hard lump
- Retraction of nipple
- Nipple discharge—blood stained or serous
- Peau d'orange appearance (orange peel–like appearance)
- Ulceration of skin over the tumor
- Fixity of lump to skin or breast tissue or underlying structures
- Destruction of nipple (Paget disease)
- Satellite nodules
- Axillary lymph node enlargement (lymphatic spread)
- Supraclavicular lymph node enlargement (lymphatic spread)
- Lower backache due to metastasis into the lumber spine
- Bony metastases in carcinoma breast (in descending order): Lumbar vertebra, femur, thoracic vertebra, rib cage, and skull
- Lymphedema of upper limb or arm due to lymphatic blockage
- Hepatomegaly
- Ascites
- Brain metastasis

4. How will you investigate carcinoma breast?

- FNAC or biopsy
  - FNAC is simple, rapid, and accurate if both operator and cytopathologist are experts; however, it cannot differentiate between in situ and invasive diseases.
  - If FNAC is inconclusive, then Trucut biopsy is performed. It can differentiate between in situ and invasive diseases and also provide information about tumor grade and receptor status.
  - Other modalities are incisional or excisional biopsy.

- Mammography: 0.1 cGy delivered. Features suggestive of malignancy on mammography are the following:
  - Microcalcification
  - Asymmetry of breasts
  - Skin thickening
  - Mass effect
  - Nipple inversion
- USG: It helps in deciding whether lesion is cystic or solid; it may also be used to direct the needle biopsy by FNAC or Trucut biopsy.
- CT scan
  - CT chest: Pulmonary complaints such as cough or hemoptysis
  - CT chest, abdomen, pelvis with bone scan: Locally advanced breast cancer or stage IV cancer (PET CT is an alternative investigation).
  - CT scan abdomen: Abdominal pain, raised alkaline phosphatase, liver dysfunction, and abnormal abdominal or pelvic examination.
- MRI: It is used for locally advanced breast cancer for which neoadjuvant treatment is being considered.
- X-ray
  - X-ray chest: It is used for lung metastasis.
  - X-ray lumbosacral spine: It is used only in symptomatic cases. Bone scan is better for detection of bony metastasis.
- Liver function tests
  - Serum alkaline phosphatase and calcium: Bone metastases

5. Describe staging of carcinoma breast.

A TNM staging* is given in Table 13.3.[8]

- *Stage I*
  - *A*: T1N0M0
  - *B*: T0 or T1, N1mi, M0 (mi: micrometastases)

Table 13.3 TNM Staging for Breast Cancer

T	N	M
0: No evidence of primary tumor Tis: Ductal carcinoma in situ Tis (Paget): Paget disease of nipple T1: Tumor < 2 cm T2: Tumor > 2 cm but ≤ 5 cm T3: Tumor > 5 cm T4: Tumor of any size with direct extension to chest wall and/or to the skin. Invasion of dermis alone does not qualify for T4 T4a: Extension of chest wall (not including only pectoralis muscle adherence/invasion) T4b: Edema and ulceration (including peau d'orange) of skin and satellite nodule that does not meet the criteria for inflammatory carcinoma T4c: T4a + T4b T4d: Inflammatory carcinoma	N0: No regional lymph node metastases by clinical and imaging method N1: Mobile ipsilateral axillary node (levels I and II) N2: Fix or matted ipsilateral axillary node (levels I and II) or in absence of clinically evident axillary node, ipsilateral internal mammary node metastasis N2a: Fix or matted ipsilateral axillary node (levels I and II) N2b: In absence of clinically evident axillary node, ipsilateral internal mammary node metastasis N3: Ipsilateral infraclavicular node (level III) with or without level I and II nodes or ipsilateral axillary (levels I and II) and internal mammary node or supraclavicular node (ipsilateral) with or without axillary or internal mammary node N3a: Ipsilateral infraclavicular node (level III) with or without level I and II nodes N3b: Ipsilateral axillary (levels I and II) and internal mammary node N3c: Supraclavicular node (ipsilateral) with or without axillary or internal mammary node	M0: No distant metastasis M1: Distant metastasis

*Highlights of eighth edition classification[8]

For T stage: Lobular carcinoma in situ is a benign entity and not included in Tis; T4b macroscopic satellite tumor nodules to the skin are separate from the primary tumor. Molecular biomarkers such as HER-2, ER, and PR are added in the prognostic classification system.

- *Stage II*
  - *A*: T2N0M0, T1N1M0, and T0N1M0
  - *B*: T2N1M0 and T3N0M0
- *Stage III*
  - *A*: T0N2M0, T1–2N2M0, and T3N1–2M0
  - *B*: T4N0–2M0
  - *C*: Any TN3M0
- *Stage IV*: Any T and any N with M1

T4 is stage IIIB and N3 is stage IIIC.

- Anything that comes under M1 is considered as stage IV.
- Metastases to lymph node other than supraclavicular in the cervical lymph node group and contralateral axillary node are defined as M1.
- In pathological staging, N1, 1–3 axillary nodes; N2, 4–9 axillary nodes; and N3: >10 lymph node involvement.

6. How will you treat carcinoma breast?

A
- Nowadays, trend is changing from mastectomy to breast conservation surgery (BCS).
- BCSs are the following:
  - Lumpectomy
  - Wide excision with 1-cm margin
  - Quadrantectomy
- Indications for BCS are the following:
  - Patient's wish
  - Breast to tumor ratio (if tumor is small and breast is large, breast conservation option can be considered, but if tumor is large and breast is small, this is not a feasible option)
  - Histological subtype other than invasive carcinoma
  - Can manage patients with extensive intraductal involvement with BCS if negative margin is possible
  - Lymph node positivity not precluding BCS
  - Family history of breast cancer not a contraindication for BCS
- Contraindications for BCS: Refer Chapter 6, *Operative Procedures* for absolute contraindications.
  - Scleroderma and active systemic lupus erythematosus are relative contraindications.

7. Describe stage-wise management of carcinoma breast.

 Early invasive (Stages I, IIA, and IIB)

- BCS with axillary lymph node dissection (ALND) or BCS with sentinel node biopsy (SNB) and if positive lymph node, ALND is performed.
- If clinically palpable axillary lymphadenopathy and confirmed metastatic on FNA or biopsy, go for ALND.

Indications for chemotherapy

- Node positive
- Patients with >1-cm tumor
- Node-negative tumor of >0.5 cm when adverse prognostic features are present (high nuclear and high histological grade, lymphovascular invasion, HER-2/neu overexpression or amplification, hormone receptor–negative tumor, elevated Ki 67 expression, and high percentage of cells in S phase)
- Triple-negative breast cancer with 0.5 cm (chemotherapy is the only option in this case)

Endocrine treatment

- Only patients with hormone receptor–positive tumor
- Aromatase inhibitors for 5 years in postmenopausal females (it blocks peripheral synthesis of estrogen and is effective only in postmenopausal women)
- Tamoxifen being the drug of choice in premenopausal women

Advanced locoregional breast cancer (IIIA and IIIB)

- Workup for metastatic disease such as bone scan, PET or CT scan, or elevated serum tumor marker such as alkaline phosphatase
- Neoadjuvant systemic therapy: Systemic chemotherapy preferred over endocrine therapy even in case of receptor-positive status (HER-2–positive status should be treated with neoadjuvant therapy directed against HER-2 [trastuzumab with or without pertuzumab] along with chemotherapy; if complete or partial response, surgery)

- If no response: Alternate systemic therapy and individualized locoregional treatment
- Surgery for stage III disease being modified radical mastectomy followed by chemotherapy and radiotherapy
- Systemic chemotherapy and radiotherapy for grossly involved internal mammary nodes

Distant metastases

- *Hormone receptor positive with no life-threatening condition or visceral metastases*: Hormonal therapy
- *Hormone receptor negative*: Adjuvant chemotherapy
- *Metastases with primary in situ*: Systemic treatment; surgery for primary indicated only in case of primary tumor progression

8. Which are the common chemotherapy regimens used in carcinoma breast?

A Chemotherapy is used as either adjuvant or neoadjuvant systemic therapy. Adjuvant chemotherapy is given after completion of surgery, preferably within 6 weeks of surgery. Indications for adjuvant chemotherapy and neoadjuvant chemotherapy are given in Answer 7.

For better understanding, indications for neoadjuvant chemotherapy are summarized here (Box 13.2).

Box 13.2 Indications for neoadjuvant chemotherapy

- Stages IIIA and IIIB
- Stage I or II: If BCS not possible due to a high tumor-to-breast ratio, or poor cosmetic outcome due to tumor location; (smaller (T1c) triple-negative breast cancers or HER2-positive cancers
- Temporary contraindications for operative surgery

Six-monthly cycles of chemotherapy are employed. Before starting chemotherapy, CBC should be recorded. If TLC < 4000, chemotherapy should not be given and the count should be improved with granulocyte colony-stimulating factor.

Common chemotherapy regimens are as follows:

- *CMF*: Cyclophosphamide, methotrexate, and 5-FU
- *CAF*: Cyclophosphamide, adriamycin, and 5-FU
- *MMM*: Mitomycin-C, mitoxantrone, and methotrexate
- *Taxol*: Paclitaxel and docetaxel

Adriamycin is cardiotoxic. Baseline echocardiography and ECG should be done before starting adriamycin.

9. Describe the hormonal therapy in carcinoma breast.

A
- Commonly used drugs are tamoxifen, anastrozole, and letrozole.
- Indication: Only patients with estrogen or progesterone receptor–positive status should be given hormonal therapy.
- In postmenopausal women, the source of estrogen is fat, through peripheral conversion with the help of aromatase. So aromatase inhibitors instead of tamoxifen would be a better option and adverse effects associated with tamoxifen, such as DVT, hot flushes, vomiting (most common side effect), endometrial carcinoma, cataract, and menstrual irregularities, can be avoided.
- Tamoxifen has estrogenic as well as antiestrogenic actions.
- Dose is 20 mg OD for 5 years.

As aromatase inhibitors are associated with increase in the bone density loss, prior to commencement of the treatment, bone density scan should be performed.

10. What are the indications for radiotherapy?

A
- Positive margin in MRM
- BCS
- Node positive: Four in number
- T3 and T4 lesions
- Internal mammary node positive
- Inadequate or no ALND

11. Mention the biological agents used in the treatment of carcinoma of the breast.

A
- Known as trastuzumab (Herceptin) in a Her-2neu–positive patient: Monoclonal antibody against HER-2neu (c-erb-B2)[9]
- Lapatinib and pertuzumab: Tyrosine kinase inhibitor
- CK4/CDK6 inhibitor for ER-positive lesions

LYMPH NODE

TUBERCULOSIS (Fig. 13.18)

- *Identification*
  - Matted with central caseation

VIVA QUESTIONS

1. Describe diagnosis of TB lymphadenopathy.

- FNAC: Central caseation with epithelioid cells, giant cells, and lymphocytes
- Mantoux test
- ESR
- CBC—lymphocytosis
- Lymph node biopsy
- A cartridge-based nucleic acid amplification test (CBNAAT) performed to rule out rifampicin resistance and categorized as microbiologically confirmed drug-sensitive TB or RIF-resistant TB (revised RNTCP guideline, 2017)

2. Describe treatment for TB lymphadenopathy.

A Treatment is same as given in Question no. 6 on page 283.[1]

- Surgery indicated in the following cases:
  - When diagnosis is in doubt
  - Collar stud abscess
  - Tubercular sinus
  - Unresolved lymph node after treatment

CERVICAL LYMPHADENOPATHY

Clinical examination

- Acute condition: Painful tender nodes

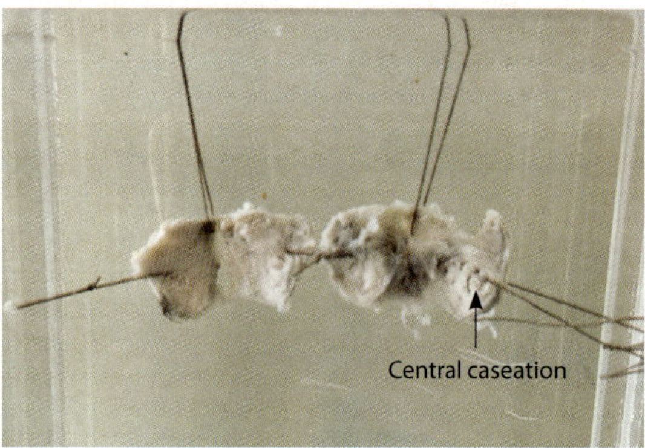

Figure 13.18 Tuberculous lymph node.

- Chronic cases
  - *For tuberculosis*: Nontender, matted, ulcer, sinus, level II
  - *For secondaries in neck*: Hard, discrete, irregular surface
  - *Symptoms of primary lymphoma*: Nontender, discrete, rubbery, posterior triangle, absence of primary

Investigations

- FNAC: FNAC helpful in diagnosis, which may show Koch's, malignancy, lymphoma, etc.
- Biopsy: If FNAC inconclusive, then go for incisional or excisional biopsy
- Endoscopy: In case of secondaries in neck, pan endoscopy (nasopharyngoscopy, bronchoscopy, esophagoscopy) used to search for primary

VIVA QUESTIONS

1. What are the causes of cervical lymphadenopathy?

A

- Acute lymphadenitis
- Chronic lymphadenitis
  - *Bacterial*: Tuberculosis and syphilis
  - *Viral*: LGV
  - *Parasitic*: Filarial
  - *Fungal*: Blastomycosis
- Malignancy
  - *Primary*: Hodgkin lymphoma and non-Hodgkin lymphoma
  - *Secondary*: Carcinoma and melanoma

2. What are the causes of generalized lymphadenopathy?

A

- HIV
- Tuberculosis
- Lymphoma
- Leukemia
- Infectious mononucleosis
- Brucellosis
- Toxoplasmosis

3. What are the levels of lymph node as given by Memorial Sloan Kettering Cancer Center, USA?

A

- *Level I*: Submental (Ia) and submandibular node (Ib)
- *Level II*: Upper jugular
  - *IIa*: Jugulodigastric node
  - *IIb*: Submuscular recess
- *Level III*: Midjugular—inferior to hyoid and superior to cricoids

- *Level IV*: Lower jugular—inferior to cricoid and superior to clavicle
- *Level V*: Posterior triangle
  - *Va*: Inferior and medial to splenius capitis and trapezius and superior to spinal accessory nerve
  - *Vb*: Inferior to spinal accessory nerve and superior to clavicle
- *Level VI*: Anterior triangle of neck, inferior to hyoid, and superior to suprasternal notch
- *Level VII*: Paratracheal nodes; inferior to suprasternal notch in the upper mediastinum

4. How many lymph nodes are there in the body?

A There are 800 lymph nodes in the body, out of which 400 are in head and neck.

5. How will you manage secondaries in the neck?

A Squamous cell carcinoma

- *N1 (single, ipsilateral node, <3 cm)*: MRND or SND
- *N2a (single, ipsilateral node, >3 or <6 cm) in upper and midneck*: RT. In case of partial response to therapy, neck dissection is performed 6–8 weeks after completion of radiation therapy.
- *N2b (multiple, ipsilateral nodes, <6 cm)*: RT, or concomitant CT/RT, followed by neck dissection after 6–8 weeks of completion of radiation therapy
- *N3 (massive or bilateral nodes)*:
  - RT alone or concurrent RT (CCRT) used
  - In case of perineural and vascular invasion, extracapsular spread, and multiple lymph nodes, neck dissection + radiation or chemoradiation is used.
  - Five-year survival rate in case of carotid encasement and fixation to important surrounding structures such as prevertebral muscle is very low and morbidity associated with carotid resection and important structure resection must be weighed carefully prior to surgery. Debulking is not advocated as it does not improve survival.
- Squamous cell carcinoma of lower cervical and supraclavicular node or adenocarcinoma (look for thyroid and parotid): RT alone used (poor survival).

For neck dissection, refer Chapter 16, *Frequently Asked Questions*.

HODGKIN LYMPHOMA (Fig. 13.19)

- *Identification*
  - Discrete noncaseating lymph node

VIVA QUESTIONS

1. Describe the presentation of a patient with Hodgkin lymphoma.

A
- Hodgkin disease is marked by enlargement of the lymph nodes, spleen, and liver.
- Age: It is bimodal, and occurs in early 20s or in the 50s.
- Sex: In nodular sclerosing, female preponderance is present; in other types, male preponderance is present.
- It is associated with EB virus and HIV.
- Clinical presentation is as follows:
  - Painless, progressive cervical lymphadenopathy (nontender with rubbery consistency)
  - Mostly axial lymphatic system involved; possibility of involvement of other lymph node regions (axillary, inguinal, mediastinal, retroperitoneal)
  - Hepatosplenomegaly

Figure 13.19 Hodgkin lymphoma (lymph node).

- Bone pains
- Pruritus

2. Describe Rye classification.

A Rye classification

- Nodular sclerosing (most common)
- Lymphocyte predominant (best prognosis)
- Lymphocyte depletion (worst prognosis)
- Mixed cellularity

WHO classification

In addition to types of Rye classification, the WHO added nodular lymphocyte predominant.

- Pathological diagnosis by Reed–Sternberg cells and lacunar cells

3. Describe Cotswold staging.

A Stage description

I: Single lymph node region or lymphoid structure involved

II: Two or more lymph node regions contiguous or noncontiguous on the same side of diaphragm

III: Involvement of lymph nodes on both sides of diaphragm

- Splenic, hilar, coeliac, or portal nodes
- Para-aortic, iliac, or mesenteric nodes

IV: Extranodal site such as lung, liver, bone marrow, skin, and GI tract or any organ or tissue other than lymph nodes or Waldeyer's ring

A: No symptoms

B: Fever, night sweats, and unexplained weight loss >10% of body weight

X: Bulky disease (mediastinal mass >one-third of transverse chest diameter)

E: Single extranodal site that is contiguous or proximal to a known nodal site

CS: Clinical stage

PS: Pathological stage

4. Describe diagnosis of a patient with Hodgkin lymphoma.

A

- Complete blood count
- Peripheral smear for cell morphology
- Screening for hepatitis B and C and test for HIV
- Serum level of cytokines such as IL-6, IL-10, and IL-2 correlating with tumor burden, systemic manifestation, and overall outcome of the disease
- Biopsy: Excision biopsy of the involved lymph node the preferred or Trucut biopsy (confirmatory immunophenotype with immunohistochemistry is performed routinely)
- Limited value of FNAC
- PET CT preferred for initial staging of Hodgkin lymphoma: Chest, abdomen, and pelvis (PET-CT also helps in identifying bone involvement)
- CT neck/chest/abdomen/pelvis: Enlarged lymph nodes, hepatomegaly or splenomegaly, lung mass or nodules, and pleural effusions
- Bone scan: If there is bone pain or elevated serum alkaline phosphatase
- If CNS involvement suspected, lumber puncture and/or MRI
- Evaluation of cardiac and pulmonary functions prior to chemotherapy

5. Describe treatment for Hodgkin lymphoma.

A Definition of favorable disease according to the European Organization for the Research and Treatment of Cancer (EORTC) is as follows:

- Limited-stage disease, age younger than 50 years, no bulky mediastinal adenopathy, ESR <50 mm/h
- No 'B' symptoms (or an ESR <30 mm/h with B symptoms), three or fewer sites of involvement

Treatment is according to latest NCCN guidelines[10]

Radiation therapy

- Involved-field radiation (IFRT) (commonly used modality): Radiation to all of the clinically involved regions
- Involved-node radiation (INRT): Radiation to involve nodal volumes plus a <5-cm margin of healthy tissue

Induction chemotherapy

Induction regimens for treatment for Hodgkin lymphoma are as follows:

- ABVD (adriamycin [doxorubicin], bleomycin, vinblastine, dacarbazine) every 4 weeks for six cycles or more (most commonly used regimen):
  - *Adriamycin*: 25 mg/m^2, days 1 and 15
  - *Bleomycin*: 10 mg/m^2, days 1 and 15

- *Vinblastine*: 6 mg/m^2, days 1 and 15
- *Dacarbazine*: 375 mg/m^2, days 1 and 15
- MOPP (mechlorethamine, vincristine, procarbazine, prednisone) every 4 weeks for six cycles or more
- Stanford V (doxorubicin, vinblastine, mustard, bleomycin, vincristine, etoposide, prednisone) plus radiation therapy to bulky sites 2–4 weeks following the end of chemotherapy
- BEACOPP (bleomycin, etoposide, doxorubicin, cyclophosphamide, vincristine, procarbazine, prednisone) every 21 days for eight or more cycles

Salvage chemotherapy

If induction chemotherapy fails, salvage chemotherapy is used:

- ICE (ifosfamide, carboplatin, etoposide)
- DHAP (cisplatin, cytarabine, prednisone)
- ESHAP (etoposide, methylprednisolone, cytarabine, cisplatin)

Early stage with favorable factors (stage I or II)

- Chemotherapy plus radiation or chemotherapy alone (however, combination treatment is superior over chemotherapy alone)
- ABVD followed by radiation

Early stage with unfavorable factors (stage I or II)

- *Early stage unfavorable, no bulky mediastinal disease*: Two cycles of ABVD or Stanford V or BEACOPP + ISRT
- *Early stage unfavorable, with bulky mediastinal disease*: ABVD for four cycles or Stanford V regimen for three cycles or escalated BEACOPP for two cycles + ABVD for two cycles followed by ISRT

Advanced disease

- *Advanced stage without bulky disease*: ABVD for six cycles without radiation therapy
- *Advanced stage with bulky disease*: ABVD for six cycles with IFRT to original sites of bulky disease

Acceptable alternative regimen for chemotherapy is BEACOPP or Stanford V.

Treatment of nodular lymphocyte-predominant Hodgkin lymphoma

- *Early stage*: Local excision + IFRT or close observation
- *Advanced*: R-CHOP (rituximab, cyclophosphamide, doxorubicin, vincristine, prednisone)

6. What are differences between Hodgkin and non-Hodgkin lymphoma?

	Hodgkin lymphoma	**Non-Hodgkin lymphoma**
Age	Bimodal peak, one in younger and one in elderly age group	Elderly
Lymph node involvement	Cervical group mainly involved	Retroperitoneal and mediastinal lymph node. Supratrochlear may be involved
Fever and pruritus	Common	Rare
Respiratory and GI involvement	Rare	Common
General condition	Good	Poor

MISCELLANEOUS

SQUAMOUS CELL CARCINOMA OF THE FOOT (Fig. 13.20)

- *Identification*
  - Cauliflower-like growth over the foot

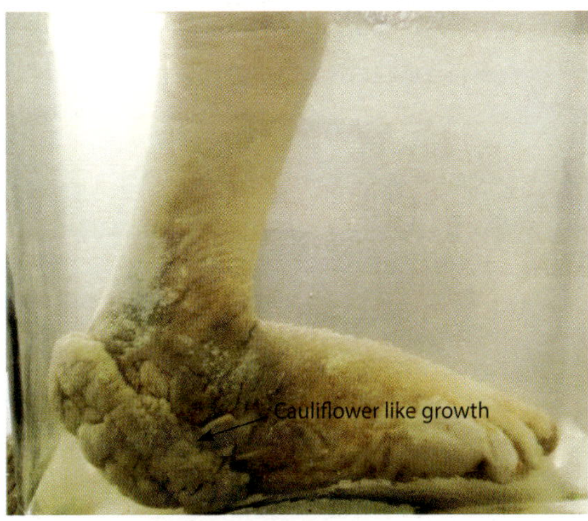

Figure 13.20 Squamous cell carcinoma.

  - Arises from any part of the skin or mucous membrane lined by squamous epithelium
  - Arises from keratinocytes of epidermis
  - Second most common malignancy of skin after basal cell carcinoma
- Common sites: Parts exposed to sun such as face, pinna, forearm, and lower leg
- Lymphatic spread common

VIVA QUESTIONS

1. **Describe the predisposing conditions for the carcinoma of the foot.**

A
- Solar keratosis
- Burn scar
- Chronic osteomyelitis
- Ionizing radiation
- Psoralen (PUVA)
- HPV-16 and -18 infections
- Family history
- Inherited disorder such as xeroderma pigmentosum, epidermolysis bullosa, albinism, and epidermodysplasia verruciformis
- Smoking
- Chronic nonhealing ulcer or wound
- Coal, tar, etc.
- ABO blood group
- Drugs such as voriconazole and oral contraceptive pills
- De novo (rare)

2. **Describe Broder's classification of the carcinoma of the foot.**

A
- *Grade I*: <25% cells anaplastic
- *Grade II*: 25–50% cells anaplastic
- *Grade III*: 50–75% cells anaplastic
- *Grade IV*: >75% cells anaplastic

3. **List the high-risk factors associated with metastases or leads to recurrence.**

A Risk factors according to NCCN guidelines:[11]
- Size >20 mm on trunk and extremity, >10 mm on cheeks, forehead, scalp, neck, and pretibial, and >6 mm on the mask area of the face (eyelid, eye brow, vermilion, etc.)
- Depth >2 mm or Clark level IV or V
- Moderate to poorly differentiated carcinoma
- Recurrent and rapidly growing tumor
- Tumor in immunocompromised patient
- Acanthocytic, adenosquamous, or desmoplastic variety
- Vascular and nerve involvement
- Tumor on previously irradiated site

4. **What is the treatment of the carcinoma of the foot?**

A For low-grade lesions and lesions <2 cm, wide excision with 4-mm margin is recommended, and for high-grade lesions, 6-mm margin is recommended.

Low-risk group
- Options are surgical excision (4–6 mm margin), cryosurgery, electrosurgery, radiation (small, well-defined tumor around the lips, nose, and eyelid: For cosmetic reason).
- For Bowen's disease: Topical 5-FU, photodynamic therapy, or imiquimod are other options.

High-risk group
- Surgery
  - Wide excision (10-mm margin) or MOHS micrographic surgery
  - MOHS micrographic surgery the treatment of choice in the following conditions:
    - It is used in the case of >2-cm lesions, areas where cosmetic and function preservation is critical, poorly differentiated lesions, and verrucous carcinomas.
  - Prophylactic lymph node dissection is not advisable. If lymph nodes are involved, then block dissection is recommended.
- Radiotherapy
  - If lymph nodes are enlarged, hard, and fixed to the surrounding structure, palliative radiation is the only treatment available. Other indications for radiation are as follows: Not fit for surgery, small growth, no involvement of muscle, cartilage, and bone, positive surgical margin, perineural histology, and multiple recurrences.
  - Poorly differentiated carcinoma is treated with radiotherapy.
- Systemic chemotherapy

Cisplatin-based chemotherapy is used in patients with distant metastases or locally advanced disease that cannot be managed with surgery or radiation therapy. Platinum-based chemotherapy has also been combined with cetuximab or panitumumab (antitumor activity and target epidermal growth factor receptor) may be more effective than chemotherapy alone.

MADURA MYCOSIS (MADURA FOOT) (Fig. 13.21)

- *Identification*
  - Multiple, small discharging sinus with granules
  - Indurated swelling
  - Commonly occurs over the foot

VIVA QUESTIONS

1. What are the causative agents for Madura mycosis?

A
- *Molds*: *Madurella mycetomatis* along with *Trematosphaeria grisea*, *Falciformispora senegalensis*, and *Scedosporium apiospermum* species complex (>90% cases) (eumycetoma) (at least 39 hyaline and pigmented species of molds cause eumycetoma)
- *Filamentous bacteria*: *Nocardia* and *Actinomyces* species (actinomycetoma)

2. What is 'mycetoma belt'?

A Mycetoma predominately occurs in the mycetoma belt in the region between the latitudes of 15 degrees south and 30 degrees north.

3. What is portal of entry?

A Portal of entry is minor trauma mostly over the foot.

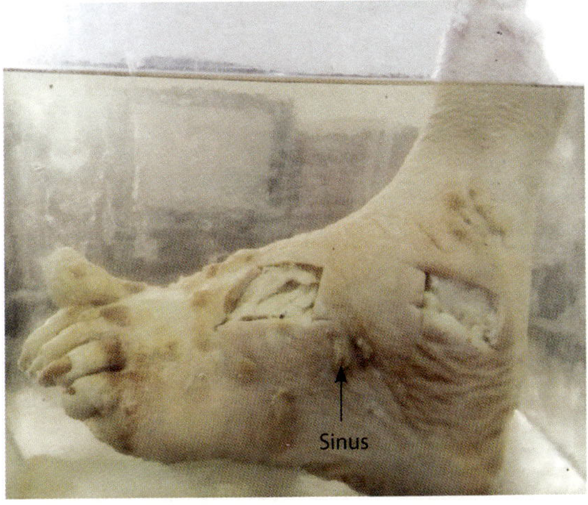

Figure 13.21 Madura foot.

4. What are the clinical features of Madura foot?

A
- Tumor, sinus tracts, and macroscopic grains represent characteristic triad of either eumycetoma or actinomycetoma.
- Black grains indicate fungal infection while white to yellow grains indicate either fungal or bacterial infection.
- Most common site is feet followed by leg and hand.
- It start as small, painless, subcutaneous, firm nodule over dorsum of foot. Lesions extend and coalesce to form a large swelling that evolves into necrotic abscesses and draining sinus tracts.
- It may involve adjacent structures such as lymphatics, muscles, and bone.

5. How will you diagnose and treat Madura mycosis?

A Diagnosis
- Deep biopsy
  - Type I reaction—grains surrounded by a layer of polymorphonuclear leukocytes. Outside the neutrophil, there is granulation tissue containing and outermost zone is fibrous tissue.
  - Type II reaction—neutrophil is replaced by macrophages and giant cells.
  - Type III reaction—it consists of epithelioid granuloma with Langhans giant cells.
- FNAC—it is simple, rapid, and sensitive.
- Plain X-ray local part (involved foot) is done to check involvement of bone.
- USG: It helps to distinguish between eumycetoma (grains produce sharp, bright, hyper-reflective echoes) and actinomycetoma (grains are less distinct).
- CT scan: It is more sensitive than conventional X-ray to detect early bone involvement.
- MRI: It helps in:
  - Early diagnosis even in absence of sinus tract
  - In assessing bone destruction, periosteal reaction, and soft-tissue involvement ('dot-in-circle sign' is highly characteristic and indicates the presence of grain)
  - Better assessment of soft tissue involvement
- Fungal culture on Sabouraud medium is helpful.

- Culture of discharge with 10% KOH is also helpful.
- Polymerase chain reaction and DNA sequencing: They help in identification of species.

Treatment

- Medical treatment
  - For fungal mycetoma: Itraconazole, ketoconazole, or voriconazole. It is given up to a year. It helps in localizing disease and makes the surgical excision possible. Posaconazole is used for refractory cases.
  - For actinomycetoma: Combination of amikacin sulfate with co-trimoxazole is the treatment of choice. Co-amoxiclav, rifampicin, and gentamicin are second-line drugs.
- Surgical treatment
  - If there is no improvement with drugs, it requires wide local excision and debulking. At least 6 months of antifungal should be given prior to consideration for surgery.
  - Amputation can be considered only in severe and progressive disability.

References

1. Chaudhuri AD. Recent changes in technical and operational guidelines for tuberculosis control programme in India—2016: A paradigm shift in tuberculosis control. J Assoc Chest Physicians 2017;5:1–9.
2. Miura F, Okamoto K, Takada T. Tokyo Guidelines 2018: initial management of acute biliary infection and flowchart for acute cholangitis. J Hepatobiliary Pancreat Sci 2018;25(1):31–40.
3. Warttig S, Ward S, Rogers G; Guideline Development Group. Diagnosis and management of gallstone disease: Summary of NICE guidance. BMJ 2014;349:g6241.
4. Fong Y, Fortner J, Sun RL, et al. Clinical score for predicting recurrence after hepatic resection for metastatic colorectal cancer: analysis of 1001 consecutive cases. Ann Surg 1999;230:309–21.
5. Rini BI, McKiernan JM, Chang SS, et al. Kidney. In: Amin MB, ed. AJCC Cancer Staging Manual, 8th edn. New York: Springer, 2017, p. 739.
6. Mellon JK. Kidney and urethra. In: Bailey and Love's Short Practice of Surgery, 27th edn. London, UK: CRC Press, Taylor and Francis; 2018: 1398–1422.
7. Piccart M, Gathani T, Zardavas D, et al. Cancer of the breast. In: Oxford Textbook of Oncology, 3rd edn. Oxford: Oxford University Press; 2016:546.
8. Amin MB, Edge SB, Greene FL, et al, eds. AJCC Cancer Staging Manual, 8th edn. New York: Springer, 2017.
9. Sainsbury RC. The breast. In: Bailey and Love's Short Practice of Surgery, 27th edn. London, UK: CRC Press, Taylor and Francis; 2018: 860–883.
10. National Comprehensive Cancer Network (NCCN) guidelines. Available at www.nccn.org. Last accessed on November, 2017.
11. Bichakjian CK, Alam M, Andersen J, et al. NCCN Clinical Practice Guidelines in Oncology (NCCN Guidelines): Basal Cell and Squamous Cell Skin Cancers, Version I.2013. Pennsylvania: National Comprehensive Cancer Network; 2013.

CHAPTER 14

Drugs

There are so many drugs in pharmacology. Here are included essential emergency drugs as well as antibiotics. Emergency drugs are useful in treating emergency in the ward as well as operation theater. Antibiotics are essential to prevent or treat infection associated with surgery. Knowledge of these drugs is important to prevent morbidity and mortality associated with surgical condition.

ATROPINE

It blocks all types of muscarinic receptors (M1–M5). It is a competitive antagonist; glycopyrrolate is its synthetic derivative. It is absorbed through eye, GI tract, mucous membrane, and skin. It is metabolized in the liver and excreted unchanged in the urine. Its effect on various systems is as follows:

- CNS
  - Stimulant
- CVS
  - Increased heart rate
  - Usually causes tachycardia without significant change in blood pressure; causes paradoxical bradycardia in small doses
- Smooth muscle
  - It reduces the tone of motility of the gut; it also reduces the tone of the ureter. It is a potent bronchodilator. It also causes relaxation of bladder musculature and bile duct muscle.
- Glands
  - Inhibition of secretion from sweat and salivary, bronchial, and lachrymal glands
- Local anesthetic
  - It is also a mild local anesthetic.

DICYCLOMINE

It is antispasmodic and antiemetic.

DROTAVERINE

It is nonanticholinergic smooth muscle relaxant. It inhibits phosphodiesterase 4.

HYOSCINE BUTYLBROMIDE

Antispasmodic

Side Effects

- Dry mouth
- Tachycardia
- Dry and hot skin
- Constipation
- Allergic reaction and urinary retention
- Psychotic symptoms

Contraindications

- Absolute
  - Pediatric patients
  - Acute glaucoma
  - Gastric outlet obstruction
- Relative
  - It should be used with precaution in the elderly (fear of retention of urine) and patients with chronic respiratory problem (dries up the secretion).

Uses

- Preanesthetic medication
  - Reduces bronchial and salivary secretion, prevents laryngospasm as well as vasovagal attack, and prevents halothane-induced ventricular arrhythmia
- It is also used to counteract bradycardia in hypersensitive carotid sinus and partial heart block.
- It is used before pleural tapping, ascitic tapping, and intercostal drainage insertion.
- It is used as an antidote for organophosphorus poisoning.
- Neuromuscular blockade reversal: It is administered with neostigmine or with edrophonium.

It is available as a 0.6-mg/mL injection ampoule and a 6-mg/mL vial.

ADRENALINE

It is a direct sympathomimetic. It is an α as well as a β agonist. Its effect on various systems is as follows:

- CVS
  - Positive chronotropic (increases heart rate) and positive inotropic (increases force of contraction) action, increased cardiac output, increased systolic blood pressure, and decreased diastolic blood pressure
- Smooth muscle
  - It is bronchodilator and it also helps in relaxation of uterine smooth muscle and detrusor muscle.
- Secretion
  - Inhibition of secretion from salivary, bronchial, and sweat glands
- Metabolic
  - It causes glycogenolysis and leads to hyperglycemia; lipolysis: Increased free fatty acid and hyperkalemia.

Side Effects

- Palpitation, anxiety, hypertension, and tachycardia
- Anginal pain
- Injection site local necrosis
- Acute pulmonary edema in cardiac compromised patients

Uses

- Cardiac arrest
- Anaphylactic shock (adrenaline 0.5 mg IV slowly along with hydrocortisone, O_2 inhalation, and IV fluid)
- Hemostasis: 1:10,000 or 1:20,000 solution pack used to control local superficial bleeding such as post hemorrhoidectomy, dental procedure, and epistaxis
- Bronchial asthma
- Combination with local anesthetic: Prolongs the action of local anesthetic because of its vasoconstrictor effect

Contraindications

- Cannot be used with halothane
- Hypertension
- Hyperthyroid
- Anxiety
- IHD

NORADRENALINE

It causes rise in both systolic and diastolic blood pressure. It has a positive inotropic as well as a positive chronotropic effect; it decreases exocrine secretion. It is available as 2 mg/mL solution.

Use

Shock

DOPAMINE

Dopamine is D1, D2, as well as α and β_1 agonist.

D1 receptor is present in the renal and mesenteric blood vessels; it produces vasodilatation.

Its effect on CVS is as follows:

- Positive inotropic and positive chronotropic action, and increased cardiac output and systolic blood pressure

It has a dose-dependent action:

- *Low dose (2–5 µg/kg/min)*: It causes vasodilatation in coronary, mesenteric, and renal vessels (D1 receptor), diuresis, and natriuresis
- *Moderate dose (5–10 µg/kg/min)*: Positive inotropic action, little positive chronotropic action, and raised systolic blood pressure (β_1 receptor)
- *Large dose (>10 µg/kg/min)*: Vasoconstriction (α_1 receptor)

Side Effects

- Local necrosis in case of extravasations
- Nausea and vomiting
- Possibility of angina and arrhythmia due to high dose

Use

- Cardiogenic or septic shock

It is given in infusion or drip. It is diluted with normal saline. It is started as 2.5 µg/kg/min and gradually increased up to 20 µg/kg/min depending on the response and then gradually tapered off. It should not be continued for more than 3 days (tachyphylaxis). Its dose is regulated by monitoring BP and urine output.

It is available as 5-mL ampoule, 40 mg/mL.

DOBUTAMINE

It is an α and a β agonist. It does not act on dopaminergic receptor. It has mainly positive inotropic effect (force of contraction and cardiac output increase).

There is no significant chronotropic effect or change in peripheral resistance.

Use

- Cardiac failure accompanying MI or surgery

It is available as 250 mg in 20-mL ampoule, 2.5–10 μg/min.

MEPHENTERMINE

It has α and β action as well as helps in release of noradrenaline. It is a cardiac stimulant and vasoconstrictor. It increases blood pressure by increasing cardiac output and peripheral resistance.

Use

- Prevents and treats hypotension due to spinal anesthesia or surgical intervention

One ampoule contains 15 mg/mL solution while 10-mL vial contains 30 mg/mL solution. A total of 15 mg is given IV and repeated as required.

SODIUM BICARBONATE

Each ampoule contains 25 mL of 7.5% sodium bicarbonate, 22.5 mEq sodium, and 22.5 mEq bicarbonate.

Dose calculation (mEq/L) = 0.5 × weight (kg) × ([desired HCO_3]–actual HCO_3])

Uses

- Metabolic acidosis
- Cardiac arrest
- Hyperkalemia

Metabolic acidosis should be corrected slowly and only if pH is <7.0 or when bicarbonate level <10–12 mEq/mL.

Normal 50 mEq is given (4 g sodium bicarbonate). Per 100 mL contains 7.5 g. So 50 mL is given. It should be mixed with D5% because of its irritative effect.

Half of the deficit is corrected in the first 4 hours and the rest over 24 hours.

Side Effects

- Alkalosis
- Hypokalemia (never correct acidosis without correcting hypokalemia)
- Hypocalcemia
- Pulmonary edema
- Gastric distension and belching
- Hypernatremia

Bicarbonate can cause rise in pCO_2 level as well as rise in blood lactate level, so it should be used with care.

CALCIUM GLUCONATE

One ampoule contains 10%, 10 mL solution; calcium gluconate contains 90 (4.6 mEq) mg of elemental calcium.

Calcium gluconate is used because of its action to stabilize the cardiac membrane potential.

Uses

- Hypocalcemia
- Hyperkalemia
- Hypermagnesemia
- Cardiac arrest in presence of above-mentioned three conditions
- Beta-blocker and calcium channel blocker toxicity
- Citrate toxicity

Ionized calcium <3.2 mg/dL with cardiovascular or neurological manifestation should be treated urgently.

Ten percent, 10 mL containing 90 mg of elemental calcium diluted in 10 mL saline given over 10 minutes raises the serum calcium by 0.5 mg/dL.

Calcium starts falling after half an hour, so bolus should be followed by infusion. A total of 500–2000 mg of calcium gluconate diluted in 500 mL dextrose is given over 6 hours.

In hyperkalemia with ECG changes and serum potassium >7 mEq/L, calcium gluconate should be given 10 mL, 10% IV over 5 minutes. It can be repeated after 5 minutes.

Side Effects

- GI upset
- Hypotension
- Bradycardia
- Extravasation necrosis

In treatment of hypocalcemia, it is important to note that if associated hyperphosphatemia or hypomagnesemia is present, it should be corrected first.

Physiological compensatory mechanism helps in preserving ionized calcium in case of massive blood transfusion. Hypocalcemia observed is transient and prolonged only in case of hypothermia and renal and liver failure. Ionized calcium should be monitored and replaced when clinically indicated during massive blood transfusion.[1] Routine use of calcium gluconate is not justified.

HYDROCORTISONE

Uses

- Critical illness–related corticosteroid insufficiency (major trauma, septic shock)
- Septic shock: Relative adrenal insufficiency (not responsive to fluid and vasopressure)
- Thyrotoxic crisis (inhibits T4 conversion to T3)
- Chronic autoimmune thyroiditis
- Myxedema coma
- Fulminant vasculitis
- ITP
- Organ transplantation
- Anaphylactic shock
- Ulcerative colitis, either oral or retention enema
- Severe allergic reaction
- Malignancy: In combined chemotherapy in ALL; in advanced malignancy provides symptomatic relief by increasing appetite and controlling secondary hypercalcemia

Side Effects

- Peptic ulcer
- Delayed wound healing
- Hyperglycemia
- Skin fragility and easy bruising
- Hypertension
- Growth retardation
- Proximal myopathy and osteoporosis
- HPA axis suppression
- Susceptibility to infection

It is available as hydrocortisone hemisuccinate powder in a bulb containing 100 mg of drugs.

POTASSIUM CHLORIDE (KCl)

Uses

- Hypokalemia

In nondiabetic and normal renal function: 0.6 mmol/kg/h infusion in saline.

In patients with acute kidney injury: 0.3 mmol/kg/h.

DKA with diabetes mellitus: 0.2 mmol/kg/h.

A 10-mL ampoule contains 150 mg/mL of KCl. One gram of KCl is equivalent to 13.4 mmol of potassium.

A total of 50 mmoL/day or 4 g is sufficient to prevent depletion and 100 mmol/day is sufficient to treat deficiency.

Side Effects

- Arrhythmia
- Bleeding
- Hyperkalemia
- GI disturbance
- Cardiac arrest

ANTIBIOTICS

Principles governing the use of antibiotics in surgery are the following:

- Before starting antibiotics, suspect the possible causative organism.
- Obtain culture of blood, urine, sputum, pus, or any other relevant sample prior to initiating empirical antibiotics.
- Use narrow-spectrum antibiotic whenever possible.
- Use for optimal duration: Prophylaxis is limited to single-dose, empirical therapy (3–5 days).
  - *Monomicrobial infection*: UTI, 3–5 days; bacteremia, 7–14 days; osteomyelitis, 6–12 weeks
  - *Peritonitis*: Penetrating GI trauma with minimal contamination, 3–5 days; perforated or gangrenous appendicitis, 5–7 days; perforated viscus with moderate degree of contamination, 7–14 days
- Combination of broad spectrum antibiotics is justifiable in case of suspected severe polymicrobial infection.
- In clean and clean-contaminated procedures, do not administer additional prophylactic

antimicrobial agent doses after the surgical incision is closed in the operating room, even in the presence of a drain.[2]

- Antibiotics are not substitute for drainage of surgical infection.
- They are used in procedures associated with ingress of significant numbers of organisms (colonic surgery) or in whom the consequences of any type of infection due to the said process would be life-threatening (prosthetic valvular graft).
- Do not apply topical antimicrobial agents to the incision for the prevention of surgical site infection (SSI).[2]
- Only spreading infection or evidence of systemic infection requires use of antimicrobial agents (Table 14.1).

Table 14.1 Commonly Used Antimicrobials in Surgery

Drugs	**Mechanism of action**	**Organism**	**Side effects**	**Clinical uses**
Penicillin	Inhibition of cell wall synthesis	*Streptococci, staphylococci, gonococci* *Pneumococci, Clostridium, Bacteroides fragilis, Treponema, and Actinomyces* (most Gram-positive cocci, and bacilli, anaerobes, and spirochetes)	GI upset Allergic reaction Hematuria, albuminuria, hemolytic reaction Local irritability	Streptococcal infection, pneumococcal infection, meningococcal infection, gonorrhea, syphilis, anthrax, actinomycosis Gas gangrene
Amoxiclav	Inhibits cell wall synthesis	β-Lactam–producing resistant organisms such as *Staphylococcus aureus, E. coli, Proteus, Klebsiella, B. fragilis, Salmonella*	Diarrhea Allergic reaction Candidal infection	Urinary, respiratory, intra-abdominal, and gynecological sepsis Cellulitis Superficial skin infection Human and animal bite
Mezlocillin and azlocillin	Inhibit cell wall synthesis	*E. coli, Klebsiella, Salmonella, Pseudomonas*		Burns UTI Sepsis Their main role is in severe mixed infection in immunocompromised patients
Cephalosporin	Inhibits cell wall synthesis	First generation (cephalexin, cefazolin, cephalothin, cefadroxil): Gram-positive organisms and limited Gram-negative enteric organisms—*E. coli, Klebsiella*, and indole-negative *Proteus*	Hypersensitivity Altered LFT Neutropenia (mainly with ceftazidime) Bleeding due to hypoprothrombinemia (ceftriaxone and cefoperazone) Nephrotoxicity Colitis	Prophylaxis in surgery and postoperative infection Used as an alternative to penicillin Urinary infection: Ceftriaxone, cefotaxime, cefoperazone, cefuroxime

(*Continued*)

(*Continued*)

		Second generation (cefaclor, cefamandole, cefuroxime): First generation plus respiratory Gram-negative organisms Third generation (cefotaxime, cefoperazone, ceftriaxone, ceftazidime, cefixime, cefpodoxime): Mainly Gram-negative organisms Cefoperazone and ceftazidime: *Pseudomonas* Fourth generation (cefepime, cefoxitin, cefotetan) Cefepime: Antipseudomonal and Gram-positive coverage Cefoxitin and cefotetan: Second generation plus more active against anaerobes	Disulfiram-like reaction mainly with cefoperazone	Gram-negative septicemia: Combined with aminoglycoside Typhoid: Ceftriaxone
Aminoglycoside, gentamicin, amikacin	Cause misreading of mRNA code and affect permeability Binding and inhibition of 30s ribosomal unit	*Pseudomonas aeruginosa*, *Proteus*, *E. coli*, *Klebsiella*, *Enterobacter* Main feature with amikacin is that it is resistant to bacterial aminoglycoside-inactivating enzymes No antianaerobic activity *Enterococci*: Only Gram-positive organisms where it is drug of choice with either penicillin or vancomycin	Nephrotoxicity Ototoxicity Neuromuscular blockade	Septic shock with Gram-negative bacillary bacteremia Pneumonia UTI Septic burns Intra-abdominal infection
Fluoroquinolones, ciprofloxacin, levofloxacin, moxifloxacin	Inhibit DNA gyrase	Gram-positive cocci, bacilli, including MRSA, Gram-negative cocci and bacilli They are resistant to anaerobes	GI upset Dizziness, headache Allergic reaction Prolong QT interval Tendinitis Arthropathy Retinal detachment Leukopenia Neutrophilia	UTI Prostatitis STD GI infection Respiratory tract infection Bone and soft-tissue infection Skin and soft-tissue infection Their widespread use leads to resistant organisms

(*Continued*)

(*Continued*)

Carbapenems, imipenem, meropenem, ertapenem	Inhibit cell wall synthesis	Broad-spectrum Gram-positive and Gram-negative organisms and anaerobes Not active against MRSA Imipenem is hydrolyzed in the kidney by renal dehydropeptidase to toxic metabolite. To prevent this injury, imipenem is paired with cilastatin	Seizure	ESBL-resistant UTI Serious mixed abdominal infection Ertapenem has a longer half-life as compared to other carbapenems (4 hours vs. 1 hour) 1 g IV or IM OD suitable
Nitroimidazole, metronidazole, tinidazole, ornidazole, secnidazole	Interfere with DNA function Production of toxic metabolite	Anaerobic bacteria such as *B. fragilis*, *Clostridium difficile*, and *H. pylori* *E. histolytica* and other protozoa	GI upset Headache, dizziness Peripheral neuropathy on prolonged use	Prophylaxis and treatment of anaerobic infection after surgical procedure such as abdominal, colorectal, and pelvic surgery Pseudomembranous enterocolitis Amoebic liver abscess Amoebic colitis *H. pylori* infection
Vancomycin	Inhibits 50s ribosomal activity (protein synthesis inhibition)	MRSA, *Streptococcus viridans*, *Enterococcus*	Allergic reaction Nephrotoxic Ototoxicity Red man syndrome (histamine release due to rapid IV) Neutropenia, thrombocytopenia	MRSA infection Orally it is used for pseudomembranous enterocolitis
Macrolide, azithromycin, clarithromycin	Inhibit protein synthesis	Clarithromycin: *Mycobacterium avium complex*, atypical mycobacteria, Gram-positive cocci, *H. pylori*	GI upset Allergic reaction	Skin and soft tissue infection *H. pylori* infection in combination Atypical mycobacterial infection
Aztreonam	Inhibits cell wall synthesis	*H. influenza*, *Pseudomonas*, and Gram-negative bacilli No Gram-positive or antianaerobic activity	Same as penicillin	Serious hospital-acquired infections such as urinary, gastrointestinal, and biliary infections It can also be used in patients allergic to penicillin or cephalosporin
Clindamycin	Inhibits protein synthesis	Gram-positive cocci High activity against anaerobes (*B. fragilis*) Drug of choice for anaerobic lung abscess and invasive streptococcal infection	Allergic reaction Pseudomembranous enterocolitis	Abdominal, pelvic infection caused by anaerobic and mixed infections

(*Continued*)

(*Continued*)

Daptomycin	Binds bacterial membrane, results in depolarization, lysis	Active against aerobic, Gram-positive organisms such as MRSA and VRE	Myopathy	Serious infection caused by MRSA, VRE
Linezolid	Inhibits protein synthesis	MRSA, VRSA, VRE, *B. fragilis*	Mild abdominal pain, GI upset, headache, and allergic reaction Thrombocytopenia, pure red cell aplasia, pancytopenia Tongue discoloration Peripheral neuropathy Lactic acidosis Optic neuropathy	Uncomplicated skin and soft-tissue infection caused by MSSA, *Streptococcus pyogenes* Complicated skin and soft- tissue infection caused by MSSA, MRSA, especially diabetic foot without osteomyelitis Hospital-acquired infection Specially indicated for multidrug-resistant organisms such as MRSA and VRE Advantage: 100% bioavailability in oral as well as injectable forms
Colistin, polymyxin B	Interact with lipid A content of LPS, disruption of cell membrane increases permeability	Gram-negative bacilli or cocci including *Pseudomonas*, *A. baumannii*, *K. pneumoniae*, and *Enterobacter* *Proteus* is highly resistant Polymyxin B does not require dose modification in presence of renal insufficiency	Nephrotoxicity Neurotoxicity	Gram-negative septicemia
Trimethoprim–sulfamethoxazole	Inhibition of purine and DNA synthesis by inhibition of dihydrofolate reductase	*S. aureus*, *S. pyogenes*, *Streptococcus pneumoniae*, *M. catarrhalis*, *E. coli*, *P. mirabilis*, *N. gonorrhoeae*	Allergic reaction, GI upset Hypouricemia Sweet syndrome TEN Methemoglobinemia Pancytopenia Pseudomembranous colitis Hepatitis Cholestatic jaundice	UTI Respiratory tract infection Skin and soft-tissue infection GI infection *P. jirovecii* infection

(*Continued*)

(*Continued*)

Nitrofurantoin	Inhibition of ribosomal translation, bacterial DNA damage, and interference with Krebs cycle	*E. coli*, VRE, *S. aureus*, and *Staphylococcus saprophyticus*	GI upset Allergic reaction Hepatitis Peripheral neuropathy SIRS Acute pulmonary reactions such as fever, cough, myalgia, pleural effusion Headache	Acute uncomplicated and complicated UTI such as cystitis and pyelonephritis Prophylaxis of recurrent UTI
Tigecycline	Inhibits bacterial protein synthesis	Gram-positive and Gram-negative bacteria Anaerobes, atypical bacteria such as C. *pneumoniae* and C. *trachomatis* Mycobacteria and *Nocardia* (rapidly growing mycobacteria such as *M. fortuitum* and *M. abscessus*)	GI upset Hepatotoxicity Pancreatitis Headache Dizziness	Skin and soft-tissue infection Intra-abdominal infection Respiratory tract infection

References

1. Hassan F, Cooney RN. Hypocalcemia and hypercalcemia. In: Textbook of Critical Care. Vincent JL, Abraham E, Kochanek P, Moore FA, Fink MP, eds, 7th edn. Philadelphia: Elsevier.
2. Berríos-Torres SI, Umscheid CA, Bratzler DW, et al. Centers for disease control and prevention guideline for the prevention of surgical site infection. JAMA Surg 2017;152(8):784–91.

CHAPTER 15

Endoscopy

Endoscopy is a diagnostic and/therapeutic procedure used to examine body's interior using an instrument inserted through a natural body opening or incision. Through the endoscope one is able to see lesions and other surface conditions, take photographs, take biopsies, and retrieve foreign objects. Endoscopy includes the upper gastrointestinal endoscopy, colonoscopy, and bronchoscopy.

UPPER GI ENDOSCOPY

- This procedure involves visualization of mucosa of the upper GI tract, up to the second part of the duodenum.
- The instrument commonly used nowadays is a fiber-optic video endoscope, forward viewing 110 cm.

Preparation

- The patients are asked to fast for 6–8 hours for solids and 2–4 hours for liquids.
- Antibiotic prophylaxis is routinely not recommended, but for those who are at a high risk for developing bacterial endocarditis, single IV injection of co-amoxiclav should be administered before the procedure.
- If therapeutic intervention is planned, recent coagulation profile and platelet count should be within the safe range.
- Patients with chronic liver disease and ascites undergoing sclerotherapy should receive antibiotic prophylaxis.
- Patients who require percutaneous endoscopic gastrostomy (PEG) are also at a high risk for infection and need prophylactic antibiotics.
- Most diagnostic endoscopies can be performed under pharyngeal local anesthesia or without sedation; however, some endoscopists routinely use a combination of narcotics and benzodiazepines to provide sedation.
- Monitoring is required before, during, and after the procedure. Level of consciousness, vital signs, degree of pain, and respiratory status are routinely monitored.
- Supplemental nasal oxygen is required to decrease the frequency of desaturation.

Indications

- Diagnostic
  - Alarming symptoms for upper GI malignancy
    - Dysphagia
    - Persistent vomiting
    - Hematemesis/melena
    - Unexplained weight loss
    - Recent-onset dyspepsia after 55 years
    - Weight loss
    - Upper abdominal lump
    - Unexplained abdominal pain
    - Worsening dyspepsia
    - Abnormal findings on CT/MRI/USG
  - Hematemesis and melena of other etiology
  - Odynophagia
  - Signs and symptoms suggestive of GERD (persistent long-term reflux, odynophagia, or dyspepsia unresponsive to 6-week treatment in primary care)
  - To confirm the healing of esophageal and gastric ulcer
  - Surveillance of Barrett esophagus, gastric dysplasia, familial adenomatous polyposis (FAP; risk of duodenal polyp), esophagogastric varices
  - In corrosive poisoning, to assess the extent of injury (within 24–48 hours of corrosive ingestion)
- Therapeutic
  - Management of bleeding lesions such as varices and ulcer
  - Removal or ablation of malignant and premalignant lesions

- Management of upper GI obstruction with self-expanding metallic stents (SEMS)
- Enteral access of feeding (PEG, nasojejunal tube placement)
- Removal of foreign body

Contraindications

- Absolute
  - Recent MI
  - Pneumonia
  - Recent foregut surgical procedure
- Relative
  - Coagulopathy

Complications

These are rare, 1:1000.

- Most complications are related to sedation and patients' comorbidity (aspiration and cardiorespiratory complication).
- Perforation is rare but associated with most therapeutic procedures such as stricture dilatation, polypectomy, and mucosal resection if performed by inexperienced personnel.
- It can occur from the existing lesion like varices or from the biopsy or polypectomy site.
- There are three main complications associated with PEG: local infection, perforation/fistula, or tube dislodgement.

Operative Procedure

- First, spray local anesthetic inside the throat.
- Make the patient lie in left lateral position.
- Keep mouth piece or bite guard.
- Introduce the scope after applying lignocaine jelly over it.
- Look for the tongue–palate junction.
- Look for the pyriform fossa.
- Gently introduce the scope, while asking the patient to swallow.
- Then, gradually progress and visualize the esophagus, stomach, and duodenum.
- While removing the scope, do retroversion and capture the image of the gastroesophageal junction.
- Inspect the mucosa properly while withdrawing the scope (Figs 15.1–15.15).

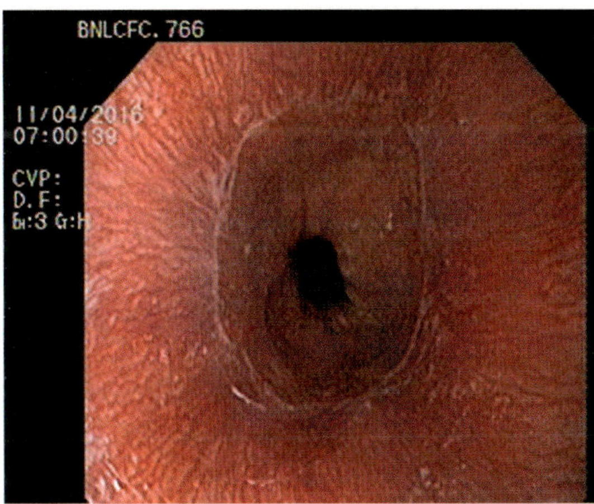

Figure 15.1 Normal squamocolumnar junction.

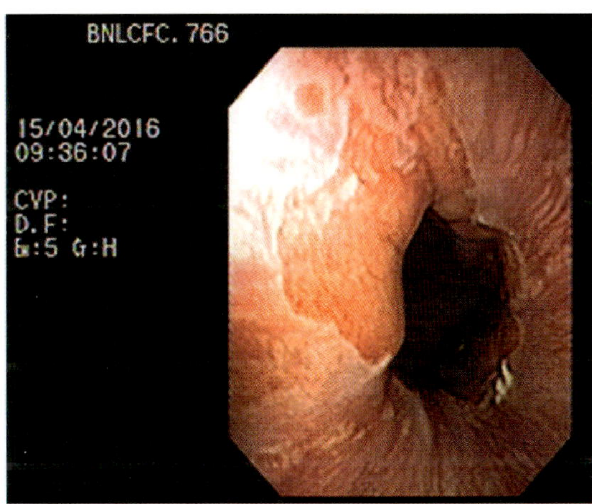

Figure 15.2 Barrett esophagus.

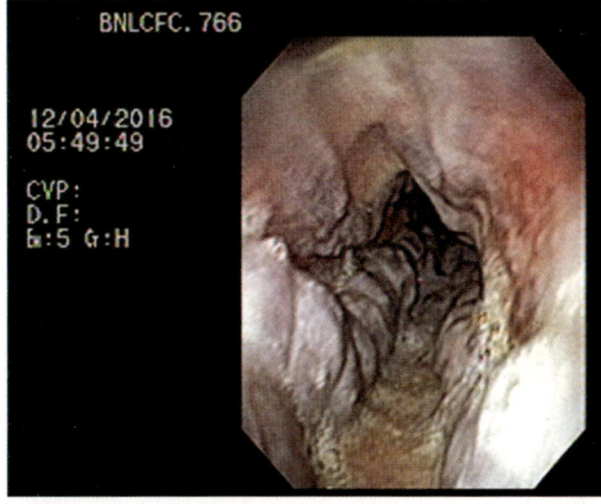

Figure 15.3 Esophageal varices.

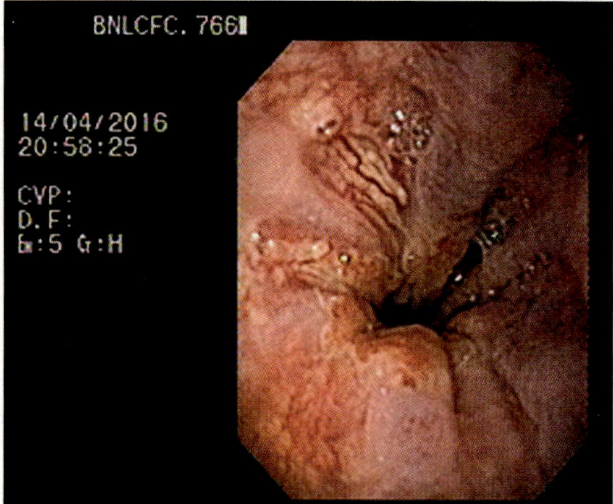

Figure 15.4 Reflux esophagitis.

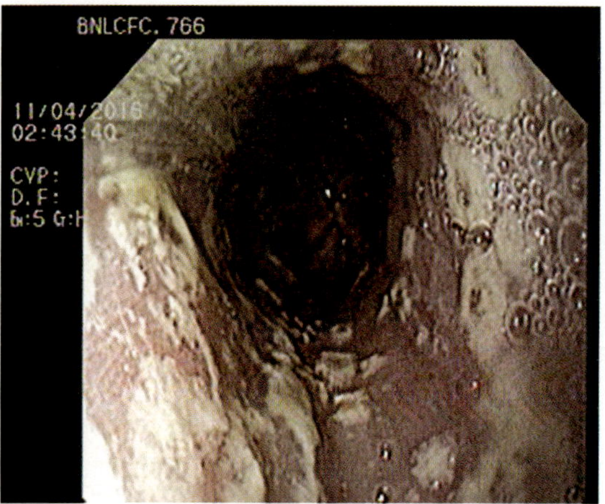

Figure 15.5 Esophageal candidiasis.

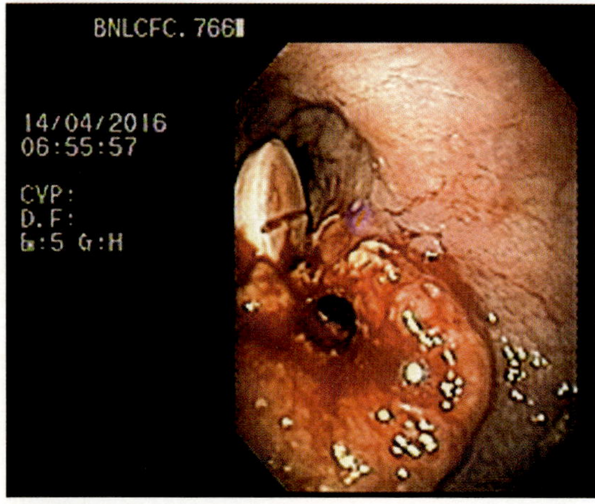

Figure 15.6 Esophageal cancer.

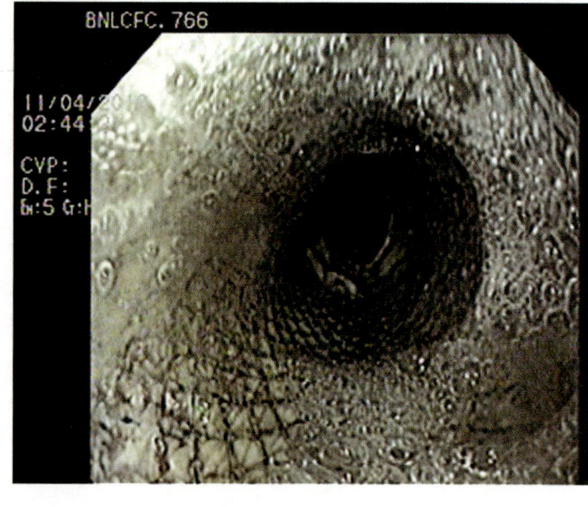

Figure 15.7 Esophageal stent.

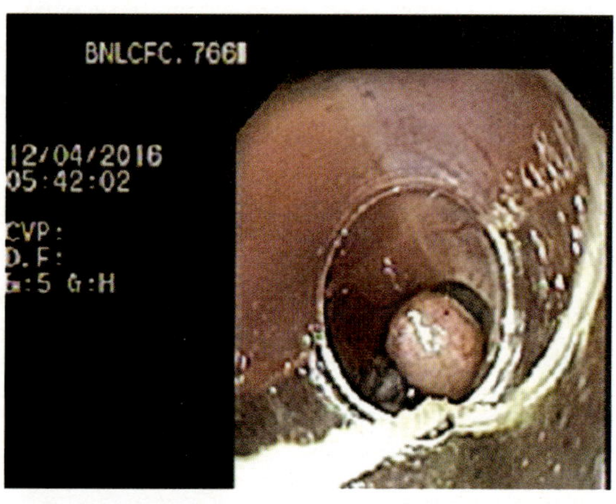

Figure 15.8 Endoscopic variceal ligation (EVL).

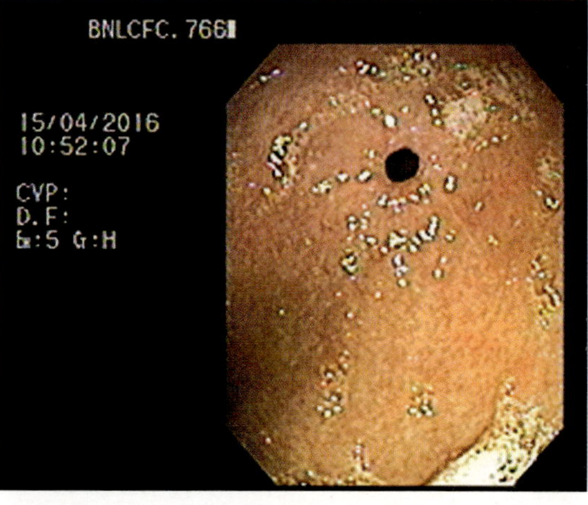

Figure 15.9 Gastric antrum.

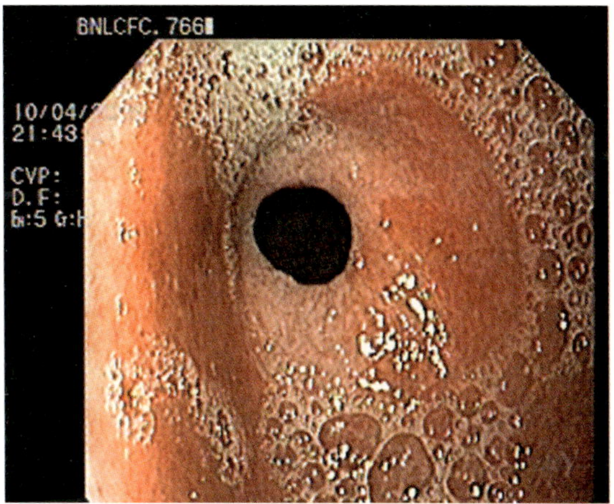

Figure 15.10 Antral gastritis.

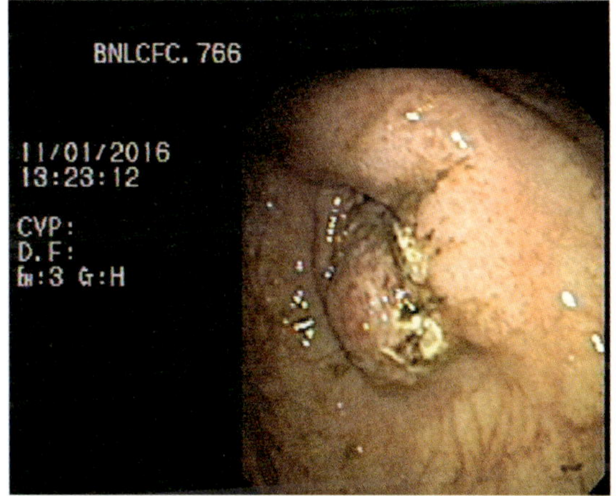

Figure 15.11 Gastric cancer.

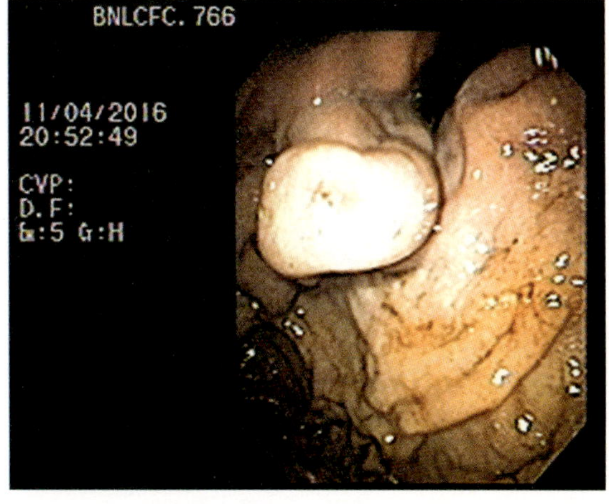

Figure 15.12 Fundal varix.

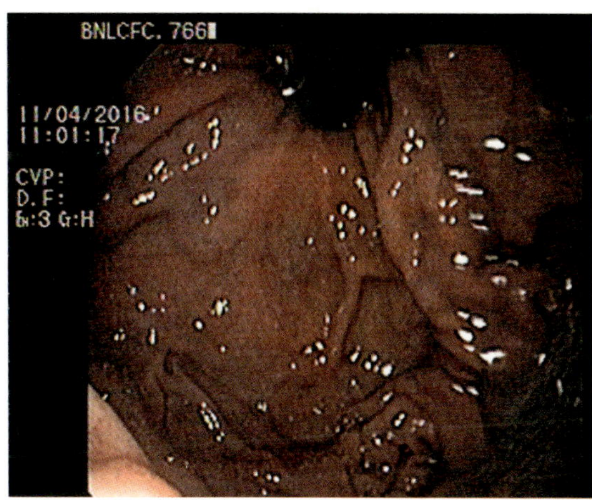

Figure 15.13 Gastric fundus in J position.

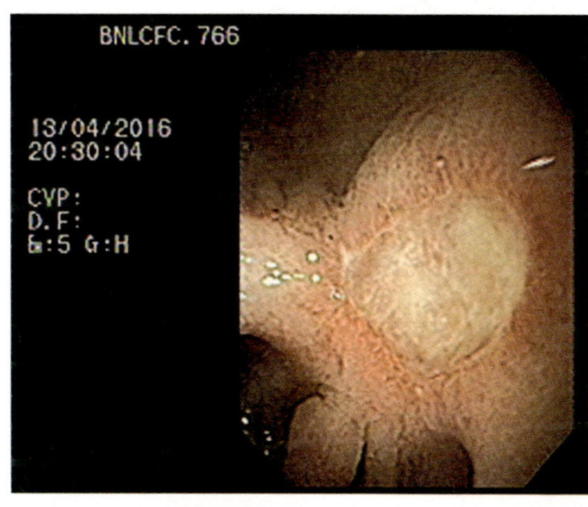

Figure 15.14 Duodenal ulcer.

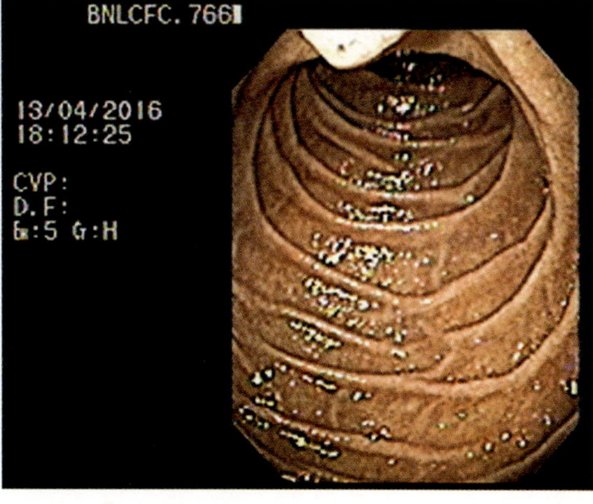

Figure 15.15 Second part of duodenum.

COLONOSCOPY

It should be done under sedation.

Preparation

Preparation is the same as for any major colonic surgery.

- Low-residue diet or clear liquid is followed for at least 1 day in elective colonoscopy.
- Enema alone is sufficient for sigmoidoscopy. Diverticular disease and presence of stricture require full bowel preparation using polyethylene glycol solution.
- Drinking extra clear fluid is better. Medication containing iron should be stopped at least 4 days back.
- Split-dose regimen (2 L + 2 L): Half of the polyethylene glycol 3350 solution is given in the prior evening and half on the morning of the day of procedure. This is preferred as compared to nonsplit (morning) dose regimen.
- Sodium picosulfate split-dose regimen is also equally effective.
- Patients with obstruction, perforation, dysphagia, severe diarrhea, and hemodynamic instability are contraindications for bowel preparation.
- Preprocedure antibiotic is usually not recommended. Antibiotics can be given to those with a high risk for infective endocarditis.

Procedure

- Colonoscope is inserted through anal canal and visualization is performed till cecum in most cases and if required terminal ileum is examined.
- Scope is maneuvered by seeing the wall of the colon on TV.
- Air, water, and suction can be applied to provide a clear field of vision. The goal is to reach up to cecum.
- Visualization of appendiceal opening, ileocecal valve, and transillumination over right inguinal region suggest that goal has been achieved.
- Mucosa is usually inspected while withdrawal and it should take at least 6 minutes.
- Length of the scope is 160 cm.

Indications

- Diagnostic
  - Unexplained lower GI bleed
  - Inflammatory bowel disease
  - Fecal occult blood positive
  - High risk for carcinoma of colon
  - Chronic persistent diarrhea
  - Abnormality found on CT or barium enema examination
  - Chronic constipation
  - Patients with carcinoma (to check for synchronous malignancy)
  - Preoperative and intraoperative localization of lesion
  - Surveillance of IBD and follow-up after polypectomy or cancer
- Therapeutic
  - Dilation of stricture/stent placement
  - Hemostasis, in case of a bleeding lesion
  - Reduction of sigmoid volvulus
  - Polypectomy
  - Decompression and tube placement in pseudo obstruction (Ogilvie syndrome)
  - Endoscopic submucosal dissection for early colorectal malignancy (not recommended for invasive cancer)

Contraindications

- Absolute
  - Acute diverticulitis
  - Peritonitis
  - Toxic megacolon
- Relative
  - First 3 months after MI
  - Ascites
  - Peritoneal dialysis

Complications

Factors associated with colonoscopic complications include elderly patients, active colitis, extensive diverticulitis, internal hernia, and therapeutic colonoscopy. Some complications are as follows:

- Perforation: It occurs due to excessive shaft tip pressure (mechanical pressure) and excessive air insufflations (barotrauma) in severe diverticular disease and electrocautery injury. Full-length colonoscopy in the presence of severe colitis or polypectomy is associated with 1% risk of perforation. Small perforation can be closed using hemoclip.
- Hemorrhage: Polypectomy is associated with 1–2% risk of bleeding. Submucosal injection of

adrenaline and hemoclip can be used to control bleeding. Repeat colonoscopy is advised for continued or recurrent bleeding, transfusion requirement, and hemodynamic instability

- Transmission of infection can occur.
- Abdominal distention and pain: It can occur due to intraluminal gas. It can be minimized by evacuating air while withdrawal and insufflating CO_2 instead of room air as it is rapidly absorbed.
- Postpolypectomy coagulation syndrome: Transmural electrocoagulation injury with microperforation during polypectomy, usually sessile, leads to localized pain secondary to peritoneal irritation along with fever, tachycardia, and leukocytosis. There is no evidence of diffuse peritonitis or overt perforation. Management includes intravenous antibiotics, bowel rest, and hydration with intravenous fluid.
- Splenic rupture and small bowel obstruction are extremely rare.
- Complications related to bowel preparation are the following: Nausea, bloating, malaise, and rarely syncope. Use of phosphate-based preparation is associated with chronic renal failure due to precipitation of phosphate crystals in the renal tubule. PEG-based preparation is associated with electrolyte imbalance (Figs 15.16–15.22).

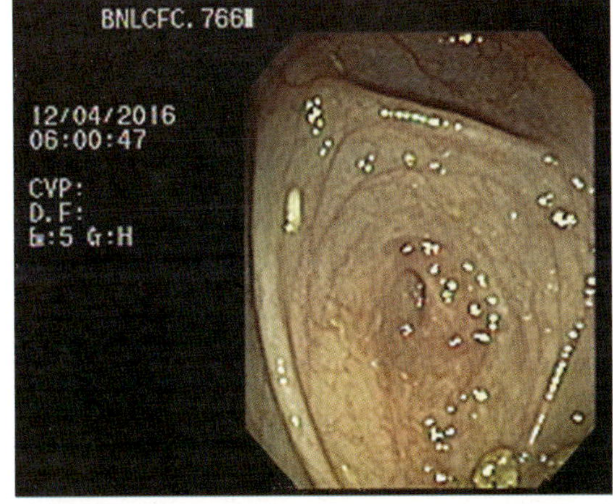

Figure 15.16 Normal appendicular opening.

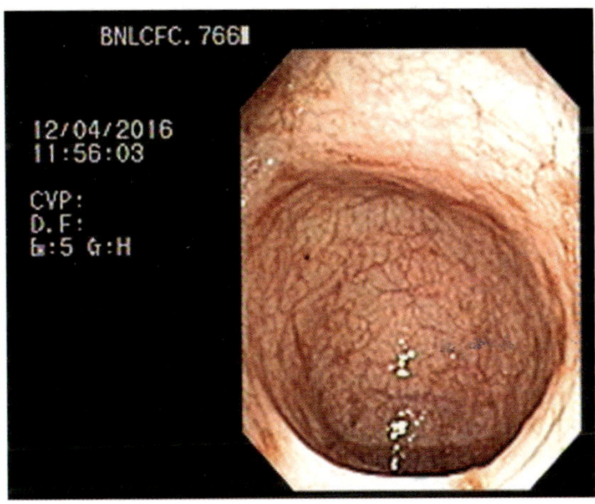

Figure 15.17 Normal terminal ileum.

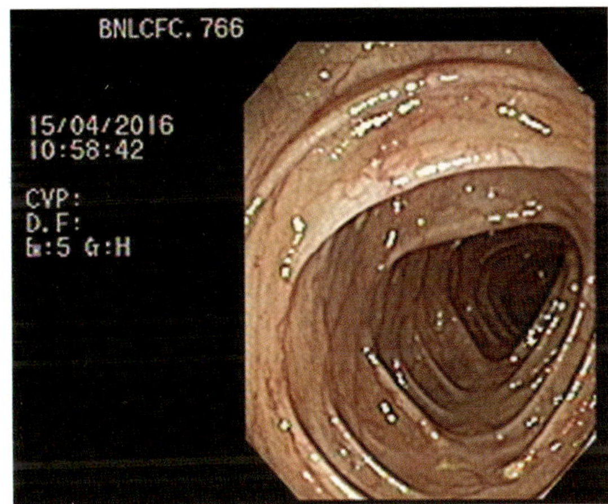

Figure 15.18 Normal transverse colon.

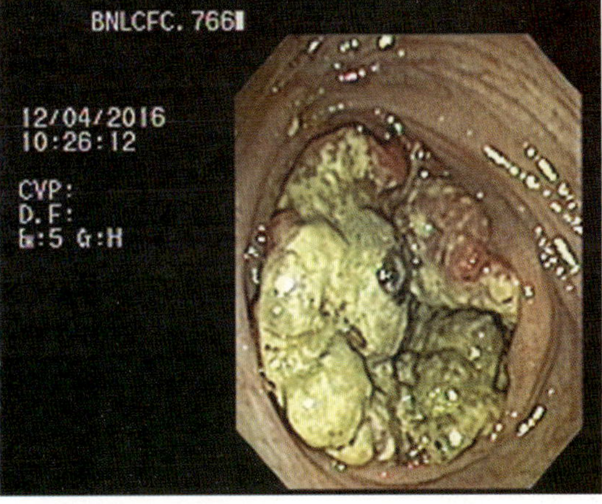

Figure 15.19 Colon cancer.

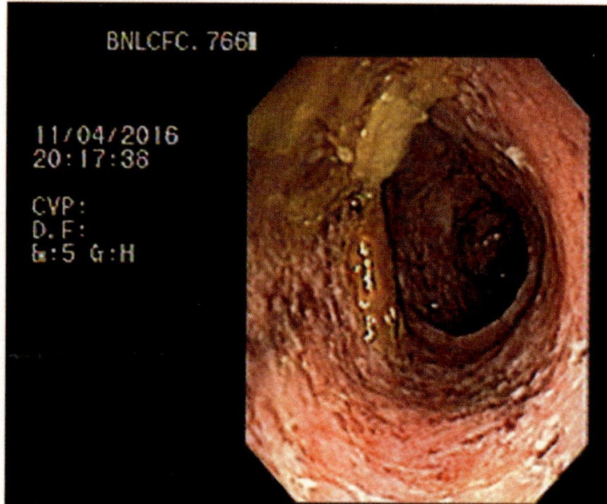

Figure 15.20 Ulcerative colitis.

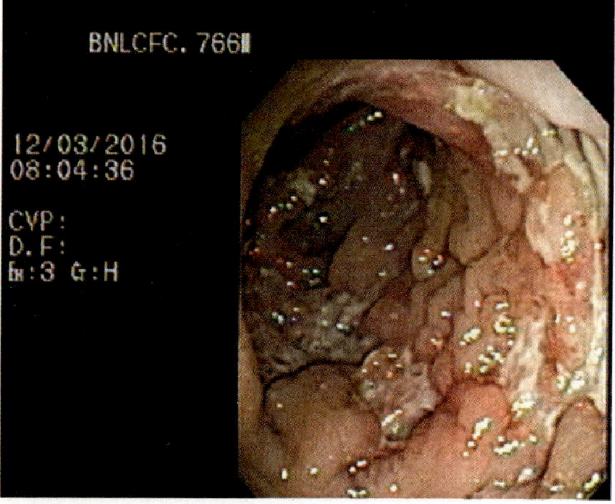

Figure 15.21 Crohn disease.

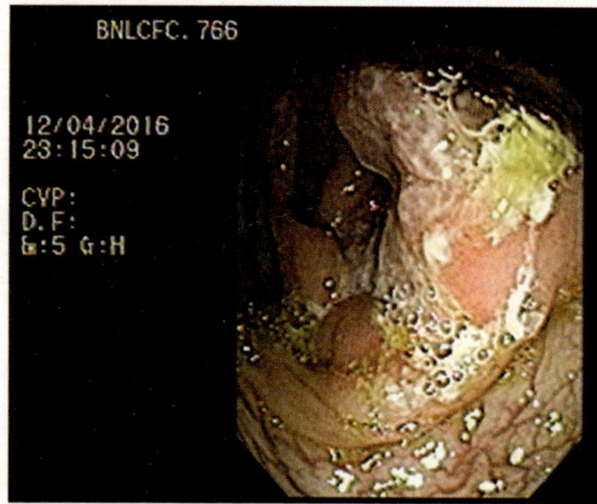

Figure 15.22 Ileocecal Koch's.

SMALL BOWEL ENTEROSCOPY

The areas which cannot be evaluated by conventional upper GI endoscopy and colonoscopy can be evaluated by either capsule endoscopy or small bowel enteroscopy. Sonde endoscopy has the ability to examine entire small bowel but it has limitations of long examinations time (6–8 hours), inability to perform therapeutic procedure, and risk of perforation. Nowadays, the techniques used for small bowel endoscopy include double balloon or single balloon enteroscopy.

Indications

- Diagnostic
  - Occult GI blood loss
  - Overt blood loss per rectum (cryptic hemorrhage)
  - Investigation of malabsorption syndrome
  - Crohn disease
  - Small bowel tumors
  - Surveillance for neoplasia in patients with polyposis syndrome such as FAP
- Therapeutic
  - Hemostasis with argon plasma coagulation, vasoconstrictor injection, clipping
  - Dilatation of inflammatory or fibrotic stricture
  - Resection of polypoid lesion

Procedure

- CO_2 is used instead of air.
- The principle is to fix the scope with a soft balloon and it is inflated and deflated serially as The scope advances.
- It fully evaluates The small intestine and obtains tissue biopsy.
- Therapeutic procedure for hemorrhage, obstruction, and occult neoplasia can be performed.
- In case of unsuccessful colonoscopy, it helps in evaluating full colon along with small bowel.

Complications

- Bleeding
- Perforation
- Pancreatitis
- Complications related to sedation

ENDOSCOPIC RETROGRADE CHOLANGIOPANCREATOGRAPHY (ERCP)

Indications

- Stone in the common bile duct
- Endobiliary stenting in cases of obstructive jaundice (the only definite indications for drainage of bile duct in patients awaiting surgery are cholangitis and intractable itching)
- Stenting in case of benign or malignant stricture, fistulae, postoperative bile leak, or large common bile duct stone
- Nasobiliary drainage in acute cholangitis
- Permanent metal biliary stent as a palliative procedure in inoperable periampullary malignancy
- Brush cytology in suspected malignancy of common bile duct
- Evaluation and treatment of sphincter of Oddi dysfunction
- Endoscopic pseudocyst drainage
- Treatment of complications of chronic pancreatitis such as stricture or stone
- To recover migrated stent, hemobilia investigated, choledochoscopy performed, and parasite removed
- Treatment of ampullary adenoma

Preparation

- NBM overnight
- Antibiotic prophylaxis
- Bowel preparation
- If bleeding profile is altered, then Inj. vitamin K IM once daily for 3 days

Procedure

- For ERCP, side-viewing scope is used.
- The patient is placed in left lateral position, and turned to prone position once in the second part of duodenum. Once in the second part of duodenum, the scope is gently pulled backward to achieve a straight and short loop position for better visualization and cannulation of the duct.
- Cannulation is best achieved when ampulla is at the 11 o'clock position.

  Two main devices are used—guidewire and sphincterotome. Once guidewire is seen in the common bile duct, sphincterotome is passed over the guidewire. Sphincterotomy is performed using Eendocut mode in the cautery machine. Therapeutic procedure such as stone extraction, stenting, and nasobiliary drainage can be performed.
- Postoperative observation is done for 24 hours.

Complications[1]

Early

- Bleeding
  - May be associated with sphincterotomy, ampullectomy, balloon dilatation after sphincterotomy, and pseudocyst drainage
  - May be immediate or delayed beyond 1–2 weeks
  - Prevention and management
    - Coagulopathy should be corrected.
    - Blended current should be used for sphincterotomy.
    - Balloon dilatation should be used instead of sphincterotomy in patients with irreversible coagulopathy and severe portal hypertension.
    - At the time of procedure, it can be controlled by the following: Balloon tamponade, thermal coagulation, endoclip placement, or injection sclerotherapy. If it is unsuccessful, embolization of gastroduodenal artery provides hemostasis.
- Perforation: It can be retroduodenal perforation, guidewire perforation, perforation anywhere in the upper GI tract, and perforation due to migrated stent. It occurs when the cut of sphincterotomy extends beyond the junction of CBD and duodenal wall. It is usually managed conservatively as acute abdomen by measures such as NBM, IV antibiotics, and adequate hydration. If the condition worsens, then surgical exploration is performed
- Pancreatitis: It is the most common complication. Young age, suspected sphincter of Oddi dysfunction, history of post-ERCP pancreatitis, difficult or failed cannulation, pancreatic sphincterotomy, and pancreatic duct injection are the risk factors for post-ERCP pancreatitis. It typically presents as pancreatic pain with a three fold rise in serum amylase at 24 hours. The different types of post ERCP pancreatitis are as follows: mild pancreatitis, <3-night stay; moderate, 4- to 9-night stay; and severe, >10-night stay and those who require ICU admission. It can be prevented by gentle cannulation of the desired duct

with minimal contrast injection, wire-guided cannulation as compared to contrast-guided cannulation, avoiding excessive coagulation near the pancreatic orifice, rectal administration of diclofenac or indomethacin, topical adrenaline, somatostatin IV bolus or infusion >12 hours, and pancreatic duct stenting

- Infection: Cholangitis occurs if contrast is injected proximal to the obstructed system. It is due to failure to provide adequate drainage in patients with obstructed system such as stone and stricture, nosocomial infection, cholecystitis, and pancreatic sepsis. Prophylactic antibiotics help to prevent infection. Delayed infection is usually due to blocked stent. It is routine practice to change the stent every 3–4 months
- Complications of anesthesia

Late

- Related to stent: Blockage, migration, and ductal damage
- Related to sphincterotomy: Sphincterotomy leads to bacterial contamination of bile which leads to pigment stone formation. Pancreatic sphincterotomy is associated with restenosis and recurrent pancreatitis.

Diagnostic ERCP is not used nowadays because of availability of MRCP.

Advantages of MRCP

- No contrast is required. Complications associated with contrast are thus avoided.
- Complications associated with invasive procedures, such as perforation, hemorrhage, and pancreatitis, can be avoided.
- Accurate anatomy above and below the obstruction can be seen.
- It is a cost-effective procedure.

ENDOSCOPIC ULTRASOUND

In routine endoscopy, views are limited to the mucosa. Submucosal or extraintestinal pathology cannot be assessed. This limitation can be overcome by EUS.

In this technique, the ultrasound probe is mounted at the end of an endoscope. Frequency is 7.5–12 MHz.

Improvement in the endoscope design that allows transducer and receiver to travel along the tortuous and long path, multiple frequency option availability, and treatment protocol based on accurate staging make the EUS an invaluable tool in the upper GI endoscopy.

Indications

- Diagnostic
  - Staging of upper GI and hepatobiliary malignancy
  - Diagnosis of microliths in the biliary system
  - Diagnosis of early pancreatitis, CBD stone, anastomotic stricture assessment, which also helps to decide whether the tumor is amenable to endoscopic mucosal resection (EMR) or not
  - Biopsy from submucosal lesion of upper GI tract, paraesophageal lymph node, portal lymph node, pancreaticobiliary malignancy, and drainage of pancreatic pseudocyst
- Therapeutic
  - Drainage of pseudocyst
  - Celiac plexus block in chronic pancreatitis
  - Botulinum toxin injection in achalasia
  - Botulinum toxin for the treatment of obesity (muscularis propria of the antrum)
  - Cholangiopancreatography (in case of failed ERCP or in altered anatomy): Transgastric or transduodenal drainage
  - Fine needle tattoo for small pancreatic tumor
- Main limitations are cost and training issue.
- Complications are oversedation, hemorrhage, and perforation.

CAPSULE ENDOSCOPY

- With a routine upper GI scope, we can visualize up to the second part of duodenum and with a lower GI scope we can visualize up to the ileocecal junction. The remaining major portion of small bowel can be visualized with the help of capsule endoscopy.
- Other small bowel scopes are also available, such as Sonde scope.

Preparation

The patient should be NBM for 12 hours, oral iron should be stopped 3 days prior to study, and bowel preparation may help in better visualization of terminal ileum.

Three basic components of the procedure are as follows: An ingestible capsule, a portable data recorder, and a workstation equipped with image processing software.

Capsule will take around 50,000 images. Reconstruction will take around 2 hours.

Dummy patency capsule: It can be tracked via a handheld device; it dissolves after 40 hours if it gets impacted.

Available capsules:

- Small bowel capsules
  - PillCam SB
  - EndoCapsule
  - MiRo capsule
  - CapsoCam
- Esophageal capsule: It is used for detection of mucosal disease in patients with heartburn and screening of esophageal varices.
  - PillCam ESO
- Colonic capsule: It is used for screening of colon cancer.
  - PillCam Colon
  - Advantage: Non-invasive procedure
  - Disadvantages
    - High cost
    - Failure to localize the area
    - Failure to progress in case of stricture
    - Gets stuck within diverticula

Indications

- Diseases of the small bowel
- Malabsorption syndrome
- Crohn disease
- Polyps
- Obscure GI bleed

Contraindications[2]

- Absolute
  - Small bowel stricture
- Relative
  - Severe gastroparesis and pseudo-obstruction
  - Swallowing disorder

In future, capsules will be available which will take biopsy and deliver thermal energy for vascular lesions.

VIRTUAL COLONOSCOPY (CT COLOGRAPHY)

- This technique involves a combination of spiral CT and 3D reconstruction to display mucosal surface and lumen of colon.

  Steps in virtual colonoscopy include the following: Bowel preparation, air insufflations, image acquisition, image processing, and interpretation.
- Bowel preparation is the same as for any major colonic surgery.
- Small lesions, up to 5 mm, can be detected.
- It is a noninvasive procedure.
- Two hundred milliliters of air is inflated into the rectum and images are taken with two to three breath holdings, within 2–3 minutes.

Advantages over conventional colonoscopy

- There is less discomfort and shorter examination time.
- It provides three-dimensional images.
- There is less risk of perforation.
- More than 72% of patients prefer CTC as a screening procedure as compared to 5% who prefer conventional colonoscopy.
- More patients preferred repeat procedure with CTC.

Limitations

- Only diagnostic
- Small risk of perforation
- Long-term risk of radiation exposure

ADVANCES IN IMAGING IN GI ENDOSCOPY[2]

- *Narrow band imaging*: Most scopes now come with a switch which helps in converting standard to narrow band which uses filtered light to enhance the mucosal surface, especially capillary network. It helps in differentiating squamous from nonsquamous epithelium, so helps in identifying Barrett esophagus. Adenoma and carcinoma appear dark brown against blue-green background because of their rich capillary network. It uses two bands of light: (a) blue (for superficial capillary) at 415 nm and (b) green (subepithelial vessels) at 540 nm. In combination, both produce extremely high-contrast images
- *Chromoendoscopy*: Topical application of stains or pigments improves tissue localization,

characteristics, and diagnosis. It detects subtle mucosal abnormalities. Several agents have been used and include methylene blue, indigo carmine, Congo red, and Lugol's solution

- *Confocal fluorescence microendoscopy*: It achieves histological images at the time of endoscopy
- *Magnification endoscopy*: It may be used alone or in combination with NBI and chromoendoscopy to achieve near-cellular definition of mucosal surface
- Optical coherence tomography
- Autofluorescence
- Light scattering spectroscopy

References

1. Freeman ML. Adverse events of ERCP: prediction, prevention, and management. In: ERCP, 2nd edn. Barron TH, Kozarek RA, Carr-locke DL, eds. Philadelphia: Elsevier, 2013, pp 57–65.
2. Lindsay JO, Woodland P. Gastrointestinal endoscopy. In: Bailey and Love Short Practice of Surgery. Williams NS, O'Connell PR, McCaskie, eds, 27th edn. FL: CRC press, Taylor and Francis, 2018, 216–33.

CHAPTER 16

Frequently Asked Questions

GENERAL SURGERY

1. How will you diagnose and treat disseminated intravascular coagulation (DIC)?

A Diagnosis

There is no single test that diagnoses the DIC. The following finding may suggest DIC:

- Prolonged aPTT, PT, or thrombin time
- Decreased fibrinogen
- Increased fibrin degradation products (FDPs) or D-dimer assay
- Sudden fall in platelets ($<100\times10^9$/L)
- Fragmented red cells on peripheral smear (schistocytes)
- Bleeding and/or thrombotic complications

Treatment

DIC treatment involves the following:

- Treatment of primary medical or surgical cause
- IV fluids to maintain perfusion
- Use of plasma expanders
- Platelet concentrate should be given in setting of bleeding; target is 20,000–30,000/mm^3 (in most cases) or >50,000/mm^3 (intracranial or life-threatening hemorrhage); higher level may be desired in patients undergoing major surgery or invasive procedure.
- Fresh frozen plasma (FFP) should be given to patients with significant bleeding or prolonged PT and aPTT to replace hemostatic factors in active bleeding.
- Cryoprecipitate may be given when fibrinogen level is <80–100 mg/dL. Fibrinogen concentrate or platelet concentrate may be required.
- Heparin is not useful in acute DIC but may help in arterial or venous thromboembolism. It should be used only when platelet count is >50,000/mm^3 or there is no CNS or GI bleed. It should not be used in abruptio placentae or other obstetric conditions.
- Epsilon-aminocaproic acid (EACA) is not useful in acute DIC. It is useful only in profuse bleeding not responding to other conventional treatment. PT, aPTT, fibrogen, and platelet count should be monitored every 6 hours in acute DIC.

2. What is the basic difference between a tropic and a trophic ulcer?

A A trophic ulcer is associated with a neurogenic cause while a tropic ulcer is associated with malnutrition.

3. How much is the increase in percentage of hemoglobin after administering 1 unit of whole blood and 1 unit of PCV?

A One unit of whole blood increases hemoglobin by 0.5–1 g%, while 1 unit of PCV increases hemoglobin by 1–1.5 g%.

4. Which is the best fluid for replacement in case of burns? Describe in brief about commonly used formula for fluid resuscitation.

A
- Ringer lactate
- Ringer with 5% dextrose should be recommended for children younger than 2 years
- Fluid is replaced according to the Parkland formula (Baxter formula): 4 × total body surface area (TBSA) burns (%) × weight (kg).
- Half of the fluid should be supplemented within the first 8 hours and the remaining in the next 16 hours; time is calculated from the time of accident, not from the time of admission of the patient
- Urine output is the best indicator of monitoring fluid therapy in burns

Resuscitation targets are as follows:

- Urine output: 0.5–1 mL/kg/h
- Pulse: Easily palpable peripheral pulse
- Sensorium: Patient should be easily arousable

- SBP >100 mmHg
- Base deficit <2

Other formulas used for fluid resuscitation:
- Modified Brooke: 2 mL/kg × TBSA burns (%)
- Rule of tens: TBSA burns (%) × 10 = fluid rate (mL/h) (for 40–80 kg)

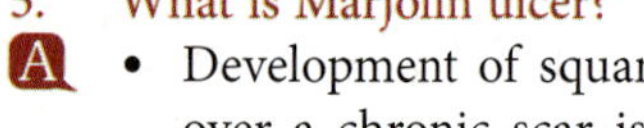

5. What is Marjolin ulcer?

- Development of squamous cell carcinoma over a chronic scar is known as Marjolin ulcer. Presence of overturned wound edges indicates malignant transformation.
- Peculiarity: It is slow growing due to absence of blood vessels.
- It is painless due to absence of nerve fibers.
- Lymph nodes are not enlarged due to absence of lymphatics.
- Biopsy from wound edges is recommended.
- Excision with 0.5- to 1.0-cm margin is recommended.

6. What is Pott puffy tumor?

Osteomyelitis of the skull (frontal bone) associated with subperiosteal swelling and edema

7. Describe in brief about keloid.

Keloid is made up of dense collagen. The most common site is presternal area followed by back, shoulder, and earlobe.

Treatment
- Intralesional injection of steroid (triamcinolone) (treatment of choice)
- Silicones in combination with pressure garment or intralesional 5-FU, bleomycin, and verapamil also effective
- Cryotherapy alone
- Laser therapy: Can also use pulsed dye laser (PDL) and neodymium–yttrium–aluminum–garnet (Nd:YAG) laser to treat keloid

In case of failure of these treatments:
- Excision with adjuvant electron beam irradiation or brachytherapy with iridium-192 can be attempted to reduce recurrence.
- Excision along with perioperative intralesional steroid or 5-FU also helps to reduce the recurrence.
- Five percent imiquimod topical cream can be used postsurgery to reduce recurrence.
- Cryotherapy can also be used to reduce recurrence.

8. Which is the best disinfectant?

Soap and water constitute the best disinfectant, and hand washing is the most important preventive measure for infection.

9. What are characteristics of malignant melanoma?

- *Most common*: Superficial spreading
- *Least common*: Acral lentiginous
- *Most malignant*: Nodular variety and acral lentiginous
- *Good prognosis*: Lentigo maligna melanoma
- *Most common site*
  - *Males*: Lower back
  - *Females*: Leg
- *Risk factors*
  - Family history
  - Benign nevi
  - Race
  - Sunlight exposure
  - Fair complexion
- *Diagnosis*: Excision biopsy
- Sentinel lymph node biopsy (SLNB) is recommended for 1- to 4-mm thick melanoma; it is also useful in <1-mm thick melanoma with adverse features such as >1 mitosis/mm and ulcerated
- Suspect malignancy in benign mole when the following are present: (a) asymmetry, (b) bleeding, (c) color change, (d) diameter expansion, and (e) elevation

Treatment
- *Stage I*: <1-mm thick, wide local excision with 1-cm margin
- *Stage II*: 1- to 4-mm thick, margin 2 cm, SLNB
- *Stage III*: >4-mm thick, margin 2 cm, SLNB optional (there is no evidence that margin more than 2 cm is beneficial)

10. What are various stages of tuberculoid lymph node?

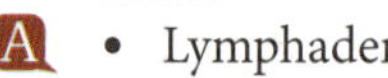

- Lymphadenitis
- Perilymphadenitis
- Cold abscess
- Collar stud abscess
- Sinus or ulcer

11. What are the various types of edges of ulcers?

A
- *Undermined*: Tuberculoid ulcer, amoebic ulcer, pyoderma gangrenosum, and some form of pressure ulcer
- *Sloping*: Healing ulcer and venous ulcer
- *Raised and rolled out*: Basal cell carcinoma
- *Raised and everted*: Squamous cell carcinoma
- *Punched out*: Trophic ulcer and arterial ulcer

12. What are different types of hemorrhage? How will you identify different types of bleeding and various methods of hemostasis?

A Types of hemorrhage
- *Primary*: Occurs during surgery; direct trauma to vessel
- *Reactionary*: Occurs within the first 24–48 hours of surgery due to slippage of ligature or wearing-off effect of anesthesia and dislodgement of clot
- *Secondary*: Occurs 7–14 days after surgery, secondary to infection

Identification of types of bleeding
- *Arterial*: Bright red, pulsatile, and spurter
- *Venous*: Dark red, copious, and continuous
- *Capillary*: Bright red and oozing

Methods of hemostasis
- Pressure: Temporary pressure with thumb
- Position: In venous bleeding from venous ulcers, elevation of the limb may be the only thing required
- Packing: Packing or pressure used in prostatectomy and abscess cavity
- Tourniquets for limb surgery
- Hemostatic clamp
- Sclerotherapy for bleeding esophageal varices
- Diathermy: Cauterization of small bleeders
- Ligature: Small vessels
- Transfixation: Small vessels
- Clip: Ligaclip in cholecystectomy for cystic artery or other small blood vessels
- Adrenaline pack: 1:1000 dilute solution used
- Thrombin: Local hemostatic
- Gelatin sponge (gel foam) or fibrin sealant
- Harmonic scalpel: Cuts and coagulates simultaneously at a vibration of 55 kHz; converts electric current to mechanical energy
- Vessel-sealing device (LigaSure™): Can cut and coagulate vessels up to 7-mm diameter
- Laser, photocoagulation, and argon beam coagulation
- Embolization: Can intentionally place hemostatic agent inside the vessel to stop bleeding or occlude the blood supply to the tumor

13. A patient is brought to casualty with severe hypotension due to ruptured aortic aneurysm. The patient is nearly dying and there is no time to cross-match the blood. Which blood group should the medical officer demand?

A O-negative

14. What are the complications of blood transfusion?

A *Transfusion reaction* occurs due to use of incompatible blood or use of blood that has already hemolyzed or crossed expiry date. It can be classified as infectious hazards, noninfectious hazards, and hazards associated with massive blood transfusion.[1] Diagnosis is based on a high index of clinical suspicion, hemoglobinuria, and positive Coombs test.

Infectious hazards*

Transmission of infections
- HBV
- HCV
- HIV
- Human T-cell lymphotropic virus
- West Nile virus
- Chagas disease
- Zika virus
- Malaria
- Bacterial infection
- Parasitic infection
- *Toxoplasma*

Noninfectious hazards
- *Pyrexia:* It occurs due to the presence of pyrogen and is managed by administration of antihistamines and antipyretics.
- *Allergic reaction*: It occurs due to the presence of plasma products. It can be prevented by giving leukocyte-depleted

* Pathogen-reduction technology inactivates potential infectious agents in the blood component. It inactivates virus, bacteria, and parasite. It is available in the USA for plasma and platelets.

blood. It can occur with any blood product but is more commonly associated with FFP and platelets.
- *Mild*: Rash, urticaria, and flushing
- *Severe*: Anaphylactic shock
- *Treatment*: Stop transfusion, administer antihistamines, in severe cases steroids and epinephrine

- *Transfusion-associated circulatory overload (TACO)*: It is common in patients with severe anemia and older patients with underlying heart disease. It is characterized by cardiogenic pulmonary edema resulting in acute respiratory distress. It presents as acute or worsening pulmonary edema within 6 hours of transfusion.
  - *Clinical features*: Dyspnea, coughs, rales, and pedal edema
  - *Treatment*: Diuretics and symptomatic, oxygen, phlebotomy, and increased transfusion time (4 hours)
- *Transfusion-related acute lung injury (TRALI)*: It is noncardiogenic pulmonary edema related to transfusion of any plasma-containing blood products. It occurs within 6 hours of transfusion.
  - *Cause*: Antigranulocyte or anti–class I or class III MHC antibody
  - *Symptoms*: Fever, rigors, and bilateral pulmonary infiltrates
  - *Treatment*
    - Transfusion discontinued
    - Supplemental oxygen
    - Mechanical ventilation
- Hemolytic transfusion reaction
  - *Acute (<24 hours)*: It is due to ABO incompatibility. There is intravascular destruction of red blood cells, and consequent hemoglobinemia and hemoglobinuria. Clinical features include fever, rigor, loin pain, oliguria, hypotension, and jaundice. Treatment is as follows:
    - Transfusion stopped
    - A sample of the recipient blood sent to the blood bank along with suspected unit for comparison with the pretransfusion sample
    - Per urethral catheterization
    - Adequate hydration
    - Symptomatic treatment
    - Mannitol and frusemide SOS
    - Bicarbonate to alkalinize urine

In anaesthetized patients, diffuse bleeding and hypotension is the cardinal sign of acute transfusion reaction.

  - *Delayed (3–21 days after transfusion)*: It is due to antibody to Rhesus factor (Rh factor); it occurs after 3–21 days. Extravascular hemolysis occurs. Clinical features include anemia, jaundice, and hematuria. Treatment is as follows:
    - Corticosteroid, immunoglobulin or rituximab
    - Supportive measures to maintain fluid balance and erythropoietin may be required in patients who develop anemia due to renal failure
- *Transfusion-associated graft-versus-host disease*: This occurs due to engraftment of viable donor T cells from the blood component in a susceptible recipient. Clinical features include rash, watery diarrhea, fever, anorexia, and vomiting. Liver function test abnormality is prevented by irradiation of blood components, which inactivates T cells. Treatment is corticosteroid and cytotoxic agent.
- *Transfusion-associated iron overload*: It occurs in patients who require long-term red-cell support such as those with congenital or acquired anemia. Each unit of packed red cells contains about 250 mg of iron. Heart, liver, and endocrine organs are affected leading to cardiomyopathy, cirrhosis, and diabetes. Diagnosis is by liver biopsy, magnetic resonance imaging, or serum ferritin testing. Chelation therapy is the main treatment approach.
- *Immunomodulation*: Blood is a proven immunosuppressant. Its effect is due to

altered leukocyte antigen presentation and a shift to the T-helper type 2 phenotype. It increases the risk of infection. Risk increases after 1 unit and almost certainly after 15 units of transfusion.

- *Complications due to IV line*
  - Infection
  - Thrombophlebitis
  - Air embolism
- *DIC*: It occurs due to ABO incompatibility.
  - Dilutional thrombocytopenia
  - Dilution of factor V and factor VIII necessary for clotting
- *Metabolic complications*
  - Increased level of serum hydrogen and potassium
  - Decreased 2,3–diphosphoglycerate level
  - Hypocalcemia
  - Metabolic alkalosis

Complications due to massive transfusion

Massive transfusion refers to single transfusion of >2.5 or >5 L in 24 hours. It can also be defined as transfusion of more than 10 units of packed red blood cell within 24 hours.

- Hyperkalemia: Due to RBC lysis
- Hypothermia: Blood must be warm before transfusion
- Citrate toxicity
- Metabolic alkalosis

15. What are the complications of typhoid fever? Describe the classical presentation and tests in brief that help in diagnosis of typhoid fever.

A Classical presentation

Classical presentation of typhoid fever is relative bradycardia and neutropenia with relative lymphocytosis. Lipopolysaccharide endotoxin is responsible for neutropenia with splenomegaly.

Complications

Most complications of typhoid occur in the third week of fever and are as follows:

- Gastrointestinal tract (GIT)
  - Paralytic ileus (most common)
  - Hemorrhage (second most common)
  - Perforation (most common cause of ileal perforation in tropical countries)
  - Cholecystitis
  - Splenic abscess
- Genitourinary tract (GUT)
  - Cystitis
  - Orchitis
- CVS
  - Endocarditis
  - Myocarditis
- CNS
  - Meningitis
  - Encephalitis
- Blood
  - Anemia
  - Thrombocytopenia
- Bone
  - Osteomyelitis

Diagnosis

For diagnosis of typhoid, following tests will be positive:

- *First week*: Blood culture
- *Second week*: Agglutination test (serum Widal)
- *Third week*: Stool culture
- *Fourth week*: Urine culture

16. Which is the usual mode of spread of soft-tissue sarcoma and which sarcoma spreads by lymphatic route?

A
- *Soft-tissue sarcoma*: Blood (lung) is the usual mode of spread of soft-tissue sarcoma. However, the most common site of metastasis in retroperitoneal sarcoma is liver.
- *Lymphatic spread*: Lymphatic spread occurs in the following:
  - Clear cell sarcoma
  - Rhabdomyosarcoma
  - Angiosarcoma
  - Epithelioid sarcoma
  - Malignant fibrous histiocytoma
  - Synovial sarcoma

Pearls

- Tensile strength of the wound never becomes that of normal skin. At the end of the first week, wound acquires approximately 10% of the tensile strength of normal skin. It increases rapidly over the next 4 weeks and then increases gradually up to the third month and then reaches a plateau of 70–80% of the normal skin.
- *Wound healing*
  - *First day*: Neutrophil
  - *Second day*: Epithelial cells
  - *Third day*: Macrophage
  - *Fifth day*: Granulation tissue and neovascularization
  - *Second week*: Collagen and fibroblast
  - *First month*: Scar (connective tissue)
- The most common site for rhabdomyosarcoma is orbit.
- Malignant fibrous histiocytoma is the most common soft-tissue tumor of the adult.
- Malignant change in retroperitoneal lipoma may present with abdominal pain, renal failure, and weight loss or may be asymptomatic.
- Immunohistochemical marker used for rhabdomyosarcoma is desmin.
- The most common malignancy in an HIV-positive individual is NHL followed by Kaposi sarcoma. Kaposi sarcoma consists of asymptomatic purple to brown bruises and progress of spot, plaque, or nodule. The most common site is extremities. It is locally aggressive. Radiation and intralesional chemotherapeutic injection are the primary treatment. Surgery is reserved for bowel obstruction or airway obstruction.
- Dermatofibrosarcoma protuberans is a low-grade sarcoma commonly seen on trunk. It presents as smooth flesh-colored nodule in or beneath the skin in midadult life. It is positive for CD34. Wide local excision with 2- to 4-cm margin is the treatment of choice. Imatinib is the first-line treatment for advanced disease.
- Thrombocytopenia is the most common coagulopathy in surgical patients.
- If patients with fracture shaft femur develop dyspnea, bleeding, and petechial hemorrhage in the chest after 2 days, it is due to fat embolism.
- Primary hemorrhage develops at the time of surgery, reactionary within 24 hours, and secondary hemorrhage is between 7 and 14 days of surgery.
- Venous air embolism is seen in neurosurgical procedure (mostly posterior fossa surgery) performed in sitting position. Other causes of venous air embolism are the following: Surgery of head and neck, diagnostic and therapeutic air injection, obstetric procedure, accidental entry of air into vein, laparoscopy, and central venous catheter. Give 100% oxygen and place the patient in left lateral decubitus and head-low position.
- Radial artery is the preferred artery for cannulation. It is used to measure arterial blood gas analysis.
- Intra-abdominal pressure (IAP) during laparoscopy is 12–15 mmHg.
- The most commonly used gas for laparoscopy is CO_2 and flow of gas is 1 L/min.
- Shoulder pain in laparoscopy is due to CO_2 retention leading to irritation of diaphragm.
- Morbid obesity is body mass index (BMI) >40. Patients having BMI >40 or >35 with comorbid condition are candidates for surgery.
- Surgery for obesity includes the following: Vertical banded gastroplasty (restrictive), Roux-en-Y gastric bypass (mostly restrictive/malabsorptive), and biliopancreatic diversion with duodenal switch (largely malabsorptive).
- The most common immediate cause of death following bariatric surgery is peritonitis following anastomotic leak and cause of death within 30 days is pulmonary embolism.

- John Hunter introduced catgut in the surgery. Catgut is prepared from the submucosa of sheep intestine and is preserved in isopropyl alcohol.
- Polydioxanone (PDS) undergoes hydrolysis and complete absorption.
- Polyamide polymer is the raw material used for nylon suture.
- Infections caused by organisms are the following:
  - *Cellulitis/lymphangitis*: *Streptococcus pyogenes*
  - *Erysipelas*: Streptococci
  - *Necrotizing fasciitis (synergistic gangrene)*: Polymicrobial, most common being group A beta-hemolytic streptococci
  - *Carbuncle*: *Staphylococcus aureus*
  - *Tetanus*: *Clostridium tetani*
  - *Yaws*: *Treponema pertenue*
  - *Gas gangrene*: *Clostridium perfringens*
- Bowen disease is intraepithelial neoplasia (carcinoma in situ); its sites are the following: Skin or mucous membrane of mouth, anal canal, and genitalia.
- Actinic keratosis is the most common premalignant condition of skin.
- Breslow's method is more accurate as compared to Clark's level for predicting risk of metastatic disease.
- Intravascular thrombosis produces hemorrhagic skin infarction in children known as purpura fulminans.
- Nodular form is the most common type of basal cell carcinoma. Although basal cell carcinoma is radiosensitive, location of the tumor precludes its use. Surgical excision is the treatment of choice.
- According to recent NCCN guidelines, 4- to 6-mm margin for low risk and 10-mm margin for high risk is adequate for squamous and basal cell carcinoma.
- High-risk factors for SCC and BCC are the following: Size >2 cm on trunk and extremity, >1 cm on forehead and neck, and >6 mm on the central face. Rapid growth rate, immunosuppression, recurrence, poorly defined border, and presence of neurological symptoms are high-risk factors. On histology, moderate or poorly differentiated malignancy and perineural or vascular invasions are high-risk cases.
- The current favored method of bowel anastomosis is single layer extramucosal because it causes least tissue necrosis and luminal narrowing. It must include submucosa that has high collagen content and the most stable layer of anastomosis. It is popularized by Norman Matheson.
- Stapler used for MIPH is circular cutting stapler.
- Lambert is a seromuscular suture.
- In case of discrepancy in diameter of bowel while anastomosis, correction is made with cut into the antimesenteric border (Cheatle split) of the distal bowel.
- Bowel preparation prior to surgery provides little benefit. Meticulous prevention of spillage of intestinal content must be followed.
- Polypropylene is the ideal suture for vascular anastomosis. Needle must pass from within outwards.
- In surgical patients, malnutrition is best assessed by midarm circumference.
- The most common type of shock in emergency room is hypovolemic.
- The most common type of shock in surgical practice is hypovolemic.
- Hemorrhagic shock is classified according to blood volume lost:
  - *Class 1*: <15%
  - *Class 2*: 15–30%
  - *Class 3*: 30–40%
  - *Class 4*: >40%
- In neurogenic shock (head and spinal injury), interruption of sympathetic drive to heart leads to hypotension, warm extremity, decreased heart rate (bradycardia), flaccidity, and loss of reflexes.
- Release of endotoxins and activation of immune systems leads to vasodilation, hypotension, and high cardiac output in septic shock.

- Skin incisions are made along the Langer's line. Transverse abdominal incision is associated with better scar and less postoperative complications. The 22 number blades are used for abdominal incision.
- To minimize the risk of wound dehiscence or incisional hernia, the length of suture material used should be at least four times the length of incision to be closed.
- Abdominal wall closure requires delayed absorbable suture such as polydioxanone (PDS). Nonabsorbable suture such as polypropylene is associated with increased pain and sinus tract formation and does not have any significant difference in wound complications.
- A continuous suture of delayed absorbable suture with mass closure is the preferred method of abdominal wound closure.
- In the past, clindamycin was the most common antibiotic responsible for *Clostridium difficile* infection but nowadays, fluoroquinolones are the most prone toward increased risk to cause *C. difficile* infection.
- Drains should not be placed through end of incision but they are inserted through a separate incision to decrease the chance of wound infection.
- Capacitance coupling is the cause of an accidental electrical injury to the intraperitoneal structure during laparoscopy surgery.
- Bipolar diathermy is the choice for microsurgery and delicate procedure.
- Sequence of repair in hand injury
  - Wound debridement
  - Identification of artery, vein, and nerve
  - Bone stabilization
  - Extensor tendon repair
  - Flexor tendon repair
  - Vascular anastomosis
  - Nerve repair
  - Skin repair
- Typhoid ulcers are parallel to the long axis of bowel and in the lower ileum.

GASTROINTESTINAL TRACT

17. Write a short note about Zenker diverticulum.

A Zenker diverticulum is pharyngoesophageal pouch.

Location
- Between the transverse fiber of the cricopharyngeus muscle below and the oblique fibers of the inferior constrictor above, a triangular area contains a few muscle fibers and is referred to as Killian's triangle or dehiscence.
- The mucosa of the hypopharynx bulges from this space and forms diverticulum.

Clinical features
- Initially the patient may have a sensation of stickiness in the throat, irritation, cough, and intermittent dysphagia (globus).
- The following manifest when it enlarges: Dysphagia, regurgitation, and swelling in left side of neck.
- Chronic aspiration and repetitive respiratory infection (pneumonia), and lung abscess are common.

Investigation

A barium esophagogram with special attention to the oropharyngeal phase of swallowing is the best test to diagnose this condition.

Treatment
- Cricopharyngeal myotomy with either diverticulopexy or diverticulectomy is the treatment of choice.
- Endoscopic cricopharyngotomy and diverticulotomy using special diverticuloscope and endoscopic linear stapler to divide the septum between esophagus and diverticulum (Dohlman procedure) is the most effective for larger diverticulum >2 cm.

18. What is the etiology of achalasia cardia and its clinical features and treatment?

A Etiology
- Loss of ganglion cells in the myenteric (Auerbach) plexus (inhibitory myenteric neuron secretes VIP and nitric oxide; their loss leads to failure of relaxation of LES)
- Infection of neurons by virus (herpes zoster)
- Autoimmune: CD3/CD8 lymphocyte

Clinical features

Men and women are equally affected. It affects all ages; however, the common age is between 20 and 50 years.

- Progressive dysphagia (most common)
- Regurgitation common during night and may result in overspill in the trachea (pneumonia, lung abscess)
- Heartburn
- Hiccups
- Halitosis
- Chest pain
- Weight loss

Occasional dysphagia, regurgitation, and halitosis suggest Zenker diverticulum; it is best diagnosed by barium swallow.

Criteria for severity

If diameter of esophagus is:

- *<4 cm*: Mild achalasia cardia
- *4–6 cm*: Moderate achalasia cardia
- *>6 cm*: Severe achalasia cardia

Diagnostic criteria for achalasia

- Increased LES pressure
- Absent or incomplete relaxation of LES
- Absent peristalsis in the body of the esophagus
- Increased intraluminal pressure

Barium swallow is the investigation of choice in anatomical disorder and manometry is the investigation of choice for motility disorder of esophagus.

Pseudoachalasia: Tumor infiltration and tight stricture in distal esophagus will lead to similar manifestations.

Treatment

- Medical
  - Calcium channel blockers
  - Nitrates
  - Sildenafil
- Endoscopic
  - Injection botulinum toxin into LES. It provides temporary relief; repeat injection may be required. Repeated injection may complicate the future surgery.
  - Pneumatic dilation using Rigiflex balloon is the main alternative to surgery but has a risk of perforation.
  - Per oral endoscopic myotomy (POEM): It involves the opening of esophageal mucosa 10 cm above the LES with needle knife electrosurgery through endoscope. A large submucosal tunnel is created and circular muscle fibers are divided in the distal esophagus, LES, and proximal stomach, keeping the mucosa intact. Mucosa is closed with endoclip at the site of opening.
- Surgical
  - Modified Heller cardiomyotomy (open or laparoscopic or robotic) with partial fundoplication (in original description of Heller cardiomyotomy, both anterior and posterior muscle fibers were divided; only the longitudinal division of the anterior muscle fibers was performed in modified procedure)

19. What are the types of Barrett esophagus and how will you treat this condition?

Barrett esophagus is a columnar lined segment of esophagus of any length visible on upper gastrointestinal endoscopy. It is premalignant, leads to adenocarcinoma, and follows metaplasia–dysplasia–carcinoma sequence. It represents end-stage form of severe reflux esophagitis due to chronic gastroesophageal reflux disease (GERD).

The most common type is intestinal metaplasia.

Types

- Long segment (>3 cm)
- Short segment (<3 cm)
- Ultrashort segment (just at cardia)

Barrett's ulcer, stricture, and adenocarcinoma are the complications.

Treatment

- *Barrett's metaplasia (nondysplastic)*
  - Endoscopy every 3–5 years
  - PPI
- *Barrett's low-grade dysplasia*
  - High-dose PPI for 8–10 weeks
  - Four-quadrant biopsy at 1-cm interval recommended

- Endoscopic eradication or ablation for any mucosal irregularities (radiofrequency ablation, photodynamic therapy, and endoscopic mucosal resection)
- Repeat endoscopy with high-resolution white light endoscopy

- *Barrett's high-grade dysplasia*
  - American College of Gastroenterology statement: Esophagectomy is no longer necessary for the treatment of high-grade dysplasia because lymph node metastasis is unlikely.
  - Modalities of treatment for high-grade dysplasia include the following:
    - Photodynamic therapy
    - Radiofrequency ablation (most commonly used)
    - Cryotherapy
    - Endoscopic mucosal resection (EMR) and submucosal dissection

20. What is dysphagia lusoria?

A It is constriction due to vascular ring at aortic arch or great vessels, often due to aberrant great vessels, which leads to dysphagia.

Causes

- Anomalous right aortic arch and double aortic arch (most common cause)
- Abnormal right subclavian artery (arteria lusoria)

Diagnosis

By either barium or endoscopy. HRCT or angiography identifies vascular anomaly.

Treatment

In case of progressive dysphagia, treatment is thoracoscopic ligation and division of aberrant great vessel.

21. What is Schatzki ring?

- It is a thin, web-like projection at the squamocolumnar junction.
- It is diagnosed by endoscopy.
- Episodic dysphagia to solid food is a common presentation.
- Treatment: In patients without reflux, esophageal dilatation is performed. Patients with proven reflux require antireflux surgery.

22. What is Boerhaave syndrome?

- It is spontaneous perforation of esophagus at distal one-third.
- Perforation is due to barotrauma because of forceful vomiting against closed glottis.
- Patients present with severe chest pain and respiratory distress.

Diagnosis

- Chest X-ray: Air in the mediastinum, pleura, or peritoneum and pleural effusion
- Contrast swallow or contrast CT: The site of perforation confirmed

Treatment

- Broad-spectrum antibiotics
- Early presentation within 6 hours: Primary repair
- After 12 hours: Local tissue used to buttress the repair such as gastric fundus, intercostal muscle, or pericardium
- Large septic load associated with pleural and mediastinal contamination: T-tube within esophagus with properly kept drain and feeding jejunostomy

The most common site of iatrogenic perforation is cervical esophagus.

23. Which are the most common type of hiatus hernia and complication of hiatus hernia?

A Sliding hernia is the most common type of hiatus hernia and reflux esophagitis is the most common complication.

24. Describe important points about carcinoma esophagus.

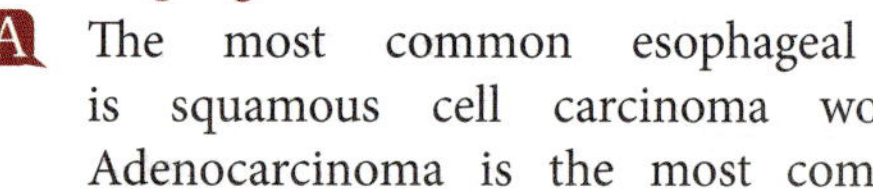

A The most common esophageal cancer is squamous cell carcinoma worldwide. Adenocarcinoma is the most common in the United States. The most common site is middle one-third.

Risk factors

- Risk factors for squamous cell carcinoma are as follows:
  - Alcohol
  - Tobacco
  - Low dietary fiber
  - Fresh fruits
  - Poverty
  - Achalasia
  - Caustic injury

- History of head and neck cancer
- History of radiation for breast cancer
- Achalasia
- Plummer–Vinson syndrome
- Tylosis
- Polyaromatic hydrocarbons
- Nutritional deficiency
- HPV infection
- *H. pylori* infection
- Occupational exposure
- Red meat consumption
- Hot food and beverages
- Risk factors for adenocarcinoma are as follows:
  - Tobacco
  - GERD
  - Barrett esophagus
  - Obesity
  - History of radiation therapy for breast cancer
  - Male patients
  - Caucasian
  - Western countries
- *H. pylori* infection, HPV infection, and aspirin use are associated with decreased risk of adenocarcinoma.
- Aspirin use, GERD, and obesity are associated with decreased risk of squamous cell carcinoma. Diet rich in β-carotene, vitamin E, and selenium helps to reduce the incidence of squamous cell carcinoma.

Clinical features

- Dysphagia (most common symptom)
- Weight loss
- Anorexia
- Chest pain
- Halitosis
- Odynophagia
- Horner's syndrome, hoarseness of voice, chronic spinal pain, diaphragmatic paralysis, and palpable lymph node suggest advanced disease

Classification

Siewert and Stein classification is for gastroesophageal junction tumor. They are of three types:

I: Esophageal
II: Cardiac
III: Subcardiac

Investigations

- Endoscopy is the investigation of choice for diagnosis.
- CT of the chest and abdomen is the first line of staging for distant metastases and local spread.
- In the absence of distance metastases, EUS is the investigation of choice for T and N staging.
- Ultrasonography of the abdomen: It helps to see for liver metastases.
- Bronchoscopy: It helps to see involvement of the main airway in patients with upper two-third malignancy.
- Positron emission tomography with CT: It helps in identification of distant metastases. Persistent PET activity after neoadjuvant therapy is a poor prognostic sign.

Treatment

Squamous cell carcinoma is radiosensitive and treated initially with chemoradiation while adenocarcinoma is treated with surgery.

- Stages 0 (Tis): For high-grade dysplasia and tumors that are limited to the mucosa <2 cm in size with well to moderate differentiation and no lymphovascular invasion, EMR is performed.
- Stages I and II (T2) (involvement of lamina propria, submucosal and muscularis propria): Ivor Lewis 2 stage esophagectomy (middle third) or transhiatal esophagectomy (more suitable for lower esophageal and GE junction tumor). Upper esophageal tumor requires three-stage esophagectomy. Resection margin is 10 cm proximal and 5 cm distal. Gastric tube conduit (based on right gastric and right gastroepiploic artery) is used to restore continuity.
- Neoadjuvant chemotherapy is indicated in stages II (T3) and III (involvement of adventia with or without lymph node involvement). Cisplatin and 5-FU for three cycles are used as neoadjuvant chemotherapy. Adjuvant treatment should be given to patients with positive margin, macroscopic residual disease, and poorly differentiated carcinoma.

- Criteria for unresectability: Distant metastases and extraregional lymph node involvement (para-aortic and mesenteric lymphadenopathy). Celiac node, mediastinal node, and supraclavicular node are considered regional node irrespective of tumor location.
- Locally advanced disease: It can be treated by palliative stenting using self-expandable metal stents (SEMS), laser ablation, or photocoagulation for dysphagia.
- Malignant tracheoesophageal fistula is best treated by SEMS.
- Combined chemotherapy and radiation is superior to chemotherapy alone in locally advanced disease.
- Metastatic disease: Epirubicin, 5-FU, and cisplatin are used. Another regimen is capecitabine and oxaliplatin with epirubicin.
- Trastuzumab, with 5-FU and cisplatin in case of HER2-positive GEJ tumor, is also used for treatment.

Prognosis

Polypoidal morphology has the best prognosis.

25. **What is infantile hypertrophic pyloric stenosis? What are its characteristics?**

A
- It occurs in first born full-term infant.
- The male:female ratio is 4:1.
- There is seasonal variation; it is more common in winter. There may be genetic predisposition; erythromycin use in early infancy and prone position are likely to be associated. Bottle feeding and maternal smoking are also associated with increased risk after the fourth week of birth.

Clinical features

- Nonbilious projectile vomiting immediately after feeding
- Signs of dehydration
- Weight loss
- Hypochloremic hypokalemic alkalosis with paradoxical aciduria
- Olive-shaped lump felt while feeding or under sedation (2.5 cm)
- Visible left to right peristalsis

Circular fibers are affected more.

Diagnosis

- USG being investigation of choice, criteria for US diagnosis are channel length of >19 mm, pyloric thickness >4 mm, and pyloric diameter >14 mm. Target sign is present on transverse view.
- Contrast radiology: Persistent narrowing and elongation of pyloric canal bird beak and shoulder sign are also noted.

Treatment

- The patient is kept NBM.
- Correct fluid and electrolyte balance by giving 5% dextrose with 0.45% saline with added potassium of 2–4 mEq/kg for 24 hours at a rate of 150–175 mL/kg. Correction usually takes 48 hours.
- Child must be adequately rehydrated; urine output >1 mL/kg/h is a sign of adequate rehydration.
- Fredet-Ramstedt operation (pyloromyotomy): It involves open (by either right upper quadrant or periumbilical incision) or laparoscopic surgery.
- Postoperative feeding is started with electrolyte solution and gradually increased to breast milk.

Complications of surgery

These include perforation (mucosal perforation is treated by repair and nasogastric drainage), hemorrhage, wound infection, and incomplete myotomy (persistent vomiting after 3 days of surgery indicates incomplete myotomy).

26. **Enumerate the causes of upper GI bleeding. Describe Forrest classification and investigation of upper GI bleeding.**

A Upper GI bleeding means bleeding proximal to ligament of Treitz.

Causes

- Duodenal ulcer is the most common cause.
- Gastric ulcer
- Gastritis
- Esophagitis
- Esophageal varices
- Iatrogenic: Following endoscopy or upper GI surgery. PEG or endoscopic sphincterotomy may be associated with bleeding. Bleeding from the staple or suture line is also a known complication following upper GI surgery.

- Mallory–Weiss tear: Longitudinal tear involves gastric mucosa near squamocolumnar junction usually 2 cm from the gastroesophageal junction on the lesser curvature. It is due to sufficient increased IAP pushing the gastric cardia in the thoracic cavity that results in a longitudinal tear. Hiatus hernia coexists in >75% of cases. A typical young alcoholic male presents with a history of initial vomiting and retching followed by hematemesis with fresh red blood. Endoscopy is used to confirm the diagnosis and retroflexion or J maneuver is important to look at the cardia and GE junction. Patient is initially managed with twice-daily IV PPI. Usually self-limited, continuous bleeding may require endoscopic band ligation, hemoclip, or thermocoagulation. Angiographic embolization is indicated in patients who had failed endoscopic management. High gastrotomy and suture of the tear is required if the above-mentioned measure fails.
- Gastric antral vascular ectasia (GAVE): GAVE is also known as a 'watermelon stomach' due to its typical appearance that resembles the surface of a watermelon. Dilated tortuous blood vessels are seen in the antrum and converge toward the pylorus. Women are more commonly affected. GAVE may be associated with connective tissue disorder and/or liver disease. It most commonly presents with occult blood loss and anemia. Upper GI endoscopy is the investigation of choice. Argon plasma coagulation (APC) is the treatment of choice. PPI cover for 1 month is recommended. In patients with portal hypertension (PHT), transjugular intrahepatic portosystemic shunt (TIPS) may be considered. In patients refractory to APC, antrectomy is recommended.
- Carcinoma stomach
- Dieulafoy lesion (abnormally large tortuous submucosal artery in the stomach): Dieulafoy lesion is located in the stomach within 6–10 cm of the cardia on the lesser curvature but may be present anywhere in the GI tract from stomach onwards. Males are more commonly affected. Sudden, massive, painless hematemesis is the common presentation. It may be recurrent. Contact thermal ablation with heater probe with or without adrenaline is the most effective treatment. Other methods are the following: Endoscopic clipping or banding. In case of failure of above-mentioned methods, either angiographic coil embolization (preferred method) or wedge resection may be employed.

Uncommon causes

- Aortoenteric fistula
- Hemobilia
- Hemosuccus pancreaticus
- Bleeding disorder is present.

Investigation

- Upper GI scopy is the investigation of choice.
- Less than 5 mL/min bleeding is required to produce 'blush' on angiography.
- A total of 60 mL of blood is required to produce single black-colored stool.

Forrest classification for risk of rebleeding

- *I*: Active bleeding
  - Spurting or pulsatile bleeding (90%)
  - Oozing (30%)
- *II*: Sign of hemorrhage without active bleeding
  - Visible vessel (50–100%)
  - Adherent clot (20%)
  - Black dot or hematin on the ulcer (<5%)
- *III*: Fibrin-covered ulcer with no hemorrhage (<5%)

27. What is Zollinger–Ellison syndrome (ZES)?

A
- It is a disorder in which tumors of the pancreatic islet cells produce large amounts of gastrin, leading to excess acid in the stomach and a peptic ulcer.
- The most common site is duodenal loop. It is a tumor of G cells present in the Brunner's glands of duodenum. At the time of diagnosis, more than 60% of tumors are malignant. Duodenal gastrinoma tends to spread to lymph node and pancreatic primary tends to spread to the liver.

Clinical features

Abdominal pain (most common), GERD, and diarrhea. More than 85–90% of patients have a peptic ulcer. Most ulcers are in the first part of duodenum. Atypical location of ulcer should prompt an evaluation of gastrinoma.

Features that indicate gastrinoma are the following:

- Peptic ulcer resistant to treatment
- Ulcer distal to the duodenum
- Diarrhea responding to PPI
- Enlarged gastric folds
- Erosive esophagitis not responding to PPI
- Family history of peptic ulcer disease
- Above-mentioned feature plus endocrinopathy
- Above-mentioned feature plus family history of neuroendocrine tumor

Diagnosis

- Presence of serum gastrin >1000 pg/mL suggests ZES.
- When serum gastrin level is 100–1000 pg/mL, *secretin stimulation test* is helpful in differentiating it from other causes of hypergastrinemia. If serum gastrin level increases by 200 pg/mL over 1 hour, it suggests ZES.
- In presence of hypergastrinemia (serum gastrin level > 100–150 pg/mL), basal acid output (BAO) >15 mEq/L indicates ZES. (Normal BAO is 5 mEq/L.)
- Exclude MEN I: Measure serum ionized calcium and parathyroid hormone level.
- Gastric pH 2 or less and gastrin level more than 10-fold elevated is almost diagnostic of ZES.
- Various other modalities such as CT scan abdomen, USG abdomen, and endoscopic ultrasound help in diagnosing this condition.
- Imaging study of choice is somatostatin receptor scintigraphy (octreotide scan).
  - Currently preoperative imaging study of choice is ^{68}Ga-DOTATATE PET/CT scan. It images more than 90% primary as well as metastatic tumors.
- Gastrinoma is commonly seen in gastrinoma triangle (Passaro's triangle), bounded by the junction of cystic duct and CBD, second and third parts of duodenum, and neck and body of pancreas.

Treatment

- Control of acid hypersecretion is the primary treatment.
- Localization of gastrinoma: Initial test to localize is CECT abdomen and pelvis with fine cuts through the pancreas. CECT plus octreotide scan/DOTATATE scan is superior as compared to CECT alone. Dual-phase MRI with delayed images may also help in localizing the primary tumor as well as metastatic liver lesion. An octreotide scan helps in preoperative localization of tumor. EUS is an alternative investigation in the case where CECT and octreotide scans fail to localize the lesion. Secretin arteriography is advised when investigation mentioned above fails to detect the lesion. ^{68}Ga-DOTATATE PET/CT is recently introduced in the armamentarium for localizing gastrinoma. The last option is exploration and intraoperative sonography. Treatment depends on the location of the gastrinoma:
  - Pancreatic
    - Small, well capsulated: Enucleation with lymph node dissection
    - Large, uncapsulated, and deep within the gland and located in the body and tail: Resection
  - Duodenal
    - <5 mm: Enucleation
    - Large tumor: Full-thickness excision of the duodenal wall
- Gastrinoma with primary hyperparathyroidism (MEN I) requires parathyroidectomy (3 and 0.5 parathyroid gland removed) for better control of acid secretion. In patients with liver metastases, chemotherapy using streptozotocin and doxorubicin plus or minus 5-FU, systemic removal of all resectable disease (cytoreductive surgery), somatostatin analogue, biotherapy with interferon, hepatic embolization alone or with chemotherapy, and liver transplantation are performed.
- In MEN I, surgery is recommended only if tumor size >2 cm.

Prognosis

- Duodenal gastrinoma has a good prognosis as compared to pancreatic gastrinoma.
- The best predictor of survival is the presence or absence of liver metastases and the most common cause of death is liver metastases.

28. What is Ménétrier disease?

A
- Premalignant condition
- Protein-losing gastropathy
- Due to overexpression of TGF-alpha
- Proximal stomach biopsy showing hyperplasia of mucus-secreting cells
- Treatment: Gastrectomy

29. Enumerate the risk factors for carcinoma stomach.

A Carcinoma stomach is the fourth most common cause of death due to cancer; it is more common in Japan and China. Risk factors are as follows:

- >50 years
- Males > females
- Lower socioeconomic classes
- *H. pylori* infection
- Pernicious anemia
- Diet high in salt and pickles (nitrates)
- Tobacco
- Epstein–Barr virus
- Gastric atrophy
- Previous gastrectomy
- Gastric adenoma
- Gastric remnant cancer
- Ménétrier disease
- Genetics: *p53* and *COX-2* genes
- Association with mutation in e-cadherin and overexpression of epidermal growth factor and vascular endothelial growth factor
- Loss of heterozygosity in *bcl-2* gene
- Premalignant conditions
  - Polyps
  - Atrophic gastritis
  - Intestinal metaplasia
  - Benign gastric ulcer

30. Describe in brief about gastrointestinal stromal tumor (GIST).

A The most common site for GIST is stomach. GIST is a mesenchymal tumor.

It arises from the interstitial cell of Cajal (gastrointestinal pacemaker cell).

Mutation in *KIT* gene or platelet-derived growth factor receptor alpha (PDGFRA) is responsible for development of GIST.

It expresses CD117 antigen (KIT).

The most common mode of spread is hematogenous to the peritoneal surface of liver. Tumor size > 2 cm and mitosis >5–10/HPF are the two most important prognostic factors.

Symptoms

Clinical presentation in descending order:

- Acute or subacute gastrointestinal bleeding (overt or occult)
- Incidentaloma
- Abdominal pain
- Abdominal lump
- Obstruction

Dysphagia and early satiety are nonspecific symptoms.

Syndrome-associated GIST is multifocal, is commonly found in small bowel, and has an indolent course.

Neurofibromatosis and autosomal dominant syndrome of Carney–Stratakis: GIST associated with extra-adrenal paragangliomas.

Investigations

- CECT is ideal for primary tumor and staging (imaging modality of choice).
- Upper GI endoscopy and EUS-guided biopsy are helpful.
- PET CT is recommended for recurrent GIST.

Treatment

Preoperative EUS-guided biopsy is not mandatory in case of strongly suspected and resectable lesion.

- For tumor >2 cm in size: Resection with 2-cm margin
- En bloc resection of the structure involved without lymphadenectomy (lymph node metastasis is rare)
- 1–2 cm size: Resections if symptomatic and endoscopic follow-up for asymptomatic
- Larger tumor that requires multivisceral resection or borderline resectable (metastatic or locally advanced): Treated with imatinib preoperatively for

3–6 months followed by surgery (sunitinib malate is used in patients with imatinib refractory GIST)
- Adjuvant imatinib indicated in a large tumor with higher malignant potential

31. What are various classifications for carcinoma stomach and most common site for cancer?

A
- *WHO classification*
  - Adenocarcinoma
    - Papillary
    - Tubular
    - Mucinous
    - Signet ring cell
  - Adenosquamous carcinoma
  - Squamous cell carcinoma
  - Small cell carcinoma
  - Undifferentiated carcinoma
  - Others
- *Lauren classification*
  - Intestinal gastric cancer
  - Diffuse gastric cancer
- *Other classifications (Japanese)*
  - *Early*: Limited to mucosa and submucosa with or without lymph node
    - *Type I*: Protruding
    - *Type II*: Superficial
      - Elevated
      - Flat
      - Depressed
    - *Type III*: Excavated
  - *Late*: Involves muscularis
- *Borrmann classification*
  - Polypoid
  - Ulcerated with elevated margin
  - Crateriform
  - Diffuse infiltrative
- *Ming classification*: Expanding and infiltrative
- *Site*: The most common site being proximal stomach

32. Give a brief account of superior mesenteric artery syndrome or Wilkie syndrome.

A
- It is a rare problem, common in young asthenic females.
- The most common cause is chronic immobilization with weight loss and body cast.
- Postprandial pain and epigastric discomfort with weight loss and distension is the common presentation.
- Critically ill patients, such as those with spinal trauma, head injury, burns, and HIV, are at high risk.
- It is also known as *cast syndrome* because of its relation with spinal trauma and hip spica.
- Various theories have been suggested, but the commonly accepted are the following:
  - Narrowing of aortomesenteric angle from 25–60° to 6–15° which leads to extrinsic compression of third part of duodenum
  - Loss of mesenteric and retroperitoneal pad of fat

Diagnosis
- Hypotonic duodenography
- Upper GI endoscopy
- Endoscopic ultrasound
- CT abdomen with angiography: Duodenal obstruction (third part), an aortomesenteric artery angle of ≤25°, and aortomesenteric distance ≤8 mm.

Treatment
- Conservative
  - Improve nutritional status (weight gain). Option can be nasojejunal tube feeding or TPN to restore aortomesenteric fat. It is followed by frequent, small meals.
  - Turn to the left, or in prone or knee–chest position.
- *Surgery*: It is indicated in patients with failure of conservative management, or chronic disease with progressive weight loss.
  - Duodenojejunostomy (open or laparoscopy); laparoscopic duodenojejunostomy being the procedure of choice
  - Duodenal mobilization and lysis of ligament of Treitz (strong procedure)

33. Discuss briefly the presentation, diagnosis, and treatment of the blind loop syndrome.

A Blind loop syndrome occurs when the intestine is obstructed, thus slowing or stopping the progress of digested food and facilitating the growth of bacteria.

Causes
- Stricture
- Obstruction
- Jejunoileal bypass
- Diverticula

Clinical features

- Main presentation: Megaloblastic anemia (lower loop)
- Steatorrhea (higher loop)
- Weight loss
- Diarrhea
- Abdominal pain

All of the above-mentioned are due to bacterial overgrowth.

Diagnosis

- Presence of colonic bacteria in the duodenal aspirate
- Endoscopic biopsy from duodenum
- Anaerobic bacteria in the small bowel metabolizing xylose and releasing $^{14}CO_2$, which is detected in the breath (breath test)
- Serum vitamin B_{12}

Treatment

- Treatment of the cause (diverticula, fistula, stricture or malignancy, etc.)
- Broad-spectrum antibiotics (7–10 days): Rifaximin, metronidazole, and ciprofloxacin being commonly used antibiotics
- Parenteral vitamin B_{12}

34. Discuss briefly acute mesenteric ischemia.

A

- The most common type is the occlusive type.
- Most commonly, superior mesenteric artery is involved.
- The most common source is embolus.
- The patient may have a history of IHD, CVA, or valvular heart disease.
- Sudden onset of severe abdominal pain is followed by vomiting, anorexia, diarrhea, and maroon-colored stool. Severe abdominal pain out of proportion to the abdominal sign such as tenderness and guarding is the hallmark. Hypovolemic or septic shock is late presentation.
- Mucosal sloughing starts within 3 hours and full-thickness infarction by 6 hours of onset.

Investigations

- Laboratory investigations reveal marked leukocytosis, metabolic acidosis, and elevated hematocrit. Serum amylase may be elevated. Normal D-dimer level helps to exclude acute mesenteric ischemia.
- Plain X-ray shows adynamic ileus with gasless abdomen.
- Duplex USG is a noninvasive means of assessing mesenteric vessel patency.
- CT angiography and MR angiography are now routinely performed.

Treatment

- Initial treatment consists of fluid resuscitation and anticoagulation (LMWH).
- Correct metabolic acidosis.
- Catheter-directed thrombolysis with urokinase or recombinant tissue plasminogen activator with endovascular angioplasty and stenting can be safely performed within 12 hours of acute pain and without sign of peritonitis to establish blood flow.
- Surgical revascularization with laparotomy is performed for single, proximal SMA thrombosis: Transverse arteriotomy and thromboembolectomy is performed to restore flow. Bowel must be examined for viability after restoration and nonviable bowel requires resection.
- Venous thrombosis is usually improved with anticoagulation alone. In rare cases, thrombolysis and laparotomy are required.
- Nonocclusive ischemia: Remove the precipitating cause, and perform intra-arterial vasodilator therapy. Laparotomy is performed in case of peritonitis.
- After extensive intestinal resection, once patient improves, small bowel transplantation may be considered in selected patients.

35. What is short bowel syndrome? What are its causes and clinical features?

A

- Short bowel syndrome is a malabsorption disorder caused by either the surgical removal of the small intestine or the loss of its absorptive function due to diseases.
- <200 cm or $<30\%$ of the initial small bowel length is associated with short bowel syndrome (normal length: 300–600 cm). Intact ileocecal (IC) valve is very important as patients with one-third colon and IC valve may not develop short bowel syndrome until <75 cm small bowel remains. Entire jejunal resection is well tolerated while complete ileal resection is

not well tolerated because of its specialized absorptive function.[2]

Clinical features

- Diarrhea
- Dehydration
- Malnutrition

Causes

- Resection for management of Crohn disease and its complications (most common cause)
- Mesenteric vascular ischemia
- Malignancy
- Radiation injury to the small bowel
- In pediatric patients: Volvulus, necrotizing enterocolitis, and atresia of intestine

Modalities of management of short bowel syndrome[3]

- Antidiarrheal medications (loperamide) and cholestyramine that help to reduce diarrhea due to bile salt malabsorption
- Enteral and parenteral supplementation of vitamins and trace elements
- Drugs that improve intestinal adaption: Growth hormone, glutamine, and glucagon-like peptide 2 agonist
- Home TPN
- Intestinal lengthening procedure
  - Longitudinal intestinal lengthening and tailoring (LILT)
  - Serial transverse enteroplasty procedure (STEP)
- Small intestinal transplantation: Metabolic complications of TPN (liver dysfunction, metabolic bone disease, and renal stone) can be considered as an indication for small intestinal transplantation

36. What are the clinical presentations of a patient with Peutz-Jeghers syndrome (PJS)? Mention in brief about diagnosis and treatment.

A
- It presents with pigmentation of lips and oral mucosa.
- Multiple hamartomatous polyps are present throughout gastrointestinal tract.
- It is most common in jejunum.
- The gene *STK11* on chromosome 19 is responsible.
- Lifetime risk of cancer (37–93%) colon and pancreatic cancer is common. Gastrointestinal cancer is associated with PJS and the most common site for extraintestinal cancer is breast.
- Diagnosis of PJS: It involves two or more histologically confirmed PJ polyps, and any number of PJ polyps in patients with mucocutaneous pigmentations or in patients with family history of PJS.
- Resection is required only for severe and persistent or recurrent hemorrhage or obstruction.

37. What is radiation enteritis? Describe its clinical features and treatment.

A Radiation enteritis is inflammation of the lining of the small intestine due to radiation therapy. It may be acute or chronic.[4]

- Acute: 2–4 weeks
  - *Mechanism*: Apoptosis
  - *Causes of symptoms*: Malabsorption and bacterial overgrowth
  - *Clinical features*: Nausea, vomiting, diarrhea, crampy abdominal pain, and tenesmus
- Chronic: 6–24 months
  - *Mechanism*: Vasculitis
  - *Causes of symptoms*: Obstruction, fistula, internal failure, and neoplasia
  - *Clinical features*: Partial small bowel obstruction, perforation, rectal bleeding, diarrhea, malabsorption, steatorrhea, anorexia, fistula, and fecal incontinence

Predisposing conditions

- Higher radiation dose
- Short course of radiation
- Concurrent chemotherapy
- Prior intestinal surgery
- Volume of small bowel in the field
- Diabetes
- IBD
- Smoking
- Hypertension

Diagnostic workup

- Hematological and biochemical profile
- Tumor markers

- Clinical examination of perineal area to look for dermatitis, fistulae, and mass
- Sigmoidoscopy and colonoscopy: Endoscopic findings include erythema, ulceration, telangiectasia, friability, and necrosis
- Sigmoidoscopic and colonoscopic biopsy
- Can use CT colonography or barium enema as an alternative to colonoscopy
- Capsule endoscopy: Identifies mucosal edema, atrophy, stricture, and bleeding in chronic case

Treatment[3]

- Medical
  - Low-residue, low-fat diet
  - Antidiarrheals
  - Cholestyramine: For bile acid malabsorption
  - Antibiotics (rifaximin, metronidazole): In case of bacterial overgrowth
  - Hyperbaric oxygen: Neoangiogenesis and revascularization
- Endoscopic procedure: Endoscopic therapy such as APC, thermal coagulation, and cryoablation
- Surgery: Resection to be considered only in life-threatening conditions
  - Severe bleeding not controlled with other therapies: Resect/ileostomy
  - Perforation: Resect/ileostomy
  - Stricture: Bypass, resect/reanastomosis or ileostomy, stricturoplasty
  - Fistulae
    - Enterocutaneous: Resect/reanastomosis
    - Enterovaginal/enterovesical: Bypass, resect/reanastomosis or ileostomy, reconstruct

Either ileostomy or colostomy is the best and safest procedure.

38. What is Meckel diverticulum? Describe its clinical features, diagnosis, and treatment.

A
- Meckel diverticulum is a congenital pouch (diverticulum), approximately 2 inches in length, which develops in some persons at the lower end of the small intestine. It is the most common congenital malformation of the gastrointestinal tract.
- It is described by the *rule of 2*:
  - Incidence: 2%
  - Two inches long
  - Two feet away from the ileocecal valve
  - Male:female ratio of occurrence = 2:1
  - Two types of ectopic tissue: Gastric and pancreatic
  - More common before 2 years of age
  - Two centimeters in diameter

Clinical features

The most common feature is inflammation or infection that mimics appendicitis. Meckel diverticulum is frequently suspected, often sought for but seldom found. It is located on the antimesenteric border of the small bowel. It presents with the following features (in descending order of frequency of occurrence):

- Hemorrhage
- Intussusceptions
- Diverticulitis
- Peptic ulcer disease
- Intestinal obstruction
- Perforation
- Malignant change (rare)

Intestinal obstruction is the most common presentation in pediatric population.

Diagnosis

- *CT abdomen*: It is not very helpful.
- *Radionuclide scanning (^{99m}Tc pertechnetate)*: It is the most common and accurate noninvasive study. Use of cimetidine decreases the peptic acid secretion without affecting radionuclide uptake. It increases the sensitivity of the scan up to 95%.

  In case of high clinical suspicion and negative Meckel's scan: Single photon emission computed tomography/computed tomography (SPECT/CT) helps in localizing the lesion.
- *Angiography and RBC-labeled scan in the setting of bleeding*: These are performed in acute hemorrhage.

Treatment

- *Symptomatic*: Resection and anastomosis
- *Asymptomatic*: Diverticulectomy indicated (Box 16.1)

Box 16.1 Indications for prophylactic diverticulectomy

- Palpable, heterotopia
- Narrow base, scarring, or adhesion
- Young patient
- Male sex
- 2 cm in length

Nowadays, the trend is changing toward increasing use of Meckel diverticulectomy in incidentally found cases, as there is low complication rate with this operation.

39. Which are the various sites for colonic diverticula? Describe etiology and clinical features of diverticular disease.

A Sites

- Sigmoid colon, followed by
- Descending colon
- Transverse colon
- Ascending colon

Etiology

- Low-fiber diet
- High-carbohydrate and high-protein diet

Clinical features

- Asymptomatic (most common)
- Diverticulitis leading to abdominal pain
- Peridiverticular abscess
- Hemorrhage
- Obstruction: Either due to progressive fibrosis or adjacent small bowel may adhere to inflamed colonic diverticula
- Perforation
- Generalized peritonitis
- Colovesical fistula

40. Describe briefly meconium ileus (MI).

- It refers to intestinal obstruction in a newborn child following the thickening of meconium.
- It is associated with cystic fibrosis.
- It may be simple MI (there is no associated GI pathology) or complex MI (associated with GI pathology such as perforation, atresia, or volvulus).
- Gastrografin enema is performed for diagnosis—microcolon with some meconium flecks.
- Plain radiograph shows ground-glass appearance.
- Enema containing saline, diatrizoate meglumine, or acetylcysteine may disperse the meconium in simple MI.
- If obstruction is not relieved or complex MI is present, then laparotomy is indicated: Enterotomy and irrigation with saline or *N*-acetylcysteine.
- Bishop–Koop operation: It refers to resection of the most dilated segment with end-to-side anastomosis of the colon to ileum and ileostomy.

41. Discuss briefly the treatment of ulcerative colitis.

Mild attack

Less than four episodes of diarrhea or dysentery, rare passage of blood or mucus, and no systemic symptoms:

- Oral 5-ASA (mesalamine, balsalazide, and olsalazine)
- 5-ASA enema (deliver drug up to splenic flexure and used in left-sided UC, proctosigmoiditis, and proctitis)
- Suppository (deliver drug to the distal 10–15 cm and used in ulcerative proctitis)
- Steroid enema
- Maintenance with oral or topical 5-ASA

Moderate attack

More than four episodes of diarrhea with daily passage of blood or mucus with minimal systemic symptoms; C-reactive protein (CRP) and ESR may be elevated:

- Same as mild disease but if not improved:
  - Prednisolone: 40 mg/day for first week, followed by 30 mg/day for next week; then 20 mg/day for 1 month
- In patients with steroid refractory disease or intolerance to 5-ASA or azathioprine:
  - May use anti-TNF (tumor necrosis factor) antibody
  - Infliximab (IFX)
  - Adalimumab (ADA)
  - Golimumab (GOL)
  - Maintenance with oral 5-ASA or topical 5-ASA
  - Azathioprine in patients with steroid dependency
  - Combination of IFX, ADA, or GOL with azathioprine in steroid-resistant cases and those who responded to IFX, ADA, or GOL

Severe attack

More than six episodes of diarrhea, with systemic signs such as fever, tachycardia, anemia hypoalbuminemia, elevated CRP, and ESR:

- NBM
- Intravenous hydrocortisone 100 mg 6 hourly
- IV cyclosporine
- IFX
- Maintenance with azathioprine in patients who responded to steroid or cyclosporine
- Combination of azathioprine and IFX for those who responded to IFX
- Rescue therapy: Vedolizumab (integrin inhibitor)—reducing the need for emergency colectomy

  Fulminant colitis: >10 times bloody diarrhea with persistent bleeding, abdominal pain, systemic toxicity, anemia, hypoalbuminemia, and toxic megacolon

Indications for surgery

- Elective
  - No response to optimal medical therapy
  - Inability to tolerate medical therapy
  - Steroid-dependent disease
  - Severe dysplasia or malignancy on follow-up colonoscopy
  - Significant risk of developing malignancy (↑ with pancolitis)
  - Extraintestinal manifestation
- Emergency
  - Severe hemorrhage
  - Toxic megacolon (other causes for toxic megacolon are Crohn disease, amoebic colitis, and salmonellosis)
  - Fulminant colitis not responding to medical management

Surgery

- Procedure of choice is restorative proctocolectomy with ileal pouch anal anastomosis (IPAA).
- For emergency, total proctocolectomy with ileostomy is the treatment of choice followed by IPAA in the next stage.

> Remission is defined as ≤3 stools/day without bleeding per rectum or systemic sign.

42. What is pouchitis?

 It refers to nonspecific inflammation of the mucosa of the pouch of ileum treated by IPAA.

It is due to stasis and overgrowth of anaerobic bacteria.

Clinical presentation

- Increased stool frequency
- Fever
- Weight loss
- Stomal or anal bleeding
- Dehydration

Diagnosis

Clinical symptoms and endoscopy finding

Treatment

- Antibiotics are provided for 14 days (e.g., metronidazole, ciprofloxacin, or rifaximin).
- Antibiotic refractory pouchitis: Obtain culture and sensitivity to guide antibiotic therapy. Four weeks' course of ciprofloxacin and metronidazole or rifaximin is followed.
- Antibiotic-dependent pouchitis (three relapses per year): Consider giving probiotics as maintenance therapy or chronic low-dose antibiotics, either ciprofloxacin or rifaximin.
- Budesonide enema may help.
- Chronic or recurrent pouchitis: It refers to combination of treatment such as rifaximin plus metronidazole or ciprofloxacin with metronidazole.
- If it fails to respond, search for *C. difficile* infection or CMV infection. Treat accordingly.
- Chronic refractory pouchitis may respond to azathioprine or infliximab.

43. Which are the common causes of lower GI bleeding?

- Anorectal disease (piles and fissure)
- Diverticulosis
- Angiodysplasia
- Polyp and cancer
- Enterocolitis

44. Which are the common sites for carcinoid tumor (argentaffinoma)?

A The sites in descending order of importance are as follows:

- Appendix
- Ileum
- Rectum

45. Which finding is the hallmark of Hirschsprung disease? Describe important points in this disease.

A
- Lack of ganglion cells in myenteric plexus with hypertrophic nerve fibers is diagnostic of Hirschsprung disease.
- The most common site is rectosigmoid characterized by absence of ganglion cells in the myenteric and submucosal plexus with hypertrophied nerve trunk.
- Full-thickness rectal biopsy is the gold standard for diagnosis.
- Findings on contrast study: Transition zone and aganglionic segment are contracted.

Treatment
- Short-segment disease is treated by extended myectomy.
- Long-segment disease requires temporary colostomy followed by Swenson, Martin, Duhamel, or Soave procedure.

46. What is the best treatment for a patient with carcinoma left side of colon presented in emergency as an obstruction?

A Hartmann procedure (resection of colon or rectum, colostomy, distal colon or rectum left as a blind pouch)

47. Mention treatment of colonic pseudo-obstruction in short.

A
- Exclude mechanical cause usually by gastrografin enema or CECT.
- Decrease narcotic as tolerated or stop if possible.
- Conservative measures in small or large bowel obstruction such as bowel rest, nasogastric decompression with nil by mouth, resuscitation, and correction of electrolyte are important. Eighty percent of patients improve with these measures.
- Colonoscopic decompression is performed in nonresponders to above-mentioned measures.
- IV neostigmine (2 mg IV over 3–5 minutes) is also effective. It is a reversible acetylcholine esterase inhibitor. It increases colonic motility by accentuating action of acetylcholine on muscarinic parasympathetic fibers. Second dose can be given to those who have not responded to the first dose or if recurrence occurs.
- Total colectomy with end ileostomy is indicated in patients with perforation, peritonitis, or prolonged distention unresponsive to above-mentioned treatment unless the comorbid conditions preclude operative intervention.[5]

48. How will you treat operable rectal cancer and anal cancer?

A Investigations

After clinical diagnosis, biopsy confirmation is first performed via colonoscopy.

Then general evaluation is performed:
- CEA
- CT abdomen, pelvis, and chest: Tumor plus distant metastases
- MRI and EUS: Locoregional staging
- PET CT for distant metastases

Treatment

The treatment for rectal cancer (in operative case) is as follows:
- Early rectal cancer (T1–T2, N0) (stage I) (tumor up to muscularis propria)
  - Upper and middle rectum: LAR
  - Lower rectum: *Total mesorectal excision* (TME) or APR
  - Can manage T1 with favorable features with TME or transanal minimally invasive surgery (TAMIS)
- Locally advanced (T3, T4, N0, N+) (stages II and III) (tumor invading serosa, nonperitonealized perirectal tissue [T3], perforated tumor or invading adjacent structure [T4], three perirectal nodes)
  - *Upper and middle rectum*: Chemoradiotherapy followed by LAR
  - *Lower rectum*: Chemoradiation followed by TME or APR
- Distant metastases (any T, any N, and M1) (stage IV):
  - *Symptomatic*: Chemoradiation or palliative procedures such as stent, laser ablation, endocavitory radiation, and diverting stoma
  - *Asymptomatic*: Chemotherapy; restage: If resectable; and single metastases: Resect
  - *Not resectable*: Chemotherapy continued

49. Discuss differential diagnosis of lump in RIF.

A Appendicular lump

- History of pain in RIF, anorexia, nausea, and fever
- Short duration
- Young and middle age
- Intra-abdominal
- Firm

Carcinoma cecum

- Middle to old age
- Anemia
- Lump in RIF
- Intra-abdominal
- Firm to hard
- Features of spread, such as lymphadenopathy, ascites, and liver enlargement

Ileocecal Koch

- Young to middle age
- Pain in RIF
- Alternate diarrhea and constipation
- Subacute intestinal obstruction
- Intra-abdominal lump
- Ascites
- Mesenteric lymphadenopathy
- Constitutional symptoms of Koch

Ameboma

- History of diarrhea/dysentery
- Dull, aching pain in RIF
- Intra-abdominal lump
- Firm
- Mucus in stool

Retroperitoneal lump

- Asymptomatic
- Vague, dull, aching pain
- Urinary complaints
- Hard
- Fixed, if not kidney that is initially mobile and in later stages becomes fixed
- Weight loss and constitutional symptoms

50. Which are the most common tumor of spleen and most common benign tumor of spleen?

A
- The most common tumor of spleen is lymphoma.
- The most common benign tumor is hemangioma.

51. What are the nonsurgical causes of acute abdomen?

A
- Ischemic heart disease
- Pleurisy
- Diabetic crises
- Porphyria
- Sickle cell anemia
- Hemophilia

52. Name factors related to burst abdomen.

A
- Infection
- Steroid use
- Metabolic conditions such as jaundice and uremia
- Acute postoperative conditions
  - Acute gastric dilatation (best prevented by nasogastric tube)
  - Prolonged ileus
  - Acute postoperative cough
  - Mechanical ventilation
- Nutritional status: Anemia, hypoproteinemia, and obesity
- Poor surgical technique
  - Tension on suture line
  - Use of absorbable suture

53. Highlight the important points about carcinoma anal canal.

A Carcinoma anal canal

- The most common is squamous cell carcinoma.
- Bleeding P/R is the most common symptom followed by pain and sensation of anal mass.

Investigations

- Locoregional staging: MRI rectum and pelvis with or without endoscopic ultrasound
- Distant metastases: CT chest, abdomen pelvis, and FDG/PET CT

Treatment

- <1-cm tumor not involving sphincter: Local excision ± chemoradiation. Chemoregimen used is mitomycin plus 5-FU.
- Up to 5-cm lesion can be treated with radiation.
- >5-cm lesion, involving adjacent structure or ipsilateral inguinal node, can be treated with chemoradiation.
- Metastatic disease is treated with cisplatin plus 5-FU.

Pearls

- Diaphragm develops from septum transversum (forming central tendon and some muscle tissue), pleuroperitoneal membranous folds, thoracic body wall mesoderm, and esophageal mesenchyme. All contribute to the formation of muscular rim and esophageal crura.
- Left posterolateral congenital diaphragmatic hernia (CDH) is Bochdalek hernia.
- Morgagni hernias appear on either side (usually right anterior) of the xiphisternum.
- Respiratory distress, cyanosis, scaphoid abdomen, tracheal deviation, and mediastinal shift are typical of CDH.
- Endotracheal intubation with IPPV is ideal for CDH. Bag and mask ventilation is contraindicated as it invariably causes gastric distention.
- Cause of death in CDH is lung hypoplasia.
- The most common site for foreign body impaction is above the cricopharynx (narrowest portion of esophagus).
- The most common cause of esophageal perforation is iatrogenic caused by endoscopy (esophageal instrumentation such as dilatation of stricture and achalasia) and site is cervical esophagus.
- The most common site for spontaneous esophageal perforation (Boerhaave syndrome) is left posterolateral site of the distal esophagus.
- Mackler's triad is seen in spontaneous esophageal perforation (Boerhaave syndrome) (vomiting, chest pain, and subcutaneous emphysema).
- Multidetector CT is ideal for detecting presence, site, and cause of alimentary tract perforation including esophageal perforation. The collection of air and fluid in the mediastinum, pleural effusion, pneumocardium, and pneumoperitoneum are important diagnostic findings. CT is ideal because contrast esophagogram identifies esophageal perforation but not its complications such as mediastinitis, pneumonia, empyema, lung abscess, and fistula. Water-soluble contrast is preferred.
- Symptoms of mucosal damage produced by the abnormal reflux of stomach content in the esophagus is defined as GERD. Typical and atypical symptoms define GERD. Typical symptoms are the following: dysphagia, heartburn, and regurgitation. Atypical symptoms are the following: Cough, hoarseness, asthma, tooth decay, and aspiration pneumonia.
- Candidates for surgery in GERD are those who demonstrate the following: Symptoms improve on medical therapy, typical symptoms, and abnormal esophageal acid exposure determined by 24-hour pH monitoring (off PPI) (multichannel intraluminal impedance [MII]).
- Esophageal manometry (investigation of choice for motility disorder) helps in identifying achalasia and aids in selecting partial or full fundoplication.
- Barium esophagogram (investigation of choice for anatomical disorder) and upper GI endoscopy should be performed as a preoperative evaluation test.
- Lower esophageal sphincter pressure is decreased by the following (ADSP): A, alcohol; D, drugs such as barbiturate, diazepam, CCB, morphine, and theophylline; S, smoking; and P, prostaglandin and progesterone.
- Leiomyoma is the most common benign tumor of esophagus and accounts for two-third of all benign esophageal tumors. Dysphagia and pain are the most common symptoms. Pyrosis and weight loss are other symptoms. EUSFNA is ideal for diagnosis. Immunohistochemical stains are positive for desmin and actin but negative for CD34 and CD117. Indications for surgery are as follows: symptomatic, a progressive increase in size, uncertainty of diagnosis, ulceration of the tumor, and regional lymph node enlargement. Asymptomatic patients should be followed with EUS every 1–2 years.
- The commonest cause of mortality after Ivor Lewis operation is anastomotic leak.

- POEMS stands for polyneuropathy, organomegaly, endocrinopathy, M-protein, and skin changes.
- Gastroduodenal artery is the most common cause of bleeding in duodenal ulcer while left gastric artery is involved in gastric ulcer.
- The commonest cause of death in peptic ulcer patients is bleeding.
- Curling ulcer is seen in the body and fundus in burn patients.
- Organoaxial gastric volvulus is common as compared to mesenteroaxial gastric volvulus. Organoaxial volvulus is associated with diaphragmatic defect. Characteristic feature of volvulus is Borchardt's triad: Upper abdominal pain, retching, and inability to pass nasogastric tube.
- Interstitial cell of Cajal is a gastric pacemaker cell and located in the body along the greater curvature of the stomach.
- Brunner gland is the submucosal gland in the duodenum.
- The most common cause of gastric outlet obstruction is carcinoma of the stomach.
- *H. pylori* is a Gram-negative bacterium that has urease and *urel* gene to overcome gastric acid and survives on human gastric mucosa.
- Diseases associated with *H. pylori* are the following: Duodenal ulcer, gastric ulcer, gastric cancer, gastric mucosa–associated lymphoid tissue (MALT) lymphoma, atrophic gastritis, intestinal metaplasia, antrum predominant gastritis, and corpus predominant pangastritis.
- Proximal gastric cancer is associated with obesity and higher socioeconomic status. Selenium, aspirin, fresh fruits, and vitamin C may be protective against gastric cancer.
- The most common type of mesenteric cyst is chylolymphatic cyst. Treatment is enucleation.
- Enterogenous mesenteric cyst requires resection and anastomosis.
- Acute mesenteric lymphadenitis is associated with *Yersinia* infection. It is a syndrome associated with right lower abdominal pain and mesenteric lymph node enlargement with normal appendix. *Campylobacter jejuni* is also equally associated.
- Idiopathic retroperitoneal fibrosis is known as Ormond disease.
- In retroperitoneal fibrosis, lower one-third of ureter is the most commonly involved. The most common symptom is back pain.
- The commonest cause of intestinal obstruction is postoperative adhesion—X-ray abdomen standing is the best investigation for diagnosis of acute obstruction.
- Hypokalemia is the most common electrolyte disturbance leading to paralytic ileus. Small intestine is the first organ to recover from paralytic ileus.
- Pelvic abscess is the most common intra-abdominal abscess. CT-guided drainage is the preferred treatment.
- Adenoma is of three types: Tubular, tubulovillous, and villous. Tubular adenoma is the most common and villous adenoma is the most invasive. Villous adenoma is primarily diagnosed by colonoscopy. Clinical presentation is watery diarrhea, hypokalemia, hyponatremia, hypochloremia, and metabolic acidosis.
- The most common type of anorectal abscess is perianal; fistula is intersphincteric and fissure is posterior fissure-in-ano (6 o'clock).
- The most common site for extramammary Paget disease is an anogenital region. Perianal region is the most commonly involved and pruritus is the most common symptom. It may be associated with underlying eccrine or apocrine carcinoma. Anorectal malignancy is associated with it in 33–86% of cases. Wide local excision is the treatment of choice. Invasive disease requires APR and delayed margin positive requires re-excision.
- The most common cause of bleeding in colonoscopy is postpolypectomy.

- Raspberry tumor is umbilical adenoma and is congenital due to partially unobliterated vitellointestinal duct. Treatment is ligation.
- Desmoid tumor is locally aggressive low-grade sarcoma. Fifty percent of the tumors develop over extremities. Rest are located on the abdominal wall or retroperitoneum. Desmoid tumor arises from the musculoaponeurotic sheath of the abdominal wall/abdominal desmoids are associated with pregnancy. Estrogen stimulates the growth of desmoids. Surgical trauma is also an important etiological factor. It has been reported in FAP. Plasmodial cell mass with or without central myxomatous change is found in desmoid tumor.
- Local resection with wide margin is the treatment of choice for desmoid tumor. Radiation is recommended for unresectable or an adjuvant following surgery for recurrent disease. Tamoxifen is also found to be beneficial; chemotherapy should be reserved for nonresponders to the above-mentioned treatment.
- Cecum is the widest portion of colon and thinnest wall so it is most vulnerable for perforation and least vulnerable for colonic obstruction, while sigmoid colon is narrowest and extremely mobile; this explains why obstruction is common in sigmoid and sigmoid colon pathology may occasionally present as right-sided abdominal pain.
- Antiperistalsis is seen in proximal colon.
- The most common organism in colon is *Bacteroides* while the most common aerobe is *Escherichia coli.*
- Colon absorbs water, sodium, and chloride while it secretes potassium.
- Lack of short-chain fatty acid due to diversion of fecal stream by either ileostomy or colostomy produces diversion colitis. Short-chain fatty acids are an important source of energy as well as important for active transport of sodium.
- Nitrogen, oxygen, carbon dioxide, hydrogen, and methane are the major components of intestinal gas.
- Length of various scopes is as follows: Sigmoidoscopy, 60 cm; colonoscope, 160 cm.
- Hemorrhage of 0.5–1.0 mL/min can be localized by angiography and technetium-labeled RBC scan detects 0.1 mL/h.
- Angiodysplasia of the colon is almost always confined to the cecum or ascending colon (cecum is the most common site).
- The most common site for colonic diverticula is sigmoid colon. Colonic diverticula is the most common cause of massive GI bleed in elderly patients.
- The most common site for colonic ischemia is splenic flexure.
- Mercedes procedure is done where there is a discrepancy between ileum size and stoma.
- Guy rope technique is used to evert the necessary length of bowel for ileostomy.
- An early postoperative complication of ileostomy is necrosis. However, the most common complication is skin irritation.
- The most common complication of either loop or end colostomy is parastomal hernia.
- Toxic megacolon is associated with ulcerative colitis, Crohn disease, and pseudomembranous colitis. It is defined by systemic toxicity such as tachycardia, fever, colonic diameter >6 cm associated with distension of abdomen, decreased bowel sound, and constipation or obstipation. Triad of toxicity is the indication for intervention: Tachycardia, fever, and increased WBC count. Total abdominal colectomy with preservation of the rectum is the treatment of choice.
- Preferred operation for rectal prolapse is abdominal rectopexy (either suture or prostatic sling [Ripstein and Wells rectopexy]) with or without sigmoid resection.

- Another abdominal operation for rectal prolapse is Moschcowitz repair (reduction of perineal hernia and repair of cul-de-sac).
- For high-risk patients in rectal prolapse, treatment is Altemeier procedure or perineal rectosigmoidectomy. And another perianal operation is Delorme: Tightening of the anus with various prosthetic materials and reefing the rectal mucosa.
- The most common predisposing condition for sigmoid volvulus is excessive mobility of the sigmoid colon. Torsion in volvulus is counterclockwise and should be at least 180° to produce a clinically significant obstruction. Plain X-ray abdomen shows omega sign, bent inner tube sign, or coffee bean appearance with convexity of loop lying in the right upper abdomen. Water-soluble contrast study reveals bird's beak appearance. CT scan shows whirl sign. Detorsion with sigmoidoscopy is followed by elective sigmoid colectomy in the absence of signs and symptoms of peritonitis. In case of strangulation, gangrene, or perforation, sigmoid colectomy with end ileostomy is performed.
- Colon becomes massively dilated in the absence of mechanic obstruction and is known as colonic pseudo-obstruction or *Ogilvie syndrome*. It is usually associated with narcotic use, bed rest, and comorbid condition in hospitalized patients.
- The most common cause of splenomegaly is cirrhosis of liver followed by lymphoma and infections such as AIDS and endocarditis.
- For rectal cancer: Depth of penetration of bowel wall is the best indicator to assess the tendency of colonic carcinoma to metastasize and in case of carcinoma of rectum it is best assessed by transrectal ultrasonography (TRUS). Endorectal ultrasound is best for T1 and T2 identification. MRI is for advanced T stage and N stage, response to neoadjuvant chemotherapy, and assessment of circumferential resection margin. For extent of large lesion and recurrent lesion, pelvic MRI or pelvic CT scan, and PET scan are performed.
- In case of profuse lower GI bleeding, the investigation of choice is selective arteriography.
- In ulcerative colitis: Prophylactic proctocolectomy in patients with more than 10 years of ulcerative colitis with no dysplasia is controversial.
  - *Proponents*: Multiple biopsies do not exclude dysplasia or malignancy throughout the colonic mucosa.
  - *Opponents*: There is a relative low risk of developing malignancy in a patient with all biopsies negative.
- Right-sided diverticula are more likely to bleed; so common sources of bleeding in diverticula are superior mesenteric vessels.
- Oxalate absorption is more from the small intestine; massive bowel resection leads to formation of oxalate stones.
- Acute abdominal pain along with metabolic acidosis in any patient is suggestive of acute mesenteric ischemia until proven otherwise.
- *Carney triad* is GIST + endocrine tumor + pulmonary chondromas.

HEPATOBILIARY SYSTEM

54. Describe anatomy of liver.

- The functional unit of liver is hepatic lobule and contains central hepatic vein and portal triad.
- Liver parenchyma is entirely covered by Glissonian capsule except in posterior surface, which is a bare area.
- Liver is divided into two hemilivers by Cantlie line. It runs from gallbladder fossa to IVC. Hemiliver is supplied by hepatic artery, portal vein, and bile duct. Liver is divided into four sections: Right anterior and right posterior sections and left medial

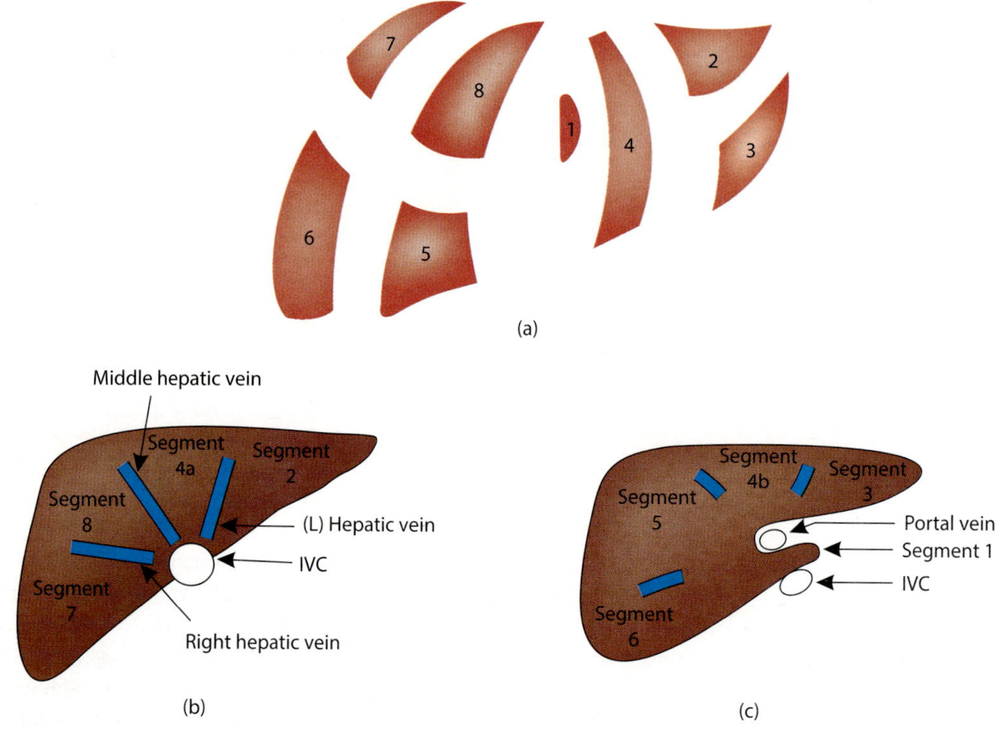

Figure 16.1 (a) Segmental anatomy of liver. (b) View of liver in CECT abdomen. (c) View of liver at portal vein level in CECT abdomen. *Courtesy*: Dr Vismit Joshipura, Consultant GI surgeon, Ahmedabad.

and left lateral sections. Segments of liver are described by Couinaud (Fig. 16.1).

- Eighty percent of the blood supply is from portal vein and the rest is from the hepatic artery.
- Right anterior section consists of segments V and VIII.
- Right posterior section consists of segments VI and VII.
- Left lateral section consists of segments II and III.
- Left medial section consists of segment IV.
- Segment I is the caudate lobe of liver and has independent supply of hepatic and portal veins and directly drains into IVC.
- Caudate lobe drains into right and left hepatic ducts in 80% of cases.
- Falciform ligament divides left lobe into medial segment (segment IV) and lateral segment (segments II and III).
- The liver is supplied by common hepatic artery.
- Right portal vein supplies right lobe and left portal vein supplies segments II, III, and IV.
- Hepatic vein drains the blood into IVC.
- Left hepatic vein drains segments II and III.
- Middle hepatic vein drains segments IV and V/VIII.
- Right hepatic vein drains segments V/VIII and VI/VII.
- The bile duct, portal vein, and hepatic artery (portal triad) are contained within lesser omentum (hepatoduodenal ligament). The bile duct lies lateral to the hepatic artery and both are anterior to portal vein (Mickey Mouse view on ultrasonography).
- Right hepatic duct is entirely intrahepatic while left hepatic duct has a long extrahepatic course.
- Hepatic stellate cells or Ito cells are found in space of Disse. It has a high lipid content and its major function is storage of vitamin A.
- The major function of hepatic Kupffer cells is phagocytosis.

55. Describe the risk factors, clinical features, and management of hepatocellular carcinoma.

A Risk factors

- Age: 50–60 years
- Males > females
- HBV (>50% os cases)
- HCV
- Positive family history
- Genetic factors
- Obesity and metabolic syndrome
- Diabetes
- Radiation exposure and immunosuppression such as HIV and post-transplant immunosuppression
- Cirrhosis
- Smoking
- Alcohol
- Aflatoxin
- Nitrates
- Vinyl chloride
- Oral contraceptive pills
- α_1-Antitrypsin deficiency

Pathology

It has a tropism for portal vein.

Clinical presentation

- Right upper quadrant pain being the most common symptom
- Generalized malaise
- Anorexia
- Fever
- Weight loss
- Palpable mass (hepatomegaly)
- Friction rub or bruit over the liver
- Jaundice (less common)
- PHT
- Budd–Chiari syndrome (BCS)
- Rarely, hypovolemic shock due to rupture intraperitoneal hemorrhage
- May present with paraneoplastic manifestations (Box 16.2)

Box 16.2 Paraneoplastic manifestations

- Hypercalcemia or hypoglycemia (commonest presentation)
- Hypercholesterolemia
- Erythrocytosis
- Watery diarrhea
- Cutaneous manifestations (dermatomyositis, pemphigus, porphyria cutanea tarda, etc.)

Diagnosis

- USG: It is the primary modality of investigation.
- Triphasic helical CT or MRI with contrast help in the determination of extent of tumor, presence of vascular invasion, and tumor thrombi. HCC is hypervascular in arterial phase and hypodense during delayed phase. It has a tendency to invade portal vein. Presence of portal vein thrombosis is highly suggestive of HCC.
- American Association for the Study of Liver Diseases (AASLD) guidelines for diagnosis are:
  - A mass found incidentally on USG in the setting of a patient with known hepatitis B or cirrhosis is likely to be HCC.
  - <1-cm mass: Repeat USG at 3- to 6-month interval. In case of static nodule for 2 years, follow routine surveillance.
  - >1-cm mass: If CECT or dynamic MRI abdomen is suggestive of typical HCC, then no further investigation is required. If not typical of HCC, go for either second CT/MRI or biopsy. If second imaging is also negative, perform biopsy.
- Tumor marker: *Serum α-fetoprotein* (AFP) <20 ng/mL is normal. AFP level >200 ng/mL is suggestive of HCC. At higher cutoff values (>500 ng/mL), specificity increases but sensitivity decreases. Other tumor markers are microRNA, des-gama-carboxy prothrombin, glypican-3, and human carboxylesterase.
- Percutaneous needle biopsy is indicated only when the patient requires nonoperative management. It is not recommended for obvious diagnosis.
- Liver function tests are also helpful.
- Indocyanine green clearance test helps to know hepatic blood flow. It is for functional assessment of the liver and deciding suitability of resection.
- PET scan also helps in the diagnosis.

Treatment

Patient selection is done for surgical resection. Liver resection and transplantation are the curative options.

- Resection of liver
  - All noncirrhotic patients should be considered for resection.
  - In fit patients, operatibility will be decided by tumor location and its relation to the vessels.
  - Well-compensated cirrhosis with no PHT can also be considered for resection.
  - Solitary liver mass, 10 cm, confined to the liver and without vascular invasion can be treated by hepatic resection. Operative goal is to achieve 1-cm margin of normal liver.
- Liver transplantation
  - *Milan criteria*: These were used traditionally. Patients with solitary lesion <5 cm or three lesions <3 cm are candidates for orthotopic liver transplantation.
  - Now, San Francisco criteria are used: Patients with single lesion ≤6.5 cm or two to three lesions not exceeding 4.5 cm with total diameter of ≤8 cm are candidates for liver transplantation.
  - Technically unresectable and recurrent HCC is another indication.
- Other modalities for treatment
  - Intratumoral percutaneous injection of alcohol is suitable in lesions <4 cm and Child's class B or C.
  - Radiofrequency ablation in <3-cm tumor. RFA is now the main ablative therapy using microwave technology for the following:
    - Single <2-cm nodule with increased bilirubin and portal pressure
    - Three nodules ≤3 cm with associated disease
- Other techniques of ablation are the following:
  - Cryoablation, laser, and microwave are used.
  - High-intensity focused ultrasound (HIFU) is under development.
  - Transarterial chemoembolization (TACE): More than 3.5-cm tumor. Lipiodol is used with chemotherapy. Drug-eluting beads containing doxorubicin are also used for TACE.
  - Chemosaturation: Chemotherapy to the liver is delivered for 30 minutes. Suprahepatic and suprarenal IVC is blocked with balloon and all the branches of celiac axis that allow chemotherapy to enter extrahepatic site must be occluded via chemoembolization coil.
  - Sorafenib is the standard of care in advanced HCC. It inhibits cell proliferation and vascular endothelial growth factor receptor (VEGFR).
- Supportive treatment is as follows:
  - Antiangiogenesis factor (bevacizumab) damages the formation of feeding vessels.
  - Erlotinib, an epidermal growth factor receptor inhibitor (EGFR), is used.
- Systemic chemotherapy
  - Doxorubicin
  - Cisplatin
  - Mitomycin
  - 5-Fluorouracil

- Focal nodular hyperplasia can be diagnosed with high accuracy by using nuclear imaging, because it contains functioning reticuloendothelial cells and hepatocytes.
- Decreased uptake is seen in HCC.
- Fibrolamellar HCC
  - Does not produce AFP
  - Calcification differentiating FHCC to FNH
  - Associated with elevated neurotensin level
  - Occurs in young adults
  - Well demarcated and nonencapsulated—good prognosis
  - Not associated with cirrhosis
  - Resectable

56. What is PHT? Discuss etiology and management of acute variceal bleeding.

- PHT
  - Normal portal pressure: 5–10 mmHg
  - PHT: >10 mmHg
  - Esophageal varices: >12 mmHg
  - Possibility of rupture greater if PHT is more than 15 mmHg

Normal hepatic venous pressure gradient (HVPG) is 3–5 mmHg; 5–9.5 mmHg is the silent stage of PHT. HVPG >10 mmHg indicates clinically significant PHT. Varices develop at HVPG of 12 mmHg. Acceptable target for treatment is HVPG below 12 mmHg.

Etiology

- *Presinusoidal*
  - Portal vein thrombosis
  - Splenic vein thrombosis
  - Congenital hepatic fibrosis
  - Noncirrhotic portal fibrosis
  - Extrinsic compression (tumor, lymph node)
- *Sinusoidal*
  - Cirrhosis
  - Fatty liver
  - Wilson disease
  - Idiopathic PHT
  - Schistosomiasis
- *Postsinusoidal*
  - BCS
  - CCF
  - Constrictive pericarditis

Management of acute variceal bleeding

- Color Doppler is the investigation of choice in PHT.
- Establish large-bore IV access (two-IV access is ideal) and withdraw blood sample for BGCM (blood group cross matching), hematocrit, Hb, creatinine, and LFT
- Consider for ICU admission as the condition deteriorates rapidly.
- Resuscitation with IV fluids
- Consider for FFP and vitamin K (INR >1.4:2 units FFP and 10 mg vitamin K).
- Give IV PPI and stop NSAIDs.
- Give O negative blood if the patient is hypotensive (if critically ill); otherwise wait till group-specific blood is obtained. Goal of transfusion: 7 g/dL.
- Catheterize and maintain input–output chart.
- Monitor TPR, BP, and urine output (urine output should be at least 0.5 mL/kg/h).
- Maintain systolic blood pressure of 100 mmHg. Optimal blood pressure at which endoscopy can be safely performed is 70 mmHg.
- Use endotracheal intubation to prevent bronchial aspiration of stomach content and blood prior to endoscopy particularly in patients with severe hematemesis and associated hepatic encephalopathy.
- Establish diagnosis by emergency endoscopy (within 12 hours of acute variceal bleed). Delayed endoscopy >12 hours increases the rebleeding and mortality.
- Fluoroquinolones or cephalosporin is associated with decreasing infectious complications.
- Vasoactive drugs should be started and continued for 2–5 days.
- Vasopressin, terlipressin, and somatostatin are given. Terlipressin is the only drug found to improve survival. Dose is 2 mg bolus every 4–6 hours for the first 2 days or till the bleeding is controlled, and then the dose is reduced to half. ECG is mandatory as terlipressin has cardiac side effect.
- Somatostatin is given as infusion (250 µg bolus followed by 250 µg/h infusion).
- Octreotide is given as 50 µg bolus followed by 50 µg/h infusion.
- Endoscopic therapy includes endoscopic variceal ligation (EVL) and sclerotherapy.
- *TIPS*: It is the method of choice for emergency decompression in acute variceal bleeding not responding to pharmacological or endoscopic methods.
- In refractory acute variceal bleeding, perform balloon tamponade procedure with the help of Sengstaken–Blakemore or Minnesota tube; the effect is due to compression of the collateral veins at the cardia of the stomach; it can be used as a bridge therapy to TIPS.
- EVL and nonselective beta-blockers (NSBB) ± nitrates are used for secondary prophylaxis.
- Nowadays, shunt and nonshunt surgical procedures are rarely performed.

- The most common cause of death in cirrhosis is hepatic failure followed by variceal bleed.
- The most common cause of left-sided PHT (due to splenic vein thrombosis) is pancreatitis. The most common cause of isolated gastric varix is left-sided PHT. Splenectomy is the treatment of choice.

57. Describe etiology, types, and clinical presentations of Budd–Chiari syndrome (BCS) and its management.

A BCS is hepatic venous outflow obstruction, independent of level (from small hepatic vein to IVC with the right atrium) or mechanism of obstruction. Exceptions are cardiac and pericardial diseases.

Primary BCS is obstruction within the vein and secondary is venous obstruction due to compression or invasion by a lesion that originates outside of the vein (e.g., malignancy).

Etiology

- Chronic myeloproliferative disease
- Carcinoma
- Contraception
- Conception
- Coagulation (hyper)
- Congenital web in IVC
- Idiopathic

Myeloproliferative disorders (MPDs) are the leading causal factors. The most commonly associated MPD is polycythemia vera. Major causes for secondary BCS are malignancy and infection.

Types

- Acute: Total occlusion of hepatic blood flow
- Acute on chronic
- Subacute: Partial occlusion over several weeks
- Chronic: Usually present with PHT or liver failure

The most common form is subacute or chronic.

Clinical presentation

- Abdominal pain in right hypochondrium (RHC)
- Fever
- Hepatomegaly
- Ascites (most common initial presentation)
- Tenderness in RHC
- GI bleed
- Fulminant hepatic failure
- Hepatic encephalopathy
- Hepatorenal syndrome

Diagnosis

- SAAG >1.1 and ascitic fluid protein >2.5 g/dL are consistent with BCS.
- Real-time color and pulsed Doppler is the investigation of choice.
- MRI with gadolinium is the excellent investigation. However, it does not show the direction of blood flow.
- Venography with transvenous biopsy is performed.
- Liver biopsy reveals zone 3 congestion.

Treatment

- Anticoagulation for all
- Control of ascites (low-sodium diet, diuretics, and albumin)
- Treatment of the cause
- Thrombolytic therapy (either systemic or direct in the vein)
- Angioplasty: For IVC web and stenosis of short hepatic vein
- TIPS: As a bridge to liver transplant

- Liver transplantation is performed in case of acute BCS with fulminant hepatic failure and end-stage liver disease after chronic BCS.
- Portosystemic shunt surgery is performed for subacute cases and with favorable cause.
- Denver shunt is for ascites and LeVeen shunt is between peritoneum and superior vena cava and is for ascites.

58. Describe liver abscess.

A
- The most common type of liver abscess worldwide is amebic; the most common type in the developed world is pyogenic; hydatid is common in sheep-rearing countries.
- The common organism causing pyogenic liver abscess is *E. coli* (most common) followed by Klebsiellae, enterococci, and *Bacteroides*. Biliary tract sepsis is the commonest source followed by portal venous, for example, appendicitis.

- Amebic liver abscess is caused by *Entamoeba histolytica*. Trophozoite reaches liver through portal vein. It is solitary and in right lobe liver. Amebic abscess contains anchovy sauce fluids of necrotic hepatocyte and trophozoites.
- Right upper abdominal pain (most common symptom in amebic abscess), fever (most common presentation in pyogenic abscess), malaise, anorexia, hiccups, and jaundice are the symptoms while tender hepatomegaly, jaundice, reactive pleural effusion, atelectasis, and fever are the signs of liver abscess.

Treatment

- *Amebic abscess*: Metronidazole followed by diloxanide furoate; indications for aspiration: Left lobe large abscess, abscess >6 cm size, infected abscess, pregnancy, and failure of medical management
- *Pyogenic liver abscess*: Treatment of the cause, percutaneous aspiration and drainage, and antibiotics according to culture and sensitivity

59. What is Murphy's sonographic sign?

A Tenderness is revealed over the gallbladder by sonographic probe.

60. Describe the morphology of chronic cholecystitis.

A
- Contracted or distended
- Cholesterosis
- Mucosal outpouching to the muscularis (Rokitansky–Aschoff sinuses)

61. What is Charcot's triad? What does it suggest? How does it develop?

A
- Pain
- Fever with chills
- Jaundice

The triad is suggestive of cholangitis.

Development of cholangitis requires the following: Bacterobilia, stagnant bile, and increased intrabiliary pressure more than 20 cm H_2O. Partial biliary obstruction is more commonly associated with cholangitis than complete biliary obstruction as complete obstruction is less likely to be associated with bacterobilia.

62. What is Reynolds pentad?

A It is a combination of fever, jaundice, pain, septicemia, and disorientation.

63. What is HIDA scan?

A Technetium-99m–labeled derivative of dimethyl iminodiacetic acid is used for diagnosis of the following:
- Acute cholecystitis (gallbladder fails to fill)
- Obstruction at ampulla
- Biliary leak

64. What is Mirizzi syndrome?

A Impaction of stone in the cystic duct or neck of gallbladder leads to mechanical or inflammatory compression or obstruction of CBD or CHD. As a result of the ongoing process, it leads to development of cholecystocholedochal or cholecystoenteric fistula (Table 16.1) (Fig. 16.2).

65. What are the common causes of postcholecystectomy symptoms?

A
- Retained or recurrent stone
- Long stump of cystic duct
- Biliary dysfunction
- Bile duct stricture

66. What are the indications for prophylactic cholecystectomy?

A Usually asymptomatic gallstone requires only conservative management, but surgery (prophylactic cholecystectomy) is indicated in the following situations:
- Porcelain gallbladder (controversial) (Towfigh et al.[6] evaluated the pathology slides of 10,000 patients for evidence of calcification and carcinoma of gallbladder; no one had a carcinoma gallbladder)
- Gallbladder polyp >1 cm
- Large stone >3 cm size
- Gallbladder stone with polyp (irrespective of size)
- Pima Indian population
- Patients with sickle cell anemia or hereditary spherocytosis
- Bariatric surgery (controversial)
- Candidates for organ transplantation or immunosuppressed individuals
- Pediatric patients with gallstone
- Patients with intestinal carcinoid syndrome requiring long-term somatostatin therapy

Table 16.1 Modified Mirizzi Classification[7,8]

Type	Description	Treatment
I	Extrinsic compression of the common bile duct by an impacted gallstone	Subtotal or total cholecystectomy
II	Cholecystobiliary fistula secondary to an eroded gallstone involving one-third of the circumference of the common bile duct	Subtotal cholecystectomy. Leave 5 mm gallbladder wall around fistula in order to aid in closure of the destroyed bile duct. Separate incision is kept over the bile duct distal to fistula protected by T tube
III	Cholecystobiliary fistula involving two-thirds of the circumference of the common bile duct	Subtotal cholecystectomy. Leave 1 cm gallbladder wall around the fistula. Bilioenteric anastomosis to the duodenum or a Roux-en-Y hepaticojejunostomy can be performed in second stage if required
IV	Cholecystobiliary fistula comprising the whole circumference of the common bile duct	Subtotal cholecystectomy with Roux-en-Y hepaticojejunostomy
V	Any type plus a cholecystoenteric fistula	
Va	Without gallstone ileus	Division and simple suture with an absorbable material of the bilioenteric fistulae over the implicated viscera (duodenum, stomach, colon, or small bowel) and cholecystectomy, either total or subtotal according to the presence of a cholecystobiliary fistula or simple external compression of the bile duct
Vb	With gallstone ileus	Treat gallstone ileus first and later on after 3 months definitive surgery of the gallbladder depending on type of fistula

(somatostatin inhibits cholecystokinin, decreases gallbladder contractibility, and promotes lithogenesis)

- Short gut syndrome requiring long-term TPN
- Gastric cancer surgery (it avoids reoperation in case of acute acalculous cholecystitis and avoids complex ERCP procedure or exploration in the presence of Roux-en-Y anatomy in case of cholangitis or CBD stone)

67. Enumerate etiology and clinical features of hemobilia.

A Etiology

- Accidental liver trauma: Blunt or penetrating
- Iatrogenic (the most common cause of hemobilia; endoscopic, percutaneous, or operative liver procedure; most cases are due to percutaneous liver biopsy, percutaneous cholangiography, or percutaneous biliary drainage [most common cause]; ERCP with sphincterotomy also causes hemobilia)
- Hepatic malignancy
  - Vascular and inflammatory
- CBD stone
  - *Ascaris* infestation

Clinical features

Quincke's triad:

- Right upper abdominal pain
- Jaundice
- Upper GI bleeding

Treatment

- *Minor*: Treated conservatively
- *Significant*: As with any severe bleeding, resuscitation, and reversal of coagulopathy
- *Intervention radiology*: Nonselective embolization of left or right hepatic artery
- Surgery
  - Ligation of bleeding vessel
  - Excision of pseudoaneurysm
  - Liver resection

But most of the patients are critically ill, and cannot withstand major surgical procedure.

Nowadays, transcatheter arterial embolization is the treatment of choice and covered biliary stent is treatment for post-ERCP bleeding.

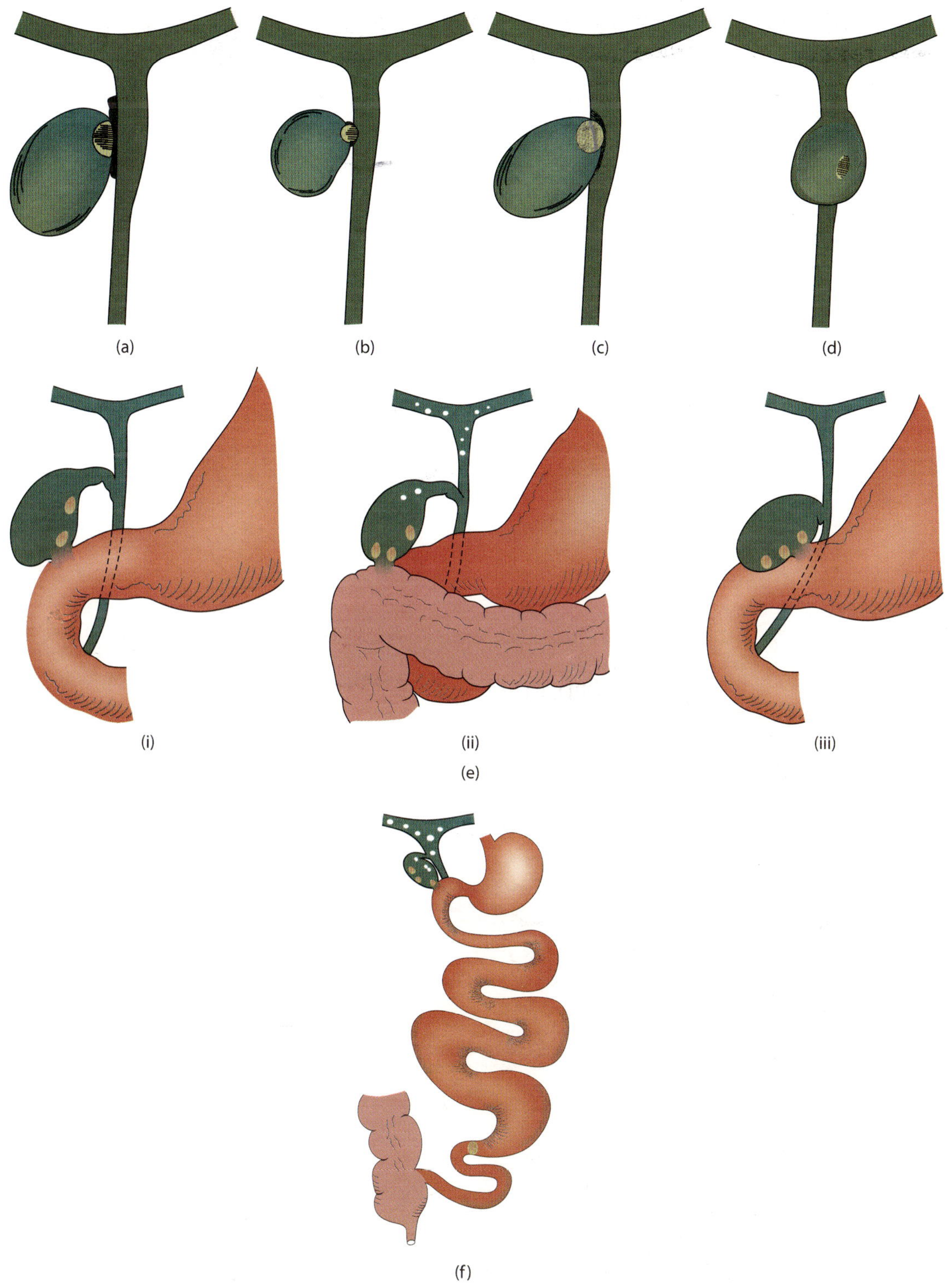

Figure 16.2 Type I to Vb—Mirizzi syndrome. (a) Type I, (b) Type II, (c) Type III, (d) Type IV; (e) Type Va: (i) cholecystoduodenal fistula, (ii) cholecystocolonic fistula, (iii) cholecystogastric fistula; (f) Type Vb: gallstone ileus. *Courtesy*: Dr Vismit Joshipura, Consultant GI surgeon, Ahmedabad.

68. Which part of the common bile duct is most likely to be injured in laparoscopic cholecystectomy? Describe the various classifications used for bile duct injury.

A
- Upper part (near junction and proximal to it)
- Stewart-Way classification of bile duct injury
  - *Class I (least common injury, 6%)*: It refers to incomplete transection of CBD with no tissue loss. CBD is mistaken for cystic duct but is recognized. Cystic duct incision is extended into common bile duct for cholangiogram.
  - *Class II*: It refers to incomplete transection of common hepatic duct with resultant stricture or fistula. There is lateral damage to CHD from cautery or clip. Visibility is poor due to associated bleeding.
  - *Class III (most common type, 62%)*: It refers to complete transection of CBD, including cystic duct—common duct junction. CBD is mistaken for cystic duct but is not recognized. CBD, CHD, RHD, and LHD are transected and/or resected.
  - *Class IV*: It refers to complete or incomplete transection of right hepatic duct. RHD or right sectoral duct is mistaken for cystic duct. Right hepatic artery is mistaken for cystic artery and RHD and RHA transected. There is lateral damage to RHD from clip or cautery.
- Strasberg classification[9] (Fig. 16.3)
  - *A*: Bile leak from the cystic duct stump or minor biliary radical from gallbladder fossa
  - *B*: Right posterior sectoral duct occluded
  - *C*: Bile leak from the right posterior sectoral duct
  - *D*: Bile leak from the main bile duct without major tissue loss
  - *E*:
    - *E1 (Bismuth Type I)*: Transection >2 cm from the hilus
    - *E2 (Bismuth Type II)*: Transection <2 cm from the hilus
    - *E3 (Bismuth Type III)*: Transection in the hilum
    - *E4 (Bismuth Type IV)*: Separation of major ducts in the hilum
    - *E5 (Bismuth Type V)*: Type C injury plus injury in the hilum
    - *E6*: Complete excision of the extrahepatic duct involving hilus

69. Discuss briefly gallstone ileus.

A
- Gallstone ileus causes mechanical bowel obstruction through impaction of a gallstone in the terminal ileum. It is more common in women of age 70 years.
- The most common site of obstruction is at the IC valve[10]
- Biliary enteric fistula is most common between GB and duodenum; it will lead to passage of stone.
- Stone size is >2.5 cm.
- It presents with obstruction.
- It is associated with tumbling stone phenomenon: varied location of pain throughout the abdomen due to intermittent obstruction at various locations (due to ball valve effect).
- Rigler's triad: It refers to dilated small bowel, stone, and pneumobilia (seen in 20–50% of patients) on a plain radiograph (two of these signs are pathognomonic for gallstone ileus).
- CT is more sensitive and able to diagnose other stones within GI tract (imaging modality of choice).

Treatment

- The obstruction can be relieved through proximal longitudinal enterotomy, milking of the stone upstream , stone removal, and transverse closure. A careful inspection of whole small bowel is performed to search for another stone as recurrence rate because of missed stone is 5–10% within 30 days.
- Low-risk individuals (ASA grades I and II) should have definitive biliary procedure in a single stage along with enterotomy (either cholecystectomy and fistula

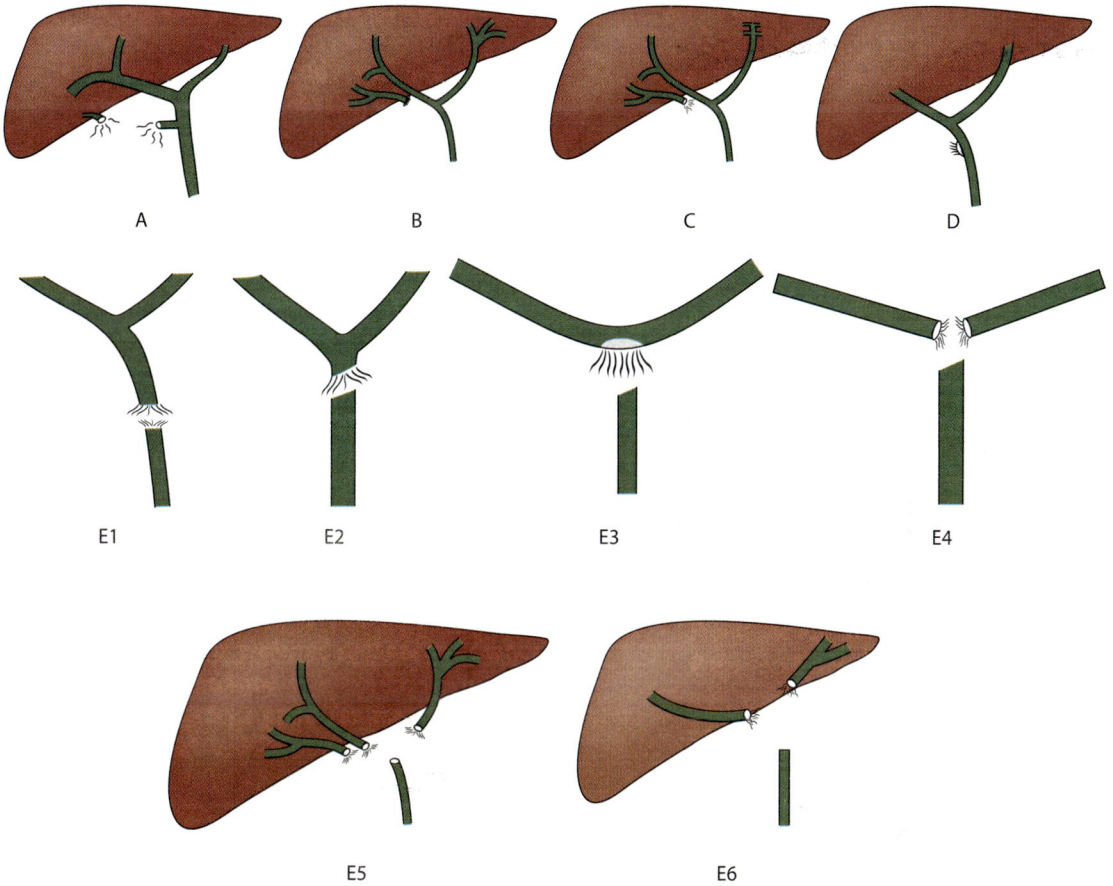

Figure 16.3 A to E6: Strasberg classification of bile duct injury. *Courtesy*: Dr Vismit Joshipura, Consultant GI surgeon, Ahmedabad.

closure or cholecystectomy with bile duct exploration).

- High-risk individuals (ASA grades III and IV): Enterolithotomy alone is performed and definitive biliary procedure is deferred in the next stage once condition improves.

70. What are the indications for common bile duct exploration?

A Nowadays, the procedure of choice for CBD stone is laparoscopic CBD exploration at the time of laparoscopic cholecystectomy. Many centers use ERCP for CBD stone preoperatively. Preoperative MRCP is ideal to look for CBD pathology. In case of preoperative diagnosis of CBD stone, laparoscopic CBD exploration is advised to complete the procedure in a single stage. Palpable stone in the CBD or filling defect on intraoperative cholangiogram is an indication of laparoscopic CBD exploration. However, in certain conditions, preoperative ERCP is ideal:

- Cholangitis
- Gallstone pancreatitis
- Dilated CBD more than 8 mm and jaundice (to rule out malignancy)

Open CBD exploration is nowadays rarely performed.

71. Describe in short about gallbladder cancer.

A 

Risk factors

Risk factors for carcinoma gallbladder are the following:

- Long-standing gallstone (larger stone is more likely; gallstone more than 20 years; risk is 1%)

- Anomalous pancreaticobiliary duct junction
- Single adenoma in more than 50 years and >1 cm
- Bacterial infection: *Salmonella typhi* and *H. pylori*
- PSC
- UC
- Drugs: Methyldopa, isoniazid
- Women with long-standing estrogen exposure
- Heavy metal and radon exposure; chemicals
- Obesity
- Choledochal cyst or anomalous pancreatobiliary junction
- Genetic associated with Gardener syndrome, HNPCC, neurofibromatosis, etc.

Clinical features
- Asymptomatic
- Symptoms of gallstone
- Weight loss and jaundice
- Mass or lump
- Ascites

Diagnosis
- USG: Gallbladder cancer is suspected in the following features on USG—mural thickening or calcification, a mass projecting into the lumen of the gallbladder, fixed mass in the gallbladder, loss of the plane between the gallbladder and the liver, or liver infiltration
- CT scan, MRI/MRCP: To confirm the diagnosis and to know the local extend and distant metastases
- EUS: Helps in detection and differential diagnosis of polyp and local staging
- PET CT and CT chest: For staging completion
- CA 19-9: Is tumor marker
- Preoperative suspicion of gallbladder cancer is in the following cases: asymmetric wall thickening, polyp > 1 cm, or mass lesion.

Common types, site, and mode of spread

The most common type of carcinoma gallbladder is diffuse infiltrative type. The most common histological type is adenocarcinoma.

The most common site is fundus of gallbladder and direct hepatic invasion is the most common mode of spread followed by lymph node.

Treatment
- Incidental detection of cancer GB after cholecystectomy (Tis or T 1a): Lamina propria invasion with cystic duct margin free—no surgery. If margin is involved, bile duct excision with lymphadenectomy is performed.
- Perimuscular connective tissue involvement (T2): Hepatic resection 4b and 5 segments and regional lymphadenectomy. If duct margin is positive, excision of the bile duct is performed.
- On-table identification requires the following: Frozen section; conversion to radical cholecystectomy.
- T3 (serosal invasion or perforation or single extrahepatic organ involvement): Radical resection with excision of organ involved is performed.

For locally advanced and metastatic gallbladder cancer, treatment is as follows:
- Palliation such as hepaticojejunostomy or stenting for jaundice
- Chemotherapy such as gemcitabine and cisplatin

PANCREAS

72. Describe etiology, clinical features, complications, and management of acute pancreatitis.

A Atlanta definition: Acute pancreatitis is an acute inflammatory process of pancreas with variable involvement of other regional tissues or remote organ system.

Etiology
- Alcohol (ethyl alcohol, methyl alcohol)
- Gallstone and other obstructive lesions such as parasites, duodenal diverticulum, annular pancreas, and choledochocele
- Collagen vascular disease
- Drugs: Corticosteroids, thiazide, estrogen, didanosine, anti-HIV drugs, and azathioprine
- Post-ERCP—Familial hereditary, genetic
- Hypertriglyceridemia
- Hyperparathyroidism

- Hypercalcemia: Idiopathic
- Infection: Viral and parasitic
- Ischemia (emboli to pancreatic blood vessels, hypotension)
- Tumors: Intraductal papillary mucinous neoplasm (IPMN) and ductal adenocarcinoma
- Toxin: Jamaican scorpion venom
- Organophosphorus insecticide
- Trauma: External and surgical
- Vasculitis

Clinical features

Severity of pancreatitis according to Atlanta definition (2012):

- *Mild acute pancreatitis*: No organ failure or no local or systemic complication
- *Moderate acute pancreatitis*: Transient organ failure and local or systemic complication without persistent organ failure
- *Severe acute pancreatitis*: Persistent organ failure more than 48 hours

Symptoms

- Severe abdominal pain radiating to back
- Nausea, vomiting, and retching

Signs

- Tenderness over epigastric region and periumbilical region
- Tachycardia
- Grey Turner sign: Discoloration on the flanks
- Cullen sign: Discoloration around umbilicus
- Fox sign: Discoloration below inguinal ligaments or at the base of the pelvis
- Jaundice
- Hypotension
- ARDS

Investigations

- Serum amylase: A value greater than four times of the normal value is suggestive of pancreatitis. p-Type isoenzyme is helpful. It rapidly increases in the first 24 hours, gradually increases over the next 48 hours, then plateaus, and then gradually declines. After 7 days, it comes to normal.

  Other conditions causing increased serum amylase are as follows: Acute cholecystitis, peritonitis, perforation, ruptured aortic aneurysm, salpingitis, burns, DKA, ruptured ectopic pregnancy, and mesenteric ischemia.
- Serum lipase: Values >3 times of the normal value suggest pancreatitis. Other conditions causing elevated lipase level are cholecystitis, bone fracture, and perforation.
- CRP: A value of >150 mg/L or worsening clinical state with persistent organ failure indicates severity.
- BUN: On admission or after 24 hours >20 mg/dL or any rise within 24 hours indicates poor prognosis. It is the most valuable single routine laboratory test to predict mortality in acute pancreatitis.
- Hematocrit and creatinine: Hematocrit <45% and creatinine >1.8 indicate possibility of severe pancreatitis or necrosis.
- Procalcitonin: It helps to differentiate mild from severe pancreatitis within the first 24 hours of symptom onset.
- Other markers indicate severity but are not readily available: Interleukin-6, polymorphonuclear leukocyte elastase, phospholipase A2, and urinary trypsinogen activation peptide.
- Organ failure is the most significant prognostic factor in severe acute pancreatitis. Plasma D-dimer is a surrogate marker for future organ dysfunction.
- Hyperglycemia is also helpful.
- Hypocalcaemia can be performed.
- Altered LFT is also helpful.
- X-ray
  - Colon cutoff sign
  - Renal halo sign
  - Calcified gallbladder
- USG: Its main role is to diagnose gallstone, dilated CBD, and acute cholecystitis:
  - Pancreatic edema
  - Peripancreatic fluid collection
  - Abscess
  - Pseudocyst
- CT scan: It is routinely not recommended for the diagnosis of pancreatitis, but helps to diagnose complications of pancreatitis, such as necrosis, abscess, pseudocyst, gangrene, and ascites. It is performed in case of diagnostic uncertainty or

differentiates between interstitial and necrotic pancreatitis. It is not recommended in early 48 hours. It should be performed if the patient is not improving after 48 hours and/or in the presence of a suspected complication; it will identify the area of necrosis as a nonenhancement after IV contrast (if more than 30% of pancreatic parenchyma and >3 cm of area do not enhance, it indicates necrosis). CT-guided aspiration is performed if necrosis is present and patients did not improve on routine measure. It helps to differentiate sterile pancreatic necrosis from infected necrosis.

- MRI: Indications are moderate renal dysfunction and/or allergy to IV contrast media.
- Various scoring systems are available to judge the severity of pancreatitis, such as Ranson criteria, Glasgow scale, and Acute Physiology and Chronic Health Evaluation (APACHE) II score.

Management

- Maintaining hemodynamic stability and urine output >30–60 cm^3/h is of prime importance:
  - NBM
  - TPR monitoring
- Catheterize the patient: Input/output charting
- Oxygen saturation <90% requires supplemental oxygen by either nasal prongs or face mask.
- Establish large-caliber IV access. Perform resuscitation with IV crystalloid. Lactated ringer is the fluid of choice due to its bicarbonate content. It prevents metabolic acidosis.
- Patients with acute severe pancreatitis should be managed in ICU.
- Aggressive fluid resuscitation is beneficial in the first 12 hours. After 24 hours, aggressive fluid replacement may not be beneficial. A total of 250–500 mL/h fluid should be given within the first 48 hours depending on BMI (5–10 mL/kg/h). Care should be taken in patients with cardiac and renal problem and elderly patients. CVP is used to determine volume status. Six-hourly assessment of fluid requirement should be done for the first 48 hours and goal should be to decrease the BUN.
- Pain is the cardinal symptom and its relief is priority. Mild pain is managed with nonsteroidal anti-inflammatory drugs such as diclofenac sodium 50 mg/6–8 hours and severe pain is managed with opioids such as tramadol or buprenorphine IV. If required, antispasmodic dicyclomine can also be given.
- If hypotension persists even after aggressive fluid resuscitation, IV dopamine may help to maintain systolic blood pressure (it does not impair microcirculation to the pancreas).
- American College of Gastroenterology (ACG) guidelines on management of acute pancreatitis (2013) do not support the use of prophylactic antibiotic even in the presence of sterile necrotizing pancreatitis. Antibiotics should be used for cholangitis, pneumonia, catheter-associated infection, UTI, and bacteremia. They should be given in infected necrosis (CT-guided FNA for Gram stain and culture). Antibiotics used should have a better penetration in pancreatic tissue such as carbapenem, quinolones, and metronidazole (ACG, 2013[11]).
- Patients with cholangitis require early ERCP within 24 hours. Gallstone pancreatitis lacks evidence of cholangitis and persistent biliary obstruction should not undergo ERCP. MRCP or EUS is advised in the absence of cholangitis, if CBD stone is suspected (ACG, 2013).
- Nutrition: In mild acute pancreatitis, oral feeding can be given if there is no nausea and vomiting, and abdominal pain subsides. A low-fat, solid diet is as safe as clear liquid. In severe pancreatitis, enteral feeding is preferred. Nasogastric feeding is as safe as nasojejunal feeding (ACG guidelines, 2013).
- In patients with gallstone, cholecystectomy should be performed before discharge to prevent recurrence. In patients with necrotizing pancreatitis with collection,

cholecystectomy should be differed till the inflammation subsides.

- In patients with asymptomatic pseudocyst or necrosis, intervention is not required.
- In symptomatic patients with infected necrosis, minimally invasive, either endoscopic or laparoscopic, method is preferred.
- In asymptomatic infected necrosis, intervention is delayed for at least 4 weeks.

Complications

- Local
  - Necrosis
  - Abscess
  - Pseudocyst
  - Ascites
  - Phlegmon
  - Pancreatic fistula
  - Splenic complication (thrombosis, infarction, pseudocyst, hematoma)
  - Compression or fistulization of bowel, most commonly left sided
  - GI bleeding due to varices secondary to splenic vein thrombosis, splenic or portal vein rupture, pseudoaneurysm of splenic artery, hemorrhage in pseudocyst, and postnecrosectomy bleeding
- *Systemic*: It may involve any system of the body and can lead to failure of one system or multiorgan failure.
  - Renal failure: Oliguria
  - Respiratory failure: Arterial hypoxemia
  - Cardiac failure
  - CNS: Confusion, coma, and alcohol withdrawal syndrome
  - Hypocalcemia
  - Hyperglycemia
  - Hypokalemia and hypomagnesemia
  - Abdominal compartment syndrome (ACS)
  - DIC and fat necrosis: Intra-abdominal saponification and subcutaneous fat necrosis
  - Retinopathy (Purtscher retinopathy)
  - Psychosis (pancreatic encephalopathy)

73. Describe pseudopancreatic cyst.

- It refers to a peripancreatic cystic lesion that is well circumscribed and contains amylase-rich fluid with no associated tissue necrosis and is lined by a wall of fibrous or granulation tissue that is present for 4 or more weeks after disease onset. If It is postnecrotic collection that contains necrosum, when mature it is best termed as walled-off pancreatic necrosis (WOPN).
- It is suspected when acute pancreatitis fails to resolve after a week or when after initial improvement, symptoms return.
- Disruption of the pancreatic duct secondary to acute pancreatitis, trauma, or duct obstruction in chronic pancreatitis leads to accumulation of pancreatic secretion.

Classification (Dégidio)

- *Type I*: Acute postnecrotic, pancreatic duct normal with no communication with cyst; percutaneous drainage
- *Type II*: Acute on chronic, pancreatic duct abnormal without stricture, 50–50 duct–cyst communication, internal drainage or resection
- *Type III*: Chronic pancreatitis, pancreatic duct stricture, with cyst duct communication, and internal drainage with duct decompression

Common sites of occurrence

These are the body and tail of pancreas, but it can develop anywhere from mediastinum to scrotum.

Other common locations are the following: Chest, left lobe of liver, spleen, and rarely kidney.

Diagnosis

- USG, which is the initial investigation to diagnose pseudocyst.
- CT abdomen
  - Size, shape, and wall thickness
  - Content of cyst, which can also demonstrate the following:
    - Necrosis
    - Chronic pancreatitis, duct diameter, or ductal stone and calcification
  - Triphasic helical CT (it delineates regional vascular anatomy and abnormality such as pseudoaneurysm in arteries and thrombosis, cavernous transformation, or formation of varices in the vein)

- MRI: It is the best tool for morphological characteristics; MRCP may be used to know the pancreatic and biliary duct anatomy and communication of the cyst with the ductal system.
- EUS: It is superior to other investigations in distinguishing pseudocyst from other pancreatic lesions. Calcification in the cyst wall is highly suggestive of cystadenoma rather than pseudocyst. It also allows aspiration of fluid for analysis: Fluid should be sent for amylase, CEA, and cytology. Low CEA (<400 ng/mL) and amylase >5000 units/Ml usually indicate pseudocyst. Cytology reveals inflammatory cells.

Complications

- Rupture (into the bowel and peritoneum)
- Infection (abscess, sepsis)
- Bleeding (erosion of the vessel, hemorrhage in the cyst, and hemoperitoneum)
- Pressure effect from enlargement such as obstructive jaundice and bowel obstruction

Treatment

Cysts of >6 cm size and >12-week duration, cysts in context with chronic pancreatitis, and symptomatic cysts of any size are less likely to resolve spontaneously.

- *Indications of intervention*
  - Symptomatic cyst
  - Complication of cyst
  - When there is need to differentiate between cyst and neoplasm
- Treatment options
  - USG/CT-guided drainage: It is usually avoided because of high likelihood of recurrence and external pancreatic fistula.
  - Endoscopic stent placement
    - Transpapillary (when communication between cyst and pancreatic duct is evident)
    - Transgastric or transduodenal
    - Endoscopic drainage contraindicated when wall thickness is more than 1 cm and large intervening vessels or varices evident on EUS
  - Surgical drainage: It can be performed either laparoscopically or by open surgery.
    - *Cyst in head*: Cystogastrostomy
    - *Cyst in body*: Cystojejunostomy
    - *Cyst in tail*: Distal pancreatectomy

The commonest complication is infection.

74. What is periampullary region?

- Head of pancreas
- Ampulla of Vater
- Distal CBD
- Duodenum (2 cm area surrounding the ampulla of Vater)

75. Mention in brief about bilhemia.

Bilhemia is because of biliovenous fistula.

Causes

- High intrabiliary pressure due to obstructing CBD lesion
- Trauma with central liver rupture
- Iatrogenic penetrating injury with percutaneous therapeutic intervention (most common)
- Gallstone eroding into venous system

Diagnosis

- Bilirubin level can rise dramatically with direct hyperbilirubinemia without substantial rise in liver enzymes.
- ERCP is the investigation of choice.

Treatment

- Endoscopic biliary stenting to lower intrabiliary pressure is the treatment of choice.
- Gallstone bilhemia requires surgical intervention in the form of hepatic resection.

76. Give a brief account of annular pancreas.

- Annular pancreas is because of faulty rotation of ventral pancreatic bud around the posterior aspect of angle of duodenum.
- Clinical features are of duodenal obstruction.
- Associated anomalies are the following: Duodenal atresia (40%), intestinal malrotation, or trisomy 21 (15–25%).
- X-ray findings: Double bubble sign.
- ERCP is the investigation of choice.

Treatment

Duodenoduodenostomy. It is preferred over duodenojejunostomy because of lower incidence of postoperative complications such as blind loop syndrome or obstruction.

77. Describe in brief risk factors, classification, clinical features, and investigation of chronic pancreatitis.

A Risk factors for chronic pancreatitis

- Alcohol
- Pancreatic duct obstruction from stricture (trauma, acute pancreatitis, or carcinoma)
- Cigarette smoking
- Hyperparathyroidism
- Hyperlipidemia
- Malnutrition, ingestion of cyanogenic glycosides, and exposure to hydrocarbon
- Genetics (serine protease inhibitor Kazal type 1 [*SPINK1*] alteration is responsible)

Singer and Chari classification for chronic pancreatitis

- Calcific (alcohol, tropical, hyperlipidemia, idiopathic)
- Obstructive (tumor, stricture, trauma)
- Inflammatory
- Autoimmune
- Asymptomatic pancreatic fibrosis

Clinical features

- Epigastric pain is the most common symptom and is because of ductal hypertension, parenchymal process (inflammation), or neural involvement.
- Steatorrhea (first functional sign of pancreatic insufficiency) (stool fat >7 g/day) is associated with weight loss.
- Diabetes is usually present.

Investigation

- USG is the initial investigation followed by HRCT or MRCP; it is a method used to detect changes in pancreatitis such as duct dilatation, calcification, calculus diseases, inflammation, and cystic changes.
- ERCP is the gold standard for detection of changes in chronic pancreatitis. However, because of its risk of post-ERCP pancreatitis, its use is limited. EUS is equally good in detecting advanced lesion and may be more sensitive in detecting mild disease.
- Fecal elastase 1 is a noninvasive method to diagnose exocrine insufficiency of pancreas (<100 µg/g indicates insufficiency).
- ERCP is the most useful test to diagnose pancreatic duct leak or fistula. Bowel rest along with TPN and somatostatin analogue octreotide helps in closure of fistula in more than 50% of cases.

Tropical pancreatitis is associated with mutation in *SPINK1* gene. Seen in tropical countries, the patient is malnourished and extremely emaciated, and sometimes cyanotic discoloration of lips can also be seen. Patients may have a family history.

Idiopathic pancreatitis: There is no family history, young patients, and mutation in *SPINK1* or *CFTR* gene.

78. Describe carcinoma of pancreas.

A

- Risk factors for carcinoma pancreas are as follows:
  - More common in males and individuals >60 years of age
  - African-Americans
  - Family history
  - Hereditary syndrome
  - Genetic factors: Lynch syndrome, ataxia telengiectasia, Peutz–Jeghers syndrome, FAP, familial breast–ovarian cancer syndrome
  - Cigarette smoking, which doubles the risk
  - Chronic pancreatitis >5 years
  - Type II DM
  - Coffee and alcohol
  - High-calorie intake
  - Non–O blood group
  - Mutation in *K-ras* proto-oncogene
- The most common type of carcinoma pancreas is ductal adenocarcinoma.

> - Presentation of jaundice and weight loss along with pancreatic mass and/or distal CBD structure should be considered malignancy unless proved otherwise and tissue diagnosis is not mandatory.
> - Tissue diagnosis is required in patients who require neoadjuvant therapy, suspected neuroendocrine tumor, lymphoma, and cystic lesion.

Clinical features in various modes of presentation

- *Carcinoma head of pancreas*
  - Most common site (between bile duct and main pancreatic duct [60–70%])

  - More commonly present with obstructive jaundice
  - Weight loss
  - Pain
  - Gallbladder palpable (according to Courvoiser law) (in 1890, Ludwig Courvoisier described an observation that patients with painless jaundice and a palpable gallbladder often have a malignant obstruction of the common bile duct; this is known as 'Courvoisier law')
- *Periampullary carcinoma*
  - Pain
  - Jaundice
  - Anorexia
  - Weight loss
- *Body and tail*
  - Frequent pain
  - Weight loss
  - Anorexia
  - Splenomegaly

Adverse prognostic factors in pancreas carcinoma

- Age >70
- Presence of type 1 diabetes
- CA 19-9 >400 units/mL
- T4 lesion
- Distant metastases
- Lymph node ratio >0.2
- G3 (poorly differentiated)

Diagnosis

- USG: It is usually the first test and very sensitive for gallbladder and bile duct pathology.
- CA 19-9 is also helpful.
- Pancreatic protocol multidetector, dynamic, contrast-enhanced CT scan with dedicated arterial and venous phase and 3D reconstruction is the single most versatile and cost-effective investigation for diagnosing and staging pancreatic cancer.
- PET scan helps to differentiate chronic pancreatitis from pancreatic cancer.
- EUS: Small pancreatic mass that cannot be seen on CT. It helps in transluminal biopsy. Precise visualization of mass, surrounding vascular anatomy, biliary and pancreatic ducts, and peripancreatic lymph node can be better seen on EUS.
- Although biopsy is not mandatory for surgery, it is very helpful when neoadjuvant therapy is planned. Other indications for preoperative biopsy: Patient unfit to undergo a major resection, or suspected metastatic disease. EUS-guided fine needle aspiration (FNA) is the best modality for obtaining a tissue diagnosis, even if the tumor is poorly visualized by other imaging modalities.
- Diagnostic laparoscopy: With the use of ultrasonography, it improves the accuracy up to 98% for resectability.
- Staging laparoscopy should be reserved for tumors >4 cm on left side, markedly elevated CA 19-9 (>1000 units/mL), small indeterminate liver, or peritoneal lesions seen on CT that are too small to investigate with biopsy or PET CT.
- ERCP: It is not routinely used. Stenting is advised in patients with intractable pruritis, cholangitis, and coagulopathy.

Treatment

- Signs that suggest advance malignancy are the following:
  - Ascites
  - Left supraclavicular lymph node enlargement
  - Sister Mary Joseph nodule
  - Blumer shelf
- Criteria for resectability and unresectability in carcinoma head of pancreas (Society of Abdominal Radiology/American Pancreatic Association):
  - *Potentially resectable*
    - No distant metastatic disease
    - Normal fat plane around SMA, celiac axis, and hepatic artery
    - Patent portal vein/superior mesenteric vein or <180° contact without vein contour regularity
  - *Unresectable*
    - Tumor abuts >180° of the celiac axis and hepatic or superior mesenteric artery

  - Solid tumor contact with the first jejunal SMA branch
  - Unreconstructable SMV/PV due to tumor involvement or occlusion
  - Contact with the most proximal draining jejunal branch into SMV
  - Enlarged lymph node outside the boundaries of resection (nonregional lymph node)
  - Distant metastases
  - Ascites
- *Borderline resectable*
  - Tumor abuts ≤180° of SMA circumference
  - Very small liver lesion, 1 mm, that is difficult to recognize as metastasis or biopsy
  - Solid tumor contact with CHA without extension into celiac artery or bifurcation of the hepatic artery to allow safe and complete resection and reconstruction
  - Short-segment occlusion of portal vein/superior mesenteric vein with normal proximal/distal segment
  - Solid tumor contact with IVC
- Surgery
  - Standard of care for pancreatic head and periampullary malignancy: Pylorus-preserving pancreaticoduodenectomy (PPPD), which includes removal of pancreatic head, duodenum, and distal part of bile duct. Reconstruction is with choledochojejunostomy, pancreatojejunostomy, and duodenojejunostomy. Cholecystectomy is also performed.
  - Original Kausch–Whipple operation includes removal of the gastric antrum and reconstruction with gastrojejunostomy. It is still performed in the case of tumor close to infiltrating stomach or duodenum.
  - PPPD (pylorus-preserving Kausch–Whipple operation) is more physiological and there is no difference in recurrence rate and overall survival. It is the procedure of choice nowadays.
  - For body and tail:
    - Distal pancreatectomy with splenectomy
  - Total pancreatectomy is indicated in the following situation:
    - Multifocal tumor and too inflamed or too friable pancreas in body and tail to achieve safe bowel anastomosis
- Complications of pancreatic surgery
  - Pancreatic fistula
  - Early and late postoperative bleeding
  - Delayed gastric emptying
- Most patients with surgery receive adjuvant chemotherapy using either 5-FU or gemcitabine.
- Palliation for unresectable tumor
  - Obstructive jaundice
    - Biliary stenting, either plastic or covered metallic biliary stent. Metallic biliary stent should be used in a patient who is expected to live more than 6 months.
    - Operative palliation includes the following: Hepaticojejunostomy.
  - Gastric outlet obstruction
    - It includes endoscopic gastroduodenal metallic stenting.
    - Operative palliation includes gastrojejunostomy that is retrocolic and isoperistaltic.
  - Pain
    - Stepwise escalation of analgesia
    - Chemical splanchnicectomy: 20 mL of 50% ethanol or saline through spinal needle on either side of aorta at the level of celiac plexus
    - CT-guided celiac plexus nerve block or external beam radiotherapy
  - Steatorrhea: It includes enzymatic supplementation.
  - Diabetes: It includes insulin or oral hypoglycemic agents.
  - Chemotherapy is given in biopsy-proven ductal adenocarcinoma.

Summary of management

- Chemotherapy is 5-FU based or gemcitabine based (6–10 cycles).
- Radiation is intensity-modulated or image-guided radiotherapy.
- Resectable: Resect. R0, chemotherapy followed by radiation; and R1, radiation followed by chemotherapy.
- Borderline resectable: Resect. Rest is same as resectable or neoadjuvant induction chemotherapy followed by restaging. If there are no distant metastases, resect and the rest is same as resectable. If there are distant metastases, give chemotherapy.
- Unresectable: Induction chemotherapy followed by chemoradiation. After restaging if there are no metastases, resect; if metastases are present, give chemotherapy.
- Distant metastases: Give chemotherapy.

79. What is Whipple's triad?

A
- Whipple's triad refers to three conditions necessary for proving hypoglycemia as the cause of a person's symptoms.
- Whipple's triad seen in insulinoma:
  - Fasting hypoglycemic symptoms
  - Blood glucose <50 mg/dL
  - Relief of symptoms on administrating glucose
- Insulinoma is the most common functional endocrine tumor of pancreas.
- Elevated serum insulin level and C-peptide level help in diagnosis.
- CT and EUS localize insulinoma.
- Most insulinomas can be enucleated except those >2 cm and those close to main pancreatic duct which require either distal pancreatectomy or pancreaticoduodenectomy.

80. In which malignancies is migratory superficial thrombophlebitis seen?

A
- Pancreatic malignancy
- Gastrointestinal malignancies
- Lung cancer

81. What is IPMN? Write in brief about IPMN.

A
- The expansion of the acronym 'IPMN' is intraductal papillary mucinous neoplasm.
- The most common site is head of pancreas within duct.
- MRCP shows diffuse duct dilatation with atrophy of pancreatic parenchyma.
- Mucin can be seen coming out of the ampulla on ERCP known as *fish-eye lesion* and is virtually diagnostic of IPMN.
- Three types of IPMN
  - Main duct
  - Side branch
  - Mixed
- Symptoms
  - Pain
  - Recurrent pancreatitis
  - Signs of pancreatic insufficiency
- High-risk features
  - Mural nodule
  - Dilated main duct
  - Positive cytology
  - CEA >200 in cyst fluid
- Treatment
  - Observation annually with EUS
    - <1-cm side branch IPMN
    - One- to 2-cm side branch IPMN without high-risk features
  - Resection
    - All main duct IPMN and branch duct IPMN >3 cm
    - One- to 2-cm IPMN with high-risk feature[12]

Pearls

- Okuda staging system is for HCC and includes bilirubin, albumin, tumor size, and ascites.
- Rare presentation of HCC is the following: Intraperitoneal rupture, BCS, jaundice, and pyrexia of unknown origin (PUO).
- Secondaries in liver are hypoechoic in pancreatic cancer, breast cancer, and lung cancer and hyperechoic in colon, RCC, and neuroendocrine. Calcified metastasis is seen in mucinous adenocarcinoma of colon and ovarian malignancy.
- The most common hepatic primary tumor in childhood is hepatoblastoma. The most common presentation is abdominal lump. AFP is elevated. CT findings are vascular with calcification.
- Electrolyte abnormalities in cirrhotic patients are the following: Hyponatremia, hypokalemia, and metabolic alkalosis.

- Moth-eaten or worm-eaten filling defect is seen in esophageal varices on barium esophagogram or barium swallow.
- Endoscopic therapy failure in varices is defined as failure of two consecutive sclerotherapy or band ligation to control bleeding.
- Child–Turcotte–Pugh score includes the following: Bilirubin, albumin, encephalopathy, ascites, and international normalized ratio or prothrombin time. It has 5–15 points. It is a principal predictor of operative risk.
- MELD score uses bilirubin, creatinine, and INR.
- TIPS is a side-to-side intrahepatic portocaval shunt. It is placed between hepatic and portal veins. It is indicated for the following: Acute or recurrent variceal bleed, BCS, refractory ascites, and hepatic hydrothorax.
- Hepatopulmonary syndrome, right-sided heart failure, polycystic liver disease, and pulmonary hypertension are contraindications for TIPS.
- Complications of TIPS are the following: Hepatic encephalopathy and shunt stenosis (can be reduced by coated stent).
- The most serious immediate complication of TIPS is intra-abdominal hemorrhage.
- Indications of liver transplantation in descending order are the following: Hepatitis C infection, hepatitis B infection, alcoholic liver disease, cryptogenic or nonalcoholic steatohepatitis, cholestatic disorder, and HCC.
- The major indication for pediatric liver transplantation is biliary atresia following a failed Kasai procedure followed by α_1-antitrypsin deficiency.
- The most common cause of death in liver transplantation is sepsis.
- Pringle maneuver is compression of the portal triad structure at the hepatoduodenal ligament with noncrushing vascular clamp or between finger and thumb for hepatic inflow control. Clamp time should be limited to 15–20 minutes and declamping for 3–5 minutes in between. Some authorities believe that it can be safely applied for 30–60 minutes without ischemic damage. If bleeding stops, it is assumed to come from portal vein or hepatic artery and if it persists, it is assumed to arise from IVC or hepatic vein. If liver bleeding is not possible to control with local measures including packing, this maneuver is used.
- The most common benign tumor/most common incidentaloma/most common nodule of liver is hemangioma.
- Hemangioma appears as nodular enhancement on CECT. MRI shows classical light bulb sign.
- Hepatic adenoma is associated with oral contraceptive pills. Right upper abdominal pain is the most common symptom. It is devoid of bile duct component. USG and CT are diagnostic. Biopsy is contraindicated due to extreme vascular nature. Cessation of oral contraceptive pills is associated with tumor regression. It has a malignant potential. The symptomatic tumors are best resected.
- Kasabach–Merritt syndrome includes the following: Cavernous hemangioma, consumption coagulopathy, and thrombocytopenia.
- Spleen is the organ most commonly involved in blunt abdominal trauma. Liver is the second commonly involved organ.
- Liver followed by small bowel is the most often involved organ by stab injury and gunshot injury involves most commonly small bowel followed by colon and liver.
- Indications of laparotomy in blunt trauma are the following:
  - Hemodynamic instability
  - Peritoneal irritation
  - Pneumoperitoneum
  - Evidence of diaphragmatic injury
  - Persistent GI bleeding in either nasogastric tube or vomitus
- Indications of laparotomy in penetrating injury are the following:
  - Same as above-mentioned plus evisceration and implementation in situ

- Regeneration of the liver can be complete within 4–6 months after hepatectomy. Eighty percent of the liver can be resected without compromising its function.
- FNH contains hepatic as well as Kupffer cells while adenoma is devoid of Kupffer cells.
- FNH is the second common benign tumor of liver (first is hemangioma) and it has no malignant potential. A sulfur colloid liver scan taken up by Kupffer cells shows hot spot with spoke wheel pattern and is diagnostic.
- Vitamin K is corrected in patients with obstructive jaundice.
- Liver biopsy is done through the eighth intercostal space midaxillary line.
- Honeycomb liver is seen in actinomycosis of liver. It is caused by *Actinomyces israelii*; it reaches liver via portal vein from cecum or via hepatic artery from faciocervical region. Treatment is penicillin.
- NCPF is intrahepatic presinusoidal obstruction.
- Hydatid cyst is caused by *Echinococcus granulosus* (dog tapeworm). Sheep, cattle, and humans are the intermediate hosts. Segment VII is most commonly involved. Hydatid fluid is clear with high specific gravity (1.005–1.009) and contains hooklets and scolices. Commonly it ruptures into intrabiliary tree. Diagnosis is confirmed by eosinophilia on blood examination and serological test for antibodies to hydatid antigen in ELISA. CT findings are floating membrane within cyst with multiple septa. Treatment includes surgery or puncture, aspiration, injection, and respiration (PAIR).
- USG is the investigation of choice for gallbladder and liver pathology. Initial investigation of choice for biliary obstruction is USG.
- Radiolucent stone, normal-functioning gallbladder, and small stones can also be treated by medical management. Problems with medical management are the following: High chance of recurrence, prolonged treatment, <70% response rate, and side effects of drug treatment.
- Duodenal bulb obstruction due to gallstone is known as Bouveret syndrome.
- In case of a stone in the neck of gallbladder, bile is absorbed but mucus secretion continues, which leads to large tense globular mass in right upper quadrant. Early cholecystectomy is the treatment of choice.
- The most common site for pancreaticoenteral fistula in chronic pancreatitis is transverse colon or splenic flexure.
- Necrolytic migratory dermatitis along with diabetes raises the suspicion of glucagonoma. Serum glucagon >500 pg/mL is diagnostic. Common sites for dermatitis are the following: Lower abdomen, perineum, circumoral, and feet.
- WDHA syndrome is watery diarrhea, hypokalemia, and achlorhydria; it is also known as vasoactive intestinal peptide-secreting tumor or VIPoma. The most common site is distal pancreas. EUS is the most sensitive method for localizing tumor.
- Jaundice is the most common symptom of ampullary and pancreatic head tumor.
- Splenic abscess: Treatment involves treatment of the cause and percutaneous drainage. Splenectomy is indicated where interventional radiology facility is not available.
- Perfusion defect in the spleen on CECT indicates splenic infarct. Treatment is conservative. Splenectomy should be considered in case of development of abscess.
- Embolization and endovascular stenting is the mainstay of treatment in splenic artery aneurysm.
- A future liver reserve (FLR) of 25 % of the preoperative volume is sufficient to prevent postoperative liver failure in liver resection. Exceptions are patients with impaired liver function including those who have chemotherapy-induced liver damage and may require larger FLR.
- Communication with biliary system is contraindication to PAIR technique for liver hydatid cyst.
- Recurrent variceal bleed secondary to splenic or portal vein thrombosis is treated by splenectomy and gastroesophageal devascularization.

GENITOURINARY SYSTEM

82. Which is the most common malformation of genitourinary tract? Describe in brief about the most common malformation.

A
- The most common congenital malformation of genitourinary tract is hypospadias (1:300). In 70% of cases, it is distal penile or coronal. Undescended testis and inguinal hernia are associated anomalies.
- Circumcision should be avoided.
- Healthy, full-term boy 3 months or older can be considered for repair.[13]
- The ideal age for repair is 6–12 months.
- The aim of repair is cosmetic, improvement of sexual function and correction of urinary stream.
- Operations
  - Denis-Browne
  - Meatal advancement and granuloplasty (MAGPI)
  - ASOPA technique
- The most common complication of surgery is urethral fistula. Other complications are urethral stricture and meatal stenosis.

83. What are the differentiating points between neuroblastoma and Wilms tumor?

A
- Neuroblastoma is tumor of adrenal gland. Foci of calcification, bone metastasis, and not being located within kidney (as shown on CT scan abdomen) are the characteristics of neuroblastoma, while the Wilms tumor is located within kidney and is shown to invade inferior vena cava and aorta.
- Urine shows catecholamines and their breakdown products in neuroblastoma.

84. What are the causes of hematuria and how will you investigate a case of hematuria?

A
- Presence of three or more RBCs per high-power field is known as microhematuria.
- Any visible blood in urine is indicative of gross hematuria.

Causes of hematuria

- Stone in the kidney, ureter, bladder, and urethra
- Tumor of kidney, ureter, bladder, and urethra
- Tuberculosis of urinary tract
- Trauma to the urinary tract
- Other causes: Benign prostatic hyperplasia (BPH), prostatitis, and coagulation disorder
- Nephrological causes such as IGA nephropathy and Alport syndrome
- Embolization of renal vessels leading to infarction of kidney (you can remember the causes as the acronym STONE)

Investigations

- Urine routine and microscopy to find out hematuria and infection. If history and physical examination indicate infections, menstruation, and recent urological procedure, repeat urine examination after treatment of other causes. If they come negative, no further investigation is needed.
- Urine culture and sensitivity to identify organism and its sensitive antibiotics
- Renal function testing and cystoscopy imaging, concurrent nephrological workup if proteinuria, red cell morphology, and other signs indicate nephrogenic cause
  - Patients >35 years of age and having other risk factors should undergo cystoscopy.
  - Patients <35 years of age without risk factors and clinical suspicion of bladder cancer and urethral pathology should not undergo cystoscopy.
  - Multiphasic computed tomography urogram is the imaging study of choice for evaluation of asymptomatic hematuria.
  - MR urogram should be done in case of renal insufficiency, contrast allergy, and pregnancy.
  - In patients with contraindications to MR such as pacemaker and significant renal compromise, noncontrast CT or USG in conjunction with retrograde pyelography should be done.
  - Urine cytology is suggested for initial negative workup in suspected urothelial malignancy and symptomatic hematuria.
- USG KUB to identify stone, tumor, and its sequelae
- Flexible ureteroscopy to find out source in the ureter

- Terminal hematuria is seen in bladder pathology.
- Initial hematuria is seen in urethral pathology.
- Blood mixed with urine is seen in renal, prerenal, or ureteric pathology.

85. Enumerate types of radiolucent stones in the kidney.

A
- Uric acid
- Triamterene
- Indinavir
- Xanthine

86. What is Dietl crisis?

A
- It is a manifestation of hydronephrosis.
- It is a triad of typical renal pain, swelling in the loin, and disappearance of swelling after passing urine.

87. Describe briefly genitourinary tuberculosis.

A
- Frequency of urination is the earliest symptom.
- Urine shows sterile pyuria.
- Intravenous urography (IVU) is the earliest method of diagnosis.
- Cystoscopy reveals 'golf-hole ureter.'
- Gross appearances are as follows
  - *Kidney*: Putty kidney, hydronephrosis, pyonephrosis, perinephric abscess, and miliary tubercle
  - *Ureter*: Stricture
  - *Bladder*: Thimble bladder
  - *Prostate*: Calcification
  - *Vas*: Beaded
- Antitubercular treatment is the mainstay of management.
- Surgery may be required depending on the mechanical problems such as stricture and thimble bladder.

88. What are the different types of RCC?

A
- Clear cell carcinoma
- Chromophobe carcinoma
- Papillary carcinoma
- Granular carcinoma
- Sarcomatoid carcinoma (worst prognosis)

89. Enumerate the etiology of RCC.

A
- Tobacco and smoking (most important risk factors)
- Viral infection
- Asbestos exposure
- ESRD
- Analgesic nephropathy
- Obesity
- High fat and protein, low fruits and vegetables
- Family history
- Association with VHL
- Kidney transplantation
- Acquired cystic kidney disease

90. Discuss briefly the characteristics of ureterocele.

A It is cystic enlargement of the intraluminal part of ureter.

Mechanism

Congenital atresia of ureteric orifice. Persistent membrane is present between the ureteral bud and the urogenital sinus.

Clinical presentation

- Hydronephrosis
- Pyelonephritis
- Stone
- Bladder outlet obstruction
- Possibility of large ureterocele as intralabial mass in newborn

Investigations

- Excretory urography (IVP, IVU) (adder head appearance)
- Cystoscopy: Translucent cyst enlarging and collapsing as urine flows in from the upper ureter

Treatment

- Surgical excision with reimplantation of the ureter being the treatment of choice
- Endoscopic diathermy incision for stone in the ureterocele. The complication of diathermy incision is vesicoureteric reflux (VUR) that may require ureteric reimplantation.
- Advanced unilateral case with hydronephrosis or pyonephrosis: Nephrectomy

91. Discuss briefly carcinoma bladder.

A
- Most common: Transitional cell carcinoma
- In bilharzia: Squamous cell carcinoma
- Persistent urachus: Adenocarcinoma
- Most common site: 60% lateral wall of bladder; 30% base or trigone of bladder
- Most common symptom: Painless gross hematuria
- Most important investigation: Contrast-enhanced CT scan of abdomen and pelvis

Management guidelines

- Nonmuscle invasive cancer:[14] Biopsy obtained to confirm grade and eradicate all visible tumor in case of abnormal growth on scanning but not proven cancer (transurethral resection of bladder tumor [TURBT]); TURBT repeated in case of incomplete resection, high-grade, pathological T1, or there is no muscle in specimen)
  - *Low-risk (solitary small volume, low-grade Ta)*: Surveillance cystoscopy (3–6 months) intervals
  - *Intermediate risk (multifocal and/or large-volume low-grade Ta, recurrence at 3 months)*: Adjuvant intravesical (6-week induction) bacillus Calmette–Guerin (BCG) (preferred) or mitomycin, surveillance cystoscopy and cytology (3–6 months) intervals, upper tract imaging every 2 years or as indicated
  - *High risk (high-grade Ta, all T1, CIS)*: Adjuvant intravesical BCG (6-week induction followed by maintenance), close surveillance cystoscopy, cytology, and upper tract imaging; early cystectomy considered in selected patients
- Muscle invasive bladder cancer
  - T2–T4a, NO, and MO: Radical cystectomy with bilateral pelvic node dissection
  - T3–T4 or node positive disease: Adjuvant chemotherapy for recommended
  - Can also consider cisplatin-based neoadjuvant chemotherapy in case of clinical T2–T4a disease (NCCN guidelines)
- In metastatic disease, can use MVAC or GC or peclitaxel and docetaxel; can use radiotherapy metastatic pain and spinal cord compression and no role of surgery

92. Which electrolyte abnormality is associated with ureterosigmoidostomy?

A Hyperchloremic acidosis with potassium depletion

93. How will you manage testicular tumors?

A Investigations

- Ultrasound scrotum
- Serum markers (LDH, β-hCG, α-fetoprotein)
- X-ray chest
- CT chest, abdomen, and pelvis for confirmed testicular cancer

Treatment

- Urgent high inguinal orchiectomy (radical orchiectomy) is performed in all stages.
- Trans-scrotal biopsy or orchiectomy is absolutely contraindicated.
- All patients who require treatment such as chemotherapy, retroperitoneal lymph node dissection (RPLND), or radiation therapy should be offered sperm banking.

Other indications for orchiectomy are the following:

- Carcinoma prostate (subcapsular orchiectomy)
- Metastatic male breast cancer
- Nonviable testis in testicular torsion

- Seminoma
  - *Stage I*
    - *Surveillance*: Negative serum markers without detectable metastasis
    - *Chemotherapy*: Single agent carboplatin
    - *Radiotherapy*: Infradiaphragmatic para-aortic node in patients with prior scrotal surgery; ipsilateral iliac nodes should be included
  - *Stage IS*
    - Infradiaphragmatic radiotherapy to para-aortic node in patients with prior scrotal surgery; ipsilateral iliac nodes should be included.
  - *Stages IIA and IIB*
    - Three cycles of bleomycin, etoposide, and cisplatin (BEP) chemotherapy or four cycles of etoposide and cisplatin (EP)
    - Radiation as in stage I if not suitable for chemotherapy
  - *Stages IIC and III*
    - Three cycles of BEP chemotherapy or four cycles of EP
- Nonseminomatous germ cell tumors
  - Treatment dependent on lymphovascular invasion, presence of embryonal histology (50% or more), absence of yolk sac histology, and tumor stage >T1

- Stage I without above-mentioned factors: Surveillance, two cycles of BEP, or open nerve-sparing RPLND in high-volume center
- Stage IS: Three cycles of BEP
- Stages IIA and IIB
  - *Normal markers*: Three cycles of BEP or RPLND (nerve sparing)
  - *Elevated markers*: Low risk, three cycles of BEP; and high risk, four cycles of BEP
- Stages IIC and III
  - Low risk, three cycles of BEP; and high risk, four cycles BEP
- Management postchemotherapy
  - CT after 2 months of last cycle
  - No residual disease and normal markers: Surveillance
  - No residual disease with elevated markers: Chemotherapy such as two cycles of TIP and VeIP
  - Residual disease: RPLND

- Irrespective of histology
  - If enlarged retroperitoneal lymph node is present, then combination of chemotherapy followed by serum markers and CT scan is followed.
  - Small-volume tumors usually resolve and large-volume tumors usually require further chemotherapy and retroperitoneal dissection.
  - Combination chemotherapy includes four cycles of cisplatin, bleomycin, and etoposide.

94. **Which is the best indication of testicular biopsy in case of male infertility?**

A Azoospermia

95. **What is varicocele? Discuss its characteristics and management.**

A
- Varicocele is varicosity of the pampiniform plexus of the spermatic cord, forming a scrotal swelling.
- It is more common on the left side because:
  - Left testicular vein (LTV) is longer.
  - LTV is open at right angle to the left renal vein.
  - LTV opens in front of left suprarenal vein (effect of catecholamine).
  - LTV is sandwiched between superior mesenteric artery and aorta (nutcracker phenomenon).
  - Loaded colon leads to increased venous pressure in the left renal vein.
  - There is absence of valves or valvular incompetence of left internal spermatic vein at its junction with the left renal vein.
- Collateral venous anastomosis is present.
- In those patients who develop sudden onset of varicocele, not decreasing in size on elevating the scrotum, and those with right-sided varicocele, retroperitoneal neoplasm should be suspected.
- Grading
  - *Grade 0*: Subclinical—nonpalpable and visualized only by color Doppler study
  - *Grade I*: Thrill palpable on Valsalva maneuver
  - *Grade II*: Bag of worm-like feeling on palpation
  - *Grade III*: Is a visible varicocele

Clinical features

- Adolescent age
- Tall, thin boy
- Scrotal swelling
- Pain
- Possibility of testis being soft on palpation along with varicocele

Investigation

Color Doppler scrotum and semen analysis: Testicular volume is important. Loss of testicular volume is associated with varicocele.

Treatment

- Conservative: Scrotal support and symptomatic treatment
- Radiographic embolization of gonadal vein: It is the first line of treatment. Its advantage is to identify venous collateralization as a route of outflow and reflux.[3]

Indications for intervention

- Significant left or bilateral hypotrophy of testis
- Testicular pain
- Abnormal semen analysis in patients older than 18 years of age

- Radiographic embolization of gonadal vein the first line of treatment (its advantage is to identify venous collateralization as a route of outflow and reflux)[3]
- Indications of operation: If radiographic embolization is not possible or varicocele recurs, operative—microsurgical varicocelectomy (open or laparoscopic) and Palomo operation (testicular vein is ligated in the *retroperitoneum* as it comes through the internal ring)

96. What are common premalignant lesions of penis? Discuss common penile carcinomas, and their diagnosis and treatment.

A Premalignant lesions of penis

- Leukoplakia of glans
- Long-standing genital warts
- Paget disease of penis

Most common type of penile carcinoma

Squamous cell carcinoma associated with HPV 16 and smoking

Jackson staging

- *Stage I*: Confined to glans and prepuceal skin
- *Stage II*: Involvement of shaft of penis
- *Stage III*: Operable inguinal lymph node
- *Stage IV*: Inoperable inguinal lymph node

Diagnosis

Diagnosis is by biopsy. In all stages, CT abdomen and pelvis are required to rule out inguinal lymphadenopathy and abdominal lymphadenopathy

Treatment[3]

- Recently, penile preserving surgery is preferred with excision of much lower margin as compared to traditional 2-cm margin.
- For tumor involving glans penis: Glansectomy. More advanced tumors require partial penectomy
- Total penectomy for lesions involving shaft or very large lesions
- In younger patients with prepuceal involvement: Circumcision and close follow-up. Treatment of inguinal lymph node is delayed for 3 weeks after treatment of primary lesion. Infected node subsides with antibiotic therapy. Inguinal block dissection is indicated in case of FNAC-positive node or in case of nonpalpable node and sentinel lymph node biopsy-positive node.
- In younger patients with lesion <3 cm: Radiotherapy to avoid partial penectomy
- Possibility of treatment of stages 3 and 4 with adjuvant chemotherapy with VBM (vincristine, methotrexate, and bleomycin)

The cause of death is torrential bleeding from femoral or external iliac artery as growth from inguinal lymph node erodes these vessels.

97. What is the common presentation of posterior urethral valve? How will you manage it?

A Posterior urethral valve is a fold of urothelium extending distally from prostatic urethra to external sphincter.

- Type I PUV: It originates from abnormal insertion and absorption of the distal-most part of the Wolffian ducts during bladder development.*
- Type III PUV: A membrane in the posterior part of urethra arises from incomplete canalization between the anterior and the posterior urethra.

Clinical presentation

Straining and dribbling of urine with recurrent UTI is a common presentation.

Other clinical manifestations:

- Asymptomatic
- Palpable mass
- ESRD
- VUR

Investigations

- USG KUB
- Voiding cystourethrogram (VCUG, MCU), which shows distended posterior urethra, thick-walled bladder, and VUR (investigation of choice)
- Renal scan to assess renal function
- Urodynamic study to know about associated voiding dysfunction

---

*Type II is actually a dissection artifact and is no longer considered PU valve.

Treatment
- Prophylactic antibiotics
- Per urethral catheterization with feeding tube
- Transurethral valve ablation if creatinine is normal
- If creatinine raised, suprapubic drainage and ablation of valve later on

The most serious outcome of this condition is pulmonary hypoplasia due to intrauterine oligohydramnios and is the most common cause of death.

98. A patient is brought to the hospital with a history of road traffic accident 6 hours back. A few drops of blood were noted in the external urethral meatus. He had not passed urine and his bladder was palpable per abdomen. What is the probable diagnosis?

A Diagnosis

Urethral injury: Bulbar urethral injury being the most common urethral injury

Clinical features
- Retention of urine
- Perineal hematoma
- Bleeding from the external urethral meatus

Treatment
- Suprapubic cystostomy
- Cystoscopic guided silicon per urethral catheterization

99. Discuss etiopathology, clinical features, and management of BPH.

A Etiology
- As age advances, level of testosterone in the body decreases, so the relative level of estrogen rises. Estrogen sensitizes the prostatic tissue to the growth-promoting effect of dihydrotestosterone, which is formed from testosterone with the help of 5-alpha reductase.
- Periurethral transitional zone is involved.
- The disease primarily affects the stroma.

Clinical features
- Frequency of urine
- Urgency
- Nocturia
- Urge incontinence
- Nocturnal incontinence
- Poor stream
- Dribbling urine
- Hesitancy

Diagnosis
- Clinical features plus per rectal examination
  - Prostate size
  - Median sulcus
  - Upper border
  - Consistency
  - Mucosa can be assessed

Normally it is smooth, firm, and elastic in consistency. Hard prostate and induration or nodule on prostate indicates malignancy.
- *USG KUB and prostate*
  - Prostatic size
  - Volume
    - Postvoid residual urine
      - Assessment of median lobe projection
  - Hydronephrosis and hydroureter
- *Blood*: Serum creatinine and blood urea
- *Urine*: To rule out UTI or hematuria
- *Uroflowmetry*: To judge the severity of bladder outlet obstruction (Q_{max} <10 mL/s indicates obstruction)
- *Urodynamic study*: To differentiate between obstruction and neurogenic bladder (voiding pressure >80 cm H_2O suggests obstruction)

Complications
- Acute retention
- Chronic retention
- Impaired bladder emptying, leading to infection and stone formation
- Hematuria
- Hydronephrosis and hydroureter
- Retention with overflow

Treatment
- *Conservative*
  - Patients with mild symptoms
  - Good flow rate
  - Patients with postvoid residual urine <80 cm^3
- *Medical management*
  - It includes mainly two groups of drugs, alpha blockers and 5-alpha reductase inhibitors.

- Alpha blockers act by releasing tension on smooth muscles and 5-alpha reductase inhibitors act by decreasing the size of the gland.
- Combination of alpha blockers and 5-alpha reductase inhibitors significantly reduces risk of progression of BPH.
- Alpha blockers
  - *Nonselective*: An example is phenoxybenzamine.
  - *α_1 blockers*: These include prazosin, alfuzosin, and indoramin.
  - *Long-acting α_1*: Terazosin, doxazosin, and alfuzosin. Alfuzosin is associated with less adverse drug reaction and blood pressure changes, so it has been described as uroselective. Hypertension and LUTS or BPH is treated with doxazosin or carvedilol (recently found to be both β and selective α_1 blocker).
  - *Subtype selective*: Tamsulosin, silodosin, and naftopidil. Abnormal ejaculation is the common side effect associated with tamsulosin and silodosin.
- 5-Alpha reductase inhibitors are finasteride and dutasteride.

- *Surgery*
  - Surgery is indicated in patients who do not respond to conservative management, and for complications of BPH (recurrent UTI, refractory urinary retention, recurrent gross hematuria, bladder stone, and renal failure).
  - Options are the following:
    - TURP: This is the gold standard; risk of TURP syndrome. Absorption of hypotonic irrigating solution leads to hypervolemia and hyponatremia. Risk is increased with increased operative time >90 minutes and >75 g prostate. Most commonly used solution is 1.5% glycine. The most distal landmark in TURP is verumontanum just proximal to external sphincter. Treatment of TURP syndrome is diuretics and in severe cases hypertonic saline (3%).
      - *Complications of TURP*: Bleeding, perforation of bladder, prostatic capsule, retrograde ejaculation, impotence, and incontinence
      - *Late complications*: Bladder neck stenosis and urethral stricture
    - Open prostatectomy: It is suprapubic (Freyer), retropubic (Millin), and perineal (Young).
    - Transurethral needle ablation (TUNA): It is done for lateral lobe enlargement; <60 g prostate.
    - Transurethral incision of prostate (TUIP): Incision is kept at 5 and 7 o'clock position; very small prostate <35 g.
    - Holmium laser enucleation of prostate (HoLEP)
    - Prostate ablation and vaporization
    - Transurethral microwave thermotherapy (TUMT) can be used.
    - Water-induced thermotherapy (WIT) is also helpful.
    - Intraurethral stent: It is used in patients with significant comorbidity.

100. Discuss etiopathology, clinical features, and management of carcinoma prostate.

- It is the most common malignancy after the age of 65 years in males.
- Average age is 72 years.
- Hormonal environment: Synergistic stimulation of prostate by both hormones; estrogen acts to sensitize the prostatic tissue to growth-promoting effect of dihydrotestosterone derived from the plasma testosterone.
- Family history is obtained.
- There is mutation in chromosome no. 1.
- It is more common in North Americans.
- It occurs in the peripheral zone.

Histology

Adenocarcinoma

Clinical features

Early disease is asymptomatic; later it shows the following:

- Signs of bladder outlet obstruction
- Bone pain

- Hematuria
- Hydronephrosis
- Renal failure
- Ankle edema

Spread

- *Direct*: It spreads to the surrounding structures.
- *Lymphatics*: The most common is obturator node; others are internal iliac nodes and external iliac nodes.
- *Hematogenous*: Bone—lumbar spine and pelvis, and involvement of axial skeleton mainly. It gives rise to osteoblastic (sclerotic) secondaries and it is the most common primary for secondaries in bone.

Investigations

- Digital rectal examination (DRE): It includes hard prostate or nodular prostate, shallow median sulcus.
- Tumor markers
  - S. PSA: It is a glycoprotein that is serine protease.
    - Function: It helps in liquefaction of semen.
    - Normal value: It is <4 nmol/mL.
    - Value 4–10 indicates equivocal.
    - Value >10 indicates suspicion.
    - If value >20, bone scan is advisable.
    - If value >35, malignancy is confirmed.
    - As PSA is also elevated in BPH, other parameters to be considered are the following: Free PSA, PSA velocity, and PSA density.
    - Patients with PSA<4 nmol/mL (20% chance of having prostate cancer) and between 4 and 10 nmol/mL (25% chance of having prostate cancer) are also likely to have a prostate cancer. Biopsy is advised if PSA >3 nmol/mL[3]
    - It is very useful in postoperative cases to detect early recurrence.
  - Human kallikrein 2: It shares 80% amino acid homology and exhibits similar specificity for prostatic tissue.
- Biopsy:
  - In case of suspicion of carcinoma prostate, by either DRE or PSA, biopsy is advisable.
  - Double sextant (12- or 13-core) biopsy is taken with automated gun per rectally. Transrectal ultrasound (TRUS) guided is preferred.
  - Prophylactic antibiotics: Ciprofloxacin is given before the procedure.
  - Complications: These include bleeding, urinary retention, and vasovagal shock.
- Other tests required are the following: TRUS, liver function test, renal function test, and bone scan in symptomatic patients or PSA >20. Other indications for bone scan are the following: Gleason score ≥8, patients with severe low back bony pain, clinical stage T3 or T4, raised calcium or alkaline phosphatase.
- CT and MRI abdomen pelvis are performed if PSA >20 and >T2 or Gleason score >8.
- AJCC staging of carcinoma prostate is shown in Box 16.3.

Treatment

Treatment according to risk stratification

- Low risk
  - *Life expectancy <5 years*: No intervention
  - *Five to 10 years*: Active surveillance

Box 16.3 AJCC staging of carcinoma prostate

- *T1*: Incidentally found tumor on prostatectomy specimen
  - 1a: <5% of tissue involved
  - 1b: >5% of the tissue involved
  - 1c: Impalpable tumor found following elevated PSA
- *T2*
  - 2a: On DRE palpable nodule confined within one lobe
  - 2b: Involving both lobes
- *T3*: Extension beyond capsule
  - 3a: Unilateral or bilateral extension
  - 3b: Seminal vesicle involvement
- *T4*: Fixed tumor or involving adjacent structure such as rectum or pelvic wall
  - *Low*: T1–T2a, GS <6, and PSA <10
  - *Intermediate*: T2b, GS 7, and PSA 10–20
  - *High*: >T2c, GS 8–10, and PSA >20

- *>10 years*: Radical prostatectomy and radiotherapy (external beam or brachytherapy 40–60 Gy for 4–6 weeks)
  - *Radical prostatectomy*: Complications include impotence and incontinence.
  - *Radiotherapy*: Complications include rectal pain, dysuria, rectal bleeding, and sexual dysfunction. Complication rate is less for brachytherapy as compared to that in XRT.
- Intermediate risk
  - *Life expectancy <5 years*: No intervention
  - *Five to 10 years*: Active surveillance, radical prostatectomy, or external beam radiation with 6 months of androgen-blocking therapy
  - *>10 years*: Radical prostatectomy with lymph node dissection or external beam radiation with 6 months of androgen blockage treatment
- High risk
  - External beam radiation with 18 months of androgen blockage treatment or radical prostatectomy with lymph node dissection is considered.
  - Bilateral orchidectomy or high-dose bicalutamide may be an option in unfit patients.
  - Recurrence after RP may be treated with salvage EBRT and after radiation may be treated with salvage RP.
- Advanced disease
  - Bilateral orchiectomy is done.
  - GnRH analogue is used.
  - Complete blockage requires addition of antiandrogens (flutamide and bicalutamide to block androgen from the adrenal medulla).
  - If the patient develops spinal cord compression, urgent decompression must be done.
    - Start with high-dose steroid, EBRT, and laminectomy.
  - In case of urinary obstruction, observe if there is mild dysfunction, and perform TURP if there is moderate dysfunction.
  - In case of hydronephrosis or hydroureter, DJ stent or PCN is used.
  - In case of bone pain, NSAIDs, nerve block, and systemic strontium are used.
- Castration-resistant prostate cancer (CRPC)
  - Nonmetastatic: Observation or ketoconazole, steroids, etc.
  - Metastatic (asymptomatic): Abiraterone with prednisone, enzalutamide, and systemic chemotherapy (docetaxel with prednisone)
  - Symptomatic with good performance status: Docetaxel with prednisone
  - Poor performance status: Abiraterone with prednisone or enzalutamide
  - All patients who receive ADT to be given vitamin D and calcium supplements
  - Patients with metastatic CRPC to be given antibodies such as denosumab every month to reduce bone-related complications, or in the absence of denosumab, zoledronic acid given.

101. What is priapism? Describe its etiology, investigation, and treatment.

A It is persistent, painful erection of penis lasting more than 4 hours and unrelated to sexual stimulation.

Types

- *Low flow*: Acute, painful, veno-occlusive, lasting for several hours (most common) (ischemic)
  - Decreased arterial flow → hypoxia → acidosis → edema leads to impotence and fibrosis if not treated within time and occasionally results in frank necrosis
- *High flow*: Arterial, painless, traumatic due to cavernous artery–corporal body fistula (nonischemic)

Etiology

- Idiopathic
- Sickle cell anemia
- Leukemia
- Trauma (high flow)
- Intracavernosal injection for erectile dysfunction
- Drugs such as anticoagulants
- Malignancy

- Cocaine abuse
- TPN

Investigation

Color Doppler study is especially useful in high-flow type and helps in confirming and localizing the fistula.

Treatment

- Management of low-flow or ischemic priapism
  - Exclude underlying cause.
  - It is a urological emergency, because if decompression is not achieved within 8 hours, the patient will end up with permanent erectile failure.
  - Oral baclofen or pseudoephedrine is used.
  - Aspiration of thick and viscid blood with 18-gauge needle and irrigation of corporal bodies with intracavernosal injection of phenylephrine 200 mg in 20 mL saline are performed.
  - Oxygen supplementation and adequate hydration are important in patients with sickle cell disease.
  - If priapism lasts more than 2–3 days, following measures should be taken.
    - The first choice is distal cavernoglanular shunt using Tru-Cut needle (winter shunt). Al-Ghorab shunt is the most effective distal shunt but it is more invasive and it includes excision of the tunica albuginea at the tip of the the corpus cavernosum.
    - In case of failure of distal shunt, proximal shunt is used by making window between the corpus cavernosum and the corpus spongiosum (Quackels shunt) or by anastomosis of the saphenous vein to one of the corpora cavernosa (Grayhack shunt).
- High-flow priapism
  - It is managed conservatively and resolves spontaneously many a time. However, selective pudendal artery embolization by autologous blood clot or gel foam is useful.

102. Describe the incidence and types of undescended testis. How is this condition diagnosed and treated?

- It is more common in premature babies.
- Incidence is 3% in full-term babies and 30% in preterm babies.
- At 1 year, incidence is around 1%.

Types

- *Cryptochidism*: It refers to failure of testis to descend down into the scrotum.
- *Ectopic testis*: Testis is located outside the normal path. Common sites are superficial inguinal pouch (most common location), scrotal, femoral, and perineal.
- *Nonpalpable testis*: Testis is not palpable in the physical examination. It may be absent, atrophic, or missed on physical examination.
- *Retractile testis*: Testis is withdrawn outside the scrotum by active cremasteric reflex, but can be brought down easily in orthotopic position.

Phases of testicular descent

- *Transabdominal*: Adjacent to the kidney by the 8th week and migration does not begin until about the 23rd week
- *Transinguinal*: Till 28th week
- *Extracanalicular*: 28th–32nd weeks

Testosterone and androgen stimulate the development of the gubernaculums and testicular descent in the second and third trimesters.

Effects of cryptorchidism

- Infertility
- Neoplasia (most common is seminoma)
- Hernia
- Testicular torsion
- Pain
- Epididymo-orchitis (in right side, it may mimic appendicitis)

Diagnosis

- History, physical examination, USG, CT, and MRI are performed.

- Diagnostic laparoscopy: In case of intra-abdominal testis.
- Bilateral nonpalpable testes
  - HCG stimulation test: It induces production of testosterone and confirms the presence of at least one testis.
  - If basal GnRH and FSH are increased, then no further investigation is required in prepubertal boys.

Treatment

- It is treated with the help of orchidopexy. Aims are as follows:
  - It is done for cosmetic purposes.
  - Complications such as hernia and torsion can be prevented or reduced.
  - It facilitates diagnosis of malignancy and improves testicular function as early orchidopexy helps restore testicular growth.
- Orchidopexy is ideally done after the age of 6 months as spontaneous descent after 6 months is less likely.[15] Average age is 1 year.
  - Single- or two-stage Fowler–Stephens orchiopexy can be considered when testis cannot be brought down in a single sitting.
  - Transcrotal orchidopexy: Low palpable undescended testis can be managed (superior scrotal, median raphe, and/or transverse scrotal incision can be used).
  - Laparoscopic or open transabdominal orchidopexy: Abdominal testes can be managed.
  - If opposite testis is normal and there is failure to bring down the testis, then do orchiectomy.
  - Hormonal therapy is considered only in the case of hypogonadism.

103. What are the predisposing conditions and clinical presentation of torsion of testis? How will you diagnose and manage the condition?

A *Four varieties*

- Acute intravaginal spermatic cord torsion
- Intermittent intravaginal torsion
- Extravaginal spermatic cord torsion
- Torsion of the appendix of testis

Predisposing conditions

- Inversion of the testis (most common predisposing condition)
- High investment of tunica vaginalis (bell in a clapper testis)
- Long mesorchium

Clinical presentation

- It occurs in young adults.
- It is more common on the left side.
- Past history of similar event may be present.
- There is severe pain in the scrotum and iliac fossae.
- Elevation of scrotum aggravates the pain.
- Pain may be less acute or absent in some cases.
- Nausea and vomiting may be present in up to 60% of cases.

D/D from epididymo-orchitis

- In epididymo-orchitis, elevation will relieve the pain (Prehn sign).
- Technetium-99m pertechnetate scan shows increased uptake in epididymo-orchitis, while decreased uptake in torsion.
- Scrotum and testis are severely tender.
- Opposite testis may have horizontal lie.
- The cremasteric reflex is lost (good indicator).

Investigations

- Perform scrotal Doppler to see the blood supply. There is reduced or absent Doppler waveform or heterogeneity as compared to in opposite testis.
- High-resolution USG: Using 10- to 20-MHz probe, the cord twist may be identified as a snail-shaped mass proximal to the testis.
- Urine (routine and microscopy): It is sterile and acellular.

Management

- Acute intravaginal spermatic cord torsion
  - Prompt surgical exploration is warranted. >80% of the testes can be salvaged if surgery is performed within 6 hours. At the same time, opposite testis may be explored and fixed to the dartos fascia. Once the testis is

detorsed, check for viability and if found viable, orchiopexy should be performed.
- The testes are fixed to the dartos fascia with small, nonabsorbable sutures on their medial, lateral, and dependent portions.
- Orchiectomy is indicated only in case of clearly gangrenous or necrotic testes.
- If not viable, then go for orchiectomy with opposite orchiopexy.

• *Intermittent intravaginal torsion*
  - It may last for minutes to hours.
  - Pain may be associated with swelling, nausea, and vomiting.
  - A whirlpool sign or an abnormal boggy spermatic cord and pseudomass below the torsion cord indicates intermittent torsion.
  - Diagnosis: High index of suspicion is required and can be possible in few cases only.
  - Treatment: It is treated by bilateral prophylactic orchidopexy.

• *Extravaginal torsion*
  - It occurs before fixation of the tunica vaginalis and dartos within the scrotum.
  - Prenatal USG may show torsion.
  - Treatment is same as that of intravaginal torsion.

• *Torsion of appendix of testis*
  - It is common in 7- to 12-year-old boys.
  - It may be due to trauma and testicular enlargement.
  - Tender nodule, scrotal edema, and blue dot sign (discoloration of the upper pole of testis) may be seen.
  - Color Doppler is diagnostic.
  - It is mostly self-limited. Surgery is indicated only for diagnostic dilemma and prolonged, recurrent, and severe pain.[16]

104. Which is the major source of bleeding during prostatectomy?

A Dorsal vein complex

105. Which is the most sensitive diagnostic modality for ureteric stone in colic?

A Noncontrast spiral CT scan

Pearls

- Congenital posterior urethral obstruction due to muscular hypertrophy and bladder neck stenosis is referred to as Marion disease.
- Catheter-associated UTIs are the most common nosocomial infection. *E. coli* is the most common organism associated with UTI (85% community acquired and 50% hospital acquired).
- Staghorn calculus or struvite stone or infection stone is made up of triple phosphate (magnesium ammonium phosphate), is smooth, and occurs only in association with infection by urea-splitting organisms such as *Proteus* and *Klebsiella*. Laminated and irregularly shaped stone is calcium oxalate.
- Pain of stone in the upper ureter is referred to testis, that in the midureter is referred to iliac fossa, and that in the lower ureter is referred to thigh and scrotum.
- The most common renal stone is calcium oxalate.
- The most common bladder stone is uric acid.
- The most common prostatic calculus is calcium phosphate.
- The most common cause of emphysematous pyelonephritis is *E. coli*.
- Stone associated with laxative abuse is ammonium acid urate.
- Drugs associated with stone formation are the following: Indinavir, guaifenesin, ephedrine, and thiazide.
- Anatomic abnormalities associated with stone formation are as follows: PUJ obstruction, horseshoe kidney, calyceal diverticulum, and medullary sponge kidney.
- Urine culture should be performed in patients with infection related to calculi or UTI.
- Predisposing conditions commonly associated with renal papillary necrosis are the following: Diabetes mellitus, pyelonephritis, urinary tract obstruction, analgesic abuse, and sickle cell anemia.[17]

- Antibiotic prophylaxis is not recommended prior to urinary catheterization. Transrectal prostatic biopsy requires prophylactic antibiotics.
- Shock wave lithotripsy is recommended for stone up to 1 cm in size in kidney. Nowadays, flexible URS has an excellent safety with efficacy superior to SWL; contraindications to SWL are as follows: Pregnancy, uncorrected bleeding diasthesis, untreated UTI, distal obstruction, aneurysm near the stone, and inability to locate or target the stone.[18]
- One- to 2-cm stone within kidney: SWL is indicated if stone is not in the lower pole, attenuation <900 HU, skin to stone distance <10 m, and there is no history of SWL-resistant minerals such as cystine, calcium oxalate monohydrate, and brushite.[18] Flexible URS or PCNL is a good choice.
- For renal stone >2 cm, matrix stone, and calyceal diverticular stone, PCNL is considered first-line treatment.
- Upper ureteric stone is managed with PCNL or flexible URS and lower ureteric stone with URS.
- Sterile pyuria is seen in renal tuberculosis, atypical mycobacteria, and *Chlamydia trachomatis*.
- Emphysematous pyelonephritis is seen in diabetic patients. *E. coli* is the most common organism. Fever, vomiting, and flank pain are the usual presentations. CT is the investigation of choice. It is a surgical emergency. Resuscitation and broad-spectrum antibiotics are used if kidney is functioning. Nephrectomy is indicated in patients who do not improve after few days of therapy and in case of nonfunctioning kidney. Obstructed kidney must be drained.
- Unilateral chronic renal infection leads to diffuse destruction of kidney known as xanthogranulomatous pyelonephritis. The common organism associated with xanthogranulomatous pyelonephritis is *Proteus*. Factors associated are renal stone, obstruction, and infection. Most patients present with flank pain and fever with chills. Kidney is massively enlarged. CT is the investigation of choice. Nephrectomy is the treatment of choice.[17]
- Acute pyelonephritis presents with fever with chills and unilateral or bilateral flank pain. Urine analysis reveals plenty of pus cells and leukocyte or granular cast in urinary tract is suggestive of acute pyelonephritis. Urine culture and blood culture should be obtained. *E. coli* is the most common cause.
- The most common predisposing factor for chronic pyelonephritis is VUR.
- Goblet sign and stipple sign seen in transitional cell carcinoma are best demonstrated by RGP. CT IVP is the investigation of choice for renal pelvis malignancy. Nephroureterectomy is the treatment.
- Motor vehicular accident is the most common cause of renal injury. Hematuria is the best sign for renal injury. CECT is the investigation of choice. Urinoma is the most common complication.
- The earliest sign of genitourinary tuberculosis on IVU is moth-eaten calyx. Other signs on IVU are thimble bladder and ureteric stricture.
- Primary bladder calculi are most common in children younger than 10 years. They are associated with dehydration and low protein intake. Ammonium acid urate is the most common type of stone seen in primary bladder stone.
- The most common cause of bladder calcification is schistosomiasis. Urinary frequency is the most common symptom. Sandy patches on cystoscopy and fetal head appearance on plain radiography are diagnostic. Praziquantel is the drug of choice.

- Hunner's ulcer or interstitial cystitis is seen in women with increased frequency of urine. Cystoscopy shows linear ulceration in the fundus with reduced bladder capacity to 60 mL. Hydrostatic dilatation and dimethyl sulfoxide instillation help in relieving symptoms in some patients.
- The most common presentation of ureterocele is UTI. On IVU, adder head or cobra head appearance is seen while on cystoscopy enlarging and collapsing cyst is seen as urine passes.
- VUR is the most common inheritable disease of GU tract. Investigation of choice is MCU and the investigation of choice for pyelonephritis and renal scarring is DMSA scan.
- Ureter identified by peristalsis. Narrowing of the ureter is seen at the following: PUJ, pelvic brim (crossing of iliac vessel), juxtaposition of vas or broad ligament, VUJ, and ureteric orifice.
- Autonephrectomy is seen in renal tuberculosis.
- Flap of bladder wall fashioned into tube to bridge the gap between ureter and bladder in ureteric injury (lower ureteric reconstruction) is a Boari operation.
- BPH develops in a transition zone while ca prostate develops in a peripheral zone.
- In male infertility, absence of fructose on semen analysis indicates obstruction of vas deferens or seminal vesicle agenesis. The next line of investigation is transrectal USG.
- Verumontanum is the single most important landmark in TURP. It is a distal landmark for prostate resection and proximal limit of external sphincter.
- Adenocarcinoma of the prostate is the most common cancer in males.
- Hard, irregular, or nodular prostate with shallow median sulcus raises the suspicion of ca prostate. It should be followed by sPSA. TRUS-guided biopsy is indicated in such cases.

BREAST

106. What are causes of weight loss in breast pathology?

A Carcinoma breast, TB of breast, and TB of chest wall leading to retromammary abscess

107. What is tethering and fixity?

A
- *Tethering*: Involvement of Astley Cooper ligament pulls the skin inwards, creating a dimple or puckering over the breast. The overlying skin is movable and not involved by tumor.
- *Fixity*: It refers to infiltration of skin or chest wall by tumor. Skin is not free if it is fixed.

108. What are the causes of retraction of nipple?

A Retraction occurring early in puberty is known as inversion. Problems with inversion are the following: Problem with breast-feeding and infection. It is due to shortening of subareolar duct. A patient who seeks correction should be clearly explained about postoperative complications such as altered sensation, necrosis, and retraction due to fibrosis.

Recent retraction are of two types and are of pathological importance:

- *Slit-like*: Duct ectasia and periductal mastitis
- *Circumferential*: Is due to malignancy

109. What is sentinel lymph node?

A
- The first lymph node to drain a tumor is known as the sentinel node.
  - Intraoperative identification is done by using either isosulfan blue dye or technetium-labeled sulfur colloid or albumin.
  - Dual tracer technique is superior in identifying sentinel node as compared to blue dye. Subareolar injection technique is superior in identifying sentinel node in the presence of multifocal and multicentric disease.
  - Intraoperative evaluation is done by frozen section.
- For carcinoma breast, level I lymph node and for carcinoma gallbladder, lymph node of Lund is sentinel node.

- SLNB is helpful in the following:
  - Carcinoma breast
  - Malignant melanoma
  - Carcinoma penis (sentinel node of Cabanas)

110. What are the various types of discharge from the breast and their causes?

Discharge	Cause
Serous	Fibrocystic disease and duct ectasia
Purulent	Infection
Milk	Lactation, galactocele, galactorrhea, milk fistula
Bloody	Duct papilloma and carcinoma
Green or black	Duct ectasia

111. Which condition of breast will lead to popcorn calcification on mammography?

Fibroadenoma

112. An 18-year-old girl presented with firm, nontender, mobile lump in right breast. What will be the findings on FNAC?

- Tightly arranged ductal epithelia cells with discohesive bare nuclei are present, which suggest fibroadenoma.
- Nontender, firm, mobile lump in an 18-year-old female suggests fibroadenoma.

113. Mention in brief about Phyllodes tumor.

It is also known as serocystic disease of Brodie or cystosarcoma phyllodes.

Cystosarcoma phyllodes is a misnomer as it is rarely cystic and very rarely develops features of sarcoma.

Types

- Benign
- Borderline
- Malignant

Clinical presentation

It presents as a large breast lump with uneven bosselated surface in women older than 40 years. Skin ulcer due to pressure necrosis may be present; it is mobile over chest wall.

Pathology

- Cut surface reveals leaf-like (phyllodes) appearance. Stroma is more cellular as compared to fibroadenoma and always monoclonal on molecular technique.
- Presence of mitosis and invasive foci indicates malignancy. The most malignant tumor reveals liposarcomatous and rhabdomyosarcomatous components. It is metastasized via bloodstream.

Treatment

- *Small tumor*: Wide excision
- *Massive tumor*: Mastectomy without axillary dissection
- *Other indications for mastectomy in phyllodes tumor*: Recurrent tumor and malignant type

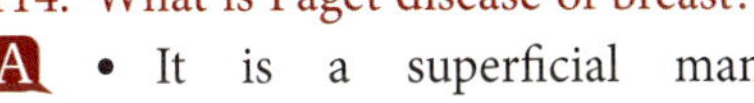

114. What is Paget disease of breast?

- It is a superficial manifestation of underlying breast malignancy. Most patients have an underlying ductal either in situ or invasive malignancy. Lump may or may not be palpable.
- Intraductal spread of the cancer cell to the nipple is responsible for nipple involvement
- It presents as an eczema-like condition, but this is usually unilateral and does not respond to steroid, and itching is not a prominent feature.

Investigations

- Mammography is done to rule out occult multicentric disease supplemented by MRI if breast is dense.
- Biopsy reveals characteristic malignant cell with 'fried egg' appearance in nipple skin or Paget cells.
- Paget disease is differentiated from superficial spreading melanoma by CEA positivity.

Treatment

It is treated by simple mastectomy.

Other treatment options are follows:

- Nipple with lump is removed, followed by radiation.
- Axillary dissection is warranted in case of invasive malignancy.

The other pathology of breast where simple mastectomy is done is large cystosarcoma phylloides; for a small lesion, wide excision is the treatment.

115. What is Mondor disease?

- Thrombophlebitis of superficial veins of breast and chest
- Cord-like feel; on elevation of arm, characteristic groove seen.
- Lateral thoracic vein, the thoracoepigastric vein, and/or superficial epigastric vein may be involved.
- Treatment
  - Restriction of arm movement
  - Anti-inflammatory drugs
  - Hot water fomentation
  - Should be followed for 4–6 weeks; if no improvement, then excision of inflamed segment needed

116. Which are the prognostic factors in carcinoma breast?

- Tumor size: Size usually correlates with lymph node involvement
- Lymph node status: Strong independent risk factor (even small tumor with positive node has poor prognosis as compared to large tumor with negative node)
- Pathological grading and type: Because of interobservor variation, grade removed from the prognostic factors by recent TNM staging
- Estrogen receptor [ER]/progesterone receptor [PR] status: Positive (good prognosis)
- Lymphovascular invasion: Presence indicating poor prognosis
- HER2 (human epidermal growth factor receptor)/neu (C-erbB2) status: Overexpression (poor prognosis)
- Proliferation markers (Ki-67)
- Mitotic index

117. Which tumor may occur in residual breast after breast conservation surgery and radiotherapy?

A Angiosarcoma, probably associated with chronic lymphedema following radiotherapy

Peau d'orange appearance is due to blockage of subdermal lymphatics.

118. Describe the etiology and treatment of gynecomastia.

A It is because of excess circulating estrogen in relation to testosterone.

Causes

- *Physiological*: Neonates, puberty, and old age
- *Pathological*: Klinefelter syndrome, primary testicular tumor, liver disease (cirrhosis), hyperthyroidism or hypothyroidism, testicular trauma, orchitis, cryptorchidism, and renal failure
- *Drugs*: Digoxin, spironolactone, anabolic steroids, cimetidine, estrogen, ketoconazole, verapamil, theophylline, reserpine, diazepam, tricyclic antidepressants, and frusemide

Grading

- *1*: Mild
- *2a*: Moderate without skin redundancy
- *2b*: Moderate with skin redundancy
- *3*: Marked with ptosis

Treatment

- Reassurance
- Treatment of the cause
- If progressing, subcutaneous mastectomy
- Liposuction

119. What is Zuska disease?

A It is a condition of recurrent retroareolar infections and abscesses and is also known as recurrent periductal mastitis. Smoking is a risk factor. Antibiotics and incision and drainage, if required, are the treatment options.

120. Which is the best myocutaneous flap for reconstruction of breast after MRM?

A The acronym 'TRAM' denotes transverse rectus abdominis myocutaneous flap. Reconstruction should never be done prior to radiotherapy.

Silicon implant is the most common method of breast reconstruction and it should be placed beneath the pectoralis major.

Pearls

- Triple assessment for carcinoma breast includes the following: Clinical examination, radiological imaging (USG/mammography), and pathology (FNAC/Tru-Cut biopsy/biopsy). The positive predictive value is >99.9%.
- Forty-five years is the age at which screening mammogram is advised (American Cancer Society [ACS] recommendation). The ACS recommends yearly screening until age 55, and then decreasing to every 2 years. The NHS recommends mammogram at the age of 50 and 3-yearly mammography between 50 and 70 years of age.
- MRI is used for screening when patients are very high risk or radiation is hazardous (Li–Fraumeni syndrome).
- Risk assessment models for ca breast include the following: Gail model and Claus model.
- The most common cause of blood-stained nipple discharge is duct papilloma and that of greenish discharge is duct ectasia.
- The most common presentation of lobular carcinoma of breast is breast mass with ill-defined margin.
- Breast cancer is the most common cancer of women in the world.
- The most common location for carcinoma breast is upper and outer quadrant (60%).
- Invasive lobular carcinoma is usually bilateral, multifocal, and multicentric.
- Breast cancer with the best prognosis is tubular variety. Distant metastases are rare and 5-year survival is almost 100%.
- Breast cancer with the worst prognosis is inflammatory carcinoma.
- Molecular classification of breast is based on gene expression profiling.
- Peau d'orange appearance is due to obstruction of the subdermal lymphatics because of lymphatic permeation by tumor cells. It may occasionally be seen in chronic abscess.
- FNAC is the first investigation and the best investigation is Tru-Cut biopsy.
- The most common site of distant metastases in breast cancer is lumbar vertebra.
- The most common cause of death in carcinoma breast is pleural effusion.
- Van Nuys Prognostic Index is used for DCIS and Nottingham Prognostic Index is used to select the patients for adjuvant treatment.
- Chest wall involvement in carcinoma breast includes involvement of ribs, intercostal muscles, and serratus anterior muscle. Involvement of pectoralis major muscle is not considered as chest wall involvement.
- Axillary node clearance boundaries are the following:
  - *Superior*: Axillary vein
  - *Medial*: Chest wall
  - *Posterior*: Latissimus dorsi, teres major, and subscapularis
  - *Lateral*: Axillary skin
  - *Anterior*: Pectoralis major and minor muscles
- Breast conservation surgery means removal of tumor plus at least 1 cm of normal breast tissue. Sentinel node biopsy is required in breast conservation surgery to decide whether axilla needs clearance or not.
- The best single marker for prognosis in carcinoma breast is axillary lymph node involvement.
- The axillary nodes act not as a reservoir of breast malignancy but as a marker for metastatic potential.
- Intercostobrachial nerve damage during axillary dissection leads to intercostobrachial neuralgia or postmastectomy pain syndrome. It is characterized by circumscribed numbness of the medial aspect of the ipsilateral upper arm. Pain in the axilla and anterior chest wall is also seen in this condition.
- Long thoracic nerve injury leads to winged scapula.
- Medial and lateral thoracic nerve injury leads to pectoralis atrophy.

- Thoracodorsal nerve injury weakens the internal rotation and abduction of the shoulder.
- The first and second perforating arteries are too large for cautery and need to be ligated.
- If axillary vein is injured, it has to be repaired as ligation is associated with chronic edema.
- In pregnancy, mastectomy is a more suitable option for cancer of the breast as compared to breast conservation surgery. Radiotherapy is must in breast conservation surgery. In pregnancy, radiotherapy is contraindicated.
- Chemotherapy is avoided in the first trimester of pregnancy and hormonal therapy is usually not required as most tumors are hormone receptor negative in pregnancy.
- For male breast cancer: 20% preceded by gynecomastia. Radiation exposure and excess estrogens are predisposing conditions. Invasive duct carcinoma is the most common. It is more likely to involve pectoral muscle due to scanty breast tissue. It is more likely to present as advanced disease. Stage-to-stage treatment is same as that of female breast cancer. The most common procedure is modified radical mastectomy.
- Sarcoma of the breast is usually spindle cell variety and treatment is mastectomy followed by radiation.

VASCULAR SYSTEM

121. What is Buerger disease? List the etiological factors.

A Thromboangiitis obliterans (TAO) or Buerger disease, or von Winiwarter–Buerger syndrome, is a progressive, chronic, inflammatory, nonatherosclerotic, thrombotic, segmental obliterative, tobacco-associated vasculopathy primarily involving small-sized and medium-sized arteries of predominantly young male smokers, veins, and nerves of the upper and lower extremities. It may also be associated with thrombophlebitis of the superficial and deep vein, and Raynaud syndrome. It is characterized by inflammatory changes leading to arterial thrombus with preserved internal elastic lamina.

Etiology

- *Smoking*: It leads to Buerger disease.
- *Genetics*: It may play an important role in making smokers more susceptible to disease. HLA-A9, HLA-DR4, and HLA-B5 have been associated with TAO.
- *Hypercoagulability*: Various factors such as coagulation mechanism and hyperhomocysteinemia may be implicated. Patients with TAO have increased hematocrit and blood viscosity, and reduced red cell deformability and platelet activation. Higher median plasma activity of factor VII, factor VIII, factor XI, fibrinogen, and homocysteine has been reported in patients with TAO.
- *Endothelial dysfunction*: Endothelium-dependent vasodilatation is impaired in TAO. Nitroglycerin-induced vasodilatations are similar, indicating that endothelium is involved rather than smooth muscle.
- *Autoimmunity*: T-cell–mediated cellular immunity and B-cell–mediated humoral immunity associated with macrophage activation or dendritic cell activation in the intima of the vessels play an important role.
- *Oral infection*: Higher incidence of apical periodontitis in patients with TAO and same bacteria may also be demonstrated in affected arteries.[19]

122. What are the diagnostic criteria for Buerger disease? Mention the various treatment options for it.

A Shionoya's criteria for diagnosis of Buerger disease

- Age <50 years
- History of smoking
- Upper limb involvement or phlebitis migrans
- Infrapopliteal arterial occlusive lesion
- Absence of atherosclerotic risk factors other than smoking

Clinical features

- Foot, arch, and calf claudication (intermittent claudication: Muscular pain of the affected limb on walking or exercise worsened on increasing level of effort and relieved by rest)
- Migratory superficial thrombophlebitis
- Burning pain in the feet or hand
- Trophic nail changes
- Ischemic ulcer
- Digital gangrene
- Possibility of absence of anterior tibial, posterior tibial, dorsalis pedis, radial, and ulnar arterial pulsation
- Normal brachial and femoral pulsation
- Abnormal Allen test with ischemic ulceration in lower limb highly suggestive of Buerger disease

Diagnosis of Buerger disease

- Ankle brachial pressure index (ABPI)
  - It is a simple, reliable, and accurate test. It requires handheld Doppler and sphygmomanometer.
  - ABPI is calculated as highest systolic blood pressure at the ankle/highest systolic brachial pressure.
  - Values
    - *Normal*: 1.0
    - *Arterial obstruction*: <0.9
    - *Rest pain*: <0.5
    - *Imminent necrosis*: <0.3
  - Limitations
    - Artificial high reading may be seen in calcified vessels like in diabetes. So ABPI >1.3 in diabetes necessitates toe pressure measurement.
    - Non–flow-limiting iliac obstruction with typical claudication pain may have a normal ABPI and require exercise ABPI measurement.
    - It does not provide information about the location of the disease.
- Toe pressure <30 mmHg indicating severe ischemia
- Four-limb segmental arterial pressure and pulse volume: Normal above knee joint and markedly reduced distally
- Digital plethysmography: Abnormal
- Arterial duplex scan: Cork screw collateral (snake sign or dot sign) in continuous wave Doppler
- Transcutaneous oxygen pressure
- Digital subtraction angiography: It helps in diagnosis as well as excludes the proximal lesion
  - Segmental involvement
  - Distal artery involvement severe with normal proximal artery without evidence of atherosclerosis and collateralization around the area of occlusion (Martorell sign or tree root or spider leg deformity)
- Can also use gadolinium-enhanced MR angiography or 64-slice MDCT angiography to diagnose
- Electrocardiography, echocardiography, and abdominal ultrasonography to rule out proximal source of emboli
- Laboratory test to exclude connective tissue disorder and hypercoagulable state
- Routine tests such as CBC, RBS, renal function, and liver function test
- Thyroid function test
- Lipid profile
- Coagulation screen
- Autoimmune screening
- Serological markers, etc.
- Biopsy of skin nodule or involved segment of artery indicated when age is more than 45 and unusual presentation is present in the form of either proximal artery involvement or central nervous system disease

Treatment

- Smoking cessation including passive smoking able to arrest the disease but not reverse it
- Exercise therapy
- Foot and hand hygiene
- Pain: Narcotic analgesic
- Reverse Trendelenburg position for severe ischemic rest pain
- Nonsteroidal anti-inflammatory drugs
- Antiplatelet agents such as aspirin
- Cilostazol: Phosphodiesterase 3 inhibitor with mild antiplatelet properties

- Statins: Pleiotropic effect—improve endothelial function and decrease oxidative stress and inflammation
- Prostaglandin analogue: Vasodilator and antiplatelet—iloprost
- Endothelin 1 receptor antagonist: Endothelin 1, a potent vasoconstrictor, acting via ETA and ETB receptors; bosentan a dual receptor antagonist; oral treatment beneficial in patients with ulceration and rest pain
- Hyperhomocysteinemia: Folate
- Intermittent pneumatic compression
- Chemical sympathectomy: Guanethidine, an adrenergic blocker and using multiple sessions of IV regional blockade by Bier's technique, helpful in ischemic rest pain, ulceration, and gangrene
- Endovascular treatment
  - Selective intra-arterial thrombolysis with urokinase or streptokinase or percutaneous subintimal angioplasty
- Surgical options
  - Debridement, omental transfer (for rest pain, nonhealing ulcer, or both), and implantable electrical spinal cord stimulation address neurogenic component of pain.
  - *Lumbar or thoracic sympathectomy*: Provides short-term pain relief and promotes ulcer healing, and has no value in management of intermittent claudication (blood flow through the skin of the affected limb will not improve as vessels are already maximally dilated in ischemic area; in unilateral lumbar sympathectomy sympathetic ganglia L1, L2, L3, and sometimes L4 removed and in bilateral lumbar sympathectomy L1 of one side is preserved)
  - *Therapeutic angiogenesis*: Bone marrow-derived mononuclear cell therapy, intramedullary K-nail-stimulated angiogenesis, tibial fenestration at six sites, and EPC mobilization with H-GCSF
  - *Amputation*: If all of the above-mentioned measures fail[19]

123. Mention in short about Rutherford and Baker classification and Fontaine staging for PAD.

A See Table 16.2.

Table 16.2 Rutherford and Baker Classification

Grade	Category	Presentation
0	0	Asymptomatic
I	1	Mild claudication
	2	Moderate
	3	Severe
II	4	Ischemic rest pain
III	5	Minor tissue loss: Nonhealing ulcer, focal gangrene
IV	6	Major tissue loss: Above metatarsal level, no longer salvageable

Fontaine staging:

Stage I: Asymptomatic

Stage IIA: Mild claudication

Stage IIB: Moderate to severe claudication

Stage III: Ischemic rest pain

Stage IV: Ulceration or gangrene

124. Describe arteriovenous fistula.

A
- It is an abnormal communication between artery and vein.
- It can be congenital or acquired.

Effects

- *Local*: Vein becomes arterialized—dilated, tortuous, and thick walled.
- On palpation: Thrill.
- Auscultation: Machinery murmur.
- *Nicoladoni sign or Branham sign*: Pressure on the artery proximal to fistula reduces the swelling and ceases thrill and bruit.
- *Effect on blood system and heart*: It leads to increased cardiac output, left ventricular enlargement, and sometimes heart failure.

Surgical arteriovenous fistula is created for hemodialysis.

Principle

- Upper extremity, nondominant hand is preferred.
- Fistula should be created as distal as possible, to preserve the proximal site for future access.
- Autogenous AV access is preferred as compared to nonautogenous graft because

of superior patency and lower complication rate.
- Lower limb and body wall are the last resort in case of exhausted upper extremity venous access.

Three types
- Autogenous primary: Commonly performed autogenous primary is radiocephalic (Brescia–Cimino fistula) at the wrist because of its high patency, longevity, and low incidence of postsurgical complications. Cephalic vein is preferred because of its lateral location and minimal dissection. Ulnar artery is not preferred because of its distance from cephalic vein.
- Autogenous secondary: It is less commonly performed because its long-term patency rate has been disappointing. Basilic vein or great saphenous vein may be harvested. It may be end (vein) to side or side to side. End to side is preferred as it has less chance of steal syndrome.
- Nonautogenous graft: The most commonly used graft is PTFE. It is indicated when suitable veins are not available or suitable vein length is not available. Other forms of fistula are as follows: Brachiocephalic, transposed basilica or brachiobrachial, and forearm basilic vein. It may be of the following types: Loop forearm, straight forearm, upper arm AV graft, lower limb AV graft, and hemodialysis-reliable outflow graft. In hemodialysis-reliable outflow graft, upper extremity graft is connected to a thoracic component and extended to the cavoatrial junction.

Complications of fistula for hemodialysis
- Thrombosis, infection, nonmaturation, venous hypertension, pseudoaneurysm, high-output cardiac failure, and seroma can occur.
- Steal syndrome: Ischemic monomelic neuropathy—diversion of blood flow into AVF leads to decreased blood flow in the hand. It leads to ischemia of the nerve and produces neurological deficit deficits of the median, ulnar, and radial nerves. The patients may initially present with cool, pale, numb, or painful digits that can progress to nerve damage and distal necrosis. Patients may also present with weakness or paralysis despite a warm hand and palpable radial and ulnar pulses.

Treatment

Narrowing of the access conduit (banding) to revascularization procedures such as distal revascularization/interval ligation to ligation access.[20]

125. Describe in detail about thoracic outlet syndrome.

A Thoracic outlet syndrome is characterized by pain, paresthesia, and weakness in hand and arm due to compression of neurovascular bundle at the thoracic outlet.
- Boundaries of outlet
  - *Roof*: Subclavius muscle
  - *Floor*: Superior surface of the first rib
  - *Front*: Manubrium sterni
  - *Posterior*: Spine
- Three anatomical spaces
  - Scalene triangle (above clavicle): It is bounded by anterior scalene muscle (ASM) and middle scalene muscle (MSM) on each side and first rib at base and contains only subclavian artery and brachial plexus.
  - Pectoralis minor space is present below clavicle.
  - Costoclavicular space (between clavicle and first rib): Its compression leads to subclavian vein obstruction.
- Contents of the thoracic outlet
  - Nerve: Brachial plexus (C5–C8 plus T1), phrenic nerve, long thoracic nerve, dorsal scapular nerve, and cervical sympathetic nerve chain
  - Artery and vein: Subclavian and axillary vessels
  - Scalene muscle (which originates from the transverse process of cervical spine and inserts into the first rib) and pectoralis minor muscle (which originates from the anterior surface of third, fourth, and fifth ribs and inserts into the coracoid process of scapula)

Predisposing anatomical condition with hyperextension neck injury is associated with neurogenic TOS.

Predisposing conditions

- Narrow scalene triangle (average width is 1.1 cm)
- Interdigitating fiber between ASM and MSM
- High emergence of C5 and C6 nerve roots
- Adherence of ASM and MSM to C5 and C6 nerve roots
- Cervical rib and first anomalous rib
- Hyperextension neck injury produces scalene muscle scarring and compresses brachial plexus. Whiplash injury in road traffic accidents is common, followed by fall on the slippery floors.
- Repetitive stress injury: Swimming, weight lifting, keyboard entry, and working in an awkward position repeatedly also associated with NTOS
- Spontaneous neurogenic TOS rare (cervical rib is the underlying cause in most cases)

Popular theories for TOS—congenital band, splitting of ASM fiber around C5 and C6, and presence of scalene minimus muscle are actually not associated with TOS. This is based on the observation that they are commonly found in normal population.

Clinical features

- Neurogenic (95%): Cervicobrachial pain, history of tingling, numbness, and weakness in the hand exacerbated by arm overhead (compromised thoracic outlet), and dangling (stretch brachial plexus) are present.
- There is obliteration of pulse with arm abduction.
- Gilliatt–Sumner hand: It involves weakness and atrophy of the thenar, hypothenar, and interossei intrinsic hand muscles. There is hyperesthesia in median and ulnar antebrachial cutaneous distribution, but normal median nerve sensation.
- Arterial: It is usually due to thromboemboli from poststenotic arterial aneurysm or intimal lesion. Arm and hand ischemia (diffuse pain, poikilothermia, pallor, decreased pulse), effort fatigue of arm and hand, and Raynaud phenomenon in a small number of cases are present.
- Venous: Effort thrombosis of subclavian and axillary veins leads to arm engorgement and swelling (Paget–Schroetter syndrome). It is common in swimmers, weight lifters, and volleyball players. Duplex USG or contrast venography (where USG is not available) is performed.
- Patients may have a disuse edema and extreme hypersensitivity of the affected arm.

Pathology

Acute and chronic inflammation following hyperextension injury that leads to fibrosis and persistent muscle spasm

Various tests for diagnosis

- *Adson or scalene test*: There is 90° abduction with external rotation and head is rotated toward same side, which leads to loss of radial pulse and drop in blood pressure in upper extremity. Reliability is improved when the test is combined with arterial duplex.
- *Roos stress test*: Draw the shoulder backwards and raise arm to horizontal position with elbow flexed to 90° to occlude the radial pulse and symptoms are reproduced with 3-minute rapid opening and closing of hand.
- *Halsted test (costoclavicular test, military position)*: Drawing the shoulder downward and backward causes obliteration of radial pulse and symptoms are reproduced when shoulder is displaced caudally.
- *Wright test*: Occludes the radial pulse and symptoms are reproduced when ipsilateral arm is abducted cranially for 1 minute and elbow is extended.

Diagnosis

- TOS is a diagnosis of exclusion and is clinical diagnosis
- Tenderness over scalene muscle and supraclavicular fossa of the affected side
- Pain and tenderness of anterior and posterior shoulder region
- Headache
- CT cervical and thoracic region
- Nerve conduction study

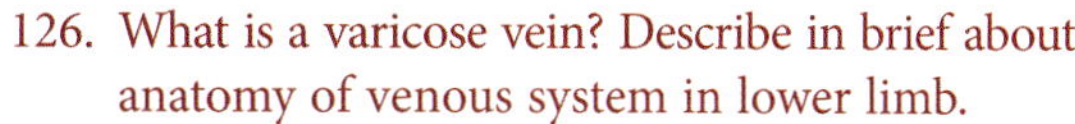

Treatment

- Physical therapy being the mainstay of treatment
- Lifestyle modification: Posture training
- If lifestyle modification and physical therapy fail: CT-guided scalene block with local anesthetic—will cause relaxation of ASM and allow the first rib to drop and relieve pressure on brachial plexus
- Symptoms relieved also by botulinum toxin injection into muscle
- Surgery: If physiotherapy fails
  - Resection of the first rib
  - Division of costoclavicular ligament
  - Resection of ASM and MSM
  - Vascular and brachial plexus decompression
  - Sympathectomy C8–T3

126. What is a varicose vein? Describe in brief about anatomy of venous system in lower limb.

A Definition

Varicose vein: A dilated, tortuous, bulging, superficial vein measuring usually more than 4 mm in diameter

Anatomy

Veins of the lower limb can be divided into three systems (Fig. 16.4):

- *Deep*: Deep to deep fascia and runs parallel to the tibia and femur
- *Superficial*: Is between deep fascia and skin
- *Perforating*: Is also known as connecting vein and joins deep veins to the superficial vein

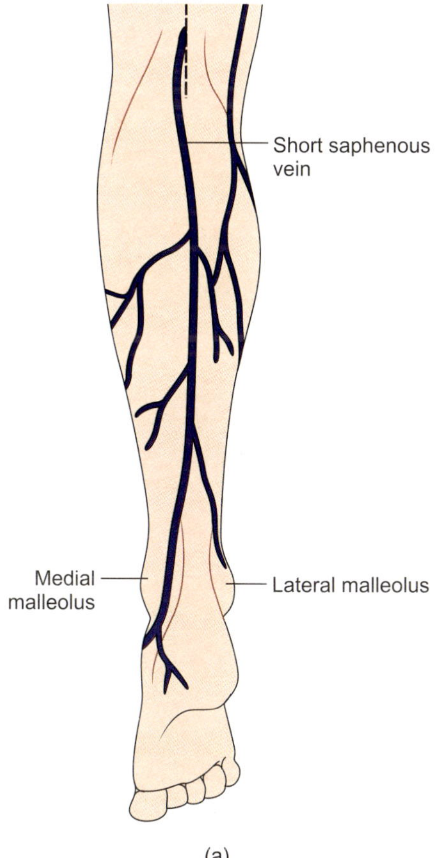

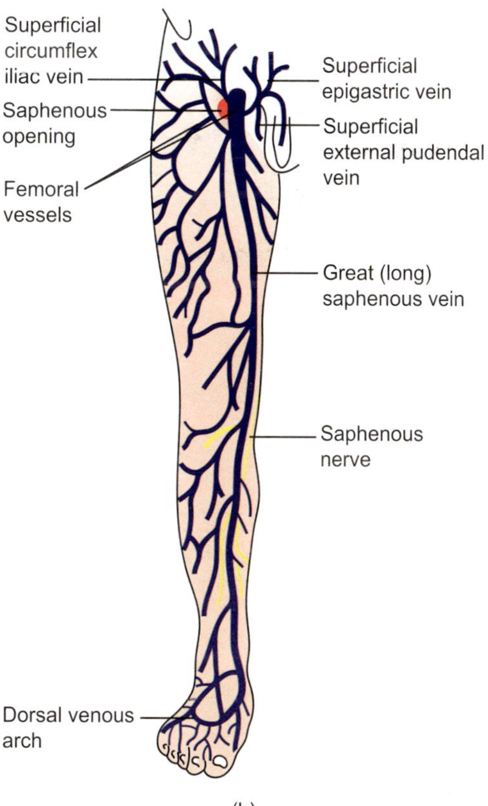

Figure 16.4 (a) Short (small) saphenous vein of the right lower limb and its tributaries. (b) Great saphenous vein and its tributaries. *Source*: Singh, DR. Essentials of Anatomy for Dentistry Students, 2 edn. New Delhi: Wolters Kluwer India, 2017.

Deep veins

Principal return of blood flow from the lower limbs is through deep veins.

- Crural veins (vein accompanying anterior tibial, posterior tibial, and peroneal arteries) are interconnected and join to form popliteal vein. As popliteal vein ascends, it becomes femoral vein in the thigh and near the groin femoral vein joins the deep femoral to form a common femoral vein that ascends to become external iliac proximal to inguinal ligaments.
- Great saphenous vein: It is the longest vein of the body. Its caliber is 3–4 mm. It starts from the medial side of the dorsum of foot from dorsal venous arch and courses proximally on the medial side of calf as marginal medial vein and runs along the saphenous nerve. At knee, it is found in the medial aspect of popliteal space and runs along the anteromedial thigh to join common femoral vein by passing through well-defined fossa ovalis 4 cm inferior and lateral to pubic tubercle. This termination point is referred to as saphenofemoral junction. It contains 10–20 valves.

Tributaries

- In the leg: The posterior arch vein, the anterior superficial tibial vein, and the medial superficial pedal vein
- The posterior arch vein (Leonardo vein [posterior accessory saphenous vein]) being a major tributary just below knee
- In the thigh: Receives one or two tributaries from the anterior and posterior accessory great saphenous veins
- At fossa ovalis: Superficial epigastric, superficial circumflex iliac, and external pudendal

Small saphenous vein

- It is the second largest vein of the lower limb.
- It contains 7–10 valves.
- It starts from the lateral aspect of dorsum of the foot and runs along the lateral margin as lateral marginal vein. As it ascends in the calf, it enters the deep fascia and ascends between heads of gastrocnemius muscle. Its termination is variable and described by Kosinski.
  - *Normal*: To join popliteal vein 5 cm below the knee crease
  - *High*: In midthigh, in muscular vein or GSV
  - *Low*: Ends in deep vein of calf or deep sural muscular vein or GSV

Sural nerve courses along the SSV in distal calf and is at risk at the time of endovascular ablation.

Vein of Giacomini

The thigh extension of small saphenous vein runs in the posterior part of thigh and connects with the GSV.

Perforating veins

There are approximately 150 perforating veins in the lower limb. However, only few are clinically important. The medial calf perforator is the most important. Perforating vein connects superficial to the deep vein.

Perforators in lower leg

- Medial aspect of ankle and leg: Posterior tibial perforators (previously known as Cockett perforator). They connect posterior arch vein with posterior tibial vein. These perforators are further classified as lower, middle, and upper.
- Anteromedial portion of calf: It contains paratibial perforator (previously known as Boyd perforator).
- Midthigh: Superior perforator of femoral canal (previously known as Dodd and Hunterian perforators) connects GSV to the femoral vein.
- Distal thigh: Inferior perforators of femoral canal (previously known as Dodd and Hunterian perforators) connect GSV to the popliteal vein.
- Intergemellar perforator (previously known as midcalf perforator of May) connects small saphenous vein to soleal veins.
- Para-Achillean perforator (previously known as perforator of Bassi) connects SSV to peroneal veins.

Reticular vein

1- to 3-mm diameter, thin-walled, blue venules in superficial compartment constitute the reticular vein.

Telangiectases

0.1- to 1-mm diameter, dilated venules, capillaries, or arterioles are termed telangiectases.

127. What are the various theories suggested for pathophysiology of varicose vein?

A Ambulatory venous hypertension

At rest in erect position, superficial and deep venous systems have the same hydrostatic pressure that is equal to weight of column of blood between the point of measurement and the right atrium. During contraction of calf muscle, there is a transient rise in deep venous pressure. This propels blood cephalad. Competent valve closed during the process prevents blood transmission from the deep to superficial vein and during relaxation, valve opens and pressure in the deep vein falls abruptly and blood rushes from superficial to deep vein.

Failure to decrease the superficial venous pressure approximately 20 mmHg on walking is called ambulatory venous hypertension.

Water hammer effect

Changes of chronic venous insufficiency are related to velocity of reflux (water hammer effect). High pressure is transmitted during Valsalva to the skin and ulcer through perforating vein in the presence of normal ambulatory venous pressure.

Fibrin cuff or ECM cuff or trap hypothesis

Venous hypertension leads to damage to the capillaries and associated inflammation leads to deposition of fibrin, collagen, and fibronectin and forms a pericapillary fibrin cuff. The cuff is formed by ECM protein. The fibrin cuff does not act as a barrier to diffusion of oxygen. The cuff traps TGF-β_1 and α_2 macroglobulins in its interstices and these are not available for healing and regeneration of skin and subcutaneous tissue and lead to skin changes such as ulceration and lipodermatosclerosis.

White cell trapping hypothesis

Reduced blood flow on standing leads to reduced shear rate in microcirculation and favors white cell margination or trapping and trapped white cell activates and releases proteolytic enzymes, free radicals, cytokines, and chemotactic factors as well as causes capillary plugging and as an end result leads to tissue hypoxia and damage to the tissue.

128. Why are skin changes common in gaiter area?

A The area between lower border of soleus muscle and ankle is known as gaiter area.

- This area is located farthest from the heart and has a high venous pressure even in a normal person.
- It has a relatively poor arterial supply.
- There is extra load in this area when foot muscle pump acts.

Skin changes in chronic venous insufficiency are as follows:

- Ankle flare or corona phlebectatica is present.
- Eczema and pigmentation: Due to high venous pressure, venules rupture and blood extravasates in the tissue and hemosiderin pigment is responsible for itching and pigmentation.
- Lipodermatosclerosis: It is sclerosing panniculitis located on the area with maximum venous pressure. It indicates severe CVI and is characterized by localized chronic inflammation and fibrosis of skin and subcutaneous tissue and can produce fibrosis and contracture of tendo-Achilles.
- Ulceration: It is present in the gaiter area.

129. Mention the treatment of varicose vein.

A Nonsurgical

- Infected ulcer: It is treated by antibiotics.
- Limb elevation is helpful.
- Compression therapy is also an effective treatment.
- Elastic compression stocking (class 1: 14–17 mmHg pressure; class 2: 18–24 mmHg; and class 3: 25–35 mmHg)
  - It provides graded compression of the leg and opposes the hydrostatic forces of venous hypertension.
  - It is donned in the morning and removed at bed time. It significantly

improves symptoms of varicose vein and aids in ulcer healing but one must be explained. It is not going to correct abnormal venous hemodynamic and it must be worn once ulcer is healed to prevent recurrence.
 - It reduces pain, swelling, and pigmentation and improves activity.
- *Unna boot*: Gauze paste contains zinc, calamine, and glycerin. It is nonelastic compression and needs to be changed once or twice a week. It prevents further breakdown of skin.
- *Pneumatic compression*: It provides sequential compression and is used to treat venous insufficiency and helps in prevention of DVT.
- *Topical dressing*: Topical steroids may be used for eczematous dermatitis. Hydrocolloid and hydrogel dressing may be used for ulcer. For infected ulcer, silver-impregnated dressing is used. Biological human skin substitute and extracellular matrix consisting of small intestinal submucosa may be used in difficult-to-heal ulcers. It should be used for the shortest period. It may be counterproductive. It is toxic to fibroblasts.
- *Pharmacotherapy*: Drugs used are coumarins, flavonoids, saponosides, and other plant extracts. They are venoactive drugs and improve venous tone and decrease capillary permeability. Flavonoids are the most commonly used.
- *Exercises*: Structured graded exercise program may be beneficial to improve calf muscle pump as a supplemental to medical or surgical therapy.
- *Foam sclerotherapy*: Detergent destroys the lipid membranes of endothelial cells and causes shedding, thrombosis, fibrosis, and obliteration of vein. The procedure is performed under ultrasound guidance. The most commonly used sclerosant is sodium tetradecyl sulfate. Tessari method that utilizes two syringes connected with three-way taps is used. 1:3 to 1:4 ratio of sclerosant and air is drawn into single syringe, and then oscillated vigorously for 10–20 times. After emptying the vein by limb elevation, starting with small reticular vein and ending in large vein, it should be injected as soon as possible after vigorous oscillation. At one site maximum 2 mL and in single session not more than 12 mL sclerosant should be injected. Compression bandage is applied for 7–10 days. Patients should walk 30 minutes after the procedure.
 - *Contraindications*: These include history of allergy to sclerosant, contraceptive pills (high risk for DVT), acute thrombophlebitis, uncertainty of diagnosis, obese immobile patients, pregnant patients, and massive incompetence in saphenous vein (better treated surgically and sclerosant will give only temporary relief).
- *Endovenous laser ablation*: Insertion of laser fiber into suitable incompetent vein with subsequent thermal ablation. Diluted lignocaine with adrenaline and bicarbonate warmed up to body temperature is injected to produce tumescent anesthesia. It provides analgesia, compresses the vein, increases contact area between vein wall and fiber of laser, protects nerve and skin by causing hydrodissection, and acts as a heat sink. Laser ablation treats only junctional and truncal incompetence. Concomitant or subsequent phlebectomy or sclerotherapy is advised for rapid improvement.
- *Radiofrequency ablation*: It is associated with less pain and bruising. Bipolar catheter is used to generate thermal energy. It generates 85–120°C temperature with 2–4 W power to ablate the vein.
- *Endovenous glue*: Cyanoacrylate adhesive is applied through catheter placed within lumen of the vein.

Surgery

- Principle
 - Elimination of source of incompetence: Flush ligation at its origin with deep vein
 - Removing the principal pathway of incompetence: Long single channel, one of the saphenous veins stripping

- Removing the tributaries: Multiple small-incision phlebectomy
- Elimination of perforating vein
- Procedures
  - Saphenofemoral ligation and long saphenous vein stripping: Stripping will reduce the chances of recurrent varicose vein. Stripped up to the knee level: Stripping up to ankle will lead to saphenous nerve injury and produce cutaneous anesthesia or unpleasant traction neuritis. It is advisable to pass the stripper from below.
  - Saphenopopliteal junction ligation and small saphenous stripping are helpful.
  - Perforator ligation: In uncomplicated varicose vein, small, duplex-guided incision is used for perforator ligation and in patients with skin pigmentation, subfascial endoscopic perforator ligation (SEPS) is indicated.
  - Phlebectomy: It is performed via a small incision using mosquito forceps and phlebectomy hook.[21]

130. Which is the absolute contraindication for varicose vein surgery?

A Deep vein thrombosis (in presence of DVT, superficial vein is the only vein which drains the blood)

Superficial thrombophlebitis is seen commonly after IV infusion.

131. What is Virchow's triad?

A Virchow's triad includes the following: Venous stasis, endothelial injury, and hypercoagulability of blood.

- This triad predisposes to thrombus formation.
- Investigation of choice for DVT: It consists of duplex ultrasound scan of venous system in lower limb or color Doppler.

132. Describe in detail about treatment of DVT.

A General measures to prevent DVT

- Early ambulation
- Adequate hydration
- Active flexion–extension exercise
- Adequate analgesia
- Limb elevation

Mechanical methods

- Graduated elastic compression or active compression with pneumatic compression devices (foot pump)
- Intermittent pneumatic compression of the extremity

Treatments

- Initial guideline was strict bed rest and limb elevation. However, a recent study shows that ambulation is associated with early improvement in pain and swelling. Bed rest is not associated with significant reduction in PE. Ambulation is recommended as tolerated.
- Anticoagulants: Start either UFH or LMWH along with an oral anticoagulant on the basis of documented DVT or in case of very strong suspicion.
  - Overlap for 5–10 days (till INR is between 2.0 and 3.0 for 2 consecutive days).
  - Initial dose is 80 units/kg bolus followed by 18 units/kg/hour infusion.
  - Monitor aPTT
  - aPTT
    - *<35*: 80 units/kg bolus followed by 4 units/kg infusion
    - *40–70*: No change
    - *70–90*: 2 units/kg/h
    - *>90*: Stop infusion for 1 hour, and then 3 units/kg/h
    - Alternatively heparin can be given 5000 IU bolus followed by 17,500 IU sc BD. Achieve INR 2.5–3.5.
  - LMWH: When given subcutaneously, it has a better bioavailability, has predictable pharmacokinetics and pharmacodynamics, and is more consistent. It is cost-effective and patients can be managed with the help of outpatient treatment. It does not require routine monitoring of coagulation profile except platelet count. Dose needs to be titrated in renal insufficiency. It can be given OD or BD subcutaneously.
  - Fondaparinux: It is a selective anti-Xa; it gives 5, 7.5, and 10 mg subcutaneously OD depending on weight.

- Direct factor Xa inhibitor: Rivaroxaban and apixaban can be used for long-term treatment with better profile.
- There should be an overlap of at least 3–5 days before discontinuing heparin.
- IVC filter is recommended by American College of Chest Physicians in only those with venous thrombolism and having contraindication to anticoagulant, complications of anticoagulant, and recurrent DVT despite adequate anticoagulation. The most common complication of IVC filter is insertion site thrombosis.
- Catheter-directed thrombolysis is indicated in migration of DVT resulting in severe PE and hemodynamic instability, and potentially lifesaving thrombolytics should be considered.[22]
- Long-term treatment: Oral anticoagulants such as warfarin and acenocoumarol should be given for at least 3 months to prevent thrombus extension and recurrent DVT. High-risk patients require >3-month treatment.

133. A patient presented in the casualty with bleeding from the ruptured varicose vein at the ankle. What will you do as a first line of management?

A Elevation of limb

134. Describe clinical features, management, and surgical complications of diabetic foot.

A Clinical features

- Diabetic patients suffer from microangiopathy, neuropathy, and high glucose load in the tissue leading to decreased resistance to infection.
- Autonomic neuropathy leads to decrease in sweating → dry skin → fissure → infection.
- Sensory neuropathy leads to decrease in sensation → unawareness of trauma → repeated trauma → ulcer. Semmes Weinstein monofilament is used to check sensory neuropathy. Inability to perceive 10 g SWM indicates large fiber neuropathy.
- Vasculopathy leads to decrease in blood supply, so healing of the ulcer is delayed.
- Diabetic foot may present in a spectrum of conditions from cellulitis to chronic osteomyelitis.
  - Cellulitis: Group A streptococci and *S. aureus*
  - Deep infection: Gram-negative organisms and anaerobes
  - Acute osteomyelitis
  - Chronic osteomyelitis: Group A and group B streptococci and *B. fragilis*

International Working Group Diabetic Foot risk classification

- *Group 0*: No neuropathy, no peripheral arterial problem, and no joint deformity or immobility
- *Group 1*: Peripheral neuropathy, no peripheral arterial problem, and no joint deformity or immobility
- *Group 2*: Peripheral neuropathy, foot deformity and limited joint mobility, and/or peripheral arterial disease
- *Group 3*: History of ulcer, amputation, or Charcot joint

Diabetic ulcer severity score

	0	**1**
Dorsalis pedis palpable	Yes	No
Bone involvement	No	Yes
Site	Toe	Foot
Number	Single	Multiple

The maximum score is 4; as the score increases, severity of condition becomes greater.

Wagner ulcer classification

- *0*: No open wound; may have cellulitis
- *1*: Superficial diabetic ulcer (partial or full thickness)
- *2*: Ulcer extending into ligaments, tendons, and joint capsules, deep fascia without abscess or osteomyelitis
- *3*: Deep ulcer with abscess, osteomyelitis, or joint sepsis
- *4*: Gangrene localized to toe, forefoot, or heel
- *5*: Extensive gangrene involving whole foot

Neuropathic foot or neuroischemic foot

- *Neuropathic foot*: It is warm and well perfused with bounding pulse. Dry skin and ulceration develop over sole of foot due to secondary infection. Charcot joint is present.

- *Neuroischemic foot*: It refers to cool foot with pulseless and poor perfusion. It is associated with swelling. Ulceration is seen on the edges of foot; plantar ulceration is rare. It is more often tender and painful. Claudication and rest pain are present. Skin blanches on elevation and reddens on dependency.

Natural history of diabetes

Stages of diabetic foot

- *1*: Normal—asymptomatic normal foot
- *2*: High risk—neuropathy, ischemia, callus, and deformity
- *3*: Ulcer—may be neuropathic or neuroischemic ulcer
- *4*: Infection—cellulitis or infected pus discharge
- *5*: Necrosis—may be dry or wet necrosis
- *6*: Unsalvageable

Diagnosis of diabetes (according to the American Diabetic Association criteria)

In any patient with typical hyperglycemic symptoms (polyuria, polydipsia, and weigh loss) with the following:

- RBS >200 mg/dL
- FBS >126 mg/dL
- PG_2BS >200 mg/dL after 75 g of glucose load

In 2010, the ADA introduced HbA1c as a diagnostic criterion: HbA1c >6.5% or 48 mmol/mol is considered as diabetes.

In asymptomatic patients or patients with intercurrent illness, repeat test is necessary to establish diagnosis.

Fasting blood sugar is the preferred test as compared to PG_2BS examination.

Treatment

- Superficial infection is treated with antibiotics mostly covering Gram-positive organisms and anaerobes.
- Deep infection requires debridement and daily dressing.
- In presence of slough, use EUSOL bath daily.
- Collagenase can also be used as a debriding agent.
- Perform pressure offloading.

Stage 2 management

High risk with no current ulceration

- *General advice about foot care in diabetes*
  - Do not walk barefoot.
  - Do daily inspection of foot.
  - Wash feet daily with warm and not hot water, and dry carefully.
  - Do not cut corn or callosity.
  - Trim the toe nails straight across.
  - Apply emollient over dry skin.
  - Regular review by podiatrician as well as self-monitoring is essential.
- *Modification of footwear or special footwear*
  - This is performed if there are abnormalities with foot pressure or problems with pressure loading on certain part of the foot.
  - Padded socks reduce the trauma.
  - Wear footwear indoor as well as outdoor.
  - Wear shoes with a large room for toes.
  - Inspect footwear before putting them on for foreign body.

Management of stage 3 and above

- Optimization of blood glucose is a must.
- Improve nutritional status.
- Perform debridement of wound including callus and dead skin regularly with usually scalpel and forceps. Use of chemical agent should be limited as it may damage normal healthy tissue. Sterile maggots may be effective. After debridement, apply proper dressing.
- Infection control: It may localize sinus, osteomyelitis, or systemic infection. All infections or ulcers should be considered deep and/or involving bone unless proved otherwise. Culture and sensitivity is obtained and antibiotics used are according to local guidelines. Commonly used antibiotics are the following: Co-amoxiclav, clindamycin, metronidazole, and linezolid.
- Plain radiograph may help to diagnose osteomyelitis.
- If debridement and antibiotics fail to control the osteomyelitis, resection or amputation is required.
- Pressure offloading and trauma reduction
  - Suitable shoes and insoles help to relieve the pressure.

  - Pneumatic boot or total contact cast may allow patients to be mobile with pressure offloading.
- If there is a coexisting vascular disease, bypassing grafting or angioplasty gives excellent results.
- Failure of vascular intervention in the presence of vascular disease needs amputation; below-knee amputation is preferred.
- Charcot foot: Foot should be immobilized to prevent joint destruction. Use nonwalking plaster cast or air cast type of boot for at least 3 months (to allow bone repair or remodeling).

Surgical complications of diabetes

- Skin: Boil, abscess, carbuncle, and cellulitis
- Vascular: Vasculopathy
- Neurogenic: Neuropathy
- Gastroparesis
- Genitourinary: Impotence and neurogenic bladder

135. Mention in brief about abdominal aortic aneurysm (AAA).

A Fifty percent or more dilatation of localized segment of artery is an aneurysm. <50% is an ectasia. Abdominal aorta (AA) is the most common site and in aorta, infrarenal aorta is the most commonly involved. Popliteal artery is the most commonly involved peripheral vessel.

Risk factors

- Male gender
- Family history of AAA
- Increasing age
- Smoking
- Hypertension
- Hypercholesterolemia

Types

- True aneurysm contains all three layers of vessel wall. False (pseudo) aneurysm is due to trauma.
- True aneurysm is because of atherosclerosis, infection (mycotic), or collagen vascular disease.
- Infected aneurysm is because of either septic emboli or contiguous spread. Commonly involved organisms are *Salmonella, H. influenzae, Staphylococcus (most common organism), Mycobacterium tuberculosis, and Treponema*. The most commonly involved artery is femoral.
- Mycotic aneurysm is usually saccular and has a high risk for rupture.

Symptoms

- Majority of the patients are asymptomatic and diagnosed incidentally
- Back or lumbar pain
- Malaise, fever, weakness, weight loss, night sweat (inflammatory or mycotic aneurysm)
- Abdominal lump (pulsatile)
- Acute or chronic lower extremity ischemia due to thromboembolism (trash foot due to microemboli leads to patchy area of ischemia on the plantar aspect of foot)
- Compression of duodenum: Early satiety and nausea and compression of the urinary bladder (frequency of micturation)
- Rupture is associated with lumbar pain, rapid onset, unexplained hypotension (hemodynamic instability), and pulsatile abdominal mass
- Aortocaval (high output cardiac failure), aortoiliac, and aortoenteric fistula (fourth part duodenum, massive GI bleed)
- Rupture into the urinary bladder or ureter is associated with gross hematuria and erosion into adjacent vertebra leads to severe back pain.

Risk of rupture increases with increased diameter.

Diagnosis

- Clinical examination: Palpation of aneurysm above umbilicus suggests AAA. Severe tenderness on palpation suggests inflammatory or mycotic aneurysm.
- CBC, CRP, ESR, and antibody to *Salmonella* are suggested in inflammatory aneurysm.
- USG abdomen: It is the most frequent investigation used for screening and serial monitoring of AAA.

- CT angiography is the gold standard for evaluating AAAs. It defines the extent of AAA and relation to the visceral arteries.
- MR angiography also helps in the diagnosis.

Medical management

- Control of risk factors for rupture such as smoking cessation
- Exercise
- Statin therapy
- ACE inhibitors
- Antibiotics (it has been suspected that *C. pneumoniae* has a role in AAA development)
- NSAIDs (indomethacin inhibits the aneurismal growth)
- Immunosuppressants and antioxidants
- Control of blood pressure and treatment of COPD

Endovascular repair

Elective repair: For asymptomatic:

- Diameter is >5.5 cm for male or >5 cm for female and >4.5 cm with growth rate 0.5 cm/6 months.
- It may be open or laparoscopic.
- Endovascular repair with stent graft: Complication specific to endovascular repair is endoleak that is defined as failure to exclude aneurysmal sac fully from arterial blood flow.

Urgent repair is indicated in symptomatic AAA.[23]

136. Write a short note on celiac plexus block.

A Celiac plexus is located at T12–L1 behind the stomach and in front of crura of diaphragm and lies on the anterolateral surface of aorta. It includes sympathetic innervations from the splanchnic nerve (greater and lesser) and parasympathetic innervations from the vagus.

Indications

- Severe intractable pain secondary to malignancy of pancreas and upper GI malignancy
- Severe intractable pain of chronic pancreatitis

Three techniques

- Direct at the end of laparoscopy or laparotomy
- Percutaneous fluoroscopy guided
- EUS guided

Technique

- First, local anesthetic is injected and if pain relief is achieved, then it is repeated with neurolytic agent.
- Agents used: These are alcohol or phenol.

Side effects

- Orthostatic hypotension (most common)
- Diarrhea (common)
- Interscapular back pain
- Hiccups
- Pleurisy
- Hematuria
- Transient motor paralysis
- Paraplegia

137. List the risk factors for DVT.

 Family history is the single most important risk factor for DVT.

Other risk factors are as follows:

- Surgery (total hip replacement has the highest incidence followed by hip fracture and total knee replacement; general surgery, gynecology, and urosurgery are history of VTE)
- Advanced age
- Cancer and its treatment
- Oral contraceptive pills
- Pregnancy
- Postpartum period
- Age >40 years, history of VTE, bed rest >5 days, stroke, and MI
- Cardiac and respiratory failure
- IBD
- Nephritic syndrome
- Antiphospholipid antibody syndrome
- Factor V Leiden, protein C and protein S deficiency, prothrombin gene mutation, and antithrombin deficiency
- Major extremity trauma
- MPD
- Central venous catheterization
- Raloxifene

Pearls

- Inflow disease (aortoiliac occlusive disease) and outflow disease (femoropopliteal occlusive disease and runoff disease) constitute tibial peroneal occlusive disease.
- Butcher's thigh is an accidental injury to major vessels such as femoral artery and vein in thigh or groin.
- Acute arterial occlusion is characterized by the following: Pain, pallor, pulselessness, paralysis, paresthesia, and poikilothermia (6 Ps). Rutherford classification of acute lower limb ischemia:
  - *Class I*: Viable (no loss)
  - *Class II*
    - *Threatened (marginal)*: Sensory loss
    - *Threatened (immediate)*: Sensory with some motor loss
  - *Class III*: Irreversible paralysis
- The most common presentation is pain and the most common cause is atherosclerosis.
- The triad of intermittent claudication, impotence, and absent femoral pulse is associated with aortoiliac occlusion and is known as Leriche syndrome.
- In neurogenic claudication, cessation of activity will not relieve the pain immediately; it may take 30–60 minutes for symptomatic relief. Leaning forward straightens the lumbar lordosis and relieves the pain. It is due to spinal canal stenosis and also referred to as pseudoclaudication.
- Fogarty catheter is used for embolectomy.
- In addition to Buerger disease, lumbar sympathectomy is indicated in the following: Hyperhidrosis, acrocyanosis, causalgia, nonbypassable atherosclerotic occlusion or rest pain, and Raynaud disease.
- Effect of sympathectomy depends on smoking cessation. It provides short-term relief of pain and promotes ulcer healing.
- The most common complication of lumbar sympathectomy is neuralgia. Bilateral L1 ganglionectomy is associated with retrograde ejaculation and sterility.
- The presence of rest pain or ischemic skin lesions (ulcerations or gangrene) more than 2 weeks with ankle systolic pressure <50 mmHg or toe systolic pressure <30 mmHg is known as critical limb ischemia (TransAtlantic Inter-Society Consensus conference definition). ABPI <0.5 indicates critical limb ischemia.
- Arterial ulcer is located on the distal digits (in between toes) or lateral surface of ankle (around the malleoli) with punched-out appearance. It is painful and distal pulse is not palpable. Hanging the limb will relieve the pain in arterial insufficiency.
- The most common splanchnic artery aneurysm is splenic.
- FAA is focal dilatation more than 1.5 times of the adjacent artery. It may be true or false. False FAA is more common and is because of femoral artery catheterization. It may present as pulsatile groin mass or pressure effect on the surrounding structure. Duplex USG confirms the diagnosis. Yin–yang sign on color flow indicates pseudoaneurysm (equal filling of FAA with antegrade and retrograde swirling of blood flow).
- Traditionally true FAA >2.5 cm in size was considered an indication for repair. True FAA <3.5 cm is very low risk for rupture, so currently indication for repair is >3.5 cm for true FAA and >3 mm^3 for pseudoaneurysm. Open surgical repair is currently the standard of care.
- PAA is bilateral in 50–70% of cases. Symptomatic aneurysm, aneurysm >2 cm in diameter, and mural thrombus are indications for repair.
- Severe stenosis or high-grade occlusion of the first part of subclavian artery proximal to patent vertebral artery causes reverse flow to supply the arm. Stealing of blood from the posterior cerebral circulation down the vertebral artery supplies the arm. There is a feeling of light-headedness and syncope or presyncope often with visual symptoms (diplopia) on arm exercise. CT angiography confirms the diagnosis. Angioplasty or stenting of the lesion or bypass graft will establish the flow.

- For infrainguinal bypass or femoropopliteal bypass, the best graft is autogenous saphenous vein and Dacron graft is best suited for aortoiliac bypass.
- Seldinger technique is used for cannulation of vessels for angiography and angioplasty. Commonly used vessel for angiography and plasty is femoral vessels.
- The most commonly used vessel for arterial cannulation and monitoring is radial artery.
- Superficial venous thrombophlebitis, air travel >6 hours, and diabetes are associated with slightly increased risk of VTE.[19]
- Phlegmasia alba dolens: DVT with sparing of the collaterals leads to blanching, edema, and discomfort. There is some degree of venous return maintained due to sparing of collaterals.
- Phlegmasia cerulea dolens: DVT extending into collaterals leads to limb pain, swelling, and cyanosis.

HEAD AND NECK

138. What is ranula?

- It is a retention cyst of gland of Blandin and Nuhn. It looks like frog belly.
- It has two varieties:
  - Simple (on the floor of mouth)
  - Plunging (present as a neck mass)
- On examination:
  - Unilocular and smooth
  - Bluish discoloration
  - Transillumination: Positive
  - Plunging ranula is ballottable and cross-fluctuation positive.
- Treatment: It involves complete excision or marsupialization.

139. What is cystic hygroma? Write a brief note on cystic hygroma.

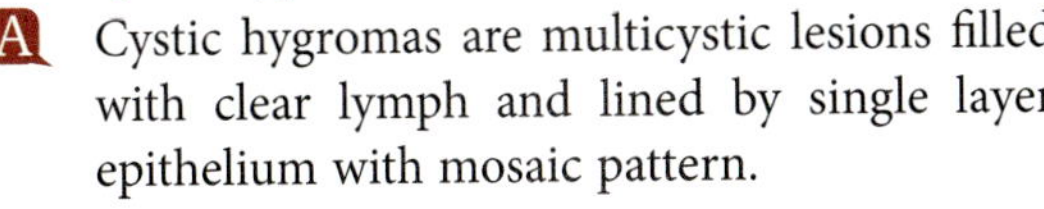

Cystic hygromas are multicystic lesions filled with clear lymph and lined by single layer epithelium with mosaic pattern.

Location

- Posterior neck (lymphatic jugular sac) is the most common location.
- Cheek, axilla, mediastinum, and groin are the other sites.

Clinical features

- Usual age of presentation: Neonate or early infancy. However, 50% may be present at birth.
- It is usually unilateral but may be bilateral, soft, and partially compressible. It increases in size when the child cries or coughs.
- It is brilliantly translucent.
- Prenatal USG and fetal MRI may sometime help in management at the time of delivery.
- Sometimes, it may be large enough to obstruct the labor.
- Large cyst may obstruct airway and require either aspiration or tracheostomy.

Complications

- Infection
- Hemorrhage

Treatment

- Excision is the treatment of choice.
- Injection of sclerosant may not be helpful as it is multicystic but helps in reducing the size of lesion (OK-432, Picibanil).

140. Write a short note on branchial cyst.

Origin

It develops from the vestigial remnant of second branchial cleft.

It is lined by squamous epithelium and contains thick, turbid, and cholesterol crystal-rich fluid.

Clinical features

- Age of presentation is usually the first two decades of life.
- Location: It is present at the anterior border of sternocleidomastoid at the junction of upper and middle third.
- It is a smooth, painless, slowly growing mass in lateral neck.
- It is fluctuant and may transilluminate.
- Cyst becomes infected and is tender at the time of inflammation.
- At the time of inflammation, ultrasound and FNAC differentiate it from tuberculous abscess.

Treatment

- Complete excision of the cyst and the tract is performed when the lesion is quiescent.

- Any infection and inflammation must be treated first.
- Hypoglossal, glossopharyngeal, and spinal accessory nerves (SAN) must be identified positively and preserved.

141. Write a short note on solitary thyroid nodule (STN).

A
- The most common cause of STN is colloid nodule followed by adenoma. Other causes of STN include simple cyst, multinodular goiter, Hashimoto thyroiditis, and malignancy.
- Solitary thyroid nodule is a palpable, painless, discrete swelling in the midline of the neck that moves with deglutition.
- Presence of pain indicates intrathyroidal bleeding or hemorrhage, thyroiditis, and/or malignancy.
- It presents with pressure symptoms such as dysphagia and dyspnea.
- Hoarseness of voice suggests involvement of recurrent laryngeal nerve.
- History
  - Proper history about onset, duration, and progress of the swelling, symptoms of hypothyroidism, hyperthyroidism, and malignancy should be inquired. History of pressure symptoms is also important.
  - Past history of radiation exposure as well as family or personal history of thyroid or other malignancy is important.
- In physical examination, gland is best palpated from behind with the neck in mild extension position. Important points to be examined are the following:
  - Thyroid: Size, symmetry, and consistency
  - Nodule: Size, location, consistency, and mobility
  - Lymph node: Size, location, and mobility
  - Presence of tracheal deviation and substernal or retrosternal extension

Investigations

- Serum TSH: Most patients are euthyroid. It is the initial investigation.
- Serum thyroglobulin: It is raised in metastatic thyroid cancer. It is useful in patients who have undergone total thyroidectomy for malignancy for follow-up.
- Serum calcitonin: It is useful in follow-up of medullary carcinoma of thyroid.
- The most important investigation in any case of thyroid swelling is *FNAC*, which is the investigation of choice too. A 23-gauge needle is used and the procedure can be performed with or without USG guidance.
- *USG*: It differentiates solid from cystic nodules, detects nonpalpable nodules and lymph nodes, and guides FNAC.
- *US elastography*: It detects tissue stiffness noninvasively; malignant nodule is hard and deformed less as compared to the surrounding thyroid tissue.
- *CT or MRI*: It is indicated in large, fixed, and retrosternal lesions.
- *Thyroid scan*: The only indication is follicular thyroid nodule on FNAC with suppressed TSH.

Management

Management of dominant or solitary thyroid nodule is divided into six categories according to Bethesda criteria:

- *Nondiagnostic (10–15%) (technical error, acellular, blood, clotting artifact, or cyst fluid)*: FNA repeated with USG guidance
- *Benign (70%)*
  - *Cystic*: Aspirate. If recurrence is present three times, perform surgery (thyroidectomy).
  - *Solid*: Colloid nodule. Observe for an increase in size (more than 50% increase in volume or pressure symptoms ± FNAB—thyroidectomy).
- *AUS (atypia of undetermined significance)/FLUS (follicular lesion of undetermined significance)*: FNAB repeated
- *Follicular neoplasm or suspicious for FN (assessment of malignancy on the basis of capsular and vascular invasion)*: Lobectomy followed by completion thyroidectomy if follicular cancer or follicular variant of papillary cancer on tissue diagnosis
- *Suspicious for malignancy*: Lobectomy or near-total or total thyroidectomy
- *Malignancy (5%)*: Near-total or total thyroidectomy

142. Describe in short about thyroid malignancy.

A Types of thyroid malignancy:

- Papillary (80%)
- Follicular (10%)
- Hurthle cell carcinoma (3%)
- Medullary carcinoma (5%)
- Anaplastic (1%)
- Lymphoma (<1%)
- Metastatic (common primary are RCC > breast > lung)

Papillary

- Thirty to 40 years of age
- Common in females (2:1)
- Predominant malignancy of thyroid in children and those exposed to external beam radiation
- Slow-growing midline neck swelling
- Lymph node metastasis common (lymphatic spread)
- Pressure symptoms such as dysphagia and dyspnea indicating advanced malignancy
- Distant metastases less common and lung the most common site for distant metastases
- Thyroid malignancy with best prognosis
- FNAC diagnostic
- Histopathology: Papillary projection, Orphan Annie eye nuclei, and psammoma body; multifocal
- Prognosis
  - AGES, MACIS, AMES, TNM, ATA (American Thyroid Association) and De Groot
    - AGES (age, histological grade, extrathyroidal invasion, size) (young patients with well-differentiated tumor without metastases and small-sized lesions have a good prognosis)
    - MACIS (metastases, age, completeness of resection, extrathyroidal invasion, size)
    - AMES (age, metastases, extrathyroidal extension, size) (age <50 and size < 5 cm provide a good prognosis)

Follicular carcinoma

- It occurs in females older than 50 years.
- The ratio of females to males is 3:1.
- There is painless midline neck swelling.
- History of rapid increase in size may be present.
- Pain may be due to hemorrhage within nodule.
- Large tumor in an older male is likely to be malignant.
- Preoperative diagnosis with FNAC is difficult unless distant metastases are present.
- The most common site of metastases is bone.
- Histopathology
  - Follicles ++, lumen does not contain colloid.
  - Capsular and vascular invasion are seen.

Hurthle cell cancer

- It is a subtype of follicular cancer.
- Hurthle cell tumor is more likely to be multifocal and bilateral, does not take up RAI, and is more likely to metastasize to lymph node as well as distant site.

Management of differentiating thyroid cancer (papillary, follicular, and Hurthle cell cancer; Tables 16.3 and 16.4)[24,25]

- Multifocal papillary microcarcinoma (<5 foci): Lobectomy and isthmectomy
- Multifocal papillary microcarcinoma (>5 foci): Total thyroidectomy
- In patient initially operated with lobectomy and pathology shows >5 foci: Completion thyroidectomy
- For thyroid cancer with lateral or central lymph node metastases: Therapeutic regional lymph node dissection
- For large tumor and tumor with high-risk features: Prophylactic central compartment lymph node dissection
- Postoperative radioiodine ablation indicated in patients with high-risk and intermediate-risk criteria

Table 16.3 American Thyroid Association Risk Stratification System[25]

Risk	Criteria
Low	Papillary thyroid cancer confined to thyroid
Intermediate	Regional metastases, extrathyroidal extension, aggressive histology, vascular invasion
High	Distant metastases and gross extrathyroidal extension

Table 16.4 American Thyroid Association and NCCN Guidelines[24,25]

Size	Extrathyroidal extension	Lymph node involvement	Surgery
<1 cm	No	No	Lobectomy
1–4 cm	No	No	Lobectomy or total thyroidectomy (contralateral lobe involvement, suspected future administration of radioiodine for follow-up)
>4 cm			Total thyroidectomy
Any size	Yes	No	Total thyroidectomy
Any size	No	Yes	Total thyroidectomy
Any size with history of radiation exposure in childhood			Total thyroidectomy

- T4 supplementation: Suppresses TSH and reduces growth stimulus for any residual thyroid tissue (for low risk maintain TSH between 0.1 and 0.5 mU/L and for high risk <0.1 milliunits/L)
- External beam radiation and chemotherapy for unresectable, recurrent, metastatic disease

Anaplastic

- It has a female preponderance, in seventh to eighth decades.
- There are rapid increases in long-standing painless swelling and it may become painful.
- Pressure symptoms are present.
- Cervical lymphadenopathy ++, distant metastases may be present.
- On FNAC: Giant and multinucleated cells are seen.
- It is the most aggressive thyroid cancer.
- Most of the patients do not survive beyond 6 months.
- CT, MRI, and/or PET-CT should be obtained to decide resectability.
- Treatment
  - Total thyroidectomy with node dissection is performed.
  - Invasion of local structure precludes resection (dysphagia, hoarseness of voice, and respiratory compromise).
  - Radiation should be given to patients with good performance status and no evidence of distant metastases.

Lymphoma

- There is painless neck swelling, may present as ARDS.
- It is B-cell–type NHL.
- Most lymphomas occur in the background of lymphocytic thyroiditis.
- It is suspected on FNAC but for immunohistological study either core or open biopsy is indicated.
- Treatment
  - Good prognosis being no cervical lymph node involvement
  - CHOP (cyclophosphamide, doxorubicin, vincristine, and prednisone) chemotherapy regimen
  - Highly sensitive to radiotherapy

143. Enumerate important features of medullary thyroid carcinoma (MTC).

- Arises from the parafollicular C cells of thyroid; C cells derived from ultimobranchial body and secrete calcitonin
- Mostly sporadic
- May be associated with MEN IIA and MEN IIB
- Fifty to 60 years of age; female:male, 1.5:1
- Neck mass
- Diarrhea
- Cervical lymphadenopathy
- Pressure symptoms such as dysphagia and dyspnea
- Distant metastases such as liver and bone (osteoblastic)

Diagnosis

- Increased serum calcitonin (>0.08 ng/mL) (CEA and calcitonin gene–related peptide may be positive)
- Amyloid stroma in FNAC

- Does not take up radioactive iodine as it is not TSH dependent

Treatment

- In all cases before surgery, pheochromocytoma must be excluded by measuring urinary catecholamine levels.
- No cervical lymph node involved: Total thyroidectomy + prophylactic central lymph node dissection (lymph node dissection is not indicated in small intrathyroidal lesion and preoperative serum calcitonin <20 pg/mL)
- If cervical node involvement is present: Total thyroidectomy plus bilateral central compartment dissection plus dissection of the involved lateral neck compartment(s). Calcitonin > 200 pg/mL indicates prophylactic dissection of uninvolved lateral neck.
- Prophylactic total thyroidectomy is indicated in patients with RET proto-oncogene mutation (familial).
- Prophylactic lobectomy is adequate for sporadic cases.

144. Describe in brief about retrosternal goiter.

- Retrosternal goiter is said to be present when more than 50% of thyroid tissue is below the thoracic inlet. It is usually discovered on routine X-ray chest and dyspnea is the most common presentation.
- It is common in short-necked individuals and males with strong pretracheal muscles.
- Pemberton sign: Retrosternal goiter may lead to compression over superior vena cava, leading to dilated veins over anterior chest wall. This may become more prominent when arm is raised above the head.
- Scabbard trachea: Flattening of trachea caused by compression. It is seen in any swelling that causes long-term tracheal compression such as thyroid cancer, laryngeal cancer, thyroiditis, and goiter.

Types

- *Substernal*: Part of nodule palpable in the neck
- *Plunging*: On increased intrathoracic pressure, thyroid gland forced in the neck
- *Pure intrathoracic*: Will not come in the neck when intrathoracic pressure increased

Treatment

Surgical removal through cervical incision (incision on the neck)

145. What is Plummer disease?

- Solitary thyroid nodule presenting as secondary thyrotoxicosis
- Single hyperfunctioning nodule
- Most nodules attaining size up to 3 cm
- RAI scan: Hot nodule (hot nodule: Increased activity within nodule than that within surrounding normal thyroid,) on scan in Plummer disease

Other nodules seen on scan are the following:
- *Warm nodule*: Same activity within nodule as that within surrounding normal thyroid
- *Cold nodule*: Activity within nodule less as compared to that within surrounding normal thyroid tissue (malignancy, post-FNAC, hemorrhage within colloid degeneration)

Treatment

- Smaller nodule: Antithyroid drugs
- Larger nodule: Higher dose of antithyroid drugs
- Lobectomy and isthmusectomy required by young patients with larger nodules

146. What is tubercle of Zuckerkandl and organ of Zuckerkandl?

- *Tubercle of Zuckerkandl*: It is a posterior extension of lateral lobe of thyroid gland near ligament of Berry. It is pointing toward the RLN nerve.
- *Organ of Zuckerkandl*: It is a small mass of chromaffin cells derived from neural crest located along the aorta, beginning just above the superior mesenteric artery and extending to the level of the aortic bifurcation. The highest concentration is seen at the origin of the inferior mesenteric artery. It is one of the common sites for extra-adrenal pheochromocytoma.

147. Describe eye signs in thyrotoxicosis.

Mild

Sympathetic overactivity leads to mild signs.

- *Stellwag sign*: First sign—Starring look with infrequent blinking and wide palpebral fissure
- *Von Graefe sign*: Lid lag

- *Dalrymple sign*: Lid retraction leading to visible upper sclera

Moderate

Joffroy sign: Absence of wrinkling of forehead (retro-orbital tissue accumulation)

Severe

Mobius sign: Inability to converge the eyeball (intraocular accumulation and paralysis of muscle)

Progressive eye signs

- Keratitis, chemosis, epiphora, opthalmoplegia, and orbital hemorrhage; papilledema and corneal ulcer are present in most severe cases.
- Severe and progressive ophthalmopathy is known as malignant exophthalmos and eye may be destroyed. Ophthalmopathy is because of antibody-mediated effects on ocular muscles.

Other clinical features of primary thyrotoxicosis

- *Signs*: Tachycardia, tremors, hot–moist palm, bruit, and agitation, hyperreflexia, systolic hypertension, and muscle weakness
- *Symptoms*: Weight loss in spite of good appetite, heat intolerance, nervousness, fatigue, perspiration, palpitation, and menstrual irregularity

148. Describe thyrotoxic crisis.

A
- It is an acute exacerbation of hyperthyroidism. It is mostly because of inadequate preparation in hyperthyroid patients for thyroid or other surgery.
- Other precipitating conditions are the following: Infection, acute medical illness, acute psychosis, parturition, trauma, high dose of iodine, and discontinuation of antithyroid medication.
- Clinical manifestations are the following: Restlessness, dehydration, hyperpyrexia, agitation, cardiac failure, and atrial fibrillation.
- Treatment: Treatment is directed against the precipitating causes, the systemic disturbance, the thyroid gland, and the peripheral effect of thyroid hormones. ICU admission is required (Table 16.5).[26]

149. A complete head and neck examination is normal except in level II cervical lymph node. But the fine needle aspiration cytology report suggests squamous cell carcinoma. How will you proceed?

A
- Carry out triple or pan endoscopy: Esophagoscopy, bronchoscopy, and nasal endoscopy.
- If this is also normal, carry out blind biopsy from the nasopharynx, tonsils, pyriform sinus, and base of the tongue.

150. In which conditions are Hurthle cells seen?

A
- Hashimoto thyroiditis
- Follicular carcinoma of thyroid
- Hurthle cell adenoma of thyroid

151. What is MEN?

A
- MEN stands for multiple endocrine neoplasia.
- Multiple endocrine neoplasia type I (MEN I): Wermer syndrome—involvement of parathyroid, pituitary, and pancreas (3 P's).

Table 16.5 Management of Thyrotoxic Crisis

Treatment directed against systemic disturbance	Treatment directed against thyroid gland	Treatment directed against continuing effect of thyroid hormone in periphery
• Cooling the patient with ice pack and acetaminophen • Supportive: Oxygen and vasopressors • IV fluid, glucose, and vitamins for dehydration and poor nutrition • Diuretic for cardiac failure • Sedation for restlessness • Digoxin for atrial fibrillation	Reduction of thyroid hormone secretion and production • *Inhibition of synthesis*: Propyl thiouracil and methimazole • *Inhibition of secretion*: Iodide and lithium carbonate	Amelioration of peripheral action of thyroid hormone • *Inhibition of extrathyroidal conversion of T4 to T3*: Propylthiouracil, propranolol • *Removal of T4 or T3 from serum*: Cholestyramine, hemodialysis, plasmapheresis, and hemoperfusion

- MEN II: MTC and pheochromocytoma
  - *Type A*: Hyperparathyroidism (Sipple syndrome)
  - *Type B*: Mucosal neuroma of tongue and marfanoid body habitus

152. How will you clinically diagnose thyroglossal cyst? What is its treatment?

A Clinical diagnosis

- Usual age of presentation is 15–30 years.
- Anterior midline swelling
- Most common site being subhyoid
- Movement with deglutition present (any thyroid swelling, pretracheal and paratracheal nodes, and subhyoid bursa also move with deglutition)
- Movement with protrusion of tongue present

Complications

Recurrent infection, fistula, and papillary carcinoma

Treatment

Sistrunk operation—en bloc cystectomy with removal of the central hyoid bone

153. A 45-year-old patient is operated for solitary thyroid nodule and in the ward he develops severe dyspnea. What is the treatment of choice?

A Open the stitch of operative site, because the likely cause is oozing of blood from vessels or thyroid bed producing hematoma and causing respiratory tract compression. Identify it and ligate and cauterize it.

154. In how many days does hypocalcemia develop usually following thyroid surgery?

A Within 2–5 days

155. Describe in brief about different types of thyroiditis.

A Acute thyroiditis

- Pain in the neck
- Dysphagia
- Fever
- Chills
- Usually follows URTI
- Cause: Streptococci and staphylococci
- Treatment: Antibiotics and surgical drainage; and thyroidectomy if persistent abscess or failure of open drainage

Subacute (granulomatous) (De Quervain) (giant cell) thyroiditis

- It occurs in association with HLA-B35.
- It usually follows upper respiratory tract infection.
- There is gradual or sudden appearance of pain in the region of thyroid gland with or without fever and typically pain radiates to the angle of jaw or ear of the affected side. Moving or turning of the head, coughing, and swallowing may aggravate the pain.
- ESR is markedly raised (>100 mm/h).
- Radioactive iodine uptake is decreased.
- Antithyroid antibodies are low with thyroid function tests such as T3, T4, and TSH value depending on the stage.
- Serum Tg level is high.
- It is self-limiting and has a classical progression: Hyperthyroid → euthyroid → hypothyroid → euthyroid.
- In mild cases, aspirin and other nonsteroidal anti-inflammatory drugs work to control the symptoms. For acute and painful cases, steroid is given daily 10–20 mg for 7 days and this is followed by gradual tapering.
- In case of thyroid failure (if TSH is not suppressed), thyroxine is given.

Hashimoto thyroiditis (chronic lymphocytic)

- It is the most common inflammatory condition of thyroid.
- It is the most common cause of hypothyroidism where iodine is sufficient.
- It is autoimmune.
- It is perimenopausal.
- It is associated with other autoimmune disorders; most commonly it is asymptomatic.
- Transient hyperthyroidism f/b inevitable and permanent hypothyroidism.
- There is thyroid swelling with or without pain. Swelling is moderate in size and firm in consistency, and pyramidal lobe may be palpable.
- Twenty percent of patients are having hypothyroidism and 5% may have hyperthyroidism (hashitoxicosis).
- Antimicrosomal (TPO), antithyroglobulin, and anti–TSH receptor antibodies are elevated.

- A rare but serious complication is lymphoma.
- Thyroid follicles are lined by Hurthle or Askanazy cells (pathognomonic).
- Raised TSH with thyroid autoantibodies confirms the diagnosis. In case of doubt, perform FNAC.
- Treatment
  - If thyroid function is normal and goiter is small with raised antibody titers, no treatment is given.
  - Thyroxine: Hypothyroidism and large symptomatic goiter may improve with hormone therapy.
  - Levothyroxine is indicated in patients with TSH level >10 milliunits/L and patients with TSH of 5–10 milliunits/L in the presence of goiter or anti-TPO antibody.
  - Steroid: It is used if goiter increases despite hormonal replacement.
  - In case of no improvement or pressure symptoms or increase in size of swelling, surgery is required.

Riedel thyroiditis (fibrosing)

- It is probably autoimmune. It is probably a collagen disease.
- The thyroid gland is hard and woody.
- Hypothyroidism is present.
- It may be associated with other fibrosing conditions of the body such as sclerosing cholangitis, fibrosing mediastinitis, retroperitoneal fibrosis, and periorbital and retro-orbital fibrosis.
- Thyroid glandular tissue is replaced by fibrous tissue.
- Diagnosis is confirmed by open thyroid biopsy as gland is fibrous and being extremely hard makes FNAC inadequate.
- Treatment
  - Isthmectomy to relieve pressure symptoms and to rule out malignancy
  - High-dose steroid, tamoxifen, and thyroxine
  - Mycophenolate mofetil, which attenuates the inflammatory process and leads to improvement

156. What is Pendred syndrome?

A It is due to defect in the sulfate transport protein on chromosome 7q and associated with sensory neural hearing loss with goiter.

157. What is carotid body tumor (paragangliomas)? Describe its clinical features, diagnosis, and management.

A

- Carotid body tumor is also known as chemodectoma or potato tumor.
- It is a nonchromaffin paraganglioma, occurs in the fifth decade, and is unilateral at the site of carotid bifurcation.
- It arises from branchiomeric paraganglia.
- It is more common at high altitude because of chronic hypoxia. It leads to carotid body hyperplasia.

Clinical features

- It is a painless, firm, rubbery, round, slowly growing, and pulsatile swelling. Bruit may be occasionally present.
- It moves laterally and medially (side to side) but not in cephalocaudal plane (Fontaine sign).

Investigations

- Duplex scanning of the carotid region is the investigation of choice.
- Carotid arteriogram: Lyre sign—splaying of external and internal carotid arteries
- MRI: 'Salt and pepper' appearance on T2-weighted image
- FNAC and biopsy contraindicated

Treatment

Except in old and unfit patients, treatment is excision of the tumor.

- *3-cm tumor*: Requires preoperative embolization
- *>5-cm tumor*: Requires concurrent carotid artery replacement

Complications of excision

- Cranial nerve injury (most common is superior laryngeal nerve)
- First bite syndrome: Pain at the beginning of mastication
- Bilateral removal associated with wide fluctuation in blood pressure due to baroreceptor failure

Pearls

- The metabolic effects of the thyroid hormones are because of free T3 and free T4 (0.3% and 0.03% of total circulating hormone).
- Parafollicular C cells secrete calcitonin.
- Dose of T4 is once daily while that of T3 is three times a day.
- Recombinant human TSH is used to maximize iodine uptake as an alternative to thyroid hormone withdrawal.
- Indications for CT scan in thyroid
  - Retrosternal goiter, malignancy of thyroid, and rarely in case of recurrent thyroid swelling
- ^{123}I (half-life 12–14 hours) and 131 I (half-life 8–10 days) are used for radioisotope scanning.
- ^{123}I is used to screen lingual thyroid and other thyroid swellings while 131I is used to detect and treat patients with differentiated thyroid malignancy for metastases.
- Cold nodules are more likely to be malignant as compared to warm or hot nodules (20% vs. <5%).
- PET CT is used to detect metastases in patients with thyroid cancer selectively and it is also of value in case of Tg-positive and radioactive iodine-negative tumor.
- For toxic multinodular goiter, the best treatment is surgery, either near-total or total thyroidectomy.
- For treatment of small toxic adenoma, antithyroid drugs or radioactive iodine is effective, while for treatment of large toxic adenoma, surgery (lobectomy and isthmectomy) is required.
- Diffuse toxic goiter: Antithyroid drugs, radioiodine, and surgery are required. Most patients respond well to initial antithyroid drugs with radioiodine for relapse. Pregnancy, large goiter, progressive eye signs, and the patient's refusal for radioiodine are indications for surgery.
- Recurrent thyrotoxicosis after surgery: Radioiodine is the choice. Antithyorid drugs may be used in patients who want to have children.
- Jod–Basedow effect is iodine-induced hyperthyroidism and Wolff–Chaikoff effect is iodine-induced hypothyroidism.
- Cardiovascular manifestation of thyrotoxicosis: Sinus tachycardia is most common even during sleep. Other manifestations are loud first heart sound, aortic systolic murmur and Means–Lerman scratch (systolic scratch), orthopnea, exercise intolerance, hyperdynamic precordium, and third heart sound. The stages of development of
- thyrotoxic arrhythmias of are multiple extrasystoles, paroxysmal atrial tachycardia, paroxysmal atrial fibrillation, and persistent atrial fibrillation not responding to digoxin.
- Severe muscular weakness (myopathy), pretibial myxedema (thyroid dermopathy), subperiosteal bone formation and swelling of metacarpals (thyroid acropachy), and eye signs are also seen in thyrotoxicosis.
- In secondary thyrotoxicosis, CVS manifestations are common as compared to eye signs. Secondary thyrotoxicosis is more common in old age and sympathetic activity affects heart more while primary thyrotoxicosis is a disease of the young.
- Secondary thyrotoxicosis develops from either MNG or adenoma. Manifestations are the following: Edema feet, dyspnea, orthopnea, and presence of only lid lag and lid retraction.
- Respiratory manifestations in thyrotoxicosis: These include dyspnea, respiratory muscle weakness, decreased vital capacity, increased ventilation, oxygen uptake, and carbon dioxide production.
- Neurological manifestations in thyrotoxicosis: These include hyperactivity, emotional lability, anxiety, persistent fine tremor, distractibility, and rarely chorea.
- Dancing carotid may be seen in thyrotoxicosis and aortic regurgitation.
- Ultrasensitive TSH assay is the most sensitive investigation to diagnose hyperthyroidism or hypothyroidism. It is also useful to monitor response of treatment.

- Anti-TPO antibodies are the most accurate test to determine diagnosis of Hashimoto thyroiditis.
- Serum thyroglobulin is useful for differentiating thyroid cancer and destructive thyroiditis.

PARATHYROID GLAND

158. Mention in short about anatomy of parathyroid gland and its functions.

- There are four parathyroid glands. Supernumerary glands can also be seen. As many as eight glands have been reported.
- They are small, 2–5 mm.
- There are two superior and two inferior glands.
- Superior glands are dorsal to the RLN at the level of cricoid cartilage.
- Inferior glands are ventral to the RLN.
- They are derived from III and IV branchial pouches.
- Superior glands are derived from IV branchial pouch and inferior glands are derived from III branchial pouch
- There are two types of cells: Chief cells (generate parathyroid hormone) and oxyphil cells (no known function).
- They may be seen in ectopic location.
- Inferior gland has a higher propensity for ectopic location. The most common location for superior gland is superior mediastinum and that for inferior gland is thymus.

Blood supply

All four glands are supplied by inferior thyroid artery.

Functions of parathyroid

- Maintains calcium homeostasis
- Increases osteoclast and blast activity
- Increases GI absorption and decreases renal absorption of calcium
- Increases hydroxylation of 25-hydroxy vitamin D in kidney

159. Mention about types of hyperparathyroidism (HPT), and its investigation and treatment.

Primary

- In primary hyperparathyroidism, the primary abnormality is parathyroid tissue leading to inappropriate production of PTH.
- The common cause of primary HPT is adenoma (90%); other causes are hyperplasia and carcinoma.
- The pentads of symptoms are painful bones, kidney stones, abdominal groans, psychic moans, and fatigue overtones in primary hyperparathyroidism.
- Renal manifestations are as follows: Renal stone, hypercalciuria, nephrocalcinosis, and chronic renal failure.
- Bone manifestations are as follows: Salt and pepper appearance of skull (osteitis fibrosa cystica) and brown tumor of long bones.
- Neurological changes are as follows: Confusion and mental status changes.

Secondary

- It is due to increase in level of PTH in response to low calcium level.
- Causes are as follows: Chronic renal failure, hungry bone syndrome, aluminum toxicity, malabsorption syndrome, and vitamin D–deficient rickets.
- Hyperphosphatemia impairs the renal 1-α-hydroxylase, decreases 1,25(OH)2D production, and directly stimulates synthesis and secretion of PTH from parathyroid. FGF23 (fibroblast growth factor 23) plays an important role in hyperphosphatemia by impairing Na^+-dependent phosphate transport in both intestinal and renal brush border membranes.

Tertiary

- It is due to autonomously elevated PTH secondary to long-standing secondary hyperparathyroidism.
- Chronic stimulation in sHPT leads to hypertrophy of parathyroid gland and in some patients it becomes resistant to normal feedback mechanism and autonomously produces PTH.
- End-stage renal disease requires hemodialysis or later on renal transplantation.

Investigations

- Biochemical abnormality in primary HPT
  - The following are increased: Calcium, intact PTH, chloride, and chloride:phosphate ratio.

  - Uric acid, alkaline phosphatase, 1,25-dihydroxyvitamin D_3, and urinary calcium may be normal or increased.
  - Magnesium and phosphate may be decreased.
- Localization studies
  - USG and sestamibi scan (88%) sensitive
  - Four dimensional CT(4D-CT): CT is a three-dimension technique. The fourth dimension is number of changes over time in enhancement after IV contrast administration.

Management

- Primary
  - Symptomatic hyperparathyroidism patients benefit from parathyroidectomy while management of asymptomatic primary hyperparathyroidism is controversial.
  - NIH consensus conference (2009) guidelines for parathyroidectomy in asymptomatic primary HPT:
    - Serum calcium >1 mg/dL above the upper normal limit
    - Bone mineral density (BMD) measured at any three sites (lumbar, spine, and radius) being 2.5SD below for those who are gender- and race-matched but not age-matched controls
    - Creatinine clearance <60 cm^3/min
    - Age <50 years
    - In those in whom long-term medical surveillance not possible or desirable
  - Medical management: It is indicated for those who do not meet the criteria for surgery, are not fit for surgery, or refuse surgery.
    - Adequate hydration
    - Bisphosphonates
    - Raloxifene
    - Cinacalcet hydrochloride
    - Percutaneous ethanol ablation
- Secondary
  - SHPT is not a surgical problem.
    - Treatment of the cause
    - Vitamin D deficiency: Vitamin D supplementation
    - Management of CKD
    - Cinacalcet
  - Indications of parathyroidectomy in SHPT
    - Patients' wish
    - Medical observation not possible
    - Calcium phosphorus products >70 mg^2/dL^2
    - Failed optimum medical management (PTH >800 pg/mL)
    - Severe symptomatic SHPT: Severe pruritis, pathological bone fracture, musculoskeletal pain, calciphylaxis, and severe vascular calcification
- Tertiary
  - THPT is primarily a surgical problem.
  - Severe hypercalcemia, symptomatic hyperparathyroidism, and high risk for fracture require surgery.

160. When should parathyroid carcinoma be suspected? Give an account of its management.

A *HRPT2* (now known as *CDC73*) gene mutation leading to inactivation of parafibromin plays an important role in pathogenesis.

When to suspect?

- Severe hypercalcemia >14 mg/dL
- Raised PTH >5 times normal
- Severe symptoms
- Glands more likely to be palpable than their benign counterparts

The hallmark of carcinoma is invasiveness. FNAC should be performed. Frozen section is unreliable.

Kidney stones are seen in more than 60% of patients and bone diseases in 90% of patients. Thirty percent of patients have nodal metastases on presentation.

Treatment

- En bloc resection of parathyroid and thyroid lobectomy with overlying musculature and node dissection are performed when indicated.
- Adjuvant or palliative radiation may be indicated.
- For disseminated disease, management of hypercalcemia includes rehydration, bisphosphonates, cinacalcet, calcitonin, and glucocorticoids.

- Most recently, antiparathyroid hormone immunotherapy is found to be useful in case of refractory hypercalcemia secondary to parathyroid cancer with pulmonary metastases.
- Persistent hypercalcemia following surgery is a poor prognostic indicator.
- Recurrent hypercalcemia is a good marker for local recurrence or metastases.

Pearls

- Complications of parathyroid surgery are the following:
  - Persistent (failure of calcium and PTH to normalize in initial 6 months of surgery) or recurrent hyperparathyroidism (recurrence of hypercalcemia after 6 months)
  - Hypocalcemia
  - Hypoparathyroidism
  - Recurrent laryngeal nerve injury: Temporary or permanent
  - Bleeding
  - Infections
- Persistent hyperparathyroidism is because of either missed adenoma or ectopic glands.
- Recurrent hyperparathyroidism is because of missed pathology, hyperplasia in autotransplanted tissue, parathyromatosis, and development of new adenoma.
- Acute hypoparathyroidism is because of removal, trauma, or devascularization of parathyroid gland at the time of surgery and may present as circumoral tingling or paresthesia, digital numbness, carpopedal spasm and cardiac arrhythmia, seizure, laryngospasm, bronchospasm, Chvostek sign, Trousseau sign, and prolonged QT interval.
- High-frequency ultrasound is the first investigation to identify enlarged parathyroid gland. Technetium-99m (^{99m}Tc)–labeled sestamibi isotope scan identifies 75% of abnormal glands. The area must include mediastinum to locate ectopic parathyroid gland.
- CT, PET, and MRI are not warranted prior to first-time parathyroid surgery.
- Advanced malignancy is the most common cause of hypercalcemia.
- Urgent near-total parathyroidectomy is indicated in neonatal hyperparathyroidism.
- Hypercalcemic crisis is a life-threatening condition present as nausea, vomiting, lethargy, muscle weakness, arrhythmia, confusion, decreased level of consciousness, and acute renal failure. Serum calcium level is usually above 14.0 mg/dL. The most common cause is malignancy-induced hypercalcemia. Other causes are the following: PHPT, parathyroid malignancy, and granulomatous diseases. It requires admission in ICU, airway management, cardiac monitoring, rehydration, and frusemide once urine output >100 mL/h. Other drugs such as bisphosphonates, calcitonin, glucocorticoids, plicamycin, and cinacalcet can be used.
- Hemodialysis may be of benefit in severe and refractory hypercalcemia. Parathyroidectomy is done in PHPT once the patient is adequately resuscitated, electrolyte is corrected, and localization study is complete.
- Failure of PTH level to fall by at least 50% within 10 minutes after excision of adenoma should prompt bilateral neck exploration.
- Vitamin D is metabolized in the liver to 25-hydroxy vitamin D and further hydroxylation in liver produces 1,25-dihydroxyvitamin D in kidney, which is the most metabolically active vitamin D. The main function is absorption of calcium and phosphate from gut and resorption of calcium from bone.
- Calcitonin is an antihypercalcemic hormone.
- Target organs of PTH are the following: Bone, kidney, and gut.
- Thiazide diuretic may be used to unmask PHPT in case of borderline hypercalcemia as it causes hypercalcemia by decreasing renal clearance of calcium.

ADRENAL GLAND

161. Write in short about anatomy of adrenal gland.

- It is located at the upper pole of kidney and is a paired retroperitoneal organ.
- Weight is approximately 4 g.
- Size is 5 × 3 × 1 cm.
- It has an outer cortex (90%) and an inner medulla (10%).
- Cortex has three zones:
  1. *Zona glomerulosa*: Aldosterone secretion—stimulated by renin–angiotensin system and raised serum potassium
  2. *Zona fasciculata*: Cortisol—stimulated by ACTH from anterior pituitary
  3. *Zona reticularis*: Secretes adrenal androgen
- Medulla produces catecholamines such as adrenaline and noradrenalin.
- Blood supply: This is through arteries—superior adrenal branch of inferior phrenic artery, middle adrenal branch from aorta, and inferior adrenal branch from renal artery.
- Venous drainage
  - Right adrenal vein drains into the vena cava.
  - Left adrenal vein drains into the left renal vein.

162. Mention in detail about pheochromocytoma.

- It arises from chromaffin cells of adrenal medulla.
- Extra-adrenal sites are as follows: Organ of Zuckerkandl, hilum of the liver and kidney, paravertebral ganglia, posterior mediastinum, and urinary bladder.
- Classical symptom triad is the following: Headache, sweating, and palpitation. In the presence of hypertension, it is highly sensitive and specific.
- Hypertension is the most common feature.
- Rule of 10 is as follows:
  - Ten percent extra-adrenal
  - Ten percent bilateral
  - Ten percent children
  - Ten percent familial
  - Ten percent malignant
  - Ten percent recurring after surgical removal
  - Ten percent multiple
  - Ten percent benign sporadic
  - Ten percent asymptomatic

It may be suspected in the following:

- Patients with severe hypertension
- Patients with resistant hypertension
- Hypertensive pediatric patients
- Patients with hypertension with adrenergic spells such as headache, anxiety, pallor, diaphoresis, tachycardia, and palpitation
- Hypertension in patients younger than 20 years of age
- Patients with a family history of pheochromocytoma
- Patients with multiple endocrine neoplasia types 2A and 2B, and any hypertensive patient with MTC
- Patients with pressor response during surgery or anesthesia
- Patients with a history of GIST or pulmonary chondromas (Carney triad)

Diagnosis

- Plasma fractionated metanephrines
- Measurement of catecholamines and fractionated metanephrines in 24-hour urine collection
- CT scanning being the imaging test of choice
- T2-weighted MRI also useful
- Functional imaging with ^{123}I-metaiodobenzylguanidine (MIBG) and is very specific for both extra- and intra-adrenalin pheochromocytoma

Treatment

- Laparoscopic adrenalectomy is helpful.
- Preoperatively hypertension is controlled with phenoxybenzamine (α-blocker) (10 mg BD). Dose may be as high as 90 mg/day. Patients with tachycardia or dysrhythmias may be treated with beta-blockers such as atenolol or metoprolol. Beta-blockers should never be given until successful α-blockade has been achieved. Unopposed α-stimulation may lead to hypertensive crisis.
- Intraoperative exacerbation of hypertension is controlled with esmolol or sodium nitroprusside.

163. Write a short note on adrenal incidentaloma.

A
- Nonfunctioning cortical adenoma is the most common incidentaloma.
- The first priority is to determine whether mass is functional or nonfunctional.
- Hyperaldosteronism
  - Overproduction of aldosterone from zona glomerulosa. Conn syndrome is when it is due to adrenal adenoma. It should be considered in patients with hypertension and hypokalemia. Plasma aldosterone to renin ratio >20 is diagnostic of hyperaldosteronism.
- Hypercortisolism
  - Hypercortisolism from any cause is known as Cushing syndrome.
  - Overproduction of cortisol is from zona fasciculate.
  - Twenty-four-hour urinary cortisol (>100 µg) and low-dose overnight dexamethasone test (plasma cortisol at 8.00 a.m. >5 µg) are useful for diagnosis.
- Pheochromocytoma
  - Detailed in the above-mentioned question

Treatment

- <4-cm nonfunctioning incidentaloma and benign appearing on imaging: Observation
- Functioning lesion, lesion more than 5 cm, and atypical appearance on imaging: Adrenalectomy

Pearls

- Malignant pheochromocytoma refers to tumor >5 cm and extra-adrenal tumor, and patients harboring succinate dehydrogenase B mutation are likely to have malignant pheochromocytoma. Malignant pheochromocytoma secretes dopamine and homovanillic acid. Malignancy is usually diagnosed by invasion of surrounding structure and distant metastases. The most common site of metastases is bone. Treatment is resection followed by chemotherapy. Tyrosine kinase inhibitors such as α-methyl-*para*-tyrosine may be helpful to control the symptoms. Chemotherapy includes cyclophosphamide, vincristine, doxorubicin, and dacarbazine. High-dose ^{131}I-MIBG is used to treat metastatic disease. Radiotherapy is done for palliation of bone metastases.
- Factors precipitating crisis in pheochromocytoma are the following: Surgery, exercise, straining, sexual intercourse, and drugs (tricyclic antidepressant, IV contrast, unopposed B blocker, anesthetics, opiates, glucagon, metoclopramide, and glucagon).
- Costovertebral angle pain and tenderness seen in acute adrenal insufficiency is termed Rogoff sign.
- In bilateral adrenalectomy, steroid is given after excision of both adrenal glands.
- The most common cause of Cushing syndrome is iatrogenic (steroid administration).
- The most common endogenous cause is bilateral adrenal hyperplasia.
- The most common cause of Addison disease in India is tuberculosis.
- The most common cause of primary adrenal insufficiency worldwide is autoimmunity.
- Common physical signs for adrenal insufficiency are hypotension and hyperpigmentation while laboratory findings are hyponatremia and hyperkalemia.
- Bilateral adrenal infarction associated with meningococcal sepsis is known as the Waterhouse–Friderichsen syndrome.
- Chronic adrenal insufficiency is associated with hyperpigmentation of skin and oral mucosa because of increased level of proopiomelanocortin level.
- A homogenous mass with low attenuation value (<10 HU) prior to contrast administration is likely to have benign adenoma.
- Chemical synergies between ACTH and melanocyte-stimulating hormone produce hyperpigmentation due to continued ACTH production at high level after failed pituitary surgery for adenoma and bilateral adrenalectomy (Nelson syndrome).

SALIVARY GLAND

164. Describe in brief anatomy of salivary gland.

A

- Major salivary glands are the following: Parotid, submandibular, and sublingual. All major salivary glands are two in number.
- Minor salivary glands are 450 in number and found in lips, cheeks, retromolar area, palate, and floor of mouth. The highest density is found within palate.
- Parotid gland is a serous gland and its duct known as Stensen duct that opens in mucosa in front of the upper second molar. Eighty-five percent of the salivary gland tumors arise from the parotid; most of them are benign and the most common is pleomorphic adenoma. Parotid gland lies on the carotid sheath and the XI and XII nerves, and extends forward over the masseter muscle. It is bounded superiorly by zygomatic arch, inferiorly by SCM, anteriorly by masseter muscle, and posteriorly by external auditory canal and the mastoid process.
- Important structures in relation to parotid gland are the following: Branches of facial nerve, terminal branch of external carotid artery, retromandibular vein, and intraparotid lymph node.
- Submandibular gland is a mixed gland (serous + mucous). Its duct is known as Wharton duct that opens in the floor of the mouth just lateral to the frenulum. Fifty percent of tumors arising within submandibular gland are benign. Important structures in relation to gland are the following: anterior facial vein, facial artery, and three nerves (marginal mandibular, hypoglossal, and lingual).
- Sublingual and minor salivary glands: They are mucous glands and duct known as Rivinus duct and Bartholin ducts. Fifty percent of tumors of the sublingual gland are malignant while 75% of the minor salivary gland tumors are malignant.
- The most common malignant tumor is mucoepidermoid carcinoma.

165. What is Frey syndrome? Describe its diagnosis, prevention, and treatment.

Frey syndrome is a food-related syndrome. There is redness and sweating on the cheek area adjacent to the ear when a person eats, sees, or even thinks about certain kinds of food that produce strong salivation. It is due to damage to the auriculotemporal nerve. It is also known as auriculotemporal syndrome or gustatory sweating. Secretory parasympathetic fibers of the parotid gland are thought to communicate with sympathetic fibers of sweat gland and blood vessels of the skin overlying parotid region. This leads to sweating and flushing of the skin over that region.

Diagnosis

- Minor's starch–iodine test: Apply starch and iodine over parotid region; it turns blue on exposure to sweat.
- Stress thermography test shows cold spot on the same side.

Prevention

Application of barrier between skin and parotid bed

- Superficial musculoaponeurotic flap
- Temporoparietofacial flap
- Artificial membrane

Treatment

- Antiperspirant (aluminum chloride)
- Botulinum toxin local injection (most effective and can be performed on OPD bases)
- Tympanic neurectomy

166. Describe in brief about complications of parotid surgery.

- *Complications of parotid surgery*
  - Hemorrhage

> Other causes of salivary fistula are the following—spontaneous rupture of parotid abscess, inadvertent incision of abscess, and penetrating injury; sialography is the investigation and the treatment is Newman and Seabrook operation.

  - Salivary fistula (sialocele): After parotid surgery, mostly it is due to gland disruption rather than duct and maintaining close suction drainage for 5–7 days will help to facilitate adhesion between parotid parenchyma and skin flap. Repeated aspiration and compression dressing for 2 weeks is done. Anticholinergic drugs may also be administered. In refractory cases, the following are helpful: low-dose radiation, completion parotidectomy, botulinum injection, and tympanic neurectomy.

- Facial nerve injury
- Greater auricular nerve damage
- Cosmetic

167. What is the contraindication for sialography? Why is infection more common in parotid and stone more common in submandibular gland?

A
- Sialography is contraindicated in acute sialadenitis and contrast allergy.
- Infection is more common in parotid gland due to straight course of duct and less viscid secretion; because of the same reason, stone formation is less as compared to that in submandibular gland.

Indications for sialography are the following: Salivary duct stone and chronic sialadenitis.

168. Describe briefly the pathology, diagnosis, and treatment of pleomorphic adenoma.

A
- It is the most common salivary gland tumor.
- The most common site is tail of parotid gland.
- It is also known as mixed parotid tumor (benign).

Pathology

It contains two types of cells—epithelial cells and myoepithelial cells.

- Pseudopodia are present that extend beyond the central tumor (high possibility of recurrence).
- Hemorrhage, necrosis, and calcification are occasionally present.

Clinical features

- It occurs at around 40 years of age.
- Sex: There is slight preponderance of females.
- It is a painless, slow-growing tumor most commonly seen in the parotid, but can also occur in submandibular and minor salivary gland.
- It is located below, posterior and superior to the angle of mandible.
- Three to 5% of patients may undergo malignant change, known as carcinoma ex pleomorphic adenoma, which is firm in consistency and has well-demarcated edges.
- It is not fixed to the underlying tissue or overlying skin.
- There is no lymphadenopathy and no facial nerve involvement.

Rapid tumor growth, metastases to cervical nodes, deep fixation such as fixation to mastoid tip, and facial nerve weakness and pain are strongly suggestive of malignant transformation.

Diagnosis

- FNAC
- Spiral CT scan and MRI
  - MRI is the most sensitive study to determine the exact relationship of the mass with facial nerve and depicts better soft-tissue anatomy. It is also helpful in distinguishing inflammatory from neoplastic condition as well as may better discern an inferior tail of parotid mass from upper cervical nodes.
  - CT is superior for evaluation of bony structure.
- PET scan (in some cases it may help in evaluation of suspected recurrent parotid cancer, lymph node metastases, and distant metastases)

Treatment

Superficial parotidectomy (Patey's operation) is used to treat pleomorphic adenoma.

169. What is Warthin tumor? Describe its clinical features and treatment.

A It is a benign parotid tumor. It is also known as papillary cystadenoma lymphomatosum and adenolymphoma.

Clinical features

- Age: >60 years
- Males > females
- More common in cigarette smokers
- Ten percent bilateral
- Soft to firm in consistency

- Located slightly below the location of pleomorphic adenoma
- Never undergoes malignant changes
- Papillary projections with tall columnar cells present
- Hot spot on Tc scan

Treatment

Superficial parotidectomy is done.

170. Which parotid tumor spreads through neural sheath?

A Adenoid cystic carcinoma of parotid

- Adenoid cystic carcinoma has skip metastases in the nerve.
- The rate of treatment failure is high because of skip metastases.
- Local recurrence is high.
- There is postoperative radiation in high-risk patients.

171. What are the indications for postoperative radiation in salivary gland tumor?

A The indications are high-grade histology, positive or close surgical margin, perineural invasion, regional metastases, large primary tumor, preoperative facial nerve dysfunction, direct invasion of regional structures, cervical lymphadenopathy, and presence of extraglandular disease.

172. What are the causes of bilateral enlargement of parotid gland?

A
- Alcohol
- Amyloidosis
- Acromegaly
- Cirrhosis
- Chronic pancreatitis
- Diabetes mellitus
- Sjögren syndrome
- Sarcoidosis
- Viral infections such as HIV cytomegalovirus and mumps

Pearls

- Characteristics of parotid swelling are the following: Below, behind, and slightly in front of the ear lobule in the region of parotid, ear lobule pushed upwards, curtain sign (swelling cannot be moved above zygomatic bone), obliteration of retromandibular furrow, and is superficial to the masseter.
- Faciovenous plane of Patey: This plane contains retromandibular vein and posterior facial vein. Facial nerve lies superficial to this plane and external carotid artery divides into superficial temporal artery and maxillary artery is deep to this plane.
- Stafne bone cyst is the most common ectopic salivary tissue and does not require any treatment. It is found at the angle of mandible due to bony invasion of the juxtaposed submandibular gland.
- Snowstorm appearance is characteristic of recurrent parotitis in children. It responds well to a short course of antibiotic.
- Chronic parotitis in children is classical of HIV.
- Major landmarks of facial nerve are the following: 1 cm deep and below the tip of the inferior portion of cartilaginous canal (Conley point), inferomedial to the tragal point, upper border of the posterior belly of digastrics, and lateral to the styloid process; the stylomastoid artery lies immediately lateral to the nerve.
- If facial nerve is involved in the tumor, excision is performed with nerve grafts, either auriculotemporal or sural nerve.
- The pleomorphic adenoma contains epithelial cells, myoepithelial cells, mucoid material, and cartilage; hence, it is also known as mixed parotid tumor.
- Malignant potential varies for the different salivary glands:
  - *Parotid*: 10–20% malignant
  - *Submandibular*: 50%
  - *Sublingual*: 85%
  - *Minor salivary gland*: 90%
- The most common neoplasm of salivary gland is pleomorphic adenoma; the most common neoplasm of salivary gland in children is hemangioma.
- The most common malignant tumor of salivary gland is mucoepidermoid carcinoma and the most common malignant tumor of minor salivary gland is adenoid cystic carcinoma (common site is hard palate).

- Acinic cell carcinoma is a low-grade malignancy mostly affecting women and almost exclusively seen in parotid gland. It may involve the regional nodes and treatment is radical excision.
- Ackerman tumor is a variant of well-differentiated squamous cell carcinoma that may develop in mucosal surface of upper aerodigestive tract. It has a multifocal warty appearance and surgery is the mainstay of treatment.
- Submandibular salivary gland duct (Wharton duct) has a long, curved, and upward course and secretion of submandibular gland is highly viscid than that of parotid gland, which makes it more vulnerable for stone formation. Eighty percent of the stones are radiopaque. Pain and swelling in submandibular region aggravated by food or sucking lemon is associated with duct stone. If the stone is in the duct in the floor of mouth distal to the lingual nerve, longitudinal incision over the duct and removal of stone are done. If the stone is distal to the lingual nerve, submandibular gland excision, removal of stone, and closure of duct under vision are done.
- *S. aureus* and *Streptococcus viridans* are the two most common organisms responsible for bacterial parotitis. Fluid, analgesic, and antibiotics are the main treatment. If it becomes fluctuant, aspiration is performed. If incision is required, it should be short and low.

TRAUMA

173. What is triage?

A Triage allocation of the victims is done on the basis of their severity of injury, possibility of survival, and urgency of treatment.

- *Black (expectant is hopeless, dead)*: Pulseless, no breathing
- *Red color (immediate)*: Critical patients (severe facial trauma, tension pneumothorax, flail chest, etc.)
- *Yellow (delayed)*: Serious, not life threatening (compound fracture, pelvic fracture, degloving injury, and ruptured abdominal viscus)
- *Green (minimal)*: Ambulatory patients (minor laceration, sprain, and simple fracture)

174. Describe metabolic response in patients with injury.

A Changes in plasma

- Increased
  - ACTH and GH
  - Cortisol and adrenalin
  - Glucagon
  - Aldosterone
  - Vasopressin
  - Renin–angiotensin
  - IL-1, IL-6, IL-8, and TNF-α
- Decreased
  - Insulin
  - IGF-1
  - T3
  - Testosterone

Changes in body metabolism

Increased

- Adipocyte
- Lipolysis
- Hepatic gluconeogenesis
- Skeletal muscle and protein degradation
- Hepatic acute phase protein synthesis (positive reactant CRP ↑ and negative reactant albumin ↓)

Phases in trauma

- *Catabolism*: Is associated with lipolysis, proteolysis hyperglycemia, and wound healing due to stress hormone such as cortisol, catecholamine, and glucagon and volume control hormone aldosterone, ADH, and rennin–angiotensin
- *Early anabolic phase*: Gain in muscle strength (positive nitrogen balance)
- *Late anabolic phase*: Gain in weight (positive caloric balance)

175. Describe in short about initial management of trauma. Also give a short account of trauma scoring system.

A Primary survey for trauma

- *Mnemonic for primary survey*: It is ABCDE.

- *Airway and cervical spine protection*: Look for airway obstruction and injury. Ask the patients to speak. Ability to speak indicates patent airway. If the patient is not able to speak, suspect either neurological injury or airway trauma. Abnormal breathing, tachypnea, and severe facial trauma may need special attention for airway. Suctioning helps patients in clearing airway. In case of unstable patients, establish airway by endotracheal intubation; other options are the following: Oropharyngeal airway, LMA, cricothyroidotomy, or tracheostomy. Until proved, all patients are assumed to have cervical spine injury and cervical spine protection with hard collar and maintenance of the log roll technique for all movements of the patients is considered.
- *Breathing*: Physical examination and pulse oximetry. Supplemental oxygen and ventilation are provided. Following life-threatening conditions should be identified immediately:
  - Tension pneumothorax: Respiratory distress along with hypotension, deviation of the trachea, decreased breath sound, cardiovascular compromise, and surgical emphysema signify tension pneumothorax. Needle decompression with a wide-bore needle in either second intercostal space at the midclavicular line or fifth intercostal space at the anterior axillary line (according to recent study, this is preferred) is performed. Tube thoracostomy before X-ray is advised.
  - Massive hemithorax: Tube thoracostomy is performed.
  - Pulmonary contusion: Mechanical ventilation is performed.
  - Open pneumothorax: Closure of the wound and tube thoracostomy to remote site is performed.
  - Flail chest: Tube thoracostomy and pain management is performed. If required, mechanical ventilation is done.
- *Circulation*: After airway and breathing, the next priority is the circulation. Examine the patients for signs of shock (tachycardia, tachypnea, hypotension, weak pulse, cool extremities, diaphoresis, and decreased urine output). Four life-threatening conditions during assessment of circulation include massive hemithorax, massive hemoperitoneum, cardiac tamponade, and mechanically unstable pelvic fracture.
  - Establish two large-bore IV lines; infuse 1–2 L crystalloid and watch for response.
  - Assess for the site of blood loss. Main sites are the following: Long bone fracture, pelvic fracture, abdomen, and chest.
    - *Long bone fracture*: Reduced and splinted
    - *Chest*: Tube thoracostomy and if sign of ongoing blood loss, thoracotomy
    - *Cardiac tamponade*: <100 mL blood enough to produce tamponade (the classical Beck's triad [dilated neck veins, muffled heart sound, and decline in arterial pressure] is not seen; immediate pericardiocentesis is performed; failure of this requires immediate thoracotomy and opening of pericardium)
    - *Abdomen*: Focused abdominal sonography for trauma (FAST) scan—laparotomy required by hemodynamically unstable patients with intraperitoneal bleed
- *Disability or neurological condition*: Glasgow Coma Scale is assessed. A value of 15 is normal; 13–15, mild; 9–12, moderate; and <8, severe injury. Hypoxia, hypercarbia, and hypovolemia induce mental changes. Neurogenic shock is manifested by hypotension and relative bradycardia. Treatment is fluid and inotropes.
- *Exposure and environmental control*: All clothes must be removed for seriously injured patients to allow an adequate examination and intervention. A core body temperature must be measured in seriously injured patients and must be maintained normal. Warm blankets, increased room temperature, heated fluid administration, and body warmers help in correcting hypothermia.

Secondary survey

- It may be delayed until after operating room in unstable patients or in extremis.
- Head-to-toe examination is done. This includes back and front and right to left approach with detailed examination.
- Axilla and perineal area need special attention.
- AMPLET history: This includes allergy, medications currently taken, past history, last meal, event related to injury, and tetanus status.
- Imaging is done.

Tertiary survey

- Repeat primary and secondary survey to rule out missed or occult injury within 24 hours.
- Create an injury problem list with specifications of trauma care consultant handing it.

<C>ABCDE is probably more ideal than ABCDE protocol, where C stands for control of life-threatening external hemorrhage. It is easy to diagnose and easy to treat. Major trauma centers in the United Kingdom follow these principles.

Various systems used in trauma

- Abbreviated Injury Score: Is based on anatomic region and is foundation for development of many scoring systems.
- Glasgow Coma Scale: Eye opening, motor response, and verbal response
- Revised Trauma Score: Includes Glasgow Coma Scale, systolic blood pressure, and respiratory rate
- Organ Injury Scale
- Trauma and Injury Severity Score: Includes Revised Trauma Score, Injury Severity score, age, and mechanism of injury
- Mangled Extremity Severity Score: Includes age, shock, limb ischemia, and energy that caused the injury

176. Write a short note on blunt abdominal trauma.

A
- Mechanism of injury: compression, shearing force, increased IAP
- The most commonly injured organ is spleen and the most common organ injury in penetrating trauma is small bowel.
- Common locations for small bowel injury are duodenojejunal junction and ileocecal junction.
- The most commonly involved organ in seat belt injury is mesentery.

Management

- Unstable patients
  - If patient is hemodynamically unstable → distended abdomen → laparotomy
  - Unstable → no obvious sign → FAST or diagnostic peritoneal lavage (DPL) → positive → laparotomy
  - FAST and DPL if negative → observe and evaluate
- Stable patients
  - History, physical examination, radiological assessment, and blood test
    - *Normal examination*: Serial examination
    - *Equivocal*: CT or DPL or FAST; if positive, selective management; in case of negative, observation
    - *Peritoneal sign*: Laparotomy

Indications for urgent laparotomy in blunt abdominal injury

- Pneumoperitoneum
- Positive DPL (particularly important in hypotensive unstable patients with multiple injuries; >10 mL blood on aspiration and RBCs; >100,000/mL, WBCs >500/mL, amylase >19 IU/L, alkaline phosphatase level >2 IU/L, and bilirubin level >0.01 mg/dL indicate positive DPL)
- Peritonitis
- Unexplained hypovolemia

Choice of incision for blunt abdominal trauma is midline laparotomy.

177. Write a short note on damage control surgery.

A It includes abbreviated laparotomy, temporary packing, and closure of abdomen in order to blunt the response to massive hemorrhage and prolonged shock.

Indications

- Coagulopathy, acidosis, and hypothermia all interacting with each other in a vicious cycle and resulting in ongoing hemorrhage and death (it is known as triad of death; presence of any of these is an indication for abbreviated laparotomy)

- Multiple intra-abdominal injury, multicompartment (abdomen and thorax) injury, and severe intracranial injury; old-aged and debilitated patients who cannot tolerate prolonged anesthesia

For intra-abdominal hypertension and abdominal compartment syndrome refer Chapter 7.

Parts of damage control

- *Damage control 0 (DC 0)*: Rapid transport to definitive care
- *Damage control 1 (DC 1)*: Rapid control of hemorrhage and contamination
- *Damage control 2 (DC 2)*: Resuscitation—shifting to ICU and correction of acidosis, coagulopathy, and hypothermia
- *Damage control 3 (DC 3)*: Return to OR for definitive repair
- *Damage control 4 (DC 4)*: Definitive abdominal closure (this includes patients in whom abdomen was not possible to close safely due to increased IAP and contamination requiring repeated washout in DC 3)

178. What are the effects of abdominal compartment syndrome? How will you manage it?

Physiological effects

- Compression over IVC → decreased preload → decreased cardiac output → hypotension
- Decreased venous return → organ ischemia → bowel and hepatic necrosis
- Decreased thoracic cavity compliance → hypoventilation and increased airway pressure
- Compression of kidney → oliguria

Management

- *Grades 1 and 2*: Nasogastric decompression, sedation, and diuresis. Failure of conservative management requires decompressive laparotomy.
- *Grade 3*: If sign of organ failure is present, decompressive laparotomy is performed and if not present, then close monitoring and neuromuscular blockade are performed.
- *Grade 4*: Decompressive laparotomy is performed.

179. Give a brief account of flail chest.

- The condition of three or more ribs fractured at two or more places is known as flail chest.
- It is a paradoxical movement of chest wall during respiration.
- When sternum is part of flail chest due to involvement of costochondral or costosternal joint, it is known as sternal flail chest.
- Alteration in chest wall mechanics leads to impairment of tidal volume and ability to clear the cough.
- Pulmonary contusion produces hypoxia.
- Pain prevents adequate pulmonary toilet.
- Combination of all of these produces hypoventilation, atelectasis, and pneumonia.

Management

- Pain control is the most important: Parenteral narcotic and patient-controlled analgesia. Thoracic epidural, intercostal nerve block, and if ICD in situ, then intrapleural local analgesia can be given. Thoracic epidural is the effective way of managing pain.
- Oxygen administration and physiotherapy are helpful.
- Patients with pulmonary contusion who develop hypoxia and hypercarbia and severe alteration in chest wall mechanics require mechanical ventilation.
- Selected cases of isolated severe chest injury and pulmonary contusion may benefit from rib fixation.

180. Steering wheel injury on chest of a young man reveals multiple fractures of ribs and paradoxical movement with severe respiratory distress. X-ray shows lung contusion on right side without pneumothorax or hemothorax. What is the initial treatment of choice?

- Use endotracheal intubation and mechanical ventilation, because from history it seems we are dealing with a case of flail chest.

- Flail chest: It refers to fracture of two or more ribs at two places on either one side of the chest or either side of sternum.
- Local control of chest pain with epidural analgesia is the most important in small segments, while in more severe cases use IPPV till fracture becomes less mobile (up to 3 weeks).

Indications of thoracotomy:
- ICD output >1.5 L/24 hours
- ICD output >200 mL/h for 3 hours
- Rupture of bronchus, aorta, esophagus, or diaphragm
- Penetrating chest injury with cardiac tamponade (engorged neck vein, pallor, rapid pulse, faint heart sound, and pulsus paradoxus)
- Emergency room thoracotomy (for cardiac arrest)

181. A 5-year-old child presented with splenic trauma in the casualty. Vitals on admission are as follows: Pulse, 84/min; blood pressure, normal; and there is no respiratory distress. What is the treatment of choice?

A Conservative (observation)

Kehr sign is positive in splenic injury (due to hemoperitoneum).

182. A patient presented with tenderness over the cervical spine region in the trauma center. What first step would you like to take as a medical officer?

A Immobilize the spine before ABC of management with either manual or Philadelphia collar.

Pearls

- Hypotension in spinal injury is due to loss of sympathetic vasomotor tone. The patient is having bradycardia from unbalanced vagal input. Atropine may be used to treat bradycardia and systolic blood pressure should be maintained >90 mmHg to maintain spinal perfusion.
- Spinal cord injury without radiographic abnormality (SCIWORA) is common in children and rare in adults.
- Patients with spinal cord injury presented within 8 hours of the injury should be treated with high-dose methylprednisolone. Methylprednisolone is not indicated in patients with penetrating spinal cord injury.
- CNS rhinorrhea is due to fracture of the ethmoidal or frontal sinus in base of anterior cranial fossa and otorrhea is due to fracture of petrous temporal bone.
- Periorbital bruising is raccoon eyes associated with subconjunctival hemorrhage and is seen in anterior cranial fossa fracture.
- Battle sign is a patch of bruising behind the ear and seen in petrous temporal bone fracture.
- Headache, vomiting, and decreased levels of consciousness are the cardinal indicators of raised intracranial pressure (ICP).
- Extradural hematoma (EDH) is due to laceration of middle meningeal artery and associated with lucid interval. There is a transient loss of consciousness followed by recovery to normal, and then rapid deterioration leads to unconsciousness and coma (lucid interval). Hematoma collects over time and initially ICP is maintained due to compensatory mechanism but in later phase brain shift occurs with raised ICP and patients deteriorate. It is associated with skull base fracture in the region of pterion. CT scan shows biconvex hematoma that does not cross the suture line and treatment is craniotomy.
- Subdural hematoma (SDH) is due to laceration of cortical vessel in association with severe cortical contusion and blood collects between dura and arachnoid membrane. It has no lucid interval and poor prognosis as compared to EDH. It has a crescent-shaped high-density collection on CT scan. Craniotomy is the mainstay of treatment.
- Indications for immediate intervention in neck injuries are the following: Hemodynamic instability and ongoing external bleed.

- There are three zones in the neck: Zone I, sternal notch to cricoid cartilage; zone II, cricoid cartilage to angle of mandible; and zone III, area cephalad to angle of mandible. Zone I injury is often associated with great vessel injury.
- Tracheobronchial injury is the most common cause of death in blunt chest trauma.
- In severe traumatic injury, the sequence of repair is as follows: Bone, extensor tendon, flexure tendon, artery, vein, nerve, and skin.
- Patients on left-sided chest and abdominal trauma with fluid in the peritoneum and sign of hypotension are most likely to have splenic injury. They should have a referred pain over shoulder tip due to diaphragmatic irritation due to blood collection.
- The most common injury in chest trauma is rib fracture. Fracture of lower rib like 9–12 ribs is associated with liver injury on the right side and splenic injury on the left side and that of upper rib like 1–3 ribs is associated with vascular injuries. The best approach in thoracic trauma is anterolateral thoracotomy.
- Sudden death in superficial neck injury is due to air embolism through external jugular vein.
- The most commonly involved organ in blast injury is tympanic membrane and the least is liver, and the most commonly affected organ in underwater explosion with head out is GIT and that fully underwater is tympanic membrane.
- A patient with stab injury to anterior abdominal wall with omental protrusion is hemodynamically stable and shows no sign of peritoneal irritation. Initial management is CECT abdomen.
- Any penetrating injury below fifth intercostal space should raise the suspicion of diaphragmatic injury. Tip of the nasogastric tube next to the heart on X-ray confirms the diagnosis. The most accurate method of evaluation is VATS or laparoscopy. Operative repair is done in all cases to prevent herniation of intra-abdominal content as abdomen is at positive pressure and thorax is at negative pressure. Laparoscopy is ideal for repair as it allows diagnosing additional hollow viscus injury. The most commonly herniated organ is stomach followed by spleen. In blunt trauma, diaphragmatic injury is more common on the left side as liver diffuses some of the energy on the right side.
- Bleeding occurs from five major sites in trauma: *One* on the floor—bleeding due to external (skin) trauma; and *four* more—chest, abdomen, pelvis, and extremities (fracture).
- Hemorrhage is the cause of death in chest injury.
- CT scan chest has replaced angiography as an investigation of choice for thoracic aortic injury. The most common source of bleeding in chest trauma is intercostal or internal mammary.
- Thoracic aorta is fixed distal to the ligamentum arteriosum just distal to origin of the left subclavian artery and the common site for rupture. Asymmetry of upper and lower limb blood pressure with chest wall contusion may indicate rupture. Chest X-ray may reveal widened mediastinum. CT is the preferred investigation.
- Severe subcutaneous emphysema with respiratory compromise indicates tracheobronchial injury.
- Blunt cardiac injury or myocardial contusion cannot be diagnosed reliably. Arrhythmia and pump failure are the indications for myocardial contusion. Normal ECG reliably rules out cardiac contusion.
- FAST will not reliably detect less than 100 mL of free blood.
- Cullen sign in patients with right lower chest and upper abdomen is due to tracking of blood through ligamentum teres to the umbilicus and indicates liver trauma. CECT abdomen will grade the injury and hemodynamically stable patients are managed conservatively.

- The four Ps for management of liver injury are as follows: Push, pringle, plug, and pack. Pringle maneuver is the occlusion of the portal triad using vascular clamp through the foramen of Winslow with the aid of left index finger. It can be applied for 60 minutes without significant hepatic damage. Alternatively, it can be released intermittently. Ideally, one should attempt to perfuse liver every 15 minutes for 5 minutes.
- Blood in the nasogastric tube in penetrating trauma usually indicates stomach injury.
- Isolated duodenal injury is rare and usually associated with pancreatic injury. It is difficult to diagnose as it is a retroperitoneal structure. Sometimes gas in the periduodenal space on CT is the only sign.
- Small bowel injury requires urgent repair; large bowel injury with little contamination and satisfactory viability can be repaired primarily while patients with extensive contamination and doubtful viability, and unstable patients require defunctioning stoma. Intraperitoneal rectal injury can be managed as colonic injury and extraperitoneal injury requires either defunctioning stoma with closure of the distal end (Hartmann procedure) or loop colostomy.
- To rule out bladder injury, in cystogram, at least 400 mL contrast should be used. Two views in two occasions are ideal, anteroposterior and lateral in full bladder and postvoid film.
- Cycle handlebar injury in a 10-year-old boy 15 days back and now presented with epigastric mass indicates traumatic pseudocyst of pancreas.
- In renal injury, sometimes IVU is performed to know the function of the opposite kidney. A patient who is hemodynamically stable but is having persistent hematuria is a candidate for renal angiogram and may benefit from embolization.
- The most common cause of reduced GCS in alcoholics is hypoglycemia. Other causes are hypoperfusion and drug abuse.

MISCELLANEOUS

183. In India, which is the most common cause of unilateral lymphedema of lower limb?

A Filariasis

184. Rhabdomyosarcoma of which site is likely to have poor prognosis?

A Rhabdomyosarcoma of extremity is usually associated with alveolar histology and found to have a poor prognosis (most common sites for rhabdomyosarcoma are head and neck).

185. Which are the more common retroperitoneal tumors?

A
- Lymphoma
- Retroperitoneal sarcoma

The most common structure involved in retroperitoneal fibrosis is ureter.

186. In which malignant conditions is screening beneficial?

A
- Carcinoma cervix
- Carcinoma breast
- Carcinoma oral cavity
- Carcinoma colon and rectum

187. During bilateral adrenalectomy, when should intraoperative dose of corticosteroid be given?

A After removal of both glands

188. What is Pancoast tumor?

A
- It is a tumor located in the apex of lung.
- Shoulder pain radiates to the ulnar distribution of extremity.
- First and second ribs are involved.
- It may produce Horner syndrome.

189. What is the best time for repair of cleft lip and cleft palate?

A Cleft lip is repaired at the age of around 3 months and palate at around 12 months.

For repair of cleft lip, follow 'rule of ten': 10 weeks of age, 10 lb weight, and 10 g/dL hemoglobin.

190. Which is the most common cause of subarachnoid hemorrhage (SAH)? Mention the most common site for SAH. Which investigations help in diagnosis?

A
- Berry aneurysm rupture. The patient presents with worst ever headache he or she experienced in his or her life.

- The most common site is junction of anterior communicating artery with anterior cerebral artery.
- Lumbar puncture is diagnostic.
- CT brain is the investigation of choice.

191. Which vessel is most likely to be injured in extradural hematoma and SDH? Which is the best indicator of prognosis in head injury?

A Extradural hematoma

- Middle meningeal vessel is most likely to be injured.
- On CT scan, it appears as biconvex lentiform opacity.

Subdural hematoma

The most likely injured vessel is anterior cerebral vessel and it appears as concavoconvex crescentic opacity on CT scan.

Indicator of prognosis in head injury

The best indicator of head injury prognosis is Glasgow Coma Scale. Maximum in the scale is 15 and minimum is 3.

- Eye opening, 4
- Verbal response, 5
- Motor response, 6

192. Which is the most common malignancy in adult males in India?

A
- Oropharyngeal malignancy (most common site is buccal mucosa)
- Most common premalignant condition being leukoplakia

193. What are the causes of left supraclavicular lymph node enlargement in malignancy?

A Causes

- Lung cancer
- Breast cancer
- GI malignancy
- Pancreatic cancer
- Ovarian malignancy
- Testicular malignancy

Painless hard lump in the left supraclavicular region is usually due to metastatic lymph node.

- FNAC or biopsy is required.
- If it is squamous cell carcinoma, the likely primary site is lung.
- If it is adenocarcinoma, the likely primary site is GI malignancy.

194. What are the various types of neck dissections?

A
- *Radical neck dissection (RND) (Crile's)*: Level I–V lymph nodes + sternocleidomastoid muscle (SCM) + internal jugular vein (IJV) + spinal accessory nerve (SAN)
- *MRND (functional neck dissection)*: Level I–V lymph nodes (preserve SCM, IJV, SAN)
  - *Type 1*: Preserves SAN
  - *Type 2*: Preserves SAN and IJV
  - *Type 3*: Preserves SAN, IJV, and SCM
- *Selective neck dissection (SND)*
  - Preservation of lymphatic compartment that is removed in classical RND
  - Supraomohyoid: Levels I–III (oral malignancy)
  - Lateral neck: Levels II– IV (laryngeal malignancy)
  - Posterolateral: Levels II–V (thyroid malignancy)
  - Central compartment: Level VI

Blow-out carotid is a complication of RND. Other conditions where carotid blow-out is seen are the following: Radiation-induced necrosis, recurrent tumor, and pharyngocutaneous fistula.

Medial cutaneous nerve of arm injury during RND leads to loss of sensation in the medial side of the arm.

References

1. Carson JL, Triulzi DJ, Ness PM. Indications for and adverse effects of red-cell transfusion. N Engl J Med 2017;377:1261.
2. Leinicke JA, Wise PE. Small intestine. In: Klingensmith ME, Vemuri C, Fayanju OM, et al (editors). The Washington Manual of Surgery, 7th edn. Philadelphia: Wolters Kluwer; 2016:339–56.
3. Carlson GL, Epstein J. The small intestine. In: Williams NS, O' Connell PR, McCaskie A (editors). Bailey and Love Short Practice of Surgery, 27th edn. Florida: CRC Press, Taylor and Francis; 2018:1240–57.

4. Patel AD, Thompson JS. Radiation enteritis. In: Yeo CJ (editor). Shackelford's Surgery of the Alimentary Tract, 8th edn. Philadelphia, Elsevier; 2017 (E-book).
5. Mitchem JB, Hunt SR. Colon and rectum. In: Klingensmith ME, Vemuri C, Fayanju OM, et al (editors). The Washington Manual of Surgery, 7th edn. Philadelphia: Wolters Kluwer; 2016:422–45.
6. Towfigh S, McFadden DW, Cortina GR, et al. Porcelain gallbladder is not associated with gallbladder carcinoma. Am Surg 2001;67:7–10.
7. Csendes A, Muñoz C, Albán M. Síndrome de Mirizzi–Fístula colecistobiliar, una nueva clasificación. Rev Chil Cir 2007;59(Suppl):63-4.
8. Marcelo A, Beltrán MA. Mirizzi syndrome: History, current knowledge and proposal of a simplified classification. World J Gastroenterol 2012;18(34):4639–50.
9. Strasberg SM, Hertl M, Soper NJ. An analysis of the problem of biliary injury during laparoscopic cholecystectomy. J Am Coll Surg 1995;180:101-25.
10. Johnston LE, Hanks JB. Small bowel obstruction. In: Yeo CJ (editor). Shackelford's Surgery of the Alimentary Tract, 8th edn. Philadelphia: Elsevier; 2017 (E-book).
11. Tenner S, DeWitt J, Baillie J, et al. American College of Gastroenterology Guideline: management of acute pancreatitis. Am J Gastroenterol 2013;108(9):1400–15;1416.
12. Fisher WE, Anderson DK, Windsor JA, Saluja AK, Brunicardi. Pancreas. In: Brunicardi FC, Anderson DK, Billiar TR, et al, eds. Schwartz's Principle of Surgery, 10th edn. New York: McGraw-Hill, 2015, 1341–422.
13. Campbell-Walsh Urology, 11th ed.
14. Alkhateeb S, Al-Mansour M, Alotaibi M, et al. Saudi Oncology Society and Saudi Urology Association combined clinical management guidelines for urothelial cell carcinoma of the urinary bladder. Urol Ann 2016;8(2):131-5.
15. Barthold JS, Hagerty JA. Etiology, diagnosis, and management of undescended testis testis. In: Wein AJ, Kavoussi LR, Partin AW, Peters CA, editors. Campbell-Walsh Urology. 11th ed. Philadelphia: Elsevier; 2016. p.3430-52.
16. Palmer LS, Palmer JS. Management of abnormalities of the external genitilia in boys. In: Wein AJ, Kavoussi LR, Partin AW, Peters CA, eds. Campbell-Walsh Urology, 11th edn. Philadelphia: Elsevier; 2016, 3368–98.
17. Schaeffer AJ, Matulewicz, Klump DJ. Infection of the urinary tract. In: Wein AJ, Kavoussi LR, Partin AW, Peters CA, eds. Campbell-Walsh Urology, 11th edn. Philadelphia: Elsevier; 2016, 237–303.
18. Leavitt DA, Rosette JJ, Hoening DM. Strategies for non medical management of upper urinary tract calculi. In: Wein AJ, Kavoussi LR, Partin AW, Peters CA, eds. Campbell-Walsh Urology, 11th edn. Philadelphia: Elsevier; 2016, 1235–59.
19. Akar AR, Durdu S. Thromboangiitis obliterans. In: Cronenwett JL, Wayne Johnston K, eds. Rutherford's Vascular Surgery, 8th edn. Philadelphia: Elsevier; 2014, 1167–86.
20. Olitan OK, Hollinger EF. Dialysis access. In: Saclarides TJ, Myers JA, Millikan KW (editors). Common Surgical Disease, 3rd edn. New York: Springer; 2015:83-90.
21. Chatter IC, Carradice D. Venous disorder. In: Williams NS, O'Connell PR, McCaskie A (editors). Bailey and Love Short Practice of Surgery, 27th edn. Florida: CRC Press, Taylor and Francis; 2018:969-94.
22. Kearon C, Akl EA, Comerota AJ, et al. Antithrombotic therapy for VTE disease: Antithrombotic Therapy and Prevention of Thrombosis, 9th ed: American College of Chest Physicians Evidence-Based Clinical Practice Guidelines. Chest 2012;141:e419S–96S.
23. Loftus I. Abdominal aortic aneurysm. In: Thompson M, Boyle J, Brohi K, Cheshire N, eds. Oxford Textbook of Vascular Surgery, 1st edn. New York: Oxford University Press; 2016, 467–568.
24. Haugen BR, Alexander EK, Bible KC, et al. 2015 American Thyroid Association Management Guidelines for Adult Patients with Thyroid Nodules and Differentiated Thyroid Cancer: The American Thyroid Association Guidelines Task Force on Thyroid Nodules and Differentiated Thyroid Cancer. Thyroid 2016;26:1.
25. National Comprehensive Cancer Network (NCCN). NCCN Clinical practice guidelines in oncology. http://www.nccn.org/professionals/physician_gls/f_guidelines.asp
26. Gwiezdzinska JK, Wartofsky. Thyrotoxic storm. In: Wass JAH, Stewart PM, eds. Oxford Textbook of Endocrinology and Diabetes, 2nd ed. Oxford: Oxford University Press; 2011, 454–60.

Index

A

M

R

S

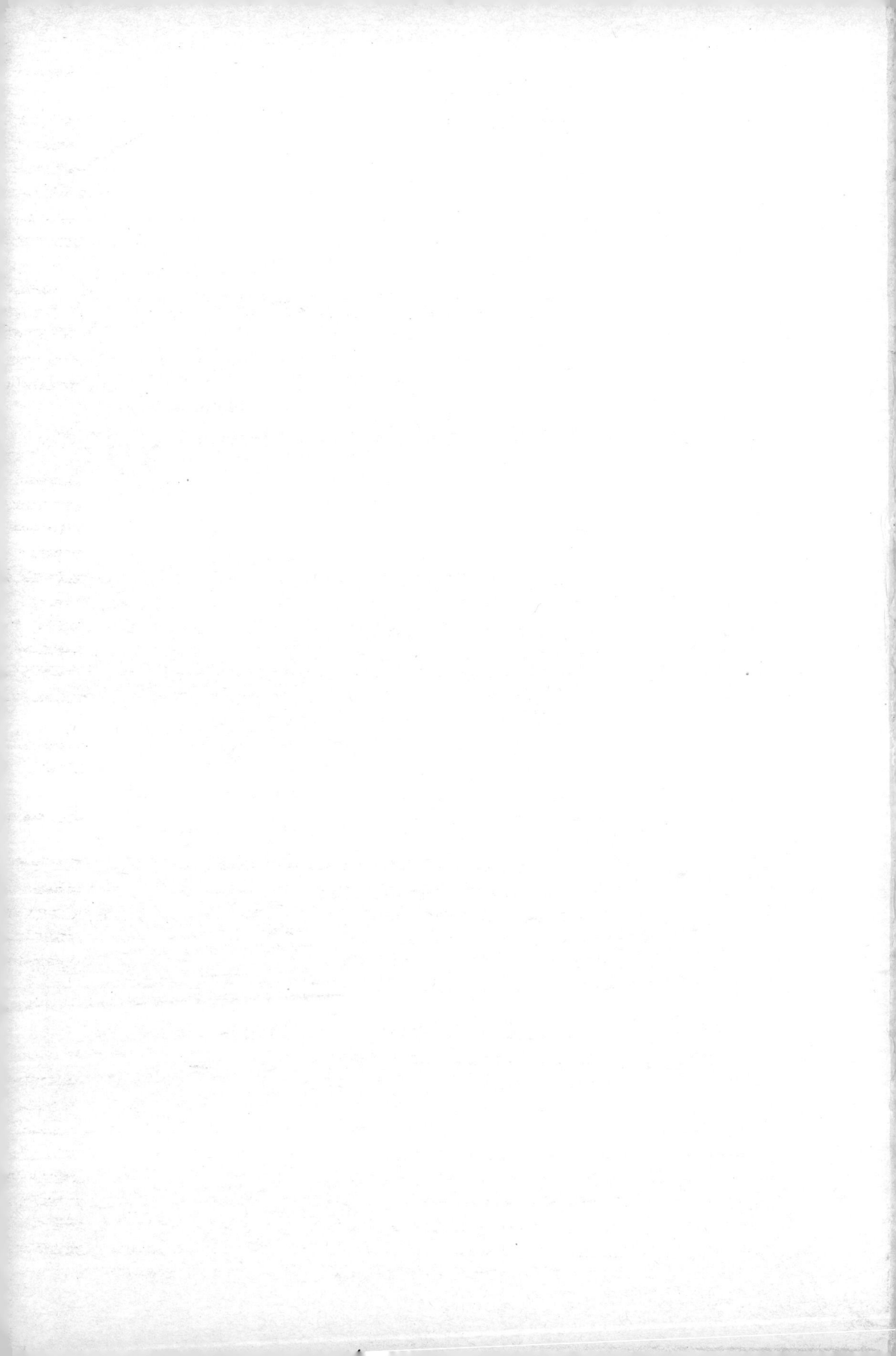